Published by

**MELROSE
BOOKS**

An Imprint of Melrose Press Limited
St Thomas Place, Ely
Cambridgeshire
CB7 4GG, UK
www.melrosebooks.co.uk

FIRST EDITION

Cover designed by Catherine McIntyre

ISBN   978-1-907732-70-6

Printed and bound in Great Britain by:
TJ International Ltd, Padstow, Cornwall

MIX
Paper from
responsible sources
FSC
www.fsc.org   FSC® C013056

I LIKE TO WALK IN THIS FIELD

BY

PATRICK DAVIDSON

CONTENTS

PART ONE

PART TWO

PART THREE

PART FOUR

PART ONE

A FURROW LONG BEGUN

I

A stab of flame in the night sky. Fraser Baird could hear the gunshot crackling in the hills around him many times in later life. It was there, in his boy's bank of memory, for long years after the wind-driven rain had smothered it.

Some months off being four years old, Fraser felt that the circumstances of the scene were wholly understandable in terms of what must surely come, the very way of life that he would follow, just like his father. Able to go out of a winter's afternoon and shoot a duck or a rabbit, and have it retrieved by his very own dog, maybe still by good old Argo, as he, Fraser, came to be a grown-up too. He would know all the farmers, too, and they would know him, but in what capacity, he wasn't quite sure yet. It was all very solid in his mind.

As one of the very earliest pictures held within his mind from later years' total recall, Fraser could feel again the penetrating cold and stillness, could see the windows of the old stone house yellow-lit in the darkening winter's afternoon, could harbour in the warm certainty of himself the security of those things familiar in his grandfather's clatter of buckets and tools, in his old man's intermittent low grumble as he talked to the hens and calves at their shutting-up for the night.

Fraser knew his grandfather as Grandpa Teatime, from everyone's call for him to come to the house for a hot drink and a scone off the griddle in the afternoon. The hens, Fraser knew from fine acquaintance, would be responding to Grandpa Teatime's presence with a low seep-seep-seep from their perches in the hen house that smelt strongly of creosote.

Hungering for his father to come home, Fraser felt the tension of high expectation. He shivered in the grip of long runs of uncontrollable snatches by his leg and stomach muscles. Standing in the angle of the high drystane dyke, his mother could not immediately see where he was, or forever come running out to see what was keeping him. There would be those smells about his father's person which he enfolded in his olfactory library: warm leather of

3

the car seat, wet dogs' rankness, the peculiarly man's mixture of tweed jacket and plus fours, sweat and pipe tobacco, surgical spirit, cows and gun oil. For his father not to have these invisible proofs of identity about his person would have been seriously alarming.

The essentials for this day's high point had been set, unexpectedly for Fraser, at the breakfast table. His father had asked Fraser's mother, almost casually, "Mary, would you mind making up a piece, a few sandwiches of some kind, to take with me? I've been invited to shoot at Haugh of Birkfaulds, Tommy Anderson's place, and they'll go on there until about two o'clock afore we stop for a meal."

Fraser at once ceased his absorption with creating islands of porridge and rivers of milk. This matter of his father going shooting, today, this was of serious importance. His father might well invite him to help clean his shotgun on coming home, but what other tantalising activities, anything to do with shooting, might come his way? He eyed his father with visible intensity, easily perceived by both his mother and father. His sister Jean was not in the slightest concerned. Well, she was a girl, she was at school.

Alec Baird, country veterinary surgeon, leant across the table, pushing the jar of home-made marmalade out of the way, towards his father, who was reading the previous day's Aberdeen Press & Journal, spectacles on the end of his nose. He had fed the hens before coming in for breakfast. Fraser could smell the dust of hens' litter on him. Now, what was his father going to say? He had started to say something, and having done so, tried to suppress an outright laugh:

"Look, Fraser–" at which Fraser nearly leapt off his chair, raised with cushions to be the same as grown-ups at the table.

"Now, pay attention, young squire. If I get home early enough, and the weather's right, how about you and I having a go at the duck? It'll be a good night for them on the pool, if the weather's closing in."

Fraser felt waves of tingling energy coursing up through all of his body, whirling around his brain and then down through his legs like lightning. Going to the duck? There would be some shooting then. Great. He paid renewed attention to the porridge and milk. Table manners were tiresome, constantly being drummed into him, if not by his mother, then annoyingly by his sister as well. Fraser glowered at her.

"Mind and clean your shoes!" he growled at his sister Jean in a perfect tonal imitation of their grandfather. He would have to be quick to get breakfast out of the way, get down off his chair and leave the table; to help his father load gun and cartridges into the car was an important task. It came before anything else.

4

Now, with the winter's day darkening by the minute, Fraser wanted and willed and wished for his father to come home. Running behind the car as it swung into the yard, Fraser could tell by his father's silhouette that he was still in his shooting clothes, that he was stiff, and probably a bit tired too. Turning to him, one foot still on the running board, his father spoke very quietly in the near-darkness.

"That's a good fellow, Fraser. Are you all set to go to the river? Come away then."

Fraser put up his hand to be grasped, hearing the solid clicking of cartridges being dropped by his father's other hand into his jacket pocket.

"Hold on. Run and tell your mother what we're doing, all right?"

"Aye, all right, Daddy."

Fraser whirled, banged his way past the back door, shouting loudly for his mother's attention. Come on, come ON, LISTEN!

"All set then?"

"Aye, Daddy."

"Right, away we go."

Still holding Fraser's hand in his own, his father tucked the Boss twelve-bore shotgun over his other arm, in the crook of his elbow. It had already been used that day. Fraser could tell by the smell; he knew this without conscious thought.

As they stepped quietly down to the pool, which released gleams from its blackness in the closing dusk, rain slanted on their upturned faces and both could smell the river to their front as they listened, heads tilted.

A thrash of wings and loud quacking caused Fraser to let go at once, his hand released by his father, the two or three mallard now stretching out in alarm for distance and safety in the darkness. He sensed his father's movement, his taking a single step forward, almost leisurely, firing once. A black form dropped to the report, smacked against the water's glitter, and splashed. While his father went forward a few paces to direct Argo, the black Labrador retriever, Fraser was left to hold the emptied gun, stock to the ground, cold steel barrels clasped tightly to his chest and cheeks.

Carrying the fat drake through the garden and into the warmth of the kitchen passage, with few words passing between father, son and dog, left a solid imprint on all of Fraser's senses. The smells, sounds and colours of the duck's taking were deeply imprinted, long after the day and the deed.

In the kitchen, with the Triplex range ruddy in steady heat behind her, his mother's comments had been mildly congratulatory.

"Well, you two, and who did the shooting?"

"Daddy did – he shot it. It's for eating."

"Oh, aye, an' Argo brought it back, 'cos he can see in the dark time."

Nods and looks were exchanged above his head as gun, scarves and glossy mallard drake were handed about and disposed of. Fraser's richly nourished senses swam into the contentment of a hot drink, clothes being tugged off and falling into bed. One hand was cunningly and covertly preserved in its unwashed state, redolent of oils from duck and gun, and held close to his nose until sleep relaxed the soft, grubby fingers.

In sleep, the faintest sensations were crystallised, to await their recall by the smallest manner of things yet unseen; a sound, a smell, a touch, the current of life carried the hardly-breathing form on into a stream, which by its course and composition was already flowing steadily towards events predetermined by that earliest remembered afternoon of childhood.

With the warm lights of the kitchen passage bright behind her, Fraser's mother called out to her husband, who had his back towards her, busily occupied in his car.

"Have you more to do, or can you come in for your tea now? I've had mine with the children, but your father insisted on waiting. He's aye late in coming in, anyway. It's ready now."

"Well, I have milk reports somewhere in here to be made up, but – ach, they'll keep."

Alec Baird slammed the car door shut in the steady rain that now glistened on his face and moustache, and turning, head down, made for the warmth and meal waiting in the kitchen. Alec looked towards his wife, questioning, as he tugged off his boots.

"Was the wee cratur out there, waiting for me all that while?"

"That he was, and – Alec! Determined did you say? Huh! He just would not listen, or come in or anything. He had to wait for his father! Well, I just hope that the two of you found it all worthwhile."

"Aye, of course it was, Mary. By God, this is hot! Anyway, the wee soul has been craiking on at me for long enough to take him down to the duck; it fitted in fine."

The faintest asperity in his wife's comments, as she moved from ironing to kitchen range and back again, was dissolved by her husband's pleasure in his meal, and then the clatter of nailed boots as the children's grandfather came into the kitchen, bringing a sudden sharpness of colder air with his clothes and presence. Any words passed were amiable but perfunctory, the principal

6

engagement of both being the hot meal in front of the two men. Fraser's mother, preoccupied with the repetitive movements of smoothing, ironing and folding away, gave her husband and his stocky, strong-featured father only occasional attention; their manner of talking and the content of it were entirely familiar to her. A splatter of wind-driven rain against the tall sash window made them all look up in surprise at the intensity of the night's weather. Only an hour or so back it had been admittedly very cold but bearable outside, and there had been no hesitation in taking a small boy out to flight duck. Even in the warm kitchen, Mary and Alec Baird could hear the steady hissing of rain on the flagstones of the yard outside.

The older man took large mouthfuls of mashed turnip, potatoes and mince, and chewed his food with obvious satisfaction.

"Aye, man, you're for the Ardoch beasts in the morning, then, Alec? I'm thinking those heifers'll take some handling, but you'll have plenty of helpers, surely?" Chuckling to himself, Fraser's grandfather patted his pockets for his pipe and tobacco. His daughter-in-law stiffened in patent irritation, with a look to her husband that was more than questioning.

"Well, if it's a day like yon," – Fraser's father nodded to the streaming window panes – "then I shall need Fraser to keep the test forms and anything else dry and out of the muck about the place. You ken fine what it's like there, Father, near as many folk running about as there are beasts, and not one of them of any use. Fraser can easily sit in the car if it's all that wet."

The boy's mother interjected, more than brusquely:

"Fraser will do no such thing! It's Bella's day off tomorrow, and I'd planned to take him with me on the bus into the town, and then go along to Shelagh's place for tea in the afternoon. Remember, Alec?" She smiled, and added quickly, "You've had him out shooting today for a start, so turning him into a wee cowboy can just wait for another day. Besides, he could quite well have other things he wants to do. He's got to have some time with his sister, and other people, grown-ups, although you may not think so! Anyway, you two go away through the house, and I'll be through in just a minute. All this can be put by for Bella when she comes back in."

She looked up as their chair legs scraped the red-tiled floor.

"Grandpa, did you bring in more logs before the rain came on? Put some on the fire when you go through, please."

The look that she directed at her husband was unnecessary: he knew that she wanted him to stay behind for some comment on something that he, or his father, or even young Fraser, had done, or not done. Or some other dashed thing. He sat at the untidy table, undisturbed and relaxed with satisfaction at the day well dealt with. He had really enjoyed the day's shooting, amongst farmers and friends all well-known to him. And himself to them. That in itself was a fine feeling, too.

Mary's father-in-law took his pipe and presence and the newspaper into the hall, a rumble of words, heavy footfalls and a door opening and closing to mark his movements.

"You know, Alec, I don't think that you should just expect Fraser to do all the things that–"

"All the things that I like doing? Ach, away you go, Mary. You know perfectly well that he's been going on at me this past while about going out with Argo and the gun. He can see the dashed things better than I can! Man, if you'd just seen him carrying that mallard drake all the way up from the river!"

Her husband shook his head from side to side, with snorts of amusement at the picture, gasping, "He would persist in gripping it by its neck. The stupid cratur's beak was over his left ear somewhere, and still its rear end was trailing in amongst his feet. Every few steps, he'd give it an almighty howdge up again, with wings and feathers all over his face!"

His mirth got the better of him, and he leaned backwards on the elm kitchen chair, shaking with laughter, tears spilling down his cheeks and his moustache. His wife was equally affected, and began to laugh, too, in spite of her earlier irritation about something that was now imperfectly recalled, if at all.

"Yes, he's clearly another Baird if ever there was, Alec. I was watching him out there with your father. Leaning on the fork, Grandpa's special graip, and giving him all his orders, just like some of your old farmer-bodies."

They both started to laugh, Mary Baird leaning on her husband's shoulder as they inclined towards one another. But she straightened up and coughed determinedly, declaiming in what Alec called her "Morningsehd ehccent. Purest Edinburgh, y'know":

"But you must agree, he's far too young for all this going around with you, holding things at herd tests, and hearing goodness knows what language. Believe me, he gets plenty of gems from your father – I hear them, you don't! The next thing'll be the two of them going out with the gun while you're away from home, and I don't think that either of them should be getting any ideas in that direction. Come on, let's go through to the fire."

Mary Baird turned to the door, but her husband sat on at the table, his legs in serviceable tweed plus fours and thick hand-knitted stockings stretched out below.

"Mary? What you said just now about the two of them... I can just see them, Fraser in front, of course, measuring his length over another duck or some muckle great hare, and ordering Father and Argo about: 'Come in to heel, you miserable brute!'"

He rubbed his stockinged soles along the red tiles, laughing delightedly. Exasperated, Mary turned back to him.

"But, can't you see, that's just what I'm trying to tell you? Anyway, both he and Jean are to come with me to Shelagh's tomorrow, so that should do them a power of good, don't you think?"

"Oh, couldn't be better!" He affected an even more pronounced parody of his wife's unconscious Edinburgh manner of speaking: "The effaict of her prehsence on our delaitful wee bairns will prove ehbsolootly dehvastating, mai deah!"

In sudden temper, Mary flounced out into the hall with a final "Oh, you're quite impossible, the lot of you!" She shut the door forcefully behind her, but not so quickly that she didn't hear her husband's added "That's it! Impossible!" and another burst of laughter as he rose to follow her into the hall.

The night's lash of rain, now steady over the Aberdeenshire river valley and low hills, blurred what chinks of light there were from the windows up and down the gables of the granite-built house. The three generations harboured there, coming to comfort in their sleep, and with their attached satisfactions, memories and hopes, were all at different levels in their lives, like the small gleams of light shining through the night's storm.

II

As a faithful and diligent attendant to his father's commitments and enthusiasms, Fraser felt that he would surely arrive at the same stage of easy competence in ever so many things, such as the shooting of the mallard drake. There was no reason to doubt that he, Fraser Baird, would do all these things, and he felt quite assured that this would be so, sticking out his jaw in determined pursuit of each day's occupations, proof of the resolution there in his inner mind.

As an admittedly young boy, his continuous rather than episodic recall of events from earliest years commenced with a slightly older, more general view of things, framed forever by the sunlight of a perpetual summer morning. Fraser felt sure that his continuity of recall all really started when, quite suddenly, they had moved as a family down into England. They settled in there as spring was lazily easing into the summer months of 1933.

Events so unlikely to happen in his view of their family being the most stable of quantities, it seemed to Fraser, and further, quite unconsidered in any of his daily absorptions, had uplifted and transported his parents, his sister Jean and himself, far to the south, into the English Midlands, at an immeasurable distance from his birthplace and home in rural Aberdeenshire. It was almost, Fraser confided to Innes McAndrew, their farmer neighbour's son of similar age, a few days before their removal to the south, "As though we're going to go and live in another country somewhere."

He tackled his mother repeatedly about this, this maladjustment tugging at his boy's mind. Things did not seem tidy, or in their right, familiar places.

"Mummy, why is Daddy having to go to England to make cows and things better down there? Are they different from the ones up here in Scotland? They're prob'ly not so good as Mr 'Candrew's ones. I hope that Grandpa Teatime is still going to be with us down there?"

In his boy's mind, Jim McAndrew's cattle, their appearance, calves and easy tolerance of his, Fraser's, overtures to friendliness, constituted the yardstick of all that was desirable in bovine companions. And his grandfather's physical presence would naturally and surely have to be a reassuring part of this moving business.

10

"Are we really going to stay down there? Do you and Daddy and Jean know where we're all going to live? What is it called?"

"Melford. I think you'll like it, once we're settled in."

His mother turned to him, with some concern that this uprooting be accommodated in her son's mind; there was little doubt that he was disturbed, reluctant to let go his attachment to such things as Mr McAndrew's fine glossy cows, his grandfather's daily regime of things needing to be done, the proximity of the river in all its sounds and smells.

"Look, your father's been asked to go down there to help make some very good cows and calves and other animals better again after a difficult illness. He'll be needing you to help him, once you're a wee bit bigger. Now, just try and understand this, Fraser: your grandfather's not coming all that way south with us. He's going to have his own wee place here, some miles up the river, with his own friends close by, and hens and things of course."

"Melford. Melford?" It sounded all right, but Fraser struggled to find form and some kind of mental dimensions for the end-point of all this upheaval and packing up of everything stable and familiar. He found it difficult and tiring. This was not a definite thing that could be picked up, handled and regarded for its usefulness in doing things, such as Grandpa Teatime's wheelbarrow, or the milk can, taken across the calves' wee park for milk from the McAndrews' dairy every day, cool and echoing of voices with water flowing down over the corrugated cooler. In Fraser's mind, you knew exactly where you were with things like that.

Melford, a county town of the English Midlands, was, in 1933, the year of their coming down from the North, a place of predictable, steady rhythms, mostly those of the farming year. This point made for a welcome easing in his mind, Fraser felt. He had already seen some laden cattle floats making their way into the Melford auction mart, so that was all right.

That morning in their home on the outskirts of the town, as his mother pulled on his shirt, the sounds and smells were those of early morning, quite distinct and sharp in their nature and composition as the sun rose to its slow morning heat. He jumped up and down on his rumpled bed, clamouring in the manner of an insistent puppy, asking of her, "Am I four now, really four years old?"

"Yes, young fellermelad, you're all that, and a right wee man with it! Yammer, yammer – that's you!"

His mother laughed, from a sudden well of shared happiness.

Well satisfied and entered into the actual day and importance of being four years old, Fraser looked for his newly acquainted and nearby friend Hedley

Dunn. The warmth of that May morning enriched the details of their tiny picture, and for a substantial time afterwards, particularly when viewed through the concentrating lens of memory. Two small figures in corduroy shorts, squatting on the tussocks lining a dusty lane.

Both were awaiting predictable developments of the morning, the most interesting one being the appearance along the curving lane of Mr Middleton and his milk float. Mr Middleton was a daily happening not to be missed. He sold milk by the pint and half-pint dipper from churns, all the way into and out of town from his dairy holding south of the main LMS railway line.

"It's really a good thing that we know when it's his morning time, isn't it, Hedley?"

Hedley's answer to this was to quote a useful authority:

"Prob'ly, but my father says the real brains of Mr Middleton's milk round are in that horse's backside."

"What eckzackly does that mean? Your father? I mean, no – the horse?"

Horse or man, the milk delivery routine was varied only on Sundays, when a slightly earlier delivery time ensured that his horse and trap would not delay churchgoing customers. Charlie, a big bay gelding, was always between the shafts, there were always four ten-gallon churns in the well of the trap, each with assorted quart, pint and half-pint dippers clunking inside its rim, and Mr Middleton always wore cord breeches with polished leather leggings, a long brown stockman's coat, and a somewhat grease-blackened cloth cap. He would solemnly pass command of Charlie to Fraser by handing over the reins, slippery with leather soap and milk splashes, and point him forward to stand amongst the dribbles and pools of cloudy water on the ribbed wooden floor of the float, with his nose to the curlicued iron rail on the gaily painted curved dashboard. Hedley preferred to walk beside the ever-tolerant Charlie and the high black and yellow-painted wheels. In motion, when going from stop to stop, they flickered in the sunlight, and even on dull days, it seemed to Fraser that they spun their spokes in reverse, if you looked at them in a certain way with half-shut eyes.

"Hey, Hedley, look at them like this!"

"Come on now, young man, get up to the front and tek' up them reins." Mr Middleton was kindly, but his tone brooked no delay in getting on with the morning's round, if that's what this young lad was so intent on doing.

Fraser mimicked Mr Middleton's throaty grunt to Charlie, to which the gelding twitched back an ear and one non-committal hoof but stood still, undeceived. Twenty yards further along the lane, walking on quickly with his back to the boys, Charlie and trap, Mr Middleton slapped his leg in the greasy

12

brown coat and gave a nod to one side, and Charlie at once walked on, one ear looking to his master, one ear cocked back to the small figure with the reins.

Accepted between them was Fraser's need to be physically involved with the whole business of horse, harness and milk, while Hedley's contentment lay with solemn observation, with due consideration of options.

That morning in May, they pursued their customary conversations about the dispensation of milk, small change and pleasantries by Mr Middleton, had run the roadside gravel through their fists, and had indulged in rambling, half-comic song of loosely narrative nature, to round off that part of the day's activities.

"Just nonsense songs," Hedley's mother called them, amused and entertained by their unpredictable content. The songs had no neat scan, but easy scope. Their companionship pleased her.

Having fulfilled serious partnership with Mr Middleton, having noted the blazers and tunics converging on the railings of the Girls High School across the rough water meadow, the two small figures were set to explore the satisfactions of another day of comfortable certainty and expectation in the English Midlands, in that early summer of 1933.

At this time of a summer's morning, their respective fathers' preoccupations were of an interesting mix. Hedley's father, Tom Dunn, was Town Clerk of the county town, while Fraser's father had been appointed county veterinary officer the previous year.

The two families were part of a small neighbourly enclave, more of the country than the town, which lay off a little-used farm lane overlooking flower-hazed meadows flanking the river. The lane wound past the large gardens of the houses so placed, and through a gate, to disappear into an undisturbed thicket of hawthorn, damson and blackthorn bushes which offered concealment to small boys and cattle alike. At four years old, Fraser had already got to know the embowered ways in and out of this little-known bit of rough pasture very well indeed.

The Dunns and the Bairds, both families being incomers from harder north country backgrounds, were close neighbours. Although Tom and Marjorie Dunn had come from no farther than Yorkshire, they shared with the Baird family come from much farther north, in Aberdeenshire, the cheerful recognition that on the face of it, life in the English Midlands was far more comfortably secure and socially active than anywhere much north of Newcastle. Alec Baird's keen professional interest in the factors promoting tuberculosis in cattle and human populations, together with publication of some of his findings on the matter, had more or less presented him as being the best person qualified to tackle this pressing health problem. As the County Council woke up to the urgent need to deal with this all-too-prevalent and insidious disease in dairy herds throughout the county, they had cast around for the right man to tackle it. A local Member of Parliament, alive to this health issue in farming and familiar with the background of sound Scottish farming practice, had brought the name of Alec Baird, Fraser and Jean's father, to the attention of the right ears. But playing around the knees of his father's friends and colleagues, and listening, as they all discussed his appointment not long before the move, Fraser had needed some basic things sorted out to his satisfaction, too.

"Daddy, are cows in England different from other cows that live on farms up here?"

"No, but they often get certain infections which they can pass on to the people, men and women, and their children like you two, who look after them on the farm, and then pass it on to more cows or calves. And on to pigs as well."

Fraser looked at his father steadily.

"Mummy, I think that Daddy looks tired. Is he going to have to work really hard down there?" Fraser turned to his father once again. "So, are you and us going to go down there to make them better, and do things to stop the 'fection?"

"Well, not that easily, but there's going to be a lot of very hard work, and I shall need you to help when I, when you and I, that is, go to farms to do tests."

Fraser felt only slightly mollified by this prospect of a working partnership at this Melford place, whatever it might turn out to be, and to immediately get on with the business of going with his father to these farms which apparently needed his help. Right, he would be ready as soon as they got this moving business out of the way.

III

C lose to teatime, and pushing open the door into the kitchen of their new home just outside the town of Melford, Alec Baird's ill-tempered expressions of frustration became familiar to Fraser and his mother, afternoon teatime usually being when they came together. Fraser was not yet at the primary school across the field, and his sister was frequently with school friends at their homes, or on her own way home, once released from the school gates.

"These damned small farmers down here are their own worst enemy; some of their byres or cowsheds are absolutely appalling, unbloodygodly, I can tell you. Try to speak to them about simple things like washing their blasted hands, or cleaning the muck off the udders!" Fraser's father gave an explosive, sardonic laugh and went on, "Going into these places, Mary, there are times when I don't know where the blazes to start, by God."

Mary Baird cocked an anxious eye at Fraser, never far away when his father came home, at the same time making a pursed mouth at her husband's free use of what she called "some choice terms". Fraser was not unfamiliar with most of them; it was how a grown-up used them that was interesting: "unbloodygodly". Now, that sounded a really useful expression of practical worth. Fraser went upstairs to the bathroom, stood in front of his father's shaving mirror, and tried it, with suitably growly voice, a few times. There had to be an occasion to use it. He would try to have it ready. It would make his father laugh, and that was always a good thing. He would tell his friend Hedley about it in the morning. Ha! Unbloodygodly!

The move hadn't turned out too bad or difficult to accommodate, Fraser felt. True, both he and Hedley Dunn, with only the width of a well-tended garden separating their daily friendship (the Dunns actually employed a gardener, Mr Bristol, who Fraser found to be an unusual and intriguing quantity, particularly having shown him, Fraser, his tattoos), lost their respective fathers in the mornings: one to agenda and Local Orders within the Town Hall chambers, court meetings and pragmatic fulfilment of legality, the other to farms and cowsheds, markets and slaughter-houses of a largely pastoral district which had changed little since the adoption of more productive farming practices of the mid eighteen-hundreds.

The lane with its fields and comfortable homes was Fraser's province, with intermittent and absorbing glimpses of the farming and veterinary matters which made up his father's day once away in his car after breakfast. In the August that followed Fraser's fourth birthday, however, listening to his parents' discussions above him as he held amicable conversation with Argo the retriever, Fraser and his friend Hedley became aware of formal education as an imminent reality. This "Going to school" business sounded like an ominous and threatening quantity. School, it seemed, was something that was actually going to happen soon.

Brant Hall lay across the water meadows from Fraser's home, its Georgian elevations in pale, elegant tranquillity amongst the beech trees, lawns and gravelled walks surrounding it. Fraser's mother had taken him for an introductory visit, "to get him used to the idea". So far as he, Fraser Baird, was concerned, "the idea" was already firmly rejected.

"Come along, don't hang back like that, Fraser. You'll have to meet Miss Wheeler anyway. She probably has umpteen things which will interest you. Don't you think so?"

Looking down at the object of her one-way conversation, Mary Baird felt amused, but rather more uncertain about how this grafting-on of all that Miss Wheeler stood for in Fraser's darkly suspicious mind would be attended by any measure of success.

"Does she know anything about cows and horses and things?" had been his last question as they set off.

Within Brant Hall's orderly process of education, the first class for new pupils was allowed comparative freedom, in the abundant sunlight of the bay-windowed morning room of the departed Pearce family. Where Colonel Wentworth Pearce, DSO, MC, had been wont to stand, lean in breeches and glittering gaiters, contemplating elegant trees planted by his forebears, the view, and the number of male Pearces killed in Afghan, African and Boer campaigns and the 1914–1918 War, there was now a low play and modelling table for those who would be brought together as a group by Miss Wheeler. She prided herself as being competent in divining the nature of each and every one of these children as they entered into "her" school. And then moulding them to her own gentle, but inescapable vision of how these very young persons should behave, and grow up.

Fraser's disparaging eye perceived in an instant that the be-smocked children babbling amongst themselves, and moving a set of miniature farm animals about, had no idea of how proper farming should be conducted. With a brusqueness to demonstrate that he knew how things should be, and to take charge of the purposeless situation, he did just that. This was just like seeing how his father absorbed every visible detail in all of the farmyards that they drove into, even before he got out of the car.

"These are the milking cows. They'd have been milked by now, so they have to go out, and they all go together, into this field. Here, give me that gate, that's better."

The seemingly identical children already in bonds of coteries unknown and unheeded by Fraser, fell back in silent, thumb-sucking regard as he established order and meaning.

"Where's the cowman? He feeds the calves after milking time. He does the bull, too. But they have to be inside. My father knows all of the farmers. I go round with him a lot, really. No, don't put that there. Let me put it straight. The sheep shouldn't be on the road; the milk lorry's coming quite soon, so they'll have to be moved. Where's the farmer's dog – that's his job?"

Totally absorbed, he did not perceive the steady regard of Miss Wheeler, to whom the other children were now looking in expectation of admonishment for "bossiness", or "not sharing". She stood with Fraser's evidently discomfited mother, in quiet appraisal of a clearly determined small boy who knew very well what he was doing. His companion, the Dunn boy, Hedley, she reflected, looked for all the world like a King's Counsel in mannikin form, nodding in grave approval as his client pleaded his case. Noting Fraser's dogged progress towards completion of his farmyard arrangement, Miss Wheeler further decided that the notion of young Fraser Baird doing anything remotely like pleading his own case was highly unlikely. She was about to say something to him of her own wishes, but paused. She could clearly see that here was a quantity, a will, which might well present her with the need for thought, in the way of her teaching day, if not a certain readjustment.

Following closely behind all that he had gathered from grown-ups about how going to school had to be suffered, Fraser had hoped that this surprisingly liberal regime would continue the following morning, but his father had grasped his hand with firmness and alacrity immediately after breakfast.

"You'll be all right then, squire? There'll be any number of new things to see and do today, just as fine as coming out with me, or Mr Middleton's milk float, or whatever! Come on, I'll see you across to the gate."

Fraser tolerated about rather more than an hour and a half of the first period that morning before he decided that this was a good time to quietly leave. He had exhausted the rather meagre possibilities on offer from Miss Wheeler of practical, interesting things to be looked into. Fraser had looked across at his friend Hedley, who was paying more attention to the teacher. No, this was just a private concern of his own. And there was all this pulling and tugging and being turned around first thing in the morning in the cloakroom by the old woman whose breath smelled strongly of peppermints as she grasped one foot after another for jerky manipulation of her gleaming buttonhook, or even more impatient attempts to tie small laces, and her systematic encasement of each compliant body and face in a small green apron which she tugged and tied at the back.

"I shouldn't be having to do this for all of you, you know, with my tired old hands as they are!"

Fraser felt that such a degree of invasion of his independence, every morning by the looks of things, was not necessary. For one thing, he could tie his shoelaces himself. With one last jerk, Miss Wheeler spun him round, in ill temper. Fraser looked at the network of small, angry veins which threaded mostly all of her face; her nose was spectacularly so inflamed. She had the same sort of sweetish smell as his mother and father's drinks cabinet in the sitting room. Where the various bottles jostled together, Fraser knew, there were sticky rings on the metal tray; their smell was just like this old woman – maybe she kept her bottles in a cupboard like that, too.

What was this Miss Wheeler saying now? "Children, we're going to have some jolly good games in a moment – we'll need to be in two teams."

This teams nonsense was pointless and unnecessary. That was quite enough. Fraser quietly faded his presence to insignificance at the back of the class, shuffling backwards until round the angle of the cloakroom recess. He hung the silly apron thing on a hook, any hook, never mind this names business.

With quiet intention, he swung open the heavy door which led to a cobbled yard, with coach-houses and stables, stilled in their desuetude of many years. The latch was difficult to open without a pronounced hard clack. He had looked at it carefully before, and tried it. He knew that once behind the garden's beech hedge he was out of sight from the front of Brant Hall and its schoolrooms. The milk cows' meadow beside the river looked friendly and inviting, as always.

A red roan Shorthorn cow with ridged horns tore off some coarse timothy grass, swinging her head up as the small figure in flannel shorts and dark jersey appeared; she had seen and heard him many times before, and grazed on uninterestedly, stamping sideways at flies on her udder. Fraser slouched along close to the outermost cattle, hands in his pockets, singing and talking to himself, and considering concealment once he achieved the gap made by himself and Hedley in the elm and hawthorn hedge of his parents' garden. It was, he knew, overlooked from upstairs windows. His final place of concealment in the roomy kennel of Sam, his father's Staffordshire bull terrier, and unusually at home on this day, was an act of inspiration and strategy.

Discovery was precluded by rapidly deciding to come out, with an abundance of small pieces of broken straw all through his clothes, in particular the V-necked jumper bought specially by his mother for starting at school, as soon as Fraser heard the sound of his father's car swinging in from the lane through the gates. His parents' heated exchange was carried out above him, as he stood between them, with his father's hand heavy and warm on his head and neck. His mother was distraught, angry, taking repeated puffs from her cigarette, and pointing jerkily with it at the school gates.

"Not a word from that woman, nothing seen of him for goodness knows how long before they rang across here. Heaven knows, I was at my wits' end where to look. That damned teacher never thought to come here herself; she just sent yon stupid old Mrs Something-or-other, bobbing and curtseying like a daft thing before I could get a word out of her, Alec."

In his mother's high temper and rage, there were tears close, too, Fraser knew without looking up.

"Well, does it really matter all that much now, anyway? He must have been quite badly put about with himself to do what he did, Mary."

"Right, so now that he's home again, or rather within our sight, just how do you propose to handle this episode, this defiance of his, hmm? For that's really what it boils down to, Alec, just straight out, downright typical defiance." She looked round wildly, searching for a measure of her worry and distress, with tears wet on her cheeks. "Your son is just another obstinate wee Baird, so he is!"

With no discernible movement of his most serious face, his father slid one non-committal eye down towards Fraser, who, by identical process, rolled one anxious eye imperceptibly upwards, neither wishing to be detected as not giving the most serious of attention to the raging figure confronting them. With the faintest quiver of his moustache, Alec Baird started to say something, thought better of it, and after a grunted "Ach, well," spoke in the sternest of manner:

"Listen to me, young Fraser, d'you hear? Do exactly as your mother tells you, this very instant. Go inside, get cleaned up and come back out here to me, but before you go, stand here and say that you're very sorry for all the trouble that you've caused. Go on!"

I Like to Walk in This Field

The effect of his statement of contrition was somewhat spoiled by Sam the bull terrier's perception that a trip to some farm or other was in the offing, from his master's slightest inclination to the car and other bodily signs, and Fraser's "Yes, Daddy, I'm sorry," was cut off by impartial slobbering and grinning at the level of Fraser's straw-speckled new pullover, and then Sam's strong nudging of man and boy towards the car.

"Right, in you go, and get cleaned up. You can come with me to the Brassingtons' place. There's a job there that'll just fit in fine; I need to check the new heifers there. If you are quiet and do exactly as I say, you can come along with me, right? But firstly, you and I shall go across and have you apologise in person to Miss Wheeler."

Fraser made a dark face of embarrassment and irritation at his sister, as she turned in from the gates for a hurried dinner time meal.

Her "What's he done now?" was not clearly answered.

"Oh, for that, you'ld better ask his father!" Jean's mother snapped out curtly, flouncing back into the house, head up and very angry.

The episode of rejection of school had ended, conceding victory to no one. Formal education had plainly got off to a bad start, but there was the acceptable escape, offered by his father, to the outer, sensible world of farmers and farming that had some meaning and purpose to it. That prospect, so far as Fraser could judge, was one that would always be there. This school business that everyone went on about would have to be fitted in somewhere. It might not last for as long as people said that it would.

IV

This moving of himself, his older sister Jean and his parents from Aberdeenshire to an unknown place in the English Midlands had been something that Fraser eventually conceded was in the nature of a needful thing for his parents to do, to fulfil his father's appointment as the county veterinary officer, but nonetheless, the actual mechanics of the translocation held interesting elements of, so far as Fraser was involved, not really knowing what things were going to be different from family life in his Scottish river valley home, or indeed, what quantities might turn out to be much the same.

But one development had most definitely not been foreseen. Fraser very soon realised that, with the move accomplished, his early years with his mother, father and sister in Melford were dogged by a pattern of seasonal, difficult ill health.

Melford was surrounded by the water meadows of two rivers, in the joining of whose gentle waters the town lay, spreading this way and that, largely unchanging for the past many years, and tied to the farming year in its commerce and community. With spring and summer, the ground of the county heated up quickly, being mostly a medium-to-open loam, with odd pockets of gravel overlying sand. The mild winds from Shropshire and the Welsh marches carried a medley of rich, clean scents from hedgerows in whose mediaeval origins seven or more species of one-time woodland trees could be identified amongst the melange of leaf and limb. Hawthorn, chestnut, hazel, field maple, elm, ash... a hundred years of age attached to the presence of each different tree, all added together, gave the approximate life of most hedges. So it said in his little book History in Hedgerows with good illustrations, cherished by Fraser as a birthday gift some time after the family's settling into their life in the Midland county. He knew and had memorised the different leaves and winter twigs before being able to read all of the text. A little later in the spring months, early summer really, another, lighter fragrance from oats or tillering wheat coming into leaf would escape into the lanes winding their way out of Melford.

Hay time in the county was marked by the towering foliage of elm and ash in the field hedges: dusty cascades of leaves suspended over glossy grain crops in a heat which was always humid, although not necessarily overwhelming.

In the summer's warmth, the streets of the town were more likely to have the scents of privet blossom, tulips, lilac and wallflowers, and the smells of the two stock markets, the bakeries and tanning works, rather than acrid discharge of any large industrial processes or exhaust fumes billowing from the busier roads.

Apart from the presence of some withered-looking men wheezing on benches in the square beside the river, their arms rigid and extended to their knees for support, there was little apparent reason for Melford, in summer, let alone at any other time of year, to have a reputation as being "bad for chests".

"Daddy, what's the matter with those men? Can't they go and work or something?"

"No, young man, those poor fellows cannot work; they're soldiers that were badly gassed in the war."

"Oh, I see," Fraser said, but didn't, really. Gassed? He put this unknown quantity carefully aside for exploration at another time.

By late autumn and winter, however, when mists and thick fog thickened and layered out silently from water meadows, the two rivers and canal, it was an entirely different matter. These vapours linked and thickened as the winter afternoon light faded, enshrouding the entire town street by street, rolling out again only to meet cold air currents coming in from the surrounding higher ground, and then settling, dense and implacable, as freezing point came in and dropped still lower, with the dusk thickening to darkness.

Traffic of all kinds was slowed on these days, more so if night temperatures had produced black ice. Practically the only vehicles moving with any care were coalmen's carts and milk and bakers' vans, with pointed frost nails in the shoes of their cobs and vanner horses chipping and squeaking on ice. Hoar frost lay on their manes and heavy rope nosebags. Coming into town from farm visits, Alec Baird could only detect otherwise familiar roads and lanes by drive entrances, by leafless trees stark and mysterious in the rank fog, and an increasing rawness in his nostrils as he approached the centre and north end of town where a handful of factories were located. Hard by these lay the county prison, its three storeys pale and silent in the fog.

On such days, farmers stayed at home, busying themselves and their men in dusty barns and grain stores. A few working prisoners would attempt unplanned escape into silent and freezing, unfamiliar countryside, and Fraser Baird knew that he would predictably be gripped by rasping bronchitis and asthma before midday.

Dr McKay had visited, examined, consulted and prescribed so many times for this reason that it became something of a tired and wry exchange between

22

all involved with each episode. A tall, lean, rather peremptory person, he would enter the house by the front door after the briefest of flicks to the knocker, and be halfway into Fraser's bedroom, stooping, rapidly searching for respiratory rales with stethoscope in nicotine-stained fingers, by the time that it took Mary Baird to run upstairs.

"Taken to your bed again, young man? I thought you were always out digging, or helping your father, or something. Breathe deeply, again."

"We try everything possible, doctor, to prevent these bouts. But he always ends up like this, whether it's going from heat to cold or vice versa. And will he ever cover himself up? You'll have to be the one to tell him that, doctor!"

In addition to a breathless, meaningless jollity irritating to both physician and patient alike, there was always a detectable disclaimer of further responsibility in his mother's outbursts, just as there was a more than faint acerbity in the doctor's response between rapid, repeated placings of his stethoscope.

"Open mouth, breathe normally. Cough. Hmm. I think that we've established – well, I certainly have – that the bronchitis and repeated respiratory episodes he's had – that's it, as deeply as you can – undoubtedly set the scene for all this, when you moved down from the clear cold air of Aberdeenshire to the murky, mucky days down here. No air movement, you know. Breathe deeply once more, young man. All right, cover up now."

Dr McKay was already in movement towards the bedroom door and landing.

"Is there anything in the Melford air, doctor, or do we just have to thole all this, time after time?"

Normally, his mother would use these Scots terms and then, for the benefit of the unknowing, heavily underline them with lengthy explanations; it was a form of patronisation which Fraser recognised immediately and with each and any such occasion, squirmed inwardly in embarrassment. Why did she have to do it? But their doctor was an Ayrshire man and understood these words. And his mother.

Still stooping, he swung his case behind his back and considered the polish of his black Derby shoes.

"I believe that if you were to get away from here, outside the town, about five or six miles at least, or more, up where there's more air movement in the winter months especially, this would help him, or at least reduce the frequency of the attacks. Talk it over with your canny veterinary husband, Alec. He may grow out of it, but it does create a lot of strain. And that affects growth, too, y'know."

He handed Fraser's mother a prescription in a rapid interplay of hands, silver fountain pen, pad, case and coat, and left while giving out curt injunctions about spitting up phlegm and not going outside. Mary Baird went back upstairs, looking at but not reading the spidery notation for cocillana compound and adrenaline inhalant solution. Fraser was twisted round on one hip, supported on an arm extended in front of him, the skin over collarbones and throat flicking deeply inwards and holding there with each wheezing inspiration.

"I'll have to discuss this with your father, otherwise you're going to be in bed all winter, every winter, my lad!"

To make up for the censure and severity of this observation, Fraser would then be asked (predictably, he knew), if there was anything in particular that he wanted to read, or eat, before his mother returned downstairs. The day would then crawl past, punctuated by occasional sounds from the lane or fields outside his window. He was usually too desperately hard-up for breath to get up out of bed to see what any of the farm men might be doing; even a very few minutes of such harmless interest (and getting cold), as he now very well knew, would only serve to extend the long, laboured night hours into a torture of time that should have slipped past in sleep. Many times, as his eyelids drooped and closed, he found on wakening in the stilled house that he was propped up in exactly the same upright position that he had adopted as the day had demanded some hours before.

V

As the matter of daily schooling grew to be accepted, even tolerated, or sometimes found to be quite interesting, with something new to read, for example, Fraser was made just as welcome and accepted in his friend Hedley's home after school as he was in his own. There was a continual exchange of ideas, speculative pursuit of matters as yet unexplained and a degree of more than just juvenile humour. A lot of their activities were shared, and individual wants quite comfortably fitted in. The unused grazing between the Dunns' large garden and the grounds of Brant Hall bore evidence to their enquiring minds and feet, with narrow tracks into the stands of giant hogweed, cow parsley, clumps of dog roses and overgrown elderberry. There they sat on or sprawled around tufts of stemmy cocksfoot, reviewing matters present or intended. In this, the two boys were frequently accompanied by Argo, the Bairds' Labrador retriever. Sam, stout-bodied Staffordshire bull terrier, nearly always went off in the car with Fraser's father, rolling a malicious eye from the open car window at farm dogs to fight or bitches to subdue. To the boys' retreat below the hedge came the sounds of the town behind and the farm land before them, gentled by willows, poplars and majestic elms. For all this companionship along ditches, hedges and farm tracks, there were few days on which Fraser did not manage to go with his father, in the late afternoon, or after tea, to some farm or other, as "his father's little shadder", as one amused farmer put it. Whatever the matter in hand, Fraser unconsciously assumed the same deep absorption as the men around him, within farm buildings or out from them, according to season. Where he was unsure as to the direction of their talk, careful and silent attention at their elbows usually provided an answer.

In this way, watching dairy cows downed with milk fever after calving, his father's calm assessment of some demanding situation, or holding the box that contained the impedimenta for tuberculin testing, and drawing his fingers back from calves' rasping tongues while milk samples were being taken from their dams, Fraser observed and noted the rhythms of bulling, calving, milking and breeding again, and all of the endless feeding and mucking out that had to be carried out with dairy cows, come health or illness, high summer or winter's cold clench of the land.

25

I Like to Walk in This Field

Fraser could see that farming engaged the countryside to ordered effect, and he began to feel a comfortable and confident familiarity with seasonal smells and fragrances, subtle variations in the texture of elm, ash, beech and hawthorn, even knowing the different sounds of their foliage in the winds of spring, summer and autumn. Coupled with this awareness came an accuracy of feeling for the strength and quality of sunlight at certain times of day. Farming was to be his whole life, Fraser determined. This decision did not demand any sustained effort of thought or doubt, and was thus already firmly established in his mind's review of things; it was a part of himself, Fraser Baird. No question about it; how tiresome these grown-ups could be, with their stooping and looming over him with their fatuous questions: "And what are you going to be when you grow up, young man?"

He could tell from the simpering, mock-concerned expression on their face exactly what they were going to come out with.

Thus it seemed to Fraser that from the very morning of having established the solid achievement of being four years old, and daily partnership with Hedley, life continued to present an expanding potential that he could never entirely harvest in the days available. He became increasingly familiar with all that went on at the many farms where he could see that his father was a well-liked and respected person of some authority, at all levels of country and county society. From about nine years old or so, and surviving some fractious passages at school ("Daddy, I told the teacher that the bit we had to read about how fields were made was all wrong"), Fraser satisfied himself as able to conduct an entirely sensible and practical conversation with many of his father's farmers, and their farm workers, while they stood in a cobwebbed cowshed, awaiting the outcome of his father's examination, or as they walked over a field to view some part of a herd, or to look at a single animal. It was all intensely absorbing. With frequent recourse to a rather well-thumbed copy of British Breeds of Livestock on his father's desk, Fraser knew he could recognise the features of most breeds of cattle: Shorthorn, Hereford, Red Poll, Jersey, Blue Albion, Friesian, Ayrshire, even some Longhorns, and thus come to be able to identify them fairly closely as occasions arose.

On a late afternoon in the autumn of 1938 Fraser went along with his father on a round of three herd visits, in that area of smallish family farms which lay to the west of Melford. They were all dairy places, under contract to the United Dairies creamery to put a certain number of ten-gallon milk cans on their respective roadside stands for the milk lorry to uplift, or on to the local railway station platform, every single morning, for every day of the year.

Fraser walked carefully just a pace behind his father and Mr Hopton of Tanners Copse Farm as they set off across the yard, set with blue-glazed engineering bricks to run off the dung and washings from the cobbles and flags of cowsheds, milkhouse and stable. That's funny, Fraser muttered inside his mind, Mr Hopton takes much shorter steps than my father, but seems to go a lot quicker.

He tried this different step himself, getting completely mixed up with his feet in wellingtons. "You'm all buggered up," was what some of the farm men he knew would say. Fraser snorted with sudden laughter, and his father turned half-round, curious, but said nothing.

They were going to look at the milking herd, and the home-bred replacement heifers. A dozen or so of the latter were needed every year, so Mr Hopton was saying to his father, as replacements after calving mishaps, old age or barrenness in the herd of forty-odd milkers. On these expeditions Fraser was now well aware of, and curious about, his father's interest in checking to see the level of general health and condition before he made the first test for evidence of tuberculosis in the herd.

"Well then, Stanley, and how did the harvest make out this season?"

"Ooh, good enough, Mr Baird, good enough! We'd ploughed in that owd cow pasture at back o' Little Henry's, an' a danged good do that were, an' all. Them owd cows 'as just milked perfeck on that extra bit o' feed, an' a twist of 'ay. Very satisfactory, h'indeed, Ah'll say."

Stanley Hopton limped slightly off his left leg, the consequence of a carting accident with a skittish mare, and a poor job of setting by an inept doctor. His left boot and leather legging always squeaked a little with each pivoting turn of the splayed ankle and foot. Fraser watched silently as Stanley Hopton halted, gazing intently at his beasts from below a tugged-down cap brim, thumbs with black-rimmed nails hooked into the old shiny waistcoat below his brown milking coat. He had that look about him, particularly his eyes, sliding apparently guilelessly sideways, that signalled to Fraser that this Mr Hopton was going to try out the depth of his father's knowledge about something, something about these heifers that both men were solemnly regarding.

Perhaps if I look at each one carefully, without Daddy and Mr Hopton noticing, Fraser thought, I'll spot something myself.

He stuck his hands in his trouser pockets, like Mr Hopton, and tried to look knowing. It would have been even better if he'd had a cap to pull down over his eyes and frown darkly. His father was speaking, carefully.

"Certainly these ladies look to be in tremendous order, Stanley. Any poor doers would really stand out. You could carry another half-dozen or so on this heavier land, d'you think?"

"Ooh, ah... an' yew an' the boy a-gooin' to 'elp milk 'em, hey?"

A twisted sideways grin, pulled round and down in the direction of father and son. The milking in Stanley Hopton's herd, and hundreds of those like it, was all done by hand, and not all farms could rely upon two or three good, steady hand milkers, twice a day, or be clean with it, either. There was talk at farmers' meetings and livestock markets of this new vacuum milking machine. Lots of cleaning and sterilisation to be done, if you took it on. Manus, it was called, with a little vacuum pump off the electric; a pulsator, they called it.

They turned away to the gate of the heifers' enclosure. Even Fraser's young eye could see that the hedging, gate and posts were all more robust and well maintained here, and he knew that any heifers either had the bull running with them, or were most positively and necessarily separated from him until of a certain age or size. Fraser walked behind the two men a little way into the field, some partridges whirring in sudden flight from their scratching place below the high thorn hedge, lifting and dropping on set wings into the field neighbouring Little Henry's. In that slowly softening November dusk, a cock pheasant cok-cok-upped twice, and flustered up to roost somewhere behind them. Most likely in that bushy old willow with the ivy, thought Fraser, and there would be a cluster of neat white and greyish-black droppings below the branch in the morning. The black and white and some roan heifers, trusting yet fearful, extended muzzles to blow raspy breaths, almost cross-eyed in their curiosity about the three figures in front of them. Jostling and shouldering each other heavily out of place, they stared and snorted.

"Coom on, then, young man... tell us when they'm a-gooin' ter calve, an' all!"

Suppressing a measure of sudden surprise, but with due gravity, Fraser frowned intensely at the beasts. His father stood, silent, watching with his own curiosity contained at this unforeseen opportunity to assess his son's understanding of what were really quite basic and yet adult matters.

Fraser had been in possession of the fact for some time that it took nine months from service to calving. Sows and ewes were different, how much he wasn't certain, yet. Part guess, part intuition, part retention of matters previously seen or heard about calving down in the back-end, his answer sent Stanley Hopton into splutters of amazement.

"Looks to me, Mr Hopton," he said with another scowling, careful look at flanks and little fatness as yet about their undeveloped udders, "looks to me as though they could be about seven months in-calf. I think."

"Well, Ah'll be danged! He's right, an' all – the young bugger! Ah'll be blowed! Wait'll Ah tell the missis: 'seven months in-calf, I think'! 'Ow old is 'e then, Mr Baird?"

Alec smiled and smothered his own snorts of surprise and laughter. "Oh, learning, I would say, Stanley, still learning!"

Both men laughed then, and Stanley clapped the boy about the shoulders, pulling him into the brown coat smelling of calves, milk and meal. Later, in their noisy preoccupation with tying-up, feeding and preparing to set about milking, the Hopton father and sons set in place another colourful and vigorous imprint into Fraser's mind and memory, by stopping to listen and exclaim in great good nature over "the vet's young lad 'ere, knowin' them 'eifers to the month, mark you, to the bloody month! We will 'ave to watch oursen' when 'e's aroun', never mind 'is dad!"

VI

Fraser's experiences on moving on from the small primary place to the big, noisy grammar school had not been good. Things within the regime that now surrounded him, and his good friend Hedley, Fraser found difficult and in some respects, distinctly unpleasant, due in large part to the treatment meted out to him by one of the schoolmasters in particular. The other boys in the class stuck their own name on this master, Mr Sutton-Fleck – "Mutton-Flit". In terms of roving, acid sarcasm, on bad days he went far beyond the bland soubriquet.

Two or three weeks after starting his first new term there in September, with endless entering of his name in registers, classes, teams and school houses (What on earth was the point of all this blooming "house" business? Couldn't anyone manage their school day by themselves without even more meaningless names and labels? he muttered to himself), Fraser felt his hearing floating away from the sound of his form master's voice in the first period after school dinners.

Crikey, Mr Ripley's voice sounds as though he is in an echo chamber or something, Fraser wondered, in a strange detachment, and at the same moment was overwhelmed by unstoppable coughing, which made his head split. Aching, he doubled up over his desk, and as the rigours shook him fiercely, coughing with a strange fluting severity, he put up his hand, supporting his head and neck with the other.

"Please sir, I think that I'll have to go home."

Mr Ripley's "Come out here and let me see you," was innately suspicious at first.

Fraser discovered that the only way he could get up and go forward was to hang on to each of the other boys' desks in front of him in turn. Looking at him, some of them made dramatic play of recoiling in disgust, retching and mouthing low-voiced "Plague! Plague!" in rising clamour.

The school nurse, Nurse Broome, a part-time, lumpy, officious woman, was summoned to the classroom. All the pupils knew that she smoked heavily in the corridor to the games pavilion and whose husband, the coke boiler man, took bets from the staff to the bookmaker in his dinner break. Fraser was accompanied by Nurse Broome to the treatment room and directed to lie or attempt to do so between bouts of coughing, on a high, slippery couch thing. He felt really ill, hot and headachy, and close to vomiting up his midday meal.

His father appeared in the first aid treatment room, bringing with him a waft of outside air, sunlight, and cigarette smoke as well. He took Fraser's wrist with cool, firm fingers. The school nurse uttered a babble of words which amused Fraser, light-headed as he was; he laughed and immediately shook with bizarre whoops of coughing.

"Mrs Broome, did you take his temperature?"

"Of course I did, Mr Baird; one hundred and one point six. He really should be seen at the infirmary. I'll speak to Mr Pullen, the Headmaster–"

"No need, please don't bother; he's going home with me. Right, can you make it to the car? Here, hold on to me. I've spoken with Doctor McKay, Mrs Broome. He's coming over in minutes."

By mid-afternoon Fraser, worn out with unstoppable bouts of coughing and gasping, regarded Dr McKay dully, registering the latter's statement that "...your young lad here, he's almost certainly got whooping cough, and it's been incubating for some days. This is the worst phase, but his resistance to other infections will be low for some months, I'm afraid. So, and listen to me, Fraser: no getting over-tired, no getting chilled or attempting things beyond your strength. And – rejoicings, no doubt – no school for at least three to four weeks."

Fraser swung his eyes to his father and mother. His father's expression "unbloodygodly", popped into his disordered mind and he laughed weakly, but was overtaken at once with compulsive coughing. No one would know what had amused him, he could hardly remember what it had been himself.

"Here you are, Alec, prescriptions; anti-tussive, sedative to let him get some sleep, day or night, definitely no sudden changes in temperature. He should start to build up some antibodies in about ten days or so, but secondaries are the danger; you don't need me to tell you that, Alec. Bordetella pertussis, remember it? I've prescribed sulphadimidine tablets, M.& B.639, to combat that possibility."

Fraser was surprised to feel Dr McKay's fingers on his shoulder, suddenly compassionate and with concern in his eyes.

"Now, young man, you're taking a bit of a battering. If you must cough, try lying on your side and letting this rotten sort of rasping hoot just slide out of you. Don't fight it. What do you like doing best – going out with your father? Well..." – he glanced at Fraser's father – "...once you're on the mend

31

and when he's in the byre or cowshed, you just sit tight, and mind the car, right?"

The whooping cough hung fire for only a few days, but then progressed inexorably into acute bronchitis and bad broncho-spasm along with it. I feel like a prisoner inside a body that has tight bands round it, Fraser thought, hunched up in blankets beside the kitchen range. Visits from Hedley at a sort of stage-managed careful distance, with repeated injunctions about "immunity" and "contagious", were the only relief from his mother's severity of watch: "What are you getting up for now?" or, "Can you not find something else to read without going through the whole house?"

To satisfy his mother, Fraser turned to Cherry Kearton's British Birds, a ponderous volume, but the illustrations were all in faded sepia, and his energy level faded rapidly. He curled up in the old sagging armchair at the kitchen fire, slipping into sleep at what, for him, was a most improbable time of day. Given normal steady health, that is. He missed getting outside to work.

It was well over a month before Fraser felt that going back to school could be handled. Dr McKay extended that for another ten days. By the time that he had picked up the timetable of subjects, feeling very strange indeed, Fraser saw that a vast and distant plain extended before him of unknown quantities, in maths in particular, which, seen from his isolated position of not knowing how to attempt them, left him feeling choked with frustration.

Due to the sarcasm and baiting of the tart-tongued Mr Sutton-Fleck, Fraser found this rock of mathematical impotence to be a barrier to him for years, this teacher being not only of polished algebraic paradigm, but of acid malice towards those pupils who did not instantly comprehend and apply his equations and theorems. Sutton-Fleck honed this weapon upon Fraser from the day of his return to classes.

"Ah, boys, our primitive from wild Caledonia has graced us with his lowering brow. Baird, are you now well?"

"Yes, sir, I hope so, sir."

"Can we therefore hope that you will join us in elucidation of some quite simple, nay, primitive – ha! that should suit you – steps in elementary algebra, for example? Good."

Some of the other boys had confided in Fraser, before this maths lesson, that they did not only bandy around the usual soubriquet in respect of the master. With wild fearful eyes, they told Fraser there were some who were so scarred by his attacks they now called him "Mutton-Shit". As the bell rang to go in, there had been an undercurrent of tension, even fear.

32

Sutton-Fleck at once took the class into matters totally beyond Fraser's understanding. When problems to be solved for homework were finally chalked up, Fraser felt waves of sullen, silent resentment within himself.

"Please sir, I don't know how to do these problems."

"But Baird, we've all followed my lucid steps; even the most simple amongst us have grasped the necessary principles, haven't you, boys?"

There was a muted chorus of "Yes, sir!" from rows of faces, knowing and fearful of the inescapable degradation from this most hated of persons, unavoidable in each day's lessons.

"Ah, Baird, do tell me, no, do tell us, what your problem is concerning my problems. Come on, stand up, Baird!"

"Sir, I've been off for nearly two months. Everyone else is way in front of me. I need–"

The master held up his hand.

"Ah, Baird, what you're really trying to say – isn't he, boys? – is that you, our dour Scotchman, is really incapable of applying your strange, Scotch brain to really quite simple matters of basic logic and so on. Sit down, Baird. Ah, boys, we have a difficulty here, but we mustn't let it or rather him, hold us back, must we?"

It took countless miserable hours of mental and dogged stamina for Fraser to achieve, mainly with his mother's help, some small degree of success in prying open only a very narrow path of understanding. Algebra was a pointless pathway into purgatory.

On Monday mornings, Fraser knew that he would be the focus of Sutton-Fleck's biting sarcasm because he had been mentally exhausted after a weekend of attempting to solve many of the infuriating set problems. What was the point in them, anyway?

In the spring, pale sunlight stretching the afternoon, Fraser waited for the local bus home, freed from school and the implacable misery of maths for another day. Ted Parsons, son of a publican whose noisy bar and eating house The Rising Sun lay next to the livestock market, and known as "Piggy Parsnip" in school, came up to Fraser, gazed at him belligerently through pale, almost albino eyelashes (You look just like a weaner pig, complete with bubbles of spittle at your lips, Fraser reflected), snatched off Fraser's school cap, and spun it by the brim on to the top of a cattle float lumbering into the market yard, chanting, "Scotchman, Scotchman, you ain't no fucking swot-man!", rotating a levelled forefinger, nails chewed to their raw quick, level with his close-cropped skull.

Any other boy's weakness was nourishment to Piggy; Fraser had seen umpteen episodes, tears and fists flying and all, but singled out for the Parsons treatment, this afternoon, was a jolt of more than surprise. It was a flag-up for something that demanded taking drastic and final action, now, otherwise there would be more of it. Oh, well, Piggy, my lad. Parsnip, Arsenip or whatever the dratted creature's name was, he was sneering at him, Fraser, from only a few hateful inches away.

"Don't they 'ave no fucking numbers an' sums and things wheer you cums from, eh?"

Fraser regarded Parsons dispassionately and with a slow fury. Here it was, that which needed to be done, and he could and would do it. Lots of digging over the big vegetable garden and sawing logs had made him tough and strong again. Carefully setting down his satchel, he turned round, and taking a sudden fistful of Piggy Parsons' blazer, shirt and tie, close up, Fraser punched him really hard, twice, on his nose and mouth. Still keeping a hold, and seeing another cattle float coming out, Fraser whipped off Parsons' school cap, flicking it directly under the rear double wheels as they splashed through a puddle of cattle and pig urine. He then punched Parsons once more, hard, on the side of his head. While he still had control and a grasp on this odious creature, another opportunity occurred to Fraser, causing him to grin savagely.

"Listen, not only do you look like a silly bloody parsnip, but you're as thick and white as one as well." Giving Parsons or Parsnip an enraged shake, Fraser added, "Just don't you ever try that on me again!" and flung him loose, in the way of a stockyard man with his stick.

"That's the way, young 'un; you've larn't him a lesson of sorts! Hold on there, the mart fellers'll have your cap in a jiffy!"

The man grinned at Fraser, as he turned, in flat cap and a stockman's coat, and whistled to one of the men with a fork, pointing upwards. He came back, still grinning.

"'Ere you are, young master, and as fer you!" He applied a swift, flat-booted kick to the bleeding, bawling Parsons. "Goo on, yer blubbin' bully! I knows your old man, and he'll hear of this!"

Suddenly, impossible algebra, unbloodygodly algebra and pointless maths seemed much less of an insuperable burden to Fraser. Seems to me, he cheered his inner resolve as the conductress took his school return ticket, the best thing is to get on and do the things you know you can do, such as punching Piggy Parsons on the nose! The conductress, seeing Fraser grinning fiercely, felt her own lips shaping in amusement, to their mutual surprise, so she winked at him, but not quite knowing herself what all this was about.

There remained the comforting, albeit tenuous, fact that school and maths and Sutton-Fleck couldn't go on forever, that he would make his own way into much more important matters without unbloodygodly algebra.

VII

Some time after Fraser and his father's visit to take a look at Stanley Hopton's young dairy heifers, Alec Baird arranged to make a follow-up call, to go through improving the milk-handling way of things at Tanners Copse Farm, and also to set a date for the herd tuberculosis test. He knew that the possibility of machine milking was being rotated in Stanley Hopton's mind, with great caution.

After all was done, and the afternoon light fading rapidly, there had been a noisily cheerful airing of opinions between all the men in the kitchen, with Mrs Hopton dispensing tea, common sense and good humour in her continuous circuits of the massive scrubbed white kitchen table. Mr Hopton, sucking his tea from his capacious blue and white mug, beckoned Fraser over to him with a hand from within his tattered and stained jacket, the frayed silk linings hanging out beyond the cuffs.

"Now, then, young Fraser 'ere, you'll mind as to them 'eifers as you hit right on the nail as to calving? Well, one of 'em in particular, she put on a bit too much condition, and was the very devil an' all to get calved. Gets too fat inside, you see. Took us some days to get 'er back on 'er pins again. So, you just mind on that when you'm a-runnin' your own place, come time."

Fraser could feel the warmth of Mr Hopton's regard, talking to him man to man, as though he was another farmer.

The misted hollows were frosty as Alec Baird drove home through deep-hedged lanes now quite familiar to Fraser, sitting beside him, watching the headlights probing verges, ditches and well-laid hedges. Fraser was content to remain silent, running the very satisfying events of the late afternoon through his personal mental picture screen again, in detail. Reflecting on his nerve-racking anxiety for some way to figure how long those skittish heifers had been in-calf caused Fraser to grin with an inner delight at getting that bit right, anyway! This was broken into by his father's "Getting a feel for how young beasts like that are managed, are you, Fraser?"

"Well, yes, Daddy, but it's a bit difficult, 'cos each place is different."

"Aye, that's true, but how d'you mean? Different in what way?"

Fraser was entirely happy to elaborate upon what, in his eyes, made each farm that his father drove into, and the farming family therein, different, and vastly interesting. His father broke in again:

"Look, we've a little while before we get home, and seeing that you're obviously getting the hang of this farming business, I want the two of us to take this wee while to bring into your own grasp of things about where you, and I, and my father, your old Grandpa Teatime, and so on, have all sprung from, way up there in what folk down here call 'Bonny Scotland'!"

Fraser's father added the last bit with a sort of semi-sardonic curl to his tongue. They both smiled.

In the warm companionship of the rumbling car, Fraser turned sideways on the leather car seat to regard his father's features more closely, washed with light from occasional car headlamps.

"Daddy, quite a lot of my friends at school keep asking, 'Where do you come from? You're Scotch, aren't you?'"

"So, what do you tell them?"

"Well, I tell them Scotland, of course, and they go on about why do I say they have to pronounce Peter Strachan's name with a proper 'ch' in the middle, instead of that silly Strackan way. But none of them have the faintest idea where Aberdeenshire is, huh!"

His father laughed outright, choking it short with an angry "Get over the blasted road a bit, you idle bugger, damn you!" and pulling the wheel round suddenly. An elderly saloon and equally elderly staring driver deviated only slightly and grudgingly from the middle of the lane, in crepuscular complacency.

"What I mean, Daddy, is where do all my ancestors, where does Grandpa, come from? Where does everyone else in our family come from? Were any of them farmers? Have I ever been there?"

Fraser felt that there was never enough detailed, easy-to-follow conversation about the places and people which must lie behind such sideways snippets as "Your great-grandfather was a master with bringing on good horses" or "Oh, aye, Sandy? He married yon lassie from down in Fife; they were into a place of their own and them only twenty-four or so – tireless workers the two of them". Where were these places, were they all farms, what were they called, had his father been there, or what?

As he was moving all these place- and face-less quantities around in his head, trying to come out with the best way to pick up the continuous thread of connections, his father said, "Look, do you want to go straight home, and we'll have a talk about all this, get your mother on about her family as well, after tea? Some unusual characters on her side too. Or how about going in here for half an hour? I see an old friend's car across there." He jabbed a finger beyond the low eaves of The Dog In Doublet public house, where two or three cars were parked, bumpers to a trough in the stable yard. Looking at them, Fraser was fairly sure that they were all farmers' cars. There was a big, rough-looking Austin Sixteen saloon, a Humber Snipe and a Rover, and a Wolseley saloon.

Alec Baird, his energies suddenly at low ebb, looked across at Fraser. "Well?"

"Well, I'm not really old enough. D'you want me to come in too? I can easily stay in the car, Daddy, if you want me to?"

"No, come on. Dinna be daft, at the age you are, around ten years or eleven or whatever? We'll both just go in the back way, where all the best folk go! Come on, Roger and Joan Boxall will be here at this time of day, and we'll have a bite or something in their sitting-room, right?"

Their two car doors slammed in unison. The Standard saloon looked even more dusty and worn in the yard lights. Fraser wondered why his father, normally so particular about his tools, instruments and things, seldom washed or even polished the car, like other people did. In a way, it was a tool, too, best kept in good nick as all hand tools should be.

It was quite dark, but windows and doors gave out golden light and cheerful voices. Going round the far gable of the inn, they passed below a substantial sandstone archway with rust-thickened hinge-pins set in the masonry, Alec Baird confidently turning left into a stone-flagged passage and immediately knocking on a heavy oak door which had 'TRADE & OFFICE' painted on it. He went straight in.

"Hallo! By God, it's Alec! Come in, come in, and the young man with you? Capital, capital!"

A bustling man's figure in thick socks, breeches and open-necked shirt, Roger Boxall, landlord, almost pulled them into the busy room by the cheerful force of his welcome. Everyone was lively, animated, noisy, a lot of hand-shaking and laughter springing up. Fraser felt himself smiling happily, too. The low-ceilinged room and its occupants were really interesting. The warmth of welcome enfolded everybody within it.

Whatever the title given to the room, Trade, Office, or any other designation for the business of running an inn or public house, it all felt very fine to Fraser, looking around as his father was engrossed with all these other people claiming his attention. Although not large, it really was a sort of sitting room-cum-office with strong evidences of involvement in all kinds of country and farming matters.

A large roll-top desk and typewriter against one wall, below a long window, gaily curtained with hunting scenes, lots of pictures and mounted photographs, a deep, well-used fireplace in smoke-blackened brick, logs burning steadily, shotguns in a glass-fronted cabinet with a large calendar hanging on the brass handle, a brace of mounted pheasants in a case on top of low bookshelves, the hen bird an albino, the cock a handsome melanistic fellow in dark, almost purply green. Fraser felt himself grinning in pleasure at such an abundance of really satisfying surroundings.

Shrinking from appearing over-familiar or forward in his father's eyes, Fraser purposely hung back a pace whilst the circle of people opened up from their comfortable places around the wide hearth. There was, he felt in its enfolding, an immediate ease of friendship, which of a sudden, made his whole spine ripple and then relax. Three smooth-haired terriers of stumpy-tailed curiosity and brown gleaming eyes came running to sniff at his trousers and hands, one placing neat paws on his knee to lick his fingers.

He took his time to look at the many pictures round the entire room: teams of Shire horses at ploughing matches; a man with thick hide mitts, a gleaming billhook and a wide grin laying a dense hawthorn hedge; and another, larger, photograph of the inn at an earlier time, with an immensely long slab-sided charabanc and a happy froth of women wearing over-large hats and men with stiff collars and bushy moustaches. By golly, they all looked so specially dressed up! There was much more, of times past and present.

Roger Boxall, who had welcomed them with such evident pleasure, was one of three men there, and a tall, fair-haired smiling woman in a bright jumper and fawn slacks, who rose and having put an arm round Fraser's father and given him a resounding kiss, laughing, turned and spoke directly to Fraser, hands on her hips.

"Well, what a jolly fine thing to have you two appear; we were just having a bite to eat before the bar gets busy, Alec and – what's your name? – Fraser? Now, that's great. You can tell me what you and your father would like to have. Something to lay the dust, and a sandwich or two? Cold meat and pickles, or a pork pie? Or maybe the whole jolly lot, if I know anything about young men's appetites!" She gave Fraser a capable wink and a sideways nod, smiling in an open companionable way, which made him smile in response.

"Come along. You and I'll put it all together in the kitchen, and you know that I'm Joan, Joan Boxall. That fellow with all the gab is Roger, my wonderful husband."

As he followed her into the kitchen, she paused, holding on to him in the doorway, and snapped a finger at the young man who was listening to what was being discussed between Fraser's father and the third man, standing back to the fire. "Handley! I say, Handley!" She got his attention and demanded he come to her across the room with a forceful toss of her head. "Listen, my lad, there's a party of farmers from Uttoxeter coming in fifteen minutes, remember? No, of course, you don't. Now listen to me. This is Fraser Baird. Say hello to him, then go smartly to the cellar and make sure that you're drawing Mears Ale from that new barrel, and – come HERE, I'm not finished!"

Joan Boxall took Handley's available ear in her fingers and turned his head this way and that, not over-gently, but Handley was grinning and wincing.

"Now, see to the pump, put logs on the fire in the snug and get a fresh platter of cheese and biscuits on the bar, right? Gor, if you only had brains as well as looks, you'ld be my hero! Go on! And it's your stint at the bar!"

Joan Boxall impelled Fraser in front of her, pointed him to an easy chair next the big stove. She whirled round and sought of him, "Right, check with me all those jobs which I just told Hopeless Handley to get on with, before I go batty. One word only, OK? Go on!"

"All right, er, Mrs Boxall–"

"Hey, come on! You and I can do better than that. Joan will be fine."

He started again. "Pump, new barrel, er, Mears, logs, more cheese and biscuits and, don't forget, it's your stint at the bar!"

Joan Boxall folded up with laughter, grinning and wiping her eyes and managed to get out, between giggles, "Oh, me, oh, my! Well, what shall we take through to those fellows through there, clacking like a flock of rooks?"

She swung open the door of the biggest refrigerator Fraser had ever seen, with "Prestcold" on the front, and beckoned him to take a succession of things from her hands. She's a really nice, pretty woman, Fraser decided, wondering how she kept herself so fit and slim; so many other women he had encountered, accompanying his father, were stout, and moved with repeated complaints of joints, knees and other things, faces and features pulled down in permanent registry of pain or protest, groaning about everything, it seemed to him.

His father turned from the other grown-up, who was not a tall man. Thickset, with heavy horn-rimmed glasses, and plus fours in a strong check, he seemed to spread a certain measure of authority about him. Alec Baird motioned Fraser forward amongst them.

"Fraser, shake hands with Doctor Dallas. You were asking where your grandfather, and his father and mother came from. Well, your great-grandfather, that's Grandpa Teatime's father, and Doctor Dallas's grandfather, they both came from the same wee place, hardly a village, Auchrannet, away up in Ross-shire. And likely their fathers before them. Isn't that so, Leslie?"

The smaller quieter man extended a firm warm hand to Fraser, patting the fireside settle beside him.

"So, Fraser Baird, tell me why you're so taken up with where your forefathers came from, and yet, here's you, and myself forbye, away down here in the soft old ways of England, eh? I can tell you all about your father's roots, and you're already another wee shoot growing from that particular family tree."

Fraser was instantly intrigued by the doctor's pronounciation of "growing" as in the "grow" of "growl". Also, by his instant familiarity with his, Fraser's, ancestors.

Joan Boxall came swiftly across to their seats by the fire, set down a laden tray between them all, and then, smiling at Fraser, told him:

"Our Doctor Dallas here likes to talk about people, but most of all about his beautiful Aberdeen Angus cattle. Isn't that so, Doctor? We shuffle along to his surgery when we feel poorly, Fraser, and he just tells us 'You're all as soft as muck!' Anyway, eat up, gentlemen. Here's a shandy for you, Fraser, and our doctor's usual 'afternoon tonic'!"

There was the briefest flicker of a wink from her, and a casual wave to her husband Roger, telephone to his ear, writing at the desk. A terrier bitch came across, and having reassured herself as to the existing dog smell about his person, jumped up and delicately curled herself into Fraser's body and thighs.

"Right, young man, and about what fine age would you be? Ten and a bit, nearly eleven, you say? Well, a verra useful time to be knowing about so many things. Let me get a start. A family is much like a very large, round onion, with ever so many layers, so let's see if we can peel off some of the layers between us, and put names to them, eh?"

As of a sudden illuminating thought, it appeared to Fraser, Doctor Dallas beckoned Joan Boxall over to them, asking her to bring him a fine big onion, as though such a request was entirely normal in any conversation about family matters. On her prompt return, he took the firm onion, regarding it thoughtfully, turning it over as he continued to recall Fraser's antecedents back from obscurity.

"Your grandfather, or Grandpa Teatime as you call him, his own father was Hector Baird, and he came down into Aberdeenshire from Wester Ross about 1853. That's a good bit less than a hundred years ago, and here we are, speaking aboot it..." – (I really enjoy it when he pops in these much better ways of saying a word, Fraser thought, savouring this last one, but keeping very attentive) – "... speaking aboot it as though it was only last month.

"So, here's your grandfather's father, Hector Baird. He started his working life by having to leave the wee village school, scholars all in one room, when he would have been only a year or two older than you, to help his father on a poor-like miserable wretch of a place. The very name of it spelt slavery. Are you bringing these figures of your family forward into your own mind, now, Fraser?" the doctor asked, horn-rimmed spectacles glinting at him in kindly reassuring fashion.

Fraser nodded, not speaking, not wanting to let such men of unknown times and tribulations slip voicelessly back into their long silence again. The doctor took up this family history again.

"So here's Hector, father to your Grandpa Teatime, working with his father on this wee croft up in Ross-shire. Hector's own father, Fraser, had to pay rent for this, this servitude, to a demanding owner or laird, who was half-brother to the Devil, by God. He had his heel hard down on all his tenants, poor as they were."

Absorbed in the doctor's going in reverse back from the present into an inconceivable past, Fraser chewed his sandwiches. The crusty white bread and cold tongue was delicious. Doctor Dallas carried on again, his eyes large behind the heavy glasses.

"Now, you're wondering how, where and so on. Well, let's take a wee look into this fine stout onion. It'll make a'thing clear to both of us, right?"

Doctor Dallas had taken out a well-whetted pocket knife, with a dark horn handle. Very carefully, he cut the onion from crackling crown straight down to the compact root, slightly to one side of centre. Some grains of earth crumbled from the onion's whiskery roots on to his checked plus fours. Even more carefully, he gently pried into prominence the pale green shoot at the very centre of the compact half-onion.

"Here you are, now, Fraser Baird, a family's generations are wholly like the skins of an onion. This fine strong shoot could rightly be yourself, Fraser, as the youngest generation, and the skins round it, each separate skin is a father, a grandfather and a great-grandfather. Now, you show me which layers would be your father, your grandfather and then, your great-grandfather, Hector."

Fraser took the offered knife, and with its tip, pointed in sequence to the three onion skins enclosing his own suddenly important single shoot in the heart. "Man, you've got it right away! Is that not fine!" The doctor sounded so delighted, and Fraser felt himself both very young and yet flushed at being brought forth as an important layer in the structure, the continuity of his family, the Baird family. Now, things began to feel solid! Doctor Dallas settled easily in his chair and carried on in friendly narrative; they were comrades in discovery.

"Your father and I, Fraser, we are of the same layer of family onion skin out from the centre bit, of two separate families or onions, if you like. Now, let's go to the layer outside of your grandfather. Your father and I, we're of much the same age. So, my grandfather was therefore the same layer as your father's grandfather, because your father and I are close in age, right? And, mind, what was your grandfather's own father's name again? Hector, that's right; Hector Baird. So, if you're following me, and you're the layer or centre shoot inside from your father, that makes Hector Baird, from Wester Ross, your great-grandfather. My grandfather was ages with your great-grandfather Hector; they were at the same wee school together."

As of a sudden importance, the doctor held his knife to one side, speaking quietly but seriously to Fraser. "Now, here's a thing you would do well to mind. In some families, just as in the onion that we've shown can represent them, the outer layers of a family may have worked very diligently to build up a fine, solid business, with inheritance assured to the fine young shoot at the heart of it all. For reasons which are never clear at the time, young man, that fine strong shoot at the centre can get into a state of rot and idleness, and wastes away a' the hard work and industry his forebears may have gathered for the future, his future, and the whole family collapses. Can you see that?"

Fraser nodded, quite in accord; he had heard his parents talking about such things, in a mixture of puzzlement and disbelief, even disgust.

"So, Fraser, my lad, as a grown man, just you mind to keep your distance from disasters like that in any family, otherwise you'll get dragged into a gey rotten onion which has a black spot hidden awa' at its centre, and failure follows on as night follows day."

Fraser's father broke away from Roger Boxall, and carrying his glass, Mears Local Ale in it, Fraser guessed, he carried on where Leslie Dallas had paused, with a harsh tone to face and voice which Fraser, startled, had not experienced from him before.

"Aye, your great grandfather Hector had to leave his schooling at only twelve years old, and agree to help his father on the land, with so many days' toil for that greedy brute of a laird they all suffered from up there. My God!"

Fraser turned from one to the other grown man, who stood eyeing each other in silent cognisance of something which, in recall, had marked them both.

"Fraser, we have to be away home damned quickly, but let me tell you some more in this family history of ours, of yours now, seeing that Doctor Dallas here has started. Your great-grandfather, Hector Baird, came down into Aberdeenshire on his own two feet, and took on as an apprentice to the blacksmith at Crookfauld, on the Deveron, and at the same time, taking back into cultivation a badly run-down croft or small farm. He was a devil for work, by all accounts."

"This was Grandpa Teatime's father? Did this Hector Baird then live all of his life up at home, in Aberdeenshire, Daddy?"

Startled and yet pleased in an unforeseen way, Alec Baird reflected that, well, now, here's my own son, Fraser, speaking of his first four years or so before we came down here as "home". Well, I'll be damned! Some imprints really lie deeply, so they do!

Joan Boxall had stopped, standing quietly behind the close group of two men and the boy, listening, watching.

"Fraser, the tragedy was that your Hector, father to Grandpa Teatime, had a woefully short life. At twenty-three, he was killed one dark winter's morning by going up the wrong side of a part-blind Clydesdale gelding, in the stable. The gelding was frightened, apparently knocked him down and killed him with his heavy shod hooves. And your grandfather, Hector's first child along with his wife Grace Moir as she was, was just a wee bairn, weeks old, lying beside his mother, in the drawer out of a chest. That was your Grandpa Teatime's start in life, with his father newly dead, a young widowed mother and damned little else. So, you see, some of the layers in a family onion go on for a lifetime. Others, like your great-grandfather Hector, get cut short."

Alec Baird was clearly disturbed in the telling of it, his eyes were hard, intense. He swirled the last of the ale in his glass, tossed it back and making ready to leave, bumped into Joan Boxall, both of them exclaiming, holding each others' forearms tightly. Her eyes were wide, concerned, tears brimming, caring about both of these Scots men come into their local life from an altogether harsher way of life, almost in a different country, the way they spoke of it.

Doctor Leslie Dallas rose, gripping Fraser by his shoulder.

"Young man, let me add a postscript to your father's story. After your great-grandfather was killed by that brute of a gelding, things did not go easily for your father's family, and neither did they for mine. Parents for both of us made huge sacrifices to give each of us the chance to use our country-bred young brains to the result, Great War or no Great War, that here we are, proud of our achievements. In each of our families, there were deaths and good men getting killed. Those that survived and kept the thread intact, worked a' the hours God sent them." The doctor set down his glass carefully, his eyes on an inner travail. "We all have a story in us and it seldom turns out to be what it looks like at first meeting, eh, Fraser? Take heed of all that your father tells ye. He's a bonny fechter, like me, eh, Alec? And just you mind this, young Fraser: your father and your grandfather have both nourished you to be the fine strong young shoot that you are and will be to your family. Now be on your way, but think back on this wee while's finding out things together, eh? And haste ye back, Fraser!"

Goodbyes were suddenly necessary to everyone, in haste. Roger Boxall came out of the bar, happy of face with all these good friends around him.

"Make haste home, Alec my veterinary friend; you've stayed too long, but I shall telephone Mary, and tell her that you had to see to, ah, to a difficult case with a previous history, right, Joan?" Shaking hands with Fraser, he clapped him on the shoulder, and wheeled back to the hum of the smoky bar. Joan Boxall shook hands likewise with Fraser, putting an arm across his shoulders as they all stood in a group in the warm, cheerful room.

"Come back again Fraser. It's been a pleasure to have you and your father here." Her eyes and smile were initially for him, but extended quickly to his father. There was a warmth, a quickening in her there for him; Fraser could see that. Quite clearly. Just a wee bit flustered, Alec Baird turned to him.

"Right, Fraser, my lad, we've got some explaining to do. Your mother'll be in a right state, no doubt. My God, man, look at the time!"

As Alec Baird reversed the car and then accelerated out of the dusty stable yard of The Dog In Doublet, the two figures in the lamplit doorway waved, both holding their arms upraised in companionship, and then turned away, to attend to their exercise of commerce.

"Daddy, is it mostly farmers who go there, to the Boxalls? A good job that Doctor Dallas was there, wasn't it? I've learnt more today than I've ever heard before about things. Can we have another talk sometime, please?" And then, surprising himself, both of them, with the car's familiar rumbling steady in the night air: "Don't worry, Daddy, I'll tell Mummy how difficult it was for us to get away."

Alec Baird grinned, silently, and put a warm, heavy hand to lie upon his son's knee on the car seat beside him as they made their way homewards.

The Bairds moved out and up onto higher ground in the early spring of 1938, away from Melford's low meadows and rank winter mists, to The Leys, a spacious Victorian family property in ruddy weathered brick, the one-time manager's house to the surrounding Brockwood House estate. There now was undoubtedly plenty of air movement around their new home, which sat on a plateau of farm land within visual reaching-out distance to the rolling outlines of the thickly wooded Chase, where there were three kinds of deer, his father informed Fraser. The hazy obscurity of the county town's spires and smoke now lay over six or seven miles' distance to the north. The old castle, hardly discernible beyond woodland, lay away to their left, or north-west, guarding the way into the town from Shropshire and the Welsh marches.

To Fraser, quietly but hugely excited, the actual day on which they all moved in to The Leys was not at first marked by the right things happening in the right way. To his mind, there seemed to be a feeling of nobody actually getting things moving. After all, wasn't that what a removal was supposed to be all about? Fraser grinned slightly at his own perverse humour. He tugged at his sister's sleeve as they all got out of the car, taking in entirely new surroundings.

"Hey, d'you know what? I don't think these blinking people know we're supposed to be coming to live here. Look at 'em, nothing going on."

The outgoing tenants, Captain Sadleir, RN (ret.), and his wife, seemed to have made no preparations whatsoever until the last day of their occupation. It all became an enormous confusion in the front drive, contents of two removal vans spilling out over lawn and borders. Fraser registered the fact that before she even got out of the car, his mother gave warning that by flashing, accusative eyes, pursed lips and severity of look, fault had already been found and was probably going to be attributed to someone, at any moment. The two parties of removal men mingled, manoeuvred and back-stepped in increasing frustration. Half-draped furniture belonging to both households stood on the lawn, giving the impression, thought Fraser, that tables, chairs and cabinets were silently and disparagingly looking each other up and down in mute but eloquent criticism. The furnishings of both families looked jumbled up, lacking the purpose of their ordinary usefulness.

Captain Sadleir stood on the porch steps, sucking his pipe. He smiled faintly, as though the task of clearing up behind his disorderly tenancy could hardly be any real concern of his.

"Aha! Baird and Mrs. Baird! Morning, morning. Bit of a fray. I think that Rose has got it all sorted out, somewhere. Shouldn't be too long before we can let go fore and aft and pull away."

He smiled genially, making inconsequential jabs with his pipe stem, and had almost to be motioned to one side to let them pass into the clamour inside the house.

Fraser and his sister Jean went to explore upstairs. Their shoes pluffed up little explosions of heavy dust from the underfelts exposed on the treads. Drawn to light flooding through the open door of a bedroom, Fraser went in eagerly, curious about the view over the fields. The scene in the room was completely unexpected and beyond anything in his experience. Afterwards, he knew that he would be able to recall every detail, particularly the smells within that bedroom, improbably held for years in the chemistry of his memory.

Within the large, well-proportioned room, there were three single beds, still made up with bedclothes and quilts. Amongst their pillows and counterpanes lay an indeterminate number of dogs, in watchful silence. On one bed, beside three greyhounds, Mrs Rose Sadleir sat smoking, in a long dressing gown over a jumper and tweed skirt, several strings of pearls and wearing fleece-lined flying boots. She and Fraser looked at each other, carefully, through the coils of cigarette smoke. There were other dogs on other beds. That red dressing gown, Fraser reflected, shows up all those marks and stains very badly indeed.

"Very upsetting, young man, is it not?"

"Upsetting?"

"Yes, these brutes." She flicked an eye sideways and down at the trio of greyhounds. "They don't like it one bit, y'know. Have to sit down here and steady 'em up. Me too, ha!"

Her eyes screwed themselves into amazing puckers which seemed to express different degrees of detached amusement. Cigarette ash was on her dressing gown, her skirt, everywhere. The sunlight withered in the thick smoke. Her cough somehow escaped sideways past the smouldering cigarette without more ash dropping from it.

Fraser counted seven dogs on the soiled, greasy bedclothes. Below the beds, he recognised the spines and covers of familiar magazines in stacked piles: The Field, Picture Post, The London Illustrated News. Bit funny, he thought, about this "steady them up" business. Perhaps there had been a mistake about the actual day. He turned round, went downstairs quietly and outside.

The actual departure of the Sadleirs and their dogs (rather like two tugs towing a jostling of barges, Fraser thought), was only made possible by Alec Baird's determined sending of their own removal men off to the nearest pub with a handful of loose change. He took his wife and Jean down the lane to the farmhouse of the Harris family, and then set off side by side with Fraser for one of the latter's greatest satisfactions, a walk through the fields, any fields, with his father.

"Any idea why Jack Harris hasn't ploughed this lot yet, Fraser?" A subtle test of his son's awareness of important things like this, a recall of his own innate rural inventory at the same age on his parents' farm.

"No, not exactly. Is it something to do with having to lift all these mangolds now, before the ground gets really wet and they get frosted?"

"No, not exactly." (A faint quiver of his father's neat ginger moustache – he couldn't resist the parodying of his son's reply a few seconds previously.) "It's because all these weeds and second growth from the fallen ears of wheat will very likely be eaten off by Jack's ewes, that's why. Big, greedy Masham brutes."

"Hey, Daddy! Look at Argo, he's pointing something! Bet you it's a pheasant. Oh! It's gone. But it was really dark-coloured, Daddy. Is that one of Mr Williams' ones, you know, the ones that Harry Owen reared?"

"No, I doubt it, squire; that's what I told you is called a melanistic mutant. To finish off about the sheep, though, this piece of land, about seven acres, I would guess, is pretty stony, and the main reason that Jack Harris does this is to leave plenty of muck on it once the sheep are off. Stiffens it up a bit. Plough in all the muck and green stuff and drill it before the end of the year, and that helps the next crop. Wheat again, very likely."

"We'll need to do something like that with our place, then, won't we, Daddy?"

"Oh, aye, and I can just see those great muckle Shires of Jack's wheeling round our departed friends the Sadleirs' Brussels sprouts, with the plough behind... and landing up stuck inside a henhouse!" They both burst out laughing at that picture in their minds. "Come on, then, Fraser, me lad. Time to be moving into our place, not standing out here painting ridiculous pictures!"

Coming out of the field, with the comfortable feeling of being already much at home, with things around them that they both fully understood, they found that their own furnishings were now steadily coming out of the bulky removal van, 'Shore Porters Society. Est.1498' on its side panels. The Aberdeen-based van had been on a return trip from the south, and Fraser's father knew and liked them as a known and familiar link with the family's background in Scotland. A fire had been lit in the kitchen range, all Mrs Sadleir's cigarette ends having been cleaned out, and a general inspection could now be made with freedom, with a feeling of some excitement. Even Jean looked a bit more excited, Fraser could see, and about time, for Heaven's sake!

Fraser was told that the bedroom he had discovered earlier, still with echoes of "...have to steady 'em up a bit. Me too, ha!" and with two windows looking out over fields to the north and east, was to be his. It still had three narrow brass beds, abandoned, with bedding, now being dismantled, and all the signs were that this had indeed been the sleeping place for the Sadleirs' dogs. Everything of the room smelled strongly of stale dog, and cigarette smoke. The stacked magazines were still there, lots of them.

The Harrises at the farm had put one of their workers' wives up to give a hand with giving floors a good scrub where necessary; she was so engaged when Fraser walked in eagerly.

"Bin 'aving a good look round the Guv'nor's field with your Dad, then? Yew'll meet my man, Watty. 'E'll keep yew roight – keeps every one of us roight, Ah'll tell yew!"

She burst into a laugh of great proportions, and swilled some more soapy water on to the floor, grinning at Fraser with a sideways nod of her head. At once, Fraser felt thoroughly at ease with this cheery woman. Maybe her man Watty would employ terms like "unbloodygodly".

Outside, the Khaki Campbell and Aylesbury ducks, which Alec Baird had agreed to buy from the Sadleirs, quacked and quapped nervously, heads and necks stretched high in the air and nervous, their black eyes glistening and wary. Their querulous, head-bobbing refusal to enter the long, low poultry house against the north wall was due to the fact that Tim, the Bairds' half-grown collie, more commonly called Tam, had discovered that the duck manure of years inside the shed was riddled with rats' burrows and galleries. A large population of the occupants was in residence at the moment of joyful discovery. Emulating the strategies of his Russian namesake General Timoshenko, as depicted in some of the same magazines that the Sadleirs had left behind, Tim or Tam was ploughing up the warren of holes and pursuing the rats by sheer force of muzzzle and shoulders, sending slabs of caked rat and duck muck flying to all sides as the rats literally ran up the brick and wooden walls. The noise was uproarious. And very cheerful, thought Fraser.

Fraser Baird's recall of that day was forever compounded of beds and quilts, discarded but still smelling of geyhounds, fires being lit in as many rooms as possible, gas lamps flaring cheerfully from wall brackets (they were connected to the Brockwood estate gas plant), and the turmoil of dogs, ducks and rats in the gathering darkness.

The scratch high tea-cum-supper was a noisy and cheerful affair. One of the removal men came from Edinburgh, and he chatted pleasantly of things and places familiar to Fraser's parents as he unpacked tea chests and boxes. Their new farmer neighbour, Jack Harris, wheeled into the yard in a large trap piled high with sawn logs. A can of milk dangled from his hand as he stepped heavily down from the rear of the horse-drawn trap. Tying the reins in a loose loop on the hames of the horse's collar, he enjoined her with a loud "Hey hup, then, Dansh 'ooman, shtand there!" as he turned to greet them all.

"Ho, Alec, 'ave yew got it h'all shorted h'out, then? By word, yew've got as many pershonsh 'ere ash would work a threshing box, Ah desshay, an' leave shum to sshpare!"

Jack Harris, solid yeoman farmer in boots, leggings and breeches, possessed unmistakeable presence. He also had a roughness of vocal dysfunction which gave all of his robust way of speech an extra vigour, and he embellished A's, O's and E's with a liberal supply of H's for even greater impact upon the recipient. Fraser decided at once that he wholeheartedly liked, and warmed to, this big, ruddy-faced man with these gushing explosions thrusting their way between other, quite ordinary words. From previous visits with his father to the Harris farm, and the conversation overheard between his parents, Fraser was aware that this intriguing quality of speech arose from something called a cleft palate, and that it could sometimes be sorted by surgery, in a hospital, if done early enough. But sometimes it didn't always work. Well, with this hugely interesting, exciting neighbour, it produced a rugged enunciation which turned D's to G's, and other side effects, rather like a vocal firework of continual performance. Jack's universal exclamation of pleasure, surprise, wrath or amazement came out as "Bluggy 'ELL!" rather than the normal version, which (as Fraser had found when he tried it out), sounded rather prissy and effete by comparison. There was a rough and ready man's expression of vigour with this "bluggy 'ell!" business!

"Well, Mary, theer'sh shome stuff 'ere ash Marcia's shent up. She'll be glad to 'ave yew come h'over if yew'm needing owt more, once yew've shettled in an' all."

Pushing his cap back off his forehead, Jack smiled warmly at Fraser through a jumble-up of teeth, accepted a ham sandwich from his mother, and a glass of whisky from his father, and spoke on:

"Young Frayshyurr, eh, h'are yew gooin' to be gaffer of thish place? H'I'll need to watch my shtep now, Alec, with h'all youm bluggy heckshpertsh sho bluggy closhe-to!"

Jack had heard in the county town cattle market of the vet's young son being so danged close to those heifers' calving time. He let out a bellow of laughter, and noisily took in a swallow of this good whisky.

Fraser was greatly delighted with Jack Harris's unique pronounciation of his name; it was like having another kind of identity! "I can give you a hand any time that I'm not at school, Mr Harris!"

"Theer now, that'sh bluggy good for a shtart. Ah'll tell Marcia, an' she'll 'ave yew shtay an' eat wiv h'ush. Meantime, we'd better mek' hashte an' get theshe logsh off. Goo'in' to give ush an 'and, then? Good lad. Well, Alec an'

Mary, 'ere'sh to many yearsh of good timesh, an' good neighboursh all! Hey up, then, young man, we'll mek a shtart wiv them logsh."

Working at Jack Harris' elbow in the near-darkness, with the cob mare stamping quietly in the shafts of the trap, Fraser felt that this was at once a tangible start to all those facets of farming that nourished and sustained the great need within him. The rolling terrain of Jack Harris's neatly hedged fields, their own few sheltered acres, and other farms around them, all drew together as a solid base from which to consider the best way for him to get into, and on with, this farming way of life that he craved so deeply.

Their settling-in process at The Leys took about three weeks. Once back home from school, Fraser took immense satisfaction from walking over every square yard of the five acres of garden, orchard, rough ground and coppice. There was a great deal of tidying up to be done outside, just as there had been throughout the whole house in a similar but in a much wider and productive application of tools, time and energy.

"Didn't Captain Sadleir have something to do with the Navy?" Fraser asked his father. "I always read that the Navy was very particular about things being very neat and tidy; all these photographs in the magazines show sailors cleaning and scrubbing everything. Doesn't seem to me that the Sadleirs could have been much blinking good on a ship."

His father was putting on what he called his working clothes, it being Saturday, and the two of them were going out to tackle yet another part of what Jack Harris gustily described as "Shetting th'owd bluggy placesh to rightsh, and no buggersh done damn all for bluggy yearsh, Alec!"

At weekends and into the lengthening light of those following spring months, Fraser and his father were totally given to the sustained hard work needed to set everything to those essentially Scottish rights deemed necessary by his father. Fraser felt the greatest pleasure, and pride, in watching how his father showed himself an able exponent of hitherto unsuspected skills in moving old poultry houses and abandoned pigs' arks, constructing new ones with scantling and board from the estate sawmill, and fencing in the long-neglected garden.

"How's your chest with all this lifting and heavy stuff, Fraser?"

"Oh, it's just fine, Daddy. Working outside in cool air really seems to make it work much more easily; it's just dusty or stuffy things that set it going."

"Oh, aye, young man, such as classrooms first thing on a Monday morning?"

There was a glint in Alec Baird's eye – both he and Fraser burst out laughing.

Watching her husband and Fraser from the dining room window, measuring for curtains, Mary Baird smiled, happy in the obvious satisfaction between each of them at their tasks. The move had been such a good thing, and their neighbours at the farm down the lane, Jack and Marcia Harris, they were gems of a special kind.

Their new home's position on the ridge overlooking the vale spread out below, Fraser felt, was going to provide him, and parents, and his sister Jean, too, he supposed, with a vantage point for seeing just about everything that went on in the fields and woodland that his gaze could encompass. Solid with satisfaction of all that lay before him for the whole family – by golly! – to enjoy, Fraser looked at a ruinous old shed. Repair it, pull it down, what? What would Mr Harris do with it? Hey, bluggy 'ell! – burn the bluggy thing!

The lane leading from their home at The Leys ran in a rough gravelled progression downhill, ending at its opening on to the main road to Melford. It had probably started as a well-used cart track, Fraser thought, reflecting by its curves and level bits, the easiest way for horses to take loads up or down to the Harris's farm and buildings, which lay in the angle of the lane's joining to the main road.

Apart from it being the road up to themselves, the Bairds, and one or two cottages over the brow of the hill close to the railway line and river, it was Jack Harris's way, particularly in a wet time, of getting to and from his cropping fields on the higher land of his farm. In such a fashion, the lane allowed laden horse carts and tractors to go about their journeys without cutting up the fields in a mess of mud and ruts. In the high, hawthorn-topped banks on either side, robins, wrens, dunnocks and chaffinches nested in the thick hedge bottoms; Fraser had frequent pleasure to exclaim "So that's where your wee nest lies!" and carefully ensure that the screen of grasses and hedging was neatly in place as he stepped back down to the lane.

Walking to and from the morning school bus, Fraser noted with pleasure that the mixture of gravel and compacted quarry material usually produced a continuous track of short grasses and small flowers in the middle. When sitting in his father's car on occasion and going down to the road and beyond, the tyres gave off a quieter yet more interesting drumming noise than when out on to the main road. But in a really wet time, water ran in the wheel tracks, spreading out as a pool at the end of the farm lane.

Some time in mid-July, two weeks before harvest, the lane was a watercourse from side to side. The rain was unceasing. Standing inside one of their henhouses, Fraser watched the rain sluicing off the others' roofs, with the occupants disconsolate and the ducks investigating each new pool of muddy water with relish, excited quacking and much rapid twirling of their tails.

"Go on ducks," he called loudly, "have a muddy bloody good old time!" His mother, occupied with ironing clothes which had been difficult to dry, could neither hear nor see him. A man's proper swear was necessary at times. With added grinning pleasure, he repeated, Jack Harris-fashion, "Goo on, ducksh, 'ave a bluggy good time!" The drumming on the corrugated iron roof was comforting, Fraser felt, provided that you were standing inside. He assumed Mr Harris's usual stance of legs apart, thumbs hooked into leather belt (he would have to get his own belt blackened up a bit with grease and dirt), and a bold glance that took in everything that an experienced farmer needed to know about men, cattle and crop.

His father's car swung in, driving straight into the garage-cum-tool and meal store. Fraser saw the streams of water from the wheel arches squirting out sideways as his father jogged the car up over the edge of concrete with a blip of the throttle. Even as his father, head down, turned quickly from the open garage doors to the long porch protecting the back door and dogs' kennels, Fraser could see that he was soaked. "No jobs to be done with my bold papa tonight, in all this rain. Go on, silly hens!" he muttered to the hens scratching around his muddy boots, not really displeased.

He could hear his mother's words as soon as he followed his father indoors, propping up his own wellingtons beside his father's black ones.

"Why is it, Alec, that you have to stay out in it?" She waved her arm impatiently at the downpour outside, from her position at the ironing board. "After all, it's not as though you have to, like your farming cronies. It just makes a lot more work for me when you come trailing in like that!"

"Oh, boy," Fraser mouthed quietly to Argo, pulling off his wellington socks in the kitchen, "we're off at the gallop again!"

His father's voice, with no words clear, came from the hall, presumably en route to change into dry clothes upstairs. Fraser wondered if he could swing conversation with his mother away from her seemingly ever-present prickliness towards anything connected with farming in any shape or form; it seemed to be always there in her, ready for something small to trigger it off.

"Mummy, you know that time in the spring when Daddy introduced me to his friend Doctor Dallas, where Mr and Mrs. Boxall have the pub, and gave us tea and sandwiches?" He had remembered, just in time, to say "tea" instead of shandy and drinks and things. Well, those were the sorts of things which you would be more likely to expect to get in a pub.

"Yes, I certainly do that. You were both atrociously late, and your meal here crisped to a cinder." Angrily, Mary Baird made some extra and unnecessary sweeps with the iron.

"Well, he – Doctor Dallas I mean – he knew that his grandfather and my great-grandfather were at the same school together, in Ross-shire, back in Scotland. There were even things that I didn't know about, like Grandpa Teatime's father, my great-grandfather, where he came from. He was killed by a horse, as a young man. That must have been bad."

His mother was plainly determined not to be openly paying attention to him.

"Anyway, it was all really interesting. Can you tell me a bit about all your family, please? All I know is that they were called Reid. That's right, isn't it?"

His mother laid the shirt which she had been ironing on the pile in the wide window sill. Fraser sat himself there, watching the streaming rain, savouring the warmth of clothes releasing their fresh, outdoors fragrance, content to be inside.

Straightening up, hands pressed to her back, his mother looked out of the window, seemingly not noticing the steady rain, as Fraser's father came into the living room in his stockinged soles, in dry shirt and trousers.

"Alec, our family historian here wants to know about where all my family came from. I've heard about your father's father, Fraser's great-grandfather, I suppose, getting killed by that terrible horse, but really nothing quite so terrible on my side. Or wonderful, come to that." She picked up some pillowslips then half turned. "Anyway, what do you want to know? Oh, and before I start, where's Jean, d'you know?" she asked of both of them.

"Mary, don't fuss for Heaven's sake; she's down at the Harrises, having her tea there with Eleanor. I looked in and saw them all there in the kitchen. Anyway, go on, Fraser."

Looking from one to the other of his parents, Fraser thought, it's important that I try and keep this going on the same friendly – no, interested – way that Doctor Dallas used.

"Well, what I would like to know for a start, Mummy, is were your parents, or grandparents, farmers, like Daddy's, or what? Where did they mostly live? Was that somewhere in, in Angus, if that's what it's called?"

His mother pulled up one of the dining chairs to the window and sat down, lighting a cigarette, puckering her eyes in retreat from the match's flare and smoke.

"Some of my family were, or rather became farmers, Fraser, if that's what is important to you. Ah, but let me see. The man who would have been the same age as your great-grandfather Hector Baird was a gamekeeper. Actually, he was head keeper to Lord Strathavon. That's near Forfar. Do you know where that is, Fraser?"

"Not really."

His father, sitting beside the open fire, shirt sleeves rolled up, was apparently reading The Farmer and Stockbreeder. Very quietly, without raising his head, he supplied the answer for Fraser.

"On the main line south from Aberdeen, about sixty miles. Nice county, Angus; lots of good cattle and rasps. And pheasants. Go on."

"So, Mummy, was there anything special about him? Where did he live and do his work as a keeper? He must have had a son, or daughter, to be your–"

Fraser hesitated, feeling his way up and down through what Doctor Dallas would have called his "layers" of this particular family onion. Fraser thought he'd got it right.

"– to be your father, or mother, right?"

His mother had not been paying attention.

"What was special about him, if you could call it that, was that he had an eye shot out at a shoot on the estate he worked for, and–"

She was interrupted by Fraser's "Crikey, was he killed? How did it happen?"

"Oh, the way that I mind it, with my grandmother becoming his widow, of course, was that some stupid shooting guest of the laird took a shot forward, low, which he should never have done, and pellets struck my grandfather's eye and his face, everything. Damned ignorant fool."

Not the first time that he'd heard his mother swear, but this time there was a bitterness behind it. There was silence in the room, apart from the steady rain sounds outside. His mother continued, eyes focussed within herself, cigarette smoke curling up. She started to set the stage in her inner mind for a sequence of events, a replay of matters only too familiar to her; Fraser could sense that.

"The socket of his eye became infected after he was shot, he died, and my grandmother and family of seven, with no money coming in, had to flit out of the estate house, with the laird needing to install a new keeper. They were all out of a home. That was just the way of things."

In the minds of all three of them in the room, there were silences, scenes known or envisaged.

"Where did the farming bit come in? Daddy said that all your brothers had been in farming. Where are they now? Are they still in Scotland, in Angus?"

His mother stood up abruptly, and holding her cigarette away from herself in curiously upraised fingers and forearm, recited a step-by-step description of all the pictures in her mind still in clear recall.

"When James Walker Reid died from having had his eye shot out, his widow was left with seven of a family. My own father was one of them. Nothing unusual about that in those days." She gave a sort of cynical snort, Fraser thought. "That would have been about 1890. There were four brothers, one of them was Nathaniel, my father, ultimately. He was old enough, about thirteen, to get a job of some sort, on the Strathavon estate. The other three were older; they had been in employment on local farms. That was all they knew or were schooled for. They had to leave the family home immediately, and get what employment they could scrape for. One of them landed up in the army. That was Jim." She stood, silent, saying nothing about the other three, thought Fraser.

"What happened then? Who was your mother, Mummy?"

"Oh, she was a fine, bonny woman. She came from Stirlingshire, she had been in service when my father met her. They applied for the tenancy of a not very big place, a small farm on the estate; my father was not an adventurous sort at all, he would have been in his late twenties, mebbe even thirty."

She paused, to take a long pull at her cigarette, and then ground it out in the ashtray on the window sill. She turned, to look directly at Fraser. The next part of her account was not an easy or pleasant bit to tell. He could see that from the tightening of his mother's jaw line and the rise in pitch of her voice, once she continued. Her eyes darkened.

"Folk working on farms, Fraser, have never had much success in my family. My poor dratted father worked himself into his own grave by the time that he was only forty-two. He wasn't strong enough, the place wasn't big enough to employ good men, he didn't have capital behind him to get into a bigger place. There's a hard world of difference between a farmer and a working farmer, believe me. And, poor useless soul, he got TB. Consumption of the lungs they called it then. One of the things which your own father knows a lot about!" The last few words were directed in a markedly dry tone towards his father, Fraser registered. Her voice trembled as she went on, "So, there you are, Fraser, my lad, history repeating itself in the blighted Reid family. My poor, worn out father, father to all of us, had died, and at a stroke of the estate factor's pen, no home, no income, no escape. We all just had to find what jobs we could. And a home somewhere, into the bargain."

"But, where could you all go, if someone else was needing into the farm?" Fraser asked, trying to get all these violent, upsetting scenes into the right sequence in his mind. His mother sat down heavily on the chair beside him, the ash on her cigarette unnoticed.

"There was a friend of my mother who had a good job in the telephone exchange in Edinburgh, on the switchboard. She put in a word with her supervisor for us to get jobs. We had all done well at the school; one of us got a job in the telephone exchange. We just had to take any opening that offered to get a job, get a roof over our heads and bring in some money. Mother took in piano pupils, my sisters Ellie and Marjorie, we all got jobs of one kind or another. I was lucky, I got into a bookshop. We worked hard, six o'clock finishing time everywhere, Saturdays as well, and saved enough to put our youngest sister into Varsity, to train as a teacher. Some change from the gutters and slavery on a wee farm in winter in Angus, I can tell you!"

Fraser, intent on the unfolding, unsuspected picture of a fatherless family grasping at anything that would give them a start, a living, could see that his mother appeared to be relaxed in the telling of it now. There was even a secret smile of recall trying to slip out.

"Mummy, did you manage to keep up with your brothers? Where did they go?"

His question brought the hardness came back into her features with speed. It was unpleasant to see.

"Fraser, you that would be a farmer's boy, listen to me. They all had a terribly hard time, starting with nothing but what they had learnt on the land, at a time when there was precious little else for country-reared lads to go to. They all put as much distance as possible between themselves and farm work as they possibly could."

"One of my brothers, Aden, was killed in a mining accident in South Africa, and I seldom hear from the other two; one in America in the building trade, and Sandy in Western Australia. They'd learnt their lesson about farming from their dead father, with nothing else behind them."

Mary Baird appeared to have dragged out as much as there was to tell in response to his, Fraser's, questions. Or, as much as she wanted to. But, surprising both Fraser and his mother, Alec Baird suddenly spoke up, his farming magazine laid down.

"And Mary, there was still your other brother Jack, in the Army, killed in the first year of the war. His wife or widow, rather, pens the odd letter; very odd, in fact. What for, your mother and I don't rightly know, because she just wheenges on about how she should never have married him!"

At this, Fraser was at once aware of currents of acrid friction flickering back and forwards between his parents. His mother got up, visibly disturbed by something that came, not from the moment, not from the evening of sluicing rain, but from a canker harboured from her youth. She paced between Fraser and her husband, lighting another cigarette without looking at it, Fraser noticed.

"Look, what my mother couldn't see for the life of her, her husband working himself to death, but that was clear enough to send all my worthwhile brothers as far as they could take themselves, was that this, this being bogged down in work, this slavery with cattle and beasts and feeding and mucking, working like mad souls in all weathers, and coming in dead tired, too damn well exhausted to give heed to wife or family – you men, ach! I've seen it all. And here you are, the two of you, father and son by the looks of it, getting into exactly the same damned way of life with every minute you can grab. Alec, I sometimes feel that your ever-needful band of friendly farmers means more to you than your family. Coming home at God knows what time of day or night, and so tired that I can't get a word out of you."

She choked, putting her hands to her face.

Fraser felt himself lose all blood to his face. It seemed to rush down to his stomach and beyond, and churn deeply there. This was awful and hurtful to all of them and somehow all just started up by asking about his mother's parents and grandparents. His mother straightened up, went to the door into the hall, and turned round, pointing at first to her husband, then shockingly, to Fraser.

"Going out with your father to dirty old farms in every spare moment. Everything else goes hang. I want more for you than that, Fraser, with your illnesses and school and everything." She stamped a foot to command the heat in her sentiment. "Oh, how much I hate this never-ending work, work and more damned work!"

As she choked out the last few words, Fraser's sister Jean came in from the front door, neat in school uniform.

"Oh, Mummy, you can't guess what Eleanor Harris was showing me–"

She stopped as her mother at last flung out her exposure of that which had lodged so deeply in her since childhood and later, of a father coming in white-faced and exhausted from his fields, to die in a well of bitterness.

"Mummy, Mummy, what is going on? Why are you shouting at Daddy and Fraser?"

Her mother, head down and her raven hair hanging loose around her face, said in a low and controlled voice, but totally audible in the stilled, arrested room, "Jean, I was just giving these two young men some ideas about there being other things in life than the tail end of a cow!" And then, with a flash of her normal charm and gaiety, "We were talking about family roots, and how some of them really need pulling out of the ground, not letting them grow on and on, down into family history!"

Her smile, bleary through tears though it was, relaxed at least some of the tension in all of them. In his clean dry clothes, Fraser's father tossed the magazine on to the sideboard and went outside, to find something to do in the summer rain again.

Looking blindly out of the window on to the garden, Fraser fought back his tears of distress, sufficiently sternly to note that the steady raindrops, rather like his own infuriating flow, were held by the crinkly raspberry leaves in little pools, but the apple and ash tree leaves just let it all slip off, to vanish with little trace.

THE BUSINESS OF WAR

VIII

Drawing from an increasing number of minor sources, Fraser had gathered the fact that his father, along with many of his friends and veterinary colleagues, had taken part, had actually fought, if that was the way to speak of it, in this war, the Great War, as the grown-ups called it. The proof of all this, if called for in Fraser's mind, lay with his father's three army medals in the glass-fronted cabinet in the sitting room, hectic and strangely coloured ribbons threaded through each one's small ring.

Of a Sunday morning, most Sundays in fact, Fraser knew that it was the usual practice for these friends of his father and mother, together with their wives, to appear in their various cars and join in the coffee or tea, biscuits and cheese laid out on the table in the kitchen, and to then wander, in random cheerful commentary, through to the rise and fall of conversation, laughter and cigarette and pipe smoke in the sitting room. The men tended to gravitate to the dining room, where there were copies of The Field, Veterinary Record, Farmers Weekly or other magazines of a like nature. Sometimes there were Scottish magazines as well.

Fraser really liked the company of these cheery Sunday mornings, but his sister Jean declared herself uninterested and would detach herself upstairs, purloining an armful of Picture Post as she went, or off to visit a school friend on her bicycle. By virtue of attending to such useful tasks as carrying round extra milk or sugar, or the breadboard with more cracker biscuits, Fraser managed to be at hand or elbow where the interesting exchanges were lively and free-ranging. One such morning, at the tail end of harvest in the fields outside, there was undoubtedly something holding the attention of a larger than usual number of these gathered neighbours, men and women alike. Amongst the most voluble was a man whom Fraser knew to be an old friend and veterinary colleague of his father, 'Pinto' Cockburn. Why he had attracted such a nickname, Fraser wasn't quite sure, but it had been something to do with his, Pinto's, attempt to smuggle a pony of dramatic colouring (wasn't this what was described as "painted" in books about horses?) from a circus into his landlady's digs in Edinburgh as a student, along with Fraser's father. On discovery, apparently, Pinto had assured the protesting landlady that "But ach, woman, poor beast, it needed a rest."

Further, it was disclosed with even greater hilarity amongst everyone there, the landlady had declared that "If it was a rest from the circus that the puir brute was needing, how about you an' it making a wee wigwam oot there in the front gairden; ye could mebbe train it tae ride yer motor bike as a side line!"

Now, Mr Cockburn was no longer sitting beside his fair-haired wife Marjorie, but striding about the sitting room, and hall and kitchen, voice upraised, spilling coffee from his cup into the saucer, waving his free hand (and cigarette, scattering ash), directing his fierce questions upon everyone that morning, supplying the answers himself before they could open their mouths, and becoming quite suffused about his face as he did so.

"...and, Alec, this ranting, absolute madman of an Adolf Hitler, he's at the same damned business again, been building up for it ever since the last fiasco we were in, but our gutless politicians didn't have the steel to finish the bugger off before he entered his trade as a professional warmonger. By Christ, we are in the hands of such useless, utterly bloody useless so-called leaders while this totally dangerous Fuhrer monster is busy building planes as fast as he can, going flat out to get every Jerry Jugender over the age of sixteen into Stukas or tanks, and sending them to practise their skills on those poor sods in Spain or Czechoslovakia. What in kingdom come are we thinking about?"

Other voices – everyone was gathered in the sitting room now, perched wherever they could get a seat – were suddenly joining in, speaking of places, of names that Fraser had never heard of before: Ypres, Bapaume, Lens, the Salient, Thiepval, Vimy Ridge, Pilkem, Messines. Not having seen them written down, he didn't know how to spell them. Fraser felt a driving need to fit in some more pieces of the jigsaw making up his father's little-known time in the army. He would have to look up these places in the set of Harmsworths' Universal Encyclopaedia on the bookshelf across the room from where he sat, listening, watching people's faces as they spoke with intensity about this Great War, and seemingly, another war. There were clear tones of anxiety, fear, even dark alarm in the clash of their voices.

Speaking in low-voiced aside to Fraser, his father muttered "Jugender. D'you know what that is? No? It means Hitler Youth. All the youngsters have to be–"

He was cut short by another outburst by Pinto. Overriding the swell of turbulent interjections from everyone else, Pinto Cockburn was off again.

"Do you really believe that he's going to be satisfied with invading, on this excuse of Sudetenland being a part of Germany? Na, na, Alec, put your money on Poland next. Or France or Hungary, or any other damned place where he can and will, by Christ, let his stormtroopers loose."

He bit angrily into a double cracker and cheese, and choking coughs forced him to stop, cheeks bulging. Gordon MacRae, dentist in Melford, who came from somewhere called Skye, as Fraser knew from his parents' comment, and not given to speaking without slow, careful thought on most topics, now added to the whirl of opinions.

"But hold on a minute, Pinto. Can't you see that this so-called massing of troops at borders is just a manoeuvre of sorts to get these smaller countries to accept entry of Germans as a sort of political necessity, or, what is he calling it – alignment? – amongst neighbouring countries? He undoubtedly has a thing about feeling threatened by us, or France, right?"

Fraser looked at his mother and father, in different parts of the sitting room. She was saying nothing, wary in uncertain silence, going round refilling coffee cups with a questioning look, but not speaking. His father was clearly reflecting on the surge and flow of heated declamations, and serious with it.

Pinto stood up and exploded into an even more sharply, shockingly delineated vision. "Can you not see it, man? We're going to be back into yon carnage which we endured and barely survived, pulling guns into action with terrified demented horses, trying to save the poor bloody infantry from getting hung up on uncut wire. All of us shot to hell, drowning in our own blood, if not in the hellish mud. Guns, men, bits of both, more men and horses screaming their poor heads off, if they still had them. And Hitler all the while piling up his men and machines before the ink was even dry on that, that utterly bloody useless Versailles Treaty. Treaty of Betrayal, more like. Mark my words, the lot of you, the appeasers, Halifax, Chamberlain, and that slippery swine Ribbentrop, they've all made the irreversible mistake with letting this horde of trampling Huns get as far as they have done already, by God!"

He took a gulp of tepid coffee, including Fraser in his sweep of stunned faces.

"What's coming, douce law-abiding folk that we are, is going to make the last charnel house look like a three-ring circus. We don't seem to have a single person with fire enough in his belly to stop this madman, with a taste of his own storm of terror! Blitzkreig, Stukas, tanks, stormtroopers; just what in Heaven have we allowed to pass unchecked at its very beginnings? We were, we are, all so snivellingly spineless and weak!"

Pinto, normally an equable, good-natured veterinary surgeon, positively spat out his final cry of rage:

"Reparation? Reparations? Germany coughing up to useless bloody France? Don't make me laugh! All that these Deutschers are doing is to put a socking great 'P' in front of the idiot word; they're going flat out in preparation of huge machinery for the next hellish war, and it's coming, by God!"

He went on, unstoppable:

"Stukas, tanks by the thousand and stormtroopers, in that order. It will be the very gates of Hell crashing upon us! The last slaughter was just a practice for what's coming, once again, by Heaven!"

The force of his impassioned delivery was such as to break up the company. The Cockburns were the first to leave, Pinto's wife Marjorie looking quite shaken. Fraser could feel the tension and uncertainty, the covering jollity of the terse "Bye, Mary, Alec. We're desperately concerned about the way things are going, not good to ruin your Sunday morning and hospitality like this. Very fine coffee again, Mary. Cheerio, then."

With their visitors dispersed, Fraser's mother had obvious release in her as she brought everyone's minds to bear upon preparing their usual Sunday dinner.

"C'mon, you lot, let's get dinner going." She called upstairs. "You can come on down, Jean. The visiting prophets of doom have all departed."

Fraser really liked and looked forward to this regular feature of his family's weekend. It was a sort of solid platform of satisfaction with the week past, and a measure of things to do before the week ahead. He liked working at his father's elbow in the scullery, making ready their own vegetables to go along with the roast sirloin of beef, Yorkshire pudding, horseradish sauce and trimmings. They quite frequently had someone to join them at the dining table, now being laid by Jean as her set Sunday task. A Mr Andrew Hyslop, farmer from Dumfriesshire was due to arrive at any minute. Fraser knew that he was selling attested Ayrshire heifers to a local farmer, to form a tuberculosis-free dairy herd. His father had set up the contacts between them both.

"Daddy?"

"Aye, what? Look. You've missed a parsnip. Pay attention, young man!"

"You were in this Great War, weren't you?" Fraser asked.

"I certainly was. Artillery, if you want to know. They called us the Gunners. Straight into it after my first year at Edinburgh, in the veterinary college. Nearly five years."

He straightened up, scraping knife and hands lifted from the muddy basin of water and vegetables.

"Our battery of guns was battered around all over France and Belgium, pulling eighteen-pounders in the most desperately difficult and frightening conditions for man or beast. That's what was getting our good old friend Mr Cockburn so enraged; it looks rather as though some countries in Europe are going headlong into the same madness again."

Fraser looked at his father's hands, palms lying slack on the edge of the deep sink. What kind of things did you have to do with your hands in artillery, in action? His mother was standing at the door through from the kitchen, watching him, looking fixedly at his father in a different fashion.

"Will you have to go back into all that, if this Hitler person keeps going on?" Fraser needed to pursue further the matter of his father having been a gunner.

"Ah, difficult to say, perhaps not. Come on, let's help your mother to get everything in the oven before Andrew arrives."

Their meal was well ordered, well cooked and well lubricated by some local perry and easy conversation. Andrew Hyslop had mutual friends with Fraser's mother in Angus. They had got to the stage of her apple dumpling when he mentioned that one of the dairy workers on his farm, a Territorial soldier in the Highland Light Infantry, had gone off for his annual training camp in high excitement as they had been told, all ranks, that they would be having intensive weapon training with live ammunition and night exercises together with the Ayrshire Yeomanry in light tanks and armoured cars.

At this, Fraser at once noticed the perceptible check in his mother's smooth handling of courses, crockery and directions to Jean and himself in bringing things through and taking away used plates and dishes. There was an even more noticeable check in his father's response to Andrew Hyslop's question, asked of both his parents, "And what do you good folk make of these repeated assurances by Hitler that Germany has, or rather he has, no intention of gaining more territory for the good of the Third Reich, and so on? My own suspicion is that if you gave him a penny whistle, Alec, he'ld make a damned gun out of it, double quick, and it and a thousand others would have 'KRUPP - ESSEN' stamped on the breech. He's been a long time getting ready for this, this total uproar in Europe. Ach, man, Alec, this Hitler is everyone's worst nightmare strutting into reality."

Fraser noticed his father's fingers tapping on the table, slow time. A prelude to what he was clearly considering saying to their Dumfriesshire farmer's question. Which he then delivered.

"I think that what is going to happen will be something like this: Our Mr Hitler is now a highly dangerous quantity politically, and this torrent of counter-accusations and treaties being rushed through with countries which he suspects could form an alliance against him, wherever he sends his tanks into another country – they're not worth a docken, he's just buying those essential first few hours or days of smashing power and total surprise, with another worthless piece of paper. He's building up a big store of uncertainty about when and where the German forces will pour through, anywhere in Europe. And it won't be a so-called push, more like an unstoppable flat-out destruction of everything in its path. Mark my words, all of you."

The term "unbloodygodly" fitted in neatly in Fraser's mind as he tried to visualise the exact proportions of this sudden pouring of tanks and men.

Andrew Hyslop pleaded his need to get on the road north again, the dining table was cleared, there was peace in the house, albeit with persistent recurring questions whirling round in Fraser's review of the turbulent gathering of his parents' friends earlier that day.

It was the practice, in the family, for Fraser's father and mother, and Jean, to take visitors for a saunter in casual fashion round the garden's various sections: the orchard, potatoes and green crops in neat order, the hens dust-bathing and most Sundays, it was Alec Baird's pleasure to invite everyone in this relaxed and cheerful ritual, with the geese and ducks making great splashings, and both dogs sniffing carefully for a rat or two harbouring in a pile of logs. Fraser's mother, in particular, was frequently surprised by what had been accomplished by the joint efforts of her husband and Fraser since their last walk round. Coming back to the front of the house, arm in arm with Jean, she made what she felt to be a useful suggestion:

"Right, you two men, with all the cooking and so forth, there's an abundance of hot water. How about a leisurely bath for all of us before another car-load of folk appears?" She did not seem to be overly concerned about Hitler's plans now, Fraser considered. "You go first, Jean. Don't take all the water, if you don't mind, then you two fellows run in fresh hot stuff after me," his mother directed.

His father called from the landing as he passed Fraser's bedroom door, wrapped in a large bath towel, "On you go, Fraser; there's plenty in the tap. I think your mother has laid out clean things for you."

Fraser's judgement of what was adequate for a good bath, with impromptu hair-washing at the same time (crikey, that did make the water turn grey!) was all of six minutes, or less. Passing his parents' bedroom door, Fraser saw his father perched on the edge of their bed, carefully trimming his toe nails with a pair of his curved surgical scissors. There were still some things galloping round in his, Fraser's mind, unanswered. This might be a good time. He went in, as his father was discarding the towel for clean vest and shirt.

"Daddy, you said that when you were younger, you had been in the artillery. What exactly did you do? How old were you?"

"All right, last of your questions first. I was hardly eighteen when I, we, joined up, and at just still short of nineteen we were into action for the first time. That meant we had to drive teams of six horses, harnessed in pairs, and limbered up to an eighteen-pounder gun and caisson carrying shells and fuses, batter them up hill and down dale, into battery positions, unlimber, frequently under fire ourselves, swing the guns round. We worked in batteries of four or six or more guns, laid them for targets and range, and then fired at the German infantry or their positions, whose guns were firing back at us. Usually six of us to a gun, unless one of us was wounded or had been killed. Does that answer your other question? What was it, again?"

Fraser was silent. He was looking at the spread of deep, blue-black pits down the whole musculature of one side of his father's body.

"You want to know what these are? Go on, put your finger in and press, really hard." He raised his left arm to expose and tighten the skin and ribs. Fraser slowly put a finger to one of the pits and pressed. "Go on, harder!" his father urged. "What can you feel now?" his father asked.

"It's hard, quite sort of tough round it. What are they, Daddy?"

In the most matter of fact description, the answer came in muffled words as Alec Baird pulled his clean shirt on over his head and shoulders.

"We were in action, firing over open sights, would you believe, at the Germans all along a ridge called Passchendaele. Awful bloody place, total destruction. Our battery of guns bucking and leaping as fast as we could load and fire. Horses in pickets, some way back. One of our lads needed to get to a regimental aid post in the middle of all this. I took him out of the noise and shellfire to yell into his ear how to get there. Our gun behind us took a direct hit from the German guns, killing or wounding just about everyone. The shrapnel blasted both of us with a gale of metal. Killed the fellow I was shouting directions to, and my left side took what came round him, which was still plenty. No time to get it all out, or even some of it, with all hell breaking loose around us. Hmm. So, there you are, young squire, lots of old iron in there. Doesn't bother me all that much. Anything else you were asking?"

"Daddy, what will you have to do if this Hitler person they're always going on about on the wireless, if he goes sending these soldiers into other people's countries? Will you have to go back into the army or artillery or what?"

Alec Baird buttoned his shirt and stood up, answering in a very plain, undisguised manner. "Probably not, but it takes time to equip, train, practise and move any kind of soldiers to where they may have to fight, and older men like me might not be so good at it as younger men. So, have no fear." He sat down again, wriggling his toes into clean socks. "I think that you and I going shooting rabbits with the twelve-bore is a much better idea, and for one thing they damn well don't shoot back!" He went out to the landing, whistling.

Fraser went back along to his own room. Something told him that his father had been very close to being killed himself. Damn me! Addressing his image in the mirror, Fraser pointed out to himself, "Well, if that had been the way of it, you wouldn't be here, would you, you stupid cratur?"

He turned to go downstairs, reviewing the staggering spray of pitted wounds running up and down his father's body. He would think about this now, whenever his father was doing ordinary things, like driving the car, digging in the garden, reaching round some animal or other. Or just walking. He must have been spun round like a blooming top, with such a blast of shrapnel. He would have to look up that word in the encyclopaedia, too. Once again addressing himself in a muttered monotone, as he reached the foot of the stairs, Fraser said, "Crikey, it must have been a huge number of pieces of shrapnel, like, well, like blasting a rabbit at short range with a shotgun."

Come to that, how would his father have carried on, doing such things as carrying shells around, harnessing and limbering up? How many horses did he say they had? Or just such things as getting in and out of his uniform? The reality slid into Fraser's awareness. Maybe they just wore their uniforms all the time when they were in a war.

IX

There was something different and disturbing, Fraser felt, in the manner that everyone around his home and his parents' friends were talking, all through the past week or ten days, including the farm men at the Harrises. For the farm men, that was strange, engaged as they were with the last days of harvest, in great heat and dust. There was something that they were all shunning. Fraser could feel it, like an unknown presence.

What was more difficult for him to determine was just what it was that nearly everyone amongst their friends was so strenuously avoiding talking about. It was as though they all had some sort of pressure on their thoughts that made them come out with words that were muttered and then pulled back inside their mouths or minds. It was something to do with this war business and Adolf Hitler, of which they were desperately uncertain. Or frightened. Why did he have different names or titles: Reichs Chancellor, der Fuhrer, Herr Hitler and so on?

Fraser sought out his friend Hedley about this, this laboured concealment that was so poorly practised.

"Look, do you know anything about what's happening with this Hitler madman? He seems to be threatening war or invasion or annexation with just about every country in Europe," Fraser demanded of Hedley, very seriously. He went on with more unanswered difficulties. "There seems to be a huge mix-up between Germany, Russia, France and Poland and us, saying who's going to help who if Hitler wants to start a whole lot of fighting, and all these blooming pacts and treaties flying around like, like a bookie's list at a point-to-point."

Hedley's features, nodding to Fraser's list of confusions, had assumed his almost predictable expression of careful gravity. Fraser glared at him as though he was in possession of priceless, startling information, now to be divulged man to man, no more messing around.

"Yeah, you'll make a fine hanging judge, mein freund, any blasted day! C'mon, man, are we all going to be in this war business, or what?"

Fraser felt that he had some reasonable chance of finding truth about country or countries, place and reason for it all. He had overheard Hedley's father's abrupt and heated telephone conversation, stressing that, "...of course the blasted air raid shelters come before anything else. Just damn well get on with it, man. Their dreadful bombers'll be over here in hours, never mind stupid requisition orders from me. God Almighty, man, use some initative, for Heaven's sake!"

Hedley's reply made Fraser grind his teeth.

"Well, my father is in touch with chaps in London, Foreign Office men, y'know, and it seems that Hitler has been making non-aggression pacts with Russia and other countries, so that if he does start something in Poland, these other countries won't try to stop him. At least, not all at once, my father says. Hitler's forces are too strong. Anyway, they've got the wireless on all the time at home. They think that something's going to happen soon. It's bad, Fraser."

Hedley stopped. He didn't wish, in Fraser's eyes, to be seen as just a mouthpiece for other people's opinions all the bally time.

Fraser felt not much clearer in his mind. Whatever pacts were cooked up by these Germans, or used as a sort of monstrous stalking horse, he wanted to know the likelihood of his father, and other boys' fathers too, he supposed, having to go off again to the artillery, or infantry or any dratted thing. Now, there was damned awful school coming on again, in the middle of all this tension. He felt uncertain of his own place and direction in things, with the palpable fear now clearly possessing people.

The harvest that year, 1939, had been a time of unbroken steady summer. Stackyards in farms all over the country were full. Butts of sheaves of wheat, oats and barley, all in satisfyingly solid stacks: round, rectangular, square, all aligned in perfect precision until the long dusty days of the threshing box humming between them all. Some stacks still awaited their proper pegged-in winter thatch. Fraser really savoured walking slowly along them, brushing the severely compacted straw ends with his fingers and palms. He had worked hard with the farm men all that summer holiday from school.

Fraser had spoken to his father of the fact that he now knew which sheaves gave off a different smell at different times, whether newly bindered, set up in stooks, forked on and off the wagons, or when finally rammed into endless exactitude by the men with forks on the rising stack. Their working trousers were all glazed at the knees as they knelt on the last rows of sheaves to the ridge.

Jack Harris, thumbs black with grease and arms and face tanned dark brown, accosted Fraser at the milk house in the yard.

"Now then, young Frayshyurr, youm done a right good job wiv 'arvest an' all, and I've a job youm the very feller to ashk ter dew it, that'll let the ladsh git on wiv tidyin' up an' suchlike. Cum in 'ere, young man, an' pay attention!

Firsht or shecond of Sheptember, theer's a shpecial shale of for dry cowsh, fat beashts, shpringin' 'eifersh and shuchlike, an' we've a wagon load to mek ready. 'Ow about yew goo along wiv them, shee they come off the float in good order, and check they're in the right alley for penning-up, hey? Yew know old Cyril as drivesh the lorry? Well, he'll be float driver, he'sh a reet good 'and, and yew'll manage bluggy fine atween the two on yer."

Jack regarded Fraser warmly, with his crooked grin knowing Fraser's response as a certainty.

"I'll need a list, Mr Harris, and will you have a mark or number on each one? Better speak to my father, to make sure it's OK with him."

Jack exploded in a gust of laughter, snatching off his cap in a swirl of wheat dust and chaff. "H'already h'accomplished, my word! Youm a reet partic'lar bugger an' all! Now then, down 'ere not later than sheven h'a.m. Marcia'll 'ave yew breakfust along wiv ush. H'it'll be a longish day. She'll mek up a basket for yew, shandwiches an' ginger pop, mosht like. Yew cum into the ring wiv me once they mek a shtart, and we'll run 'em through together. The motor'll be in the yard back of The Shun. Yew know where?"

Another really fine day, Fraser said to himself in satisfaction, stretching himself at the open window. He could hear partridges creaking in the stubble field beyond the small orchard they had at The Leys. The night's mist still lay low, only releasing hedges out into sunlight once their glittering skeins of spiders' webs had been pearled in droplets. Breakfast in the Harris's kitchen, he grinned in anticipation; it would be noisy and jolly, with increasing delivery of "Mek bluggy 'aste, yew men. We'm not 'ere h'all bluggy day!" as the Guv'nor scraped back his chair.

The two dogs rattled their chains, standing at their kennel with tails wagging. Fraser relented and gave them a fast clip round the outside of the poultry runs, leaving long black tracks of bruised grass. Taking his private notebook, kept for noting down unusual birds or things generally – it might come in useful for this list business – he set off at a steady lope down the lane, half past six on the kitchen clock.

The various groups of cattle drawn out from Jack Harris's dairy herd earlier that morning were loaded up the ramp to the waiting float, with a rush. As each jostling, bawling knot of cattle was harruped into the dark interior of the cattle float, either Tom or Kenneth Darlington swung in the flake gates at their heels. The Guv'nor stood outside the smaller cowshed, used as a holding pen now the milking was over. His dark regard missed nothing.

"Lewk you 'ere, Frayshyurr. These next 'unsh are a bit plain; shee ash they dunna get knocked about coming down that ramp. They'll shettle better in their mart pen wiv one of them empty ladiesh ash ish empty of a calf. Pop 'er out, mind, afore yew tek 'eifers into the ring."

Cyril Roadnight checked that everything was properly secured, peering in through the slats to see that no animal had gone down and got trampled on in the flurry of loading.

"Right, young man. Fraser is it? Well, we'll get them theer all right, providing big bad Jack 'ere let's us goo on, eh? 'Ere 'e is with the papers and suchlike."

The Foden cattle truck creaked and shuddered prodigiously as Cyril drew out of the yard, Marcia Harris's lunch basket shaking between them on the engine housing. Fraser felt the noise of the engine throughout his body happily, high in the cab as Cyril stayed in low gear for the tight turn on to the main road to Melford.

He shouted across to Fraser, declutching deftly and pulling on the worn steering wheel with visible but easy effort.

"Once they've settled down, we'll move on a bit sharper. They'll goo quiet once she's pulling steady, like." Cyril grinned at him, patting the engine housing. The whole lorry body swayed and juddered behind them as individual animals moved into more stable positions, coats steaming, eyes rolling in the press of cattle.

Fraser, feeling the importance and responsibility vested upon him by Mr Harris, tried to think how best to present these various heifers and cows to the auctioneers in tidy condition.

He looked down at the papers in his hand. His fingers were stained greenish with cow dung, just like Cyril; they were two working men, doing a skilled countryman's job. Right, here's the sale stuff. He read on:

"Two Day Sale: Springing & In-Calf Heifers. Quality Stock. Fat Cattle In No.2 Ring. Sale Starts 12 o'clock Midday. 1st.& 2nd. September, 1939."

He looked again, checking descriptions in the list clearly written in Mrs Harris's hand. Cyril glanced across at him. He always had all the necessary details in his own head anyway, and in the greasy exercise book below his driver's seat for good measure. Jack was giving this young lad (How old was he? Eleven? Twelve?) a measure of trust that all country lads were the better of, come a certain age.

Floats and wagons were reversing into the unloading bays in a steady, noisy succession, exhaust fumes heavy in the heat. Yard men in brown stockmen's coats herding groups of cattle, ears back and bawling, into central alleys, off which lay the pens connected to the main selling rings.

"'Ere's the fust lot, Fraser. You ready?" Cyril warned him, standing at the top of the ramp, stick in hand. "Last pen on the left, up theer, then, off you goo."

Fraser counted them in, swung the heavy gate behind them, one big fleshy Friesian letting out a swift kick to the bars that had him arch back his body almost without thinking. The unloading was going well. He felt competent and ready for this sort of thing, a job for an experienced man, really.

All animals penned, Cyril smacked Fraser on the shoulder, grinning.

"You 'andled them smartish, young man. I could be doin' with you some of these big days, when every bugger atween here and Holm Ash 'as a load for me, so 'ere's summat for yersen." He took Fraser's hand and slapped a half-crown into his palm. "I'll tell our friend Jack that 'e's got a good un 'ere. I can use you any day that 'e can't!" A prodigious wink and a useful piece of practical advice: "Look, see that little 'ouse next the standpipe?" He nudged Fraser with his shoulder. "Theer's pails and a long 'andled brush in there. Once them beasts 'ave settled a bit, and they know you, don't they? Well, you just goo careful like, stay outside the pen, mark you, but any as is badly soiled, give 'er a dry brush down, and then throw a splash of water at 'er, as'll run off. That's a good lad, then. Cheerio!"

The county police constable on duty for the day had noted Fraser's to-ing and fro-ing at his tasks, remarking on his steady confidence amongst the stock, not all of them to be trusted in the noise and strangeness. He strolled over, to intercept Fraser on his return from putting away pails and brush.

"Well then, young man. Cyril gone off for another load without you? Are you with him, or someone else I would know?"

"Yes sir, that's right but I'm to make sure that Mr Harris's cattle are in the right pens for the twelve o'clock ring when he gets here, which should be any time now," Fraser replied, turning to point to the lines of cars.

"All right, you are a busy fellow and no mistake, and what might your name be, if you're not one of Jack Harris's household? I know him well."

The constable was a big man, but he stood easily at Fraser's side, talking to this lad of about twelve years old, as though they were old and familiar friends. Fraser felt entirely comfortable and at ease in his presence.

"I'm Fraser Baird, sir. My father's Mr Baird, the county veterinary officer." Fraser was going to say more, but was startled by Constable Hanbury's sudden forthright declaration of surprise and pleasure.

"Well, dang me, I do declare. You're Alec Baird's son! So, between your father and Jack Harris, you have got a couple of good men to keep you right!" He hooked his thumbs in the top gilt-buttoned pockets of his black tunic, and inclined to Fraser's head and eyes, the better to impart something else of new-found friendship.

"D'you know, Fraser, my lad, many's the night your father and me, we've sat through to dawn, burning up the odd beast what goes down with anthrax. Has to be burnt to ash, you see. Ah, but you'll know all about that, being a vet's son, won't you? Well, I'll be damned!"

Turning round and straightening up with a tug at his tunic the better to resume his market day duties, both Constable Hanbury and Fraser realised, from this other person taking a firm path through the loud and lively groups of farmers, yard men and float drivers, that they were about to be joined by an impressive figure in immaculate khaki tunic and razor-sharp uniform trousers, a sergeant's three stripes and crown above them, on the sleeve of his tunic.

"Morning, gentlemen. Colour Sergeant Oldcroft. You are Constable…?" he asked, and Fraser, beside the two men, was at once sensitive to the flicker of question, recognition and response, all unspoken, between the two uniformed men. He ran his eyes along the identical campaign ribbons on the left chest of each man. There were two more on the sergeant's tunic. The ribbon colours looked the same as those carrying his father's medals in the cabinet at home.

The police constable extended his hand readily, replying, "Constable Hanbury, Colour Sarn't. And what brings you to my patch, sir? This young man, Fraser Baird, he helps me here. His father is the county's vet'nary officer."

He clapped Fraser solidly on the shoulder, eyeing the Colour Sergeant steadily. Now, Fraser sensed, the flow was strictly between the two men. He moved off a few paces, turning his back in politeness, but not wanting to abandon his connection, his easy comradeship with the policeman. Fraser could hear their conversation quite clearly.

"Constable Hanbury, I'll make no bones about it. Things over there, Germany, France and so forth, they're getting very close to flash point. Providing that you're agreeable, Constable, I want to speak to as many good strong men today as I possibly can. The Regiment, their Regiment, needs them. South Staffs, regimental depot at Lichfield. The way things are poised right now, the country needs them, needs me and even you, by God, as quickly as damn well possible!"

Fraser half turned, registering the scene: the large bulky presence of the police constable, helmet glittering above his black uniform, the ramrod-like Colour Sergeant, taut in knife-edge khaki, broad scarlet sash in a heavy knot at his right hip, tight trousers flat from the fall of his tunic to glittering toecaps, eyes strong and unblinking below his sharply peaked hat and regimental badge, the double-looped Staffordshire knot. The sergeant's webbing belt, creamy with pale blanco and gleaming flat brasses, carried a similarly blanco-ed bayonet frog at his left hip. Fraser's note of detail jogged his memeory. Wasn't the proper word for the broad sash a baldrick? He had come upon this in the family's encyclopaedia.

Around them, groups of farmers stood in knots, not talking much, but looking down at their market boots, jabbing with their sticks at the yard's dung-splashed tarmac, shaking heads, falling silent and looking away and then back again, to meet other uncertain faces.

"Go ahead. Sarn't. Try the back of The Sun. That's where most of the younger farm men take their pints when it's as warm as this. Some of 'em might be glad of a job with reg'lar hours–"

Constable Hanbury's cynical suggestion was unfinished. The sergeant's finger jabbed at Hanbury's campaign ribbons. "What lot were you with then, in that last miserable do?" he wanted to know.

"Engineers, Sarn't. Digging gun platforms, building bridges, blowin' 'em up!– "

Again, he didn't get leave to finish.

"Let me tell you this, Constable. This idiot bastard old woman Neville Chamberlain, with all his bloody appeasement. '...and I have here this piece of paper signed by Herr Hitler...'" Oldcroft's disgust was savage. He spat out his words. "He's dug us into such a fucking great hole, together with that hand-wringing, lily-livered Halifax bugger, that there's no other way out now but the poor bloody infantry, again, by Christ! I can tell you this, my men are on full mobilisation. I issued one hundred and fifty rounds per man yesterday, and Transport's on standby with ammo and field supplies since three days ago. We're going to be in it. Our politicians' sheer spineless buggering about since, since the last hellish do, has guaranteed that. Ah, but here are my bold lads. I'll need to set up shop."

A dull green fifteen-hundredweight Bedford truck, drubbing on ribbed tyres, nosed into the yard, causing everyone in the mart yard to stop in mid-flow.

"Constable, if you think on where it's all going now, and what a total bollocks-up it was the last time, well, we could be doing with solid fellows like you. Come to the depot, ask for me, and I'll get you two stripes on enlistment. And then Sergeant to follow, fast, on my say-so, Constable."

The colour sergeant flicked a speck of dung from his glazed toecap with his pace stick, took one crashing pace backwards and saluted Constable Hanbury, one-time Royal Engineer 1914–1918, with precision. Improbably, it seemed to Fraser on that warm Saturday afternoon, in the midst of bawling cattle, noisy

74

cattle floats and all, the constable drew himself to full height, left thumb down his trouser seam, and saluted back.

"Good luck, Sarn't!"

The Colour Sergeant's rejoinder, as he wheeled away, was suppressed in volume, but cutting in implication. "Yes, and by Christ, we shall all need it."

The day had changed for Fraser, from the morning's stretching of his competence with Mr Harris's cattle and lists and everything adding to his self-worth, to a strange disconnected feeling of not being able, not having a firm handle to things going on around everyone but himself, it seemed.

"I'll go and find their car," he said to himself, threading through farmers and dealers shouting instructions to drivers revving their engines, float bodies creaking with sudden unrest of the stock inside. There was an Austin Sixteen belonging to one of the Arnold Brothers, feed merchants, and then he recognised the big Humber Super Snipe belonging to Gregory Parker, cattle dealer and abattoir owner; two or three up the line was the Harris's Vauxhall, with Marcia and Eleanor sitting in it, windows open. That basket has to be returned, he remembered, carrying it to the back seat.

Marcia's "Hello, Fraser. Everything seen to, I hear?" was so welcome to Fraser, he hadn't realised how tense he had been, and she had seen his anxiety of wanting to do his best for her husband. The smell of hot leather from the sun-warmed interior of the car was infinitely reassuring. Jack appeared, smelling of sun, sweat and beer. He was cheerful. Trade had been lively, better than anticipated with all this danged war business.

As Jack Harris inched the car out through the high yard gates, newspaper vendors were speedily slapping papers into hands, backed by their large-lettered boards: 'War Imminent: Terriers Mobilised', 'Hitler: No Answer, Time Runs Out'. Everyone at the market that day now seemed to be in an almost tangible urgency to hurry home, and there listen to their wireless sets. Fraser knew that was what his parents would now be quite open about. How does a country, a whole country and everyone in it get told they've got to start a war, for Heaven's sake? Sitting on the edge of the rear seat with Eleanor Harris just at his shoulder behind him, silent, Fraser felt at a loss about everything.

The scent of roses and stocks was drawn into the car by their passing, along with the heat and dust of the day. The last newsboards they passed shouted in heavy red lettering: 'Hitler's Blitz: Poland In Flames'. Marcia Harris looked at it, then across at her husband, putting her brown hand on his thigh in his best pale market breeches.

"Well, Jack, will our lads Tom and Kenneth be of a mind to stay or go. Or what?"

Sitting where he could see the road ahead from between them, and pleased to be close to Eleanor on the back seat, Fraser felt to be included in the warmth of close-knittedness surrounding them all. Marcia turned her head a bit more, speaking directly to the two younger ones behind her.

"This man Hitler's a bad bit of work, wouldn't you say, Fraser? Have you been listening to the wireless with your Mam and Dad? Eleanor's got it set on the right station all the time. Home Service."

In the rear-view mirror, Jack's tanned face and dark brown eyes engaged those of Fraser, probably hoping for some extension of his good friend, Alec Baird's, knowing mind through his son, here with them in the car.

"What can we possibly do about such madmen as this Adolf Hitler, Jack? He's getting all these poor countries like Czechoslovakia and France and Poland in a terrible state of fear. It all seems to have been going on for at least a year." Marcia's fingers were suddenly fierce on Jack's forearm, sleeve rolled up as usual at any time.

Her husband's growl was so low and so angered, but his words were correspondingly slow, that both his wife, and Fraser and Eleanor could hear every word, with hardly any roughness in enunciation.

"I reckon the mad, deshtructive bashtard should've been cashtrated as a young 'un, and put through to killing weight, h'and 'ave done with 'im, about the time of the lasht bluggy war, my word."

His hand on the gear lever was entwined by his wife's fingers, but his hooded dark brown eyes in the mirror looked straight back into Fraser's.

"What do yew reckon, Frayshyurr?"

As Jack Harris's question hung over them, Fraser wanted to put his arms out to all of them, to be drawn into their caring about him, their family, their farm, their cattle, their countryside, to reassure them that he knew his friends of the day, Colour Sergeant Oldcroft and Constable Hanbury, would do their very best to make a stand. And maybe even his own father again, come to that.

Both Marcia and Jack detected the quiver in Fraser's voice, equally low, as he replied, "Yes, Mr Harris, I reckon."

As the car hummed smoothly on the road back to milking time and the wireless bulletins, Eleanor's hand slipped up his arm, to lie, warm, on his shoulder.

X

At a quarter past eleven on the morning of Sunday, 3rd of September, 1939, the thin, apologetic voice of the British Prime Minister, Mr Neville Chamberlain, trickled reedily from the wireless on the small oak table in the Bairds' sunlit sitting room. It was a threnody of appallingly ineffectual dithering.

"At nine o'clock this morning, Great Britain's ambassador in Berlin delivered an ultimatum to Herr Adolf Hitler. Britain has stated that unless satisfactory reassurances of German action to call off the present attack on Poland were received by eleven o'clock this morning, a state of war would exist between Great Britain and Germany.

"I am sad to say that no such assurances have been received. Now, Great Britain is at war with Germany. You can imagine what a bitter blow this is to me."

In the complete quietness of the room, Fraser and his sister sat still, observing the effect of this distanced utterance upon their parents' faces. What was remarkable to both of them, when, as adults they spoke with each other about their small, silent scene, was that the response, initially, came from and was sustained by their mother, not their father. It came as a flow of profound concern, of compassion for their father, a rare and surprising manifestation of their mother's loving and concern for him.

Fraser would recall his sister acknowledging that as families went about their business in those times, relationships between them all, his mother and father, and he and his sister Jean, were entirely normal in their frictions, difficulties of acceptable (and accepting) discipline, grudging recognition by their mother of their father's deep tiredness at the end of his day, moments of sudden hilarity when Mary Baird's sense of impish humour would raise their spirits around the meal table with tales of ridiculous pranks from her youth, only to be met with even more outrageously funny episodes from their father which reduced them all to helpless tears of laughter.

While what sounded to Fraser like a whole lot of fishy-voiced members of the government gobbled and bobbled amongst their fluting deliveries of pompous portents and grave platitudes from the wireless set, Mary Baird rose with a sudden swish of her skirt and, standing behind him, clasped both of her husband's shoulders in her hands and gently pulled his head and neck back into her own body. Without speech.

Alec Baird had drawn himself down into his big man's frame, which was now of stone, immobile. Except for his fingers, beating in an arrhythmic tattoo on the wing of the faded armchair. The nicotine-stained index finger of his right hand tapped incessantly. His light blue eyes, vacant of the moment, at a vast distance from the apologetic words which had stilled them all, appeared focussed on an far state, a scene of indescribable chaos; men and mules sucked into a monstrous soup of mud and blood to their hubs, Passchendaele, khaki oozing blood from comrades barely living, gun limbers and caissons and horses blown to unrecognisable smoking fragments.

In ghastly speed and clarity, Alec Baird's mind had wrenched open a chapter in his young man's earlier life that had propelled him into a state of bodily insult inconceivable to a callow farmer's son as he was in that month of August, 1914. He had been a first year veterinary student, in Edinburgh, enrolled in September of 1913.

The first, and as it turned out, last lecture in natural philosophy for them all in the veterinary college, had been in their second year's first week of term in the newly opened William Dick Veterinary College, Summerhall, at the east end of the Edinburgh Meadows; an eagerly anticipated event.

Farriers' sons, farmers' sons, country chemists' sons, sons of the manse, mill and market ring, they were all aware of the tide of uncertainty that washed over them, demanding their attention, demanding they abandon their studies, take into their students' hands some kind of action. Alec Baird could again picture and hear the scene in the lecture theatre that day with an entire detail that possessed him with an intensity from which he was powerless to stand back. He could hear those words of another time:

"Gentlemen," Dr Connor Aitken, their lecturer, had concluded, "we are going to stop discussion on the behaviour of gases under pressure at this point. All of you, stop taking notes, if you please."

Alec Baird was watching Dr Aitken closely. His father's farm foreman back home had always said of a beast that was an uncertain quantity both in health or otherwise, "Just ye tak' time tae add up the wee signs that are there a' the time." Was there an element of great weariness, not only in Dr Aitken's quiet instructions, but also in his stance at the lectern, one elbow, the one they already knew to be damaged in the Boer war, characteristically flat to the angled top, but also in the tension of his features?

His words came in a sequence of carefully assembled logical statements, as in the resolution of a theorem, with which he would help them, his students, to a solution. Oh, aye, but solution to what? Alec Baird asked himself, in growing tension.

He felt something springing into a hitherto unknown sensation of heightened wariness in his perception of what was taking place in the lecture theatre this fine summer's morning. He did not know what it was but sensed that he, and all his fellow students now so still along the steeply tiered benches, would every one be changed in the manner of their lives by what was coming to their ears. Alec Baird was certain of that.

"Young men, you are all probably thinking that you should be, have to be, going off to this war that is now certain to be thrust upon us. This, um, exciting, totally unnecessary war."

With a peculiarly cold twisting deep in his body, Alec knew then that a lot of them would have their faces and fortunes decided by what Dr Aitken was so clearly but wearily laying out before them from images held in his own mind. He was speaking to them again.

"This war – most of you have given it thought. Many of you will now be thinking that thought is not going to be enough, that you must translate it into action."

He had paused, his regard flicking along their faces, searching. Without moving his head, Alec swivelled his eyes left to the form of big Murray Coutts, farmer's son from lower down the country. He was leaning forward, unusually still, over-large knuckles and hands locked on the seat in front of him, knowing fine that his good friend Alec Baird was looking at him, but determined not to sacrifice one second of his own attention in responding. Their lecturer was drawing them to his exposition of what this war business was really about.

"Action is the blare of the trumpet to the infantryman, the shrill whistle for you to jump up out of your trenches, the compelling bugle of the cavalry. Action is..." He paused again. "If and when you choose to enlist, you will very quickly, almost certainly be a part of the action. As I did, in South Africa..."

Aitken's hand lifted, to almost casually pass over the scarred, withered muscle of the other forearm, the one laid flat to the lectern. It was now an involuntary motion, a silent marker of two Boer 8mm Mauser bullets in his elbow joint, severing nerves and blood vessels, to lodge below his diaphragm. Alec commented silently to himself, so, that arm is your legacy from being in action, something that we could damn well land up with ourselves? Or

79

worse...

Not only he but all of the students were suddenly jolted by the flat-out severity of Aitken laying it out for them in terms that cracked like a whip.

"You will find out for yourselves that going into action will be unlike anything that you can possibly imagine. And worse, such as a horse, one which you know well to be a willing brute, perhaps off a farm near to your home, screaming with its belly sliced open by shrapnel. Or, one of your companions, his brain splashed out by a sniper's bullet."

Aitken's voice and eyes hardened. This was the task that he had to go through with for his young men.

"Two things I see very clearly. There is going to be a huge demand for horses, just as there is now a sudden demand for men, and more men, to handle these horses. Both they and you are going to need all the skill, and common sense and a cool head, and sheer guts that you can summon up. I sincerely trust that, whatever decision you all come to very soon, your efforts will help many horses to survive, and that..."

Aitken paused, searching for something to touch their hearts.

"...and that their simple trusting bodies will help many..." (he quickly rejected the word "some") "...of you, gentlemen, to survive also."

In the quiet, rather dusty sitting room that morning in 1939, on the declaration of war, Alec Baird recalled with deadly clarity every word of Dr Aitken's final message for each one of them. His words had all been shocking in awfulness. His final sentences had come with a face and lips and eyes that were intense, lacking their usual good humour in pursuit of natural phenomena.

"Gentlemen, lectures are in abeyance for two weeks, so that the college here can adjust to whatever numbers of staff and students remain, in the face of growing pressures to enlist in the armed services. When you return, I sincerely trust to be here to welcome you back. Gentlemen, good day, and good luck."

With his final caring words, like an experienced piper cutting on his last note, Connor Aitken had wheeled swiftly out through the door to one side of the lecturer's dais. What Alec Baird and all the fellows around him had not heard were their lecturer's grated words in the staff corridor: "...and, by Christ, you poor devils are going to need every damned morsel of luck that's going!"

In the dim light, the shake of his head to deny tears had been unseen.

Now, on that dusty September morning of 1939, Fraser Baird felt that pictures, faces, voices, experiences unseen, were jostling for room in a place silently alive behind his father's impassive face. He tried hard to guess at some or a part of these images, but could not.

"He was killed by a German mortar attack in France."

"Who? What?" there had been no indications that dead-stop things like this, creating an improbable havoc in Fraser's mind, were even likely to happen. Or to be flung at him in the abrupt manner of his father's words for him on getting out of the car that particular afternoon.

In fact, through the months following the country's declaration of war upon Germany, Fraser had this curious feeling that so far as his own and his family's immediate surroundings were concerned, there was little actually happening that was war-like, that he could recognise as having any impact upon the whole business of their country, Great Britain, being at war. "Being at war", that was an unconnected sort of thing to hear, to say. What exactly did it mean?

But there was this persistently unsettling matter of grown-ups, adults, whatever you called them, detaching themselves from their immediate preoccupations to listen closely to bulletins on the wireless: "Here is an account of our forces' latest campaign in France", and the listener would at once, impatient with interruptions, be apart from whatever they had been doing just minutes ago, clearly concentrating on the words spinning out from the tinny loudspeaker, as though to wring out from them or it, the very essence or suspicion of a probability that the announcer did not describe, or want to.

Hedley had suggested that Fraser come round to his home for tea after school, or for dinner at midday when they were going to share some exploit in the afternoon. In Hedley's home, any "Special Bulletins From The Front Line" caused everything in the Dunn home to stop at once and Tom Dunn would quite brusquely motion everyone out of his way in order to sit really close to the wireless set in the sitting room. Fraser knew that his own father now made a practice of being near enough to one or two of the local farmers' pubs at midday, to join in the silent group of farm men in working clothes paying close attention to BBC announcer Alvar Liddell, and his reports of actions at places in North Africa, or western France or Belgium. Whether in folks' homes or in a smoky public bar, there was a feeling, attendant to these knots of men, conversation suddenly stilled, that things were not going well in the battles for possession in Africa, or France, or Belgium, and that something critical to the Allies' forces was in the forefront of everybody's attention. In the late spring of 1940, well into May, when the ground was drawing in light and warmth after the vicious clench of winter, Fraser was well aware of the farm men's bustle of preparation for the need to set-to in tilling the ground; he would get his chance to work along with them as the longer light came in. For the moment, Saturday morning was good for going out to the small orchard, and getting on with digging over the strip of ground well blackened by a couple of cockerels' moveable pens. He held on with trenching in neat spits, shaking in some extra muck; he reckoned that the ground there could stand it. At about eleven o'clock his mother came out with a mug of hot cocoa and beetroot sandwiches.

"That's a rare job you're making of some hard ground," she volunteered. "Your father's to be late coming back for his dinner. We'll wait for him, if you don't mind hanging on? He'll be greatly taken with the amount of digging that you've saved him. He does get tired by the weekend. You know that, don't you, Fraser?"

As his mother went back round the garage, Fraser took up his gleaming spade again, and muttered, half-aloud, to her rear view, "Mother dear, there's still a good bit of your own family's farming ways left in you yet, even though you do go on a bit."

He heard the rattle of his father's car, then the driver's door closed, and another opened. Oh? Something had been brought home.

By the garage, his father was standing, saying nothing, looking at a bicycle propped up against the open garage door. Fraser sensed that this unusual arrival dictated him, for the moment, to remain silent.

There was something odd about where this particular bicycle had materialised from. It was a BSA sports model with dropped handlebars sheathed in white celluloid. Fraser noted that it possessed only one brake, with a cable running to the front wheel only. That's funny; it should have two.

His father spoke to him quietly, in precise diction. "He was killed by a German mortar attack in France. There you are then, squire. Do you want it?"

Was there a shadow in his father's words, a moment for questions to be kept back?

"Gosh, yes. It looks a super bike to me. Cable brake, free wheel hub, that's great! Where, er, how... who let you have it?"

"It's Ronald Fellowes' bike. You know Mr Fellowes, who comes up to help us with the heavy digging? Well, it is, or was, his son's bike, but he won't be needing it now. He was killed in a German mortar attack on his position in France. Things in France are not going well for the British forces just now, Fraser. We're trying to evacuate as many troops as possible with every kind of ship or boat, before they all get blown to bits by the Germans' tanks and artillery. According to Mr Fellowes, Fraser, his son's unit were fighting a delaying action with very little ammunition left, at a place on the French coast called Dunkirk. Apparently they were hemmed in and badly knocked about. A great many of the lads there have either been killed or captured. One of his pals in the same unit had been picked up out of the sea and got home, and visited Archie Fellowes, to tell him how desperate things had been for them all in the last the few hours. Anyway, our Mr Fellowes said that I was to give it to you. So, there you are, young man, a bike for the asking, or really, not even the asking."

Alec Baird turned away abruptly to the house, jingling coins in his pocket. With unnecessary care, he scraped his shoes for twice as long as usual before going in by the back door.

Fraser knew Archie Fellowes to be a respected friend of his father, a maintainance engineer of some sort in the Redman Milling factory. He liked to get out in clean air, out from the dust from the grinding machines: "...it gets right into your lungs, young man. They don't switch the damn things off, and it does me good to come up here and give your dad a bit of a hand with all the work you've got here. Helps with the breathing, it does."

He would spit on his hands, in a noticeably groggly fashion, and brush the shining blade of his own spade with a deeply ingrained palm. Sometimes, acting on mutual agreement between Alec Baird and Mr Fellowes, the latter would double trench a particulary troublesome piece of ground, forking in lots of muck, with the satisfied injunction "That'll push you on a bit, see if it don't!"

The last person to ride this bike, Fraser thought, with a prickling up his scalp, is dead now. A peculiar peppery welling-up gripped him at the back of his nose and eyes, and the question flew round and round in his mind: what do people feel, where can their grief go when they are just told "Your son Ronald has just been killed" and so on? Do they get angry, or what?

Fraser ran his hands over the bicycle, held the handlebars and ran it to and fro on the concrete, making interesting tracks in the hens' meal, then wheeled it inside carefully, a dead soldier's bicycle, left behind in expectation of use when next on leave, to see his girl, to go to the pub. But hardly thinking that it would be given away to a person like me, someone he'd never seen or knew existed.

"Tell Mr Fellowes, please, Father, that I'll use it very carefully," Fraser said next morning.

I Like to Walk in This Field

"All right, I shall tell him that. It'll help him a little, I suppose, but don't make it too obvious that you're flying about on it when he comes up the next time. Ronald was killed about the twenty-fifth of this month, May, so I don't expect we shall see his father up here for some time. Into June probably."

But Archie Fellowes never cycled up to The Leys again, burnished and lightly oiled spade strapped to his crossbar, to walk round the place with Alec Baird in knowledgeable admiring comment. Fraser wondered about the hands that had held the handlebars before him. Had Mr Fellowes' son been blown to pieces? Where were his hands? What had happened to them, was there nothing left to bury? What had Ronald Fellowes been thinking about when the German mortar round killed him? Had he the smallest part of a second to deny, to fend off the ringing finality of being killed?

XI

As Melford and the countryside around it retreated further into the clench of that down-pulling everlasting winter of 1940, the only areas of bare ground to be seen lay between the two ribbons of grey, gritty ice on which Alec Baird's car tyres grated and sliddered as he made his way home up the lane. The whole of Britain was at a halt, in winter conditions unknown in the memory of most in the county, and beyond.

The anxiety dominating each day for the family, but Fraser's father in particular, by either his own or Fraser's agency, was to have a sufficiency of logs ready sawn and split, the hundred or so poultry fed and shut up for the night (with particular regard to prowling foxes), and to make the daily collection of their two milk cans from the Harris's farm. This was no burden to Fraser, he was well pleased that his taking on these familiar duties took some weight off his father's mind on his return home, usually late in the winter's day. In fact, he looked forward to it, an exercise for mind as well as for feet, as his double-socked Wellingtons felt for safe footing in existing deep ruts, or made new angles of approach around enormous drifts of snow.

Even before two o' clock in the afternoon, temperatures started to drop perceptibly, and any evidence of hedgerow bird activity would suddenly cease, after a final rally of croupy calls from early-roosting cock pheasants. Before going down into the shovel-cut defile through the lane's drifts, Fraser scattered a handful of wheat outside the doors at home, mainly for chaffinches, blackbirds, robins, the odd greenfinch and goldfinch, and hedge sparrows. If he was later than two o'clock in doing this, the intense cold would have driven all birds to their secretive roosts, and the provender would lie, chilled and enlarged with hoar frost until the following morning's light. Then, scavenging starlings and blackbirds would collect it avidly.

By mid-January all the lanes and farm roads of England, the whole of England, were obliterated by the steady, horizontally driven snow that had already built up over the theatres of war throughout Europe. Hedges were barely marked by sundry twigs, and fields over the length of the country carried a level sixteen to twenty inches of hard-packed, layered snow. Railways had ploughed and packed enormous cuttings to the height of the locomotives' shuddering smoke

85

shields and funnels. Every family, with or without a man in it, was forced back upon its home, and that alone, for resources of every nature.

With his father away, attempting in murderous conditions to isolate and control an outbreak of foot-and-mouth disease involving not only dairy herds, but many piggeries as well, and with his sister staying with school friends in the town, there remained only Fraser and his mother at home at The Leys, with the two dogs and all the poultry. At nearly twelve years old, Fraser felt that he was the person in charge of all things outside the house. Setting off down the lane in the still half-light (for all the world just like a fire-step in a trench in Russia or somewhere, he thought, inspired by the photographs "From The Eastern Front" in Illustrated or Picture Post), he always had a sense of needing to use the bitingly cold, cramped hours of daylight to their best. The welcome from the farm men in the yellow light of the cowshed and calves' pens was his looked-for fulfilment by work that somehow carried on, had to carry on, without loss of purpose, in spite of the war, in spite of winter's grasp. Fraser now felt himself to be a solid, relied-upon part of this essential activity. Watty Taimes, Jack Harris's general worker for all tasks, straightened bowed shoulders to greet him.

"Well, young Frasyur, yew'm gotten through again? Still that 'ard up your end, then? We're needin' yew for a-carrying all this danged milk, like enough. These ladies is well away on their winter feed an' suchlike."

He gave a sideways nod to the assorted Friesian and Shorthorn cows. Watty indicated that it was high time Fraser made his regular appearance at milking, and get on with the business of literally taking the weight off his unrewarded and overburdened shoulders. Walter Taimes grumbled past him, shoulders and arms corded with the burden of two over-full, slopping pails of warm milk for the sows, talking to Fraser before he drew level and still going on as he hunched out on to the ice-glazed cobbles of the yard.

"I dunno, Watty. It always seems warmer down here, but perhaps that's because you're putting out so much heat yourself, with all those shirts on!"

"Ooh ah, goo on, ye young bugger! Leave school as I 'ad tew do at your age, or afore, Fraysyur, an' yew larnt tew wear what youm bluddy well 'ad. Theer warn't nowt else, now then!"

Watty flung gusts of comment and complaint over his shoulder as he lurched into the snow-covered yard, white flakes lace-like for an instant on the black silk back panel of his waistcoat, which was wrinkled up over his breeches and showed a gap of shirt, belt and braces that were all stained with sweat.

To appease Walter into a better humour, and to help the three other men, Len Bowes and brothers Tom and Ken Darlington, Fraser said that he would carry the milk from the cowshed to the milk house for the others, to let them get on with milking, feeding and bedding down for the night. The straight-sided milk pails each held nearly five gallons when full, and a pair weighed close to one hundred pounds when they were lifted off the concrete alley behind the cows' hindquarters. He knew that his limit was about four gallons, and set off, with the pails held away from his legs to stop them slopping. Lifting the pails in the milk house was the really demanding bit.

The glittering snow on the long sloping path up to the strong light of the milk house door was treacherous for any ill-considered changes of balance or gait. Having gained the cold and echoing dairy equipment of the milk house, Fraser had to get up on an old beer crate, 'Bass Is Best' stamped into its permanently sodden wood, in order to gain height for pouring each pail into the milk vat and over the cooler. His first step in gaining lifting advantage was to carefully settle each part-full milk pail on the flat lid of a spare milk churn, and then get ready to steadily hoist it. The electric motor driving the milking machine vacuum pump putt-putted companionably in the bitterly cold darkness. Eunice, inseparable companion with the rough-coated collie Turk, sat, shivering, one forepaw raised, just on the shaft of lamplight from the milk house, waiting to go down to the two cowsheds on the off-chance of a rat or two being shaken out by the men foddering up for the night, and making all tidy.

There was a fine feeling of companionship and competence amongst all of them, men and boy, as they moved about their tasks, each mindful of the right sequence of their progression up and down the lines of milking cows with vacuum pails, hay, straw and brushes. The closing-in of yet another bitter winter's night in a long succession of many was acknowledged but given scant significance by the men. In shirts rolled to the elbow, caps pushed back from faces that were both beaded with sweat and powdered with snowflakes along their eyebrows, the four of them made ready hay and feed for the morning, checked both cows and calves with a last steady look for any movement out of the ordinary, adjusted various half-doors, and stood, shoulders to the door-post and to each other, looking out into the night for a last consideration of what might blow up by morning, before turning off the farm building lamps one by one and walking, heads and shoulders held down into the swirling eddies of snow, up the long row of stone flags to the farmhouse. The yellow light from the kitchen windows pulled them all into the warmth and substantial meal that awaited them.

At this time, the Baird home with its well-tilled garden, poultry runs and plantation was the last one on the gravelled lane that led to fields and railway, and by repeated presumption, people just assumed that no other houses lay beyond it. Fraser was quite content to let this belief continue; it sustained his strong feeling of not being dependent upon human contact, which so many folk seemed to need. All the time, it seemed. There were actually three cottages a good bit further on, close to the railway, river and canal, in that sequence. From questioning his father about their history, Fraser had learnt that each had been built for their own men by the respective owning and operating companies. The river-keeper's house, dominated by immense, pollarded willows and poplars, the lock-man's brick house by a low bridge with an oval cast-iron plate stating 'Union Canal – 1844', and the smaller cottage for the railway company's permanent way man. Each had housed innumerable families with their indifferent fortunes, and a succession of events, some droll, others more desperate.

As the winter of 1940 snowed everything to a muddled standstill throughout the entirety of Britain, these three cottage homes in their hidden valley were dependent upon all of their domestic needs being carried in on foot, or tied on to a sledge. Their occupants struggled past Fraser's home, stumbling and slipping round huge, packed drifts higher than themselves, on ice and snow polished to an alarmingly dangerous degree. By early December, the northerly and east winds, silently whispering their way across Europe, had completely filled in the little-known lane to these homes with snow upon yet more snow, leaving only the topmost twigs of hawthorn and elderberry showing. Their leafless stalks looked like pathetic flags of surrender.

Wanting to be helpful and to do man's work, Fraser started to cut a path through the drifts down to the cottages and the snow-bound folk therein, using his father's big meal-mixing shovel. This did not go unappreciated by two of the families (the third, the Barlows, being helped by the goodness of the railway staff), but the lengthy cutting he had made did not come to general knowledge until well on in late February, when milder winds brought a blustery thaw and County Council gangs were set to shovelling out the lesser-used lanes and farm roads.

Coming home from school and still having to leave his bicycle in the Harris's farm buildings (the lane was impossibly rutted for confident cycling), Fraser turned back from the Dutch barn, where newly-knifed hay lay in thin sunlight, still vividly green from its summer making, and had the expected few minutes' jocular exchange with the farm men. This was a normal and necessary part of his place of being, his daily identity as a part of the two families that were comfortably complementary to each other.

Watty would come staggering round a corner of the alley leading out to the Dutch barn, under a huge compressed forkful of hay, giving vent to his customary blustering, preposterously accusative demand for something, some rhetorical question of "rights", which, if Fraser was quick enough, could be deflected with some equally risible and impudent retort. This now predictable exchange had got to be so, that there existed a distinct measure of barbed riposte between the two protagonists, to the extent that, in Fraser's absence, Watty would enquire querulously of anyone within earshot, "Wheer's that young bugger what reckons 'e can play fast an' loose wiv me ? Theer's a thing or two 'as come into my moind since las' day, dang 'im!" and go about his work muttering and looking darkly into places where "that young bugger" might just appear.

Len Bowes, seemingly never quite fully occupied with any one task in particular and always bobbing into view from behind a stolid Shorthorn haunch, would slyly beckon one of the men to him for a quickly imparted latest piece of scandalous a-goo'ins-on in the village, sniggering so much to himself as to be unable to gasp out the final lewd details. Ken Darlington, second ploughman to his brother Tom, and who quite amiably took "Stiffy" as a reasonable mode of address, on account of his unhurried, unchanging horseman's gait, was always sufficiently steady in discharging his work in stable or cartshed as to have time for a thoughtful and useful reply to Fraser's questions on stock or farm tackle or other allied matters.

Jack Harris's nailed boots clattering on the stone slabs at the cowhouse door would create a ripple in the regulated rhythms of milking time, and cause the farm men to grin at their own sudden rejection of idleness amongst the buildings. They included Fraser as one of themselves in the good-humoured exchange that always ensued.

"Walter! H'aint yew got them fu'sht cans switched h'over yet? Milk running h'every bluggywheer, an' I 'ave to come an' bluggy well get yew!"

"Ho, yesh, an' what in buggery h'are yew othersh doin'? 'Avin' a bluggy muvversh' meetin', then? Why h'aint yew got 'em h'all workin', Frayshyur? You'm an 'andy lad wiv a shovel, the ladsh tell me. Come hon! Idle buggersh yew are an' all. Theer'sh muck h'everybluggywheer!"

Watty, fiercely protective of his rightful place in the Guv'nor's eyes, saw fit to respond with spirit.

"Huh-hu-h-hold on then, Guv'nor, hi-hit warn't young Fraser 'ere as was doin' all the t-talkin'. I was just tellin' 'im as that owd sow needs a–"

"'Ar, Walter me lad, she needsh kindly attention reet enough but not what you'm allus on about; young Leonard, neither. Make 'ashte wiv them lasht heifersh, Shtiffy! Theer'sh cowsh an' calvesh to finish, afore you shet up feed for them 'osshesh of yewrn. Look sharp then, ladsh!"

The injunction to milk heifers first, before any older cows, had stemmed directly from Alec Baird's stern dictate that any and all heifers and second-calvers should be milked before the older beasts with their pendulous udders and swollen, hacked teats, in an effort to prevent mastitis transferring by hands, udder cloths and milking plant, to younger animals, from the older, more resistant cows. As a sort of representative of his father's authority in this and such matters, Fraser frowned slightly and walked back along the rows of cows' hindquarters, scrutinising each one with gravity, as though to indicate that he certainly wouldn't allow any haphazard milking either. Stiffy, squatting with one ear and shoulder into a roan cow's flank to put on a teat cluster, winked at Fraser and grinned broadly.

"Good thing as the Guv'nor didn't know as owd Watty 'as 'is favourites, nor your old man, neither!"

Fraser grinned back in tacit conspiracy, with a solid feeling of pleasure at being accepted as one of the working men who got their work done in spite of the Guv'nor's fireworks, vets' notions, arse-freezing weather an' all. He stooped on to two carrying pails, left unheeded while Watty suckled his slobbering calves, picked both of them up with the necessary leverage of a straight back, and set off across the yard with about seven gallons or seventy pounds' weight of milk.

Watty Taimes stood in the shelter of the bottom pig pen with an old Wessex sow nudging his gaitered legs, and felt, beneath layers of clothes, a sudden cooling of his body, which was racked and knotted from many summers and winters of farm work. He squinted at Fraser's outline against the milk house light, arms and shoulders straining with each laden step.

"Gormless young booger!" he muttered, half in praise, half in truculence at someone taking on one of his jobs, by rights, but with a genuine measure of goodwill towards the lad.

Jack Harris, pausing in the darkness outside the farmhouse door, surveyed and savoured all the familiar sounds and smells of milking time, calves' feeding, hay being trailed into the cowsheds in great mounds, his Shire horses thudding in the stable, and the broad shaft of light from the milk house flooding out over the flagstones to splay at his feet. In this light, he saw Fraser stoop to let down the milk pails' weight, and knew from the scrape as they met the glistening concrete that it had taken every fibre of clenched muscle to carry them the forty yards from the main cowshed. Jack waited on silently, curious to see just how the lifting of a dead weight of forty to fifty pounds, counting the pail, would be accomplished, in order to pour the milk over the cooler. He noted, grinning to himself, that Fraser did not hesitate in kicking the Bass beer crate nearer, from there lifting the first pail two-handed onto a full ten-gallon churn, and then changing his hold to swing it up, right hand flat below to take the weight, his left one guiding the first surging flow of milk into the cooler vat, and not all over his boots and the floor. The last movement was the most difficult, lacking a grown man's build and height.

"An' no bluggy milk shpilt, eh? Yew'll do all right then, young Frayshyur," Jack muttered, without waiting to see the second pail dealt with similarly. He felt for the latch to the low door into the kitchen passage. The metal was sweating moisture, indicating a rising temperature. The cows would need half-doors left open tonight, and calves would have to be checked likewise before settling for the night. He went on into the light, heat and smells of his wife's kitchen, an English farmer husbanding his land and all those upon it; a benevolence which embraced any who, whilst not necessarily employed and paid by him on a regular basis, still showed the same bond and aptitude to the work with stock and crop. Such as this only-a-bit-more-than-twelve-years-old lad who willingly shovelled muck and barrowed it out, forked hay and straw, and carried six or seven gallons of milk at the slightest opening. Yes, by God, and willingly at that.

All over rural Britain that evening, as the final spring thaw of 1941 set in, farms, steadings and dairies were also coming to a halt. Barn doors were heaved shut, hay tossed into racks for horses and young cattle. Hobnailed boots and Wellingtons, and Army boots mysteriously released from service made their ways to cottage and farmhouse doors in the darkness that cloaked fatigue and weariness. Milk churns were rinsed in icy water and up-ended in the echoing chill of milkhouses which held the twice-daily pulse of a hitherto unforeseen prosperity. For Jack Harris and his like, matters at home were by no means unsatisfactory. Alec Baird, the Scotch vet and good neighbour that he had proved to be, had finally pushed him into applying for accredited dairy status, and the penny a gallon premium was a steady bonus, paid weekly moreover, where before there had been highly unpredictable returns from cattle, grain sales on a depressed market and little margin of profit on the back of a fat sheep, be it lamb, cast ewe or wether, competing unsuccessfully with cheap New Zealand lamb.

As light escaped briefly into the raw, moist darkness and was cut off abruptly by blackout closure upon suppertime clatter and voices, there was little to show that this coming spring might prove any different, if at all, for Fraser and the team of men so well known to him at the Harris farm. They would have scoffed, but in guarded fashion, "Ooh, ar, an' who's a-sayin all this, then?" For the moment, in their Midland Shires, hidden by snow and darkness, the distant theatres of war had little impact upon the ordered rhythms of a rural Britain that was still virtually asleep at the plough.

Melford's astonishing and seemingly overnight leap into production of every kind of ordnance to meet the material of war really defied Fraser's belated understanding of how it could all take place so quickly.

Cycling through the town to school, he frequently had encounters with military material of a huge and dramatic nature. He, his school friends and any factory-bound cyclists (what kind of shifts do they work now, he wondered?) could just as likely be held up by large pieces of equipment, field guns of ponderous calibre, on trucks or lorries, with an increasing number in dull green paint with endless nose to tail strings of tanks or Bren gun carriers hidden in blue exhaust fumes.

Hitherto, had anyone asked of Fraser, and or even his friend Hedley, for his overall view of things in the town, neither of them would have held Melford to be anything other than a self-sufficient market town, with two or three large-ish businesses and factories more or less out of the centre of the town's historical mixture of businesses, shops and family homes. One such, which always caught Fraser's interest in architectural detail, was the Swanspool Hotel, set back off the main street, with the sculpted sandstone panel bearing '1656' over the massive archway into the stable and coachhouse yard within. This and other small presences from times past were incongruous, seeming to shrink back from the abrasive processions of army vehicles, mostly going south through the town. A number of Air Force transporters added to the traffic problems, frequently making northwards after a night's fighter plane action or a raid by German bombers somewhere.

Those factories on the outskirts of the town known to Fraser and most folk by name, if not specific products, were General Electric, Midlands Castings & Components, Redman Milling Company and a few lesser subsidiary workshops and assembly plants; they all lay to the north, close to the main LMS through-railway line, goods yard and wharves on the canal.

One Saturday morning when both Hedley and Fraser had been commissioned on their bikes to doing some shopping inconvenient to their respective mothers, and found that messages had to be waited for and then collected,

Fraser suggested, "Hey, Hedley, why don't we take a look round the blighted heath where Britain's secret weapons are lurking? We can collect the victuals afterwards without having to queue, OK?" Which they did, with interesting results.

On a very infrequent previous scout around the factory area, Fraser and Hedley had remarked on the rather desultory activity amongst the web of single-line railway sidings running into and out of loading banks behind cavernous echoing factory buildings. The few railway wagons had looked almost discarded, the rails and switch-points heavily rusted from little use. Now, with the turn of the year into 1941, all that had changed dramatically. There was a substantial wire mesh barricade across the whole sidings area, with a guard hut, a green Bedford truck parked, and two men in uniform, with steel helmets and rifles. They both wore red armbands carrying 'SECURITY' in black letters. Fraser stopped his bike and looked at the first soldier, who not only looked back at him, initially silently, but then with an only slightly jocular injunction:

"Right, you trick cyclists, no perishing juvenile Fifth Columnists here. About turn and don't come back bloody nosing about here. Go on, get weaving!"

"Christ, man, Fraser," Hedley offered, out of wounded silence as they pedalled, "you would think they reckoned we had secret cameras in our saddlebags."

"Yeah, well, we might just as well had them up our arse, clicking away, as we retreated, baffled! Heil Hitler!"

As they cycled away, thwarted and yet still intrigued, and more to himself than in joint observation, Fraser voiced his surprise at the feel of the whole controlled effort now in hand.

"Crikey, this bally country is definitely at war now, isn't it?"

General Electric, beside the main railway line, had been switched from production of turbines and generators to tanks, Mark I Matildas, armed with seventeen-pounders and Vickers machine guns. They squealed their tracks and gunned their engines in single file ahead to track – and engine – testing in wired-off areas of Sutton Chase. The Redman Milling Company, previously in abrasives and grinding compounds for Black Country foundries, ran three eight-hour shifts producing explosives, shell casings and aerial flares, under strict safety practice and internal blast walls built at great speed. Universal Castings now put out a steady flow of mortar tubes, base plates, chassis and trails for mounting anti-tank guns, and ammunition caissons for a range of field guns.

Fraser had often stopped to watch employees from Rudd Brothers' three old machine shops in the centre of the town fishing for roach or perch in the river during their lunch breaks. For seventy years, as he had learnt from one of the older men, the company, a family firm, had filed, assembled and finished actions for the Birmingham shotgun and rifle trade.

Now, they assembled .303 Bren machine guns and Short Magazine Mark III Lee Enfield rifles of the same calibre. All this was done by the same quite middle-aged and even elderly men who could detect the slightest irregularity with a few slow passes of oil-engrained finger and thumb, as well as micrometer gauges, to confirm what their eyes and calloused fingers had already told them.

These weapons went out in stencilled crates. Fraser had seen them being loaded, some going overseas, others going to standing regimental army depots all over the country. Eight miles to the east, No. 17 Maintainance Unit repaired, tested and returned to service both fighter planes and bombers, their movements in and out stopped everything on the roads involved. The visual evidence of their damaged aircrafts' aerial encounters with either German ack-ack fire or fighter planes was usually very public. Occasionally, gruesomely so.

It was only after some time into the years of the war that Fraser learnt that in the case of one of these overlong trailers being entirely shrouded with roped-down tarpaulins, this was to conceal from public view an aircraft, or bits of it, so desperate was the damage to shattered metal, engines riven from their mountings and hydraulic lines hanging from charred bellies totally ripped open. There were sometimes dark, almost black, streaks where the body or bodies of aircrew had been lifted or fallen out. Not good for public morale, was the reason for this concealment Fraser understood to have been directed, according to a sergeant pilot whom his folks had invited in for a meal.

The thirty-three feet long boxwork transporters carrying fuselages, wings, engines, tail units and canopies had to use the road in and out of town for most of their journeys to the repair hangars. The inescapable but largely good-humoured congestion which ensued allowed the townsfolk ample opportunity to speculate on the gaping blackened holes and lines of shell punctures in fuselage panels, and fire-twisted engines reeking of burnt metal and oil.

Accepting a lift with his father of a morning, early, with a shoddy tyre and inner tube on his bike torn and useless, Fraser slid to the edge of the front seat in an effort to crane his head and neck upwards before coming to a halt in a long line of vehicles.

"Well, what can you see up ahead?" his father asked, deliberating about pulling out and reversing if a suitable opening offered. Above the trucks and cars in front, Fraser spotted the high tail of a fighter plane.

"Looks like a goner from–" Well, he didn't know nor could he guess from where. It looked blackened, but that could be camouflage.

Self-important servicemen in RAF uniform were walking about in the middle of it all. Swinging wide against the oncoming traffic, a square-fronted Bedford prime mover had stopped, slewed into an immediate clotting of lorries and reversing vehicles, denying further movement to peering, muttering drivers. While the RAF driver remained inside his cab, fag dangling from his lower lip, one or two aircraftmen jumped down laughing and joking and set about moving the embroiled traffic for their own passage.

"Can't you find reverse, then, mate?" from one of the aircraft fitters, in overalls, to the driver of a local bakery van.

"Ch, cum on, snappy young bugger! Ah'll find it right enough once you lads decide which side of the bluddy road you're using. Wheer did that 'un cop it?"

"Well, mate, it was like this: 'E got tangled up with all them fairy lights as 'Itler's using for... hey up! You'll be into that bleedin' shop front. Pull yer right 'and down a bit. That'll do there, dad. Come this way a bit now, Fred, easy like." This last injunction to the fag-dangling transporter driver, squinting through his own cigarette smoke.

Hands made quick, deft indications, with eyes narrowed, watching angles and wheels. The driver locked his steering to mount the right hand pavement, transmission juddering, then abruptly spun the wheel the other way. The vehicle came to a stop inches from a gaggle of factory girls, bunched together with legs on raised pedals for incidental visual exposure to the eyes of any men who were likely to reward them with welcome attention. Alec Baird inched his car in behind the girls and their bikes; there was no way forward.

"Come on, girls, move over the bed a bit. We've a lot of homework to do on this lot!" Fraser noticed that to give impetus to this impatience, the blue-clad servicemen did not lay helping hands on bicycles but certainly did so on the women riders.

"Mebbe they're needin' some right good homework an' all, Fred, eh?"

Already, an aircraftman's arm was around the waist of the nearest girl, while his hands rapidly explored what lay beneath her faded overall, to the apparently outraged gasps but obvious pleasure of the wearer. Fraser looked across at his father, who shook his head from side to side, rolling his eyes in disbelief, or was it in detached amusement?

The sudden laughter and shrieks of the factory girls echoed off the shop fronts, more traffic backed up, and a police constable materialised on the running board of the transporter. His 1914–18 campaign ribbons and uniform were a marked contrast to the grease-darkened Air Force blue of the driver.

"Where are you taking this one, Corporal?"

"Seventeen Unit. Big job, this one. Needs a new prop, new landin' gear, engine stripped... and a new pilot."

"Badly hurt, was he?"

"Dead in 'is cockpit by the time they got 'im out. Blood all over everything. Riveted to his bloody seat, poor bastard. Mad bloody Pole."

Fraser and his father heard the laconic description clearly through the open car windows.The constable dropped backwards off the running board, and looking round, took charge.

"Right then, lady, squeeze back just a little, then hard this way. Nice and slow, m'dear. That'll do nicely. Stop now. Now, sir, you over there."

The RAF roundels slid past Womens Voluntary Service drivers, shoppers and a few late schoolchildren and pensioners, leaving a sweetish smell of aviation fuel fumes, aeroplane dope and carbonised metal. With the lettering in large bold white 'CAUTION! LONG TRAILER – NO SIGNS!' the hugely long vehicle and its load receded up the road past the market, and normal traffic edged out, to take over a day from which drama had suddenly been drained.

XII

To Fraser's mind, this tangible evidence of warfare that could be seen, smelled and speculated upon, was still not easily linked to the nightly rumble of German bombers across the night skies of the countryside around him and their home. By now, of an evening, any evening, the whole family would instantly be alert to the asynchronous engine noise above them, more of a heavy, wavering vibration that signified single German bombers, or groups of them, probably off-course after a bombing run, and now making east- or southwards, back to German landing fields in the darkness, probably in France. So, what did they look like, smelled, sounded like, Fraser wondered to himself, the German ones?

The countryside and villages around had endured occasional release of bombs, either in error or confusion. On these happenings, Alec Baird was curiously adamant, Fraser thought, in that they must all get out of bed at the first sound of continuous bombing activity, and get into the cellar below the stairs, which harboured them between massive oak beams, upon these alarms. Fraser would instantly waken as he heard the cock-upping and harsh screeching of those cock pheasants that habitually roosted in the trees beyond the poultry runs. They were unfailing in their response to any rumbling of planes, bombs and anti-aircraft fire alike.

Going out in the morning after a heavy bombing raid on Wolverhampton or Birmingham, with the flat thoom-thoom-thoom of anti-aircraft guns coming up in staggered repetition through the ground and the fabric of their home, and the stale taste of broken sleep in his mouth, Fraser saw that his father had already done the feeding in the three larger henhouses; the clover was blackened where his Wellingtons had crushed the dew. The tracks of their dogs Argo and Tam went in wider, questing loops, to the pile of hawthorn and ash limbs where there was the chance of a rat or two.

"Will the German planes be coming this way every time, Daddy?" he asked his father, with a certain diffidence, idly rotating a feed bucket with the toes of his boots. His sister Jean, pulling on her school coat and hat, overheard his question from the back door, and she found a sudden intense interest in the nearby dogs' kennel.

"Difficult to know, Fraser, but, aye, they probably will. Were you frightened at all, with last night's going on? Your big sister wasn't awake enough to know where she was sleeping!" he said, lifting a questioning eyebrow at Jean, who snorted and made some unconvincing display of little interest in this commentary.

"What about Mr Harris's cows, and heifers. Are they safer inside or out?" Fraser squinted up at his father's face, wishing to appear concerned about the animals that were familiar to him now, and not at all mindful of his own exposure to German planes on their bombing runs.

"Well, it would all depend on what was going on, and where they were. Bombs have much less effect in an open field." His father's face suddenly became impassive, placing a shutter between Fraser's questions and his own thoughts, his recall of matters in another store of memory. "Now, I'll have to get going. You take out the ducks' mash, and give their troughs a hose out first. You know fine what messy beggars they are!"

In the thin morning sunlight that imparted pale colour and clarity to the fields, the tracery of elm branches and occasional bunch of out-wintering cattle, there came to Fraser a sort of jauntiness. It was a feeling of having come out of an uneven and unexpected trial of spirit with a much better showing than he felt he could have reasonably expected. He had noticed this buoyancy of feelings amongst factory workers in the town going into the tank and ammunition factories, engaging in noisy exchange as they cycled along in close bunches.

At school, lumps of jagged metal bearing fragments of threading, casting or milling marks were passed from hand to hand. Excitedly, they were identified as being from ack-ack shells or flares, or incendiary sticks, with an earnest authority that went unchallenged by boys from parts of the school area untouched by unlikely or misplaced bombs. But what changed all this jauntiness in Fraser's mind took place throughout the night of November the fourteenth 1940.

On the early evening of that day, not long after Fraser had goaded his sister to help in the task of setting up the blackout screens in all the windows, and even before the usual after-supper tidying up in the kitchen and sitting room, and then settling down to homework or wireless programmes, the vale embracing the Bairds' home and Jack Harris's farm, and all living things in it, were battened down in the darkness, overflown by endless waves of enemy aircraft whose weight and menace were only further marked by any brief interruption in their total possession of that night and its darkness. The throbbing density of the aircraft seemed to render the night even more densely black and impenetrable.

Apart from their flying on an overall southerly bearing, the German bombers did not seem to observe particular lines of approach, but filled the entire night sky. Fraser attempted to ask something of his parents. It went unheeded by both of them in their positions of acute stillness, facing each other, listening.

"Why are there so many pl–?"

His mother cut him off with one upraised hand, not altering her stance one fraction. Tilted to one side, Fraser's father shook his head in negation of any distractions from his assessment of the storm unleashed by the waves of bombers above them.

By midnight the sky was a sullen, sustained furnace. In unspoken accord and a feeling of awful apprehension, getting into heavy coats and without speaking, the whole family filed quietly out of the house and across the lane, to stand in Jack Harris's wheat stubble, looking and listening. There were none of the customary safety precautions; the focus of all the enemy's distant destruction was terrifyingly clear. Two whole cottagers' families from the lane were already there, not speaking in the darkness, faces ruddy in this diabolical light, which was not at all as a winter's night would be in blackness, but a fiery red from the huge violence to the south of their position, in a row, backs to the hedge.

What they were absorbing with all of their senses was so enormous, so brutally alien to conceivable experience (with the exception of Alec Baird, and his memory of service through the bloodiest of shot and shell), that they stood apart from one another in an unconscious seeking for freedom from close contact, to let their tumbling minds fully take in the spectacle of an English city being taken through and beyond the roaring firestorm at the gates of Hell.

As Coventry was reduced to a smoking charnel house and flames suffused the southern sky, Fraser was aware, incongruously, of the night smell of mangolds or turnips and kale. Good for holding pheasants, but not for partridges, Jack Harris and his father had agreed. He also heard the small movements of hedgerow birds behind him, restless and disturbed. A gathering wind stirred everyone to return slowly to the house. In Fraser's mind was imprinted the row of faces palely turned to the sight and rage of the leaping cauldron of war, yet with the gentle counterpoint of small birds' rustlings to their rear.

Now that the enemy bombers in the night had found their way to locations of military significance, the intercourse between people, business and trade acquitted a new vigour, a greater purpose. It certainly gave day-to-day matters a new dimension in the minds and conversation of Fraser and Hedley. Listening to the overheard exchanges between their respective fathers over occasional drinks in either of their families' sitting rooms of an evening, it was evident that the cumbersome, ineffectual machinery of commodity control and rationing was largely bypassed by all who were in any kind of trading activity at all. The more frequent and intense were the nightly bombing runs over the Midlands, the more prevalent and determined was the participation by everyone, it seemed, in activities that cheerfully and successfully brushed authority aside, usually for useful gain of some kind or another.

Fraser was usually home from school before his sister ("Well, you could get home a lot quicker if you didn't spend so much time talking on and on with Daphne, or Sonia or Margery..." (assuming an accent for each girl named) "... then missing the half-past bus, and I have to be back here to get all my jobs done, see?") and had fed all the poultry by the time that his father's Standard car came rattling up the lane.

By reason of his keenness to get home from school and do the afternoon feeding and shutting-up round of their poultry, Fraser but to a much less frequent extent his sister, had seen how wearily their father would stay seated in the car at homecoming, slumped behind the steering wheel, before climbing out stiffly and stretching his whole body and arms with a great audible yawn.

"Well, young man, which got most attention from you today, books or birds or bits of bombs?"

"Huh, I'd sooner be at home or down at the farm, with the men, than doing some of that awful stuff. We've got five broody hens now, did you know?" This was a hint that the long-awaited time to set eggs in below these hens off the lay, was now, and more fertilised eggs put into their single Glevum incubator. He, Fraser, would be in charge of the whole operation before setting off for school, turning eggs, adjusting wicks and water, crossing off days on the calendar. Twenty-one days it took for hens' eggs to hatch, and twenty-eight for duck eggs. He wasn't quite sure about turkeys. These were useful things to know.

With outward jocularity and inner fatigue put aside, his father came closer and said quietly, "There are two bags of wheat in the boot. We'll just leave them there until after supper. You and I will see to them then, all right?"

Some of the wheat stayed on the place; a good balance was passed on to one of the other local vets who also kept hens, and a half-bag of about ninety pounds they left in the boot, to go off elsewhere the next day, probably.

Many years later, Fraser recognised the extent to which the early and middle war years had proved a severe and continual strain upon his father, who to him at that time possessed tirelessness as an entirely normal attribute. Alec Baird had become increasingly well regarded by the farming community by dint of his personal interested efforts to further their husbandry systems, thus affecting profits, and other gains, greatly to the surprise of some. These farmers' ways of returning his practical input, which lay beyond purely veterinary applications, was to have someone on the farm "Put a bag of summat in the back of the vet's car, while 'e's getting hisself cleaned up."

Alec Baird's farming background had been such that he knew better than to refuse such tangible proof of these farmers' regard; instead, he had the knack of saying something deftly humorous just as he drove out of the yard, that would leave donor and recipient well pleased with services rendered on both sides. At the same time, he was coolly aware that interception by any out-of-district police car could prove dangerous to his position, if he had to justify possession of controlled commodities while working in an essential occupation. Driving away from one farm in particular, he smiled wryly to himself, being well aware of the same largesse extended to his acquaintance, the Chief Inspector of the county police force. And others...

Of rationing in general, eggs were the common currency for everything: clothes, shoes, cinema seats, food of all kinds – sugar, tea, sweets, bacon and hams – silk stockings, dress materials, even professional services from lawyers or dentists. Eggs also purchased, at an exorbitant level, alcohol in all its forms and potencies and unspecified origins. This last was suddenly lent urgent desirability, as though the nation's civil, commercial and military functions could not possibly function without it.

One winter night, Marcia Harris had walked up the lane by torchlight, to exchange some clothing coupons for a few dozen eggs in return, her own Light Sussex hens having turned broody. She also anticipated relating one of her surprising market day excursions to Fraser's mother with great relish.

"You know, Mary, when I walked into Mercer's shop, he never looked to see who I was, just whether I had a basket, and if there was anything in it!" Marcia's comely face was animated, eyes twinkling in the telling.

"Where was this? At the serving counter, with all the queue watching, as usual?" Fraser's mother already sounded anxious, her own eyes wide.

"Well, yes, and me knowing that if I didn't get my stuff handed over, he'd take the first one that had eggs, anyway. All those townspeople standing staring at me! Eleanor was with me and she dashed near ran out of the shop. She gets so uncomfortable with all this, bless her!"

Looking up from his homework, Fraser could see more than a faint smile on Marcia Harris's face and lips and a sparkle in her warm brown eyes. His mother cut in abruptly, plainly anxious for her friend and neighbour, and standby in so many ways, throughout this whole wartime trading business.

"Look, Marcia, Alec says that the police have been watching Joe Mercer's shop for some time. He's fairly sure that all those eggs, yours and mine as well, are being traded for extra petrol coupons somewhere in the Midlands. Oh, Marcia, you really are daft, doing it so openly!"

"Well, I had to make the best of it once he got started, and I just said to Mrs Mercer, 'Here's the envelope with all the right coupons. Eleanor'll get the order round the back', an she knew to make it seem in the usual way of doing things."

Marcia chuckled, including Fraser in the pleasure of the conspiracy. He really liked her, and Eleanor too, of course.

With renewed anxiety, his mother asked, "And did Eleanor get it all the right way round?"

"No, she had to run out and back to the car with her coat over the basket, get another empty one for me in the shop, and then go round to the side door with the eggs – most of them yours, Mary!"

Marcia burst out laughing, pushing her abundant dark hair up with both hands and leaning back in her chair. In so doing, she caught Fraser's interested eyes upon her, and winked at him, causing both of them to smile, but having him to look away, embarrassed for reasons he wasn't quite sure about.

"By God, Marcia, you'll have us all in the county jail yet. You're as bold as anything, but what the dickens does your Jack say about all this, you daft creature?"

There was a curious contradiction of shocked admiration in Mary Baird's query. Fraser stifled an exclamation of impatience with his mother's twittering one way and then the other.

"Well, Mary, you know as well as I do that a pretty face and a nice pair of legs used to work wonders before, but there has to be other goods along with 'em now!"

Marcia's brown eyes gleamed mischievously. Fraser was somehow well aware how much Jack Harris adored his wife, but especially for her gaiety. Hands on hips, Marcia regarded her legs reflectively for a moment, lifting her dress to swirl it this way and that, before taking up the narrative of illicit dealings again.

"That wasn't the end of it, though, Mary! Before we'd got the length of Timothy White's, this little man came out of The Dog with Jack, and ran up beside me, and sort of squeaked at me out of the side of his mouth, 'Ah, Mrs Harris? What about that set of china you wanted for a christening? It's in my car, if you've got the necessary, understand? If not, well... if not, I'm obliged to pass it on right smartish.' Just about pissing himself, he was!"

Both women snorted, and gleeful, Mary Baird felt more relaxed and going along with the improbability of it all. But, it was dangerous...

"For Heaven's sake. A full set? That would take, ooh, dozens of eggs. Marcia, you are the giddy limit!"

"Now then, Mary, my dear, hold on a moment. These little fellows in the Potteries are tricky to deal with, you know. The odd seconds or imperfect piece slipped in amongst the rest. So, I got Eleanor to go to his car and count the pieces, and I said to Jack, 'Get you out to your cousin at Stonehouse smartly, get all the eggs that Hazel has there, and a couple of table fowls, and then come back to the car park at the Station, not the hotel park, you great stupid things!'"

And so the story had gone on – a lot of laughing and chaffing, but still a wide area of resistance in Fraser's mind, as an onlooker, to the fact that all of this deception and evasion should need to be practised so wholeheartedly by people he really liked. And Jack Harris's wife had included him in the telling of her tale of knowing tricks on both sides. He had liked that, being looked upon as a, well, an almost grown-up by her. He felt curiously warmed by Marcia Harris's regard in this and other respects.

A couple of days after Marcia's tale, Fraser had an opportunity to broach with his father something that had lain in his mind, unanswered, since that evening.

"Daddy, I heard you talking with Hedley's father about how difficult it was for everyone not to get involved or mixed up with black marketeering. What exactly does that mean? Have we done it, got mixed up with it, I mean?"

Fraser regarded his father seriously. He liked to have the comfort of knowing where people and their behaviour could be accurately placed in his view of the rightness of things. He was beginning to recognise certain persons about whom he did not have a secure feeling. His father stopped his work on herd tuberculin tests at the kitchen table and leant back in his chair.

"Well, this is what I've found out: if you have a war going on, just as we have at the present, the main thing in peoples' minds and in the government of the country, is to win the battle, or series of battles, right? If we didn't make a great effort to beat the Germans in this war, we would be invaded, and you know from the wireless and in magazines that life for all of us, including young men like you, and adults such as me, would become pretty damned awful. Some would co-operate with the Germans, others would be sent to concentration camps, some who resisted would be shot. That last bit makes you think, doesn't it? Well, my lad, they've done that once already, not that long ago, and they're going flat out to do it again, but much more savagely."

Fraser jostled with things, scenes, in his mind and just nodded. His father went on, speaking man to man.

"As soon as everything and everyone is concentrating on putting every scrap of their country's resources into helping win the war, and that includes like ploughing up old grassland for wheat, producing as much food as possible, such as eggs, butter and so on, there are always people, individuals, who say to themselves, well, if I keep a little bit here, a little bit there, that's not harming anyone, and if we sell this stuff to someone else, that's helping them to carry on OK as well. But, it all gets bigger and bigger, and where you have things like petrol, desperately needed to fuel planes and tanks, all you need is one crooked fellow handling supplies in, and supplies out, to his financial gain – aye, man, selling the stuff to more men like him. We have to buy petrol and oil from other countries. We couldn't keep the air force or army going a week longer if we didn't have tankers coming in from America, Burma and so on. Multiply one crooked man in a fuel depot by thousands like him, and none of that petrol is ever going to help keep a fighter plane in the air when he's stopping us, you and me and Jean and your mother, from getting bombed to bits tomorrow night."

His father was speaking with deep feeling, his Aberdeenshire way of speaking more pronounced. Fraser wanted one last bit made clearer.

"Daddy, you know all this swapping of ration coupons for eggs and butter and bacon, what do you think about that going on?"

Alec Baird knew at once that Fraser was unhappy with this seething flow of stuff off the farms. Right, tackle it head on, or you're going to have problems, he decided at once.

"Fraser, the one thing that keeps folk going when nothing very good is happening, is that you find ways of keeping their spirits up. That's what you call 'morale'. So, if exchanging eggs for someone to make a dress, or a coat, from material that's hard to get with coupons, that's good for morale. And then Daisy Doo-Dah'll go off to the tank factory in a really cheerful mood. And that's what's keeping all of us in a good frame of mind, and the tanks and planes get turned out when we really need them. And by God, Fraser, let me tell you we need every damned one of them right now."

Fraser looked at his father curiously. Crikey, he's pretty good at keeping things straightforward and simple. As his father and mother (she had heard the last bit, and lingered) got on with their evening tasks again, Fraser wondered if anyone had taken the trouble to make all this buying and selling and swapping of petrol and eggs and meat and wheat, clear and acceptable to that pilot in the shot-up fighter plane, the poor bloody Pole, riveted in his blood-soaked seat.

XIII

For Fraser, and his own family, it seemed that the early 1940s war fields in Europe, and elsewhere, delivered intimations of death and loss to penetrate families in a fashion that made them despair in their innermost thoughts of how it was ever going to stop.

With the first crispness of green showing on the elms in the morning light, the spring of 1941 brought an easement of snow and deep frost from the land, but also the delivery of telegrams to two of the cottages along the lane, with terse words of capture and death.

Mrs Rowe, a widow, lived in a brick cottage overlooking the long, grassy slope behind Jack Harris's cowsheds. To Fraser's eye, the house and its inhabitant were grotesquely well matched: tall, gaunt and somehow ill-balanced, almost unstable. The unusual elevation of the three-storey house, height not matched in breadth, was further emphasised by the over-narrow blue brick yard at Mrs Rowe's door, with a hand pump to the well leaning drunkenly on its cracked elm mounting. She would appear whenever any person passed her gate, breaking from incoherent mumblings into a wild harangue. Her only son, Ken Rowe, was an infantryman in the Worcestershire Regiment who, before going off into active service, had left his mother with a fully grown Alsatian dog, in the mistaken belief that she needed its protection. The animal was from then on more or less permanently chained to the pump, and Mrs Rowe further incited an incipient instability in its temperament by her constant stumbling over the worn stone threshold, to shout meaninglessly at some passer-by, no matter how familiar to her, as she twisted her large, red, chapped hands in a wet sacking apron.

One Saturday morning in that spring, early summer really, Fraser and his father set off down the lane to the Harris's farm, where some heifer calves were to be disbudded, as an act of neighbourliness really, Alec having only recently convinced Jack Harris that in all respects, cattle of any age settled better where there was no bullying or horning going on between beasts in their natural state.

Fraser felt an almost proprietorial satisfaction in pointing out to his father any small changes in each field as they came to it, the latter's work well into the evening each day having prevented him from noting such things as the peewits' courtship display, last year's laid hedging clouding over in green, when Mrs Rowe rushed out of her rickety gate (in much the same state as the house, pump and person, Fraser reflected), brandishing a telegram form in his father's face.

"Tekken Ken, they 'ave. Oh, God! Our Ken's been tekken! What can you say about that, Mr Baird? Why does it 'ave to be our young 'uns wot gets token? Why aren't you other men doin' summat? Git yoursen over theer or suchlike, Ah say."

Her sobbing agitation added to her lack of bodily co-ordination, and made her stumble wildly. Fraser saw the too-large black shoes, cracked by prominent bunions and tied with string, and thought, yes, she's going to wear out all of his things as well as her own. His father stopped her in mid-flow.

"Well, then, Mrs Rowe, what exactly does the wire say about your Kenneth? Is he captured or wounded or what? May I have a look at it, please?"

Imperturbable but kindly in tone, Fraser saw that his father's way of speaking, as someone used to taking control of situations, combined with his physical stature to affect the pitiable behaviour of the bereft woman, much as a good drench of chloral hydrate would take the edge of a beast that was excited, or distressed beyond all restraint. He had seen this happen.

Mrs Rowe pushed the mangled yellow paper into his hand, the better to wrap her own in the perpetually frayed sacking at her waist. She sobbed and swayed, small rivulets of saliva escaping with every shake of her long, sallow-cheeked face.

Alec Baird read aloud, "'…regrets to inform you… your son Private Kenneth Rowe, number… captured in recent action, France… wounded.' Hmm. Well, aye, Mrs Rowe, this is a great deal better than I'd thought from the way you were going, er, describing things to me. Yes, a great deal better."

Fraser watched his father clearing his throat noisily, in overriding competition (Fraser smiled faintly, then turned to conceal it) with the medley of utterings from the woman looming in front of him.

"Your Kenneth's going to be perfectly all right. Well out of it, I would say. Just listen carefully to what I'm saying, Mrs Rowe, as we go over it together, right?"

The faintest but unmistakeable touch of asperity there in his speaking, Fraser thought, standing silently at his father's side. Submissive but with her speech still flaring wildly, Mrs Rowe gulped wetly and noisily and demanded, "But 'ow can our Ken be out of it as you're a-saying? Ooh, but 'e's wounded an' all, 'e'll die, 'e'll danged well die! They'll not feed 'im, them German Nazis, mardy beggars they'm are. Ooh, our Ken, our Ken…"

With a firm clasp on Mrs Rowe's forearm, Alec Baird stated firmly, "Look now, Mrs Rowe, Kenneth's not killed. That's one good thing for a start. For another, he's slightly wounded and he'll get a dashed sight better food in hospital. I know, I've been through all that in the last war. Are you listening to what I'm telling you, Mrs Rowe?" He breathed heavily down his nose.

Fraser observed the flickering emotions in the woman's face in solemn, interested silence. Perhaps if he stood absolutely still and squinted up into the elms and hawthorns, she wouldn't notice that he was there at all, and further unknown aspects of soldiering would be revealed to him. His father clearly knew all about this being a prisoner and wounded stuff.

Stemming further tumbling words with his upraised hand, Alec concluded "...and lastly, he won't be the only one from hereabouts. I'll bet you a pound of tea that all the rest of his pals from The Wain public house are in there with your Kenneth, having a rare time annoying the Germans in umpteen ways. If you want to send something off to Kenneth, speak to Mrs Baird; she's in the Red Cross office at Brockwood Hall."

"Ee, that 'as eased my mind ever so. And 'ere, this young man's bin a-waitin' on all this time. Quiet! You fule!" She railed at the hysterical Alsatian, choking with fury at its restraints and frustrations, at its entirely pointless existence.

"Kenneth will be back to hammer some sense..." – Fraser's father coughed loudly – "...to train that dog of yours before long, Mrs Rowe. Meanwhile, Mrs Baird will help you all that she can; we all will. And, Mrs Rowe, the only reason that I'm not over there this time, again, is that I'm better helping Jack Harris and many like him to produce the food and milk that you and all of us need to survive, than landing up behind wire along with your young Kenneth," Alec said, with an edge to his voice. "Or below it," he added, under his breath.

Fraser's father swung away from the woman, the dog, the ruinous yard, to summon Fraser with a flick of his hand, to terminate the whole encounter. They both kept a taut silence until they had rounded the bend that brought them within sight of the farm roofs and Dutch barn.

"Do you think that Mrs Rowe's son will get on all right, Daddy?" Fraser's question hinted at the unknown quantities in the whole business.

"Well, I can't say for sure. If he is badly wounded, they might repatriate him through the Red Cross. But, you know, Fraser, that chap she's making all the hullabaloo about was born an idle bugger; not a single hour's continuous work in him. Very likely he'll never give a thought to whether or not he ever sees his poor, demented mother again, or his home, or that equally demented poor brute of a dog. God knows."

Fraser pondered the business of army service, and fighting, and the inconceivable matter of being imprisoned. "In the bag", he'd heard it called by boys at school with fathers or brothers held as prisoners of war. Behind all juvenile conjecture, arose the aged woman's face, the flying spittle and the chaos of her mind. As he handed his father the disbudding implements, Fraser decided that in many ways, Mrs Rowe was infinitely more of a prisoner than her son.

Mr Henry Lawson read the War Office telegram stating that his eldest son had been killed in action in North Africa, in the customary silence of his existence. Everyone in the scatter of cottagers' houses from the Harris farm up to The Leys knew of the content of the telegram within less than an hour or two, but by what agency no one could say; Mr Henry Lawson never spoke of it from the moment of its delivery.

Surrounding the moss-grown dwelling-cum-shop, there was an atmosphere of collapse into hopelessness. Fraser felt disturbed himself. This was rendered all the more incongruous, he thought, by his unpredictable encounters with Mr Henry Lawson's younger son, in silent and intense embrace with the attractive young woman whom Fraser had recognised when she turned her face, surprised and resentful, as one of the grammar school's secretaries. The couple seemed normal enough for that sort of thing. On such unintentional exposures, usually below the poplar tree at the opening into the bridle path past The Leys, no words were spoken, no attempt to disengage from the couple's pleasant congress; just a look of blank expectation at something which had to be momentarily accommodated. It, he, would go away, and they would quietly resume.

Any attempts to question the men at the farm about further background to Mr Henry Lawson, or the son killed in Africa, had met with only rather uncertain and puzzled responses on knowing nothing of rural note about either son or for that matter, about the solitarily living father.

Watty Taimes, unfailing and usually accurate repository of all worthwhile personal histories, was at a loss. "Carn't say as I do know owt, Fraysyur; 'e never was a feller to give an 'and with bugger all 'ere, no," which was a monumental obstacle to any understanding in Watty's summing up of worth. No matter the occupation in or of the town, when hay or harvest was in need of extra, willing hands, if a man did not know to turn out; well, bugger 'im.

As for conjecture about Mr Henry Lawson's spouse, mother of the two Lawson sons so disparaged by Watty, "…never been seen in hair nor hide by none of us in this parts; arh, a right mysterious kind of a do, an' all."

Season by season, year by year, the implacable jungle of perennial plants and weeds overwhelmed ever more tightly the gappy thorn hedging, long grown thin and spindly in need to be touched by sun, but choked by ivy.

Nettles, cleavers, docks of magnificent proportions, cow parsley, bindweed, even a few tattered spindles of blackcurrant bushes, relics of a long past previous time and occupants; they all stretched to entwine up and then around window openings, enlaced over the choked gutters there, and then pulled up each new season's growth to follow blind tendrils seeking the roof and ridge.

Built in the 1870s by estate carpenters at a cost of less than a few hundreds of pounds, Mr Henry Lawson's home had initially been a gamekeeper's cottage. Its thatch had long since been stripped, or rotted, and replaced by corrugated iron sheets, made lumpy by plaques of green moss and birds' droppings, overhung with whippy laburnums and elm saplings. Speaking with the farm men, Fraser gathered that the Brockwood Estate had sold the building in the Thirties, in a very poor state of disrepair, to a local jobbing builder for about a hundred and forty pounds. He had sold it on to a then-younger Mr Lawson and his wife at a much reduced figure, it seemed, glad to get shot of endless patching up to keep out weather and sinuous, sliding tendrils seeking entry.

Hunched at his cobbler's tools, the silent worker's bow-curved figure, whose condition was due to advanced kyphosis of the spine, was only ever spoken of as "Mr Henry Lawson". Folks thus generally attempted to give him some dignity of being. He mended boots and shoes, without speech, for anyone who cared to wait in the dark room where he also sold a few packets of salt, sugar, tea and biscuits. The smell of tanned hide mingled with that of the paraffin in his lamps; the tiny squares of glass in the walls seemed reluctant to let in natural light of any duration.

Devoid of speech after the blow of his son's death, Mr Henry Lawson's acutely humped spine arched even further down over his workbench.

When anyone of the Bairds' acquaintance came to collect repaired footwear, they now saw no more than a jerked-up shoulder, a sparsely stranded scalp and his leather apron hanging by a knotted lace from around his nearly horizontal neck, unnecessry speech ignored. In the matter of payment, Mr Henry Lawson not infrequently just wrote the required sum in pencil on a scrap of paper, pushing it across the counter.

Biking up the lane one spring afternoon, Fraser stopped, to really look over the whole cottage and wilderness of growth. What was wanted here, and Fraser itched to put into action, needing orderliness on the land, any land, was some hours' good work with scythe and slashing billhook. That would sort it out, then a whacking great bonfire. Let the sun and light in. Crikey! The whole damned place, Mr Henry Lawson included, might go up! He further decided that the sagging lattice-work porch, collapsed garden gate, green with moss, catch and hinge long since broken, and the rank growth beyond it, was rather like a silent barbed wire entanglement; an enticement with possibly uncertain and maybe regrettable consequences.

Mr Henry Lawson's younger son, something to do with chemicals in the town, certainly had neither will nor stamina to tackle things around the cottage. With the few pitiful, unchanging packets of goods at his elbow, Mr Henry Lawson tap-tapped away. His speechless receipt of the telegram notifying him of his son's death had served as a draw-cord around the shrivelled fabric of his home and purpose, tightening all inward to put his unprotesting figure at the littered bench even more distant from involvements with the outside world and its war.

Waiting for his father's re-heeled shoes, Fraser believed that there had been two deaths here, but one of them was still of this world, right there in front of him, behind the oil-stained counter.

The way that things were now in Melford's capacity to manufacture articles of war, in the spring of 1942, it was no uncommon thing for Fraser and his country-bound friends to find that cycling out from the school would find them either entrapped in a stream of tanks and Bren gun carriers, or obliged to pull into the side of the main road south, and tag on behind the last roaring machine in the line.

This manifestation of war right there in amongst the seemingly trivial concerns of school life was usually in the form of steady and increasing passage of armoured vehicles and tanks up and down the long slope of Bennet's Rise, in groups of six or seven, all en route to and from the tank-testing areas deep within The Chase.

Engines of immense power, it sounded to Fraser, raced and roared in protest against the braking of tracks, sprockets and idler wheels, squealing in unison as they turned out on to the main road, over-correcting with a dip and a lurch of each tank's armoured nose plates. They would then stream out in file, accelerating on for the testing ground with a battering roar of exhausts and transmissions. Their drivers, heads out of open hatches and wearing dark goggles, seemed creatures of enviable male potency and skill.

"How d'you reckon you'ld get a job like one of those men?" he shouted at Colin Treadwell and Hedley, as they paused, feet resting on pedals, exhaust fumes coiling amongst them.

They didn't know. Hedley shook his head; Colin, from a small family farm some miles further on from the Harris's farm at the end of Fraser's lane, mouthed something that none of them could hear in the dust, fumes and engine noise. He waved his hand to indicate that they should follow on once the tail-end tank had clattered passed them.

This they did, weaving from side to side, looking over the injunctions stencilled in white on the hulls of the various tracked vehicles: 'DISENGAGE DRIVE SPROCKET TO SPLIT TRACK', 'LOCK UP TRAVERSE WHEN FUELLING' and 'AMMO. ONLY THIS HATCH'. One or two of the stream had their main guns slewed to the rear, the unspoken menace of black muzzles depressed directly in line with their bikes and bodies.

Hedley peeled off from Fraser and Colin as they drew level with the lime trees at the mouth of the little semi-rural cul-de-sac where Fraser and his family had once lived. "See you, men" and "See you, Hedley" from both Colin and Fraser, with the former adding "Und sprechen nicht den Sekreten mit ihre Maul offen!"

Hedley assumed his deprecating-of-junior-behaviour expression and pedalled on. Fraser and Colin laughed and wobbled dangerously close to each other's front wheel. "Hey up! You crazy bugger!" "Oh, get OVER!" They were both in good humour, the spring sunshine was easy and gentle on their faces.

"Your Uncle Matt has something to do with the tank line in General Electric, hasn't he?" Fraser turned to Colin in interest. He knew that until a year or so ago, Colin's uncle had worked on their farm and cattle floating business.

"Yeah, well, he's got on as an inspector, being good with welding and engines and that, but you wouldn't believe some of the rotten workmanship he has to put back on the line, Christ!"

Fraser was surprised, shocked. Bad workmanship? In the middle of the war with everything possible needed by the army? "Go on, Colin, such as?"

"Well, the night shift men, and some women fitters, when they're supposed to be working to a schedule, they're pissing about in the tea room, playing cards, taking a drag outside, all sorts of things what they're not supposed to do, blokes and these women getting together, especially considering what they get paid and all."

They both braked hurriedly; the tank in front had abruptly dropped in engine revs, then slewed on one track, corrected and took off again.

"D'you ever wonder why there's always a whole lot going out on test to The Chase gun pits in the afternoons?"

Colin turned to Fraser. "It's because Uncle Matt and the other inspectors pick up such things as unfinished welds, hatches not fitting closely, idlers not tightened up, electrics not checked through; some of them are such a fucking mess after the night shift goes off, I can tell you. They dursn't let them out on test 'til all's made good. Christ, you should hear my uncle goin' off about it; he gets fair stewed up, and it's not right."

Fraser was stunned and silent, hardly noticing Colin's carrying on homewards behind the armoured column. Whose bloody side are these factory beggars supposed to be on? I wonder if everyone else knows what goes on?

It rained steadily that night. Field work with the farm men had been put off on the Saturday morning following. Of a curiously persistent want, Fraser got on his cycling cape after seeing to outside poultry jobs, and pedalled steadily to the wooded turning off into The Chase, following fresh tank tracks to where he knew some of the gun pits and test banks for transmissions were down out of public view. There were post and wire fences which did not prevent him from looking down to where two tanks were sitting, engines idling as blue-overalled fitters climbed in and out of hatches, tools in hands. In addition to the tanks, on the edge of the much cut-up test area, was the infinitely more substantial presence of a huge Scammell tank recovery mover, rollers front and rear for the looped cables running from the winch behind the massive drawbar.

"Hmm, my lad, this could be interesting," he observed to himself.

The group of three men some forty yards to his right looked him over with a patent measure of hostility, "Young lads should know they've no place here" written all over their accusative faces. Fraser resented this. He was over thirteen – well, nearly fourteen – and keen on anything to do with how the army was equipped to do battle against the Germans.

The three men, with collars and ties as well as overalls, turned to him, clearly wanting to know his business.

"What's to do then, young man? Who told you to come poking about here, eh?"

He improvised with a coolness that surprised himself.

"My Uncle Jim's in tanks. He says the main armament on his ones…" – Crikey, what would they be? Valentines? Matildas? – "…isn't up to much on some of the Jerries' armour–"

The more truculent-looking of the three men interrupted him. "Well, you tell your Uncle Jim that we're fitting something now…" – he gestured down to the men jumping down from the idling tanks below – "…that'll blow the bloody arse off Jerry's panzers! What lot's your uncle with, anyway? He should be getting something with a whole lot more punch about it any day now."

Recalling an illustration seen in a magazine, Fraser chanced replying,

"Tank Corps, Seventh Armoured Div.," hurriedly adding, "OK, thank you," and cycled downhill out of sight and beyond further awkward questions.

Later that evening, standing with his father as they waited quietly to see if a suspect fox could be spotted issuing from the far spruce spinney, Fraser spoke of the men at the tanks' testing place, and their questioning, and his replies.

"Did they mention any specification for this improved main gun, Fraser?" His father turned to him in thoughtful enquiry.

"No, Father, but what I thought coming home was this: supposing I'd just told you this, about the improved heavier tank gun, and you said the same thing to, to someone say, who travelled to Sweden or one of these places in Europe that are not fighting, and that got passed on to the Germans. Well, they would be ready to try and get something even better themselves, or better anti-tank guns, wouldn't they?"

His father was suddenly still, immobile. He barely breathed the words, "Look, there's Mister Fox. He's slipping away to visit Edward Horne's place; all those old henhouses not properly shut up. So, you can put the gun away tonight, if you like. About this business of the tank testing men and what they told you. Well, their kindness in reassuring you about your fictitious Uncle Jim's welfare in Africa needn't have gone as far as Sweden. There are men and women, mark you, in this country right now, in the pay of the German intelligence, sifting through every damn bit of casual conversation that they hear, anywhere. They've probably been planted in this country since the mid-Thirties. And equally likely, they probably know the exact calibre and muzzle velocity of this heavier weapon before it even gets shipped out to Africa. And whose tank men's backsides are going to get brewed up then, Fraser? Sad but unpalatably true. Come on, let's go inside. It'll be time for the Nine O'Clock News."

Fraser heard the announcer's urbane tones from the wireless but did not listen; he was recalling that very afternoon's casual advice of better things for tank gunners from an artificer or ordnance man who should have known much, much better, and then Colin Treadwell's casual injunction to Hedley (Ha ha! Joke!) not to talk about secrets with his mouth open. And to cap it all, Colin's uncle unable to let supposedly finished tanks out on the road, never mind the battlefield, because the workers on the night shift were not doing their proper job, not caring. Getting paid to piss about. There was an intransigent blackness in his mind with which he found it impossible to wrestle. The whole business was unbloodygodly; weren't there really tough men who could stop all this, this threat to urgent matters of value in the country as a whole, and particularly the wholeness of the countryside and everyone in it, to see a prospect of things ever getting back to normal? Didn't Hedley's father, seemingly the person who controlled what went on in the town, know that this slack, rotten work was going on, and if he did, what was he doing about it?

Fraser, supposedly dismantling algebra problems, and scowling furiously, was trying to create pictures in his mind of what these night shift workers, men and women, in their faded blue overalls were doing when they should have been getting on with desperately needed army equipment; tanks properly assembled, mortars complete from the base plate up, small arms of every kind. If Mr Harris had been their boss or whatever in the factory, a sudden explosion of "Hey! Bluggy 'ell 'an all! What sshort of ushelesh buggersh yew damned well h'are!" would have got that lot sorted out, smartish.

PART TWO

SUMS OF THE PARTS

XIV

Vastly absorbing and stimulating as all these armaments and accoutrements of war were, the restlessness in Fraser to become a part of the imminent spring work on the land, with Watty, Stiffy, Len and the rest, and getting his orders from Mr Harris just like a regular worker, this was an infinitely stronger pull in his waking hours, the more concentrated by being constrained to the days and evenings of the springtime weekends, free of the tedium of school during the Easter holidays.

Fraser was content to accept the fact of his being well past thirteen – well, coming on for fourteen with the spring of 1942 – mainly from being ahead of most of his non-country school friends in the matter of Mr Harris and the farm men allowing him a ready place in whatever was on hand, from his willingness to take on tasks which allowed them to make up a team, or even two, for separate field or livestock jobs. He knew that if he was unaccountably absent after eight o'clock on a Saturday morning, Jack Harris would be more than vaguely annoyed, and halfway between heavy humour and downright tetchiness by the time that he arrived at where the work was going on.

He knew as a fact that, on such occasions, Watty Taimes would make the stuttering observation "Young b-b-bugger, where 'ave yew b-bin, then?" and Stiffy would grin in slow pleasure at Watty's irritation.

At home, of necessity rising earlier than the rest of the family on such Saturday mornings, Fraser kept to himself the indisputable evidence of his sister being given to smoking; the smoky stuffy smell in the sitting room and in the hall was a dead giveaway. Jean was hoping to get a place at St Andrew's University in September of the following year and on the strength of this, had lately adopted a rather superior stance, quite openly directing him to do this or that as a necessary part of her enlarging social front. It riled him that this nonsense went on; were his mother and father entirely lacking in a sense of smell, and also unaware of this blasted bossiness, right below their noses? Well, huh, that was a joke in itself!

Fraser knew that by really getting going as soon as he got up, he had little difficulty in having all his poultry jobs seen to, bringing in coal and wood for the kitchen range, have breakfast (a good, solid one. None of this affected picking at toast and now wanting coffee, if you please! Crikey, who would have a sister!) and be at the farm for eight o'clock.

He and his father moved easily around each other in the warm kitchen. Alec Baird's comments were interested and as between equals.

"Going off down to Jack's place? What's on today?"

"Don't know exactly, Father. Chester said that we'd be getting some loads of muck out, and then getting the seed drill ready."

His father smiled at the note of real pleasure in Fraser's reply.

"Sounds as though they've got you well organised already, squire! Better let your mother know where and what you're doing. Now, one egg or two? Sausages, how many? Anyway, try to be back home at a reasonable hour, or we're both in trouble, young man!"

They pulled chairs in to the kitchen table, avoiding the fuss of setting places in the dining room overlooking the orchard. In unfussy but genuine concern, his father asked, between mouthfuls, "Tell me this before you go. How are you getting on with these maths problems? Still behind with some of them?"

Fraser felt the unwelcome knot of frustration; in a tight, angry voice he answered, "Father, the biggest horrible problem is him, this so-called teacher. He never explains how to do them, and just keeps going on, and half of the class can't follow, and it's just a case of keep your head down, otherwise, if anyone asks a question, he's pouring acid all over you."

Fraser was suddenly miserable, undermined by this nebulous thing that had no obvious application in what he wanted to do. Or anyone would want to. He concentrated on having a good meal, wishing to avoid his mother's appearance and her distinctly querulous comment, "So, no doubt you're off to your mucking and milking as usual? These men, I just don't understand why you let him go off with them so much, Alec."

This never failed to arouse his sense of the ridiculous. His mother's tones printed it in his mind in large, hostile letters (probably in deep purple! he grinned inwardly) – "MUCKING AND MILKING!"

Once down the lane, off his bike and in amongst the follow-on of barrowing out the night's muck after milking (Oh yeah, just like his dratted mother went on about!), both milking cows and heifers had to be foddered up with hay in their racks, great humps of straw dragged in for bedding, and everything made tidy, especially if all hands were to be put to field work of one kind or another.

There was an easy acceptance that everyone knew what they were about. Watty would disappear behind an apparently immovable quantity of straw on the barn floor, give his pitchfork a quick double jab into it from one judicially sought angle, muttering to himself in commentary about still having to feed swill to his special sows, why couldn't yew cum down a bit earlier, Fraysyur, like enough, and there was calves to bed down an' all. With the final explosive "and H'ALL!" Watty gave a long tearing grunt and the entire body of compacted straw would be dragged along at a fast clip, out of the barn, across the yard, into the cowshed and along the concrete in one sustained head-down rush.

With Fraser following, and even perhaps Stiffy hard on his heels, having seen to his pair of Shires, there was unspoken competition amongst the three of them to be first back out of the cowshed, running the prongs of their pitchforks at an angle in front of them, to keep them sharp and burnished on concrete or stone flags. Passing each other to and fro, there was no unnecessary conversation or pointless remarks; the Guv'nor didn't think much on that nonsense when there was work to be got through, and no standing about, neither.

They were all aware of the fact that while their boss, the good ol' Guv'nor, wasn't in amongst them, he wouldn't be all that far off, keeping his infallible register of how long it would be before he needed them to be finished, clattering up the yard and brushing chaff from their sleeves, to be told their work for that day, the really important, pressing business of getting on with making the land ready. And each man's work neatly interlocked with whatever the others were doing. The Guv'nor was a master at that, by God he were.

Fraser's respect and increasing curiosity about the Guv'nor, as he achieved a deeper acceptance of Jack's overall authority and respect from the farm men, was to know how he, Jack Harris, of Staunton Farm, had grown to be the kind of man and capable farmer that he was.

This need within Fraser sprang from his strong conviction of the truth that at some time in the future, he had to become that same kind of man, entirely capable of doing any of the jobs to which he, in his own farming business, would confidently put his own men, on his own acres, with his Shire horses and tractors, and probably a dairy herd. Yes, of course, tractors, he would need more than one.

Listening to his father's talking with farmers or veterinary colleagues,

Fraser had heard him say more than a few times, "Never ask a man to do something which you can't do yourself, and get on and do it, if need be." Well, all right, how did his friend and mentor Jack Harris have so many important skills just there, ready for instant, confident demonstration? He, Fraser Baird, would jolly well find out, somehow. And achieve the same measure of burly good nature and competence, of course he would.

XV

Behind the object of Fraser's resolve, accomplished traditional husband-man though Jack Harris had proved to be, his, Jack's, earlier attempts as a younger man in courtship, marriage and procreation had proved a disaster, and nowhere more cruelly than in his own mind.

Social life as a young farmer's son in the parish of Whitton Ash had been extremely restricted, partly because his own young years and early twenties had been exactly in step with the worst depression years in English farming of the 1920s. Jack's father, on a little over eighty rented acres, hidden behind huge, matted hawthorn hedges, had no extra cash in the kitchen dresser drawer for Jack to draw on for anything approaching a bit of fun outside of the farm, where every day was given to trying to make a go of things with what little money there was.

The family fattened a few Shorthorn bullocks, milked some indifferent cows, all by hand milking of course, and sold some of the older varieties of wheat or oats, on a buyer's price in the rock-bottom market of abundant imports of grain. Jack's father, Westley Harris, laid hedges and cleaned ditches for neighbours in a bigger way of doing, to make sure that there was a bit of hard-garnered cash to handle any week-to-week misfortunes, such as a beast needing the vet, or a calf to be found to put on to a cow with her own dead at birth.

But young Jack's innate ability behind a pair of Shires and a long-breasted plough had proved some justification for money carefully spent on travel away from the family home, when he first competed at local ploughing matches, and only just into his late teenage years.

Westley Harris's comment to his wife in this developing skill was to the effect "Well, we've got something of a master coming on here, Chrissie; let's give our Jack a good bit of free rein to get into the money prizes, never mind trophies for the moment."

Young Jack's mother, Chrissie, acquiesced with just about anything that her husband Westley proposed. It went some way to deaden the pain, never lightened within her, from her not being strong or shrewish or demanding enough or all three, to absolutely insist that money be found, somewhere out of the damned farm, sell something, for God's sake, to pay for the operation to repair the boy's cleft palate before he got into the really rapid growth that boys usually shot into after about eleven or so. The time had passed, the effort was never made. Jack himself made light of it; it had become a part of his quite special rough identity.

His father would go along to the ploughing matches. These cheerful, robust male affairs nourished both of them, He would help Jack set up the marking poles and the plough for the opening furrows, and then go on to compete himself in the hedge-laying class. At one of these, in the more austere uplands in the north of the county, Jack had encountered the daughter of a publican whose noisy bar and little dining area had been the focal point for competitors and spectators alike who clattered in, carrying with them the rich smells of horse sweat, harness oil and damp, newly turned loam.

Over a period of nearly three years, the equivalent of two ploughing championships and a host of lesser events, hedge-laying and such like, Jack courted Hazel Moss of The Seven Stars public house.

Flushed with pride in the straight-cut, well-crested furrows he had set up in his class (Lea Plough; Best Setting-Up and Levelness of Work, Open), Jack turned to the matter of Hazel's apparent reserve, which was really a crippling shyness, with equally vast good humour, much as he would handle a gyppy mare in harness, or out of it.

On such occasions, Jack's direct sense of humour became something spontaneously appealing, his speech impediment hardly noticeable, and his tanned good looks undeniably attractive. The cut of well-fitting pale cord breeches, his high-waisted doeskin waistcoat barely hiding a broad plaited leather belt with brass roller buckle, and deeply polished leather leggings and boots, all of this enhanced a maleness that was positive, but not to a degree to cause offence.

Everyone who came into contact with good old Jack Harris, horse authority of repute and master ploughman, smiled in ready response to his broad grin and even broader gushing consonants and bruised vowels, but importantly, respected his skill in setting up long unwavering furrows.

Securing the lease of a hundred-and-twenty acre farm that had lain in grass for long enough to fall back into weeds, rabbits and rankness did not present difficulty; There were any number of farmers in that time struggling to make sense of cheap grain flooding in from God know's where to their, the country's farmers', detriment. Nor did the bringing of it back into hand, though some outlying fields on thin, chattery brash had been frankly abandoned. The local bank manager had been brutally direct with Jack:

"Look, you've got two burdens to handle with this place: that left behind by the outgoing tenant, a man sodden with drink, and your own monthly progress with what you can sustain in meeting the bank's charges during the first year. I shall do all that I can to both warn you of what I would deem imprudent moves on your part, and to advance you what would seem a prudent amount from the bank, should and when things do go well."

Mr Blake, local Manager for the Lichfield and Leek Bank, rose and firmly put to one side his fleeting notion of taking out his bottle of fine ruby port to seal goodwill between both parties. It would be sensible to wait for a half-year at least, to see how yet another small farmer would possibly make out. He had one last point to make to this bluff young farmer of whom everyone spoke well.

"The new Mrs Harris, is she happy to help you in all ways a good country wife should; running a poultry flock, butter making and anything you choose to bolster up the weekly cash takings? Good, I'm sure she will back you to the hilt."

Well, dang me, Jack thought, of course Hazel will get on with all these useful things; stands to reason, no need to ask about that. His mother would keep Hazel right, surely.

All of this was clear enough in Jack's impatient mind. It was a good drying day there outside the manager's stuffy office. He should be getting on with starting to put things to rights on the land, well, his land for a spell now. The priorities were self-evident, and he, Jack Harris, would attend to them with skill and muscle.

Wedlock with Hazel Moss, however, turned out to be another matter. His laughing and pretty bride, once wed, took absolutely no interest in his, in their, farming enterprises. And, a profound shock to Jack, wanted no part in it either.

Newly wed twenty-two-year-old farmer Jack Harris very soon discovered an aspect of his wife's outlook that drew him up short, in a frustration that embraced every waking hour of their living together. It also confused his mind in that his normally perceptive eye for matters present in the natures of farm folk generally had missed this one.

It presented him with serious frustrations and mysteries, to none of which did he have the keys to unlock by either intuitive or acquired right action, unlike the vigorous good husbandry so lavished on his responsive acres. His wife proved to be ever intolerant, unresponsive and remote, in that order of discovery, and Jack's direct good humour and equally forthright desire for his wife became blunted and soured. He developed a fiery sarcasm that was as much a surprise to him as to his friends and neighbours, but this was his only defence against something for which he could find no reason or understanding.

The sudden green promise of spikes of oats for which Jack had ploughed, harrowed, seeded and rolled, working long hours into the spring dusk of their first year of marriage, for the sheer pleasure of the feel of the opened-up and warming soil through his booted feet, was a powerful stimulant to mind and body. It brought a great grin to his ruddy brown face, a prickling to his scalp, and a heat and heaviness to his manhood.

"Thingsh might 'ave bluggy well bin a whole lot different," he half muttered to himself, looking out over the stubble of seven acres of red clover cut and threshed for seed in the late summer of their first year's tenancy. And, ar, by God, it had turned a tidy profit, it had, with owd Money Bags Mallinson, seed merchant, giving him a dashed good price, considering.

His voicing to himself of the satisfaction in pulling off a tricky bit of husbandry in bringing the crop to threshing in fine condition, accelerated into recall of an even greater, unlooked-for fulfilment, which now carried with it a dark rage at the seeming impossibility of any repetition.

Jack leant heavily along the top bar of the gate, bringing to memory once again the wholly surprising coupling of Hazel and himself in that same field, once the heat, noise and dust of the day's threshing had settled gently to a strong fragrance of the crop in the evening shadows; peppery it had seemed. Every detail and the surprise of it had lain long in Jack's memory.

The day's work, accomplished with the ready hands of good neighbours, had gone without stoppage. Jeff Endacote knew his Clayton and Shuttleworth threshing box down to the smallest vibration. He eased the lengthy tackle out through the field gate, the big orange-coloured Case tractor delivering easy power at low revs, and gave a final wave to Jack, his upraised arm gilded with dust in the late sun.

Quite out of expectation, Hazel had come up into the clover field earlier in that day, with basket and tea kettle.

"Well, dang me! Yew'm a treat for shore eyesh, my gal, bringin' ush a bite to eat and drink! Cum on, ladsh, we'll tek a breather, passh the bashket round, Hazel. Thish black dusht fair getsh into a beggar'sh lungsh."

And she did, in good will. Jack felt pride, great affection and many welcome feelings flooding through his entire body.

The threshing contractor's men had gathered round, in good but cautious humour. Everyone in the district knew for a fact that good owd Jack was having a difficult time with Harry Moss's lass Hazel, hardly known to tek a look sideways from whatever he was doing on the land now, to all hours.

They pulled off their caps from sweated foreheads, hair dark and plastered to their skulls, and made careful "Ta, missus" and "Yes, sugar and milk, if you please", grinning at each other through lips and eyes ringed in black dust. The head man with the mill, having made a careful job of threshing out the small tough sheaves, adjusting screens and drum speed, asked of Jack, "Did our Mr Money Bags Mallinson say as he were putting up his wagon to set the sacks on afore dew cums sneakin' in, Jack?" The dense weave of seed bags was a well known harbour to the slightest of moisture-laden dew.

"Ar, yew'm right, an' here comesh th' owd bugger, no time shpent wastin' men'sh hoursh and motor fuel shtandin' waitin' on ush, my word!"

With her husband's field quiet and emptied of tackle and men, of a sudden, Hazel had turned to him, having watched his tidying up neatly with a pitchfork round the clover stems, now sheeted against the night's dew.

"You really love this land of yours, Jack, don't you? And all this hay put up, and things put to rights. That bit over there, it is wheat, isn't it, Jack?"

Her words to him had been soft, but certain. She had very nearly added "... and you going on like a mad thing, and me wanting you to come home and be finished for once, yet dreading it when you do come in, and then after..."

Jack straightened up from setting forks and ropes to one side, looking at his wife Hazel in a silence that harboured more than just companionship. The exact number of steps to come up to her were judged as to having the need in him to slide part of her light summer dress down over her shoulder, with no further movement between them, and then to clasp her firmly as he kissed her neck, throat and naked shoulder with unhurried intensity.

"There, my love, yew'm the prettiest of dovesh to cum gleanin' here after all'sh done!"

Their pleasure was a shared thing this time, hardly spoken. How long they had lain there, Jack had no recall. He hadn't had full sight of Hazel's long comely legs until that spun out, timeless moment; their sheer beauty in the evening sun, from toe to golden bush, had astounded him.

But thereafter, rebuffed by Hazel, even physically held at a distance by her in any quiet half-hour after they had eaten a solid dinner at midday, his urgent need to pour into the very core of his wife this enormous joy of his farm, his horses, his kindling of crop, was arrested and defeated. Jack wheeled back to his acres waiting outside, the acute pain in his genitals matched by the aching resentment of his mind.

Deliberately spinning out his tidying of tools and tackle of an evening, deliberately – nay, desperately – bringing a last hidden measure of quiet good humour to Hazel's tense and wary meal offering in the kitchen, did not help.

His frank attempts to calm and warm, pacify yet arouse, brought only muffled refusals and fretful tuggings of bedclothes.

There had been some communication homewards to her parents by Hazel. Her father and mother appeared on a Monday after a particularly demanding weekend behind the bar in the pub. Her father, old Harry Moss, had known there was something up; the girl's mother went into low-voiced question and answer with their daughter on arrival, whilst he found Jack to be good enough company, walking round the farm. They had brought the makings of their dinner with them in the car. All seemed affable enough, Harry thought, but he could see that his wife had Hazel under ably exercised control.

Wasn't that what their son-in-law Jack here was known to be good at? Hosses was one thing, wimmen was another. No matter, I'll get the hearing of it all a-bed tonight; it'll be a relief to occupy myself with the driving home.

Why, Jack Harris questioned himself, as he lay listening to the dull thumping of a hind hoof from the stable, has this blight tekken root in owd Harry Moss's filly, this cold bitch lying away from me? In the darkness, his bafflement was met by Hazel's unclear defence of her actions.

"Jack, you mustn't be that angry with me, please. It's just that... that it's not right all of the time, can't you see?"

Leaning on one deeply tanned forearm, Jack tackled this with all the single-minded purpose of a terrier pulling a rat from its nest.

"Yew'm more shkittish than that owd mare o' mine out theer. Whatsh wrong wiv me now, ash yew didn't h'object afore, ash I recall?"

"Ooh, Jack, it's that it's all different," Hazel wailed. "I do try to be... to be nice to you an' all that but it was different seein' you then, at Mam and Dad's place, and now... oh, it's just not the same!" She wept and wailed by turns.

That their one union of that glorious dusk had come to pregnancy was no surprise; while it constituted a deep contentment within Jack's mind, to Hazel it became a disaster from which there was, sadly (and repeated, ad nauseam, by her mother) no retreat.

There were no further intimacies nourishing to their being man and wife, once carrying a baby was confirmed. Hazel felt that she was trapped at a crossroads from which all roads were gated, with only one carrying a notice saying 'Go Through With It'. If only her mother had said... but on that score, was there anything that her mother hadn't said? Oh, no.

During the final few weeks of Hazel's pregnancy, Harry Moss's widowed sister, Ena, came to live with them at the farm. She was capable and not unkindly disposed towards Jack. For him, the whole bluggy business was like an evil boil which came never came full enough to be lanced.

Hazel took to having small scrappy meals by herself in the parlour, pleading little appetite.

The baby, a boy, was born one rainy April evening, nearer to the turn of things around midnight. Jack's neighbour who ran a Suffolk ewe flock, had observed to him that "Come a spot of goodish rain, Jack, your missus will come to labour. Ewes and gimmers, they allus do." And so it was.

The house was overfull, with Hazel's mother, Aunt Ena, the midwife and finally Dr Leyman. He regarded Jack stolidly over his spectacles, cuffs turned back from washing and scrubbing.

"Your child is preternaturally big. I'm going to have to ease your wife's labours by incising the perineum, the birth passage; she's gone long enough and is very dry. Do you know what I'm saying? I shall suture it, but it will take some months to heal, given absolute peace and quiet, d'you understand? I mean exactly that – nothing between you and your wife now, until I say, right? Good, off you go until all is finished. And, Mr Harris…"

"Yesh?" Jack understood, but didn't. What a bluggy set-to this was coming out to be.

"Mr Harris, given care by both of you, all this will pass. It always does."

Well, the bluggy doctor was right enough in some respects, Jack believed, but not in all things, not by a long mark.

In the months after Chester's birthing, he grew in length rapidly. His conformation seemed to favour his grandmother, long and thin. And, by God, thought Jack, the boy's nature seemed to follow on in the same bluggy direction, muttering to himself as he rubbed down his pair of Shires, the house ringing with protestations of this, howls of rage at that, and outright rejection of much that his mother tried to placate him with. She had given breast feeding only a brief spell; it never satisfied Chester and left her raw in tisues bodily and otherwise.

Aunt Ena, a practical soul, had spoken to Jack in straightforward fashion as the one-and-a-half-year-old child was voicing even more frustration at trying to stumble and wretchedly clatter everywhere before able on his legs, and causing chaos in every room into which he pushed, staggered and clutched. One of Jack's ploughing trophies had been pulled down and used vigorously, if ineptly, as a hammer. Aunt Ena had to cope with all this daily friction.

"What I'm suggesting, Jack, is that Hazel and child go to her parents at The Stars until such time as he's closer to schooling. We're all being driven mad here and matters will not heal for the good as things are."

"Oh, ar, and what then? Am I a man with a wife and shon bluggy milesh away, or I goo up theer for bluggy holidaysh, or bluggy what?"

His eyes darkened with a heated frustration at not being in control of his own household. Ena placed her hand on his solid, tanned forearm. By Heavens, she thought, it takes a strong woman to handle you, my lad, and my niece is not that woman; we all could see that some time back.

"Jack, listen to me. Let the whole thing settle a while. I shall come over regular and keep things straight in the house, and I'll get you someone reasonable to make meals and so forth. Once he comes to schooling, mebbe the best place for him and his mother will be here; lots for you to teach him, away from the pub, my lad."

Under her breath, watching Jack seize upon this thread of usefulness for him, Ena added to herself, "But don't bank on our wilful Hazel doing the right thing by both of you, if I'm right."

Chester, and Aunt Ena too at regular intervals, came home, but his mother Hazel did not, after a trial run at things domestic, never mind any of the conjugal nonsense. The anger in Jack seemed to have gone out of the situation by the time that Chester Harris was seven or eight years old, an apt pupil at his father's elbow, provided that it was a mechanical matter, at which he could never achieve enough time. Jack regarded young Chester's deftness with tools with a growing pleasure, not unrelated to the fact that something of long absence in his own circumstances was beginning to burgeon too.

Of a summer's evening, Jack's neighbour Simon Ansell asked him to come over to help with the matter of a three-year-old mare that, although broken to harness and field work, was showing the corner of her eye and a wicked hoof rather more than was tolerable, or safe. Out of sheer malice, she had already lamed her partner in harness, a good steady gelding. Well, there was no call for that. Jack would set the wickedness in her to rights.

On the second consecutive evening of Jack's schooling of the mare, with the latter's growing acceptance of his handling, there was a small gallery of onlookers watching him working the mare in a number of tackled-up situations. Jack had from the start made the mare be abundantly aware that he was reading every sign of incipient viciousness from behind her, with two leading reins, as he had her tow and wheel to right or left with a length of solid sawn elm log, through the trees of the orchard. He also had a single line knotted into a savage curb chain below her normal bit.

His rasping, outraged "HeyRRRUPP! YEW BLUGGY THING, YEW!"

coupled with a crushing grip of the curb, had changed the mare's entire behaviour, as all the onlookers could see. Jack's instantaneous crackling roars of reproof were at intervals tempered with firm hands and an apple to her muzzle and determined but guarded movement around her quarters and limbs, but with the single line to the curb all the while in the clench of his elbow. The mare was showing response to commands for which she did not now attempt refusal or temper; they could all see that.

Amongst the people watching all this masterly display was Simon's sister-in-law, Marcia Holt, with her young daughter Eleanor.

In the warmth of the untidy sitting room, after Jack's final satisfying handling of the mare, rounds of sandwiches and a generous pot of hot tea were being handed round by Simon's wife Barbara, who had to suppress a smile at the evident pleasure of Jack and Marcia in being comfortably close on the settee, and winked over their heads to Simon. And – oh, my, my! – isn't our Jack in good form tonight! She, Marcia, was happily eating up every inch of this man, so confident and masterly with his horses, Barbara Ansell could see that; in fact every one in the room could see it too. Well, now!

Abed of that night, after cheery farewells in the long dusk, with friends and Jack dispersing across Simon's fields, he nuzzled into his wife's shoulder and suddenly came out with, "Well, my gal, your sister's response to good old buggered-about Jack was like her being offered a three-course meal but no cutlery supplied!"

Absent-mindedly fending off Simon's wandering hands, Barbara Ansell gave her husband's pronouncement only a moment's evaluation before coming out with her own summation. "Yes, we've got a wedding on our hands with those two, mark my words." But this was at once cut short by her noisy injunction, "Simon! SIMON! God, you're in rollicking form tonight, with all this matchmaking; you need a bit of reining-in, and a curb bit, never mind your precious filly out there. Simon, you are a devil! Oh, come on then!"

The morning following, Simon and Barbara Ansell each nursed a mug of hot tea as they spoke of the previous evening's happenings. Barbara asked of her husband, "Do you or the other fellers ever hear anything of that cheating traveller bloke that my sister was bloody soft enough to marry? How long is it now? Some sort of a reserved occupation or conscie objector, wasn't he?"

"No, come on Barbara, he's buggered off for good, drinking his commission on piddling sales of uniforms and clothing before it's in his pocket, as I do hear. And taken up with some airman's wife up North. Not a scrap of maintenance money coming back to our Marcia and young Eleanor, poor kid. Says that she's going ahead with divorce and good riddance to him."

Barbara looked across at her husband; she had a first-class man in her own marriage, and knew it.

"Well, Simon, my lusty lad, here's hoping that there's a good time coming for her, young Eleanor and our good old rascally Jack. I just know they're well suited, and we shall help them all that we can."

Looking out at the orchard, scene of the previous evening's demonstration of Jack's skills and strong temperament, Simon reflected, "Marcia could prove to be the best thing that ever happened to our Jack. Let's hope it works out both ways, just like you and me!"

He came around the table, and clasping his wife's shoulders and breasts firmly to his chest, laid his bristly chin and cheeks to his wife's soft hair.

"Simon...?"

"Yes, what?"

"Nothing, just... oh, come here, my very special Simon."

XVI

In 1943, with his fourteenth birthday satisfactorily pushed behind him, and nearing getting grown up, Fraser was gratified to discover that, where day-to-day work on Jack Harris's farm was concerned, he was now far from being spoken of as just " Oh, get the vet's lad; he'll give you a hand." Given every available term holiday, and all evenings and weekends, he was now included and indeed counted upon as a vital member of one of the teams of men representative of all those on the land who went out from home throughout the vales and villages with bustle and purpose each new morning, returning only in darkness with dragging feet and dust-rimmed eyes. This acceptance became evident one Sunday morning when Fraser was feeding young stock and heifers for Jack Harris. He had come out quietly and down the lane from his home, newspapers and wireless bulletins speaking of turbulent campaigns in North Africa, Burma and the Far East, at a vast distance from the orderly progression of warm sunny days and cool spring nights.

"Goo'in' to muck 'em out for ush an' all, are yew, Frayshyurr?"

Jack leant over the half-door, hunched shoulders broad and solid against the light of the central yard, where a light rain drizzled on pantiles and glistening flagstones. Young lad, man and animals assumed a rhythm of small movements and contacts which spoke of familiarity and trust.

"Yes, Mr Harris, once they've had their meal, I'll put them outside and muck out into the bullocks' yard. I'll give the water trough a swill out at the same time."

As the black and white heifers plucked at the racked hay, Fraser leant, sweating slightly, on the ash shaft of the fork. He and Jack looked critically at the feeding animals' feeding movements.

"That un'sh your Dad'sh shweet'eart, in't she now?" Jack flicked a brown scarred finger with a rim of black nail. "She'sh goo'in' on famoushly now, in't she?"

They both nodded their respective cap brims towards the fine-boned Ayrshire heifer. She had been calved before her dam's time, pulled out in a ditch by men struggling with ropes, from a bought-in cow that had taken fright at the end of its long road journey from Dumfriesshire, and had jumped a series of gates in

131

alarm.

From the old gig house that was now a workshop-cum-garage came a confusion of tools striking metal, raised voices and odd forceful swears. Chester and his younger stepbrother George were arguing.

"Hark at 'em, Frayshyurr! Mekkin' ready for sheed-time next week, ish our Cheshter. Can yew goo along on 'im an' tek care of the drill, fillin' an' shettin'-in an' suchlike?"

"Chester and me? I suppose so, Mr Harris. It'll mebbe just fit in with the school holiday time. You mean, you want me on the drill all the time?"

Fraser had attended to the lumbering Massey-Harris seed drill before now, to let men away at mealtimes (Chester always refusing to leave his tractor) and in the evenings before the dew pearled up on grassland and made the worked-up soil sticky, but never for a length of time that would have rendered him wholly responsible for arranging refills with the seed grain, accurate setting-in and coming off on the headlands, and prompt attention to choked seed spouts. Jack's eyes regarded him steadily from below the grease-blackened cap brim.

"Ah, my lad, that'sh it, providin' your Dad'sh agreeable."

Fraser knew that Jack Harris did not take his father's friendly support and advice on cattle matters lightly. Their good farmer neighbour was well aware that Alec Baird's view of things, particularly in the dairy herd, had put money in his, Jack's, bank balance, on many occasions, what with planning bulling times and the choice of an improving sire, and TB testing of the breeding cows and heifers. Straightening up off the half-door, Jack spoke with Fraser in workmanlike fashion.

"Yew mek' ready wiv our Cheshter, then. Stiffy'll 'arrow up behind, an' either Tom or me'll shet out sheed wiv them two h'old wagonsh. Yew'm better tek mealsh along wiv ush; there'll be little time for owt elsh."

He moved away, the agreement struck, tipping his cap back and forward in a fashion that was as much a part of him as the plaited leather belt that he wore every day in life, then abruptly swung back to Fraser.

"An' that bluggy shkewl larnin'll jusht 'ave ter goo 'ang til all'sh done!"

His harshness of delivery was belied by the sideways quirk of his mouth and crinkling of his eyes, prompting Fraser to come out with, "Oh, all right, mebbe a little bit unwell now and then, but feeling much better once I'm back on the drill!"

Jack Harris slapped his breeched leg with a resounding crack, giving vent to gusty laughter on his way up the stone flags to the kitchen door.

"Marcia, jusht 'arken to the young beggar. Ah'll be danged!"

Such was the speed and urgency of the spring work that year, that Chester Harris and Fraser ended up being virtually on their own from before sun up until long after darkness rendered accuracy of drilling in the seed corn questionable.

The sun rose from behind the tree line of elms on the far side of the valley, earlier each morning into a largely cloudless sky, and the clear, strong light thinned out mists along the hedges and water meadows. With mechanical knowledge that was in part gained by example and in part intuitive, Chester made ready the green Fordson tractor, one of two on the whole hundred and eighty acres of his father's farm. Around these two machines centred the whole operation of the actual drilling-in of seed, for apart from a four-wheeled wagon and light field tackle, most of the remaining implements had been converted to tractor draught. The exceptions were two lea ploughs by Ransomes, Sims and Jefferies and a drill plough for setting-up and splitting drills for roots or potatoes. Attempting conversion of these would have rendered the two Darlington brothers, Tom and Stiffy and their skills, utterly without exercise; denied the need for their cherished Shires, they would have left the farm.

Single drawbars of oak or ash had been fitted in place of pairs of shafts, or couples of swingle-trees. These thick hitching beams were already oil-stained and scarred by nailed boots and tools, looking as though all tackle on the land had always been this way. Most nights, the twenty-two spout Massey Harris seed drill was left on the headland, sheeted-up against dew and rain, early morning preparations consisted of filling the tractor with tractor vaporising oil (TVO), greasing all steering linkages and bushes, and loading a motley collection of drums and cans holding the day's fuel. Chester and Fraser also received pungent instructions from Jack as to identities and precise quantities of seed to be sown between different fields.

"Now then, our Chester an' Frayshyurr too, look yew 'ere. We dunna want ter bluggy well run out of sheed afore time. Thish shixteen bagsh are for finishin' off that twelve acresh of oats –'Victory', mind, sho look bluggy sharp when yewm liftin' h'out and shettin' in. We dunna want none of them fairy bluggy shirclesh, bugger it!"

Fraser at once knew that this was in jocular but pointed reference to a serious error of judgement when both Watty Taimes and he had been on the platform of the seed drill and Chester's over-fast and over-impatient turns on the headlands had caused them to drop the spouts prematurely in some instances, and too late in others. The resultant patches of either doubly thick oats and wheat, and occasional wholly bare strips, which could cause a binder's cutter-bar to either race or choke, were referred to as "Watty's fairy rings" or "farmers' ruin" by the other farm men or for that matter anyone else who looked over the hedge with a knowledgeable eye.

Thus, while the rest of the farm and the village lay in stillness before the morning's activity, Chester and Fraser were away, the four-wheeled flat wagon or dray yoked to the tractor, exhaust barking, rumbling in unaccustomed speed. Fraser stood behind Chester's left shoulder, sideways on the tractor's slotted steel platform, with the latter shouting his usual excited and unfinished phrases, wiping away the drip from his nose with a hand already smeared with grease and earth. On the wagon, proprietorially surveyed by Fraser, jiggled the drums of vaporising oil, chains, tools and any seed necessary to finish the previous evening's work, or to give them a couple of hours' start on the arrival of the horse carts bringing up the day's supply from the grain loft.

The sacks were made of tightly woven jute that gave off a particularly pleasing smell of new rope, threshed grain and seed dressing. They held one and a half hundredweights if their contents were oats, two and a quarter hundredweights if wheat. Once roughened by use, their fibres bound well together; sacks slipping in a load was unusual, provided they had been properly kneed-in together.

The green Fordson with two men roared steadily on. Looking to the rear of the wagon, Fraser could see down into the valley and along the road delineated by elm and hawthorn, to where other fields were being disc-harrowed, seeded and rolled. Tractors and implements, some horse-drawn, were distant but discernible to Fraser's eye as motes of red, yellow and blue that drew his pleased attention. Machinery and figures of men moved with a purpose that was entirely in harmony with the needs of the land at this time. Fraser grinned widely to himself; he was a known part of this! Lacking a drip from his nose, he swiped his hand across his upper lip anyway, leaning confidently against the wide mudguard and its vibrations.

"There's Reg's big MM. See that big yellow bugger. He's got his harrows hooked up behind the drill again, look yer!" shouted Chester, standing upright on the platform. His attention had been caught by a local contractor's Minneapolis Moline tractor, an immense American machine in unmistakeable brilliant yellow paintwork, part of the USA Lend-Lease donation of agricultural machinery, to equip British farmers who were lacking in machinery to boost wartime food production.

They grinned at each other against the roar of their own equipage, burnt exhaust fumes whipping about their faces, and screwed up their eyes to look where the devil-may-care figure of Reg Rowland was assembling his own set of tackle in a long sloping field. With the abundant drawbar-power of "the big yellow bugger", Reg was able to hitch up to the biggest seed drill available to him and a full set of harrows behind that, handling the whole thing with a panache and easy skill that was just Reg Rowland's style in anything that he attempted.

It seemed to Fraser that particular morning that the countryside all around him was surging with industry, great skill and enthusiasm, that the acres harboured behind hedges lay quiet but somehow eager for the ministrations of those who served the land in careful and timely ways. Well, such as Chester, himself and good old Reg! He grinned to himself with what he took to be the knowing expression of a mature, experienced farm worker.

As they filled the grain hoppers from the bulging unwieldy sacks, the spare figure of Jack Anson, gamekeeper, materialised from the corner of the twelve-acre field where he had been waiting for wood pigeons to flight in to the newly drilled corn. His previous calling of keeper on the Hands' family estate gave him a presumed continued licence, he believed, to be anywhere at any time, and for any purpose. No one saw reason to question this. In a way, his presence early and late, gun tucked over his arm, fostered the impression of his being the watchful custodian of the lane and fields on either side, with the loose cluster of homes and cottages around the Harris's Staunton Farm.

"Dew too much for you last night, lads?" Jack's scrawny larynx wobbled above the grubby celluloid collar. A gamekeeper always wore a collar and tie. His eyes were hardly visible below the peak of his cap, which was pulled down at the front between two tufts of mousy hair springing from around his ears. The roving opportunist poaching lads of the parish averred that, when viewed against an evening sky, this gave him the outline of a large, upright ferret.

"Goo'in' to finish today, Jack, with any luck," Chester rejoined, his nose drip being brushed away impatiently as he accepted a full sack swung directly down from the wagon on to the open lid of the seed drill. Not having the presumed seniority or familiarity of Chester, Fraser busied himself with cutting the hard bands of binder twine and letting the dressed grain spill between his palms into all the recesses of the two seed hoppers. From the wagon, he called to Chester, "We'll need another sack, and take an extra one on the drawbar."

As he said this, he almost knew what the likely response from the keeper would be:

"Oh, ah, and giving you the orders now, eh, Chester? Young-feller-me-lad. He'll be telling me wheer all the Frenchmen's nests are, next thing – up trees, most like!"

Jack's eyes glinted as he cackled, and cocked his head back, thumbs in waistcoat pockets. This jibe to Fraser's hurt, he now knew sprang from their unforeseen mutual encounter in a spinney where each well knew that the other was illicitly engaged, or potentially so. Fraser immediately recalled his explanation, true up to the point of sidling amongst the trees, that he had been curious to find and observe a French partridge's nest, and Jack Anson's silent acceptance of this had been an equally swift indication that the meeting had been an unlooked-for impediment to Anson's own evening affairs, conspicuously unstated.

Without stopping his handling of the seed corn, Fraser muttered to himself, "Christ, I bluggy well hate you, you blasted grubby poking-about old bastard," but continued his work with Chester without lifting his head. The drilling was far more important.

Chester and Fraser sowed all that day in Willow Piece, stopping only to refill the hoppers, adjust the bevel gears to regulate the rate of sowing, and to gulp a hurried midday meal from the basket put up by Marcia Harris that morning.

They sat with their backs to the rear wheel of the Fordson tractor, Fraser commenting to Chester, "D'you reckon we'll get this piece drilled out afore dusk, Chester?"

"Yah, no bloody fear." He wiped a drip from his nose. "Just mek sure you drop her in smartish as soon as I pull on to the straight again, right?"

Eating was best done before refuelling the tractor with TVO. The slightest drip from the neck of the fuel drums tainted fingers, food or drink forever.

By early afternoon, the wheels of both tractor and seed drill were throwing up long sprays of dried earth under a pale yet warming sun, and Fraser found that there was less need for him to be continually looking down the spouts to check that the steel shoes making each drill had not bridged with damp clods.

He was hardly aware of Stiffy coming into the field with two single-horse carts, bringing more sacks of seed and the set of link harrows for covering in. Both Chester and he had shed their heavy top coats and were barely speaking beyond the necessities when refilling, mutually possessed by the urgency to finish the twelve acres they were in, and move on to a nine-acre field which lay in perfect tilth for sowing.

It was going to be a matter of very fine adjustments of the drill's calibrations to complete the field without excess or shortfall. They deliberated on acreage and quantities remaining, as the sun started to drop lower and cast elongated shadows of men and machinery, hedgerow trees and field gates.

"Keep the spouts up whilst I reverse to slacken off the drive pinion," Chester shouted behind him with an impatient wave of his arm to Fraser, swinging sideways to release the clutch.

"Well, of course I bloody well would," Fraser grimaced to Chester's shoulders.

The drill's dog-drive coupling clack-clacked noisily in its housing as the drill was slowly backed in soft soil. They both climbed down, stiff-kneed, fatigue pulling their necks and shoulders down, dust heavy on their cheeks and eyebrows.

"OK, let's have them spanners and the big Stilson wrench."

Fraser thought, hey on a moment, wasn't this just the trick that your father got so angry about – tightening things far too much? Fraser felt torn in opposed directions, neither of 'em a good idea.

Chester guessed in a wordless moment the cause of his workmate's hesitation. His lips and nose twisted immediately with dark annoyance.

"Oh, bloody arh. I bloody well know what he's allus goin' on about! Just because you're on the buggerin' drill doesn't mean that you have to keep moanin' on an' all! C'mon, let's have the Stilson, bugger it!"

Fraser was silent, observing whether what he knew had to be correctly done in resetting the drive mechanism to the seed cups was actually going to be followed by grumpy, nose-drippy Chester, The Wonder Mechanic.

With a final, hissing grunt and backhand wipe across his top lip, Chester tightened the lock nuts on the shaft, threw the wrench to Fraser to replace in the toolbox on the drawbar, jumped up on the tractor and yanked the throttle open.

"Got enough for one more round? OK, give her some oil, then."

He let in the clutch and the big rear tyres snatched at the ground. The seed drill lurched forward and Fraser barely had time to swing up the levers to the spouts with a crash. "Stupid, mad bloody man!" he half-shouted against the clash of the coulters and roar of exhaust. With steady speed resumed and no anxieties about the flow of seed, he thought to take the long-spouted Desco oil can and liberally lubricate the whirling bevel gear assembly that drove the feed mechanism. At the moment of directing squirts of heavy oil on to the meshing pinions, several things happened which in themselves were apparently innocuous in Fraser's eyes at the time, but which in total were poised to seed tragedy for the two farm men working away in the corner of the field that spring afternoon.

"If yew dunna stop dreamin' and thinkin' on all thoshe wimmen yew'm forever a-meddlin' wiv, bluggy sheed time'll be all done with… and sho will yew, young Leonard!"

Vocal impediment or not, the threat was trumpeted out over the entire farmyard with the greatest of malicious clarity. Jack's face was brown all seasons through, but at moments of need for urgent action, it assumed a ruddy hue, a well-recognised danger signal to any beholder.

"Goo on, Guv'nor, Ah'm helping Stiffy get this load out, and the light cart with the 'arrows."

"Besht mek 'ashte then, bugger it! That sheed's to be got out to our Cheshter and Frayshyurr. Watty'sh needin' hay h'afore yew shet out to roll, and theer'sh one of youm 'osshesh half bluggy roadsh to loshin' a shoe, now then!"

Undaunted by this verbal onslaught of practical and personal aspersions around his shoulders, Kenneth Darlington, second ploughman to his brother Tom, rejoined, unhurriedly, "Right-ho, then, Guv'nor. Theer hasn't bin that much time, with them two out there on the drill goo'in' on like a pair of mad buggers!"

Stiffy or Kenneth's open face and wide grin took any sting out of the exchange. His employer re-tied the seed sacks in front of him, bolstered each one up on a knee and rammed it into place with a dexterity that was all the more remarkable for his simultaneous shouting of comment and orders to all and sundry of his band of workers.

During the last year or so, Kenneth Darlington's modest wants of life had been dramatically rearranged in their order of importance to him. When he returned of a weekend to his parents' smallholding at Little Stoke, their brick and beam cottage seemed strangely diminished by the absence of his brother Tom, now doing early training on enlisting in the local Territorial battalion. Tom had gone to work as a young carter or ploughman for Jack Harris not long after Jack and his new-found bride Marcia had come into tenancy of Staunton Farm, a goodly farm of near two hundred acres much more given to prosperity than the early days of Jack's single-handed struggle with farm and first wife, both equally cold and difficult to bring to comfort. Tom had come on to Jack's new well-set farm in the spring of 1936, joined by brother Kenneth in 1940 as he turned sixteen.

They had been together for nearly all their years, especially so as Jack's two mainstay workers.

Tom was taciturn yet considerate, while brother Kenneth was more ready to laugh or perceive a drollness in anything untoward. Notwithstanding Kenneth's soubriquet of Stiffy, bestowed by his employer with the greatest of good humour, eyeing the young ploughman's first attempts to plough in a piece of tough matted lea, both Darlingtons were hard, enduring workers, both utterly devoted to their Shire work horses: three mares, two massive geldings and a couple of two-year olds.

Now, keenly feeling a dullness to which his scanty schooling could not fit a reason or name, Ken missed the common sense and steadiness of his brother, and felt at a loss as to whether he should go home more regularly and help his dad with the place, do small tasks to ease things for his mam, and suchlike. With the beasts going out to grass now, there was much less weekend work, but his soiled shirts and dirty socks by themselves hardly merited the long solitary bike ride home; at least, not every weekend.

Marcia Harris, who kept a perceptive pulse on all their single workers who lived in – their beds were in the long gallery over the malthouse – had detected this uncertainty in young Kenneth, and felt troubled in herself. The Darlington parents were good people, with two fine lads. She was well aware that Tom, for all his quiet ways with the horses and imminent departure from the farm, had been a greater reassurance to everyone there than they had realised, with his willingness to take all orders from her husband and carry them out to the best of his skills and competence.

Without looking up from slicing the white loaf held in the angle of her left arm, Marcia heard Kenneth's footsteps coming up the flags to the kitchen door. She sliced rapidly, first spreading butter on each slice with the same whetted knife that had just cut bacon for the men's substantial meal at six o'clock.

Ken's hobnailed boots squeaked on the red tiles as he sluiced water over his face, forearms and hands. The sun, striking low in the broad kitchen window, revealed his suddenly quiet, unfocussed expression as he looked out beyond the flagged yard. Jack was at the foot of the yard, hanging over the two sows' pens where Watty Taimes was feeding meal and chat potatoes. Both were commenting on the imminent farrowing of a very large, gravid Tamworth sow, which was rubbing her shoulder and chops noisily on Watty's leather gaiters.

"Something's troubling you, I can see, Kenneth," Marcia said quietly, continuing to slice and spread. "Don't you be going off, now. It would break your poor mam's heart."

It was characteristic of Marcia that, realistically or not, she thought first of the young ploughman's parents and home life than the foreseeable effect on those at the farm here, where Kenneth was also looked upon as one of the family, in the easy tradition of pragmatic and agreeable ways for single farm men at that time.

"You know, Ken, if you get upset because your Tom's joined up, think carefully on what's best. If you both go off, well, is that going to help matters, the way you're feeling?"

139

Ken's eyes, brown, with long, dark lashes, were still uncertain. A ridiculous, appealing small curl was plastered wetly on his tanned forehead. You handsome young devil, Marcia reflected, it's a wonder you've not got some local girl into trouble before now. Not that you haven't been trying (a very small secret smile creased her cheeks), everything comes out around my table in the kitchen here, or to me and Jack talking in bed at nights.

Kenneth Darlington was aware that this was a moment of trust. Mebbe I could tell the Guv'nor's missis, mebbe she can see the best road I should go?

"It do seem so quiet-like an' all, missis. Th'owd 'osses do miss him, and I shanna leave them, but, well, what's best for me to do?"

"Ken, listen to me. You must stay on here for the present. We want you to, and get yourself a nice young wom—"

She was abruptly cut short by the door being banged open, thrust wide by Jack and then Watty, fresh from the sows' pens and their feeding after milking. As each cast his cap into its habitual place, Jack perceived at once that whatever Stiffy had been saying was in the way of receiving Marcia's full attention. In great good humour (the non-stop input of Chester and Fraser with the seed drill having wonderfully surprised him) he bent down to the sink and rolled still further shirt sleeves that were bunched tight around his upper arms, with a plentitude of oil smears, meal dust and chaff on both sleeves and weather-tanned skin.

"Missis tellin' yew ter find yourshen an 'ooman, wash she? Eeeh!"

The great frothing and blowing at the sink only partly muffled exclamations of feigned wonder.

"Ah reckon that h'our Kenneth'sh quite capable of doin' that, if young Marjorie'sh dad h'in't completely bluggy well bossh-eyed, ha!"

Behind her husband's back as he fought with a large, very grimy towel, Marcia made unmistakeable signs to Kenneth to absolutely ignore these speculative, provocative shots from her husband. Flicking her normally warm, brown eyes even more fiercely all round the table, she dared any one of them to utter a single word in response. There was no further serious attempt at conversation on that topic. Stiffy slid into his usual place on the settle beneath the window that looked out on the orchard, place of Jack's masterly hoss-breaking. Watty sat beside him, making masticatory noises of agreement with anything that anyone said, taking his plate from Marcia with a "Ta, Missis", and immediately absorbing himself in the serious task of making a very good meal.

Having eaten and savoured a plateful of ham and egg, fried bread and potatoes, Jack settled more expansively into his high-backed chair with the scarred elm seat. He was about to make some further benevolent (as he thought) and practical observations on Kenneth Darlington's amatory progress, when there came a muffled booming and vibration from the yard outside, one or two shouts, then the approach of nailed boots up the flags to the outer door. Marcia looked over to her daughter Eleanor from the gas stove, where she was already breaking in more eggs amongst the ham smoking in the wide frying pan.

"That's Chester and Fraser. Did you remember to take more eggs out of the basket, Eleanor?"

She nodded, Marcia's comely daughter was quick, foreseeing needs for everyone in the family, on the farm.

Jack belched skilfully, cheeks blown out in gustatory satisfaction. "They've done well to finish that lot," he said. "We'ld 'ave bin right shtuck wivout young Frayshyurr to shet on the drill. Hey up, yew ladsh! Cum on in and get yershen sheated. Yew lot move up if yew'm finished."

The pattern of figures along the table broke and then resettled. The two latecomers sat with their backs to the orchard window, their eyes rheumy with dust and weariness. In Fraser's head, it seemed as though the tractor still roared and blatted in his eardrums, the steel lids to the hoppers still clattered in the near darkness. Chester broke in loudly, pushing aside existing conversation to impose his own.

"That seed as you sent up only just made it, Dad. We altered the gears to the other setting and came back over the last piece to mek certain."

Unnoticed, Marcia smiled in abundant pleasure at them all. If the farm was going well, then so was her husband, and that made a great many other things in her life easier, too. She looked round at all of their cheerful weathered faces, tired but hugely pleased with their day's work.

"More tea? You know just to help yourself, Fraser, don't you? There's more ham for those that want it. George? Margaret?" Turned to her, their faces were bright with heat and conviviality, fatigue brushed aside. Chester suddenly half rose, waving his arms in high excitement, claiming their attention.

"...and then there was this bloody great yell from 'im!" He pointed to Fraser. "'The buggerin' oil can!' he yells, and holds up this thing all flat and bloody well twisted, flatter'n a duck's arse!"

Chester leant forward on the littered table hooting convulsively. Ken and Watty laughed outright, leaning back against the settle. Marcia giggled delightedly, Jack thumped the table, speechless and red-faced, Eunice the terrier leapt out from amongst their feet, barking shrilly, the youngsters jumped around, squealing at what they weren't quite sure, but joining in anyway, just as Alec Baird pushed his way into the uproarious family, farm men and dogs. Marcia attempted to make clear what the laughter was all about, wiping away the tears coursing down her cheeks.

"Ooh, Alec, these two lads, they do the daftest of things out there. They'll be the death of us yet, with all this laughing and goings-on, and, oh, mercy!" and she was off again, overwhelmed by the sheer volume of lusty good feeling and nonsense that enfolded everyone in the lamp-lit farm kitchen.

XVII

In the darkness that lay over Willow Piece, now seeded with another year's crop, the warmth shrank back into the tilth and hedge bottoms. Dew began to condense, pearl-like, on those parts of the seed drill not covered by the tarpaulin. Where the oil can had passed through the round teeth of the metal plate carrying the multiple settings for altering the seeding rate, torn out of Fraser's grasp, a fine hairline crack in the casting suddenly accommodated the stress of Chester's fiercely over-tightened lock nut no longer. With cooling of the metal, it sprang open with a sharp crack proportional to the fracture that appeared, splitting the entire cast steel disc.

Some rabbits, restless and curious on the newly sown soil, stood erect at once, thump-thumping to the sudden noise. Reassured by the total stillness and absence of footfalls or human smell, they resumed their aimless passage to the next field, flicking their paws free of clammy earth.

The seed oats, sown at four bushels to the acre, had yet to be rolled into firm contact with the loam by Kenneth Darlington and his horse roller. They began to respond to the moisture penetrating their hard shiny husks. Given some days of sunlight, germination would bring forth the faintest blush of green, and another harvest would burgeon, beckoned through spring and into summer by the ash and elm trees ringing the field.

Early morning came in with a fine drizzle, not enough to film leaves and land alike with more than a thin coat of droplets, but dampening enough to prevent Chester and Fraser from carrying on drilling in the next field awaiting their impatient industry. While they rode up from the main road on the tractor, Chester's father walked more indirectly through various of his fields. The two farm dogs, Eunice and Turk, loped around behind his legs, cataloguing the scents of each field, hedge and ditch. From the moment that his heavily hobnailed boots stepped onto the land, his feet constantly relayed information to him that complemented all that his eyes, his nose and the skin of his face and arms told him about the state of his farm's fertility.

There was a mite more moisture to the tilled earth than he had expected. As he walked deliberately in the last-sown sweeps of the seed drill, his boots picked up plaques of claggy soil, to leave light-coloured drier patches exposed, in the form of over-large clumsy boot prints. Too moist for the lads to drill on this morning, he muttered to himself, both dogs pricking their ears, terrier bitch stopping, to lift a paw, setting her sleek brown and white head to one side.

Best goo on and see how they had been looking after the hard-used Massey-Harris drill, afore owt else was put in hand. He noted that Fraser had the sense to leave the stack-cover on, and was now untying the ropes to the high steel spoked wheels to get at grease nipples and bearings.

Jack saw that Chester was fiddling with that danged breakaway hitch. This was designed to break away from the tractor's drawbar should it fetch up against something with the drill, or plough, or cultivator, hard into the ground, so Sam Clews had assured Jack in Brewis's machinery yard. The hitch carried two immensely strong coil springs linked to the jaws to encircle the drawbar pin. The jaws were closed tight with a long thick bolt and nut, which could be tightened or slackened to any desirable tension.

Jack walked on in a wide loop through the two or three acres of the corner in which the two lads busied themselves around their tackle and empty seed cart. To check if the seed oats were lying at their correct depth for easy germination and that they were there at all below the slight rib of overlap of each pass of the drill, Jack flicked up the soil with his stick. The earth crumbled satisfactorily over a slightly darker hollow where a broken tile drain had needed days of digging and re-laying last back-end, before he had been able to get Chester on with the ploughing in the spring.

At about the same moment, all three of them in the field that morning saw the shattered bevel gear disc at the end of the drill. Jack Harris' violent explosion of disbelief made clear all consequences of this, this most unacceptable of disasters. Neither he nor it could be contained.

"Jeezussh bluggy Chrisht an' h'all the buggerin' Shaints! What the bluggy infernal h'ell'sh all thish, then? Buggered the whole worksh arsh-backwardsh by the looksh on it! DAMNN YEWM BLUGGY EYESH THE WHOLE DANGED LOT ON YER, BY CHRISHT!"

His stick was rammed violently into the tilled ground and the dogs leapt backwards in a spring of white-eyed fear.

Roughly pushing Fraser's kneeling figure to one side, Jack's fingers explored the shattered drive assembly. He swung round on Chester in instant inflamed cognisance.

"Yew've tightened thish bluggy thing sho danged 'ard, my lad, there'sh scarce a shlip o' play any danged road. Never mind feeding in my bluggy h'oil can!"

144

His rage was total, with words bursting out from his thickened pulsing throat in a bellowing roar. Fraser stayed bowed down beside the drill, grease gun collapsed weakly to the ground, in sickness of disgrace at being found wanting by his mentor and wished-for model in all things manly.

"Chrisht! Yew two 'ave totally buggered the drill, put a shpanner in h'it h'alright. Yew are a couple of ushelesh bluggy fulesh, an' no mishtake. God DAMN yewr blashted 'h'eyesh!"

In a sheer coruscating fury, he raked them and the crippled implement with eyes, tongue and temper beyond any control. Heads bowed, they busied themselves with pointless, unnecessary tasks. Jack's voice raged even louder at their lowered heads and shoulders.

"Yew'd besht mek haste, both on yer, and get the bluggy thing what yew've ruined atween you tekken to piecesh, smartish. H'it'll be of little ushe today, even h'it driesh up by a meashure. And look yew h'ere, our bluggy clever Cheshter, ushe proper shpannersh what fitsh the beggarin' thing, h'includin' that danged fancy hitch yew'm allush pokin' h'at. Yew've got h'it h'all chewed ter buggery an' beyond wiv that bashtard of a ushelesh Shtilshon thing what yew'm sho h'almighty fond of. Usheless pair of buggersh an' no mishtake!"

Jack's eyes and ire raked them like the whip he used to break in obstinate two-year-olds if need be, once they had been gelded; his face was hard and flat below his severely pulled-down cap brim. Chester's face was on fire. Fraser, more abashed than he had ever known himself to be, saw that Chester was near to exploding, either into hot tears of impotent rage, or equally close to yelling back at his father, which he simply dared not attempt.

"Get that crown gear off, an' yew bring h'it down ter me, an' bluggy sharp, Frayshyurr mind. And ash fer yew, my lad, tek that bluggy tractor of yewrn an' shtart to plough that lasht bit of kale rootsh, d'yew 'ear me now?"

Frozen in Jack Harris's anger at this unlooked-for barrier to the day's work, the grouping of men, dogs and machinery moved again with these last pungent directions, which were caught by a strengthening wind from the south. It brought more rain from the valley of the Trent, and floated a string of black-headed gulls over the separating figures below them.

Patently in a fury, Chester yanked the Fordson's throttle to its fullest limit and wrenched the tractor round, his nose (and drip) twitching as his lips spat out inaudible words. The broken pieces lay at his feet in a used seed sack. Like the shattered metal therein, the rhythm of the day had been irreversibly broken and feelings were raw, disturbed. Volatile.

Every footfall of Jack Harris's crashing boots on the yard's stone flags declaimed anger, sheer choleric rage at not being able to contain this, this monstrous insult to his tight, timely direction of everything that went on in his farming operations. It would now be common knowledge that the Staunton Farm tractor and seed drill were standing idle on this best of sowing days; somebody or something was at serious fault.

"DAMN their bluggy eyesh!" he fired off yet again, turning left abruptly and feeling in the dim tiled passage for his market jacket and waistcoat. Eleanor, coming into the passage from the morning light in the low-ceilinged parlour, stiffened on sensing the violence in her stepfather, then came on, but with caution. This was not a man to brook hesitation or impediment, of any kind.

"Tell yewr Mam I've ter goo into town, if she'sh willing. Theresh time enough for some shopping if she'sh quick about h'it. Yew'd besht shee to the ladsh' dinner, sho there'll be little time for moonin' h'over that drawin' an' deshignin' an' shuchlike."

"Yes, all right, I'll tell Mam now," Eleanor could never bring herself to say "Dad" or "Father". She was grateful for the least errand to take her out of range of the palpable temper that surged around this man of strong ways and stronger wants.

He loved her mother, Eleanor was in no doubt about that, but was abundantly equally fiercely bonded to his land and its needs at all times.She whirled about, a trim and attractive seventeen-year-old girl, at a distance in all ways from her mother's husband and determined to remain at a safe distance from his wilful rejection of the fact that any of his, their, composite family might look for fulfilment beyond his fields.

Disgruntled and snappish with his stepsister, Chester snatched an early dinner and went off to higher ground, the eleven acres in front of Fraser's home, to plough in the last of the kale stumps and root drills.

He ploughed skilfully, without dropping the steady engine note from the tractor's full throttle by even one notch. Standing up on the platform, greasy with accumulated mud, he reached behind himself to adjust the two levers for controlling the level of the three-furrow Cockshutt plough and the line of draught, both according to the flow of the land below the plough as it followed the tractor across the field.

Stiffy came into the same field about midday, to harrow up earlier ploughing, the two Shire mares, Bett and Bounce, blowing wetly as the iron spikes dragged through the crust made by the night's rain. Stiffy was still feeling vaguely unsettled in his mind by events in his life to which he felt unable to put a satisfactory name. He was more than flummoxed by Madge Caldwell having

146

fended off his questing hands with unusual firmness the previous night, in the soft darkness of the Dutch barn, fragrant with hay and the crisp budding of the elms around it.

"Ken, you mustn't, no, Ken! No! That's really quite nice, but, my! You are wakening up these days, aren't you, my bold lad! With that big handsome brother away, I would've thought that you'd be too tired. Hey! Ken! KENNETH!"

Madge's remark about brother Tom suddenly moved his supposedly too-tired brother to pull her to him ardently, as if to demonstrate that he was now an individual, a man with his own ways and wants. Kenneth set in motion a pressing exploration of Madge's geography below her waist. She pummelled him vigorously, eyes flashing in the dim light that quite enhanced Ken's white teeth and black curly hair.

"No, Kenneth, you mustn't! Later, sometime, if you're good meantime. For good reason, if you know owt, you great lump!" she instructed him, quite primly and prissily at the same time.

"Oh, and what's wrong with now, Miss Perfect Marjorie? Got the rags on, or summat, 'ave you?"

"Aha, you have been learnin' your lessons, young man. Mebbe teacher'll give you a kiss, just to be going on with. Come here, Ken, but gently, mind!"

The remainder of the exchange was lost to Fraser. He had been standing below the all-seeing, stately heavily-bowed elms, watching for the pale wing-beats of the barn owls that nested in the granary above the cart sheds. In spite of limbs weary from the endless hours on the swaying backboard of the seed drill, he had been drawn back that evening, to the quiet of the farm buildings to absorb more of the noiseless grace surrounding the pair of owls and their quartering of the farm buildings in the dusk.

His father had looked up from the newspaper, asking him, "Got something else to see to? Aren't you tired enough?"

"Not, really. I want to see the young owls, if I can, when they come out on the ledge. Mebbe the parent birds will bring in some mice to them, or something."

His face was eager, happy; his father smiled, content.

Turk, rough-coated sheepdog, had rumbled in his throat at the pleasure of Fraser's caress of his head and ears, as he silently made his way out of the yard, past the dog's kennel beside the gig-house. All was utterly quiet then, as Madge and her suitor had separated, not unhappy, some things left in abeyance, it seemed to Kenneth. God, but he was tired. And more field work the next morning.

Up in the eleven acres now being steadily ploughed in by Chester on his tractor, Kenneth Darlington, happy enough in his working identity as Stiffy, harrowed on, walking loose-kneed behind his pair of horses. They breasted steadily and willingly into their sweated collars, knowing the feel of his handling and the regular resting of his hands, which communicated his directions and his mood behind them, just as their own natures and responses came back along the reins to himself. They worked well together. Kenneth was less demanding of his horses' bodily resources than the Guv'nor, whose very tone meant hard, unremitting application, although he, Ken, worked them at a steady pace that stopped for very little. The pleasures and problems of Madge occupied his mind as they stroked the harrows across the sun's broken gleam on the furrows. To his left, the tractor and three-furrow plough turned over roots, sods and earth in an unstoppable wave. Across the breadth of the field, Fraser looked up occasionally from his home jobs amongst the poultry runs generally, unattended-to during the past few days' non-stop seed drilling with Chester.

As Chester came to the end of the stint and pulled on the worn rope to trip the plough out at the marked furrow ten paces or thirty feet from the hedge, he stood up, pushing the steel seat to one side, the better to prepare for dropping it in again as he swung tractor and plough into the next opening. He did this without any expected slackening of speed of a less supremely confident, less wholly skilled tractor driver. The morning's abrasive episode with his father still rankled in his mind; dismissed to plough as a punishment, almost like, like some uppity little schoolboy. The long-handled Stilson wrench so scathingly condemned by his father lay against the angle of the mudguard; he had used it anyway, to clench up the quick-release hitch by another turn or two.

"A'right, then, you may be the bloody champion ploughman, with bloody 'osses!" he shouted of his father into the engine's steady roar, "but I'll bloody well show you how to do it with proper tackle, miserable owd bugger!" He yanked the trip rope and the gleaming plough shares and disc coulters slid into another three furrows' rippling inversion of soil and debris.

Some fifteen yards along, Chester felt that his levelling lever needed two notches to compensate for a visible dip in the land. He reached behind him for the higher of the two plough-setting levers. It was under heavy pressure from the plough bodies angling into the stiff land, and he took a tighter grip, sensing that he would need all his body weight to pull it down once the ratchet was released. This was more than correct.

As he glanced back to check his degree of adjustment, his right arm was momentarily pulled upwards by the suddenly-released lever. Chester set one Wellington-booted foot on the plough drawbar to increase his purchase. The tractor wheels bucked slightly on a knot of kale roots just as he looked behind him. His other muddied boot slipped off the greasy footplate, and he fell between tractor and plough, striking his head cruelly on the patent spring hitch as he went down.

At some level that was distant from the booming waves of pain, Chester's mind registered the hitch as being guaranteed to release itself if the implement became jammed with some unforeseen obstacle or resistance. He had previously tightened the two fat coil springs of the hitch to their maximum breakaway pressure before starting to plough, wishing to demonstrate his impressive output of acreage covered without stops for any piddling chokes, snags or suchlike.

Across the lane bordering the field with these moving figures at work, Fraser, although not a part of what was going on, felt quite satisfied that he would have his place in the team once the seed drill was rendered functional again. He knew exactly what Stiffy and Chester were doing and had the knowledge of how preparations were made for ploughing and harrowing, getting the horses' harness on correctly and so forth. The tractor had to have TVO and petrol topped up in the two separate tanks, and greased, and that was about it. Oh, and check the water level in the radiator. Yes, he could do all these tasks if need be; he turned to hosing out mucky ducks' troughs once more.

To Stiffy, the afternoon's work seemed to be going well. He noted the steam rising from Bett's haunches; she was always able to put on a bit of condition the moment you took her out of work and showed her a bite of clean grass. Thinking back to the pleasing feel of Madge Caldwell's buttocks under his hand in the sudden access to knowledge yielded from the previous evening, he called "Hoo, then, Bett" and pulled slightly to the left, to get into previously worked ground, and ease his team's draught by a fraction. As the two Shires, nodding, sidestepped neatly in unison, something different came into Stiffy's peripheral awareness.

The visual rhythm of Chester's tractor and plough continued, but strangely, inexplicably, there was no figure hunched in the seat or standing upright on the footplate, and the front wheels yawed and wandered. What the devil? Down among the plough bodies and gleaming discs, there was a dark mass that could neither be stubble nor stalks. It was too oddly coloured, too long, too much like – Jeezuss, bloody Hell! It had the length and substance of something like a human body.

Sraightening up to coil the hose, Fraser suddenly saw things happening that had no reason at first sight. Stiffy had jerked the mares to a plunging halt, and

149

one of them had squealed in fright, throwing head and collar high in protest. In the soft spring air, some gulls and a pair of carrion crows scattered in squawked alarm, the undersides of wings and bellies flashing white and grey as the man below them stumbled across the clinging loam, having thrown the long plough lines in a ragged coil over Bounce's collar and hames.

Fraser dropped all that he was doing, pelted across the lane and up the bank, the better to grasp what on earth had possessed his steady friend Stiffy in his mad abandonment of sanity, it seemed. He suddenly focussed beyond, to the tractor, swinging in a wide loop, the castor wheel to the plough clacking and jerking wildly, engine note undiminished. Where the blazes was Chester? Fraser had the answer before the question died within his throat.

Stumbling in the swinging impetus of unusually flailing boots and leggings, his breeches tightening at the knee, Stiffy heaved and rasped hoarsely for wind, and almost fell full length as he came up onto ploughed land. He wrenched himself upright with whooping lungs and tore a fingernail completely from its bed on a stone. As Stiffy, solid, stolid Kenneth Darlington to everyone outside the farm, struck at an angle across the furrows, it seemed that he would never catch up with the tractor and whatever was trailing in its random course. From an intrusive line to his left, he saw Fraser leaping across land and kale stumps like a demented madman, on a line to intercept the tractor. One of them had to.

Tractor and plough had skewed and were roaring, jangling in a swinging loop across the kale stumps. The plough was canted crazily, the castor wheel clacking in noisy derision. A Wellington boot detached itself from the inert mass below the plough frame and snagged on a kale stalk, wobbling upright in a ludicrously animated fashion as a ghastly invitation to the two figures whose arms seemed to tear at the air.

Fraser could see that Stiffy's final stumbling plunge to draw level with the tractor was beyond his physical resources. He was forced to clutch futilely at the mudguard, before falling back out of the way of the massive steel wheel and tyre. On his own swerving angle of approach, Fraser saw that if he managed to keep upright by grabbing right-handedly at the fuel tank, and fending off his body from the rear wheel, he could get a hand to the magneto lever, a sure way to interrupt everything. For one thing was a fact in Fraser's racing mind and body: Kenneth Darlington, skilled horseman and carter, did not know how to stop the engine of any tractor. In the opening seconds, it now lay with Fraser to bring the whole lumbering disaster to a halt.

The whole mass of men and machinery arrived at, and crashed into the hawthorn hedge about thirty yards further up the lane from the driveway leading to Fraser's home. The long handles of the plough clattered and shook with the impact, like steel cranes arched derisively over their mutilated burden. Lodged against the beam of the front axle was the bole of a hedge ash, about eight inches in diameter. Against this the whole power and torque of the Fordson was labouring. The front wheels had crashed obliquely through the hedge bottom and were shuddering on the lip of the bank five feet above the lane below, in sight of where, only some seconds ago, Fraser had thrown away the hose and flung himself into the field.

Both Stiffy's and Fraser's immediate grasp of things was to see that the rear wheels were beginning to jerk and spin, digging themselves further in; the plough was accordingly being crushed downwards into the ground by the huge pressure from the tractor drawbar. The cut stump of the ash tree was shuddering beneath the power thrusting at it. Its white sappy wood was revealed, bark chewed away. It was near to twisting to one side to escape from the battering of the massive front axle.

"BLOODY HELL!" Stiffy half-shouted, half-moaned. Desperate beyond control, he slammed his fist in impotent fury on the throttle linkage at the side of the engine. The exhaust crackled and barked in sudden reduction to a rumble. At the same moment precisely, Fraser wrenched at the two-way fuel cock, shutting it off completely. In spite of his action, the Fordson continued to run, exhausting the TVO still in the fuel line, exerting even greater torque. The tyres, on massive cast steel centres, still heaved and chewed sullenly at the soil, their treads slipping on stones and roots with the greater moisture so exposed. In sudden rage, Fraser flung himself up and over the wide mudguard and smashed down the magneto ignition lever.

"You mad useless BASTARD of a thing!"

The tractor engine coughed meekly and stopped.

Stiffy was the first of them to turn away from the silent tractor, to swivel his face and eyes to what lay entangled under the plough frame. The blood from his torn-off finger nail ran down his face as he put up a hand to steady the chattering of his jaw.

"Ju-Jeezuss fucking Christ."

From the other side of the tractor, winded from crashing down over the mudguard, Fraser heard Stiffy's anguished summation of his shock and impotence, at the same time registering two things: a car was coming up the lane below them, and the tractor and plough were settling still lower into the pit it had dug in its final revolutions.

In slipping from the drawbar, Chester had fallen entirely to one side of it; the crashing, bumping downwards slide of his head and shoulders had had a certain element of forward motion as the tractor roared on in gear. Unconscious by the time that his upper body had slithered to the rear of the tractor, his flaccid feet and legs, mercifully clasped together, had already been accepted, almost cradled, by the second or middle disc, skim coulter, plough body and mouldboard of the three. Their action had been to flip limbs, spine and shoulders over towards the massive steel leg carrying the first plough body, normally wholly angled into the soil, but now above it.

Chester's shoulders, neck and head, with one arm grotesquely angled upwards, had been lifted by the action of the disc coulter and scraper blade and were jammed in a welter of bloodied sods, clothing and kale stumps against the first plough's disc assembly. This appeared to have cut deeply into the sleeve and shoulder of his jacket. To both Stiffy and Fraser, Chester's face was completely obscured by a bulging mass of kale roots and sods which spewed up and over the plough frame in a great tumbling heap, as though in anger at this obstruction to their normal employment. Out of all this stuck a limp forearm and hand, the finger nails black from that morning's work on the seed drill.

The car in the lane had turned away. Christ, it was his father's car! Fraser wheeled away from where the tractor and plough were visibly angled half-through the crushed hedge, and met his father pulling himself up over the hedge bank further along.

"Fraser? I thought you... what are you doing here? Is that you, Kenneth? Having trouble with – my God, man! What in Hell's happened? Holy Christ!"

Ken was hanging on to the plough frame, hoarsely mouthing something that could hardly be understood from the strings of saliva hanging from his lips.

"Best get a bloody spade, Guv'nor. Gaffer's Chester – he's in that danged lot." Stiffy swallowed, hawked and spat with pathetic weakness, then burst out wildly, "Dunno if he's dead or what, but the plough's got 'im, bastard machine! Get yersen up 'ere smartish, Guv'nor, or we see what's best to do. Jeezuss mercy!"

Stiffy doubled up, inspirations whooping in and out of his lungs.

Alec Baird came up through the hedge in a rush, his face set and hard. "Don't touch a bloody thing, d'you hear, Fraser, Kenneth? Not a single thing. HOLY CHRIST!"

The tractor settled into the hedge bottom an audible fraction more as Alec swung himself up over the canted front wheel and tyre, seeing fully what lay behind the rear wheels. "Oh, my God!" he said, very quietly. "How long did it take you two to get... right, get in here. No! Jam that stone under the drawbar, then get in here at the front of the damned plough and start pulling off those sods. Do NOT move his arms or head once they come free. Got that Kenneth?"

Small granules of earth gathered in a sussuring ripple and rolled down into the lane. Kenneth looked from Fraser's father to the tractor, uncertain.

"Orrigh', then, Mr Baird, but what about…?"

"Never mind any other bloody thing, just do as I damned well say and nothing more, understand? Not one thing more! Good lad, Kenneth. Right! Fraser, where–" he bellowed, and turning round, almost fell over him. "Come with me, at once."

He set off at a run to the gate opposite their home. His deep gut-shaking bellow "MARY!" brought Argo and Tim barking wildly into the yard, hackles raised. With what seemed to Fraser an incalculable delay, his mother appeared, hands dusted with flour.

"Do you have to shout like that, Alec, it's positively uncouth–"

Fraser wondered in those few seconds whether this was how his father had gathered up the necessary command of things when his gun had been hit, killing the other soldier with him.

"Christ, woman, listen! Get inside, phone Angus McKay, at once, d'ye hear. Get him to come up here like the wind. Tell him…" Alec Baird let out a belly-deep gust of contained tension. "Tell him 'Compression injuries with tractor and plough, thorax and spine, serious.' Get him to come here, to this house, right? Get Angus's girl to phone for an ambulance – hospital, RAF, Army, any damned thing. GO ON!"

He gripped Fraser fiercely by the arm "Get both the digging spades, now!"

Alec Baird tore off his jacket and tie, flinging them to the ground. Fraser jumped down to get the spades at the run, almost kicking the dogs out of his way, and on impulse, grabbed the long crowbar as well.

For a moment, Alec leant upon the gate, eyes closed, weighing everything up as to what the first actions had to be. Images of fields of battle in France swarmed in his mind: men's bodies torn to pieces in shell craters, horses' guts everywhere, and those of what had been men…

He bellowed for his wife again. "Mary, send down or phone, get Jack or Marcia, tell them to get all the men and come up here to where Jack set Chester on ploughing. Doctor first, then ambulance, then every man on the place up here. GET ON, woman, for Christ's sake!"

Fraser followed his father at a hitherto unknown tearing pace. Shivering in a fashion he was powerless to control, Fraser passed one of the spades into the outstretched hand of his father, knees down beside the canted plough.

"Make anything of it, Kenneth?" asked Alec quietly. Funny how his father always called Stiffy, Kenneth, and not the other way round. Fraser pondered this for only two inconsequential seconds. Everyone's all so blooming quiet, no panic. Does this mean that Chester's dead, or what? They were all down on their knees, heads close together.

"Can you be absolutely sure, Kenneth, that this damned tractor isn't going to move on us?"

"Ar, pretty sure, Mr Baird, it's bloody well jammed an' all, now. Any road, are we goin' to get 'im out front or backways, or how then?"

Before his father could weigh that one up, Fraser pulled sharply at his rolled-up shirtsleeve. "Father, if we pulled on this lever..." – he pointed upwards with certainty – "...that'll lift the main beam and all this muck and roots with it. Stiffy and me can do it."

"Are you absolutely positive it won't go down instead of up? Is he right, Kenneth?"

"Yar, that's it, I reckon. That's the way young Chester lifts the beam an' all, for changing any share as needs it or owt else." Stiffy looked steadily at Fraser, saying nothing about his knowing that Fraser had worked both setting levers in turn, practising their functions when the plough had lain unused in the field barn across the road.

"Right, one or two notches at a time, and for heaven's sake do NOT let it come back down with you. All right, then? Only once I say 'Now'!"

Fraser's father, veterinary surgeon, one-time farmer's son, but of a period before the advent of tractors and their implements, crouched down amongst the hummocked earth and torn clothing, his freckled arms taking the weight of all that lay around the apparently lifeless form's head and shoulders.

"Right, lads, NOW! And take it slowly."

With all his weight hanging by both arms on the levelling lever, Fraser hung face to face with Stiffy, on whose features rank distress was still evident. His heavy shirt and braces reeked of old and immediate sweat, horses and Brylcreem. Blood, pulsing thickly from where the evulsed nail had been, ran in corded trails from the use of his hand to wipe away grime and sweat.

"Are you right, then, young Fraser? You tek off the ratchet whilst I pulls the bugger down." Stiffy grinned at him. He and Fraser were two grown farm men working togther now; they both knew exactly what they were going to do.

They grunted into the dead weight behind the cranked lever, and move it down they did. The entire plough frame inched upwards as they strained a notch at a time, canting over to one side the mass of plough frame, axle, discs, mouldboards and compacted debris encasing Chester's inert body. It became fractionally easier as everything slid free to the ground into the few inches of space so created.

Fraser's father, Kenneth and Fraser were surrounded in a strangely silent rush by Jack Harris, the doctor and the rest of the farm men. The tension amongst all of them on their knees beneath the acutely canted over plough, was palpable.

Jack's head and shoulders thrust through amongst them all from in front of the castor wheel of the plough, looming with all of his barely contained huge muscular power over the legs and feet that lay in the mess of mud and roots. To Fraser and everyone there, it seemed that he was preparing, with massive flexing of chest and shoulders, to take the entire dead weight of man and metal on his upper body, and bull-like, toss it aside in one convulsive heave.

Instead, resting both hands on his knees, with best cream cord market breeches squelched deeply into the churned earth and roots beneath the plough frame, he bowed his head and with a typical Jack Harris crooked grin, looked across a couple of feet at Alec Baird, friend and neighbour. The tears did not interfere with his words.

"That were danged good on yer, Alec, ter do the neshashary an' all. We'll tek our Cheshter whum then, ladsh, once h'our doctor and the vet'nary 'ere saysh the word."

For once, seldom known in the recall of all of them, Doctor Angus McKay was submissive to other men's actions in taking the first steps to resolve this tragedy. Kneeling on an old feed bag pushed in below him by Watty Taimes, his hands searched in the earth and debris with difficulty, taking vital signs, reading what he could from the little that was exposed of Chester's body. No words passed. As he crouched, looking over to his friend the vet for a few seconds in the course of his exploration of Chester's spine and pelvis, Doctor McKay flicked his eyebrows above his glasses and made the briefest of nods before turning awkwardly to Jack Harris.

"Mr Harris, there has to be the greatest of care here, the verra greatest of care, man."

Before he could add to this, Fraser's father spoke urgently to the farm men, "Go across the lane to our place, you men, to where you know Fraser mixes hens' meal, lift one of the big doors off its hinges, and bring it here quickly. Aye, Fraser, what is it? Blankets? Right, yes."

To the men, arrested as they set to run, he shouted, "Hey, look in my car, and bring the heavy horse rug from the boot. Get on with it, lads."

"Aye, Angus, carry on. I interrupted you."

The look on the doctor's features was a strange mixture of arrested professional authority and concession to swift practical planning in matters not exactly his province. Ach, well, foreseen by a fellow-countryman at least. He resumed directions.

"When I say the word, Mr Harris, we have to slide him slowly, in one steady movement, legs and arms gathered up, on to the door. Absolutely no lifting, d'you men hear me?"

The few low words exchanged between the farm men, their footfalls in bringing the door into position and sliding it in between mounds of earth shovelled clear of the plough, rendered the encompassing silence all the more critical and tense.

Its radiator scrunched into the spintered hedge, the tractor's engine released loud ticks as it cooled in the pale spring sunlight. As the group of men eased themselves out of the way of the ambulance men carrying the door to the field gate and backed-up ambulance, Stiffy's bloodied hand came round to grasp Fraser's shoulder and then his wrist. "You kept us right with them bloody handles an' all, Fraser. Thank Christ we tackled the right bugger, eh?" He pulled Fraser to him with a solid arm around his shoulders, and a sideways nod of his head, in a companionship of something which Fraser knew at once he would share with Kenneth Darlington, solid reliable ploughman, whatever the way of things for both of them.

With a strangely muted revving of engines, all involved had sped away, to hospital, surgery, homes and a dairy herd waiting to be milked. Jack had barked at Len Bowers in mid-stride to his car, "Un'ook them h'osshesh, sharpish, young Leonard, and give 'em a good rub down afore Shtiffy cumsh on down wiv 'em."

For a few minutes, there remained only Stiffy, Fraser and his father, silent in a weariness that had drained every scrap of inner resources from them all. Alec Baird looked up.

"Hold on a a moment, you men," he said. "I know that Jack would have wanted to say this to both of you, but he will himself, given the right moment. Or more like a day or two."

He stood in front of both Fraser and Kenneth Darlington, placing a darkly bloodied and dirty hand to each of their shoulders, drawing rasping breaths with great effort.

"If it had not been for what you two fellows did today, that damned piece of machinery would have killed Chester, and broken Jack for the rest of his life, and his whole family. Everyone owes you men something that they'll not be able to put in words. You knew exactly what to do, and did it, by God. None of us will ever see anything the like of this again, by God."

Watching his father saying this, Fraser could see that his father's head was bowed, not just in a sudden drain of all his energies, but also the better to hide from good old Kenneth and himself what could only be the release of trails of sweat and tears both, dripping from his moustache and cheeks. And, he knew exactly what his father was trying to say to them and somehow he couldn't. Fraser had never seen his father so crushed by unspeakable emotion. But, then, wonderfully, came the inimitable wide Stiffy grin:

"She wor a right barstard of a bloody tractor, eh, Fraser?"

In his mind's store of deeply imprinted events of that shocking day, and Chester's uncertain survival from being literally buried in the core of it, Fraser carried the picture of Jack Harris's powerful brown hands shaking like palsied things upon the clods torn away from his son's chest and face, in the waning light of a good sowing day. It also seemed to him, and spoken of by him to no one because of it being at a very private, guarded level, that he possessed an inner picture of a sort of flowing terrestial tapestry interwoven with all of the countryside that he knew, the weave of which was raised in sudden hard knots by such apparently unrelated alarums as Chester's engulfment by "that bastard of a bloody tractor and plough", by War Office telegrams being delivered to the most unlikely of cottage doors, by the sudden, almost unmarked disappearance of a man's or a young woman's known face to be a number on a scarred desert, a rolling warship or a thundering airfield.

To those whose families and homes all revolved upon the daily round of land and livestock on the Harris farm, it seemed that the feeling of relief at Chester's survival, against all odds, expanded to become a force of survival in the broadest of terms, that must now surely take the whole country through dire and threatening times. Quietly observing and storing impressions, layer by layer, that was how the whole business seemed to Fraser. He spoke little of it to Hedley; it was not to be exposed to challenge or insensitive questioning.

His, Fraser's, conviction that things were sure to change was substantiated by the daily growth of speculation spreading out from everyone around him, as to when the unavoidable massive onslaught against Germany's stamp on Europe could be contained no longer.

LEGACIES OF SCARS

XVIII

Fraser knew that he was more familiar with most parts of the Charnborough Estate than its owners, the Sefton family. He could quite easily walk to some of the farthest south fields, woodland and water meadows within forty minutes or so of leaving home. Their home, The Leys, was owned by the estate; his father paid rent for the property every six months, Fraser knew that.

In the course of his long, abundantly absorbing walkings and watchings, he had encountered and now recognised the typical signs and territories of game birds, foxes, badgers and roe deer. He had seen fallow deer only once. Courting couples were a nuisance, but they didn't wander very far, and he could usually get round them, silently. Dratted nuisance, with all their carrying on.

By the late 1800s, Charnborough Park and the Seftons were a power to be reckoned with, having estates further from Charnborough in Shropshire and Wales, much property in Manchester and London, a hereditary peerage and an easy acceptance in the House of Lords, Court circles and the country's military establishment.

The Seftons' not unattractive visages and lean cheeks were capped with many hats of office in The Park paintings, and their various roles and positions were accorded a wary respect, but usually justified.

The term "The General's Men", initially wondered about by Fraser and Hedley at first hearing, had arisen from some disaffected onlooker's wit, on viewing the field of beaters and stops assembled by Hastings, Earl Sefton, seventy-seven, to resuscitate pheasant drives on the return of his few surviving estate staff following the 1918 Armistice. In 1914, with some bewilderment, they had responded to their employer's convincingly strong entreaties that they enlist virtually en masse. Their regiments, North and South Staffs., and Shropshire Light Infantry, had suffered grievously in vicious actions throughout 1916 and 1917. Those men who eventually returned, variously wounded, chanted their ditty at opportune moments:

"Oh, the Grand Ol' Earl of Wen
He led his Wives and Men
With weary plods
He marched the Sods
'Til They buggered off Home again"

Earl Sefton's pheasants were important to him. He liked to see them about the place, to inspect any birds hatched from eggs bought-in for rearing on in the preceding season, to observe their various seasonal activities and to expect skilled marksmanship from his shooting guests when the birds curled over their pegs below high stands of beech and oak, once the leaves were off the trees. The drives, coverts and high stands of Charnborough Park were all familiar to Fraser. His longer quiet forays in the autumn-coloured vales and copses invariably took him over the tenanted farms of the estate, and, with circumspection, into the policies of The Park. There, the estate workers accepted seeing him without fuss for a number of sensible reasons. It was common knowledge that the old Earl and Fraser had met, and talked at length one day in the spring, on the subject of the dark green melanistic cock pheasant that became a predictable sight along a stream bottom and abandoned sandstone quarry.

With his favourite Westley Richards 20-gauge shotgun in the crook of an equally favoured and comfortable worn tweed jacket, the Earl had accosted Fraser with calm courtesy and gravity, both standing quietly amongst the blackened ash leaves of the autumn's fall, watching the pheasants' courtship display amongst the scratched-up leaf mould.

"Do you know what type of bird that is, young man, whoever you are? Have we met and been introduced to one another before today, hm?" enquired the elderly man, with gentle but also specific interest.

"Yessir, it's a melanistic cock. I sometimes see them when I'm out with my father. I'm Fraser Baird, sir. My father's the county veterinary officer." He added, as a final surety, "We're from Aberdeenshire, in Scotland."

In a September 1938 issue of The Field, Fraser had read an article on the origins, incidence and attractions of melanistic mutant pheasants, cocks, and hens, swivelling this way and that in his father's revolving desk chair. The Earl had also read his own copy of the same magazine in the firelit library of The Park, wondering at that time whether these variant birds and landowners such as himself would survive the unmistakeable menace of growing preparations for yet another wearisome war.

"Ah, yes, the county veterinary gentleman. Hmm. Your people must have come on the estate after Captain Sadleir, I believe. Needing a lot done to it, aahm, after they left. Come here a lot, young man?"

The older man's eyes looked calmly upon Fraser, watchful for any dissembling of purpose, his own face typically that of a Sefton; strong cheekbones above a long, lean jaw, and eyes which tended to be small, yet giving of a web of wrinkles which indicated that humour was there in gentle abundance.

He shifted his gun from forearm to shoulder, trigger guard uppermost. Fraser watched carefully, to see if the toplever or guard would become entangled in the strands of blueish wool and worn material which had accommodated the action of the gun in a comfortable woolly nest. Satisfied, Fraser felt that the Earl was expecting some further contribution from him on this matter of shared interest.

"Yes, I do come when I can; I don't work at Mr Harris's place every day unless they're needing me. And I really like to study all the game birds through different times of year; they don't always do the same thing, do they, sir?"

As though to give point to their discourse, some grey partridges creaked companionably on a stubble beyond the trees. The Earl inclined towards Fraser.

"Yes, they really are splendid to see and hear around this time, aren't they? Now, look here, Baird, ah, Fraser, isn't it? Well, don't hesitate to watch anything here that you are so plainly interested in; just tell Foss, my head keeper that I've spoken to you. I expect that you already know where he lives? Hmm, I thought so. Give my regards to your father; been a great help to us at the Home Farm. Know anything about cattle, Fraser? No doubt far more than most of us. Anyway, most welcome, young man, most welcome. Good afternoon to you."

The Earl turned, retreating almost delicately amongst the grey boles of the beech and ash trees silently waiting to gather and enfold his spare form behind them, with a final inviting lift of an eyebrow to Fraser, as though to say, "Please don't stop coming to watch my birds, y'know," and left Fraser doing just that, with unexpected interesting material to mull over on his homewards path. He decided that there was a great, solid calmness about everything to do with Charnborough Park estate, and its owner, who apparently – well no, genuinely – appreciated the small details about pheasants and things that so many other heedless folk wouldn't even know existed.

Once he grew up and made his own start in farming, it would be very useful to have as a landowner someone like the Earl who would know and understand how to support farmers on his land, where things didn't change and you could rely upon going from year to year in a confident fashion. In a sudden intuitive conviction that he would achieve exactly that place in life, Fraser vigorously booted a large weathered crust of cow dung, and maliciously alarmed a cock pheasant with his own convincing double gurrk-gurrk imitation of another cock-bird's challenge.

"Goo on, you shtupid bluggy bird!"

Fraser laughed out loud; the silly bloody thing pluffed himself up and shook, ready for, well, ready for something. Crikey!

XIX

The onslaught of the American forces upon the entire fabric of Charnborough Park was immediate, huge and heedlessly destructive. Inasmuch that Staunton Farm, the Harris family, Fraser's household and the cottage families up and down the lane were close to a couple of miles from the high wall around The Park policies, and the various estate entrances, some of them long disused, there was no word of mouth relay of armed forces of intent being anywhere in their vicinity. Curiously, the first information came with Jean, Fraser's sister's return home from having tea at one of her school friends' homes, Daphne Attwood. Her parents owned The Swanspool Hotel in the town. Jean and Daphne were together brushing up on revision; they were both trying hard to gain university entrance, albeit in different places, Jean already entered for St Andrews if her exam results were accepted. Mary Baird looked up from her Red Cross prisoner of war files, brought home from Brockwood Hall.

"Jean, what kept you this evening? Don't you feel that you've done enough for one day?"

Jean was curiously excited and to Fraser, that was unusual.

"Mummy, Daphne's father had to go back to the hotel in a rush. They're having to take in a whole lot of army officers, the town's buzzing with jeeps and trucks, phone going all the time and some of their regulars having to move out. So we got the house to ourselves, Daphne and I, but we hardly got peace to get on with steady revising. Mrs Attwood had to go back too, to arrange extra bedding, sheets and everything, and get staff back in to make meals."

Fraser was suddenly alert.

"If there's a whole lot of officers, that means there has to be men, transport, ah, heavy stuff." He ran out of naming immediate things that an army, a corps, a division or a regiment would need on the move. "Did you hear at the Attwoods where the rest of them are going to be?"

His sister, for once, was not insufferably superior in reply.

"Daphne's father said that he got the impression it was a very big unit, or whatever you call it, with loads of transport, all going through the town, coming from the Knutsford direction." Jean knew how intensely interested her brother was in anything to do with army matters. She fed him with the only other detail that she had gathered at her friend's house. "It looks as though all these officers and things are having to set up a completely new base for whatever is on the move, and it can't be all that far from Melford. Where d'you suppose they're aiming for, Fraser?"

He knew at once where this army on the move was making for, he knew it in his bones. Would the old Earl have known about this? Did any of the estate men know what was going to happen? When could he get down there, to see what was going on, and would he be able to watch something that he had never thought to come within a few miles of his home, and the farm? Was this the start of something big, starting to get ready to invade France against the Germans?

Fraser suddenly realised that his sister had said nothing about whether these officers were British, or American or infantry or tanks or artillery or what.

"Jean, did the Attwoods say anything about whether these officers and men are British forces or Americans?"

His questioning was intense. He felt the difference would be important to what was clearly going to happen all over the estate. Now that the news had been passed on, his sister had lost interest in pursuing lesser details.

"No, I don't think so. They just said a whole lot of army officers were arriving right then. It all seemed very sudden."

Fraser fumed inwardly. Oh, idiot dratted sister, yeah, of course it would; they wouldn't want the whole bally place to know what was going to happen, would they? How and when could he possibly get down there? This demanded adroit action, Fraser at once decided; this really meant business.

Down both sides of the cinder access road to the very large town water supply pumping house, abutted by well-rounded Dutch-style gables, there were innumerable American army vehicles, nose to tail, of every purpose and description. Amongst them Fraser saw three very large pieces of self-propelled artillery on tank bodies and tracks, tightly chained down on immense MACK transporters. Their sheer presence was visually overwhelming. They seemed to Fraser to be sitting there, awaiting movement to the summons, tracks clattering and clanking, to their job of killing the enemy. The whole feel of the place was now tumultuously thrown to one side by what was going on immediately outside and inside the high Charnborough estate wall on to which the pump house backed.

Both Fraser and Hedley were familiar with what normally went on within the pumping station; their previous visits had elicited a tolerance of their presence by Matt Beesley, whose entire life was given to tending his two great steam expansion engines and the pumps they drove. On a steel-plated platform level with the massive, plunging crankshafts and huge flywheels, they had licence to stand in companionable silence, absorbed in a hypnotic repetition of connecting rods, pistons and valve gear, silken smooth power thrusting the two immense flywheels spinning in endless cycles of steam and steel. Fraser needed to thrust this normality of scene out of the way, wholly absorbed by what was erupting in front of him: destruction and construction on a mammoth scale.

Having come down by himself, as likely to be less noticeable, he had passed into The Park by a little-used path known only to the keepers, now few in number. Everywhere that he could now see and hear, there was power, unlimited military machine power, directed by the unquestionable authority of gesticulating and hoarsely shouting figures in dull grey battledress tucked into high lace-up boots, and more men in trim uniform, with helmets and gaberdine jackets, presumably officers, exercising snappish directions with fingers stabbing at clipboards.

Long-disused estate drives and woodland tracks were having their desuetude penetrated by knife-like thrusts of steadily stripping bulldozer blades, the cables to their rear-mounted Le Tourneau winches twanging and whipping to the clutch controls of drivers squinting through their cigar smoke and black exhaust plumes and continually chewing gum.

Squads of men tumbled to fulfil hoarse and endless yells of command, furiously shovelling drains and tracks for snaking cables, laying steel mesh over which concrete was copiously splashed out, sections of buildings grabbed on the run and bolted up or spiked by men who almost all wore long-peaked canvas hats, carried their tools in multi-pouched leather holsters swinging from their waists and who yelled at each other, chewed gum and swore in streams of circular, repetitive obscenity.

Further into the existing driveways, white-helmeted military policemen appeared in jeeps and combat trucks, continually flagging on throbbing successions of half-tracks, high-revving GMC trucks with drab stake and canvas bodies, and engineers' equipment of proportions which made even the largest of local traction engines look puny in Fraser's eyes. All had large white five-pointed stars painted on their body panels.

Between the boles of beech trees that sheltered Fraser against the steady incoming rain, he saw Willys jeeps, Chevrolet and GMC pick-ups and some British Humber staff cars swinging over the semi-circular sweep in front of the main house, and running without hesitation on to the lawn of breathtaking smoothness, now deeply notched with dark wheel tracks.

All of this under arc lights from rumbling generators, in heavy rain driven by the spring equinox winds, men seemingly heedless of bloodied hand wounds incurred through misjudged hand signals to heavy tackle operators, and, it seemed, to Fraser, it all just went on in spite of the continually bellowed commands and interruptions from officers and NCOs of all appearances and capacities.

"Hi! You boy! Can you'all hold a line?"

Me? Hold a what? And what for? Fraser felt nonplussed. Was he going to get ordered to clear out, hold something or do something quite beyond him? The rain-soaked sergeant clambered up to him, blowing and grinning.

"Jeezz! The right feller in just the right goddam place! Here – what's yore name, young man? – Fraser? Don't sound true blue English to me, but here. See that big stout guy down by the wall where the Cat 'dozer is waitin'? OK, y'all hold this line real tight. I'll go backalong and whop in some pegs. That'll give us the straight for droppin' some of these goddam old trees. Say, what d'you call this species, anyway? Beech, huh. Ya, I guess we've got sump'n similar through the eastern States. Now, Fraser, you an' me and ol' Buster down there, we're the team. You keep that line real tight, here. Pass it around this tree here, keep real good tension on it, and then hold on to the snap clip and walk it back down to me when we gives yuh th' signal, OK?"

The instructions were clear enough; no doubt, he could manage that, but did the Earl know what was going to happen to his trees, and everything else? As the sergeant had just said to him, now loping back down to the 'dozer, Jeezz!

In puzzled credulity, Fraser saw three men, soldiers of some kind presumably, come into view in response to the sergeant's beckoning down on the flat in front of the waiting Caterpillar tractor. Each was carrying a snarling, high-revving piece of brilliantly painted machinery unknown to Fraser; heavy, they needed both hands to carry them. The men were revving them, steel bars burnished by flickering chains of hungry teeth, it seemed.

The sergeant was waving him to come on down, fast, and not forget to hold the line tight as it was reeled in. The sergeant was grinning at the soldier with the reel of line.

"'Buster, I guess we gotten ourselves a noo ree-croot here!" He pronounced "recruit" as two words. "Fraser? You boys have power or chainsaws around here? Nope? Waal, now, you stick real close to me, and watch these fellas. They can drop a big stick on a dime. Yeah, boy, just watch this!"

Fraser was aware of the steady raindrops trickling down through the sergeant's black stubble. Would British army men be allowed to go around like this? In a burst of sustained snarling power, one of the three men waved on by the sergeant, having looked critically at the angle of growth and height of his tree, took position to one side, and cut out a large orange-coloured wedge from the trunk, kicking it to one side. He stepped back, and with immediate placement, the two men remaining took positions behind and on either side of the substantial majestic beech and gave their howling saws full entry into the growing timber, horizontally and five inches higher than the extracted wedge, which they kicked out of their way.

Unheeding of the scenes of ceaseless activity behind him, Fraser was impossibly and hugely impressed to utter speechlessness by the surety and speed with which the old tree was brought creaking, smashing down amongst those behind it. As soon as it had settled, with explosive cracks as lateral branches splintered under the full weight of the fallen tree's trunk, the three men with their chainsaws moved along it in unison, blue smoke jetting out from their saws, dropping any branches in front of them with the greatest of speed and skill. The sergeant, his sergeant, was speaking to him once again.

"Waal, Fraser, sure beats them old guys with them long, two-handed whippy jobs, huh? Here, you jus' take this, with compliments from the Construction Company, 4th Armoured Regiment, an' partic-yoo-larly so from me, Sarn't 1st Class Joe Huyter," he said, pointing to the white name tag sewn on his field jacket.

The sergeant pressed a packet of Hershey bars, four dark, almost black cigars, two packs of chewing gum and a pack of Camel cigarettes into Fraser's uncertain hands, and wrapped his fingers around them all with his own rough, warm, wet fingers.

"These are for you, your pop and your mom. Look, ya did a great job. You an' me, we could mebbe be of some good purpose to each other again, huh?"

He clapped Fraser on the shoulder, stood back and saluted with a spray of raindrops and paced at speed to where the big Caterpillar D9 'dozer had already turned round one massive section of the cross-cut beech bole, and with the huge polished blade, nudged it precisely up against the back of the now widely broken-open estate wall.

Fraser felt strange and difficult responses to all that he had been an involuntary part of that afternoon. He shook himself and avoiding further involvement with the work going on without let-up, walked out by a circuitous route only faintly limned by roe deer. Patting his pockets with contents he muttered, "Hershey bars; they're OK, should last a while. I'll share them with Hedley. Now where are the dratted cigars? Better not get them squashed, or wet, damn me!"

He laughed out loud at the mental spectacle of solemnly handing over the soggy objects, and swiped the rain drip from his nose. He deliberated on this largesse.

"Bluggy rain. I'll give all the cigars to Father and the cigarettes to Mr Harris, and certainly not tell my great factory chimney sister about the fags! Split the Hersheys, and keep the chewing gum for dusty jobs at the farm."

Still some distance from his path through the fields near home, he felt a curious sense of betrayal in having been a part of this battering onslaught upon something which had lasted and probably been deeply cherished by those people of The Park who had seen it all grow through the years. And yet, he had seen ways of getting things done that were an inescapable part of having the whole of the Allied armies ready, ready for something he knew was going to be impossible to keep concealed from just about every family in the whole country. The unknown scale of the excitement of massed power gripped him again in the pit of his stomach and he shivered violently. And anyway, now he knew all about power saws. That would be useful, once he had his farm.He would get the American sergeant to show him how it worked.

XX

Due to commitments not only to certain jobs with Jack Harris's men, but also needful tasks at home that he had agreed with his father would be seen to, Fraser found that breaking off from any of these bonds to view what was sure to be going many stages further in unstoppable possession of The Park by the Americans, was not at once possible. He was in a mood of restricted independence. Some of that wet afternoon's events he passed on to his parents and sister at the supper table, not all.

"What do you get from going down there and getting in the way of these American GIs?" Jean liked to air her acquaintance with smart labels for things like American servicemen. "I'm surprised they didn't just tell you to hoof it," she added tartly.

Fraser knew from the signs that his mother was going to wade in with more condemnatory reasoning; he held his counsel. He felt that the least attention paid to this sudden availability of a whole world of male-driven military skills, machines and armaments was the best way to treat it.

"Some of the machinery they have would be quite useful for people like Mr Harris. The men are very good at working them," Fraser offered in casual fashion. He could just picture Jack Harris getting the feel of some whopping big tractor, big grin on his ruddy face, fag hanging from his lips, and keeping pushy bluggy Chester off the damned thing! He almost burst out laughing. His father cocked a quizzical eyebrow and eye but said nothing.

What was taking place on the day following therefore, might have mollified his unrest about all that tearing things down in an apparently good, major cause, but cause even deeper concern in Fraser's growing and quite accurate perception of what was good for the countryside, and what was most definitely damaging.

One of the oldest tenanted holdings on the Charnborough Estate, Old Croft Barns, was virtually unchanged in any particular of boundaries or dispositions since pre-Enclosure times. A quiet dignity of form and function embraced the thatched farmhouse, itself almost married into the farm buildings, which curtsied away from the Tudor brick chimney with a dip of ridge and tile. There was a solid brick barn with high, weathered double doors of elm giving onto an oaken threshing floor, this building completing the enclosure of a square of flagstones, cobbles and local brick, all of which flowed comfortably over and around even older different levels of ground. Change in farming practices had flowed around the holding, rather than altering ways of doing things with which everyone had been quite satisfied; it was only in the earlier years of the century that the thump-thump of threshing flails had been supplanted by the smokey power of the traction engine with its travelling threshing box.

The seventy acres that had been tilled by generations of the Cotton family lay behind hedges giving forth at least four or five species of hedgerow timber, and enclosing fields that in only two instances held more than eight acres. Ditch bottoms were cleaned, hedges laid and field gates set up with a care that spoke of good husbandry as much as for some modest profit.

Daniel Cotton, nineteen years old, enlisted in the Worcestershire Regiment in 1941. His elderly parents chose not to renew their lease, unbroken since 1819, and Mr Stanton, agent to the Charnborough Park Estate, agreed that the estate take over the fields and buildings, leaving the Cottons with their home, a few stalls for rearing calves and hens, their pony and trap, and their well-fulfilled memories of hay and harvest. All this on a simple peppercorn rent and non-repairing lease which would terminate on the death of the survivor of the couple. They were well pleased with what Mr Stanton had done for them, and the Earl, of course.

In the estate office and map room, a single-storeyed building of delicate astragals, adjunct to the east wing, American staff officers had traced those two roads embracing Old Croft Barns on a wide-based triangle as they neared to a connecting lane above the farm. The smoothly uniformed men spoke amongst themselves, with mutterings and quickening interest, noting the 1:25000 scale through coils of blue cigarette smoke. Gerald Stanton, Resident Agent, for all that he sat behind the wide map table, curiously did not somehow feel to be entirely in command of the situation, evident from restlessness in the leather chair, crossing and re-crossing his legs in a fret of unease.

The lanky Captain of Field Engineers, Lincoln Stahlmann, from Grand Rapids, Michigan, inclined deferentially to Gerald Stanton, putting his and the army's needs to the Estate Agent.

"What we're lookin' for, Mr Stanton, surr, is somewhere with real good access, to get our ree-pair units in and out faster'n a rattler. Some kinda place where we can throw a perimeter fence around the whole compound and our ree-pair guys…" – (Stanton noted that this person actually pronounced it "rEEpayah") – "…can work all hours, if that's what it's goin' to take. This Old, er, Croft Barns place seems just the kinda deal we're lookin' for. Surr."

From another direction, behind heavy rimmed spectacles which glinted and flashed in the pale light of the March afternoon came a more-than-determined pursuit of Old Croft Barns.

"Waal, now, Old Croft Barns, huh? What kinda deal can we fix there?"

This major, who seemed to be keen on fixing everything, and who now fixed Stanton with a bullish, jutting chin, displayed a congestion of multi-coloured medal and service ribbons across the left breast of his immaculately tailored and fitted gaberdine tunic. Gerald Stanton cynically reflected to himself that this person must have participated personally in one theatre of war or another, continuously, from about the age of ten. Some sort of all-American martial whirlwind. Commencing, no doubt, Gerald Stanton added to himself, acidly, with a particularly intransigent Indian tribe, perhaps two. The major broke in again.

"What about the folks there, Mr Stanton? Any of your old favourites likely to get mussed up by way of our operation in their backyard?"

The rainbow major pronounced the farm's title as something like "Aaarled Crurfft Buurrns". Stanton shuddered and spoke loudly to conceal his distaste.

"Well, no, Major. We have an old couple there, tenants for many years. Very decent folk. We, the estate, that is, take care of them, and will carry on doing so. Some of the farm buildings remain in their hands, and they will be staying on in their home. They've been there a very long time."

Major Rainbow-of-Ribbons-Go-To-War-Lucas pulled back his intimidatory features, spectacles and sartorial display of valour, declaiming with heavy enthusiasm:

"Good, real good! Anyways, surr, we've kinda looked the old place over already. It seems a fine location for our boys and their rEEpayah equipment. We would appreciate the usual go-ahead in writing from you and the Earl, of course. Don't want your old folks to get the wrong angle on our takeover, do we, huh? No, surr."

Gerald Stanton, fifty-two, imperfectly repaired tubercular subject, felt a curious sense of being challenged, threatened almost, by these men and their endless ranks of roaring machinery to make ready for waging war. Further, he felt that there was the implication that they, the go-get-'em Americans, had invited themselves over to the launching platform for invasion of Europe for the express purpose of demonstrating to the British forces just how to set about the matter.

By late afternoon, it was agreed that the American regiment would take over the major part of the buildings at Old Croft Barns for their heavy vehicle repair shop, erect a holding compound for their vehicle pool, occupying certain fields designated by Mr Stanton and outlined so in thick red crayon on Major Lucas's mapboard. The meeting between the latter and Mr and Mrs Cotton in the parlour of their small, peaceful farmhouse became stilted and devoid of easy understanding. The elderly couple had been wordlessly compliant, it seemed. Major Lucas clearly showed that he really had to be forthright and crushingly specific in enumerating how the needs of his unit were to be fulfilled. His boys were to be responsible for their actions to no one other than himself. It had all felt most disagreeable to Gerald Stanton. Painfully dictatorial.

The Earl and his agent looked at each other in the flickering firelight and tranquillity of the drawing room. Hyacinths' heavy scent overlaid the delicate aroma of tea and lemon, gilt frames, wall lights' warmth, sun-softened folds of faded curtains resting against pale walls rising into elaborate cornices. The older man spoke with care, selecting his words slowly.

"If we deny them the wider use of Old Croft Barns, Stanton, our friends…" (the Earl coughed lightly once) "…our friends will, um, simply approach us from another quarter and another level, by someone else. We did influence their thinking in that direction, I recall?"

Recalling his own unrest at the force and speed of the American negotiating officers, Gerald Stanton wanted to give vent to his employer.

"The anxiety in my mind, sir, is that, all right, they say that they will put a perimeter fence around everything they wish to occupy, but we don't know for how long that will be, and if their, er, 'facilities' expand into more roads and living quarters, and goodness knows what else. Then we are, the estate, is going to be wide open to further apprehensions by the War Ministry, and we might land up with even more than a single regiment, with married quarters, and we already hear from other sources what that brings forth."

Gerald Stanton's last sentence or two came out with a rush, his chest felt tight and painful, he felt weary and exhausted by the continuous assault by over-hearty, over-healthy bloody Americans… "our friends".

A resinous log amongst the ash and beech spat and flared, as if to underline the misgivings clearly behind Gerald Stanton's apprehensions. The Earl stood up, gracefully, yet with a careful angularity. His soft tweed jacket lacked crispness against the windows' fading light. My employer, my old Earl, Stanton thought, is showing the burden of caring for the works of his progenitors, with all their attendant joys and jaundices. This must be a drain on him, and for how long is he robust enough to accommodate all this?

Earl Sefton spoke, with a measured care in selection from his innermost thoughts, as both of them in the room knew would be so.

"Regarding the length of their stay with us, admirable Stanton, this will not, I believe, prove a burden to us beyond a certain length of time." He spoke with an unquestioned certainty. "What will prove a strain, Stanton, will be the quality of their stay. Be absolutely firm, be absolutely, ah, fair, be absolutely swift in coming to me at once if anything in your estimation of the situation warrants it. We still have the ear of the right people in the right places, hmm? Before they get out of all reasonable behaviour, these well-meaning 'friends' of ours."

The Earl smiled at his employee and they both stood up. The latter felt reassuring warmth through being included in the older man's reference to persons to whom they could turn – no, to whom the estate could turn – if these brash, demanding cousins from another continent damaged beyond recovery the more valuable and cherished products of generations of careful husbandry. Unwittingly or otherwise.

"Very good, sir, we shall all do our very best for you, and for the estate. I'm sure that there will be occasions when I shall have to come to you, if I can make it before they unleash themselves in a direction which we hadn't reckoned on, goddammit!"

How his last term of transatlantic high feeling popped out, Stanton couldn't be sure. They both laughed, for reasons that would have been totally incomprehensible to Major Lucas and his Captain of Engineers, but quite clear to those Seftons whose portraits ringed the walls of the room, their calm gaze upon their descendant and the deeply panelled door gently closing behind him, it seemed.

XXI

As for what fell upon the Cottons' nicely tended and modest farm in the next few weeks and months, no one in Fraser's extended acquaintance regarded it with anything less than downright fury and disgust. Listening to his father discussing this degradation on a telephone conversation with a practising veterinary friend further down the county, on the far side of Charnborough Estate, Fraser was shocked at the flat-out condemnation by his father of what he, Fraser, could only envisage had been going on at Old Croft Barns.

"These damned cowboys were doing WHAT with their bloody jeeps or whatever? Actually chasing the poor wretches of birds? My God, Lance, they're the most ill-disciplined, disgustingly unlikeable sub-species of rank bloody savages. I've heard some stories flying around before this lot landed on us up here, and they were enough to make your hair curl. Ach, but we only knew about their poor terrier bitch, nice wee cratur, smashed her rib cage in, absolute bastards in anyone's book. Aye, Lance, I will, I'll damn well make it my business all right."

Fraser was taken aback at how drained of good humour his father's face appeared, and at the anger in his eyes. Turning away from the telephone, he was including Fraser in the closing conversation as an equal, as another man would.

By the time that Fraser's father closed his conversation with Hugh Leversedge, dusk had drawn its skirts around the day. There was no point, Alec Baird decided, in trying to find the truth of the matter at Old Crofts Barns until another day. The same dusk came down in a merciful blanket upon the small farm and its buildings, where military control by the American personnel ensured that no local folk had access inside the eight-foot perimeter fence. Or so they believed. The farm men around knew better, silent about nightly movement of stolen tools and gasoline cans, spoils of war and that sort of stuff. But as Fraser now realised, turning away from his father's preoccupation with other calls to be made, few people in the immediate countryside around Charnborough Park harboured any illusions as to how American servicemen of all ranks, not just enlisted men, behaved when they openly held the view that the English people amongst whom they were quartered were of no account in running a war. Or, for that matter, any other goddam thing.

Inside the fence, lodged in concrete that had been shovelled around stanchions with careless liberality, damages had initially been of a minor nature and unavoidable: gateposts slewed around and broken off at ground level, a chain or so of hawthorn hedge 'dozed out in a splintered heap, later to be soused with petrol and crankcase oil, which burnt down into the very soil in a corner of the yard. An ash tree of great girth and age, featured in the Domesday land records as a sapling boundary marker where ancient woodland had been cut back, was winched out in a savage whine of unstoppable grunting power, the roots shattering in despairing gunshots, all for the ease of movement of roaring, revving trucks lodged there for repair or maintainance, where before the area of the yard had been perfectly acceptable for over a hundred years' use for Shire horses and their wagons to wheel around.

But through the winter months, damage was supplanted by a rampant wanton destruction which reached out beyond inanimate things.

Finding it too tedious to reverse out of one of the commandeered cart sheds, an "accidental engagement of forward drive" resulted in an entire rear wall being burst out, carrying with it the oak uprights supporting the hayloft above. The bricks and shattered beams were not pushed aside, but crushed into a trivial tumulus, reared over at exuberant spine-crunching speed by drivers in greasy fatigues. The Cottons' Light Sussex hens and fine silvery cockerel, released by the tearing away of their wire-netting run in the orchard, were chased in pathetic frenzy by two jeeps, the drivers yelling in a high, ululating scream, their companions standing up, field boots braced, the better to pursue them with savagely whirled garage brooms, until the birds, demented, collapsed in limp haemorrhagic bundles and were left lying on the bloodied grass, in full silent view of the Cottons at their parlour window.

Latterly, any pretence by Major Lucas of going through the motions of consulting the old couple, who now barely ventured beyond the dwelling and garden and outhouses with each and every fresh insult to their comprehension, was abandoned, with an indifference that immediately extended to his pool of drivers, mechanics and GIs of the repair pool.

In an area behind the heifers' shed that had been carefully fenced, planted with hedging quickthorns and field maple, and used for summering young calves by four generations of the Cottons, this was the handiest place for all and any rubbish from the repair bays to be dumped and burnt. The hedge thorns died, and were overrun by reversing trucks and jeeps, ultimately adding to the fire that now smouldered continually, feeding upon and adding to the poisonous sludge.

In a grave mercifully at a remove from the so-called ree-payah dee-pot, lay the body of the Cottons' smooth-haired terrier bitch Seal, retired from local hunt service in diligent pursuit of foxes, a happy and contented part of the Cottons' existence. The right ribs, spleen and liver were one massive rupture from a viciously swung tool by a corporal whose temper could not handle the bile and nausea that possessed him after a solid evening's drinking in The Wain. Seal's approach to everyone of amenable disposition was to pause, one forefoot raised and head and ears cocked to one side, awaiting further invitation to a crust from a sandwich or to pursue a hiding rat. In this manner, she had approached the figure clambering out of the inspection pit, to be sworn at and then lashed with a two-foot tyre lever. As the sniffling, gasping little dog dragged herself she knew not where, the serviceman swore continuously in obscene repetitive detail, before bending to vomit into a bin of rag waste.

Harry Weaver, licensed publican at The Wain, had been telephoned by Hugh Leversedge, veterinary practitioner for most of the Charnborough Park farm tenants and local hunt, in response to a halting, tearful call to him from Mr Cotton using a neighbour's telephone. Would he, Harry Weaver, come up with him to the Cottons' place, and see exactly the despair that surrounded them. The little bitch was dead, by all accounts. In quiet twilight, the two men buried the dead terrier below a lilac tree at the south gable of the farmhouse. They had gone into the house, cap and hat in hand, to speak with the Cottons as best they could. They would take up the whole desperate affair with the Americans the following day, find out the man responsible for finally rendering the elderly couple's life a nightmare without end.

Word of mouth passage of these latest acts of indescribable cruelty towards domestic birds and beasts flew through the night hours at bleak speed. Going to the Saturday morning milking, Fraser fell silent, astounded at the depth of savage response bursting from everyone's minds and lips. Watty Taimes was almost incoherent. Little dogs and big 'uns, Mistress Harris's fowls and his own motley perch at his cottage, they all clustered around his gaitered legs in secure benevolence at any time. Why, they was all just a normal part of things.

"M-miserable 'alf-bred bastards, orl dressed up like t-toytown soldiers. They need some thinnin' out, ar, with some on theer own f-fookin' machine guns. Ah'll bet you, young Fraser, as 'alf on 'em are bred to bluddy niggers, 'arfbreeds at the best, or worse. Bastards. We don't 'ave no bluddy need of 'em, not any road."

Fraser's father held a few moments' conversation on the phone with Hugh Leversedge:

"All right, Hugh, so you reckon there'll be no more of their moronic behaviour, eh? Did no one take responsibility for these louts? Aye, so they've been sent off camp, is that right?" His words were terse, clipped to the minimum. He turned, looking directly at Fraser as he finished speaking. "I want to have a word with Harry Weaver in any case; thank him for what he did to help you, and the Cottons. What a rotten foul business for everyone up there. A heartbreak."

Alec Baird turned to Fraser, speaking quietly but with emphasis:

"Have you got work to finish with the men at the farm? Nothing in particular? Right, I'll pick you up in an hour's time at Jack's, and take a pair of decent shoes with you on the bike."

He went through to the hall. Fraser heard his offhand words to his mother as the house and everyone therein made the customary Saturday morning dispositions.

"Mary, I'm going to the office in town. Is there anything you want me to pick up on the way back? Say now, because I'm going to speak with Harry Weaver at The Wain about this monstrous abuse at Old Croft Barns. Fraser'll be back about dinnertime, I suppose."

He cleared his throat noisily, and didn't look at Fraser as he backed the car out of the garage.

What's going on here? Fraser speculated. Why would my father want me to go along with him? And what the dickens are we going to need shoes for?

Imperceptibly, there arrived amongst the inhabitants and homes and farms of the two or three neighbouring villages a manifestation of open hostility, of rank dislike of the American servicemen. Fraser became acutely sensitive to this almost tangible, mounting feeling, and not just from his father's terse conversations with Hugh Leversedge and Jack Harris. There was now a general feeling, spreading through town and county, that all right, this gross battening onto their goodwill had somehow to be gone along with, in the need to funnel these men from a different country into the coming clamour of war, but surely not all of the practices of these bullish soldiery had to be silently accommodated, with naught said? Protest became open and strong, sometimes in highly surprising fashion.

As instructed on this morning's strange mission, Fraser climbed into his father's car, as Alec exchanged some comments with Jack and Marcia Harris. The farmer seldom missed signs of intent in folk he knew well.

"Goo'in' ter shpeak wiv h'our friend 'Arry, h'are yew h'Alec?"

Jack Harris's face was dark, concerned. Marcia looked steadily at both Fraser and his father, nodding in friendly fashion to Fraser, acknowledging his presence in this serious matter for grown-ups to sort out. She would know all about it, as well. Fraser just knew that she would, in his inside feelings' continual assessment of everything.

"Ah've known owd 'Arry for a lot of yearsh, Alec, an' by Chrisht, never before 'ave I sheen 'im sho buggerin' worked–up. He were bluggy h'inflammatory, h'and shtill inclined that way. H'it shtill ha'nt cum out on 'im yet, mark my word!"

As their car wheeled across the gravel yard outside The Wain, Fraser had the feeling that the morning had yet to move its happenings onwards in a more particular direction. Engine switched off, Fraser wanted to find out from his father where he came into things, if at all.

"Father?"

"Aye, man, what?"

"Are you and Mother and everyone else angry because nothing much seems to have been done about letting the Cottons know that they matter a lot to everyone round here?"

"What seems to be happening here, Fraser, is that these blasted Americans, these GIs as your sister is so fond of calling them, have the idea that they can do do any damned thing they wish, and not be held to account for their actions. This is going to seriously affect the way in which people all over Britain, England mainly, support them right through until they actually leave here to fight the Germans in France. If they're going to behave like this here, can you or any of us believe they're going to have any self-discipline or be of use to their officers and the folk who are in the midst of the fighting? And that bit, Fraser, is going to be really savage and nasty."

"Oh, all right, I can see that. Are we going in here? Do you need to speak privately with Mr Weaver about what happened up at the Cottons' place?"

His father looked steadily out at the yard without speaking for some quiet, sun-filled seconds, then turned and spoke quietly to Fraser.

"I want you to come with me because I think it'll be useful for you to see how to make the best of neighbours and farming folk in general, how to keep their goodwill from the other side of the fence if you like, and not be just another farm worker all of your free time. All right? Come on then with me, and get your shoes on; we both don't need to be clumping into Harry Weaver's pub with muck falling off our boots."

They passed below the low black lintel with '1679' chiselled into it. The interior of the public bar seemed at first dark and with little human presence, for all the fact that the licensee, Harry Weaver, was responding to their bringing in the morning sun and the dust from outside.

Polishing a glass, Harry nodded to both Alec Baird and to Fraser in one easy inclination, and some few words of similar unhurried manner. Fraser, his vision adjusted, noticed the three or four farm workers at a settle to his left, backs to the light, beer glasses set before them. Two of them he knew; one a more or less retired stockman from Brockwood Home Farm, the other not quite so old, who did fencing, hanging gates, cleaning ditches and hedge-laying for all farm tenants who needed his careful skills. They regarded him with ease, a friendly "Ar, all right, Fraser?" from one, and "Wiv your Guv'nor today, are you, then? That's good," from the other.

Fraser felt relieved, he knew that there was an age limit for going into pubs, but it seemed that he must either be over the age thing, or being in his father's company, on important business, made it OK. His father was speaking to Harry Weaver quietly, who had stepped down from behind the bar. Alec Baird turned to Fraser, bringing him into the shared discussion.

"Yes, he knows all about the sorry business, Harry. He heard the full measure of it when Hugh Leversedge phoned me up. I understand that the insufferable louts who did it have been sent off camp. Is that true?"

Harry Weaver was no longer relaxed with his few customers for the morning. He was intensely, deeply angered. His voice shook.

"Mr Baird, when Mr Leversedge and me went up there, it were like a bloody killing house. Blood and feathers every road, and that poor little bitch; to see 'er like that was downright hellish. Dead, of course, bled to death. But, your vet'nary colleague, Mr Hugh, was up to it. He took photographs of every damned scrap of awfulness, and made a careful note of the bitch's injuries and all that we could see afore we buried her. It's all gone up to these so-called allies of ours' commanding officer. Mr Leversedge said he'ld develop the photographs himself, at home, that very night. The county police have–"

There was a noisy unchecked interruption of vehicles turning in, revving hard, tyres scurring as they locked amongst the gravel.

The group of GIs and some NCOs fomented an instant antipathy from the moment that they burst in through the door with freewheeling obscenities peculiar to American soldiery, only just avoiding the low black lintel above the door.

Fraser just had seconds to hear his father enunciate clearly and steadily to Mr Weaver, "Harry, I'm taking a full account of this to our Chief Constable, the American CO and the Earl. I'm standing to warrant all that has taken place, so I'm backing anything that you and Mr Leversedge saw, did and said. Right?"

He had to almost shout in Harry Weaver's ear, such was the strident overflow of gratuitous comment from the looming figures clustering around the bar.

Alec Baird, with a sideways nod and raised eyebrow to the farm workers at their table, got their immediate and unspoken agreement that Fraser go and sit with them, Harry Weaver setting a tall glass of lemonade in his hand as he edged past. Fraser was curious to see that his father had taken his stance at a window to one end of the bar room, the door beside it saying 'SNUG'. He was apparently deeply interested in the three American jeeps parked outside, his back turned to the sprawling, bawling Americans. But Fraser was not deceived by his father's uninterested stance; he knew better. Something's up here, today…

The fact that he was chewing gum audibly in one side of his face obliged the last man to come in to articulate more loudly than his customary drawl, so Fraser supposed. Fraser glanced sideways at Sam Wright, the hedger and fencer, who gave an almost imperceptible lowering of his eyelids, and an even slower movement of his head from one side to the other. As plain as anything, the message was: sit tight, young man; we'll all just wait and see.

"Hey, Bub! Lookee: 'Intoxicatin' Spirits, Beers and Ales'! Why, reckon us'ld drink this lil ol' hencoop clean dry, iffen we put our good clean minds to it, yo!"

A thought struck the GI, whose abdominal bulk clearly strained the fastenings of his jeep coat:

"Hell on fire, boys, nope, we can't do that here. 'Member Captain Stahlmann told us: doan innerfere wid no local customs; they bin doin' things their way for hunners of years, goddam!"

Roars of laughter, scorn, disregard.

Slapping each other's shoulders and arms with a bullish bravado, they pushed up to the bar, sending chairs screeching along the tiled bar floor, their eyes plainly hungry for the presence of a barmaid in the room. The farm men and Fraser were equally plainly reckoned of no consequence. Harry Weaver, landlord, continued behind the bar, stolid and deliberate, a shortish man, his back view of waistcoat and balding scalp mirrored in the slightly different angles of the brewery mirrors behind the bottles arranged in groups to disguise their paucity.

By their noisy, turbulent presence, the soldiers (could they really be any good at actually fighting? Fraser reflected, recalling his father's comments outside in the car) seemed to diminish what light there was in the dim bar, and concentrate it upon their uniforms, their flushed eager faces and clustered bodies. The bulky parkas, oiled leather combat boots and fine quality uniform blouses all exuded a provision regardless of more utility wear, a way of doing things where all this came from that was incomprehensible for tired, silent farm workers to grasp, Fraser companionably of their company, stolidly regarding over their sandwiches and beer, the Americans and their behaviour.

Feeling tension growing in the pit of his stomach, Fraser thought, these men shouldn't be ramming their overweening conceit – no, arrogance – in the faces of quite ordinary working folk. Was this how they behaved at home, wherever that was?

Slightly bellicose, more than indifferent to what the response might be, the large-bellied corporal whose tunic blazed with badges, coloured patches, meaningless insignia, hunched sideways over Harry Weaver's bar.

"Waal, Pop, guess yore happy to see us come over to do th' fightin' for yuh again, huh?"

The tension rose a notch in Fraser's stomach. Sam Wright's companion, the stockman, bit slowly into his cheese and pickle sandwich and wrenched off a large piece with consummate, audible effort.

Harry Weaver shrugged diffidently to this presumption of superior military expertise, his eyelids hooded as he polished a glass for the second time, studiously making no reply.

"Guess you Limeys had to bring us in again, huh? Waal, but you ol' guys just keep right on wid the farmin' an' suchlike–"

A slim, olive-complexioned GI standing at the corporal's shoulder swivelled round in order to take centre stage as he completed the sentence, his eyes widened in feigned delight and false outrage:

"Yeah, you ol' dudes keep right on with the farming stuff, and we'll jus' keep right on with the fuck–"

His last two syllables were drowned in a howl of raucous bellows and boots being stamped, men doubled up over their tables, mugs and glasses splashing as arms and hands pounded on the oak tops.

At these downright inflammatory words, there was an immediate arresting by the farm men of their cautious drinking and raising of sandwiches. Fraser's father had turned completely round, standing in front of the bar, taking in the entire scene of the GIs clutching each other's shoulders, throwing back their heads to bellow and gasp and neigh. Directly opposite Alec Baird, Harry Weaver had swiftly placed himself at the door into the yard and street outside, which he wrenched open with a crash that had the entire door frame and thick planks vibrate. Whatever Harry's intention, planned or otherwise, Fraser instantly recognised that his father was going to bring this whole damn lot of, of companions to dog murderers and hen killers, to the most severe awareness of the universal disgust at all of their behaviour. Fraser held his breath. Sam Wright put a scarred hand across and gripped Fraser's lower arm as in a vice.

"Stop right there!" Alec Baird's voice wrenched all movement and mirth to an abrupt halt. Fraser had only ever heard this penetrating command-voice from his father once before, in the business of getting Chester Harris out from below the plough.

His father's words were low and deadly quiet. The American men were battened down into motionless silence to hear his message.

"Before any of you amateur so-called soldiers leave Mr Weaver's premises..." – (The sarcasm was like a honed knife. Fraser shivered) – "...you will listen to me, and to him. Keep all your smart talk until you get to where the Germans will be only too pleased to show you how they kill would-be soldiers like you, not hens and small dogs. Mr Weaver has something for you to see and think about, so stand exactly where you are!"

Fraser had not heard his father's voice so suffused with anger before.

"Nah then!" The publican's words slashed across their faces like a snarling, stinging whip, laid on fiercely. For all their brevity, his words carried volumes of venom and contempt. "You'll hearken to me, now, you poor useless lot, afore I throw the lot on yer out. Thirty year back, I was in the army, the British Regular Army. Professionals, I'll have you know, had been for damn near seven years. Regular, infantryman. Egypt, France, Belgium, France again. South Staffs Regiment.

"We could lay down rifle fire faster and kill more bloody Germans better than owt you may think as you can do down there..." He jerked his head to the south. "...on yer piddlin' trainin' course. Going into line, our own guns registering too far in front of us, Loos mines and pit heads, couldn't get forrard into the German trenches for wire as our guns 'ad never marked it. We wur shot into bloody raw meat by Jerry machine gunners, enfiladed. You'll find out what that means, by Christ you will. They had us, no matter which way we turned. Our lads, the whole bloody battalion, was cut to pieces. Twenty-fifth of September, Nineteen Fifteen. Our blood, their miserable swinish blood, pools of it all in the mud."

Fraser swung his gaze between Harry Weaver's stony face and the Americans. Now all turned to this barrel-chested man, gone a little bit to belly, as men who tend a bar are wont to do. His words were continuous in their deadly narrative.

"Our company was down to hardly a score of men, Worcesters some of 'em, all on us wounded. Bloody shellfire, theirs, ours, every bugger's, machine guns from all angles. All of our officers were killed, to a man. We were pinned down, no cover, getting shot to bloody bits. We'd crawled into a bit of a scrape – raise your head and your brains wur gone."

His voice lurched, and then came back in hard, stinging words that brought the crash and slaughter right there in amongst them, into the centre of the stone flags at the door.

"Two of us, me and another, we went out in all that. We went out like raging madmen to bring in my brother, just a young lad, lying out there taking bullets. That's where I got this."

Harry Weaver raised his left arm, the anger in him forcing it up in jerks against a clearly visible trembling. The hair of his armpit did not succeed in smothering the deep purple pit high in his ribs. It was livid, taut, pulling skin and tissue into a monstrous star-burst of lumpy keloid scarring. Below it, a long scything wound swept round his hip and belly to disappear, whip-like, into the waistband of his trousers. The publican turned round slowly. From his seat with the farm men, Fraser could see what the silently craning GIs at first could not: from below the left scapula, a jagged furrow of torn flesh and tissue zig-zagged low across the spine, in a final flourish of macerated body muscle.

"So, we gets to my brother, only just seventeen. He were dead. We lay for a while, and my mate strapped me up."

Harry stopped, trembling, dropping his chin to his bared chest. His eyes were tightly closed. Until they snapped open, fixing all of their faces with his own.

"There was naught else for it. When we reckoned they were changing belts on their bastardin' bloody Spandaus, we rushed at 'em by different roads, by Christ. We were bloody well screaming. Theer was a young lad had crawled in with us, a Fusilier, with 'is knee shot to buggery. He gave us covering fire. He had two rifles. We loaded both of 'em for 'im. Gave 'im all our spare ammo. A good lad."

His voice was deadly, flat, brooking not the slightest, smallest movement.

"Aarh, we got right in amongst them, the bastards. I killed two on 'em with me trenching tool, using my right arm. We killed them machine gunners any bloody way we was able."

His chuckle was throaty, risen on images past of bloody bayonets, rifles bucking them out of impalement in bone or guts with the trick, the knack, of a single shot knocking the rifle back into your hands to free the bayonet for the next bastard German sticking his weapon in your face.

"Old soldiers like us knew all the tricks, by Christ! Aar, they took badly to the bayonet. We didn't bother with taking no prisoners. When we'd used all our own cartridges, we killed the bastards with their own weapons. 'Kamarade', 'kamarade', they kept on once we were right in amongst 'em. Didn't make no odds to us."

From outside, came the present, a child's voice, a mother's reply, a house door shutting. Inside the public house, the group of men in olive uniforms was utterly stilled. They were neither of the village outside, nor of the monstrous bloodletting conjured up to confront them by this small, thickset man with his hidden, monstrous ropes of keloid scar tissue.

With a slow progression of power which brought grace into his yeoman's body, Harry Weaver extended his right palm and fingers, grasping the nearest small round table with a grip that dug into the very wood of it, and swung it off the flags, his forearm and biceps corded like ropes. He raised it to shoulder level, then with the smallest of movements, settled it noiselessly on the floor, to one side of the door standing open to the day outside. Weaver looked straight at Alec Baird. From where Fraser sat, there seemed to be some kind of a signal flick between them.

"Now then, you two lads." He indicated to the two Americans who had been most offensively free with their comments and suggestions. "I've got something here for you to take back to your mates who used our good neighbours' livestock for a bit of your USA sport."

Pointing to a basket on the window sill behind Fraser and the farm men, Harry Weaver instructed, "Just give me that basket over, young man. Theer's summat that these lads are going to take back with them."

He took out a tight handful of hens' white feathers, black and clotted with dried blood, and taking a bunch in each hand, forcibly thrust them into the pockets and open zips of the two American soldiers, and any others within arm's reach. Roughly.

"I do 'ear as that you boys had some little difference atween yourselves some years back at a place called Bull Run. Well, here's a reminder from Chicken Run. You'll have a job turning round the ill will that you've set a-goin' by your rotten, cruel ways. Americans? Aargh! What a right foul taste you've left amongst us. Goo on, get out of here!"

In a part of a second, Fraser thought, and he must have been just waiting for Mr Weaver's last word, his father cut in across everything and everyone:

"Hold it right there you men! Now, think carefully about all that you have heard here this morning. When you are actually going to have to start killing Germans, and are being seriously, savagely shot at, and your friends are lying dead, wounded or mortared into blood and guts, treat the people whose country is being destroyed, with civility and respect, as you damned well should be doing here. French, Belgian, Dutch as well as the Germans all around you; if you don't, you will pay for it dearly. A bullet is a bullet, whatever direction it comes from to knock your brains out. We have welcomed you here, now take what little is left of our goodwill with you, but behave like men, if you can, for by Christ, you will damned well need to! The reason that you're here is to kill Germans, not an old couple's few hens and a little dog just like the one you left back home. Now, clear out!"

The American soldiers struggled to find a civility that they somehow didn't have. Glasses were set down with exaggerated care and uniformed men slid past the publican with faces anxious to grasp the slightest indication of unbending, any evidence of grace, even a nod. None of these were forthcoming.

The star-painted jeeps swung away with spurts of power to their tyres and unnecessary acceleration. There was a whine of engines and gear changes that made it difficult to believe that any man had actually called out anything in their departure dust, escaping from a small, quiet man's tolerance provoked beyond all restraint, escaping from two middle-aged men's philosophy about their acts of survival in war, in another country, in a maelstrom of blood and shattered bodies.

When the three American sergeants were billeted in Fraser's parents' home at less than two hours' notice, Fraser felt his whole mind jump into a gear of seeing things present and impending in the round.

The team of two British and one American officer had swept round the gravel at the front of The Leys, late one raw, wet March afternoon as Fraser carried in logs (his mother had Mrs Kirkwood and another lady he didn't know, all on something to do with the local Caledonian Society, to have afternoon tea), and he intended to to go down to help with the afternoon milking immediately the split logs were stacked tidily.

They were there, all of them, in the hall, speaking with his mother as he sidled past them with the over-full log basket.

"…yes, that sounds splendid, Mrs Baird. And, ah, if you would care to show us the room which you feel will be suitable for the men, no doubt it will do the job, ah, excellently."

Bluggy hell, all right, Fraser me lad: unspoken but in his secured private mind as he carried out the basket. He watched the hand movements of the obviously ill-looking major in British uniform. West Surrey Regiment. He nervously shuffled a clipboard, sheets of buff-coloured forms and a half-folded six-inches-to-the-mile map, with his deeply nicotine-stained fingers. He wore the same campaign ribbons that Fraser's father possessed, and some others which he didn't know about. The other British officer was of the Intelligence Corps, a captain, with no ribbons.

They all stood around, just inside the dining room doorway, the afternoon light enlarging their silhouetted figures, and for Fraser, they suddenly made that generous-sized room feel at once congested, in a fashion he could not say had affected him ever before.

He turned and went out before they made their way outside to the hump-backed Chevrolet command truck, and for his own remedy to the feelings of vague disorder in things, made directly through the fields to the cowsheds where the milking machine vacuum motor was humming. At least nothing there had changed, or was likely to do so.

The men, just into the routine of milking, chaffed him about his unwonted silence and quite obvious preoccupation, only Watty Taimes guessing the likely cause, having seen the white-starred truck rumble determinedly up the narrow lane as he brought the cows in for milking; only one place they could be heading for up there. He noted the coming and going of the army wagon as the cows trailed the last few stalks of kale from their broad muzzles.

"Any road, young Frayshurr me lad, your mam'll do all right on it, never fear; they'll p-pay bluddy p-plenty for extra billets, and you'll mebbe 'ave some f-fun out on 'em, an' all, Ah dessay."

Watty spoke to Fraser with an almost covert assurance, stooped in the calves' pens with his sweated old cap flapping ineffectually at those that had already drunk their milk. His younger married sister Isa worked at the American army base inside The Park as a sort of housekeeper, and the army provender that found its way to her own and her brother's table was now close to being held as a rightful perquisite of the job. Watty remained incurious as to what favours Isa found it useful to bestow in order to maintain this unsolicited flow of good fortune.

Coming home from school the next day, Fraser came on his mother standing in the hall, looking rather at a loss as kitbags, valises and weapons and ammunition pouches were tossed into a heap on the lawn, and two sergeants with two other ranks were erecting bunks along two walls of the dining room. With a quickening of interest, Fraser noted the two short-stocked rifles of some unfamiliar type amongst the equipment. His father's car pulling in, or rather around, everything at the same time, added to the overriding sense of excitement, upheaval and unusual components of the day.

I Like to Walk in This Field

Even the Aylesbury ducks in their happy, messy run beside the old pool were standing nervously in a tight, taut group, heads and necks in preternatural tension, their eyes black and glistening, and tails giving little flicks of uncertainty.

With a characteristic aplomb and cheerfulness that was almost a gaiety, predictable behaviour by Fraser's mother in moments of real challenge, the three US Army technical sergeants were at once invited to join the Baird family at their tea, a meal that somehow developed into something more leisurely, more liberal, in attitudes and conversation, with even the two dogs Argo and Tam electing to sit below the bay window, ears and eyes swivelling in interest and attention to the sudden incursion of voices, body and clothing smells and ways of moving, all of which suddenly seemed to be in the process of attaching themselves to this family and home.

Fraser wondered how his sister Jean, presently in her first year up in St Andrews, would have put on one of her assumed projections of being a grown-up with casual knowledge of wordly things.Oh, yeah, "GI Jean in person!" He snorted audibly and one of the Americans looked at him with the faintest of crinkles around his eyes.

The three men were punctilious in their attention to courtesies, and it was only after some time at the comfortably disordered table that personalities behind names began to emerge into identities behind their uniforms.

There were two Donalds, Don McIlheran, a journalist with the Chicago Herald Tribune, and Donald Schrieber, a real estate salesman (how could one man be involved with something like selling an estate such as Charnborough Park? Fraser wondered. Do they have estates over in America?) from Grand Rapids, Michigan, and Andrew Runnell, a farm machinery dealer from "Well, I guess somewheres in mid-Iowa difficult to pronounce, never mind spell!"

Everyone laughed at this wry description, and from then on, with his mother truly in charge of the occasion, and his father's initial mixture of caution and heartiness proving unnecessary, there was little remaining about the three uniformed men to be uneasy about. Fraser felt relieved about this regaining of stability as the conversation, tea cups and refilled plates established an easy rhythm between all at the table, which embraced him as a part of it all, as he sat with the two dogs on either side of his chair.

He caught his father's single uplifted eyebrow and merest of questioning looks, and slipped out quietly, still a little excited by the speed of everything, to finish up the poultry jobs, and to take a quick but tensely quiet walk along the cart track above the river valley. He wanted to spy for any rabbits busily cropping in the dusk.

He carried the Lincoln Jefferies .22 BSA air rifle, given to him by one of his father's veterinary friends, and with which he had practised holding a steady sight picture until his left arm and wrist developed a shake. It was heavy, and hard to compress the piston against the spring, but was now entirely familiar in his hands. Slithering on his belly, he stalked and shot a three-quarter grown rabbit, using a high clump of nettles (he could smell their peppery presence as he inched closer) for the twenty-five yard approach.

Coming back to the house, he was not aware of the single uniformed figure motionless below the poplar at the side gate, until the sergeant started to light up a cigarette. Any turning away, Fraser sensed, would have only upset either friendly or unsettled feelings in this man. Accordingly, on the decision of a part-second, Fraser made straight for him. It was Sergeant Schrieber, and he asked him something which almost made him, Fraser, gasp at himself in inner surprise.

"Sergeant Schrieber, can you tell me why Lifesavers are called that name?"

The easy soldier, if equally surprised, did not hesitate to provide a workmanlike answer.

"Why, yeah, umm, I guess it's because they, ah, kind of save your life, as you might say, when things get unsteady. OK, let's have one, shall we?"

Gravely he proffered the silvery-papered roll to Fraser.

"You've bin hunting cotton tails, huh? Your age, back home, I was forever hunting all manner of animals. Mostly we ate 'em. Your mom going to put this one in a pie?"

He took the rabbit from Fraser's fingers, and handled it expertly; loins, hind legs and over the shoulders.

"Yeah, Fraser, isn't it? Well, wrap this one up in some pieces of bacon, onions and sweet potatoes, and you've got a feast!"

The sergeant gave back the still-warm rabbit, and leaning forward, placed the entire foil-wrapped roll of Lifesavers in Fraser's jacket pocket. They smiled at and with each other, at this very entente cordiale in the English twilight, with the lapwings whirling above them in the soft spring air.

LIVE ROUNDS NOW

XXII

It was as much of a surprise, more like an improbable awakening in Fraser's family, that these three American soldiers, destined for war, were accommodated with an ease that was open and pleasing. A great deal of this sprang from the fact that these three men, in their direct connections with the land, their American land, of course, were never more than one generation removed from it. Listening to the conversations between his mother and father and any of the "our American boys" of an evening, usually in the kitchen, plates pushed away or gathered to the scullery, Fraser came to realise that there existed a kind of definite, caring link and attitude between American city people and the farm folk left back home, growing hay and corn to feed milk cows, steers and hogs. It came over to Fraser that "back home" was a kind of anchor to which sons and daughters and their youngsters wanted to return to renew their meagre stores of the smells and sounds of the places they had almost all grown up with. In his mind's assembly of parts from the sergeants' telling of their backgrounds, Fraser found this strangely satisfying, that they expressed their valuation of this so openly and with warmth.

Bringing large packs of canned fruit, honey-baked ham and cooking fat to Mary Baird, the three men were stunned to discover that the family of which they had now become a part possessed neither refrigerator, nor a dishwasher, but that it was commonplace for most homes to have one or two stone-flagged larders, sometimes a whole series of cool and windowless store rooms, where meat, fish, milk or game would keep, unspoilt, for a number of days in summer, and indefinitely in winter.

Poking his head around the door jamb to follow Fraser's mother's movement on transfer of a typical musette bag of foodstuffs, Don McIlheran shook his head and turned away in wonder.

"Mary, ma'am, you got a whole goddam suite of cold rooms back in there."

"Don, yah ever hear of any veterinarians back home without a goldarned frig, for Chrissake?"

This between Andy Runnell and Don Schrieber as they sat on their bunks and quietly smoked after sharing supper with Alec and Mary Baird, and Fraser. It was now accepted that if they were in the house and off-duty and around at mealtimes, particularly of an evening, they were expected to pull in a chair and sit as members of the family anyway. Such mealtimes turned out to be abundant in good food and humour, and surprising and lively range of conversation.

Fraser's sister Jean had been picked up at the station in Melford, on Easter break from university. She had yet to be introduced to the three newcomers around the table, and owing something to his daily familiarity with the servicemen, Fraser was amused to find that she was now quite careful about not being so superior and condescending towards him, the young brother who was so wholly taken up with farming, would you believe, oh, la!

Jean intercepted him on the upstairs landing on her first evening at home.

"Well, I hear that you're the family authority on all things American. You'll have to clue me up, won't you?"

Fraser thought for a moment. At fifteen (nearly) he was now about as tall as his sister, and there was a subtle change in their relationship. There were one or two things she should know not to do or say.

"Yes, well, remembering how GI this and GI that was your favourite yardstick of measuring up people, or down…" – he made a grimace of unmistakeable past annoyances – "…just don't call our three good American brethren GI anything; they won't like you for that! Anything else you want to know, I'm sure they'll tell you themselves. They're really good fellows, Jean. Don't get silly or snooty with them. Mother and father think they're fine, you'll see."

The Three Musketeers, as Mary Baird called them with genuine affection, divorced from their own family lives, seemed to serve as a catalyst to far-ranging exchange and discussion in the lengthening spring evenings' drawing together round the table.

While she was at home, Jean and Fraser listened with expanding interest to fascinating experiences, viewpoints, strongly held opinions and equally great explosions of laughter, which rapidly became a feature of nearly every evening mealtime.

Intrigued, Fraser wondered at his mother's surprisingly knowledgeable discussions with Don McIlheran on the subject of his civilian life in the employ of an editor well known for his anti-British views. She expanded the origins, dogma and detail of the said McCarthy in erudite fashion, which while it raised surprise in the one-time reporter, created an even greater surprise in her husband and family. The other two sergeants listened to the spirited exchange with a rare restraint, cigarettes unheeded, intrigued to see their colleague, normally self-important in a discursive arena, on the defensive against this middle-aged woman with the unusual Scotch accent and always of such expansive hospitality.

"Don, do you know what your editor's personal views are on American troops coming over here?"

"Well, yeah, I guess I do, but not all that straight off the press since I, we, got here, Mary. He really does have to put across a kinda balanced assessment of every damned thing in this whole world war affair, not just a sort of personal stance, I would say."

Fraser at once knew that Sergeant McIlheran was hedging. From the back of the room, his sister exchanged an almost imperceptible wink with him. Considering that he knew she was longing to brazen it out and smoke along with everyone else, her acknowledgement that she saw he had some degree of perception in him other than absorption with matters agrarian, caused him to raise his eyebrows, equally imperceptibly. Their mother was not finished.

"Now, Donald McIlheran, you'll just have to recall exactly what he came out with in the editorial and a leader, all through Dunkirk," she wanted to know.

He spread out his large hands in some confusion.

"OK, OK, darn it all, I guess that I can't recall our fearless editor's sentiments exactly. What did the old turkey come out with?"

Here, Mary Baird paused. She seemed to be reaching out in her recall for the precise wording, and Fraser could see that his father's easy conversation about field guns and artillery with Andy Runnell now came to a halt while he waited for his wife's words, regarding her from below curiously hooded eyelids, his face impassive. What the heck is going on here, Fraser asked himself, ill at ease.

"Your paper's headlines were 'England's Dunkirk Her Waterloo: The Toothless Lion's Last Roars', and I can tell you how his opening paragraph went on." She looked at the men, immobile round the table, with almost a defiance in her face and eyes, needlessly honing the hurt or anger there, which would not be contained. "Can you remember, Alec? No? Well, your McCarthy opened: 'Need we even remotely consider saving the arrogant, Empire-obsessed English from what has been coming to them, and their rather small army, ever since we got them out of our hair and our Constitution.'"

Fraser was stunned, and just as clearly, so were his father and sister. Why of all things had she memorised such explosive stuff?

Fraser's father scraped his feet loudly under the table, transposing dinner and side plates with a clash and rattle of cutlery that was entirely foreign to him. The dogs looked up, alert and nervous, unsure of the changes in voices and faces. Alec Baird spoke rather loudly, in a kind of placatory rumble:

"Ach, well, now, Mary, that's no longer the point; these fellows are here, Pearl Harbour and all these torpedo attacks have put a totally different light on what the States could handle from the Axis side, and the way things are now in Europe, with Russia calling for a major attack any damned place in the west, what is desperately needed is—"

"I guess what is desperately needed is that we must all have another cup of that incredibly strong Scotch tea from you, Mary, before we have another darn Boston Tea Party right here where we're all outnumbered!"

Don Schrieber had pushed back his chair so swiftly, gathered his own and the other Don's cup and saucer in a focussed swoop across the table and positively thrust them at Fraser's mother, so that she automatically accepted them with an expression of utter surprise.

She was the first to grant the release of rapidly mounting tension in the big, sunlit kitchen, with a gay disclaimer in her mercurial change of mood.

"Ach, dinna heed me, boys. Who's for more chips. Oh dear! Sorry! French fries."

"Yeah, sure thing, Mary. We'll all have some, eh, men?"

In the general settling back in chairs and rather tentative resumption of good humour, none of them noticed Fraser's quiet withdrawal. His mother was noisily busy at the gas cooker. He sensed as much as saw the trembling of her lips, the reflected light of tears.

"Is it about Uncle Jack?' he asked her, quietly.

She nodded wordlessly.

"Don't worry, Mother, these ones couldn't have come over here to help our own soldiers until they were told. They're good men, really, and... here, I'll help you to do some more tatties, OK?"

He took her arm and pressed it to his face, near to tears himself. Jack Reid, a wild, whirling, not very robust lad, brother to his mother, had joined the Royal Scots Fusiliers in the 1920s, a door through which adventure surely beckoned. He had been wounded, captured as a corporal at St Valery, and almost at once died in captivity. There had hung, unspoken, the possibility of ill-treatment at the moment of capture, or worse. Fraser knew that was as much as his mother and father knew, nothing more. The scanty evidence of the advice through the International Red Cross had never been added to.

That evening's brief fiery episode apart, the Americans' stay with his family was pleasant enough in Fraser's inner mind, even assuming an almost family-like quality about their presence in the house, their comings and goings in a variety of military transport, and the obvious relief with which they came back to the Baird household and their bunks, after training and yet more arduous preparation for whatever everyone knew was coming.

Their battle course had suddenly been made substantially more savage and deadly. Andy Runnell had shocked everyone at the table to a sudden silence when he revealed that two men in his section had been killed that morning. Live ammunition on fixed lines of fire over the barbed wire and mud had instantly shot two soldiers who had jumped up and turned back in revolt from buried explosive charges instead of throwing themselves down. His voice shook and was over-loud as he described what had taken place.

"We had this officer come from one of your infantry regiments, Alec. He came around with most of our top-ranker officers and two of his own senior NCOs. We reckoned he'd seen a lot of combat, only had one arm. And about your age," he added, reflectively, turning his eyes to Alec Baird.

"Did you know his regiment, Andy?" Fraser's father asked.

"Well, yeah, he had KRRC on his shoulder flashes. That mean anything to you guys?"

"Aye. A great deal, Andy. Anyway, go on," Alec Baird said.

Runnell's eyes narrowed and turned again, inwards, to the images of bodies falling back upon the silent, deadly barbs.

"These two guys he had come with him; Christ, they knew their way around anything we had in small arms and heavy calibre stuff. They watched the first section get going and then this colonel, he just stopped them a small ways into it. 'Listen to me real good,' he says, voice like a whip. 'When the Germans have you in their fields of fire, running about or tackling their wire, the very smallest target they'll have is the top of your helmet. If you present them with a shoulder, a leg, an arm or your all-American backside, you will be dead meat.'"

Runnell continued, almost in awe:

"There were our guys, lying there below the wire, taking it all from this fellow with a face like a hawk, and only one goddam arm. They just goldarned knew he was a professional, he'd been there."

Andy Runnell went on, serious.

"'My two men here are going to instruct your NCOs and officers to tighten up this battle course in severity until you soldiers sweat blood, or lose it from wounds which will kill you. Live ammunition from now on, men. Those Germans know that some of you will not have paid enough serious attention to your own combat instructors or to me here, today. From now on, you had better do so. When your top man yells 'Down!' you get so far down it's painful. When you go, go like hell. They will be waiting for you. And particularly for any of you who don't drop or go fast enough. That's all.'"

Most mornings, the Three Musketeers were picked up in a combat truck or a weapons carrier driven with great hubris by a coloured private, always grinning at some vast and personal joke. Although only a four-wheeled vehicle, it was longer in wheelbase than anything locally, and having only limited steering lock due to the front-wheel drive housings, the broad-snouted machine could not make the left hand turn through the black and white gates at one attempt.

But Private First Class Clements found that by cutting the corner of the left hand bank fine, and then putting on full power, he could bounce the truck off the bank in a tearing spray of earth, stones and bruised hedging, flinging the leaping truck through the gates with only inches to spare. Swinging round on arrival with locked wheels, his grin was one of immense self-satisfaction. By now, some weeks into the sergeants being a part of daily life for the Bairds, Fraser was used to, and amused by, the men's range of response to the roaring, leaping appearance of their transport.

"Hi, ya mad coon. The plan says ya pick us up, not break us up! C'mon, turn this thing around, driver!"

Clements' grin became even wider and hugely delighted with this unfailing exchange of mortal abuse.

"Yassah, sarg'n sah, Ah'm tol' nobody can't make no decisions, sah, back there, 'til Ah gets y'all transpo'ted. Sah!" A huge grin.

McIlheran winked dramatically to Fraser, coming out with a pail of hen feed.

"Clements, yore brains are all in yore big dumb ass; get it in gear, man. C'on, let's go!"

With a rasp of transmission and heavy tyres, the truck's exhaust reverberated down the lane. To Fraser, turned round to watch their departure, it always seemed that although peace and order had taken over once again, so had a surging excitement gone, compounded of cloying exhaust fumes, rifle oil, aromatic after-shave and a large, brazen self-confidence in all things American.

On the fifth morning PFC Clements excelled himself by snapping off one gatepost with the massive fender, and shearing off the other with a flick of a rear hub as the truck slewed sideways. The three waiting sergeants were stunned, more at the fulfilment of the double trick than at the noise of the encounter, which had been considerable, with posts and gates splintered below the truck's rear fender. Clements was crowing, the star performer.

"Sarn't Schrieber, sah, Ah done knocked three whol' mimutes offen ma time up heah. Sah!" he burst out, shaking in huge satisfaction.

Sergeant Don Schrieber was lightning fast in response. Fraser thought these American guys are so quick with their reaction to unexpected events.

"Yeah? Well, hear this: Driver Clements is goin' to put those three minutes back again, by getting a repair crew up here, fast, and get this whole darned heap of trouble squared away. Oh, hi Doc! Er, Alec, don't you worry one piece about all this. Good as noo by lunch time, yessir, you bet!"

On a farm, any farm, Fraser thought privately, only incompetents broke gateposts, both of them. His father, unusually, looked quite nonplussed, and Fraser very nearly laughed out loud at his comical expression.

"Hmm, er, fine, then, Andy, but just make sure your men put them in deep enough, not less than three feet down."

"Yeah, sure thing. Clements, d'ya hear what the doc says? Noo posts, check the gates over, sink 'em in three feet. C'mon man, take it easy goin' out, for Chrissake."

In the weeks following, whatever mode of transport rumbled up to the front drive for The Three Musketeers, all became knitted into the fabric of early morning activity; Fraser saw most of their departures due to his being up early to get all the poultry fed and seen to. The whole of our family, he reflected, had become more clear-cut in its normal way of doing things through having absorbed these three men from another country and all their martial functions. Nonetheless, everyone in the house, including even my sainted sister up in St Andrews, Fraser included, were now aware that something was going to happen soon. This was clear to Fraser, and to Hedley, who stated, very aptly, Fraser thought, that the crucible of all this war and weapon training was only waiting, smoking silently, before pitched conflict. Fraser tried to conjure up a mental picture of their friendly servicemen, all or any one of them, actually in action, being wounded, being killed. He couldn't, they were now a part of this family, the Bairds, here in this un-warlike countryside of England.

Amongst themselves, and for the reassurance of those whose hospitality and friendship they valued, the American soldiery put at a careful distance the waiting for their part in the storm of war, with many episodes of boyish, unconvincing bravado, gratified if seen by others, with an easy smile and shrug of their shoulders if not. The repetitive destruction and reinstatement of the vet's gateposts, accompanied by much hilarity, was but one of their reliefs from mounting tension. Other events added to it.

One blowy cold March morning, some slight delay in Andrew Runnell's coming out from the house caused the two Donalds to remember that they urgently needed their cigarette lighters refuelled before the serious business of being soldiers got under way. "Gassing up" was the term they used, pushing past Fraser in the hall to get back into their possessions in the room with their bunks and kit.

"Hi, Fraser, mon ami. Doing the chores again? Don't you wish you had a kid brother with all these chooks to 'tend?"

Both Donalds gave Fraser a friendly slap on his shoulder; he enjoyed their manly presence and conradeship, and grinned.

"Hey, Dook, got any lighter gas in there?"

Sergeant Schrieber yanked open the the truck door and punched the driver on his thigh. A small, thickset man in stained fatigues and strap-dangling helmet, he slumped to the wheel in a parody of agony, groaned with profound presentiments of early death, then straightened his combat boot out through the open door and thumped the sergeant solidly in the chest.

"For you, hot-shot sergeant, ain't got nuthin'. For 'listed men, the ol' oil well doan nevah run dry, man. But, all in the line of dooty, Ah guess."

"Dook" Casella jumped down amongst the three NCOs, small, wiry, olive complexion and the blackest of eyes. He reached round the fender of the still-running truck and swung out a five-gallon jerrican from its carrier on the massive steel fender.

"C'mon now, all yuh country boys, close 'em up tight, git 'em all in there together, man!"

Schrieber and McIlheran held out their opened, upended lighters. Big, fat-barrelled jobs for serious smokers and men of action, Fraser surmised from where he stood in the open doors of the garage. Their fists touched as they stood backwards the better to avoid, Fraser supposed, the petrol staining their oiled boots or uniforms. Casella tilted the jerrican with patronising liberality and the petrol spilled out in dribbles over the lighters, the sergeants' hands, over the cuffs of their tunics and around their boots. Fraser saw the pinkish fluid frothing in the cold sunlight and the marbled vapours which arose around their hands and heads. He felt surprised, aghast at the flagrant waste, and then there was a prickle of something else far more frightening slamming through his stomach.

"Casella! Get the hell out of it! Back off!"

The swarthy-skinned GI swung round, astonished at the bull-like roar from Andy Runnell, who had lurched to a halt only a very few paces from where Fraser stood, choking on his words as he stabbed a shaking rigid arm and finger in violent command, not to the slewing jerrican, but at the cigarette drooping from the corner of Casella's mouth, unseen until he half-turned to face Runnell, all of them. Then, with a bellow which made everything in the yard vibrate, Runnell's hoarse commands tore into their eyes and minds:

"Git that goddam thing outta yore face! Thumb it dead! Git back from the jeezuss can!"

As Casella plucked his cigarette out and closed fingers and thumb around it with fumbling haste, the iridescent vapours around their feet ignited from a point in mid-air, it seemed to Fraser, rooted in impossible paralysis. The close knot of uniformed men arched backwards in a flailing maelstrom of smouldering cuffs, flying helmets and flaring lighters, which were flung away in arcs of flame.

Through all of this, one figure dived in lance-like precision to slam his helmet down on the unguarded spout of the jerrican and, seizing it, impelled the whole thing away in a concentrated thrust of arms, shoulders and his whole body flat to the ground.

Tongues of flame leaping from the oily gravel, the central fire and its heat could not at first be defeated, and the men were trying to save themselves in a way that lacked effective results. Fraser ran to the pile of sand and gravel kept to spread over the yard on icy mornings; his mind had leapt to accounts by school pals of how German incendiary sticks had been smothered by the ARP men using shovelfuls of sand. He grabbed the hens' mixing shovel from the bin inside the garage and attacked the heap of sand, his chest heaving and sore.

"C'mon, C'mon men! Break out those goddam trenching tools, and get with Fraser there." Andy Runnell's voice and directions were jerky and harsh.

Relieved, in the exaggerated manner of those found seriously wanting, they ran around the truck, fetching, spreading. One of them was beating out charred material around the cuffs of his tunic, which he had flung off in the first moments of yelling shock surrounding them all.

There was real anger in Donald McIlheran's shout at Casella.

"Hey, Casella, you damn near had this whole outfit in one big bejayssus goddam disaster, d'you realise that?" His outflung hand and arm took in the whole Baird home, the army truck and Fraser, still scattering sand.

To a stream of abuse, none of it in jest, Casella retrieved the jerrican flung clear of the ring of fire, checked the locking clamp on its spout and swung it back on the truck's fender. His hands, Fraser noticed, were shaking uncontrollably. Not quite meeting the eyes of the sergeants, his throaty voice had an odd, high-pitched tone to it, which did not fit with what he then said to the NCOs, with a visble effort.

"Like I said, Sergeant, you hot-shot fellas are always complainin', so I really put out for yez."

They battered him in an avalanche of flailing tunics, webbing equipment and punches which were not pulled, threw him across the driver's seat and slammed the door. Technical Sergeant Runnell had not moved from his stance with a shovel. His nostrils were white, pinched, over lips that hardly moved.

A flat command. "Casella!"

"Sergeant?"

"Shut up. Look to your front."

Runnell gathered his energies, yawned, swung round and made a 'slope arms' with the shovel, then 'present arms', extending it from the 'present' position to Fraser, who hesitantly took it from him, unsure of what was now expected of him.

"Look, young sir, I have a son back home, just about your age, Fraser, and much the same height. He wants to become a soldier. I'm telling you now what I've told him: don't ever fool around with gasoline, or it'll turn you into a tragedy in seconds. I guess that city hick Casella never got told such things."

He clasped Fraser's shoulder with a large hand, feeling its shape beneath the rough pullover, and looked at him with intensity that was palpable. Fraser knew that this caring American military man was seeing another boy, he was seeing something or everything in another place.

"You always keep that good ol' shovel close by, huh? That's a fella!"

He smiled with most of his face, but not quite matching his eyes, which were looking inwards again. The high matt green truck with large white stars on the doors revved up and spun out into the lane in a swirl of gritty dust.

It was still relatively early on this spring morning. Fraser's father had driven out to an early dairy herd visit before Fraser had come downstairs to let out the various poultry. The house and outside concerns were his own province, with his mother, and sister Jean when she was at home from university, unaware of or not sensible to the satisfactions of sound, taste and smell on such a spring morning. A large motherly Rhode Island Red hen, body feathers fluffed out, took-tooked to her five chicks, and squinting at blackened motes around Fraser's feet, pecked and scratched her way into the circle of oily gravel. Finding nothing there to justify maternal curiosity or to fill her crop, the hen and chicks moved off in hopeful fashion, past the timber garage, kennels and meal store which were all within a few paces of where fire had ballooned out from three up-turned cigarette lighters. Fraser felt drained of purpose.

A movement from the back door; his mother came out squinting into the rising sun's low rays.

"There seemed to be a lot of shouting and carrying on with your friends this morning. Are they away now?"

"Yes, Mother. They had a bit of trouble with… a leak. Is it breakfast time?"

"Aye, your breakfast's ready and waiting, come away in. Bit of a funny smell, isn't there?"

Feeling suddenly, strangely queasy, Fraser looked around himself from what felt to be a distant viewpoint, seeing the house and the buildings which abutted on to the east gable, old Tim shaking himself at the back door kennel, the workshop where his father kept all his car things. His vision of all this entirely familiar normality splintered into what might, only a few minutes previously, have been an inferno. His stomach churned and bile rose darkly into his mouth.

XXIII

As a very minor part of the throbbing concourse that possessed Britain before the assault upon German-held Europe, the American forces at Charnborough Park had swollen to an overwhelming presence of men and materiel that exuded lethal intent. There was no fashion in which the towering purpose of all this ordnance could be longer concealed. From a number of apparently inconsequential sources, Fraser had gathered that things were building up to a wholesale moving out of all of the American military units, their Three Musketeers included, to be drawn together and finally concentrated somewhere else, which last bit he didn't know.

On an afternoon when spring seemed to be unsure of its departure and summer had yet to take over with scents and smells released with heat, Hedley and Fraser, in the Dunns' sitting room, were giving not very serious attention to composing a joint effort for the geography master on local history; they both heard Hedley's father in forthright conversation with Gerald Stanton, agent at Charnborough.

"Yes, we gather that they're pulling out very soon and according to your view of things, they're giving no indication of due date, is that right?"

Both Fraser and Hedley could feel the latter's father in silent impatience as Stanton's voice made reedy commentary on what he knew and also what he didn't know about impending departure of the entire army unit for which The Park had been both their resting and testing place these past seven months or so.

Tom Dunn continued, quite testily.

"Well, don't hesitate, Mr Stanton, to have them recognise that they must put a definite date on relinquishing the special water and power supplies that we had to put in place, in such short order, and that I must have a named officer or person to accept all the county and town charges due during their stay. You must have had something similar for any charges made by the estate during the past months, surely? Oh, I see; all put through a liaison officer's hands. Well, we shall need more than that. Get me a specific agency or office, and if they won't tell you a date, how about you play the daft laddie, Mr Stanton, and suggest a cut-off date, eh?"

As the same thought struck them, both Hedley and Fraser immediately parodied a body suspended by its hair and a swift finger across the throat; they snorted and gasped, trying not to let Hedley's father hear their muffled performance of Grand Guignol, but in sassy, brassy GI mode.

Tom Dunn became demanding in specifying to Stanton what must, in his capacity as Town Clerk, be discharged before dispersal of the American forces to God knows where:

"...all local tradesmen and suppliers, don't forget the credit they had at The Swanspool Hotel, stationery from Medwins and probably laundry during the first few weeks or whatever when they descended upon us, right? Yes, I know, I know, but we cannot and will not be party to a sort of monetary fog over things once they've upped sticks and away. Right, I shall rely upon you to get as close to an actual cut-off date as you can, in the circumstances, Mr Stanton."

Hedley's father gave a bark of rough humour as he closed the conversation.

"Provided they're all cleared up at this end, they can get on with killing Germans with an easy conscience, ha!"

Late one April afternoon, at a time that caught the Baird family quite unprepared, a flurry of jeeps and combat wagons had surged into the drive and yard. The house had been stripped of all traces of the three sergeants' stay under terse, low-voiced orders which were inaudible to Mary Baird and Fraser.

The vehicles had reversed and wheeled out rapidly, the three men in the last truck looking peculiarly stricken in their near-speechless farewells to the small, shaken group in the porch. Alec Baird had appeared in the last few minutes, an unlikely occurrence; his face showed his sudden, inner concern as he quickly stepped forward to the tailgate of the truck and silently shook hands with each of the men.

Fraser avoided looking directly at the American servicemen. He felt their harsh departure from his immediate horizons of life like a wound; from them had come strengthening awareness of many things outside of his boyhood. They were taking away a large part of his growing up with them. He wondered if this part of how he had seemed to them would continue to lie, shadow-like, in their recall as they clung to survival under battle. "Live ammunition from now on, men."

That afternoon's severance of the Americans' noisy, friendly presence from the Baird family's heart had not been without some knowledge that it was going to happen very soon, but in the way of things military, with little warning.

Casting his mind back a few days before those last few unhappy minutes, there had been a party in his home, prompted by what forewarning or needs in his parents' minds, Fraser didn't know.

Their three sergeants and other American servicemen whom his mother and father had come to know and welcome mingled cheerfully with British blue-clad action-wounded and some exiles; Polish, Free French, Canadian, from other European countries, all responding to the warmth of Fraser's parents as hosts. Was it now two or three nights ago? The grand piano in the sitting room, cleared of all books, flowers and magazines, had been the centre of all the gaiety, the raised excited voices, the exchange of glasses empty and refilled, and many songs.

In his mind, acting as both a participant, however junior, but also adding to his mental repository of, well, things to be taken out and thought about, it seemed that the many songs still echoed and lingered behind the farewells as the pale dawn had come in. His mother had swung round from the keyboard, and with that small lilt of gaiety, or grieving, raised her glass "To all of our boys with us here tonight!" with their flushed faces and crumpled uniforms, showing an unnatural brightness in her eye.

"A toast to every super one of you, and here's to pastures new!"

In those sudden seconds' silence and looking down into their glasses, Alec Baird's determined " ..and haste ye back, all of you, to your homes and kin", lifted their faces, turning to their fellow men-in-arms with a tangible intensity.

Looking in from the hall, carrying a tray of sandwiches ("Prime Quality Pacific Coast Salmon, Campbell River Cannery, B.C., Canada"), it sounded to Fraser as though his father's very Scottish final words carried a note of warning into their common well of comradeship.

That night, Fraser had closed off a lot of unknown quantities in his mind, stemming from the strong emotions at large amongst the whole company; he felt himself to be almost a detached observer of something which he had earlier known was going to happen, their Americans' going away those few days later. His mother extending her open arms in last contact with a silent, white-faced Andrew Runnell, his sister Jean, (on Easter vacation from Varsity), tongue-tied at McIlheran's "Thanks a lot for lending me the bike, babe!", and all three men grasping his father's sudden hand in total, battened-down silence. For himself, they had no words, but a fast nod from Runnell to the two Donalds, a clipped "TENSHUN!" and that different, un-British outflung salute, bridging their difference in age in magnanimous fashion. They had wheeled as one, climbing up into the combat truck whose heavy treads were already taking them to that loomimg staging place, on to that portal of departure to where they would have to be three amongst thousands, all putting their lives and skills to lethal purpose. For as long as they survived.

HARVESTS OF WAR

XXIV

With the sudden, tightly controlled withdrawal of the American forces, tensions in general throughout the countryside and villages were released. In many ways, Fraser found, there were legacies accruing from their stay, of both bizarre and biological nature.

Hedley Dunn had cycled out to the Baird home one Saturday morning, firstly to go along with Fraser in a circuitous round of errands and shopping for his mother, before other more robust promises for the day. Cycling to the grocer-cum-post office at the top of the village, with basket, shopping list and the wireless battery to be recharged at the garage, they had exchanged comments upon how little their respective parents credited them with in regard to their knowing a great deal more about the GIs' non-military activities. It was in Fraser's mind in particular. He described it to Hedley as, "Christ, man, it was like an invisible tide that sucked in a whole lot of people we all know, because they just didn't know how to handle idiotically dangerous bloody rackets that were going on all the time. And then, those people that thought they knew what they were about, got into a sort of spider's web of making big money from ever so many shady businesses, like–"

Hedley broke in. They were both labouring to get up the hill, and were puffed even in lowest gear:

"Yeah, well, you should hear some of the downright criminal concerns that father knows were going on, with quite important people involved, right here in Melford. And did you know about Peter Walker's sister trying to have an abortion when she found she was pregnant, just days after they pulled out? Just about bled to death in some backstreet hag's place in Birmingham. My mother had to go with her mother to get her admitted into hospital. Gad."

Fraser thought about Ginny Walker's forever socially posturing parents, and screwed up his nose.

"Aye, well, her going on with that Yank officer wasn't exactly a state secret. Her folks will likely have her deported to, to…"

202

"Benbecula p'rhaps, Fraser?" Hedley offered, all innocent of face.

Going into the shop, chipped linoleum floor almost worn into exposed hessian, they were entertained but little surprised at the exchange in front of them.

Fraser nudged Hedley vigorously, enjoining him in a quietly and purposely pompous delivery:

"Come now, my good man – form an orderly queue, or Mrs Best here will put you out!"

Her response was nothing if not tart:

"You young lads goin' to wait 'til I'm ready?"

Mrs Best had stopped. Everything stopped, then recommenced.

"Your Valerie not serving today, then, Mrs Best?"

"No, not feeling like it today, young miss. Vaguely... Sat'days, you know."

There was a faint moue of disapproval, bafflement.

"Oh, yeees, of course. Quarter of a pound, if you can, ah, lovely, ta. Been a bit upset, I suppose, your Val?"

Neither of the two women looked directly at each other; there was a lot of play with lists, coupons, ration books and flimsy wrappings. Suddenly and with a tartness of tongue rare for the genial and buxom Mrs Best, well aware of her standing at the centre of everything that passed in the village, she said:

"And not as much upset as her dad an' me will be if colour blindness has been a large part of her trouble!"

The shop was momentarily stilled into taut silence, the two women's eyes locked together, faces set in shared condemnation. Hedley and Fraser knew all – well, most – about Valerie Best's lack of selectiveness in amatory partners, having come across her, as Hedley gravely put it, relishing the phrase "In flagrante absobloodylutely delicto" more than just once or twice, on one occasion below the yew trees of accommodating black-branched spread at the rear of the church. The summer dusk had rendered the pale uniform of the coloured GI more visible that its wearer, or part-wearer. Some months following Hedley and Fraser's presence at the conversation in the shop, they both learnt from random, unsolicited conversation in their respective homes, that Valerie Best did, in fact, give birth to a baby boy, colour golden brown, finally receiving the name Gene, the girl's parents vacillating between castigation of their precious daughter and adoration of the product of the mesalliance.

A farmer in a small way of doing, who kept a bit of everything, was charged in the County Court, Melford, with possessing War Department goods, viz. one Willys jeep engine intact in its crate, found when one of Alec Baird's assistant veterinary officers and a police constable were checking Lloyd Hanwell's suspected illegal slaughtering of pigs and selling them on for human consumption.

"Lor, Guv'nor, m'Lud, I mean, I didden know what all them bits and pieces was until my young lad – well, he clagged them altogether, like, an' there the bluddy, er, dashed thing were. As you might say, m'Lud."

Sir Colin Wheeler, TD, JP looked sourly upon Hanwell, a ray of sunlight striking motes of improbable delicacy from the pig meal and dandruff on the farmer's jacket. In the warmth of the courtroom, it and he smelled strongly of pigs. All right, you backyard Arab, I know that your baconers land on or under many a table, but Jeep engines and Seagrams rye whiskey apart, who and where is the next blasted criminal in your mendacious bloody gang?

So pondered Sir Colin on the high and disturbing probability that some of Hanwell's products were at this moment in the back premises of the small restaurant that he and his wife now owned (largely unknown to his judiciary colleagues), under a trading name skilfully selected for them by an old school chum in the catering trade, now doing extremely well in the City. Sir Colin had found that what with the flow of military and Government officials of one kind and another through Melford, their discreet business venture was doing rather well. Hmm.

"Mr Clerk, are you paying attention? I direct this case be referred, pending further questioning of the principal witness. Standing evidence insufficient; further, ah, circumstantial corroboration required, hrrm."

In Jack Harris's farm cottage, a hundred and forty years old and sagging into a comfortable position, back of the old malthouse, Watty Taimes and wife Ellen, having negotiated many useful contacts for the American unit's Captain Quartermaster at Charnborough Park, who had originally contracted with Ellen and other village wives for cleaning services at the camp, found themselves the recipients of an anonymous tightly nailed packing case, stencilled 'Mortar Base Plates, Series E2', dumped in their tiny cobbled yard a few nights before the unit pulled out.

After dragging the crate into an unused sow's pen (they had to lift the door off its rusted hinges), they made an initially cautious but progressively determined assault upon the nails, and then the contents.

Amongst the liberality of packing, in the form of three new US Army blankets, there were twenty tins, catering size, of canned goods (labels removed), a pair of new issue oiled combat boots of the best size for Watty's tortured feet, four packs of nylon stockings and a bottle of Seagram's rye whiskey.

In assaying the contents of one of the cans, and of the bottle, Watty became so grossly inflamed with cruelly stimulated appetites as to overeat on hickory-smoked ham, savagely bite his own thumb with great precision after half a mugful of whiskey, and effectively ruin the pair of nylons that Ellen had imprudently decided to try on in front of their bedroom mirror, before falling himself on their bed. Recumbent and dozing after her husband's abrupt collapse into stertorous slumber, Ellen smiled faintly at the knowledge of the various items she had previously received from the US Army, and about which her Watty knew little as to the donors... or the reasons for their gratitude.

The Americans' departing tokens of appreciation for all sorts of modest welcoming measures around the village embraced quite practical applications. Reg Rowland, the contractor and farmer, along with his eldest son, having taken out a couple of country-bred GIs to shoot ferreted rabbits, and further, with some haste having pulled out an American forces' jeep from it's nose-down resting place in a ditch some few yards from The Seven Stars pub and then taken the driver back to the farmhouse to be sobered up, which took an hour, was later visited by the North Dakota Master Sergeant. He pushed a couple of boxes of shotgun cartridges into Reg's hands, saying, "OK, Reg, yah did a slick job with that big MM mother of a tractor we-all gave yah. Here's some shells for you and yore boy to nail a bunch of them cottontails; they sure can skip along! Anyway, thanks a million for rescuing me from them Whitecaps sonsabitches, yessir!"

The cartridges were Peters Hi-Lode, with deep brass and 1 1/3oz. No.3 shot, Express Heavy Wildfowl Load. Reg's son had later carefully lined up two adult rabbits sitting outside their burrow, fired the choke barrel of his father's 12-bore (Birmingham proofed for black powder only), blew three fingers off his left hand where the barrel burst into a garland of twisted metal ribbons and received spicules of Damascus steel in his left eye, resulting in necessary extirpation three weeks later. The accident was common knowledge around the farming community within hours of it happening. Fraser learnt the details from Len Bowers at the afternoon milking. Len's father had been laying a hedge only a few fields away when he had heard the strangely muffled report and the lad's cries of pain.

Of an evening, as the golden light of the lingering day renewed the faded townhouse elegance of previous ownership of the Conservative Club, Dr McKay approached Alec Baird with purpose. They were both at the bar.

"Refresh my memory on bacteriology, Alec. For start, where did you say your three fellows' unit had been stationed before they came on to you?"

"Oh, transit camp near Chester, I believe. Have they left some sort of a problem for you? It wouldn't necessarily be anything to do with our three. They were all perfectly–"

McKay interrupted sharply, waving a hand to stem Alec's rebuttal.

"No. Look, we've got something on the go here: a nasty pus-producing bacterium something akin to a corynebacterium, or even a campylobacter, yet it's venereal and grows like kale, man, and–"

This time it was the vet's turn to interject.

"I ken fine what you're going to say, Angus: 'We've never seen anything like it in Melford before!' D'you mind if I enquire where this one has reared its wee bacterial head? Not one of my extended family of farmers' families throughout the county, surely?"

The levity had gone. From different approaches, they were both concerned.

Dr Mckay looked into the gentle spring evening fire as though he had not heard his friend's question, his eyes flat and unseeing.

"No, Alec, this is a lot closer to both of us than that. A mutual acquaintance who has travelled widely, patently in congenial company, and has apparently been far more acutely lonely or desperate or stricken than any of us thought to notice."

Angus McKay got to his feet abruptly, turning to speak in a low but forceful tone to his fellow Scot.

"The defence or façade which she has presented to the world, has been penetrated, ironically..." – his mouth gave a sardonic twist to the sexual inference – "...penetrated by something more potent and persistent than good old treponema pallidum, mark my words, Alec! And all this sorry mess as a consequence of her husband's supposed impotence from his terrible experiences in the war that you and I were in, man! The true reasons for this impotence I am verra seriously beginning to doubt."

His next words were conveyed, quietly, in patent frustration, his lips almost closed.

"And, Alec, I do not have anything in my surgery that will contain this unwelcome visitor..."

The doctor went quickly out of the room, spare, thin, not allowing himself the indulgence of further cynicism. Alec spoke absent-mindedly with some of the other club members at the bar, his mind sifting, sorting, waiting for the answer to present itself from his mental recall of community bacteriology, a shade imperfect now since qualifying, but enlarging rapidly as a consequence of the war.

The probable identity of both pathogen and patient hit him like a hammer blow, before his search process was even well begun. An expression of stolid acceptance and yet total disbelief, used by the farm folk of his youth, came to his lips: "Well, well, Alec, my lad," he mouthed, "the tides of war, they whiles leave some gey murky pools along the shore, once the tide has gone out!"

He strode out from below the period portico into the quiet evening light, barman Bird, one-time gunner of artillery in the previous war, calling out:

"Orf'ome, then, sir? Cows and things coming along all right, are they, sir?"

"Aye, Bird, they are coming along famously, as you might say. Kids and young folk with lungs rotten from TB. Some day, Bird, infected old milk cows and filthy byres will all be a thing of the past, some bloody day."

"Oh, all right, then, sir. That is good. Goo' night, then, sir!"

But, thought Fraser's father, suddenly feeling utterly drained as he swung the car out through the arch and made for home, some legacies of the boudoir damned well stay with us forever.

XXV

As harvest time in that year drew closer, with sight, sound and creamy fragrance of the waiting grain once again welcome to all of his senses, Fraser found that some experiences, unlooked-for in his own broad view of useful things to be mastered, came before him quite fortuitously.

Amongst his parents' close friends were Ken and Lucy Farne. They owned The Albion Cattle and Salvage Company, to the west of Melford by two or three miles. Hidden in a little valley off the Shrewsbury road, towards the Shropshire border, Ken Farne directed the slaughtering, meat salvage and knackery business he had inherited from his father, Noah Farne. This remarkable old gentleman had started his working life as kennel boy to the local hunt, and had rapidly recognised that where the raw product, carcases of fallen animals, were delivered to the knackery at no cost, there was very good business to be had from every particle to be sold of these animals, once converted, rendered, boiled and emulsified, with hides salted down for the tanners.

"'Refuse nothing, keep the labour costs down, look for outlets and sell some damned thing every day, Sundays and all.' That's my motto and allus has been, Kenneth, my lad; stick by it and by heavens, you'll do all right." So enjoined Noah to his rather diffident son when they came to talking about his place in the business.

Noah Farne had become something of a legend in the vales and villages for his cheerful promptitude in dealing with embarrassing errors of husbandry. Ken had been born towards the end of the 1914–1918 War, and had seen the growing dependance upon motor vehicles in every way of business as a consequence to that affair. By the time of the Thirties, Ken Farne had made a modest investment in two ex-Army lorries, equipped with winches run off the gear box, and proved his father's point; they could now bring in carcases from immeasurably greater distances, winter or summer, without the farmer losing face (and temper) from a foundered animal lying exposed to weather and public opprobium. Both lorries were smartly painted with the maxim 'PHONE FARNES: SALVAGE MAKES SENSE' and two easily remembered telephone numbers, factory and home. Although to begin with the company had only the two wagons, Ken had them conspicuously numbered 'No.7' and 'No.9'.

This quiet acumen and effective business policy allowed Kenneth Farne to venture into other businesses more suited to his and Lucy's natures, both being fairly interested in matters of social and county intercourse. Given any time away from the business, they were two people of complementary cultural interests.

Ken and Lucy Farne were a good-looking and welcome pair in the farming and county community. They both rode to hounds with the local Hunt, the annual Hunt Ball of which allowed Lucy to show off her naturally slim figure and fine blonde hair with a matching vivacity that was infectious. Her husband enjoyed his steady shooting invitations from farmers over a wide area.

The handling at the Farnes' abattoir of those cattle directed for slaughter as positive tubercular reactors by Fraser's father and his assistant VOs was consistently efficient and helpful, as was Ken Farne's quiet diplomacy a boon on troublesome occasions, to farmers and vets alike.

Lucy Farne telephoned Alec Baird one summer's evening and as with all sorts of contacts by either Ken or Lucy Farne, once mutual pleasantries had been got out of the way, Fraser was well aware that Lucy's direct way of speech always tested his father in his response to her banter of guileless innuendo; the provocation was equally testing to both of them. By intention, Fraser wondered, listening to his father's snorts of laughter?

From the exchange between his father and Lucy Farne, Fraser gathered that the latter was checking on his, Fraser's age.

"How old is he now, Alec my golden veterinary man – fifteen? Sixteen? Would he be free to put in a couple of weeks during his hols, booking-in duty at the knackery?" Lucy explained that their booking-in man had a septic hand, putting him out of action for at least ten days.

"A tremendous relief to Ken and me, if he could handle it. Usual stuff, Alec; owner, breed, sex and any tags or marks, all entered into the day book."

"Now, Alec, I know that your young man is exactly like you in many ways..."

Listening, Fraser's father could not stop himself from grinning widely in frank pleasure at Lucy's flirtatious duplicity.

"...and Kenneth and I think that your Fraser's the very fellow for the job, holidays coming up. Will you, and he, be able to help us..."

More delicious flannel, dear Lucy. He breathed heavily into the receiver.

"...by asking him, Alec? In a way which I shan't explain, you, he, both of you, will be doing this for me, really."

"Rrreally, Lucy?" And then couldn't stop himself from bursting out laughing at her giggle of delight at what she always made a point of calling his "rough

Scottish arrrr's."

He broached the matter of working for the Farnes at teatime that day.

"How do you feel about taking on this job immediately your summer holidays start, squire?"

Alarmed, Fraser looked, and felt, uncertain on two points, which he enumerated.

"Father. I don't want to let Mr Harris and the men down, 'specially when harvest's due to come on," he said.

"Aye, I can understand that. What's your other point?"

"Well, this business of checking everything that comes in, it sounds fairly responsible and I wouldn't want to make a mess of it; the Farnes would be angry or disappointed, wouldn't they?"

"Look, Fraser, you know as much as many a man about different breeds of cattle, there are only two or three kinds of sows you'll be bothered with, and if it's an injured horse, it'll have been put down before it's loaded, right? I'm sure that you'll catch up with the descriptions by a day or two, and Ken'll keep you right. Always start from the head end and muzzle, look for Min. of Ag. ear tags and their number, and which ear it's in; that's important, with cattle."

Oh, aye, that's all very fine, thought Fraser pedalling the one-time soldier's BSA bicycle with determination to be there before starting time at eight o'clock, but what the bluggy 'ell do I do if Mr Farne is not there, ay, pal?

He grinned into the strong breeze of his passing beside dusty hedges, deciding that for all-round descriptive needs, Jack Harris's customary exclamation was by far the best.

On arrival at the knackery, the foreman issued Fraser a faded, much-washed and over-large boiler suit, showed him where the men's dinner hut and lavatory were, and ran through the thumb-blackened day ledger, along with the previous month's one, for guidance. Ken Farne came and stood at his elbow as the first cattle trucks or floats creaked in, some with slop running from the tailgate, and watched how this fifteen-year old tackled the new and unlikely job.

"Yes, much like his father," Farne said to himself, smiling quietly as the odd Scottish word or pronunciation slipped in when Fraser spoke quite freely with the knackery men at their own level. He came forward quickly, putting a hand on Fraser's elbow.

"Ah, hold on, what are you putting that one in as? It's a Sussex Red, I think, even with those scurs of horns, but – go on, you're doing fine. Take time and always give a good description if you're not sure, or have the fleshers turn it over on the other side."

210

Ken Farne looked curiously at Fraser's pre-war bicycle, not knowing its history but noting the single front wheel cable brake. Hmm. Dangerous damned thing, for a young man in a hurry.

Some time after his in-at-the-deep-end spell amongst livestock in all sorts of sorry states, Fraser was astounded to find a new Triumph bicycle, Wolverhampton-made, with Sturmey-Archer three-speed gear and dynamo lighting, delivered to The Leys late one afternoon by one of the Albion Company trucks, and with a handwritten note tied to the gleaming chrome handlebars: "To 'The Flying Scotsman' with Grateful Thanks from Lucy and Ken Farne."

With delighted possession and use, everything became possible to Fraser. When he came home, and also read the writing, Lucy's writing, Alec Baird felt high up in his chest that strange fluttering of a special inner pleasure.

"You did a good job there, Fraser, young man!"

Bicycling to and from school was now perfectly acceptable, in all weathers, where the one-time belonging of the dead soldier had been a distinct hazard, with its wickedly grabbing front and only brake. Good places for both coarse and trout fishing were now definitely attainable by dint of an hour or two's energetic pedalling, especially with this great three-speed gear. Crikey! What a speed you could get up! He enjoyed cleaning every part of his split-new bicycle with an especially oily rag, burnishing the chromed rims between the spokes.

On weekends when both had completed those home tasks set by their respective parents, Fraser and Hedley now ranged far and wide over the county, and much beyond the six or seven-mile radius which they had felt was OK for the reliability of their rather worn bicycles and easily punctured wartime tyres. Hedley now had the shared use of his elder brother's Humber cycle, a very superior machine indeed, with a four-speed gear and a front hub dynamo. They felt bold and adventurous, and having hatched plans, implemented them with alacrity and anticipation.

They found and cycled through all of the Bromley villages; Abbots, Church and Long, rode to the north with its strange and raw congestion of potteries, clay works, kilns, canals and wharves, and a perceptibly harder people, different to those of the farms which Fraser felt he knew so well.

One weekend, they cycled to Lichfield and beyond, indulged their personal curiosities in every hidden aspect of that city and were thus subjected to interested questioning amongst the other members of the Dunn family at supper time that evening.

"Oh, Mummy, I do wish you'ld let me go with Hedley and Fraser on their next expedition. It wouldn't have been too far!" This heartfelt plea from

Hedley's younger sister Leonore.

"Certainly, dear, you can go along with them on their next foray – providing that they'll take you with them without bickering like polecats!"

Marjorie Dunn knew very well from her own country childhood in Wharfedale that boys and girls do not willingly mix until a certain state of gender and age. And a sort of subtle chemistry as well as a whole lot of other indefinable things.

"Anyway, and, oh! There are more hot pancakes here for any of you, and pass your cup if you want more tea. And, um, what was I going to say?"

At this point, everyone around the Dunns' generous family table made a point of dramatically raising a finger to their pursed lips and uttering a loud sustained "SSSHHH!", to the great delight of those performing, and a snort of affectionate laughter from her husband, leaning forward in the act of passing his cup to be refilled.

Marjorie Dunn coloured, slightly, dropped her eyelids in recovering her composure and continued, with just a hint of a broad smile, "This enormous distance that they've covered today, and then coming back by a different way altogether. Heaven knows how many miles they've pedalled. Do you know, either of you?"

Hedley pursed his lips and frowned. By golly, Fraser thought, every time good old Headlong Hedley does that, he does look just like a judge sending some unfortunate beggar down!

Ignoring Fraser's obvious and hardly controlled amusement, Hedley made his serious estimation.

"Um, not, not really, when we found ourselves in Shrewsbury, I think it must have been, I knew that we'd been led astray by that, ah, three-speed maniac in front of me!"

Fraser was entirely content to be laughed at, secretly savouring the looks of frank admiration bestowed upon him by Leonore, also the keener questions and conversation of her mother and father. Tom Dunn quizzed him over his heavy rimmed half-lens spectacles.

"Did you two go to see that fine old property where Johnson was born and brought up, his father's bookbinding business? Both under the same roof, you know. Good, pass your cup, and mine too, if you please, young Fraser. Thank you, my dear. And then the wonderful vaulting in the cathedral?"

Thomas Dunn, Town Clerk and keen gatherer of local history, expanded into a veritable flow of quite learned and complex detail concerning the architects and their accomplishments in the building of Lichfield Cathedral, and Fraser was enthralled. He had not known from Hedley or Hedley's father that the latter had this detailed enthusiasm about how these mediaeval structures had grown from the vision of ordinary men in old, settled towns like Lichfield.

The general conversation flowed around the littered tea table. With the mingled scents of wallflowers and tulips heavy in the warm air coming in by the open windows of the dining room, the two young men looked at each other in the satisfaction of their achievement, modest though it may have been, and aware of the fact that their exploits would no longer be of a predictable compliant and contained nature, but that they had now passed into an acceptance of being more responsible, more adult, even, and thus probably of more interest to other people in their contacts with them.

Below the table, Fraser massaged his aching upper thigh muscles very gingerly. He caught Leonore watching him, puzzled but suddenly comprehending, and winked at her. He was rewarded with a surprised grin and then a hectic flush, causing her to regard her cup and side plate with a confused intensity. In any of these fleeting expressions, Fraser thought, Leonore looks really bonny. Attractive, more like. He wasn't sure why that word felt more fitting for the tall fair girl sitting across from him.

For Fraser, opened-up routes for quite demanding cycle rides had to be displaced to one side; harvest time in that year of the Allied forces' tearing assault on the German war machine in Europe came upon everyone of the Harris farm and all around, with a steady succession of really hot days, bringing harvest on with a rush. It had the feel of going to demand the greatest of energy from everyone on or connected with the farm, if time, temper and weather would just hold for this other great battle which for farmers, had to be won every year.

By the time that the summer of 1944 was well advanced, Fraser could see that Jack Harris's standing grain crops were thickening in the ear daily. As could every other local lad, retired farm worker, local haulage contractor, agricultural equipment dealer, grain merchant, blacksmith, gamekeeper, Uncle Tom Cobley and all. It looked to yield in a bounteous fashion that would efface all bitter recollection of wet and difficult seasons during earlier, wearier war years. Fraser also knew that, being a farmer's son himself, his father always looked for the chance of a couple of hours at least to join the farm men stooking as the binders circled the standing corn, and with his gun taken into the field, to be there once the rabbits started to run as the crop shrank.

"Father, Mr Harris's eighteen acres of oats are just about ready to cut. Will you be able to come out once the rabbits get going?" Fraser asked of his father anxiously.

Alec Baird grinned. He knew and felt the same feeling of eager participation once harvesting started.

"Aye, man. We'll both be there. You can get the gun down and give it a good clean, and let me know if we need some more cartridges, right?"

Although he still employed Ken, or Stiffy, Watty Taimes, Len and a seemingly healed but humility-lacking Chester, and now young George, aged twelve, as his reg'lar work force, Fraser knew perfectly well that Jack Harris looked upon both his father "h'our good neighbour, the vet'nary" and himself also, as being a part of the extended family of his, Jack's, farming business, and definitely with roles expected of them, with their being experienced and all.

On looking back to the time when he first started to work at the farm, Fraser could claim that for a surprising succession of seasons now, he had been continually a part of the farm's growth, from an indifferently stocked permanent grassland farm, to a bustling grain and dairy place, of some purpose and plan now.

Indeed, that whole part of the county that Fraser, his parents and his sister, when at home, could survey around their home, blossomed as it had never done before in that late, hot summer, as did the sun-tanned families in the lanes leading out from the village, and in the farms and hamlets around it.

As increasing numbers of servicemen and women came home on leave, many mercifully free of physical wounds, they talked, guardedly and with no specifics, of the coming final all-out big push in German-held Europe, and in the prevailing optimistic feel of things, Marcia Harris had cajoled her husband into permitting Eleanor to attend design and art classes in Melford Technical College, one night a week, from which she returned, radiant and excited, on the last bus out of town on a Wednesday.

Her mother was now nursing another babe-in-arms, and in later years Fraser recognised that lodged in his own mind of that time, there was the powerful expression of Jack Harris' great pride and delight in his land, his gleaming Shires, his timely cultivations, his sleek and well-laid hedges, which could find no other expression than his continued and openly manifest desire for his wife, a final need to love that sprang from his immense satisfaction in creating and improving all that he husbanded, rather than from a mere everyday male want.

Like them all in that last summer of the war, Marcia was brown and darkened from the day-long sun, carrying herself with a composure and quiet beauty when she walked up to the harvest fields with heavy baskets for the men. They all worked on until first dew, apart from those who went back down at milking time, and even they came back up to the dusty harvest fields once the cows had been turned out and they had taken a hasty mug of tea, impatient to rejoin their mates in the corn field.

The scene on that afternoon in August 1944, with the grain dust rising in columns above the chattering binders, and farm men stooping tirelessly to the rhythms of stooking, was being repeated throughout the counties of England, and the Borders, and Scotland not that far behind either, so they said, according to the wireless bulletins.

By three o' clock on the second day, the eighteen acres of standing oats had been pared down to an irregular rectangle of three acres or so. The two Fordson tractors made steady inroads to the whine of their massive rear axles, but an unusually heavy dew from the cool night had made it impossible to start cutting again before midday; the binder canvases would have been soaked and straps torn out if they had been left on the four rollers. Or, as Watty put it, straightening to tip up his cap and smear away the visible film of sweat from face and brow, "They would 'ave mashed thersen to b-bloody pap, else."

Watty and Fraser had been steadily stooking together since ten in the morning, the first bouts of sheaves having been left on the stubble until then to let the grassy butts dry out.

All of this had been well seen-to in Jack Harris's mind, before he had risen from bacon and eggs and black puddings on a morning which held the promise of great heat. He swung round upon Chester, tractor driver supreme, mechanic and the Guv'nor's son.

"Yew'll tek up shome more TVO, then, Chester? Sho young Leonard doeshn't bluggy well hold all on ush up."

"Righto, Dad, but did you get me that box of knife sections for the binders? There's some on the old McCormick as needs replacin'. No other bugger thinks to check, do they now, young George? Hey, I told you to check all them sections for loose uns, and who has to do it? Bloody me, as usual."

Chester's voice rose, strident and plaintive. Since his escape from mutilation or death below the mouldboards and discs of his own plough, Chester had assumed an immunity from civility and fallibility both. His brother George rasped his tongue wetly and muttered something that had his half-brother across the table in a crash of china, his face flaring with anger, but he was halted by the torrent of orders from their father:

"Mek 'ashte, then, if yewm tractor driver, dang it! Get h'all youm tackle in h'order an' be ready when corn ish. Shee that yew greashe all them rollersh. Stiffy'll goo h'on youm binder once we've shet up last night'sh shtuff. H'I shall goo along wiv young Leonard. That'll keep 'im from gabbin' on about bugger all: 'Ooh! Ralph Wooley's got a shix-foot drive, cutsh owt, but h'our guv'nor'sh sho bluggy h'old fashioned!'"

The farmer minced comically round the laden breakfast table, nailed boots squeaking on the red tiles as he parodied the ever-whining Leonard and his local commentary. Grasping Marcia as he waltzed past her, Jack jerked her to him with a force that made her gasp and startled the children.

"H'owd fashioned am I, then, me beauty? Shome of my waysh are fairly forrard, would'en yew shay, my dear?"

Jack grinned in vast good humour, whispered something patently outrageous in his wife's ear, his brown eyes crinkling at her shock and pleasure, and clattered out into the sunlight, immediately taking in the degree of heat, Stiffy loading up a single horse and cart with binder canvases and sundry tools, Watty hurrying with final pails to sows and litters, and the dairy cooler being conspicuously over-sluiced with cold water by Leonard.

Chester had already pulled out of the yard, the Fordson's roar diminishing, but the familiar transmission whine continuing as he made up through the cows to the oat field beyond the elms and ashes on the skyline.

"Right yew h'are – yew an' Frayshyurr'll shtook, Watty, but tek a shcythe, mind, an' cut out them cornersh fusht. Shtiffy, my lad, leave h'all that shtuff wiv Chester, an' mek ready youm binder, twine an' all, then shet up sheaves wiv ush until – Hey! Leonard, cum h'out on yer hiding pace, yew carelesh weevilin' little bugger, an'shut that bluggy water h'off! Dunna yew dare leave them milk cansh h'outside, tek 'em in h'out on the shun, bugger h'it! Cum on, then, let'sh mek a bluggy shtart, fer Chrisshake!"

And so, in Fraser's reception of the mood, the harvest field had waited, uncut corn erect and watchful, it would seem, for its last few hours of readying to sun and dew, dawn and dusk, and for the men and machinery which now moved around it. They steadily produced an orderly marshalling of stooks or worked diligently on their knees at the two binders and their long sharp-filed knives and gleaming knotters, the two tractors rumbling on slack throttles behind them, all in a strong aroma of crushed oat straw, yellow grease, new binder twine and hot sun on canvases spread out on sheaves of cut corn. Fraser revelled in all these things, and through his shirt, the heat was becoming intense; deep in his body's core, he felt the solid satisfaction of being a part, a knowledgeable part of everything that was going to happen. This was going to be a day completely given over to the fulfilment of the year's work now coming to harvest!

Taking up the central two of six rows of sheaves, and walking into them butts first, Stiffy set up the first two sheaves for each stook. There was a momentary pause before ramming them down into the stubble, then Watty and Fraser coming in from both sides with pairs of sheaves clasped low on their thighs, to make up stooks of six, occasionally eight sheaves, the ends of the stooks aligned north and south for equal exposure to the heat of the sun.

Jack Harris and Len worked on similarly behind them; more than three men in a stooking team just got in each other's road, thus losing the lift-and-set swing that could be carried on all day, if need be, by two or three men well used to working closely together.

Once they had picked up each other's sequence of movements (with an initial caution which might well appear as laziness to an unknowing onlooker), they could carry on in easy conversation as they met and withdrew in the rhythm of completing each stook.

"Young gaffer desperate to get goo'in', 'is 'e, Stiffy?" Watty nodded in Chester's direction.

"Ooh, ar, mad, bloody bugger." With a slow, white-toothed grin, Stiffy added, "It'ld do him some good to tek on a bit of stookin', Ah'll wager."

Watty was tugging at three sheaves enmeshed together, a mangled confusion of oat heads, mangled straw and multiple knots.

"Gaffer'll 'ave you up on one of them binders, Ah dessay, Fraser."

No more than the slightest inclination of Stiffy's head towards Watty gave the clue that he was ribbing him, Fraser recognised, on the point that Watty was seldom given the responsibility of handling the binder's many controls and functions. Equally adroitly, and far from the first time that this sort of thing took place, for he felt a loyalty and affection for the older stockman, Fraser deflected this thrust and returned it.

"No, that's not likely, Stiffy; the only reason that the Guv'nor keeps you up there, is to keep your mind off all these women you've taken up with – hey up!"

Fraser dodged the swinging buffet from a damp sheaf, and Watty's wheezy cackle as he sputtered into the oat heads below his face confirmed that easy humour still prevailed.

Before the standing corn and bottom growth had dried, the three of them had dealt with the topics of the Standstill Order for farmworkers, the whereabouts in France of Stiffy's brother Tom, the black market trade in cars and some shrewd comments on the likelihood of Eleanor's escape to better things, from the iron hand of her stepfather's prejudice.

And as if in some welcome way promoted by their general sympathy and liking, Eleanor did appear, carrying sandwiches, baked scones and pancakes and tea, for a quick bite before working right through their usual dinner time.

I Like to Walk in This Field

The heat was intense. Under the crackling exhaust noise from the two tractors setting back into the binders' drawbars, and the younger children's excitement amongst the stooks, Fraser, fifteen, and Eleanor, nearly seventeen, were happy in friendly contact and conversation. Liking and respecting her, Fraser always felt a need to dispel any self-consciousness or shyness, with something, anything, to make Eleanor laugh, and she, in turn warmed more than a little towards the vet's rather serious son, who, she felt, surely did not have to work as hard as he did for her stepfather? Always going flat out for this selfsame man who antagonised and alarmed her sometimes, in all truth.

"Don't you find it difficult, going to classes in the evening, Eleanor?"

"No, it's wonderful!"

She wrinkled her brow and laughed, delighted. And delightfully, in Fraser's senses.

"Do you do perspective, depth, shading and things like that?"

"Yes! It's great! All of that, and lots more – principles of design, history of art, different ways with materials…"

Eleanor drew a breath of pleasure from her memory in finding this new-found and farm-divorced world. Her tautly fitted pink and white gingham frock (made by herself – Fraser had seen her kneeling on the sitting room floor with scissors and material) was filled with thrust of chest and breast which created strong feelings of more than just friendship: a sudden wish to be able and grown enough in years and, and, oh, to speed up the gap of years between himself and Eleanor, and be in some kind of place or job, secure enough to comfort and support this super young woman with the broad forehead and smiling eyes, to protect her from these explosions of near-violence by her stepfather. Fraser felt that this rejection of her wishes in life was paradoxical in a man who was basically kindly with all that he cared for and husbanded. Standing close by to Fraser now in the harvest field, Eleanor was a special person in his sensitivities.

The tractors' exhausts barked as they picked up their working engine pitch, silencing Jack's last instructions behind them, and with his outstretched hand pointing to some part of the readied machines, both men climbed up on to their high metal seats, moving levers and controls to feel the set of them, and then the forward-turning reels or bats dipped down into the standing crop, as the cutter-bars chattered their blur of severance a handsbreadth from level ground.

Eleanor gathered mugs and emptied plates into her basket. Fraser felt the quick warmth of her hand and arm in helping her and gathered close to his body's core her happy but silent smile that was just between the two of them.

Fraser maintained a hidden compartment of his life, into which no one entered bar himself. There, in quiet passages of time, he could firmly close the door behind him, to re-examine experiences, moments of unfamiliar pleasure perhaps, and see if they fitted into hitherto unoccupied spaces in assembling his mental map of good things to know about. His pleasure in Eleanor Harris's warmth of company was one such, it was always enlarging, with new feelings slipping into place.

He made off after Watty to stook on. Shedding copious splashes of sweat, the stockman asked of his co-worker, "Yore dad a-cummin' hup today, then, Fraser?"

"Probably, once he's finished the herd test at Mr Colley's place; he's got to take quarter samples from every third calver. That's so..." He grunted with the weight of two sheaves knotted together. "So he can find which ones are passing infection to the heifers, Watty."

They grappled with another bundle of mal-tied sheaves, wrenching them into singles. To Watty Taimes, all diseases were "h'infeckshun". He gave this item of Fraser's telling appropriate thought.

"This h-hinfeckshun what your dad's a-lookin' for, does 'e know which road to stop it?"

They both straightened up for necessary serious exchange. Fraser chose his words with care; he didn't know any more of the matter than he'd heard his father discussing with other vets or farmers.

"Seemingly, Watty, if you have an older cow, say, with mastitis, the infection can pass from her on a milker's hands, or the teat-cups. Hey! Look you! There's the first one!"

A rippling grey form departed the standing crop in a series of darts and changes of direction, making obvious the fact that it was an older, experienced rabbit, scut clamped tightly down. As they stopped, heads twisted over their shoulders to watch the rabbit without movement themselves, a reflex action of any shooting man (or poacher), a shot spanged out out from beneath the elms on their near side, and they saw Jack Anson breaking his gun to extract a cartridge case and reload. A well of pure excitement rose in Fraser's chest; there would surely be a deal of shooting now, and he desperately wished his father would appear in good time to be one of the standing guns.

With that single shot, sharp and flat amongst the stooks that cast little shadow now that the sun sat squarely above the harvesters, the field began to tighten in an almost palpable sensation affecting all. The final cutting of yet another field of golden corn was inescapably the scene for expression of that hunter's urge, which now possessed every man and boy gathered there, an intense determination that no rabbit should escape amongst stubble, stooks or hedgerows.

As Watty and Fraser stood, their sweat clammy and cool across back and belly, they received a peremptory enquiry from a figure hurrying into the corn field, prompting Watty to mutter, "Hey up, now, 'ere's owd Arsy Darcy Quickshot," as the smallish man made for them at the run. Watty deliberately turned away, mumbling sourly, to stoop for another couple of sheaves, revealing a sweat-blackened patch right across his back, below the old waistcoat and saturated shirt, braces, belt and heavy cord trousers. Fraser knew that all of Watty's work clothes were stained in this fashion; the habitually bowed stockman gave himself little respite, whatever the burden of work placed upon him.

The breathless arrival on the busy field was a small, slight man carrying a leg-of-mutton guncase, which he laid carefully on a sheaf of oats, and with some agitation, tugged off his jacket and re-laid the guncase on top of it, reverently. The initials A.R.R.C. on the flat of the case and across the end cap stood for Astley Renwick Ravenscore, as Fraser gathered from Watty, who added some pungent adjectives. Fraser was keen to learn more of where and how this posturing figure fitted in with Mr Harris's redoubtable approach to what he called "Ushelessh bluggy h'angersh-on".

"Who in buggery is this character, Watty, spreading his stuff all around? Does he think we're just goin' to leave that sheaf lying there for his pleasure and convenience?"

It seemed that A.R.R.C. was a distant cousin or somesuch of Jack Harris, and owned a smallish but quite good-quality furniture shop in the town. His obsession was game shooting, and complementing that, the wish to have his name hyphenated. Quite shrewdly, for he had little sense of humour in him (Fraser knew from odd references in the farm kitchen that Marcia Harris called him "That weevily little blighter") Astley felt that double-barrelling his name might not only lead to superior and useful avenues in his business, but would also yield invitations of a socially desirable nature, for him to produce the double twelve-gauge sidelock ejector by Harrison and Hussey of which he was so inordinately proud.

Astley Ravenscore ranged far and wide over cousin Jack's rented acres, with his characteristic, almost prancing gait, his cherished gun held at the high port position, all of which earned him the soubriquet "Quickshot". Amongst the farm men, this appellation, according to their mood and view of A.R.R.C.'s activities, was not infrequently modified to "Quickshit", following an encounter whereby Watty and young Leonard had surprised him, unseen themselves, squatting in the act of elimination amongst rushes, and gazing with intense pride upon his gleaming gun, propped up in front of him. They had ducked down out of view, and then proceeded to lob stones into the patch of rough cover, accompanied by artful chortles and kuk-kuks of an alarmed cock pheasant. To both men's unstoppable glee, Astley had leapt up, shirt tails flapping but otherwise effectively hobbled, and making "Daft bloody noises like a fule, an' 'is fucking trousers round 'is boots!"

Added Watty, in later recounting to delighted listeners "Oh, ar, an' if 'e'd hadden a b-b-bayonet, 'e'ld 'ave bluddy killed us,'Aybluddyarcee an' all!"

His rushing, tiptoe forays amongst the water meadows now evoked no more than a cursory "Owd Quickshit's on the prowl for fowl agen, greedy owd bugger!", and thus casually identified, he became accepted into the scene around the farm, but in a manner he little suspected.

Now, no sooner had "H'Ayarrcee" assembled stock, barrels and fore-end and had gone trotting hastily across the stubble, anxious to secure the best position for rabbits breaking cover, than the atmosphere of the whole scene changed and tightened, with Jack Harris, yeoman farmer supreme, directing the deployment of all for what was about to follow. Viewing all this, but keeping going on stooking with Watty, Fraser felt an indefinable wriggle of excitement possess him and grinned widely. Now there would be some action!

XXVI

Both tractors and binders were momentarily stopped, as the metal snouts of their red and yellow-painted dividers came low down out of the dwindling standing crop. Jack clambered down heavily from the rear-most binder, his weight causing the the whole equipage to rock, setting levers and the reel of corn batts to clatter and shake. Len Bowes was waved on in his place, taking the tractor and binder out to one side, amongst the unstooked sheaves. Both he and Jack then walked back down the crisp stubble, throwing the last three lines of sheaves into one, to open up a clean lane along which Chester and Stiffy could travel back empty along one side of the standing crop, now reduced in width to a long, narrow rectangle of rustling corn, waiting in the considerable heat of the harvest day.

The sun now felt really hot, releasing the strong smells of newly sheared oat straw and crushed oat heads to lie heavy in the afternoon air, overlaid by hot exhaust fumes, an unmistakeable melange of Brylcreem hair oil and sweat from Stiffy as he bent over the binder platform to tighten canvas straps, and the sweetish ash of pipe tobacco as Jack Anson tapped out his fill, preparatory to taking his stance at a corner where he could see down both sides of the standing corn at once. Passing and coming together at each stook in the making, Fraser picked up the sourness of Watty's body smell, both disliking and yet accepting it as an inescapable part of the man's presence when in dogged, bowed labour.

Jack bent to his tossing of sheaves to one side with vast good humour, echoing Watty's question just then put to Fraser:

"H'ish youm dad coming h'in time for a shot, then? He'd besht be h'ere shoon, elsh!"

The next fifteen minutes' excitement, Fraser knew, would prove hectic and unrepeatable until next year's harvest. He turned to George Harris, only a few years younger than himself.

"Gosh, I just hope they dunna start running for it yet. My dad really likes a good shot at them, an' he's likely to miss the whole dratted works!"

George Harris, a scaled-down replica of his father, hardly bothered to look up from throwing sheaves to one side and replied with an old farm worker's way of words in his twelve-year-old mouth:

"Rabbits'll come out anyroad. If your dad does come, you and him watch yersen for old Arsely Quickshot. My dad says he's a right grabbin' bugger, allus shewtin' at other lads' rabbits!"

This probability was accounted for in Jack Harris's disposition of everyone, children included, once throwing back of sheaves was finished. Everyone helped, trying to appear casual and offhand, in spite of a palpable air of high expectancy, of atavistic excitement.

"Now then, yew young ladsh, one on yer goo wiv each of 'em ash ish shootin, and – Ah! 'ere'sh your dad, Frayshyurr, an' all! Bluggy 'Ell, Alec, jusht come for the shootin', 'ave yer? We shall be needin' an evenin'sh shtooking from yew after all thish shport!"

The two men grinned at each other, the rough bantering belying the very solid friendship between them. The four men with guns on their forearms were joined by a fifth, Hoppy Jones, a dark-skinned Welshman, who ran a carrier's service with his cob and dray between a string of villages and Melford most days. His left arm and foot had been withered by some infantile disease, and when using his Damascus-barrelled hammer gun, he swung it in the crook of an otherwise useless limb. Jack Harris looked along at Jack Anson, and nodded.

"Jack, yew'll tek the top corner? Alec, yew'd besht goo far back and shtop any ash'll mek for them burysh in the lane. Uncle Ashtley? Hey up, pay attention, dang me! Lewk yew, dunna yew shoot any but ash goosh to th' front, walk closhe into the corn along wiv the binder, and no bluggy poachin', neither! Yew shnappin' owd bugger!" Jack added, under his breath, clearing his throat of dust and directions with a resounding spit.

Much to the open amusement and grins of everyone there, which made Fraser snort loudly down his nose behind his father's shoulder, Jack Harris glared sternly at Astley, whom he always addressed in moments of heavy humour as "Uncle", in spite of being some sort of a cousin. "Uncle" didn't pay much attention; his too-close-together eyes were swivelling busily: the first rabbit, from front or side, would be his, make no mistake. He had to make his mark amongst all these disrespectful farm folk. The barrels of his gun glittered as he raised it in order to run a finger around inside the collar and tie he always wore; these things were important.

Chester and Stiffy, tractor throttled back to a hollow rumble, were waiting at the end of the diminishing rectangle, while Leonard and Watty paused in their stooking, the better to savour the scene that everyone there knew was about to unfold.

"H'are youm h'all right, then?" Jack looked round them all: men, boys, his lads, his tractors and binders, his corn full and ripe in the sun, his whole world and work encompassed in this afternoon's harvesting, and was immensely satisfied with what he saw. From his breeches pocket, he took out two orange-coloured 12-bore cartridges, Eley Grand Prix, loaded and snapped shut the action of his shotgun and walked back, in behind the waiting binder by about three paces.

Chester was standing sideways on the tractor platform, engine throttled up now, a cigarette dangling from his lower lip, the scar on his jaw and cheek a random, ragged mess of keloid tissue, pink against his tanned face and the dust on it. Standing back from stooking, and to one side of his father, Fraser felt the most urgent and pressing need to soak up every particle of the day, and stamp it forever into a deep imprint of total recall, complete with colour, sound, smell and speech. But, how did you retain the richness, the feel of everything? CRIKEY!

In the core of his immediate pleasure, Fraser felt that at some wholly foreseeable stage in his own life, he, Fraser Baird, would be directing successful harvest operations on his own farm, with his own men – and with his own wife bringing sustenance to all. And with any great good fortune, her beauty as well.

Jack tipped back his grease-blackened cap and resettled it, setting the scene into controlled activity.

"On yer goo, then, ladsh'. Tek it nice an' easshy. Shet up youm platform, Kenneth my lad, and pull them packersh back a bit."

The last few sheaves, for the last row of stooks, were to be as neat and well-formed as his skill and eye could ensure. Just the way that good order should be.

The men waiting with their guns raised and eased their shotguns a little, the keeper shooting out his shirt sleeves in turn, not wanting his frayed cuffs to bind on sticky wrists when a sudden snap shot would present itself. The tractor angled into the corn again, with cutter bar and sprockets chattering, then became muffled as the heavy crop was sheared and the boys looked at one another with shy grins and eyes flicking everywhere at once. Eunice, the Harris's smooth-haired terrier bitch, ran from one gun to another, a forepaw raised, whining and trembling.

From where the wood pigeon was perched in the elm tree above Jack Anson, its orange-rimmed eye contracted in torpid detachment, the scene of that harvesting field was a world in miniature, with no great cause to tense and fly. Two shots in close succession from the keeper's gun immediately caused it to clatter up through the heavy foliage in search now for a roost with no figures, shots and shouts.

As the blur of the binder's oscillating knife pared off yet another six feet of the oat crop, the standing heads shook and were pulled this way and that as an alarum of rabbits ran from one side to the other. Two came flying out together from the bottom corner, one of which was shot at once by Uncle Astley, the other being missed handsomely with his left or choke barrel as it swerved under a sheaf. Jack Harris, pacing slowly behind the binder, shouted something to, or rather at Astley which made all the farm men grin, but which he didn't hear for the tractor's roar, or chose not to, his small-set eyes and pointed nose sharp with excitement.

Fraser's father, hearing the faintest of noises in the stubble behind him, swung right-handed to glimpse a large rabbit running at speed along the hedge-side row of stooks. As it came into view, and at once felt itself to be seen, leaping into the hedge bottom, Alec Baird dropped it with a snap shot made without conscious thought, swung to his front again and reloaded.

Shots now came in a crackling carronade, two or three merging into one flat report. Towards the end of the narrow strip left, those standing on the opposite side to Jack Harris saw him suddenly hold his gun high in the air by the small of the stock, the better to see what rabbits were still squatting close to him. There then exploded into the small dusty area of oats awaiting its reaping, a deafening uproar of shouts, hoarse yells:

"Hey up! Look yer, George! Behind, yew clumsy beggar! Dunna let it get away!"

"Euniss! Damn yore eyes, gerroutoffit! Euniss! Bluggy 'ell, dog!"

"Let it come, lads, let it come. Aaargh, you bugger!"

There was tumult of boys, boots, dogs, sheaves, shouts.

"Tek that un, Dad! Over there, look yer!"

George Harris jigged with need for immediate response.

Jack Anson shouted to the farmer, "Let it come, man!" only to have both his injunction and the streaking grey form crisply terminated by a shot made at extreme range, the fleeing rabbit cartwheeling twice in a visible bluffet of fur and dust. Forty yards away, Jack Harris's face broke widely in a huge grin, his teeth white against the dark shade cast by his cap brim, tipped right down over his eyes, the better to see and shoot in the fierce sunlight.

Of the three rabbits that had broken cover, young George had caught one, the terrier Eunice another and the Guv'nor had wiped old Arstly's eye by effortlessly shooting the third as it raced up the stubble, fully aware as he did so of the hawk-nosed figure marking its approach. Jack Anson muttered to himself, "Owd bugger's as greedy as 'is danged cousin Arstly" and counted his cartridges again, mindful of that evening's duck flighting at the mere.

Rabbits were now breaking cover in a stream, sensing that their long-time harbour was now a trap. Fraser had been keeping a count, but lost it after about thirty (oh, bugger it!) and concentrated on keeping a vigilant watch a couple of paces back from his father's left shoulder, who now stood with his gun propped on his left thigh, barrels to the sky. Hoppy Jones was taking careful, deliberate shots, concealing his pleasure at being included amongst the other men, to whom he was normally in the way of providing a service, by determining to make no gross errors of marksmanship, or safety.

They were all shooting now, some shots flat and cracking, whip-like, others booming, the shot twanging off the stubble. As the binder started in again, it suddenly seemed that the scurrying forms were too numerous to contain, but those that were not shot or were missed, were chased implacably by dogs and and boys, of which there were now quite a band, including the three Leighton youths, whose father was bailiff at the Home Farm. Their skills with catapult or stick were unchallenged, and sourly recognised by the Charnborough Park keeper, an older man who could do little with all his younger keepers in the armed forces.

Now, Jack Harris was marshalling his forces for the last few minutes, with only two binder widths left to cut. As the binder's drive mechanism clack-clacked behind him in turning, he waved two guns on either side of him into a wider arc, quietly motioning all boys with their sticks into a line between himself and Jack Anson as the two innermost guns. He waited until all was quiet, faces turned towards him, then called out, cupping his free hand to his darkly tanned cheek:

"Alec?"

"Aye, what?"

"Shtay wheer yew h'are. Shewt all them ash theshe other beggarsh missh, if yew can!"

Alec Baird muttered, quite audibly, "Impudent old bugger!"

Jack snickered wickedly, and Fraser caught his father winking at him, somehow without turning round. From where they all stood, sun starting to angle over the Chase woodlands, the thin strip of standing crop looked unlikely to hold more than a handful of rabbits.

Jack looked right and left, mouthed "Slowly" at walking guns and boys, and started to walk out the last stand of corn.

In about twenty yards' distance, there were perhaps that many shots. It seemed that the last few yards would prove an anti-climax, as shots dwindled to careful rights and lefts, the line halting at each shot. The walking men with guns, drawing closer together, made the odd jocular comment at any shots missed, and at that precise moment of relaxed fulfilment in every aspect of the day, there erupted a sound – a scream which jerked all of them to swing round, guns lifted high, to see what terrifying mishap could have happened to man, boy or dog.

Both dogs there looked momentarily taken aback, but in that instant of demoniacal howling, they recognised it for what it surely was and plunged stiff-legged into the corn in front of the alarmed men, growling deep-throatedly, teeth fully bared to their exposed gums. The preternaturally enlarged form that came hurtling out was that of an unbelievably huge cat, yowling and spitting open-mouthed as it launched itself, claws slicing, directly at Jack Harris's face and chest. Falling back in alarm at the blur and chaos in front of them, and in some apprehension as to the farmer's attempted use of his gun at lethally short range, Fraser registered in confused fashion that everyone was making clumsily backwards, the better to give the dogs space to leap in atavistic fury at the animal tearing Jack Harris's face and clothing.

The noise was high and inhuman. Younger children screaming, the men swearing terrible oaths, Jack roaring deeply, like an enraged bull, the dogs baying for an opening to kill. Fraser more lip-read than heard his father's injunction:

"Stand where you are, for Christ's sake."

He waved his right hand for a clear field of vision to whatever was going to be the outcome, gun held high in his left hand.

For an instant, the cat clawed into Jack's waist and chest, head arched back in a foul emission of spray and spit, resisting Jack's repeated one-armed blows as he held his gun out to one side. Fraser saw the barrels of Jack's gun come round at chest height in compulsive reflex motion to join forces with the fist battering at the cat and pulled his father's head and shoulder down with sudden alarm. Jack was possessed by purple-faced fury and rage.

"Yew bashtudd! By Christ, haaargh, yew…"

"Stand back, Jack! Get the bugger off and we'll get a shot."

Jack bellowed, his face a mess of blood and dust:

"Young George! Dunna bluggy well shtand theer, hit the fucking thing. Goo on!"

With Jack's final desperate blow to its head, the cat slewed in mid-air, slicing into Jack's forearm and waistcoat with claws which could be heard lacerating flesh and cloth alike. Both dogs leapt at the same moment, beside themselves to seize and worry, and to the stunned impotent onlookers, it appeared as though for a frozen frantic moment the enormous animal actually arrested itself in mid-air, to slash viciously downwards at their muzzles.

One such scything sweep of a hind leg, its spread of claws raking, caught the collie's face at the eye, slicing the aperture through muscle to the temporal bone, and right back to the ear. Harry Leighton ran forward, stick upraised, and delivered a blow which took the cat in the rib cage, which, solid though the impact undoubtedly was, only just deflected the cat from hugging the dog's head to its belly for savage bloody laceration in a very few seconds.

At that exact moment of impossible levitation, George Harris, his face white and tense, ran low into the melee of blood, skin and fur fixed upon his father's person, and using both fists, seized the animal by its poker-stiff tail, and ripped it loose, whirling it upwards and outwards in a twisting screeching arc out of reach by the baying dogs' teeth and jaws.

"Nah, then, ladsh – shewt the bashtard!"

The blood ran off Jack's forearm in bright red trails.

Jack Anson ran back and to one side, crying shrilly "Let her come, keep them dogs off!" and half-put up his gun as the strangely mottled cat dodged the dogs in a wild ricochet off sheaves and stooks, then came back towards the men and boys and leaped right on through the thin screen of crop that had so recently harboured it. Fraser watched intently the jerky movements of the oat-headed straw remaining. He had a fair idea of what was going to happen any second.

Bursting in a flat-out charge on the other side, escape now seemed possible to the cat, all the hated smells and enemies behind it. In its first bounding rush taking it into the last row of stooks, the cat hesitated for less than a third of a second and in that precise arrest, took an ounce and sixteenth of Number 5 shot directly in the chest and head from Hoppy Jones' carefully aligned Damascus-barrelled gun. Not having the fitness or foolishness to join the other men's jockeying for position, he had quietly and tensely waited, the stock of his gun clenched in his good right hand with a tension that made his knuckles crack.

The monstrous cat, dying, slithered to the foot of the stook, to lie in a slack disarray of limbs, muscles fasciculating, refusing to accept death from the treacherous humans and its lifetime ancient enemies, the farm dogs.

The tumultuous uproar had stunned everyone in the harvest field into breathless exhaustion, gazing wide-eyed at each other, at the corpse of the cat, so wild and vile it had been in the demented seconds before. Jack Harris held up his right forearm, bright red blood trickling the length of it, and strings of darker colour clotting on his elbow and breeches. His cap had fallen off into the trampled stubble and it seemed to Alec Baird that only once before had he seen his neighbour's features so patently in shock.

Looking at Alec, Jack declared, over-loudly, "Eee, bluggy 'ell, then, Alec, an' it wor a reet fiery bugger at the finish, eh?"

Fraser saw his father, keeping it jocular in order to mask his concern at his good friend's injuries, look Jack straight in the eyes and declare, loud enough for all to hear, "Goddammit, Jack, I do believe that you kept that monstrous bugger in there on purpose, feeding him all your damned old hens, just to give us a bit of sport! Anyway, come on over to the house, you great roaring thing. Let's take a look at your arm, and the dog as well. Christ, it's like a bloody knackery here!"

The clustered farm men surrounding them laughed delightedly, relieved that the Guv'nor and his dog would be attended to, that they'd had an afternoon of events that would live in the retelling for years to come and that the outrageous animal responsible had not escaped.

Stiffy walked over to where the stretched-out body of the cat lay, and taking hold of the last few inches of its tail, lifted it steadily until his right arm and fist were extended horizontally from the shoulder, not without some effort. It was stunningly huge.

Watty Taimes, his face screwed into a grimace of concentration, counted off the number of times that his splayed right hand, taking in about eight inches at a time, moved up the suspended carcase from nose to Stiffy's clenched fist, including the latter in his final tally:

"Six, seven, Christ, 'e's a bloody whopper, look, yer, danged near seven times. Well, Ah'll be b-b-buggered!"

His mind was clearly struggling with the required multiplication. Fraser had been counting off the mounting number of handspans; as quietly as possible, he spoke in Watty's ear:

"That's seven eights, nearly eight eights, Watty. Um, close to sixty inches." He waited a moment, then said, "About five feet and then a bit, isn't it, Watty?" Fraser wanted his good friend and mentor to be shown, not as someone who, through little schooling, was uncertain with mental calculations, but as someone who could handle a practical thing such as the size of this brute of a cat, so the Leighton lads would go home and relate, "Watty Taimes says the bloody great thing was over five feet. 'E measured it an' all!"

As Stiffy let down the slack body of the harvest field cat, joining the rest of the men preparing to set up both binders for the night, Watty adroitly regained his authoritative position, remarking, "Yer, five feet from nose to tail I makes 'im. Huge bugger, i'nt 'e?"

Young George dug Fraser hard in the ribs, grinning at him.

"So, 'oo's a reet clever 'un, then, Mister Fraser Bigsy, eh?" he said, and ducked to one side as Fraser grabbed a sheaf and buffeted him until both were breathless.

The gang of local youths had been looking curiously into the collection of rotting fragments from whence the cat had erupted in fear for its life.

"Look yer at all this 'ere, lads." The eldest of the three Leighton boys spread out the legacy of prey with the hard-scuffed out toe of his boot. "Hens' wings, partridges, ducks, bits of buggerin' rats, pheasants an' all, ev'ry danged things you could reckon on!"

Jack Anson came over, above all this idle conjecture, but curious.

"Why would it set up in the corn, Mr Anson?" asked one of the Leightons. All three possessed bright pink faces, short curly hair and slightly buck teeth. This gave an impression, entirely spurious, of boyish ingenuousness and innocence, which had misled more knowledgeable men than Jack Anson.

"To keep isself clear of all them damned snares as you idle beggars is allus setting!" Jack rejoined, with frank malice.

The rays of the sun lay longer on the land. The nature of the day was changing. There was a different rhythm, a different, easier tempo to the men's movements, a feel that now was the time for the Guv'nor to set everyone to clearing up, with the last of the field of oats finally and dramatically knocked down and safely cut. Stooking was needed to be put in hand now.

The various groups, curiosity satisfied, broke away from the focus of attention on the deceased cat, and went their ways over the stubble, leaving George and Fraser to gather the rabbits and count them under the eye of the keeper.

"No, dang it, lads, put the young 'uns separate, in the shade, dunna you paunch 'em; the flies'll be at them, else."

The total was sixty-six. Astley Ravenscore lingered, disappointed that he, the expert game shot, had not been the one to despatch the rogue cat; it would have lent interest to his meticulously kept game register, acquired with his gun (both at ridiculously low sums), from the sale of her husband's effects by an officer's widow.

Because the said widow, a trim and attractive woman in her mid-thirties, had amusedly rejected both Astley Ravenscore's offer for her late husband's gear, and his predictable but not very well practised attempts upon her person, the contents of the officer's study-cum-gunroom had gone to auction. By some connivance amongst the ring of local dealers, Astley had managed to acquire what he wanted at knock-down price, keeping the elegant sidelock ejector shotgun for himself.

Bill Sutton, dealer extraordinaire and curiously not drafted into any of the armed forces, had guessed the reason for Ravenscore's spiteful mutterings before the sale-room bell rang. Taking Astley's elbow after their carefully timed and apparently unconnected flurry of last-minute bids, and as the coterie gathered for bid sharing and pork pies with beer, he winked heavily at Astley, questioning him closely, but seemingly unconcerned about the nature of his answers.

"So, the little lady didn't accept any of your, um, special offers beforehand, eh?"

Astley looked up sharply.

"No, her figure was too much by half, and I couldn't get her to come down at the time that I tried her. Silly woman."

"By Christ!" Sutton exploded, choking on his half-masticated pie, spraying pastry particles in a blubber-lipped arc. The other dealers looked round, bundles of notes in their hands. "By Christ, lads, Astley here says that Mrs Young's figure was too much for him, and he tried to get her to come down, but... but couldn't!"

Bill Suttton doubled up in paroxysms of mirth, the others braying at him, and at Astley, whose prime motivations in life were well known: shooting of any kind, best of all without cost to himself, and a weakly implemented compulsion to attempt, or at least hint at, intimacy with any pretty woman he met in the way of business.

A part of all this was Astley's waking obsession to have his name hyphenated, and so adopted by those who knew him (they universally made a practice of telling Astley outright that they had no intention of so doing, other than in derision); it was all part of an image long nurtured in Astley's mind. Well, dash it all, shooting and pursuit of women, of a certain class, mind you, had long been recognised as pursuits of a sporting gent, and soon he would get above of just this furniture business, and become "A. Renwick-Ravenscore: Fine Art & Antiques". Known, consulted and approached with shooting invitations, perhaps sexual dalliances too... he understood this sort of thing did take place.

In the kitchen of the Bairds' home, Fraser, weary yet pleased with his duties of the day, found his father and Jack Harris sitting with glasses in hand, the low sun highlighting the contrast between Jack's tanned forearm and his broad white bandaging. Some trails of dried blood remained between his fingers, splayed over the knee of his breeches. Fraser's mother and sister Jean, home from Varsity, were preparing a larger-than-usual meal, as it was known that everyone available was to go out after tea or supper, to finish stooking out the field of oats, Watty and Len having gone down to milk shortly after the high point of noise and confusion around the killing of the feral cat.

The farmer swung round to Fraser's entry into the kitchen, his ruddy face showing great good humour.

"Ooh ar, then, Frayshyur, counted them all, 'ave yew?" He was referring to the total of rabbits shot. He took another gulp of whisky, aromatic and golden in the slanting sunlight. Fraser felt eager and of grown stature in being able to answer tidily.

"Yes, Mr Harris, me an' George did them: sixty-six, counting young 'uns, and Jack Anson got a low wood pigeon, and they're all laid out below the binder cover!" He delivered his report in a deliberately casual yet controlled fashion, belied by the obvious satisfaction in his voice.

"Good lad, yew an' me'll share 'em out to the ladsh and anyone elsh as wantsh 'em. Hey, on! Alec, thatsh ample, bluggy ample."

Jack clinked his glass to the bottle from which Alec Baird had poured a second measure, and looked on with interest as his neighbour prepared to clean and close the wound which gaped between the sheepdog's eye and ear. Alec Baird wanted to attend to this before they ate, while the edges of the wound stayed moist and likely to heal by first intention. With Fraser's help, this he now did.

"Keep his tongue pulled to the side, Fraser," said Alec Baird, and handed him the loop of bandage under firm tension. Under the chloroform mask, the dog's hind legs drummed before relaxing with a long sigh. "Keep his jaws open, squire, right, as we lift him up."

The two men gathered up the dog, Fraser being adjured sharply to "Keep that mask on a wee minute yet. We don't want any more wild animals today!" Smiles amongst them all, but kindly.

In a matter of only minutes, it seemed, his father had trimmed back the matted hair, swabbed the gaping wound dry of blood, and closed the edges with surprising deftness, using a curved needle of triangular section and forceps, drawing the margins into precise opposition.

Fraser watched his father's fingers, stained from his smoking State Express 333 cigarettes, going about the small sure movements of making sutures, closing the tissue and tying off, and felt sudden waves of tiredness making his head and neck droop. He was aware of his father's face close to his own, smelling of whisky, sunlight and sweat.

232

"OK, cut there. No! Not there, you tattie! The next one, that's it. There you are, Jack, can you keep him from scratching, think you? Let the mask off, now, Fraser, 'til we see."

His mother's voice came over their bowed heads:

"Your meal's all ready, you men. Help to set the table, Fraser, please, if you want to eat now. How's your arm, Jack? What a mess it all looked! Is it stounding a bit now?"

The farmer looked sheepish, and twirled his empty glass.

"Ar, yew'm right, there, Mary, 'tish a bit sharp-like, but yew an' Alec'll 'ave me h'all doped h'up. Jusht like bluggy owd Turk 'ere, ash I wunna feel owt!" he said, and grinned at her.

Turk was was lifted down to lie to one side of the kitchen range, there to be sniffed cautiously, then licked caringly by Eunice the terrier bitch, before she curled up amongst the flaccid limbs, while the talking and clatter of the harvest-time meal flowed on above both animals.

"You know, Mary, we have had a lot of fun, and pleasure, amongst us all, these past few years."

Marcia's summer frock was pale in the dusk at the edge of the field. After the abundant meal provided by Fraser's mother had finished with a scrape of chair legs and clatter of boots, she had stacked the crockery with Jean's assistance, and then walked out across the dusty lane in the cool of the evening, to meet with Jack's wife and younger family at the gate into the field.

Now they stood at ease, talking as they watched their menfolk and farm lads stooking out the last of that day's cutting, turning occasionally to cast an eye on the young children playing around the two sheeted-up binders and serried ranks of stooks. Two of the mothers of families from cottages in the lane were there also, their men having gone straight out to help as soon as they had cycled home from the town and taken a quick mouthful of food.

There was an almost ritualistic form and function to the whole thing: the dark-trousered men, lifting and setting to each other in solemn, repetitive sequence, a marrying of crop and craft which gave up an endless progression of closely coupled sheaves from their advancing and retreating arms. The women watching, waiting.

"Yes, Marcia, my dear, a great deal has happened to all of us, and not all as we thought it might." The older woman, Fraser's mother, given to an apparent introspection, which Fraser frequently found irritating, almost over-affected, looked out and away, with eyes pursed beyond her cigarette smoke. "I wonder how our American boys are surviving, over there. Alec doesn't seem that much concerned. I can't think why–"

She broke off, sensing that in Marcia's ranking of cares, the priorities of husband and father and family did not include worrying over departed lodgers, American or otherwise. In response, Marcia's voice was soft, considerate:

"Well, Mary, soldiers or not, your being up here and Alec giving Jack so much help and advice with things, particularly on the dairy side, we'ld have been sadly lost without you at times!" Her eyes crinkled as she recalled these times past. She turned to Mary and went on, "D'you remember how we got those dress lengths from weaselly Bill Sutton, with your eggs and mine, and that tough old devil of a turkey!"

They both laughed immoderately, tears running from their eyes. Marcia's two youngest children, Pamela and Matthew, were looking up at their mother, small hands against her thighs, giggling too, although not knowing why, or caring. From only twenty yards or so away, Fraser heard Marcia Harris's laughter, unmistakeable in its warmth. In his stomach, head and loins, he felt this rush of something dark, and happy, and... and longing. And bent to his stooking.

In the evening light, the bandages on Jack's left arm gleamed starkly white as he walked down a row of sheaves where four rows had been tossed into one, to let the binders run up and down empty. He split out the sheaves, now getting damp and clammy, with his right hand, lofting them further apart with a flick of his boot. Behind him, at a steady pace, came Watty Taimes, Fraser and his father, taking six rows and any odd ones. Going down the rows on the other side, the voices of Stiffy, Leonard (My heavens, that lad has just the most irritating laugh, Marcia thought, listening) and the voices of the two men from the cottages came quietly, in short releases, as some topic, casually discussed, would then be brought to conclusion.

Never ceasing to pick up and place, with a double heft below each arm, Stiffy spoke little with Leonard, the latter swerving from one transient intrigue to another:

"Reg Williams 'as got 'is new power drive binder, so Sam Clews told me dad. Put down the clutch in an okkerd bit an' she just teks it all in. Just what we're needing 'ere, in't it?"

Stiffy grinned, distantly, considering. "Power drive? No, we're not needin' owt like that, if you and Watty'ld just work that bloody bit 'arder with them scythes!"

Len Bowes yelped in disbelief, as Stiffy had known he would.

"Work a bit bloody 'arder? Christ, we're runnin'from one thing to the next, the Guv'nor snapping at our 'eels like an old boar badger."

"Arr, cum offit, young Bowes, youm dreamin' on about motor bikes, or wimmen, or suchlike five seconds after the Guv'nor's given you your orders; youm just the greatest, idlest, awfullest bugger as can be!"

The two men from the cottages heard all this exchange and grinned; this made a lightsome change from repetitive tasks along the permanent way of the LMS railway line in the valley below them. They felt drawn to this evening's work for the farm which lay around their homes, as a needful thing to do, for their shared rural roots. All of their parents and progenitors had worked on the land, in their time.

The two teams of men drew closer together. The stubble was darkening their boots with dew. Jack walked round the sheeted-up binders, their drawbars resting on blocks of wood, reels dropped to their lowest point in case of a sudden summer wind, and checked that extra sheaves had been placed over and around the bright steel knotter mechanisms. The binder canvases had been unstrapped and rolled up, lying on the steel platforms below the tarpaulins.

As the lines of sheaves shortened, and then finished, the men began to fall back and straighten their backs, looking back over the stooks, now near-black in their silent regular rows. A burst of laughter came from the women and children over by the gate. It was too dark to see them now. Guided by their voices, they all made their way, tired and loose in their steps, to the gate. The farm men made off to their homes or to the farmhouse, taking the two dogs with them, Turk trotting lopsidedly, his head angled to one side. Eunice ran close beside him, stopping to lick his ear, where there were still traces of dried blood in the hair.

Fraser came on his father and Jack Harris standing at the gate, looking back at the competence and completion of their work, at the detail of the day. Fraser stood quietly to one side, chewing on the sweet fibres of an oat stalk. To him, young enough to chase rabbits, yet old enough to work solidly alongside, no, as one of the accountable men in the teams putting the harvest through their hands, it seemed that the day's happenings had brought into his senses and the fibres of his being, a feeling of wholeness, to which everyone had contributed one way or another as had even, indirectly, the demise of the unfortunate cat, and from which substance the close-knit family spirit in all of them had been amply nourished that day.

The August night took possession of all within the field, as lit windows responded to voices and footsteps. The land, sheared of its crop, took in the night's stellar energies and moisture, preparing for the rotation of the earth to another season, another cycle of repair, of regeneration, of giving.

The autumn of 1944 came in quietly, and, Fraser felt, with only very gradual withdrawal from the long, sustained heat of summer. The hedgerows hung heavy with drooping clusters of scarlet haws and rosehips and an abundance of miniature red and yellow crab apples. It needed only the sight and tart smell of these last-named to bring on a tightening and drying of his taste buds as he cycled past them in early morning mists. The sun arose, pale and more lemon than yellow, silent in its upward passage, penetrating each mantle of grey mist, layer by layer.

Sudden emergence into sunlight, with his nose tingling and wet, would bring into view another few chains of hedge and ditch shot with berries of every hue or another splendidly caparisoned cock pheasant, gravely watchful amongst the lace of cobwebbed stubble. There was a particular satisfaction in being abroad in these autumn mornings, whether it was to attend to all the outside work before cycling to school, or in preparation for more meaningful activities around their home.

So far as school was concerned, and being a bit past fifteen, his firm objective of what he wanted to do and be, was, he felt, separated by an impossible distance from the desiccating progression which he was obliged to somehow get through at the grammar school.

Fraser's good friend Hedley appeared not to be trammelled by confict between school syllabus and a vision, however unshaped, of what he was likely to engage in as a grown man. He had become seriously engaged, to a rather mystifying degree, it seemed to Fraser, in all manner of in- and out-of-school activities: rugby matches, cricket, swimming, societies of one kind or another, all of which now took time where they had hitherto spent time together, and encroaching in major fashion upon weekend pursuits, providing that Fraser was free from his usual farm tasks, of course.

These divergent interests preoccupied both of them as they filed into the enclosed, dusty school hall for morning assembly, prayers and a smattering of announcements.

"What about it, Hedley? A run down to the weir at Jim Holt's place, spend some time fishing. If there's not much doing there, have tea at that place where my father goes, The Dog In Doublet, and watch old Fenton potting rabbits down in the quarry. What do you say, my fine fellow?" Fraser delivered this itinerary quietly to Hedley's head and neck in front of him, leaning forward from the edge of his chair to catch his companion's reply.

"Umm, dunno. Really." Hedley inclined his head to Fraser, eyes to his front. "Old Balmers wants another nets' practice this afternoon, going on after–"

Fraser's voice rose in his disappointment, above the scraping of chairs and feet:

"Oh, come on, Hedley! Haste we to yon fishy flume in darkest piscatorial Anglia, man! You said last week that we'ld–"

"Cut that out!" hissed a prefect over-zealously from the centre aisle.

Stung by the prefect's unwonted severity (For Heaven's sake, man, you're only Turner the blasted butcher's son! Bossy beggar that you are!), Fraser exhaled noisily through puffed cheeks, leant back in his chair, and blankly disregarded the glances of other pupils, and the staff on the platform. Nonetheless, perhaps due to his abraded sensitivity, the pronouncement by Mr Pullen, Headmaster, of the opening hymn, sounded harsh, jerky.

"We shall sing… we shall sing hymn Number 342, 'We are but corn for Heav'n to reap'."

At this point, Miss Hooper, universally referred to as "Sooper Drooper" from her enthusiastic use of the adjective and from certain over-generous womanly endowments, launched confidently at the piano into the opening bars, only to be disconcerted, or more accurately, disconnected by the Headmaster breaking in before she repeated the first measure.

"We are but corn for God, for Heav'n to rea–"

He stopped abruptly, clenching the edges of the lectern, but the pianist had plunged on and led the school and staff directly into the first verse, a ripple of dissonance as pupils looked this way and that, uncertain as to who to follow.

The morning sun striking from behind the serried heads and blazers rendered motes of dust to gold specks above their generally obedient heads, as verses were pursued, overtaken and then discarded, by young voices which were, Fraser thought, not singing himself, to be almost visible in their breaking out in variable pitch above the broad shafts of light.

Fraser and Hedley managed only a couple of questioning glances before the morning's lesson demanded silence. It made little or no sense in Fraser's mind, try as he might to satisfy himself as to what sorts of things in actual life these interminable readings were supposed to relate. Did Joseph or any of those others ever have to deal with a cow having a breech presentation calving? Or,.. or a tractor stuck in a ditch? His mind switched off, as it usually did.

The Headmaster rose and reached for the lectern. He stood, looking down at his notes, and only when there was total silence did he raise his face to the assembled school, and only then did the wetness upon his cheeks reflect in their curious eyes. As he spoke, clearly enough, the tremor in his enunciation was cruelly parodied by the visible shaking of his hands.

"In a recent naval action off the southern coast of Italy, a destroyer of His Majesty's Royal Navy was listed sunk due to torpedo damage. Among those crew killed in this action was Lieutenant Robert P-Pullen, DSO, an Old Boy of this school, and holder of…"

The speaker's head and neck bowed as though to some immeasurable, crushing force, his arms extended to the lectern shaking in rigours terrifying in their wholly public possession. Their Headmaster forced himself erect before all his pupils' stricken faces.

"Robert Pullen," he sobbed "was a distinguished scholar of this school, and was awarded a Purves Scholarship to Cambridge, where… where he enlisted… to… serve… in… this… war."

With his final tormented words, the grey-headed figure on the dais clawed notes and spectacles into an untidy bundle, levered himself with effort away from the lectern's support and limped off the platform, head held high, to push blindly through the doors leading to the main corridor and thus into release from the audible emission of shock rippling out behind him.

SHADOWS UNSPOKEN

XXVII

Not all manifestations of theatres of war were visited upon Melford in a fashion so stark and final.

With the totally surprising and welcome increase of his assistant veterinary staff by two, one invalided out from a mountain artillery unit in Burma, the other an older person needing extended recovery time from wounds suffered in North Africa, Alec Baird found an unexpected slackening of pressure, which until then had been very close to becoming intolerable. One of the two assistant veterinarians came from a part of Aberdeenshire well enough known to him, in that area called Buchan, where farming enjoyed a greater measure of fertility, and thus prosperity, than his own homeland on upper Donside. Alec grinned broadly as he drove in relaxed fashion, the sun's warmth on his arms, shirt sleeves rolled up out of the way. On his noisy return to the office from slaughterhouse duties, Lamont Findlay had brought with him one of his inimitable accounts of wildest hilarity, which, Alec suspected, only he, Lamont, could have wittingly orchestrated. It had been fairly typical of Lamont's robust and yet droll sense of humour that he had said to Alec that his main reason for enlisting, a way out of the family farm and a work-driven, domineering father, had been "Weel, Alec, man, at least I would be free to shoot at any bugger trying to get the better of me! And getting' paid for it!"

Alec recalled the entire business of Lamont's morning slaughterhouse scenario. He had leant back in his mahogany swivel chair enquiring of his assistant VO "Well, man, all your lymph glands incised and sorted out, or did you not take your breakfast this morning?"

He had spoken in apparent deepest concern, belied by only the faintest twitch of his moustache. Lamont Findlay regarded him suspiciously.

"Ach, come away man, Alec, the day's work half done, and mind, it tak's a Hielandman to get some of these dozent knackers' men moving."

He spun round a chair from a nearby desk, grappling with it rather than merely sitting down on it. "Things" tended to happen in his presence.

From long experience, usually abundantly fulfilled, both Alec and ex-Marine Mr Norman Townsleigh, general clerk, knew that some quite preposterous anecdote of Findlay's morning duties would come leaping forth, like an unstoppable tide, with great roars of laughter.

Findlay tipped his chair dangerously far back and sucked in his tea with noisy relish. "Alec, you'll mind yon auld blue beasts oot at the Lee place? Been on the place for years, and long past the best part of their lactation, and a'thing else like skim milk an' a wee bit o' whey going everybloody where; pigs, bairns, cottar hooses doon yon lane, the lot."

His boss responded easily; his county geography was detailed.

"Oh, aye, Lamont, fine that. They must have come out of the Uttoxeter mart, or maybe Nantwich, anyway. You're looking at some of the original old Blue Albion breed there, my friend."

As he poured out generous mugfuls of tea, Norman Townsleigh listened with the greatest of interest. He never failed to wonder how these vets, particularly these two Scots ones, could recall individual cows and animals in general amongst the thousands on the herd lists which he broke down meticulously and filed under herd test results.

Lamont Findlay waved a large spade-like hand in irrelevance.

"Well, never mind where they came oot o'. The three of them came in to be killed today and I did the carcase inspections this morning: neck glands and pharynx just rotten and into the crural ones, by God! Talk aboot being reactors, Ah'll be damned!"

His chair came down with a crash. The two men listening knew from wary yet delighted experience that some high point in this episode was yet to come.

"Ach, weel, yon aul' bugger Stephen Lee came in just as I was showing Ken Farne's man the incised glands, fairly typical caseation and pus. 'Them owd cows of mine wor right good 'uns,' sez Lee. 'That's owd milk fat you've got there, Mr Findlay. You was wrong to tek them.' Ye ken fine how he aye witters on. 'Ho! Milk fat?!' I sez tae him. 'What you're looking at is nae other thing but rank tuberculosis, and they're so bloody bad with it, Mr Lee, that the Ministry isnae goin' tae give ye anything at all for them!' That shut him up, Ah tell ye!"

Alec Baird and Townsleigh laughed outright; they could well picture the scene, the storm of professional outrage delivered by Lamont Findlay.

"So, when the silly daft cratur wis aye splutterin' awa', Ah yarkit him over to a bull carcase they had up on the line. 'Look at this, Mr Lee!' and showed him that damned great orchitis. Man, what a mess!"

Lamont snorted explosively into his mug of tea, but putting it away from himself abruptly, returned to his apt mimicry.

"'That's a chronic tubercular bull, Mr Lee,' Ah sez, 'and the very same condition affects the human male, more so if they're over forty! That's why we're starting to test all herd owners now, as well as the dairy workers. But, of course, ye'll ken a' aboot that, Mr Lee?' 'Ho! Bugger me!' he cries, 'but how would a feller know that 'e 'ad it, like?' By Christ, he was worried, men!"

Already, the gusts of wildest uncontainable mirth were shaking Lamont.

"'First of all, Mr Lee,' Ah sez, 'You'll no' be able to yewrrinate, and man, that's bad! But, the next thing, you'll be pissing pus! Test and slaughter, then, Mr Lee, test and slaughter; Government policy, ye ken.' Ah tell ye, he went oot o' that place so bloody fast he clean forgot aboot his precious milk fat, and the last Ah heard, along with the boys in the abattoir, he was runnin' aboot in the yard, squeaking on aboot 'Pissing pus! Pissing pus!' and his missus wis oot in the car, gaping at her man like he had flames flyin' oot of his arse! Oh, dearie me!"

The men in the room laughed uproariously, as much at the storyteller as at the episode so ably painted for them; he was thumping the table weakly with one fist, tears running down his cheeks, paroxysms of laughter choking him to near-silence before another gale possessed him.

"Oh, mighty me, Alec. D'ye ken what yon bull really was?" Lamont wiped tears away with both hands.

"No, but was it that big brute from–?"

"No, no man." There was a quick negating chop from one of Lamont's enormous hands. "It was one of those great big beasts from Simon Cook's place, that he'd tried to do with his bloodless castrators and thoroughly botched. Scirrhous cords, pockets of pus, the lot. And there wasn't a mark of tubercle aboot the bugger!"

Lamont Findlay collapsed in final speechless agonies. Alec Baird, shaking his head in wry amusement, shared with a look at ex-Marine Norman Townsleigh, who with severely pursed lips, was trying not to laugh himself.

They separated, with an easy release of great good humour generated by the younger man's anecdote, Findlay to the north of the county, to read a herd test. Alec as the senior VO went only a few miles to one of the larger dairy farms where the hundred and forty cows were already free from tuberculosis, but where there still remained the matter of accreditation status for the production of bottled milk for retail. Right now, Alec thought, starting his car, the hidden processes of this damned war are at a mysterious distance that renders them and it impossible to grasp and yet be in the centre of a man's mind all the time.

XXVIII

Driving out from the town, a persistent rattling from the near-side front wheel reminded Alec of the broken leaf in the spring of the Standard; he should go easy on right-hand bends, he reflected, turning at last on to the main road down into the southern part of the county. And hardly likely that Councillor Raymond Collier'll get that particular bit of road sorted without months of waiting, thinking back to the spine-jarring crash of his car into a deep hole made by slewing tank tracks, virtually unseen in the blackout.

Relaxed behind the wheel of the car, in the warmth of the midday sun, Alec Baird drove at ease with himself and his work, idly noting places and episodes associated with them as the countryside rolled past, broken spring or not. He commented to himself, "Aye, and just what would have happened to that daft old bugger's dairy enterprise if I hadn't sorted out his idiot way of feeding, or rather lack of it!"

Bert Parkin ran a small herd of mixed dairy breeds and a small, parsimonious mind along with it. Through the grey winter months, his practice had been to feed stale bakery goods to his lactating cows, and each spring, as a consequence, his cows were always in parlous condition, fertility markedly so. Alec grimaced to himself, thinking of the many hours spent talking with obstinate beggar Parkin over the kitchen table, stressing basic husbandry and a more sensible, balanced approach to feeding. He smiled faintly, on hearing how the miserable fellow was now claiming the radical improvement in yield, calves and everything was due to his, Albert Parkin's knowledgeable herd management.

"Hullo there, by God!" He smiled again, widely, for a different reason. The girl's figure on the bicycle, fair hair blowing and tight blue air force skirt riding above her knees, came round the bend at a more than careless angle that made Alec reflexively twitch the steering wheel, uttering an involuntary, "By Christ, young lady,you're going a damn sight too hard for safety!"

The flying cyclist was Leading Aircraftwoman Marion Richards, on the strength at the local WAAF camp. Just as her father was a calm, unhurried, pipe-smoking director of the town's cement factory, now running with night-shift production, so his eldest daughter was equally high spirited, with an infectious laugh and a zest for doing anything warranted to raise a few eyebrows. Her younger sister Pamela was as dark as Marion was fair, and on more than an isolated occasion, Alec had noted Fraser – well past fifteen now, by God! – quietly evaluating the good looks of both, under cover of his casual friendship with their brother Derek Richards.

Leaning into the bend, the speeding girl on the bike gave Alec a quick wave and her usual flashing smile, more of a grin, as she shot past him towards the town, the vet's car and its driver being known everywhere. He watched her momentarily in the rearview mirror, before the receding bend carried her out of sight. Good job the road's dry, he half-spoke to himself; that young woman's going far too damned fast.

The aptness of the term and another, now more commonly used meaning, struck him as he slowed down in anticipation of the turning off into Darsington Hall Farm, and he was still smiling in a private pleasure at involuntary images of the fair and fearless Marion, when he stopped the car to get out and stretch in the warmth, waiting for James Bolton to cross the yard towards him.

Lying at a level lower than the main road, and hidden for most of the year by a line of majestic elms, the extent of Darsington Hall Farm would come as a surprise to any person calling at the farm for their first time. The buildings ranged far back, in a succession of tiled ridges and and brick gables, and correspondingly so in rural history. It was a large and prosperous place, with solid presence and purpose in everything about it.

The enclosure into which Alec Baird drove his mud-splashed car always gave him a good feeling, but only in the same way as the nave in any cathedral of note is the most important part. Enormously broad flagstones covered the entirety of a yard which was bounded on sides and ends by an impressively long cowshed with attached dairy and milk rooms, a very large and cavernous barn, and a whole row of interrelated stables, cartsheds, loose-boxes, calf pens, root stores, malt houses, all with grain and hay lofts above, conferring upon the whole a massive dignified utility. The sole access for Alec Baird coming down off the road, was through a gatehouse, showing a clock-face above the ponderous oaken ledge-and-brace gates which stood permanently open, hung on hinge pins thicker than a man's forearm.

Facing the gatehouse, with undeniable presence, was the great brick barn, with full height-to-eaves double doors back and front, which exposed the original oaken threshing floor when opened up. Passing through beyond the gatehouse and the various field gates, led to fields, twelve hundred acres of them. Above the stone flags, deeply channelled by the slow grinding of countless iron cartwheels, sandstone quoins were equally gouged and scored from wagons' passing, over-zealously loaded, or young Shire horses clattering and pulling to one side in fright at the unusually loud noises of their loads pressing behind them.

"By heavens, Fraser would revel in seeing, getting the feel of this fine place. 'Some place indeed!' he would doubtless come out with!" Alec spoke to himself in vicarious pleasure at the idea. "I'll bring him with me, next time, that's what."

This farm square was the absolute centre of the whole place, while the gracious farmhouse occupied, as Alec Baird well knew, by the fifth generation of Boltons, an unusually perfect and well-proportioned Carolean mansion of some provenance, was modestly sited to one side, in amongst the older set of buildings, which clustered around its lawns as would a gaggle of children to the skirts of some stately matron, controlling them in gentle fashion.

Standing with one foot on the bumper and idly burnishing the radiator cap with the heel of his palm, Alec was aware of the swallows, many scores of them, conferring in great ripples of twittering from behind him on the granary roof, aware of the long stone horse trough hissing in low-key leakage from its tap, of the small sounds which signalled the presence of one, maybe two, single beasts boxed up somewhere.

"That'll be the two I asked Jim to keep back for me to have a look at." He was fairly sure.

"Ho! Alexander, my friend. Resting or making me an offer for this small, impoverished holding?"

James Bolton stood foursquare, a thickset balding bull of a man, trunk-like forearms thickly matted with a fuzz of golden hair. They regarded each other in easy amiable silence, communicating quite capably without speech. The faintest downwards beetling of the farmer's bushy eyebrows was matched by the imperceptible quiver of Alec Baird's moustache.

"Aye, man, James. The worries of wealth pressing upon you? You should take up milking a cow or two to give you that wee time for relaxation, so badly needed for a man of your age!"

The expected half-snort, half-swear burst from James Bolton just as Alec had wickedly hoped it would, and his own amusement, which he didn't try to contain, only added to the gusting manifestations of outraged dignity and striking of hands upon thighs with loud smacks like pistol shots. All this bluster and noise was entirely belied by Jim Bolton's broadest grin.

"There are times, Alec, when I suspect that my cows provide aggravating Scotch buggers like you with more interest than they do me with profit! Coming up to the house now, or after we've done? Rachel's been asking for you, as usual."

These customary thrusts having been ritually exchanged, the two men moved into joint purpose. Their respective voices came to each other indistinctly; one from the echoing coolness of the milk room as he pulled on a brown overall, Alec's comments in short queries from the rear of the car, setting out things on the dropped boot lid.

"Any change in that heifer, then, Jim? Now, where the blazes did I put it?"

"No, not really. The swelling's down, but she won't eat a damned thing that's put in front of her. Halter'll be over there. Do you want another sample?"

From the field behind the great barn came an exchange of shouts, unintelligible. A tractor engine rose to full power on a barking throttle, then died abruptly. Wood pigeons flopped and fluttered in the enormous aged sycamore before the house.

Walking behind Bolton, Alec and he paused slightly at the half-door giving on to loose boxes and stalls, with Jim Bolton's "Hey up, then, young 'uns" as a deliberate warning to the animals inside that they were coming in, their figures looming large against the day's brilliant light outside as they passed into dim coolness. There was not an unpleasant smell, compounded of meal, straw, warm dung and cattle.

In the two loose boxes, formerly single stalls for Shire mares at their foaling, were a single black and white milk cow, and two heifers, Friesians also. To the cow, an older and deep-bodied animal, this visit was something of interest maybe, a gentle diversion; she had recognised the speech and smell of the farmer from outside the box, for some minutes since he walked into the yard. She extended head and neck, and rumbled softly up into her larynx at the two men, an exhalation of bovine curiosity. Bolton suffered his hand to be noisily rasped by her tongue as he regarded the two heifers.

Mild mock alarm having been shown, the two animals stood shoulder-to-shoulder, nodding and becking in alternate curiosity and caution, muzzles held low to smell out the nature of these two human quantities. Nostrils flaring, they then retreated with a shake of the head and backwards slant of their ears, eyes looking for a possible escape route.

Beside Alec Baird, Bolton's stubby forefinger pointed from just level with his chest.

"If Bernard hadn't put a cow along with them, that blasted object would have likely wasted by now, Alec. The only thing she'll take is beet pulp and some calf nuts. Waits 'til her mate has a go, the dratted thing!" There was exasperation and frustration in Bolton's observation.

"Throw the old lady a bite of hay, Jim, and let's see the udders on the young ones a bit better. Yon one is definitely plain-looking, and she's stiff on that hind leg. You'll have noticed that, I suppose?" Below his breath Alec Baird remarked to himself, "But you damn well didn't know that, did you, Farmer Bolton? And that's unlike you, hm."

Jim Bolton was quick to see his mistake.

"By gum, and so she is, damn me! Here you are, m'lady, have a go at this."

He twisted some hay into a loose knot and threw it over the cow's back against the rails separating her from the younger animals. In walking across to investigate this, one of the heifers immediately showed that she was free-moving, the other clearly not.

Given a bit of jockeying in the loose box, Alec Baird had no great difficulty in examining the young animal's hardly developed udder, with slow, firm passes of one hand, keeping the other against the flat of her thigh for early warning of a kick in the making. His systematic palpations became more searching to the front and rear of the young heifer's vessel. Jim Bolton stroked her ear steadily.

"What do you say, back there?"

Not much delay in your questions, Alec Baird smiled to himself as he examined mainly by touch. "Did you tell me that Sam Lomax has treated her already for summer mastitis?" he wanted to know. He went on with his rear-end commentary. "There's a generalised gritty feeling high up in the glands. She still has a focus of infection from that summer mastitis; these damned flies, James. Any coughing or rasping?"

"No, just a belly cough when she rises, more from her being stale in her guts than owt else, I reckon."

Although James Bolton put a large number of farm workers to their duties every morning, and clearly had no need to tend stock in person, there was little that he did not know about any given single animal on the place.

"All right, keep her as you are for a moment. I'll take whatever I can get from each quarter." Alec eyed the other heifer as he gave instructions. "You'ld best keep this one penned up by herself, and the other one within sight of the old lady here, but not within licking distance, right?"

Alex took a shortish length of rope from his pail with sample bottles and cotton wool, slipped it round the heifer behind the swell of her belly, and tightened and tied it really hard. The heifer pranced once, then stood perfectly still.

"Are you all right there, then, Jim? I'll draw each teat for what I can get."

"Go ahead, Alec. She'll hop around a bit after our Mr Lomax's ministrations; stand HUPP, you hussy!" James Bolton's admonition was not unkindly, just necessary.

The samples were taken with little difficulty. The samples were carefully numbered: a mixture of fatty fluid, serum and cords of green, clotted cells.

Only after having cleansed his hands and forearms with water from the dairy and cresol disinfectant, did Alec Baird go back into the loose box, to make two intradermal injections of tuberculin on the flat of the neck, with two quick thrusts and a double snick, which was part-syringe, part-penetration of the hide.

James Bolton was already looking to Alec for some sort of pronouncement concerning the other, quite lively heifer, to which Alec gave a final but kindly slap on finishing a steady systematic examination.

"She's doing well, now, Jim; little after-effects to that wooden-tongue. I'll be back on Thursday to read the test on the plain lady, so just keep the three of 'em where they are, but all separated, and make a point of telling your Gerald that has to be the way of it until I tell you differently, will you?"

With typical brusqueness, Bolton questioned Alec. "TB or not, in the plain beggar?"

"Hard to say, James. Far too young for what you might term normal incidence, but I have seen cases like this, here and in the Hong Kong dairy institute. Still got the same dairy workers, no changes in the past year?"

James Bolton walked on ahead to the farmhouse, answers coming back over his shoulder in the same manner as his steps: positive, no equivocation.

"No changes on the cow side of things. Know better. Gerald moans a bit at weekends, but his young Clifford does a turn – when I tell 'im!"

He stood to one side of the wide doorway leading into a red-tiled hallway, directing Alec to carry on ahead of him. Almost audibly grinning, as his friend passed him, he added:

"No coughers or spitters allowed here, since your talk at the club the other night!"

Periodically, members of the Conservative Club were called upon to give a short presentation on any aspect of their work felt to be of general interest. At this reminder, Alec remembered having given highly diverting and entertaining observations on his experiences in linking human carriers of disease with outbreaks in farm stock, and vice versa.

"That's all very well, Jim, about these beggars that spit all round the damned place, but how d'you know until you're landed with them, eh?" He sensed, rather than saw, the farmer's ferocious grin in the dim passage. And his quick-fire response:

"Then I'ld do two things, pretty bloody smartish: give you and Angus McKay a rapid phone call, and then give him or them the boot, Labour Standstill Order be buggered, so there! Let's have some tea, Rachel!" Bolton barked in the direction of the kitchen. It always seemed to Alec that the Darsington Hall Farm kitchen was a dignified, yet simple place, filled with calmness and order.

A long, high and wide room, unrestricted by the low ceiling common to even the larger farmhouses in that part of the country, the Boltons' kitchen appeared to gather and re-diffuse the light that flooded in from the principal window, looking south over the older buildings and great barn, to the yard. The kitchen's calm and generous proportions echoed so much of all else at Darsington, comely to the beholder. Personified also, it semed, in James Bolton's wife, Rachel.

She smiled warmly as the two men came in, a tall, fair woman, not yet in her mid-forties, with a fullness of figure that verged on the ample. With her simple, drawn-back hair style, an almost shining fairness of complexion and wide-hipped summer dress, Rachel Bolton might equally well have been the central and tranquil figure, the meervrow, in some study of a Dutch kitchen two or three hundred years back.

Their movements in the afternoon's light acquired a ritualistic grace and setting in sequence, as each advanced to wash his hands, then to the table where china and cutlery had appeared smoothly, with Rachel Bolton pouring tea, adding cream and cutting wedges of cake in a series of deft but unhurried ministrations.

Watching her, Alec Baird was at once carried into vivid recall of the sensuous supplications of Krishna which he had stood before, entranced, in that strangely beautiful temple in Indo-China. It was indelibly carried in his memories of past years' living and working in Hong Kong. He relaxed at the table and spoke in a manner that reflected his pleasure in this sensation, and other things, as he looked up to her, accepting a full and fragrant cup of tea.

"Your husband James tries to convince me that he's the one in charge out there," he said, nodding sideways to the sprawl of buildings, "but I do know better, Rachel. All this afternoon tea nonsense is just so that you can give him a fresh set of orders!"

His sally made Rachel Bolton flush with delight and embarrassment mixed, truly concerned that anyone, and that Alec Baird of all people, should even think such things of her husband. Or of her.

"Oh, Alec, you do come out with such outrageous things." She sighed in deep satisfaction at the fact of wickedness of men in general, and leant heavily on Alec Baird's shoulder, teapot in hand.

"Here you are, let me fill up your cup, Alec. You must be more than thirsty, and our big son Bernard's not been near the house since mid-morning, and then comes in like a demented being!"

Alec glanced up, to provoke her with yet another, as yet unformed, assertion concerning her husband James, but decided not to, being suddenly preoccupied with the need to avert his face and gaze from the gape of Rachel's loose summer dress and obvious deep separation between her generous breasts, inclined almost directly to his eyes as she leant over with the heavy teapot.

Her husband was recounting the day's decisions about the two heifers.

"Rachel, Alec here reckons that we have a strangely nasty vessel on one of those Stanway heifers, and some more of Sam Lomax's patent drench for her mate, but hey up, man, take some more cake or sponge, before we're both chastised and chased out!"

Bolton grinned maliciously, amused at his veterinary friend's total discomfiture at suddenly having to look everywhere other than at the fullness of his wife's innocently displayed bosom, and at the same time him being the expert on all to do with mammary glands. Ha!

Rachel turned away from the table, and stepped decorously to an easy chair at the high window, sitting down prettily, relaxed yet attentive to her menfolk's needs. She turned to speak directly with Alec.

"Now, Alec, I do maintain that James does need another worker in the dairy, more so at weekends, just to see that Gerald does get time to see things done properly himself. He does get so flustered with anything extra, especially when it comes to calving time. We have had some episodes, as you might call them, haven't we, James? Some quite upsetting tantrums, throwing up his hands and a lot of temper; it does the other men no good at all."

She looked up from the work which she had in hand, edging the sleeve of a jacket with leather, and smiled anxiously at Alec. He said nothing immediately, only lifting a quizzical eyebrow at her husband, who nursed his capacious Wedgwood tea vessel in a hand which seemed merely to be a fimbriated extension of his short muscular forearm.

Alec thought to take up on Rachel's homily, her husband appearing to hear, but not to listen.

"Better an extra pair of hands, and eyes, James, than having mastitis or anything else running all through your first calvers. Our mutual friend Sam Lomax would hate you, and love you, too, for that!"

The barely suppressed amusement at his thought of the local practitioner's response to yet more troublesome mastitis cases, and debatable income accruing from same at the end of the day, made Alec Baird choke noisily, setting his cup down with a clatter. In the kitchen, relaxed in the warmth of the afternoon, they all laughed at his picture so easily conjured up. A tractor came booming through below the arch and clock, into the yard, and doors were banged about, in punctuation to raised voices. Alec Baird leant back in his chair, stretched his arms above his head, yawning in a sudden wash of weariness. James Bolton spanged his sideknife on his plate, in irritation, crumbs jerking onto the scrubbed sycamore table.

"That'll be our warriors coming in for milking." He half-rose from his chair, craning his weathered and sunburnt bald head to survey the farm men, amongst whom there were some drably uniformed prisoners of war. Seeing these set Bolton off again.

"Bloody POWs. Gerald tells 'em to do this, do that; the beggars don't understand or can't or won't, he loses his rag, lands up doing everybloodything hisself, and them standing around, watching mostly, idle buggers. I tell you this, Alec, there are some days when–"

Rachel interrupted with her gentle but quietly determined:

"James, my dear, don't get so wrought up, it'll only–"

This had the immediate effect of bringing the object of her restraint to physical volatility, swivelling round in his chair and splaying his nailed boots to either side, preparatory to probably launching himself out on to the recalcitrant milkers and POWs like a charging bull; Alec could sense this at once. Then his quite unexpected and blunt statement drew James Bolton up short, on the very point of leaping into action. The farmer and his wife fixed their surprised eyes upon Alec, waiting.

"I think that I may have the very thing for both of you. If it works out."

"The very thing for what? Me? Mastitis? Rachel?" he asked, and then, explosively "Gerald?"

Bolton's questions were verbal explosions posed between heavy sarcasm and frustration. Alec Baird quickly explained his puzzling interruption.

"No, no, Jim. Someone extra to help with the milking, or the young beasts if you like. Especially at any weekends when it's Gerald's turn to be off. How often does he get a weekend off?" Unconsciously, Alec adopted the farmer's own staccato delivery, coming to the point quickly. "My lad, Fraser, he's fifteen past now, James. Pretty strong, too. He's worked every year through for Jack Harris, next to our place."

Bolton nodded, in recognition of the name and of the farm. He was familiar with both. Alec Baird continued:

"Can't keep him at home since we went out there. Does every dashed thing that's asked of him; milking, horses, field work, feeds young cattle and pigs, the lot. Jack's even going to get him started to plough. Gets on well with the men, by all accounts. I would say that he's set for a bit more scope and responsibility, at his age."

James Bolton rose at once from his chair, going directly to where his wife had a school notebook in a drawer below the telephone, and demanded of his friend:

"What's Jack's telephone number, Alec?"

"Hmm, Whitton Ash 229. Now hold on, James, I'll have to find the moment to put this to Fraser, purely as a possibility in the first instance. Look, it might only work if it was for those certain Sundays, with maybe the Saturday as well. He'll not be willing to abandon Jack and the lads entirely; they've all been really good to him. Marcia and Jack have almost taken him in as one of the family as well as a really reliable worker on the farm along with the other men. Anyway, I'll tell Fraser to take a run over here, to see what he thinks of your ways of farming."

Alec's guileless deadpan delivery provoked a flicker of response from the farmer's eyebrows.

"Providing he's agreeable, James, Fraser will certainly work all hours. You feed him, and pay him what you think he's worth. That suit you?"

"Right-ho, Alec." Bolton straightened, undid his belt, tucked in his shirt and rebuckled the plaited leather with an impatient flick and a loud slap to his thigh. "How's he going to get here? Got a bike?"

As James Bolton spoke, already launching himself into this fortuitous proposition, Alec Baird felt a prickle of anxiety: he'd had no damned business at all to come out with this scheme without speaking about it to Fraser well beforehand. Schooling to be taken into account. Oh, damn and blast it.

James Bolton was going on again.

"Spendid then, Alec. Mind that heifer's test on Thursday – you'll be out to read it, seventy-two hours, eh? What with you and old Sam Lomax, and now your lad, this whole damn place is going to hell with bloody Scotsmen. You'll be telling me to get into Ayrshires next! Ha!"

He was out of the kitchen with a great stamping of boots, rumbling and muttering. Rachel Bolton came up to Alec as he pushed in his chair and, smiling, made a small bow to her, warmed by the friendship which flowed between the three of them.

"Well, then, Rachel."

She smiled in unaffected pleasure.

"Very well, then, Alec. You know that both of us enjoy your visits here."

Her tone of voice flowed into him as a warm benison. The hairs on his bared forearms began to prickle; he was aware of the fact (as he had been for most of his visits there), that there existed a kindling in this fine woman for him, but only just outside of her husband's awareness. Thinking of him, and his malicious grins and blustering sallies, widened Alec's smile of leave-taking into open amusement, thus taking him beyond the dangers of unspoken words and feelings behind the hand that Rachel Bolton placed on his arm.

The soft billowing of her delphinium blue frock in this warm wind which swirled around them from the yard, lent gentle pleasure to the parting contact. A more than just pretty Shires farmer's wife, standing at the door of the house from which she exercised gentle mastery upon her husband, but also all involved with the farm, their robust livelihood.

"Rachel, I get great pleasure in doing anything for Jim and yourself, and Bernard, too. Look after this lad of mine as well as you do me, and you most certainly will have another Scotsman about the place! Thanks for the tea, Rachel, just what was needed."

Crossing the yard to his car, now in shade as the sun began to dip down to the high granary ridgeline, the sounds of the milking herd and young stock being seen to generated within Alec Baird the same feeling of vigorous well-being, a well-ordered conclusion to the main farming event of the day, which it always did, regardless of location.

He decided to make one or two lesser calls on the way home, possibly into the cattle auction market office, then pick up the meat for the weekend. That would have to be his last call; anything left in the car got heated and cooled by turns, to the extent of actively promoting what bacteria were inescapably present. As he well knew, every slaughterhouse had its own little owd feller, retired slaughterman or flesher, wiping down sides and quarters of carcases with an old muttoncloth, tucked into the same hip pocket of the same overalls, every day. Ah, well, you can only change some things as you would wish, but not all. He yawned, suddenly wearied, and wanting to get finished with this day and it's not very exciting and entirely normal happenings

Preoccupied with the suddenly needful pleasure of yawning, he almost drove upon and into the obstruction and tangle of vehicles completely blocking the road ahead, at first out of sight and unsuspected round the sweeping bend at the foot of The Rise, the same road which he had taken on his way to Darsington Hall and the Boltons earlier in the day.

Slewed across the entire width of the road was a forty-foot RAF plane transporter, the square-fronted Bedford prime mover savagely wrenched into an improbable angle on the far bank. What the? A hugely violent encounter, an avoidance of another vehicle or truck, but no other likely cause to be seen. What then?

Half-turned round from the vehicles which he was holding up with one hand raised, and looking back to the savagely angled object as he turned, the police constable stooped, to speak briefly to the driver just ahead of Alec Baird, then stooping again and starting to repeat his instructions, he recognised the car and the driver. Almost with a note of relief, a contact with some known and reassuring quantity, he said:

"Ah, hullo there, Mr Baird, sir! A really bad do up front, I'm afraid. Are you making for any place near at hand? I'll try and let you through, if you don't object to some minutes' waiting. These others'll think that they need the same, you know. Hold on where you are."

Alec Baird nodded towards the strangely muted figures and vehicles ahead, including a squat recovery wagon and an RAF ambulance, raising his eyebrows to hold the constable's glance.

"Yessir, Mr Baird, a very bad accident, I can tell you. Ah, 'old on a moment, sir."

He straightened abruptly and walked purposefully back towards the knot of RAF military police uniforms, fitters in overalls and mechanics clustered round the side of the recovery truck, which was edged close into the side of the crazily tilted transporter. There were two white-coated figures, stooping, in the heart of this strange melange of men and vehicles. The nearer one straightened up, hands to the small of his back; unmistakeable signs of fatigue, defeat in his posture – Angus McKay, by God! What in God's name was going on here, Alec asked himself? RAF personnel and vehicles, medical presence, RAF police? From an immense distance, it seemed to his taut faculties that an answer was now, improbably, cruelly tendered to his leaping mind.

253

Abruptly, he backed out of the line of cars and some vans, his jaw clenched, muttering "Jessus bloody Christ!" more times than he was aware of at the time, and reversed into the nearly inaccessible (due to backed-up traffic) driveway of Morton Thwaite, one of the town's practising solicitors, continuing to mutter as he did so, in essence giving his mind something to do, "Idle damned bugger, drinking himself, his practice and family into penury. Pompous useless bastard!"

The police constable was now free and seemed glad to talk to him.

"Aye, Martin, a right nasty one by the look of things?"

There was a tangible atmosphere of exhaustion, fatigue, seeping out from the group, with curiously little sound reaching Alec and the police constable, who was well-known to him. In that moment of silence, came a cry, a sudden exclamation of desperation:

"No! No! Don't touch it. Try to get as much as we can."

Constable Martin Fox suddenly yawned, stretched to full height and shuddered visibly, very pale.

"Aye, my man, and a wee shade more thowless and weakened than that, and I'ld say you were going into shock," Alec reflected dispassionately. Fox turned towards him, away from the tangle of vehicles and men, the better to swing them out of vision. He was speaking in a monotone.

"They're trying to get everything they can, sir, that is or was a part, as you might say, of young Miss Richards – the WAAF one, you know? She got caught up below that transporter, bike and all. Got dragged for God only knows what distance before the bloody thing stopped. Says he never saw her go under."

"Oh, my God! Marion Richards!" Alec's bellow of disbelief brought heads round sharply from the scene of silent chaos.

"Holy Christ, Martin man, she was coming down... she passed me going like the wind, God in heaven! How long have they been getting her out? Is she..?" Alec Baird shivered violently, beyond suppression.

"Oh, yes, Mr Baird, they've got her away, but it took over an hour and a half; she was all bunched up over one of the wheels." Constable Fox flung an arm in the direction of a big, balloon-tyred wheel propped up against the recovery truck, with the fat tyre now grotesquely collapsed. "They had to jack up and cut, bit at a time – the chassis, I mean, Mr Baird." He qualified his words in hurried, short bursts, tipping his helmet at the oxyacetylene cylinders and cutting gear around the men's feet. "Oh, by Christ and all, Mr Baird, this is a bloody hellish war, I can tell you."

The constable turned away abruptly, pulled down the lapels of his tunic and settled his helmet with brusque sweeps of his hands. He wheeled round, hands now clasped behind his back in regulation position.

"Nurses don't run, policemen don't point – or faint." Alec sardonically and silently repeated the tired old maxim to himself, his own face, as he knew, now set in a mask.

"They got her out alive, though God only knows how. Or why, sir."

Crushed and shocked, Alec Baird stood there, his own hands in aimless progression from face to pockets, from cigarette to pockets again. At this point, Angus Mckay, doctor and friend, shouldered through the low-voiced servicemen and came up to his fellow Scot. They stared at each other, without words, then at the steel-latticed space into which the girl's living, laughing body had been scooped up and then dragged along.

"Alec, I've shot her straight into the RAF special aircrew injuries unit at Moseley Wood. They've got Francis Whitworth there. Does all the skin jobs. Grafting is his speciality. Christ, Alec! Absolutely bloody well flayed!" The doctor's temples and cheeks looked ashen in the calm sunlight of this disordered afternoon.

"Right, Angus, I hear you, but what's the point of–"

"The point of saving all the pieces, Alec?" The doctor clenched his jaw in negation. "Well, some of them are not so wee. Oh, my God, Alec…" For an instant, McKay, experienced practitioner, casualty officer some days at the infirmary, hung his head in weakness. "Some pieces of dermis might prove useful; if they have capillaries, vascular bed, substratum intact, they'll try to fix them as islands, at least with autogenous cells, flood them with saline, plasma, Ringer's with potassium and glucose… any damned thing at all if they can get even partial epithialisation started, and any chance at all of fibrin connecting everything to retain skin tissue, whatever they can try to at least limit deep keloid tissue building up. Christ, Alec, it… it would be like a mask. In happenings like this, what can a body possibly achieve?" He looked to his hands, the bloodied surgical gloves peeled off. "We did everything possible in the book to keep blood volume and tissue fluids up, but Christ, Alec! She was losing serum, plasma, every cell in her poor damned body like a running burn."

The occasions on which he flung aside his mantle of professional authority, and reverted to biting Scots Lowlands invective were so rare as to be alarming to the onlooker, even more so to his closest friends. Unless, as was the case this afternoon, Alec recognised, it was to a fellow countryman who could share the impotence that enveloped both of them.

His mind a maelstrom of plunging thoughts, Alec made a circuitous route to the south of the town along little-used farm lanes, where the car tyres threw up whorls of dust, gravel and dried muck splashes. Milked cows were starting to come out from red-tiled cowsheds into the late afternoon sun, heads low and quiet.

Gravel and grit, those young flashing legs and laughing face, all in a bloody savaged laceration – he shuddered suddenly in his seat and the car lurched to his jerk on the steering wheel. Alec felt guilty, burdened with having more or less committed his son Fraser to a work situation without so much as a word beforehand, confused now and ashamed by attempting to please Jim Bolton's comely – no, far more basic and attractive than just comely – wife Rachel, and then the treachery to all of them on the other side of decency by his visual enjoyment of Marion Richards flaunting her woman's carefree sex appeal before, before... aye, before that. Christ man, what a mess of male bloody response in half a dozen different directions. He felt soiled by his own responses, visited as never before by sexual betrayal. Oh, just get on with the ordinary things, you stupid cratur.

He drove past the Market Square, turning and wheeling around tired allotments, old tradesmen's van yards and stables, and feeling utterly drained, parked behind Albert Purves' butcher's shop.

Going into the dim coolness of the hanging part and chill cabinet to the rear of the actual shop, the sawdust on the floor smelled of hardwoods: beech, oak, ash. Titchener's sawmills most likely, he speculated. Another favoured trade customer who likes his "Purves Premium Sausages" all right, does our Bill Titchener. So, what do I do for Bert Purves that makes me a favoured customer? Alec asked of himself cynically.

When going round with his father, Fraser, well aware of his Aberdeenshire farming background, seldom found it unusual that his father would have some interested comment to make on the carcases hung from Bert Purves' overhead rail, and their probable origins. Bert Purves enjoyed these conversations, and as an observant and intelligent person, mottled cheeks and dark beady eyes to one side, he took care to follow up any of the tips that the vet proffered on fleshing, along with those cuts of meat peculiar to the Scots butchery trade.

One such novel approach concerned him, Albert Purves, being told by their Scottish veterinary friend about buying in dairy-type bull calves and bringing them on rapidly at low cost. Hmm, my goodness, looked as though it was provin' a right smartish trick, Bert had mused to himself; fust half-dozen coming on a treat. Might sell them off the hook to that army camp supply officer. Might mek a pound or two, Ah dessay. Knows his stuff, does our Scotch vet'nary.

Flicking his curved knife along the sharpening steel in a precisely executed blur, Bert at once took in the vet's restless air. Disturbed, he was, and clearly not at peace. I'll just speak to him normal like, for a start, the master butcher decided.

"The sirloin roast, and a pun' and a half of sausages, Mr Baird? All made up for you." He nodded obliquely to the chill cabinet without changing the rhythm of steel on steel: flick-flick-flick. Scuffing the sawdust on the floor, Alec Baird strode up and down and back again.

"It's a wonder that we go on eating all this meat, Albert, considering that we're only supposedly slightly more clever than slaughter animals ourselves!"

Albert Purves, Master Butcher, was deeply shocked. Very cautiously he asked, "How d'you reckon that then, Mr Baird?"

"Well, here you go every week, cutting up neat little parcels of bone, muscle fibre, ligaments, connective tissue, fat and tripes, the entire messy essentials of some poor beast's existence. We eat it, turn it exactly..." – the vet pronounced it hard, in the back of his throat: " exaaahctly" – "...into the same damned requirements for ourselves, and then what, Bert?"

"Then what, Mr Baird?" (By golly, Bert me lad, 'e is going on some today...)

"Aye, man. Doesn't do much good for us humans in the great plan of things; converting it back into the very same materials, we belch it off after a good feed if our bellies can take no more, burn or bury the bits we canna use when we're alive, and then shoot each other into so much macerated dead meat when we're inclined to have a bit of a war. Or land up as parcels of flesh as a consequence of hellish road accidents, which, by Christ, we're not clever enough to put it all back together again. So, we destroy it, ha!"

He continued to stride up and down the small shop, highly and atypically vocal about an aspect of his, Bert's, business, which in truth, he'd never considered. (Well, bugger me, he is goo'in on some today. Something seriously amiss here.)

Angus McKay's despairing words re-echoed in Alec's churning mind: "Use them as islands – try anything to epithelialise – keloid tissue like a mask", and at the same time, he was nagged at a different, deeper level by his marketing of Fraser's ill-presumed availability, just to satisfy Rachel and Jim

Bolton and linger in her beguiling presence, and then, the picture of that poor bloody girl, normally bonny enough to charm any man out of his senses, torn and shredded to the bone as he had dallied in the pleasure of his own male susceptibility to being a part of things at Darsington Hall farm. He felt sick.

"No, no splitting a bottle with you tonight, Albert, too damn tired."

Ah, now? That and something else, perceived the butcher, taking the parcel round to the side entrance, unseen from the street. These Ministry of Food bastards can be right o'kkard and vicious beggars if they catch you, even if it's just looking after your good old specials, like.

Setting squarely to his meal of black puddings, fried ham and potatoes, Albert Purves, Master Butcher and Purveyor of muscle, fat and connective tissue to his appreciative customers, propped up the Evening Standard against the teapot and stared at the double-column space plainly snatched for Late News just before going to press that afternoon:

"Local Girl Crushed: Worst Accident of the War

"Police, recovery units and RAF medical teams converged this afternoon a short distance out of town, working desperately to extricate the body of Leading Aircraftwoman Marion Richards. Dr Angus Mckay, commenting upon Miss Richards' injuries, said that she had suffered extensive lacerations, multiple fractures, had lost a great deal of blood, and was in a highly critical state following recovery from the RAF transporter involved. Cutting away the necessary framing took over two hours, during which time, Miss Richards, well known in the town's amateur dramatic society productions, along with her sister Pamela, was under continuous medical attention."

Momentarily ceasing his steady mastication, the butcher muttered in disbelief, "Well, I'll go to damnation. No wonder 'e was goo'in' on at a rate, like."

His wife cocked her head enquiringly from the kitchen sink, slungeing bloodied aprons in cold water.

"Did you say something, Bert, dear?"

Bert's pink stubby fingers drummed in fleeting irritation on the oilcloth, with their spatulate, small knife-nicks which never quite healed, fingers that were very strong from a lifetime of almost lovingly cutting down carcases which, in their component parts, were more familiar to him in their prime, fatty compliance, than those of his own wife's body. He sought to satisfy her curiosity of a moment back.

"No, my dear, not really. Just what Mr Baird the vet'nary was goin' on about. Damned right, when you think about it, war and all that. Shockin' waste of good flesh and blood any road, shockin'."

At teatime that afternoon it did not take Fraser many moments in his father's company (and by reflection, his mother's presence as well) to gather there was or had been something of sombre gravity witnessed by his father that spring afternoon. There was a tension or even a more than faint feeling of some undeniable futility, as yet unexpressed in open conversation around the table. They all waited for a word, a name or some unlikely connection to suddenly bring forth whatever it was clamped in his father's mind. Silent, attempting to appear fully occupied with passing plates and things about the meal table, Mary Baird somehow sensed it unlikely that it had anything to do with his work.

And then it happened. As soon as he, Fraser, mentioned having spent some time with Derek Richards looking at the highly engineered air raid shelter in Derek's parents' garden, now being converted into a workshop for Derek's father's machine tools, Fraser was taken aback by his father's harsh interruption.

"Fraser, listen to me. Pamela, Marion Richards – you're friendly with both of them, aren't you?"

Fraser knew at once that his father and mother too, probably, had noted his apparently casual attraction to the younger Richards girl; crikey, what was coming now? What was wrong with that, anyway?

"Pamela's and Derek's sister Marion, the WAAF lassie, was involved in a ghastly blood… very severe accident this afternoon. It is possible that she may not survive. I came on the whole aweful scene shortly after it happened this afternoon. Angus McKay had been on duty as Casualty MO. He was there. Fraser, I and your mother, want you not to be going round to the Richards family until… until we all see what happens in the next few days."

His father's face and voice were both drained. His mother was white-faced and motionless, unnaturally erect at the end of the table.

"We shall phone the Richards and let them know that Pam can stay with us here for a few nights, and Derek too, for that matter; her mother and father will be spending every minute possible at the RAF surgical unit. Try and be welcoming to them, right?"

Yes, Fraser thought, immediately quietened, and what my papa is also saying, without actually spelling it out, is, "This is definitely not a time for any girlfriend stuff with young Pamela, my lad." Given that all this awfulness had never happened, well, what would have been a time for girlfriend stuff, whatever that consisted of? And what would my strict father have been saying to me then, I wonder?

Suddenly, his mother broke into the tight circle of tension, upset of trust.

"Can you enlighten us a little, Alec?"

He did so, sparingly.

"Aye, Mary, I saw the awful aftermath of something which should never have happened to any bonny young girl, never mind our Marion."

Fraser knew at once, from the manner of his father's speaking of Marion Richards as "our", that there had been something else, not to be disclosed, that had wounded his father's innermost thoughts.

Looking at his father's features, the same disturbing facts of total uncertainty of outcome for poor Marion enveloping them all, Fraser sensed that his father had been shaken to his core. Shocking to all of them, someone whom they all knew well had been at the centre of profoundly disturbing sights and reflections that afternoon. Presenting such a question to himself, Fraser would never have thought that his father was normally given to that much introspection about anything. That was more like his mother's sort of thing, and whatever was or had been bothering his father, it certainly wasn't pressing upon her conscience.

XXIX

Seven or eight weeks after the harvest of 1944 was at last safely gathered in, stacked and thatched, there came in a trough of dank back-end days, marked by continued fog, frost and even sleety rain. Before all this wearisome wintriness seemed set in, Fraser was surprised and then faintly apprehensive about his father's no-nonsense assertion that they should both go down to speak with Jack Harris about how he, Fraser, might oblige Jim Bolton by taking on to do some weekends' relief milking and stock work. On their way down the lane in gathering dusk, his father explained the collective reasons as to why this might be a good thing for his, Fraser's, growth of experience.

"Look, Jim Bolton's got this man Gerald, second man on the Darsington dairy side; too much pressure on him when Wesley Morton has a weekend off. He's got a lot of young beasts to see to, and it's too much. Let's see if we can set up something with Jack whereby you can stand in for milking duties, say one weekend a month, or a couple of Sundays. What d'you think?"

Fraser felt that apart from the placatory undertone to his father's outline, he was at least being treated with some consideration as to his virtually grown-man place in all this. He voiced his doubts as they came in sight of the so-very-familiar farm buildings in which Fraser knew he could find his way to do any bally thing required of him by Mr Harris, or Stiffy, or Watty, for that matter, by day or by night.

"Wouldn't it look like as though, well, the farm and the men, too, are not big enough or, or grand enough for me to just keep working away? I don't want to disappoint Jack, er, Mr Harris, after all that he's passed on to me. He knows that I really want to have a farm of my own; he shows me lots of useful things."

As soon as Alec Baird responded to this not-unexpected explanation of what was in Fraser's mind, he realised that the money side of things was not an important deciding factor so far as his son was concerned.

"Jim Bolton will pay you, Fraser, and pay you well. You and he will get on famously."

Any further thrashing out of this difficult scheme was stopped, not by Jack Harris, but by Marcia Harris coming out from the harness room where she had given a cat and kittens extra milk.

261

She had been abjuring the not-yet-grown-to-size young farm cat, "Shouldn't get yourself with kittens to that damned great tom; you're too small by a long chalk, just like some of these silly young girls that come a-waltzing round, looking for fun in a pair of trousers—" when she heard Alec Baird's and Fraser's voices. She already knew exactly what they were about: coming down to speak with my Jack on this proposal cooked up by or for James Bolton, drat 'im, across at Darsington Hall Farm. Whoever had thought this one up, it all sounded a bit daft in her view of things.

She intercepted them on the path up through the orchard towards the farmhouse. If she could keep things agreeable between these three men, and that's how we all think of Fraser now, with warmth of regard for both Baird father and son, then she would or rather should, seize the moment to push both of their male minds in the right direction, before speaking with her Jack.

"What you must do, Fraser, is make it seem that Mr Bolton has been the one who asked you to help him out – no, don't say otherwise, Alec."

She placed a hand on his arm.

"And you feel that it might come in useful to let us know some of their ways of doing things over there, when you're back here – keeping us right!"

Marcia smiled warmly at both of them, close to laughing out loud, but swiftly became business-like, giving Fraser a nod in the direction of the house, and saying to Alec, "You stay on here for a moment, Alec. It's high time that our Fraser set to paddle his own canoe. We can both go inside in a minute or two, and mind, we've to be surprised and pleased with whatever the two of 'em agree to."

Jack was straight into getting this unexpected idea sorted out; young Fraser was and had been a godsend and he'd no notion of losing him just to keep Big Farmer Jim Bolton pleased to poach one of his lads for this everlasting problem of having enough men on the dairy at weekends.

"Well, Frayshyur, my lad, yewm goo'in' on ash 'ead dairyman, I do h'ear! H'and leavin' me to mek the besht of thingsh with theshe idle buggersh h'ere an' all!"

Jack's face and eyes were lively, in spite of the sting in his greeting, but Fraser did feel that he was deserting his good friend and boss, in fact all of his good friends in the fabric of what seemed just like the extended farming part of his home.

"Well, Mr Harris, it wasn't my idea actually, but father, er, Mr Bolton really, thought it would be good experience, on top of what you've taught me, to get used to working along with the men who are on the milking all the time, and taking responsibility when one of them is off."

Fraser was shivering deep in his stomach muscles; he knew perfectly well that Marcia Harris was keeping his father out of it, and wanted to be able to handle this difficult bit himself, but he would need some guidance on the timing of these days off here, and days on over there. Come on, father, stop bloody well talking out there!

"Well, my young shurr, 'ow about yew tellin' me what shhort of weekend daysh as Jim Bolton ish sheeking yew to come h'up wiv. We've gotten to rely on yew to mek up h'our shteady team. The ladsh are that well pleashed to 'ave yew work along wiv 'em, and I desshay the bluggy 'osshes know yem handsh an' all."

All spoken by Jack Harris in as jocular a fashion as he could summon, but Fraser sensed that there was a measure of more than just annoyance in his good old friend Jack Harris. This was getting bloody difficult, trying to please everyone; just what had come into his father's dratted mind to land this scheme on him?

"What Mr Bolton had in mind, Mr Harris, and has to be, to be… agreeable to you for a start," Fraser said, feeling really torn in too many different directions and not sure where or what the next sentence was going to be. "What if I could go on the dairy and milking say one Sunday every month, and a Saturday afternoon milking if someone was ill ?"

Jack Harris's response to this was short, sharp and to the point:

"Right, young man, what yew an' me h'ash to agree on, ish that in the firshht bluggy h'inshtance, we'll goo into the kitchen and write up on the calendar what daysh yewm likely to be wanted h'over theer, and then before'and, I shall shay whether or not yewm free to bugger off, depending on what the shate of the labour market ish here, by God! Dunna yew lose shight of the fact that what Jim Bolton wantsh yew to shtep in and do, real handy like, yew've larnt right here, from your Uncle Jack and h'ish merry men, my word!"

Yeah, Fraser reflected, that's all very well, but I've got to try and keep everything going at school as well. This is all getting too much.

There was enough good humour left in Jack's voice to make Fraser feel relieved; he grinned and blew out a sigh of thanks that things between them had not gone all sour. At this moment, Marcia Harris and Fraser's father stepped into the kitchen, apparently talking happily between themselves, but Fraser noticed the glance of a second that Marcia flicked quickly over her husband's face and eyes; there was instant relief from tension in her as well.

Looking at the Farmer & Stockbreeder calendar together, Jack Harris with

Fraser at his elbow fixed on a certain Sunday two weeks hence to see if this matter of split loyalties was ever going to work. In some ways which did not sit comfortably on his mind, Jack Harris privately hoped that it wouldn't.

Fraser felt that far too many people were becoming mixed up in this business of working for this unknown quantity Jim Bolton as a means of gaining wider experience. He just wished that his father hadn't set the whole damned thing going without speaking with him in the first case. There was a hard, gritty bit of dissatisfaction all through his mind; things were not fitting in together in the way that he, Fraser, would have worked towards had it been left to his own feelings. He broke into the conversation going on between Jack Harris, wife Marcia and his father.

"Look, excuse me, Father; seeing that I'm down here anyway, I think that I'll just work out the morning with the men, if that's all right?"

Almost too quickly, Marcia mended fences of angry feelings amongst all of these men.

"No need to go back up home, Fraser. Just you sit in with us at dinnertime. I'll let Mary know that you're doing your usual hefty share with the lads; they're always in good fettle when you're with them."

The direct yet unspoken need in Marcia's eyes upon Fraser for peace at a price was switched to his father to accept as a more or less satisfactory state of affairs, for the moment.

Stiffy came on Fraser in the brick barn, forking down swatches of hay for the afternoon milking and foddering. How, Fraser did not know, but all the men on the Harris farm were aware of this proposed arrangement for their own lad Fraser to be pushed into trying his hand on the Bolton place.

"Them buggers bin messing you around, 'ave they? By Christ, and you doing so 'stroad'nary well along with us. And I do 'ear that the Guv'nor's speakin' about you and me could be gooin' on wiv a spot of ploughin'.'Ow about that, then?"

Fraser felt a sudden welling up of affection, trust, companionship with all the men, even that irritating little know-all Leonard. He turned his back to Stiffy, throwing down wide dusty blankets of hay. He was near to speaking with Stiffy, but tears of confusion would have flowed had he done so. That would have been most unmanly. Ken Darlington guessed the anger in Fraser's jerky movements; not like the lad at all, so he casually turned his own back to Fraser, and looked out in general over the buildings, letting his views of such things trickle out, easy like.

"D'you know, Fraser, when I think back on all manner of things that were right bloody o'kkard to handle at the time, taken a bit at a time, there wor usually summat worth goo'in' for, even though it were a bugger to please myself, never mind other folk. Think on that. Now, you come on down off that hay mow, and give me an 'and with my special 'osses. I'll turn owd Bounce over to you for a reet good strapping, right? Come on, then. We can have a bit of talk as we goo along, them 'osses likes nothing better than a good talking as we goo's along. Funny beggars, 'osses, but they stays wiv you forever provided you treat 'em right."

Stiffy was concerned for Fraser in this argy-bargying out there with the Guv'nor an' all, and him gettin' quite raised by the sounds of things.

"That dust gettin' to you, was it?"

"More than just bloody dust, Kenneth, just... just getting pushed into things I didn't even know about, for a start."

Stiffy thumped his big brown hand on Fraser's shoulder.

"Look, I do 'ear as they've got Land Girls and some of them bloody great Yankee tractors over at Darsington; either road, you'll do well to 'ave a change. When you'm all finished of a weekend, you can come back down 'ere and tell us all about it, hey up!"

In the sudden elation (and affection) that came from he knew not where, Fraser punched Stiffy on the shoulder.

"Come on, then, Kenneth, let's talk the hind legs off your precious great 'osses; let's have a bloody good go at every damned thing, yar!"

Stiffy grinned back at him, relieved and all; the sooner the Guv'nor got Fraser here started into a spot of ploughing, well, you never know, this goo'in' off from his usual place here, to work his arse off for Jim Bolton might just fizzle out. Or summat.

Thinking on how he had handled this business of young Fraysshyur being pushed into setting on at Jim Bolton's place, Jack thought to turn to Marcia for another view of what might be best for everyone. Her response (she had been waiting patiently for just this opening) was to the point.

"Jack, you know perfectly well that Alec and Mary's lad is dead set on farming; he'll have his own place one of these days. You've taught him all he knows, now get on and let him see that he has to earn the respect of those that work for any farmer in his own right; so, you set a time to start him ploughing. That'll please our men greatly as well."

Yes, Jack reflected, that sounds bluggy good, an' all. He snickered to himself, thinking that this enticement might just turn the tables on big owd Bolton h'over theer at Darshington, by gum it might!

They started on a still quiet day in early December, when the land was at rest. Stepping down from the Bedford utility school bus with its slatted wooden seats, Fraser was intercepted on his way to pick up his bike by Eleanor Harris, smiling at him as he went into the low malthouse.

"Our dad says you've to make a start ploughing with him!"

This comely girl, this young woman whom he secretly worshipped, was clearly pleased for him and excited. But, at last, ploughing? Crikey! Himself leaning forrard over the reins, proper long-furrow ploughing. And maybe, maybe Eleanor would see him, grown to man's stature and capabilities. Straightening up beside his bike, he tried to assume a look of steady manliness, at which Eleanor had great difficulty maintaining an equally admirable (or admiring) respect.

Some months back before Eleanor's interception with her stepfather's instructions, Ken Darlington had taken Fraser the the length of a whole furrow of ploughing lea, on a day in the spring.

Placing Fraser in front of him, with the lad's hands in front of his own, the pair of Shires blew and nodded, arching their thick necks and shoulders into their collars. Fraser had had to lengthen his pace in order to match Stiffy's steady stride behind him, grinning in pleasure over Fraser's right shoulder. The whole feel of it had been deeply, profoundly satisfying, more so than anything else he had ever attempted.

Now, Eleanor regarded Fraser thoughtfully. All this fuss about him ploughing. Why was he always so taken up with work, work, just like her stepfather? She was aware that there was surely more to enjoying things, more to a different kind of life than this, this forever racing to keep up with the seasons. She really liked Fraser; there was a certain warmth and fun behind the quietness, she knew that.

"Well, come on, Fraser, Dad really misses you, you know! He says that you've got to learn proper ploughing, that is, before you get into slapdash ways with a tractor, like our Chester!"

His wide grin but evident pleasure and then confusion, made Eleanor burst out laughing. She wanted to put her arms around him and, well, somehow hug her pleasure into him, too.

For an early Saturday morning in December, the air was still, with no wind in the high elms as he sped down the lane. Jack's nailed boots rasped on the blue bricks of the stable door.

"Ho, then, young man! Ah thowt a shpot of ploughin' would get yew back where yewm bluggy well belong. H'are yew shet, then, for ush to plough on a bit? H'our Chester'll never look the way of owt in a shtable, hish h'orsshpower cooms on wheelshh! An' h'our gallant Shtiffy, here, the next bluggy thing'll be he'll tek up wiv shome shmart young filly ash'll lead him a merry dansh, h'alright, mark my wordsh! We'll do besht to be jusht yew an' me. Let'sh mek a shtart."

Immediately harnessing the two black Shires was no anxiety for Fraser. He had to drag in an old feed box to stand on when they tossed their heads as he looped the collars upside down over their ears and necks. Then the saddle with the well-greased slide, but – hey, wait a moment! He caught Stiffy grinning at him from the stable door; of course, the saddles and slides weren't needed today – the pair would be harnessed directly into respective swingle-trees. So, breechings and tail straps, then back pads to carry the chains off their flanks, all tidily strapped and snapped into each other. Stiffy interrupted him:

"Hey up, Fraser, lad, dunna just loop them chains like that; tek each one well over the other side and double it back a piece. You've a bit to goo with the Guv'nor, an' he doesn't do with them chains walloping ablow their bellies like a bugger – neither do they, old gals, hey?"

Jack Harris had explained his plan to Fraser as they walked up the two fields between the farm and the piece awaiting turning over with the plough.

"I'm goo'in' to shet yew this smallish piece ashide the twelve-acre shtubble; h'it'll do for shome feeding rape and kale an' that'll hold birdsh for next sheason, an' be handy-like for Watty an' Stiffy to cart in – won't cut no bluggy tracksh h'everybluggywheer."

The plough, made by Ransomes, Sims and Jefferies, Ipswich, of about fifty years back, lay canted to one side, left-handedly, on the headland, the mouldboard thick with yellow grease.

"Now, then, Frayshyurr, th' important bit about thish ploughing job ish leavin' enough of room for an h'eashy turn, then yer shettin-in again comesh neatly, 'cos youm 'osshes is shwung in an' ready, not sshteppin' over tracesh an' shuchlike. Yew back 'em up to the shwingle treesh, my lad, h'and we'll mek a shtart."

Fraser took hold of each bridle on the outside, really firmly, and leant into them, pushing their soft muzzles to the rear.

"Geet bak! Geet bak!" He gave a fair rendering of the Guv'nor or Stiffy – their commands all sounded much the same. Bett danced a bit with her fore-hooves, Fraser's boots well out of her range as he leaned forward. "Geet bak then, 'ooman, geet bak!"

Each mare drew its hooves back on the faded stubble, rather than taking definite paces backwards. Taking a side apiece, Jack and Fraser tackled up the chains to the swingle trees, checking backwards for twists or kinks from the flat metal hooks on the collars. Jack unlooped the reins from the near-side horn of Bounce's collar, who would be pulling on the land side, leading them back to the plough handles.

The plough's two wheels, mounted in front of the coulter, were set at two different levels; one to run in the angle of the previous furrow, the other one higher, on the unploughed or land side. Lying as it was on unploughed land, Fraser wondered how setting in to the unploughed land was to be accomplished.

"Cum in here, Frayshyurr, affront o' me for a sh-shart, an' keep yewr weight on the low shide handle," Jack said, nudging Fraser's right knee from behind with his own, "so ash she wunna dig in until yewm h'all lined up. H'are yew ready, then? Eesshee, eesshee – Bett! Bounnsh! Hoo'yup, then!"

The two mares paced easily, nodding and mouthing to get bridles and bits settled, the plough crabbing to its left due to the out-of-furrow angle. Jack and Fraser with him bore down on the offside plough handle, to keep the sliding sock-point from boring into the ground. They came to the point of swinging right-handed into the previous day's waiting furrow.

"Lookyer, dunna get in h'amongsht my feet, bugger h'it!" Jack grinned at Fraser. "Pull her h'over."

Left handle up, right one pulled down and into his groin. "Cumm hup, then! Coom hupp!"

As one, Bett and Bounce sidestepped neatly to their right, hardly moving ahead, the plough slewing round, starting to ride on the right, furrow-side wheel as the plough lined up.

From the added bearing-down pressure of Fraser and Jack Harris, there had been more resistance of the plough to desired sideways movement than the off-side mare had expected. She set down one hind leg and hoof over the taut trace, and then immediately stopped all sidestepping, passive, waiting.

Jack left the reins go slack, taking a loose turn round the curved steel brace between the long slender handles.

"Ho, then, 'ooman, good ol' gel. Good ol gel. Shtandhupp, Ah shay!"

Bounce inclined her head and eye slightly, to get a clear sight of the farmer, then stood without movement.

"Cum h'out of theer, Frayshyurr, or we short thish h'out." He put his right shoulder into the mare's haunch, slid it down to level with its knee joint,and clasped both hands round the back of the hock, directing Fraser, "Put yewr foot on the chain, an' tek it off the hook. Let h'it lay, now."

He lifted the mare's offside hock, fetlock and hoof off the ground with little

268

apparent effort; she had already adjusted her stance so as to stand in easy three-legged balance.

"Sshtan' hupp, Bounsh, o'l gel. Now bring that chain round to th'h'outshide, Frayshyurr, jusht eeshee, an' h'ook her hup agen. aarhyer!"

Fraser looked round, startled, chain in his fist.

"Yewm a daft bugger an' all! Never turn yer back to a work h'oss when yewm a–shortin' them h'out, elsh they'll plant yew one, look yer! Like ash not, sshome other carelessh bugger'll mek a mischief h'at that very moment. Cum h'on now, mek 'ashte. Tek yer mark up atween yer osshes' shouldersh, an' shtart ter feel yer plough comin' h'into yer handsh, right?"

After the second and third furrows and headland turnings, Jack Harris stood out from behind the plough, walking beside Fraser, talking him through all the repeated commands to the pair of horses, their movements and firmness of responses to the plough frame and body, which now seemed a living thing not only in his hands, but throughout his body. The plough was speaking to him.

Jack walked to one of the hedges along the top side of the two acre piece, lit a cigarette as he tested the blade of the stubby billhook he had carried up through the fields, wrapped in a sack, and watched Alec Baird's son get working with his, Jack's, pair of horses. He could see that Fraser was starting to get into the long leaning pace of a ploughman, guiding the plough into its course of work. Jack stepped up to the hawthorn hedge, and seeing, hearing all that Fraser was achieving, started to cut back the summer's growth with quick, upwards sweeps of the blade. Neither of them would be caring overmuch about breaking for dinner. He would signal his young ploughman pupil to stop before the afternoon light began to fade, give him time to get his pair back down through the fields and rubbed down in the stable. And Stiffy would doubtless overcome this urgent need to be a-courting (Jack smirked wickedly to himself at this, grunting as he sliced the billhook into stemmy stuff), and be waiting at the stable door to see that "his" precious pair be properly attended to! By the Guv'nor and young pupil an' all!

The soft jingle of the horses' traces preceded and followed Fraser's now-confident words of command. Both mares were comfortable with his words from behind them, slightly different in tone; there was an easy flow of communication between them all. Fraser allowed them a moment to blow as they came to the end of each furrow, as he looked back to see what sort of a job he was making. Could be a lot better.

A covey of partridges dropped low over the hedge, starting to chirr and creak as they jugged down in the next field. Jack knew them well since their hatching, the two old birds and five young. The birds accepted his presence and appearances as a normal part of their wary world. This was a good day to be farming, Jack thought out loud: horses, men and land all married to good purpose. Doing his bidding, in the proper and timely way of things. The pair of Shire mares, now at ease with Fraser's presence on the reins, turned neatly at their furrow's end as Jack took a pace forward to step up into another cluster of thorn and field maple.

He would set young Fraser to cart up a load of mouldy straw, to stack up all his hedge brushings and make a fine blaze at the darkening, some afternoon soon. Come to that, he would bring Marcia and the young 'uns along in the trap, and have Alec and Mary come along too. Let them see how their lad, almost like another son about the farm, had performed at the ploughing, first go. They would have a fine big blaze, bring up a drink or two to heat in the red ash and mek' a bit of a party an' all! Shee the year out in good shtyle, my word an' all!

Wiping the billhook blade with the oily sack, he turned to the two mares, their breath in vaporous nasal streams as the frost was setting in.

"Reckon to finish, then, Frayshyurr? Cum along, tek the plough along the 'eadland a piece an' we'll mek for whum. Yew've made a reet good shtart. Ah'll tell Marcia we can shtart tekkin' daysh h'off now, we've got another ploughman!"

The looping of the traces across the horses' backs, the greasing of the plough, the last look around for overlooked tools, all was done in silent amity. Their steady tramp home, Bett and Bounce comfortably nudging their shoulders in the close group along the track, the smells of horse sweat and turned earth, all of this settled down into a priceless imprint of contentment in his mind as Fraser felt Jack Harris's solid presence beside him in the dusk. But, there loomed this business of doing odd days' work for Mr Bolton; how was that going to work out?

The Shire mare Bounce leant forward and nuzzled the back of his neck with a whiskery top lip. Fraser grinned delightedly, putting a hand back to her muzzle. Jack noticed.

"Shpeakin' to yer, ish she? They do 'ave theym little tricksh, Frayshyurr, h'our ladiesh, hey 'ooman?"

They both grinned in the dusk, no words. The two Shires, the two men's figures on the field track, enfolded a tangible respect and trust which gathered them closely together with invisible bonds.

XXX

By the finish of his first Sunday's working for Mr Bolton, Fraser felt that he had not shown himself or his capabilities in the best light. At Darsington Grange there seemed always to be the need to get things done under pressure, at a constant trot. Or quicker.

His early morning run across and up and down in the dark countryside had been invigorating enough; that was all right. He had intercepted all sorts of natural emissions, in addition to seeing the sources of some of them in the cone of brilliant white light from the whirring dynamo on his rear wheel; rabbits darting across the road in infuriating sudden changes of direction, causing him to brake savagely and swear.

Warm dung smells from heifers blowing at a field gate; resting, ruminating sheep along a bank; the faint smell of ash from a fire of hedge brushings. One such air-carried smell, not natural but quite familiar, wafted into his cold-sharpened nostrils as he slowed down for the tricky, badly cambered bend just coming up to The Cross Keys public house. Stale beer, suds from the open drain where he knew a Mrs Hollister washed batches of beer glasses and plates in the yard scullery, a whiff of men's urine if it had been a busy Saturday night, with the lads needing a bit of coolth and quiet in the darkness whilst they relieved their over-full bladders against the gig-house wall.

All entirely familiar, but not very acceptable to a finicky person, if they could but guess at the source, that is. As he cycled past the pub, in the illumination of one small lamp still burning above the bar door, Fraser recalled overhearing the speculation concerning one less than well-known episode of happenings at The Keys.

As the two men, Jack Harris and a neighbouring farmer, had stood in Jack's milk house pecking over the details of a rather unusual car crash near The Cross Keys, with Fraser pouring milk over the cooler at the time, Fraser remembered Jack's fairly pungent observations.

The notably pretty daughter of one of the bigger, well-established farmers in the parish had been pulled out, badly concussed, from a damaged American army staff car lying on its side in the ditch at the very same bend. Her uniformed companion had not been formally identified, but The Cross Keys, like any other

271

local pub, had its own sources of intelligence and knew of him by much more than just name and rank.

With that peculiar, engaging sideways quirk of mouth, nose and cheek predictable to some of Jack's piercing observations, Fraser had heard him say, impediment lending pungency to his words, "We'm getting a right bad bluggy reputayshun, Joe. H'all shortsh of gamesh a'gooin' on and not all h'at that danged Golf Club bluggy placesh, neither!" He had grinned, wickedly, rolling his eye at Fraser to include him in this men's salacious conspiracy.

Joe Goodyer had turned to Jack, carefully taking his Capstan cigarette from between his lips with thumb and the only two fingers remaining on his right hand, a misjudged moment at a tractor drawbar having neatly sheared off the first two.

"Ooh, ar, then, Jack, I take it you're on about our very own wandering gel's unfortunate tip-up? Not that you were aiding and abetting in any fashion, I take it?"

"No. Allus whum by ten; ask Marcia, but I do know this about our Marjorie – that same gal's shkirt's bin ash 'igh ash 'er playmate'sh wallet could tek it, more than a few timesh, jusht ash h'it were when the ladsh got 'er pulled h'out up at The Keysh. Some smartish tidyin' h'up needed afore they could tek 'er whum, shauchy bluggy bitch an' all!"

As Fraser cycled past in the half-light of darkness before dawn, the pub was silent, shuttered, guarding its secrets and shames impartially, that strong whiff of stale beer hanging in the air and in his nostrils in the fine drizzle.

Before he had even got off his bike to wheel it inside the tool shed and workshop door, he had been noticed and brusquely shouted at by Mr Bolton.

"Get yourself into the main cowshed, young man, and be sharpish. Our wonderful Land Girl Judy whatshername hasn't shown up, Wesley's been creating something hellish, and the milk lorry'll be bloody well here afore they're all milked out, never mind put over the cooler. So you and them get moving."

From there on, Fraser felt, it had been a gallop all day. Look sharp, do this, find out that, bring in this, that and the next thing; hay, straw, mangolds, beet pulp. And don't let those clever-bugger Jerries stand about, smoking, d'you hear? Yes, he'd heard all right.

The errant or rather absent Judy had not only appeared late, with the warm smell of sleep about her, but had made a right nuisance of herself in the long cowshed as he had been intent on stripping out cows' quarters as deftly and quickly as he could, and switching teat clusters in and out of hypochlorite solution and then cold water, before squatting again, his head and cap pressed firmly into the next cow's flank, to keep up with Wesley Morton on the other side of the cows' standings.

She had damn well come prancing up to where he was pouring milk into a carrying pail, twiddling her fingers in his open shirt-neck, making eyes at him like, like a picture house poster, and going on about "Young Lochinvar flew in on his bike" or some such rubbish. She could only have been a few years older than he was, probably about the same age as his sister Jean, but clearly felt that getting on with the work shouldn't engage all of her energies. There had been a strange mixture of scents and smells about her person that he had found both annoying and yet intriguing. He couldn't put a name to her antics nor to this aura of female personality, irritated by the intrusion that it was into his determination to be a good, hard worker.

The day's pace had accelerated, Sunday and all though it was, to early afternoon, Wesley Morton's wife Dorothy, speedy enough in setting down her husband's and Fraser's dinner, but needing to know every dashed thing about him and his background, which necessitated polite response when the need was to get as much hot food into his aching stomach as possible, without unnecessary speech.

There had been the matter of his cutting and carting a load of kale, as tall as himself and shedding water on him from the waist down. Setting the mare and rubber-tyred cart back to the doors in the feed end of the cowshed had been handled easily enough, but on hearing Fraser clattering down the tailgate, the mare had not heard any injunction as to stand stll or similar, and had paced forward, trailing half the load right out across the yard. At which minute, the two German POWs in the shed grinning widely, Bernard Bolton had swung round into the yard, driving his father's big Humber Super Snipe. In exactly the same forthright challenging manner as his father, Bernard laid one arm across the steering wheel, and turned, the window wound down, to enquire of Fraser:

"Bringing it in, or taking it all back out again, Fraser?! The Guv'nor'd better not see that lot; get it bloody well forked back in there, fast, if I were you. Oh, and when that's done, you take the car round to the meal store, put two rolls of corn sacks into the boot, and then give the car a good wash and wipe down, OK?"

Crikey, and what was he supposed to do first – back the tip-cart into the cart shed, right round the back of the old barn, take the mare out and rub her down, gather up the muddy mess of kale, then get the dratted car loaded up with wheat sacks and wash the bally thing and wipe it down?

273

I Like to Walk in This Field

The long day wore on at a steady gallop. The sandwiches put up jointly between his father and himself well before half past five that Sunday morning lay uneaten in the army respirator bag hanging on the tool store door.

Engaged in cycling home at the steady rate reflecting his tiredness, Fraser flicked in his mind through to yet another abrupt appearance of Mr Bolton sen. as he and Mrs Morton and Judy were assembling milking units from the cavernous steam steriliser chest.

"Look here, young man, there's no need for you to be in here; Mrs Morton's perfectly capable of setting up the units, right?"

In his flow of terse directions, it seemed to Fraser that Mr Bolton was deliberately ignoring Judy as a reliable and useful quantity, following her tardiness on a morning when all hands were clearly needing to be putting milking through at top speed. Behind James Bolton's back, Wesley's wife made flinty-eyed faces at him, dropping her head dutifully on the second that he swung round to nod at the box beside her on the galvanised dairy bench.

"And you're remembering about those new pulsators? Good, see and fit them for this afternoon's milking; let me have the old 'uns Monday morning without fail. Fraser, you go to the house, have Mrs Bolton hand you the collection slips for October, and tally them against the cans put out on Wesley's daily totals; they sometimes try to tell us there's been a spillage of some gallons – bloody lies, I'll tell you."

He turned round with a rasp of market boots, and was half out of the milk house, when he abruptly wheeled back again and fired off another deadly shot:

"And Judy? You that's much preoccupied with problems of your figure, and other features, as I gather, go you out to Gerald fust thing Monday morning and get him to draft out a list for all his mixed feed requirements for the week, and check what's there in the meal store and what's needed. Put it all in round figures. Without fail. And, you won't have Fraser to distract you neither, right?'

This time he was out and into the yard before his last words sped over his shoulder. From there, James Bolton bellowed, "Fraser?"

"Oh, Christ," Mrs Morton implored, "don't 'ave him come back in 'ere. Get going afore there's some other small war breaks out, goo on!"

"Yes, Mr Bolton, what?" Fraser felt that he needed to show he still had limitless energies.

"Right, whatever you're doing, and afore those Jerry buggers get picked up, far too early for a Sunday's work, I'll say, get them on to moving all that Gerald needs for milling and mixing next week, so he's not running around like a flapping old woman with half a barrowful of this, and two pails of that. You can use that mare you made such a mess with this forenoon. Leave the bags in it. Right height for Gerald's bad back, and no double handling, got it?"

Crikey. Yes sir, no sir, three bags full, or shouldn't that be ten bags full, and five spares, left over in case some poor bugger dies halfway through a week's mix? Weary and yet possessed of a solid determination, Fraser set his mind to speaking with the three German prisoners of war. Which he did with a not altogether falsely assumed directness.

The three Germans who had been dropped off on that winter's Sunday morning were the complete antithesis of their Italian predecessors. There was order, discipline, almost rank, it would appear. Their boots, footsteps and bearing had purpose about them, which made even the most experienced farmworker about the place appear profoundly inept or lazy. All jobs were accomplished to rapid completion, and seeing that the Germans were near to finishing in the granary before their army truck appeared, it was time again, half past three, to be ready to milk and feed in the long warm cowshed. The now steady rain outside was making a grey, hissing curtain around the November day's meagre light.

Fraser looked down the passage into the milk house proper, where the cooler gurgled wetly to itself below the receiving vat, and the Germans were taking off rain-sodden tunics and shrugging into clean smock coats insisted upon by James Bolton for work in any of the milking herd buildings.

Looking down to the last few bubbles of milk in the milk tube, Fraser twisted off the vacuum cock and scooped up the teat cluster with a clatter before swinging the more-than-full bucket to within jostling distance of Judy's legs and wellington boots, the heavy bucket crashing to the concrete to within a wafer's thickness of her toes, intentionally.

She flung out a hip, and twirled a surprisingly well-manicured finger in Fraser's face. Wesley Morton clattered past in distracted fashion, spitting out:

"Hey up, you silly young bitch; our Mam'll have me, and you, and him, working with bloody 'andcuffs on, carryin' on like that!"

As Wesley and Fraser crowded Judy in front of them into the milk house, swinging their extremely awkward loads of full units and clusters behind her, Fraser heard James Bolton come into the cowshed from the other end, barking out sundry observations and incontrovertible flat-out statements like a rapid-fire gun levelled at them all.

"Fraser? Get these Jerries going, they're standing around watching all this horseplay; they should be moving muck, and not smoking!"

Peter Fleisschmaker, Bavarian miller/artillery bombardier, effortlessly took up a hugely heavy shovelful of muck, saying as he did so, "Hah! Herr Bolton, es ist dein Vater, nicht?"

Yeah, come on Big Peter, Fraser thought, you know bloody fine I'm not his son.

"Nein, es ist bauer, reich bauer. Ich bin nicht der Sohn; Ich bin bloody fleissig arbeiter, hier!"

It was about as much as he could hurriedly assemble from his school toolkit of basic German. The result was vastly surprising: Big Peter took him into a strong bear-hug, mock-wrestled with him in great grinning good nature, and then pronounced, one powerful fist gripping his shoulder in the friendliest of fashion, "Frehserr! Frehserr! Du bist nicht arbeiter, du bist prachtige Karl, vertsehen! Jetzt wir machen ihr ploddy vorrk, Herr Major!"

They all laughed. OK. So, they were all kamaraden on this wet, wet day on an English farm. This whole war business was indeed a funny bloody affair, Fraser decided in his weariness of mind and body that day.

He cycled home, legs weary, sweat cold on his back and belly muscles, his ex-army cape dripping water on to and into his clammy wellingtons. Christ, what a day that had been. He fingered again the flat bulge in his army tunic breast pocket. Thirty seven shillings and sixpence. So, after three such relief Sundays, he would have, um, five pounds twelve shillings and sixpence to pay into his Post Office savings book at the village Post Office after school the next day. Not bad.

After only some shortened conversation with his mother and father, finishing with the opinion that, at Darsington, "Every pound, person and bally particle there has to wash its face three times over a day, I believe, by golly!" Fraser went early to bed. His parents could clearly see that he was tired out but genuinely, generally satisfied with all this added responsibility, so they thought.

Before fatigue, released, flooded through him, Fraser tried to see what the difference was between the Boltons' way of doing things, and Jack Harris's farming. In a way that was not all that clear, it seemed to lie mainly in the fact that whereas Jack Harris took pride and a craftsman's satisfaction in the actual doing of things like breaking and working a young horse, setting in a strainer post or repairing a broken piece of tackle, James Bolton, and son Bernard too, for that matter, did not feel the need that they should do any of these things; that's what they paid the farm workers to do. Silly buggers like me, as his eyelids closed.

His dreamless sleep of exhaustion was suddenly shattered, at what time in the darkness he knew not, by a thunderous tattoo of hands, fists, distantly beating on the front door downstairs, and muffled voices in distress. Fraser jerked awake, eyes wide but sightless in the darkness surrounding the alarming swell of sounds from the front hall. Now what?

He could not get a measure of what on earth was going on outside and inside their, the Baird family's home: the furious assault on the front door was beyond alarming; it was frightening. Scrambling out of bed, pulling on his working clothes which lay on the floor as he had flopped into bed some hours before, he heard his mother speaking rapidly, forcefully to his father:

"Hold on, Alec. That's Marcia's voice. Let me go down first and I'll call you as soon as I know what's…"

She was down the stairs in a rush, barefooted, dressing gown all askew as Fraser saw from the dimly lit landing. Snapping on the hall light, she shouted loudly to Marcia, against the banging on the door, "I'm coming, I'm coming, Marcia. For God's sake, give me a moment."

Fraser leant over the banisters of the upstairs landing, his feet bare. The suddenly released shaft of light into the night and the rain was unkind in its illumination of Marcia Harris in wellingtons, nightdress and overcoat, with Eleanor huddled into her side, weeping in harsh sobs.

With a sudden savage clench around his heart at this distraught spectacle being propelled in a rush through to the kitchen, Fraser felt that this was not the time for him to appear, trying to be helpful or whatever. He went back into his bedroom, pulled on his socks and sat on his bed, but then made to go silently downstairs, to slip through the hall into the sitting room. He might be needed to kindle the fire, get some more logs or coal, or something.

From the shaded light of a bedside lamp in his parents' bedroom, his father's voice came, very quietly:

"Fraser? Come in here a moment. Just let your mother see to them first; come back up and let me know if we're needing to get the car out, or something has to be done, right?"

Mary Baird had immediately busied herself with matches, kettle, hot water bottles, tea and toast, putting her arms around Marcia and Eleanor in sudden impulse, and swaddling Eleanor's shivering bare legs in a travelling rug, in front of the poked-up kitchen range.

Marcia Harris's anxious, pent-up story of events came pouring out in total distress. It seemed that she, Marcia, had thought to make, yet again, the not unreasonable proposition to her husband that Eleanor could surely start to take art classes part-time at the town's Technical College, and she, Marcia, would bear the costs.

I Like to Walk in This Field

Jack, coming home sullenly drunk and bellicose from one of the farmers' pubs, had immediately threatened actual thrashing of his stepdaughter if… if what nobody now precisely knew, but probably by his ultimate authority in all family matters being challenged, not for the first time, at such an inopportune time by the girl's resolute mother. Marcia had intervened physically between her husband and Eleanor.

"And that was a right daft thing for me to do, Mary," she added, shaking her head.

She had then been struck, violently, by a person whom she could not truthfully say she recognised nor reacted to as her husband: an incoherent, loomimg man with diabolically darkened features, awakening and terrorising the whole family in his raging humiliation of both women.

"You know, Mary," said Marcia, her normally composed eyes and mouth twisted in confusion and shock, "he, Jack, that is, he was like a mad beast, something that you would call the vet to have put d-d-dow – Oh!"

As she realised that which she had been on the point of uttering, and the grim humour of such a demented idea, and in this veterinary household of all things, Marcia rose abruptly out of her chair drawn to the fire, in sudden hysterical laughter, which hiccupped into spasms of deep, racking sobbing.

"M-M-mmary, I thought he was going to do something terrible to her!"

Mother and daughter clung to Mary Baird, down whose cheeks tears streamed silently.

The two women, mother and daughter, slept in the Bairds' home that night, with beds hurriedly made up in Jean's bedroom, snatches of conciliatory, soothing words from Fraser's mother and a tension throughout the half-lit, half-aroused house, which persisted until well after all were settled. Alec Baird called Fraser down from his bed, and together with his mother, they conducted a low-voiced sorting out of matters in the kitchen, with the door closed.

"Look, all of us, should Jack come up here, battering on the door, demanding to see either of them, everybody stay put, right? I'll talk to him, but on no account is any of us to let him into this house."

Quietly, they went back to their beds.

Fraser lay open-eyed and staring in his bed across the landing from his sister's bedroom hurriedly adopted as a haven, a harbour for Marcia and Eleanor. He was at once aware that there was more to this violence directed upon sweet Eleanor, and her mother, than could reasonably accrue from just not liking her, or a lack of sympathy for things artistic or intellectual or anything that was not to do with farming, for Heaven's sake.

Now, there now slipped into Fraser's mind a darker side to Jack Harris's potent maleness, an unstated but outright demand that all women under his roof must bend to his ways, to his wishes, to – to his needs? What kind of needs?

What needs? In the darkness of his bedroom, now totally awake, Fraser's mind moved and split uneasily, into two areas of cognisance. On the one hand, all that he knew to be solid and unquestionable about his farmer mentor and staunch friend, the nourishment of his land and all that lay upon it – that was the whole function of Jack Harris's very existence.

But now sliding in, came this nameless, darker quantity of unknown elements. Fraser's leaping mind came to an abruptly heightened awareness, the prickling of a new perception that was flooding through him in an unwelcome tide. It was as though this episode of rage, tears and terror had released into his own being a recognition of things unspoken, unsettling. Unspeakable. Demanding a man's comprehension.

This first explosion of a man's sexual anger, sexual power, all stemming from a presumed challenge to his male authority in the first instance, now took form as an unassailable fact in Fraser's mind. Recalling some of his father's quietly voiced observations to his close friend and veterinary colleague, Sam Lomax, on the matter of Jack Harris's first marriage (the three of them, the two men, accompanied by Fraser, had been waiting on a Saturday evening's darkening for mallard to flight into a wash of water on stubbles), another province of human feelings, one which flowed darkly below everyday relationships, it seemed, began to emerge. Fraser grappled with the measure, the nature of the fact that probably in distant times, a man's wife and children were looked upon as being his property, to do as he liked with them. Suddenly, random facts conjugated with fearful violence in Fraser's wide absorption of what went on in some families; in some men's minds, those young which had firstly been gotten by another man's earlier possession of his wife and bedmate, must also be claimed and possessed, to maintain that basic blood-linked line essential for a family's wholeness, to keep it intact. Just like, like the business of breeding certain lines of livestock. That was what it was called: mating potent sires back to their own female offspring – line breeding. Fraser shivered.

Was that what was going on here?

It certainly seemed so. That was what was emerging in darkest tyranny right here and now, in the present, between good old Jack Harris and his stepdaughter Eleanor. Fraser felt deeply fearful for her, this girl whose needs in life he fully understood. And for whom he harboured the ache of impractical, loving feelings.

And if that person should refuse to bend to such domination, then to be rejected, cast out, was that what was also threatened? Well, here it was welling up, a dark current, in that very family and people and persons he liked and respected so much, and felt being a part of. Who had given of themselves and nourished him in so many ways, too. With Jack Harris's violence, what a mess things seemed to be in with the whole family, through the night's dark terrors. Fraser felt crushed and defeated with this knowledge, his respect for Jack Harris, farmer, now soiled and betrayed.

PART THREE

COMING HOME

XXXI

Whether Eleanor Harris's hunger for art in some form or another to nourish her life was fulfilled, or destroyed, as a consequence of that night of terror, was never released to Fraser's mind. He found himself summarily jolted out of what seemed to him to be reasonable enough progress towards what he knew he wanted to do with his life.

Only a few days after the unforgettable picture of Jack Harris, their friend and neighbour, as a feared, vile figure in his rage, Fraser came home from school to find his father's car already sitting in the drive. Having cycled from school, his hands were bitterly cold; he wanted to get to the kitchen fire before doing his usual poultry and firewood tasks outside. Pushing past the dogs ("Yes, yes, all right, you can get out with me – in a blooming minute!") he at once registered his mother's and father's voices; strong, interrupting each other, and yet, by their tone, remaining in accord about something. Ho, hum. They continued in half-finished sentences as he came into the kitchen and made for the fire. His mother was speaking, hardly paying any attention to his arrival.

"Alec, this is something which you must just not turn down. If you do, they'll put some younger man into the job, with less experience but more years to go, and that's the end of your yearning to get back up there. Oh, hallo, Fraser, come away in to the fire, here."

"Could I ask what's going on. What job? Who's going back where? What's the job and who's got it anyway? Where is it, here, there or where?" There was a serious, important feel about all this talk going on, and his father not even putting in his normally much longer day. That was a bit odd, for a start.

"Alec, we have to tell Fraser what's happened, quite out of the blue. It's going to make big changes for all of us."

Alec Baird pushed some officially headed pages across the table, explaining to Fraser as he did so:

"This has happened far sooner than I ever thought likely. I'm being offered the post of Senior VO for damn near a quarter of the whole of Scotland, and the

283

best bit of it, by Heavens!"

Oh, my! His father and his mother, they were both so excited! Fraser's mind was whizzing round.

"Oh, all right, Father. When is this to take place, and where to, can you tell me?"

His mother broke in eagerly, "Your father's to go to Aberdeen and be ready to start there in two months. It'll fit in fine with your sister's last two years at St Andrews, and she can just hop on to the Leuchars train for Dundee!"

From her animation, Fraser could plainly see his mother was already seeing places, old friends, possible places to make a home. Back in Scotland again! Well, that was great, and wasn't this bit of Scotland where his father had been born and grown up, and where he and his sister had been born, too? Explanations followed. His father was to be responsible for the counties of Kincardine, Aberdeen and Banff.

His mother broke in with, "Well, how do you feel about this, Fraser?"

"Right now, I don't know."

He didn't, couldn't know. Was all this going to mean changes and plans that he just couldn't encompass?

Then, whirling into his mind, came separation from the Harris farm and family, which had always been the most wonderful, solidly satisfying extension from his home at The Leys, getting his feet on the ground for all-round farming involvement as one of the whole robust family of the Harrises and all their workers. And then, parting from good old Hedley. And from Eleanor Harris. Well, one thing, it would be "Goodbye" to that sadistic damned man and his taunting and utterly pointless algebraic problems, for a start!

The continuing implications leapt in circles through his mind. Yes, of course he was pleased for his father, and his mother, for both of them, but of a sudden, Fraser was suddenly profoundly disturbed. He reached for an immediate calming in this chaos possessing his mind.

"Come on, dogs, out we go for a walk. You lot'll have to become proper Scottish dogs, for a start. Hooch aye!"

But where to go for this walk, as he set off, suddenly blinded by emotions that shook him to his core, he didn't know. Of an instant, he found that he couldn't clearly see.

XXXII

In the flurry of the planning and fulfilment of everything needed for their removal from their settled home outside Melford up to wherever they were to be living in Aberdeenshire, Fraser was more than a little surprised to find that his father, and his mother, on occasion, sought him out after school hours for decisions on this or that. Mostly on what things would need to go, and what should really be got rid of.

They were to travel north as soon as Fraser's last term at the grammar school finished. His sister Jean could join them from St Andrews in the last week of family life at The Leys, so that she could sort out her own possessions, and then all travel up together. On the matter of the big journey north, as a family, Fraser was stopped in whatever he was doing outside by his father when only a very few days remained and all manner of their poultry enterprises had been either sold or given away. He had been sorting tools and things into heaps inside the garage.

"Fraser, come out of there a moment. What d'you think we should do about the car?"

Do about the car? What was wrong with the car? Fraser asked himself. How should he know? He didn't drive the bally thing. Anyway, a wash and a grease all round and check the plugs should be OK, surely?

They both stood and looked at the Standard Twelve, well worn and dusty. His father had been driving it continuously from even before the war years and well on afterwards. His father turned to him.

"Well, what do you think, young man; it's done a huge mileage, and spares for everything are a problem."

"What sort of mileage has it done, Father?"

"Ha! Have a guess. No, never mind, just take a look at the mileometer, 'cos that's the very first thing anyone is going to check."

To Fraser's astonishment, well, mostly, it registered 157,000 miles. Crikey!

"Well, what d'you think? It's a long run away up there, best part of six hundred miles, and it's using oil like a, like one of your damn great tractors at Jim Bolton's that you're always going on about!"

There was a concerned expression on Alec Baird's face. What's going on here? Fraser asked himself.

"Using the amount of oil that it is, we're running the risk that the big-end bearings might just wear out, before we're even over the Border; then what?"

Fraser knew from accumulated facts gleaned from the men at the farm, and from working with the much larger pool of machinery at Darsington, that the big ends of the connecting rods in any engine had bearings or shells, and once they started knocking, which he had heard, the engine was as good as buggered. Or a major repair job, anyway.

Alec Baird broke into his uncertainty.

"Look, Gardner's garage has offered me ninety quid as it is, once we've finished with it here – he wants to use it for spares for another job they have. So he says. Well?"

Fraser carefully retrieved a conversation he had heard between Jack Harris and the local Vauxhall dealer in Melford, the latter keen to offer for spare wheels and tyres that Jack had hung on to. Well, worth a try?

"Father, why not chuck in all those tyres and that extra spare wheel, and ask him for a hundred pounds, or even a few quid more, say a hundred and ten?"

Alec Baird's eyebrows lifted and he then nodded in agreement.

"Well, damn me, that's a smart suggestion, Fraser, you haven't entirely wasted your time amongst our rascally farming friends! I shall tell your mother that's the best idea anyone has come up with. Anyway, we'll have a look round for a car up north and we'll just take the night train up and avoid the chance of getting stuck halfway up Shap Fell with big ends gone and knocking like a brass band!"

All things accomplished, in endless accelerating pressure, they had boarded the night train late in the summer evening as it pulled into Melford station from the south. All farewells and breaking of ties in friendship had been a painful process that morning, and the previous day. There had been a number of parties given by farming and business friends of the family. Surprising how folk felt their leaving so acutely, it seemed to Fraser. Jack and Marcia had come up specially on the last day, to make their goodbyes. Words had been difficult for everyone. Jack's very last words, along with his rough clasp to all of them, had raised a smile:

"Yew know, Alec and Mary, if it h'ant bin for all yew Scotch buggersh keepin' ush to rightsh theesh pasht yearsh, well, bluggy 'ell, we'ld h'all bin in th' bluggy shoup, mark my wordsh!" Jack took a last firm grip of Alec Baird's hand, clapped him on the shoulder, and added, "Yewm for off then, Alec? Sheein' that you beggarsh up theer 'ave shold ush all your good cowsh, yew'll be shettin'-to to breed h'up shum more, I do believe! Shee an' mek the prishe reashonable!"

The two men said no more, only tight grins between them. Jack swung round to Jean, with more instructions:

"Now, my gel, shee yew an' shtick in that college ash youm h'attending; your folksh h'ere wantsh the besht for yew, and you've shown a lot of young misshesh round thish part h'ow to work h'at what you've a mind for."

This last bit made Marcia Harris widen her eyes in brief disbelief at what her husband was saying, and she turned only slightly to Mary, pursing her lips wryly. This flicker of exchange Fraser saw and knew precisely what promoted it. When Marcia had broken from a silent embrace and tears with his mother, she had turned to Fraser, taken both his shoulders in warm hands, looked at him gently but seriously and said:

"You'll be a man shortly. Think back on all of us here at the farm. We shall miss you, you and your father, always up to some nonsense, both of you. The men are right downed at you leaving us, you know that? Eleanor wouldn't, er, couldn't come up. But if you were to write to her, she would be ever so pleased if you did so. Tell her about all the new things that you'll be seeing and doing at your new home. Tell her some of your stories from going along with your father; that will make her laugh. You will do that, for her, Fraser, promise me?"

He nodded, the tears that he had determined not to permit getting in the way, escaping from his eyelids, down his throat, trickling down his cheeks, drat them.

The Harrises had come up the lane in the trap, with the same mare, dependable old Dance, that had come up with a load of logs on that very first day that they had moved into The Leys. All those years back now.

Jack stood up, reins in his fingers, Marcia's shoulder tucked into his chest.

"Hoo up, then, Dancesh! Now, yew folksh, yew'll be shertain of a bed, the whole dang lot of yew, when yew comesh a-vishiting, jusht yew tek h'olt on that!"

Jack looked to the mare, clicking to her with his admirable gushing tongue. Holding tightly to his shoulder, Marcia waved her other hand and arm slowly to the Bairds in the sunlight, as the mare and trap wheeled and clopped briskly down the lane. Fraser turned away, a tearing pain in his chest; that'll be the last time that I go down the lane to the farm and all the men. He felt a large stout root being torn up from its nourishing bed in the ground. Damn! How daft it was for him to think it would have been there forever.

For Fraser, the train journey northwards through the summer night en route for Aberdeen proved to be a steady succession of mind-nourishing sights, sounds and smells. He was pleased that his mother and father had chosen not to take two sleeper compartments for them all; they had somehow managed to arrange themselves for sleeping, dozing or sitting and reading, with reasonable comfort, and the ten shilling note Fraser had seen his father passing to the ticket inspector shortly after they boarded the train had ensured that their previously reserved seats would not be questioned by other passengers needing a single apparently unused seat or seats. The affable ticket man had returned with a 'Reserved Compartment' sign, which he had stuck on the sliding door.

They sorted out suitcases and small stuff to give support for feet and legs, which together with a couple of rugs and rolled up coats seemed to be enough for those who wanted or needed to sleep, and very soon after pulling away from Melford and then Crewe, Mary Baird read briefly for a short while but then put down both book and cigarette, and arranged things for reasonable comfort and was quite quickly asleep, or appeared to be so. His sister Jean seemed to be reading but was clearly not all that engrossed by what she was skimming through in desultory fashion, Fraser noted. She was absorbed, looking up only as stations and signal boxes flicked past in a clatter of points and empty platforms.

Fraser sat opposite his father. They occupied the two corner seats next to the corridor windows. Shortly before slowing down for passage through Crewe Junction, Fraser responded to the silent nod of his father's head to join him in the corridor.

"Interesting stuff, isn't it, Fraser? Just about every dashed thing that comes out of Scotland by rail comes racketing through here at Crewe in all hours of the day and night, mostly the latter, in fact."

As he spoke, the train shuddered as it braked and then picked up momentum again, pulling powerfully through a web of gleaming points and interlaced rails that spread out in a vast network for acres on either side of the line they were on. The polished steel rails snaked through below innumerable signal gantries, lamps in green, red, and white light delivering visual messages which defeated Fraser's mind in relating them to the multiplicity of rail lines. On the curve to draw into the main line platform, Fraser could see the flank of the locomotive ahead of their carriage, leaning into its long load with every expression of power. It was all very exciting! Yeah, he thought, isn't this what the Froggies would term puissance? That sounded good and somehow adult and worldly, ha!

His father, leaning to the open corridor window beside him, expanded a bit more:

"Fish, grain, seed tatties, cattle and coal, engineering; this is really a major artery for all that comes pouring out of Scotland, and I sometimes wonder if it all mightily exceeds goods traffic going back up the way, bound for where we're all going to be! Anyway, it's your home country that we're heading for now, Fraser! And mine, thank Heavens."

They stood together in companionable ease as the length of the train scrunched itself to a halt, with shouts of "Croouh! Croouh! Crewe Junksh'n!" echoing off steel and glass high above them.

So the night had passed, with clatters of points wrenching the train this way and that, the fierce blow-off from the engine blatting its way through small, deserted stations and branch lines brushed aside as they spun off into the darkness.

Somewhere in the night hours, well past Carlisle, the train had come to a measured, known halt, with odd unintelligible shouts, and then much steady blowing off from not one, but two locomotives, front and rear. His father had joined him at the corridor windows on each side, let down on their leather straps. The station sign BEATTOCK was brilliantly illuminated. A porter passed below them, crying, "Beattock for Moffat! Beattock for Moffat! Alight here for Moffat!"

"They've to put on an extra engine here, to get us up over Beattock Summit. It's about sixteen hundred feet above sea level, and it needs–"

Alec Baird's next words were lost in an immense blast of noise from both locomotives; steam, smoke and ear-ringing whistle, and then a sustained, powerful lunge forwards with rapid exhaust blasts from both engines.

"We're over the Border now, aren't we?" Fraser asked his father.

Woken by the concentration of shouts and motion, Jean came in between them. In a lively parody of something that Fraser vaguely felt he should resent, she assumed a persona of some surprise to both her father and brother:

"Aye, men, ye can get yer kilts on noo, itherwise yon folks up north 'll be takin' ye furr the hated Sassenachs, ye ken!"

Alec Baird burst out laughing, and pulled Jean into him by her shoulders. Fraser said nothing, but could not entirely suppress a tight, controlled smile. Well, my fag-smoking Varsity sister ain't so blooming bad after all, he thought, and then laughed outright himself. They continued in an exchange of wildest caricature of Scots in every conceivable position in society, until Alec pleaded, tears running past his nose, "For pity's sake, dry up, you two. You'll waken your mother."

At this, the door slid open and Mary Baird joined them, stretching and yawning.

"I heard you all, capering about like a load of monkeys! Come on, let's have some of our yesterday's sandwiches and a hot drink, and as for you, Jeannie my dear, bleeding us white up there in St Andrews, if all else fails, I believe that you might do well on the stage!"

Fraser was last to go back into the fug and mess of their compartment as the train picked up speed. Ah, well, he thought, this reverse of, of what were they called, the Highland Clearances? Well, it might turn out not to be so bad after all.

The long train banged on over the Forth Bridge, somehow only barely restrained from showing its full pulling power. The North Sea lay grey and flat and unmoved to the east.

"Sturrling! Sturrling!", "Pairrth, Pairrth. Change for the Noarrth, Aiberdeen and h'Inverness!", "Sto-onehav'n, Sto-onehav'n!" All had come and gone and passed in the cold clear air where the faintest of lightening skies started to creep in with another day.

Cold but only to the extent of keeping his hands deep in his pockets, Fraser got the feeling, looking out at the stone dykes, solid clean-edged farm buildings and trimness of the fields, and then, with eye-stretching clarity, the North Sea, that things agricultural up here were more ordered than back down there in fat old Melford. He felt a stab of remorse at even thinking about everything there in such turncoat terms. His father went out, quietly, to shave; they must be getting close to the end of their long journey through the sleeping shires of Britain, well, most of them. The whole length of the train heeled over in a long triple left, right and then left again curve of the track, juddering as it braked.

"Now, then, young man, you'll see it all take shape any moment. We'll come right in behind Aberdeen Harbour and the fish market, and that is some sight, I can tell you!"

By golly, his father was excited! Ha, ha! and even ho, ho! They started to gather up cases and belongings as the train rumbled over the brilliantly silvered river.

"That has to be the Dee," Fraser muttered to himself. There were glimpses of cobbled alleys, lines of four-wheeled horse wagons backed up to loading bays, an immense set of sheer-legs rearing up somewhere in the harbour.

Now the cries along the station platform were "Ibburdeen! Ibburdeen! H'all change for the noarth!"

Well, this was the noarth, at last!

By the time that they had all assembled outside the station (why was it called the Joint Station?) the entire morning was becoming, to Fraser's senses, a succession of powerful sensations, sounds, smells, voices, potent in the extreme.

It was as though all these immensely solid buildings of great presence had voices, and they were all speaking, seriously welcoming him. The great activity all around them, of brisk two- or three-word exchanges conducted at machine-gun speed between porters, lorry drivers, railway men and postal staff, the clamour of wheeling raucous gulls, linking harbour to the city, the incessant rumble-rumble of iron-clad cart wheels on granite cobbles, the fact that his mother and father were already in cheery conversation with two men in tweeds outside, below the heavy Victorian glassed canopy – God! it all welled up from within his equally animated eagerness to soak up every nuance, every smell and sense, of, well, of glorious rightness. It was a surefire feeling of coming HOME!

One of the two men was picking up their various suitcases and placing them in the boot of a big black Austin saloon.

"We've got breakfast waiting for you, for all of us, across the road," he said, waving a hand, "and then you'll just be spending a night or two, or longer, as it pleases you, at our place for a start. Bess will just not hear of you all putting up in a hotel. So that's that settled, eh, Alec and Mary – fine that!"

Looking across the noisy concourse of the station yard stood the hotel where they were to have breakfast, an impressive crenellated granite front glinting in the strong sun. Down from it, along the harbour front, he noted what was clearly a theatre, and beyond that, an exaggeratedly larger-than-life gold or gilted facsimile shotgun, barrels up, mounted above a shopfront. Great, a gunshop!

He had to communicate this explosion of pleasure at all levels to his father and mother, they having suspected, quite rightly, that this whole business of uprooting was not sitting particularly easily in his deeper mind; they never quite knew what lay behind silence or compliance. Well, he would jolly well tell them right now exactly how he felt!

He turned to his father at the back of the car, demanding his attention for only a few seconds before this breakfast business made telling anyone anything more difficult and public. His mother was busily pointing out things to his sister. This was the moment.

"Father? Listen a moment."

"Aye, Fraser, and what do you think of it all here, eh?"

His father was in patently enormous good humour with himself, with everything. Fraser urgently wanted to break in, not a thing easily accomplished with his father. He did so, with a gusto that surprised all of them preparing to move off.

"You want to know what I think of it, here? I really like it, and… and it's just the bees' knees! It's great!"

The laughter around him was spontaneous. And relieved. A black-backed gull, splay-footed on the ridge of the station canopy, cocked a sardonic yellow iris-ed eye to one side, and extending its open beak low to the roof, croaked a harsh salute to the noisy foreshortened figures below him, and to the grey-blue hills of Don- and Deeside away to the west.

Of course, this day and everything that had preceded it, amd now what was filling up every hour, was of great importance to his father and mother, Fraser acknowledged that. But his sister took him to one side as they arrived at their newly acquainted friends' pleasant family home some miles into the country from the city; she felt that there was a need for her brother to rein in his quite surprising exuberance.

"Look, brother, just don't go rushing at things as though everything is cut and dried for your specific benefit; there's a great deal for our mother and father, for all of us, to sort out, a new home for one thing, right?"

She regarded him with what looked like, well, for her, an equally surprising absence of her usual superiority, Fraser thought.

"Right, right, I was just trying to let them know and see that so far as I was concerned, everything was–"

Jean broke in again:

"There you go again. Look, you know what Mother was always saying to both of us when we were little?"

"Oh. No, what?"

His sister produced it, whatever it was, like a trump card:

"'Where's your manners?'!"

She gave her brother a rough but tolerably affectionate scuffle round the back of his neck.

The small book of shooting and fishing essays faltered and finally collapsed, pages down, upon Fraser's chest in the high-ceilinged bedroom of his parents' friends' home. Through the open window came the strong scent of wallflowers and melodious ruckety-coo of a wood pigeon somewhere in the lime trees round the garden.

As sleep possessed him, Fraser felt it was with the greatest satisfaction that this was, after all, a good way to rediscover a different feeling about what the term "home" meant. It hadn't turned out to be too difficult a day after all. The return to Scotland was working like some sort of a catalyst where his father and mother were concerned; he was beginning to see things about them that he had never appreciated before.

Now at a remove of many hundreds of miles from the his weddedness to the Harris farm and family, from Eleanor with her quiet and growing beauty, from the pressures of high farming at Darsington, from Jack Harris with his all-purpose "Hey! Bluggy 'ell!", from… he stretched languorously and passed into the deeper sleep of a mind now comfortable with the past, to manage as best he could with all that he had learnt there and now to handle whatever lay ahead.

XXXIII

"Look, Fraser, we have to know – you have to know – what it is that you really want to do? This next year or so will be very important in whether we can all, but you particularly, make it happen. You do understand that, don't you?"

They were all sitting round the kitchen table, both of his parents, and his sister. His mother, strangely, had taken this empty moment to get back to the issue on which he, Fraser Baird, had already made his mind up some considerable time back; aye, when about four or five years old, with good old Hedley as his inseparable companion, no less.

The family having taken up the everyday matters of living once again, in Scotland, and, it seemed to Fraser, this having been accomplished with little real disturbance, the matter of his continuing senior schooling had been put quite clearly to him that it would have to go on for another year or two, or whatever it took for him to get what his father called his "Highers". Fraser held a serious mistrust of what all this further studying was going to demand of him. Much more to the point, and with some amazement, he gathered (More like, I have just been bally well told!) that a place had already been set up for him at one of the two apparently suitable schools in the city, but subject to him, Fraser, meeting with the headmaster. His father seemed to believe that this would not prove a stumbling point. Oh, yes?

Well, damn me. More than a few times, his father had kept on about "Needing to have your Highers if you ever want to go through Varsity, get a B.Sc. in agriculture, or whatever else you might take up, you never know what you might need..." and so on, and so on. He was quite clear in his own mind: get on with this last bit of schooling, do this matter of the Highers thing as best he could (dash it, he might give them all a surprise or two!), but then push on with working his way with getting experience in everything to do with running a place of his own. That was the proper way to do it: be good at all the jobs, so that when it came to him giving the men their orders for the day, they would know damn fine that he could do the job just as well as they could, or maybe even better. The same sensible provision of all-round skills would serve equally well for someone else's place, as the farm manager, you never know.

They had waited, his father and him, for only very few seconds in the library next to the college secretary's office, before being led through to the headmaster's study. Fraser's instant impression was one of vigorously channelled authority, and no rather inconsequential suggestions such as had been the way of things at the grammar school. Well, sometimes.

With a wing collar and black tie framing his face with its piercing dark eyes, meticulously trimmed moustache and similarly disciplined eyebrows, Mr Eric Cattanach seemed to have the ability to conduct a searching conversation with only very few words.

"Mr Baird! Back to the calf country? Excellent. Ah, Fraser, Fraser Baird. Good name in the north-east. Have you plans for your years after school? Farming?"

"Yes, sir. It's all that I've ever wanted to do, sir."

As Mr Cattanach shot out key words of enquiry at Fraser, he was at the same time regarding Alec Baird the father, to see if father and son were in common accord. Fraser could tell that this was a sort of finding out if there was one horse in this educational three-horse team pulling in a different direction.

"What we look to achieving here, Fraser Baird, is putting all possible resources of the college into giving each of our scholars the will of knowing how to make his brain tackle anything," said Mr Cattanach, who appeared to have the ability to look at each of them, father and himself, simultaneously, "and here, the success lies with the scholar positively wanting to do that himself. Right?"

How does farming fit in with this man's Great Plan For Life, Fraser speculated? Or more to the point, how will Mr Cattanach fit in with My Great Plan For Life? He had the greatest difficulty in containing a sort of chesty laugh, and turned away to smother it. His father and the head were into a rapid exchange of stuff about him.

"Strongest subjects, English, biology? Sciences, but not maths? Ah, whooping cough, hmm. But, fit now? We can arrange extra tuition for anything needing more depth to it."

There had been the faintest of flickers from his father's left eye, that side of his face furthest way from the light of the tall window looking out over the long drive to the gates and the janitor's black and white wooden office.

He was allotted a place in that year's Fourth year, two school years until the all-important Highers. Well, here we go again.

Cycling down the valley, weaving through the city's early morning traffic, a substantial part of it horse-drawn wagons amongst the trams and country buses, never failed to possess Fraser with a feeling of great vigour: things to be done, actions to be fitted to needs clamouring in his mind. As the sun rose seawards, Fraser's vision of things around him invested the most unlikely of subjects with a gilded halo which made him grin more than a little, knowing full well the true nature of whatever lay behind the morning's beatification.

In the last narrow wynd leading to the heavy iron-work entrance gates, the knots of cycling pupils, some wearing their own kilt or the tartan of the school's founder, would abandon bantering exchanges in fear of the burly school janitor's unerring eye and ear for perpetrators of excess in any form, vocal, sartorial or otherwise. Fraser found that the same Charlie Watt possessed a detailed and accurate inventory of pupils' names and backgrounds. He had accosted Fraser on only his second day's attendance.

"Hey, man, come on over here a minute, but you other lads haud goin'. Your day's work's waiting for you." Charlie pronounced it "waarrk". The "You other lads" did not dare look sideways. "You'll be the new lad from the south? Was your father a scholar here, name of…? Oh, right – Baird. And you'll be, ah, Fraser, Fraser Baird. A country loon, eh? Well, let me put you straight on a wee point or two: when you come in here of a morning, just mak' sure that your shoes are right well cleaned and polished. If ye dinna pay attention, it won't go well with the staff. Or with me. So, you mind my words, and leave the dubby bits of Aberdeenshire where they rightly belong, oot there in the park!"

Fraser's sudden sweep of embarrassment from the janitor's admonition was tempered by Charlie's firm but kindly grasp of his shoulder and a smile, which nonetheless emphasised his command that there would be no mucky shoes on any days following. Phfew!

Being in school, stealing out moments to watch the herring and black-backed gulls squawking and spreading their elegant white wings along the coping of the ancient school wall (Was this great brute of a wall to keep all us lot in over the years, or to keep others out, or what, exactly?), Fraser turned this and other speculations over in his not entirely scholastically occupied mind. There were pressures coming to bear upon his mind and view of the future, never previously experienced at the Melford grammar school; the feeling here was one of work, sheer sustained work, unremitting demands of work towards objectives that all of them in his class had been told had to be fulfilled. This was the inescapable Highers hurdle, the Higher School Leaving Certificate, the passport for any thoughts of Varsity entrance for those that wished it.

Only a few weeks into being one of the college's scholars, Fraser, now one of a small coterie of like-minded boys of country background, along with the rest of the class, was assembled to hear one of the senior staff members, Mr Williamson, tell each one of them what was now expected of each scholar in respect of examination subjects they would sit at the end of the next two school years. ("Yes, Baird, what were you saying about 'Do we get any time for sleeping?' A purely rhetorical comment, I presume? Well, you will get less and less of such luxury. Your brains will expand to fill idle spaces!") Meanwhile, there would be increasingly stiff test exams, they were told. The teacher, not one given to flicking his gown to one side and perching on a desk to let up for a moment in class, had detailed to each of the class, now curiously tense and anxious, exactly what subjects he had been put forward for, and at what level. He came to Fraser on his class list:

"Baird, Fraser? Pay attention. You are going to sit higher English…"

"Ah, that should be a doddle," said Fraser under his breath.

"…higher French…"

"Oh, oh, formidable!"

"…higher chemistry and physics…"

"Oh, bluggy, bluggy 'ell!"

"…and two lowers. One will have to be maths and one other, and, look, Baird, just stop that muttering, you're wasting my time and yours. That group will get you Varsity entrance, given the right amount of–"

"Wurrk!" they all chorused.

"Baird, Leslie? Right, here's your group…"

Fraser sat thinking. Well, I can probably handle the highers ones, but, bugger me, lower maths? It's even worse than it was back down in the mists of Melford. Oh,my, oh,my. The rotten, unbloodygodly algebra enemy sneaks up yet again. And I don't want to do a blasted degree in agribloodyculture!

Mr Williamson was absolutely correct in his estimation of the number of hours of homework per night that would be found necessary to keep on top of their allotted subjects. It was usually three to four, every night. This, Fraser found, left very few hours, within the rhythms of any normal household, for fulfilling his agreement with their farming neighbours to keep the rabbit population in check by any practical means. He found that by shooting, ferreting and snaring through all seasons, he could sell rabbits very profitably indeed to one or two local butchers and game dealers. Four good cleanly killed and paunched rabbits came in at a pound. That would pay for a couple of boxes or fifty shotgun cartridges, so that for the expenditure of say, five or six cartridges, the proceeds would provide a balance of a further forty-five or forty-four cartridges, with corresponding rabbit shot, and the profits were most satisfactory. His Post Office savings account was continuing the very first step towards his own farm, or own place, as they called it up here. Fraser looked at it carefully after every week's sales of rabbits or wood pigeons.

But speaking one morning in the college to his particular friend and companion on other shooting forays, Wilson Watt, Fraser asked him how he was managing to get through all this never-ending load of schoolwork that had to be completed under such a tight schedule.

"Do you honestly think, Wilson, that these damned Highers are going to be of some use in your case?"

"Huh! If you believe that I'm just going to walk into the farm in my old man's place, you don't know him! He'll still be giving the farm men their orders, and me, when I'm middle-aged and when he's about bloody well ninety, so it might be useful to have something that'll get me a job going round selling sheep dip!"

This jocular deflection of his need to find out how the other lads of similar pursuits were handling this homework business did not satisfy Fraser. He had asked around some more of his classmates, to find that whatever they did to make some extra pocket money, the load of homework dictated that it had to be tackled with alacrity, if not great energy, as soon as they got home. Gad, a man's life was hardly his own in this brave land of heather and cattle, forever being spurred on to attainments of dubious relevance.

"Well, Wilson, the only damned way that I can keep myself going on financially through selling rabbits and game, is to rise about four o'clock in the summer months anyway, go up my snare line first, and then shoot my way home and so on, to be in time for breakfast, get the bus in or get on the bike for school."

Wilson grinned and laughed outright. "Yeah, and everyone watches you fall asleep in the first period after dinner. And snoring away like a slack-mouthed idiot in class with a book propped up in front of you!"

Those winter months were something of a trial. On the impulse not to waste an hour, any hour, Fraser had cycled along to their nearest dairy farming neighbour, and asked whether he could do some part-time work in the dairy byres at the weekends.

Mr Andrew Ord, dairy farmer, a small dark man of compact body, used any terms of agreement to anything at all extremely sparingly, as though there had better be a way out, an avenue to renege on whatever might have been understood, but quite wrongly, to have been a definite contract.

Before going up the road to knock on the Ord farmhouse door and seek employment, Fraser had spoken to Charlie Geddes at the shop. Charlie was a young married man, some eight or ten years older than Fraser. He always spoke with him as an equal, and was keenly interested in his, Fraser's, marketing enterprises of rabbits and game.

"So, you took the notion to work weekends in the byre for our friend up the road, Andrew Ord? How did you get on, any luck?"

"Aye, Charlie; he seemed keen enough for me to help in the dairy byre on a Sunday, ten bob an hour."

"Well, that's a start, that you got him to hold to any figure! Let me tell you what everyone round here knows all about Andrew Ord: good farmer but he's a weaselly little bugger, not given to praise and a slavedriver to his regular men. Those that stay with him! Whatever you've settled with him, Fraser, you be ready to stick up for yourself, 'cos he goes through good men like a girning, miserable little Napoleon, and oh, man! Talk about having a short fuse? In his case it's about five seconds flat! Anyway, you stick in, you're a brave man! You're dealing with a close cousin to the Devil!"

Only after he had got this promise of work near at hand settled did it feel to Fraser that it might be good sense to speak to his father on this additional arrow in his quiver of earnings. Alec Baird had looked thoughtful, weighing up all that Fraser had told him.

"Well, if you're happy to put in this extra work, that's fine, but if you get overtired, the most important thing at your stage now is getting really confident about getting through your Highers next year. You can do any dashed thing you want once that's under your belt, but, and do take this in, young man, expending all your energies for Andrew Ord's benefit is not going to help your studies one wee bit. So, take it a week or a day at a time. That man expects his workers to march to the beat of a different drum than just about any other farmer round here. It would be a good idea to speak with your mother about this. Tell her it's just in the nature of an extra bit to top up your savings bank. She'll accept that. I hope!"

The extra bit to top up the savings bank entailed getting up in darkness and the cold in time to be at the farm ready to start milking before 4 a.m., coming back for a good breakfast, and seeing what remained of the day or weekend for work in the garden at home, or shooting game in the short winter's day with Tom, his friend the village policeman. He didn't usually find early rising a difficult assignment, it was just that sleep overcame him as soon as he sat down.

There had been episodes of a salutary nature in school, both Fraser and Wilson, and others found out, when flagrant lack of attention or even a momentary spark of rebellion or whatever, was rewarded by some painful use of the belt or tawse in cases of extreme annoyance to the master or mistress. With certain members of staff, the warning passed on to him as new to the Scottish system was succinct:

"Look Fraser, man, just keep yer heid doon and look industrious, for pity's sake, or you'll be up there, getting the belt."

Gad, should all this heavy stuff really be necessary, at our age and stage, Fraser asked of himself? Ludicrous.

Anyway, by tacit agreement with the other two Bairds in the class, he kept the heid doon and looked industrious, and wonder of wonders, he was beginning to get the confidence of tackling strange and pointless theorems in maths and trig. One of the masters, a farmer's son himself, had helped him immeasurably with his calm, here-are-the-tools-to-do-the-job approach, and it bloody well worked! But in all respects, it seemed that keeping yer heid doon and looking industrious might well apply to a dashed lot of things.

Well, now for Mr Andrew Bonaparte Ord.

XXXIV

"Hey, man! And where in blue buggery have you been until this time? Do you not have a clock of some kind at home?" Andrew Ord was in full attack. "The milk truck's needin' ready to get awa' oot, and you'll be goin' oot bloody quick unless you give Dod a load with last night's milk crates and finish off the big byre yourself! So, get that bike oot o' the road someway and yersel' bloody well moving!"

On one of his early-morning weekends on milking duty at the dairy farm, and biking along to start the milking at a quarter to four along with Dod Willox the dairyman, Fraser had crashed, body and bike, down into an exposed gaping open trench in the road, the warning barrier having blown over to God knows where. The bicycle front wheel and forks were badly buckled, a crank bent, his cheekbone cut and bruised and his overalls torn on the ragged edge of the tarmac. By the time that he limped down into the frosty farm yard, half-carrying his sorely wrecked bicycle, it was half an hour past yoking or starting time.

Like a malevolent dwarf, the thickset farmer launched himself at Fraser, verbally and almost physically. The attack continued, in front of the other men waiting for their orders in the open-fronted cartshed.

"Seeing as you think you can arsy-parsy about with yoking time, you can damned well put in your time lost this morning, scattering muck with Archie oot on the stubbles."

Archie Sutherland wasn't a robust lad, as Fraser had learnt in normal conversation in the course of any field work shared with him. He had left the school at only a few months off thirteen in order to bring in a pay for his mother; the father had just gone off. No maintainance, no money, no bugger all. At a time when good food might have made all the difference to the lad's growth, there had not been money in his mother's impoverished cottar house to provide it. He had been put to farm work, and as orraman, the least skilled and most put-upon of farm workers, one year older than Fraser, had toiled to exhaustion for four years already. Talking at times with Fraser, Archie was not embittered, for a wonder, just exhausted by a way of life for which Fraser could see only too plainly that he, Archie, really had no stamina.

Battering on with scattering the hard, frosted heaps of dung dropped in the field at five-yard intervals, Fraser soon found that he was drawing ahead of Archie, determined of nature though he was. He adopted the practice of saying to Archie, "You go on to your next one. I'll finish out this one, and catch you up. Go on." In this fashion, they worked steadily, covering for each other where the muck heaps were of unequal size.

They were working up two parallel rows of heaps, leaving a wide band of stubbles blackened with broken up lumps of muck behind and on both sides of them. They worked hard, with a steady rhythm that reduced weariness and strained back muscles but allowed no reservoir of staying power. They were getting on with the job, which in Fraser's mind had two components: getting the muck spread, right enough, but also satisfying that vicious creature back at the farmhouse. Coming to the end of those two rows, they straightened up for a moment's survey of the next two to start, and to look towards Jock Stephen ploughing in the next field. Neither of them had taken a piece or scone or a warm drink in a thermos with them; it was common knowledge on this particular place that to do so, and being seen to be stopping for a break, and emperilling the farmer's profits, meant instant dismissal. Or death, the miserable bastard!

At the precise moment of having eased their backs, to turn to the next two rows, Andrew Ord's gleaming black Austin Princess saloon (always washed and polished by any farm man within shouting distance) gently coasted to a halt at the far end of the field. And then stopped.

Archie, without looking at the car, made the observation, "Aye, the mean auld bastard, that's him snicking it oot o' gear again. He disnae like payin' for petrol!" He bent to the muck scattering.

The farmer's wife was a tall woman of statuesque build, given to smart clothes and lots of make-up to enhance what she already possessed, which was impressive. The combination of the big car, Mrs Ord driving, and her husband perched on a cushion beside her had, as Fraser had soon found out, earned the whole equipage the bandied-around title "The Princess and The Puddock", or toad, a treble-barbed cut at all three quantities sitting there at the end of the stubble field. The other men did not dare utter, or snicker aloud at this allegory, anywhere within the farm buildings.

Having done his stint, more than a few times over, to make good his disgraceful timekeeping of the early morning, Fraser went into the cartshed at twelve o'clock to retrieve his damaged bike. The other workers were coming in for their dinner. All were stopped in their tracks by a furious roar from their employer, who was leaning out of an upstairs window.

"Hey! You bloody lot, stand right there or I get down to you!"

302

The sash window was slammed down with a crash. Further uproar inside the farmhouse exploded in the shape of the farmer as a missile, flinging himself past the wrenched open door towards the men, swearing incoherently.

"Christ! The miserable bastard's goin' some today. That door's usually jammed tight shut!" muttered Jock Stephen, tractorman, standing beside Fraser.

"When I put men to scatter dung, that doesn't include time for strolling about lookin' at the fucking countryside, nor to be pricking aboot helping whoever's falling ahin. The two of you idle shargers, you should have more than fifty odd heaps scattered, easy, up to lowsing time. I've seen an old wumman scatter mair than that with a fucking toastin' fork ! What a useless band of idle cunts I have to endure to make this farm pay a pound or twa. Jeezusschristalmighty!"

There was sudden movement above, drawing the mens' eyes. Fraser saw Mrs Ord opening the same sash window, observing the scene below. This was supposed to be payday, important and respectful, not a raging volcano of obscenities. All the men were silent, faces impassive, an immobile barrier to the oaths and spittle flying from the man before them. In a loud, firm voice that Fraser hardly recognised as his own, he spoke to, or rather at their employer.

"Mr Ord, you're quite wrong: Archie and I scattered ninety-two heaps, and you can get someone else to do the byre work. That's it, I'm finished. But I want to tell you something right now: if you have to be continually checking up on how hard we all work for you, I suggest you go and speak with whoever it is face to face, not go creeping about with that idiot great car!"

The farmer choked himself into total congestion. Head down and with both fists clenched, he lurched towards Fraser, and two things happened. The other men, four in all, opened and closed, pulling Fraser and Archie backwards in amongst them, out of immediate reach of violence. In a voice never previously heard by the men, Mrs Ord barked, once, "Andra!" and then stopped directly in front of them, peremptorily elbowing her fulminating husband to one side, causing him to stumble and almost fall. From amongst her handful of pay envelopes, she thrust one out to Fraser and another to Archie. Her face was starkly white and set against the gash of lipstick on her tightly closed lips. Turning away, fiercely proud of his stand, Fraser wondered, she's quite a good-looking woman, what in heaven's name is she doing married to an obnoxious monster like that? God knows.

Unseen behind his firmly set lips and face, Fraser felt a tight clench of quivering stomach muscles, his heart pumping with a solid pulse, and a cold fury that anyone so, so obnoxious and foul-mouthed, could vent their ignorance and total ill-will upon him, but more to the point, upon poor, ill-nourished

I Like to Walk in This Field

Archie, for whom taking all the swearing and degradation had to be a part of staying in his job, any damned job. Anyway, he was fiercely steadfast that he, Fraser, had seen fit to stand up to the odious, foul-mouthed Andrew Ord. Well, another useful bit of experience to be slotted in for future reference, should another foul tempered potential employer present himself in some respect or another. But, as Fraser spoke to himself, loudly, "I reckon I can spot your kind of foulness at a couple of gunshots' distance now, ha!"

He shouldered his badly buckled bicycle and set off out of the yard for the long walk home.

XXXV

Drawing a heavy, conclusive line below the last question of that morning's Highers examination paper, Fraser exhaled a long release of concentration and contained tension. He knew that he couldn't have improved on the past two hours' input. Mr McWilliam had said that they were free to go once each of them had finished, and by golly, Fraser reiterated in his mind, I have several very pressing things needing attention, number one being the driving test at half past eleven. The very last exam paper had fitted in most helpfully, aye man!

In the really warm late May sunshine, he strode steadily down the avenue and out of college, past Charlie Watt in his janitor's black and white gate office, receiving a cheerful nod of acceptance. Charlie now looked upon "his" scholars of the Fifth and Sixth years with a more kindly eye. Wonder of wonders! Anyway. just keep going, he muttered to himself, and if you ask of me "Where are you making for, young man?" I shall strike him dumb with my casual "Oh, just off to sit my driving test, Charlie – er, Mr Watt!" That was number one on today's list.

The instructor, with whom he had done three brushing-up lessons, after school of course, had ventured, "Right, listen to me. Don't get all sorts of smart ideas. You've done a fair bit of tractor driving, I know that, and you say that you've practised reversing with your father's car. Does he know that you're doing this? No? Well, I'm putting you in for the actual test this time next week, the sooner the better. At this stage, if you don't get on with the test quickly, lads like you get over-confident and young girls go off the boil."

The actual test and subsequent Highway Code questions did not take all that long. He passed.

"Right, my man, let's get on with number two now, come along, come along there!"

This parody of some awfully decent and over-confident young man about town, uttered loudly outside the driving licence office, caused a startled shopper to swerve around him in some anxiety as to what this lad's number two might be, for heaven's sake! The gunsmith's shop and work premises lay off the main thoroughfare, down a narrow cobbled street, more like a lane or a wynd from a

305

different time. The proprietor, with whom Fraser had set up an easy relationship in the course of buying cartridges, purse nets and so forth, was a one or two steps removed relation on his father's side. Jack Harper had given the old hammer gun passed on to Fraser by a friend of his father, a careful overhaul at no charge, other than to point out, showing Fraser the proof marks, that it was proved for black powder only. He held Fraser's attention on this matter:

"Just you heed this, do not go pushing heavy stuff like Maximums through this gun of yours, Damascus barrels and all. Come to me for a decent gun as soon as you can afford it, or preferably before. If, and this is wholly unpredictable, mind you, if you do use a heavy load, you'll stand a good chance of losing a few fingers, or even an eye or a piece out of your face."

"Yes, Mr Harper, I do heed you and I've read all about this risk in the shooting magazines."

"Well, just you mind what I'm telling; nitro powder in old barrels can blow your head off!"

In the shop, with all its wonderful smells of gun oil, boxes of new cartridges and split cane rods in rows, Fraser picked up, at last, his new .22 BSA bolt action rifle, on which he had placed a deposit some weeks previously. The village constable had come round with the awaited firearm certificate, and having quizzed Fraser as to his intended use of the weapon, cheerfully enjoined him to "See and shoot as many o' the wee beggars as ye possibly can; they're a right plague on the land."

Mr Harper handed over the firearm certificate and ammunition.

"Fraser, my lad, here's two hundred rounds, and I'm giving you a bonus of fifty rounds free – to make up for all the ones that you miss! All clean head shots, I suppose?"

"That'll be right, once I get it zeroed – big difference in price from the butcher!"

Fraser grinned, even before leaving the shop with his new rifle – this has the feeling of being a really great day!

With the rifle in its slip on his shoulder and clean, buff driving licence in his pocket, Fraser instructed himself sternly, "OK, my friend, next stop in the kitting-out process!" and set off for a shop of modest frontage, not all that far in walking distance from both the gunshop and the college. The black and gilt sign declared: 'Hamish Morison, Gents Tailor & Kiltmaker. Est. 1886.'

For a variety of reasons, not all that sharp in his mind, but perhaps triggered by having noticed a really fine-looking Harris Tweed jacket carrying a 'SALE' label in the window, he had decided to really launch out and buy himself a good jacket, provided that the actual price was sensible, of course. Well, it would only make good sense to have such an item for, for good occasions, he supposed, whatever they might turn out to be. It had better do him for a lot of years ahead, at that price.

He had frequently heard friends and acquaintances recounting how they had "Got something off for cash." The jacket in a bluey-green tweed, was exciting to his fingers and sense of smell; it had been in that sale display earlier in the spring, and Fraser felt the difficulty of suppressing his broad smile of sheer pleasure! He would have a go at this cash business.

"How about you, we, I mean, rounding it off for cash, Mr Morison?"

He nearly added "sir", but sensed that would make him something of a supplicant, not the wordly fellow that he needed to appear on this fine May morning. The tailor looked at him speculatively over his half-lens spectacles. With a profound sigh, he asked:

"You wouldn't happen to be one of those canny fellows from away up in the mountains of Dee or Don, by any chance?"

He accepted the ten pounds in single pound notes from Fraser and wrapped the jacket in flat, neatly squared-off folds.

"Now, you know where we are. Make sure you come back here for anything else you might need. That jacket will serve you for a lifetime." Mr Morison paused, looking at him in a sort of measuring manner. "You know that we make kilts and kilt jackets here?"

Fraser shook his head.

"Well, we do and be sure to come to me if you've a mind to have a kilt in your own tartan. Very fine kilts they are, too."

He shook Fraser's hand in a firm, man-to-man fashion. Well, damn me, the cash thing fairly worked!

Fraser knew that it would be prudent to retrace his steps back into college, although there was no real exam pressure upon them in his class; members of staff were now, surprisingly, inclined to draw out their scholars on their plans and prospects for their respective futures.

With the jacket flat in its parcel, rifle and slip on his shoulder, but most important of the lot, his full driving licence safely in his wallet, Fraser smiled contentedly, passing Charlie with a respectful nod.

"Afternoon, Mr Watt." No more, no less. Hah! A pretty good way to round off his eighteenth birthday morning!

Listening to his good friend Wilson Watt telling his physics master of the problems of a family farm, and few hopes of succession thereto, Fraser idly ran through the events of that morning again. The driving test had been something of a close affair.

The early morning traffic had thinned considerably; country buses with shoppers and scholars long since discharged, carters with their flat wagons dispersed with loads from harbour and hauliers' depots, fish lorries sluicing out salty trails well on their way southwards. Trams whined and sang their song of steel on steel, unhurried.

"Right, you've driven this car before; you'll know where everything is, correct? Drive down to the harbour, turn left and then take the second street to your left, stop halfway up, switch off and then start again. Remember your hand signals. Drive on."

The interior of the car, a green Morris Ten, was comfortable, smelling of warm leather in the sun. OK, stop and start on a hill, steepest street in the whole bally place! Well, we should manage that, I believe, Mr Examiner.

The car was easy and responsive.

They went through a number of simple manoeuvres. The examiner said little other than directions and "Drive on" after each procedure.

"I'm going to give you an emergency stop anywhere along our route. Be ready."

Rolling gently down the main thoroughfare in third gear, the atmosphere was warm, not unfriendly; things were going fairly well. There was a zebra-striped pedestrian crossing ahead. Fraser scanned carefully for likely mothers with prams. At that same moment, at high alert for anything that the examiner might spring upon him, Fraser suddenly knew from the smallest of signs that the selfsame driving examiner sitting beside him had fallen asleep in the car's gentle warmth, clipboard slipping from his limp fingers. Jesus. He had to find an opening out of the traffic, pull in and park, and switch off. And wait.

The woman on the pavement to his left was looking and speaking forcefully to another woman beyond her, hands and arms and everything going like a windmill, but suddenly she flung her arm and shopping bag out towards the zebra crossing. She spun round and strode out on to the black and white stripes of the crossing in one head-down lunge.

Fraser stamped the clutch and brake to the floor and wrenched up the handbrake with an arm of iron. You idiot bloody woman! Three things happened in close sequence, with attendant sounds. The tyres locked and yelped, the sleeping examiner shot forward against the dashboard and windscreen, uttering a half-formed "Hey! Look out. Oh, my God!", and the woman sprawled right across the car bonnet, glaring, outraged, at Fraser, the examiner, the L-plate, the everything.

They both sat, motionless, enclosed in a strange capsule where any sounds came from a distance. From where Fraser sat, he was clear in his mind that while the overhang of the front bumper might be over the edge of the stripes on the road, the front wheels were certainly not – the very first signal to him from the flailing shopping bag had seen to that.

The woman was in furious defence of her outraged territory at the front of the car, pummelling the bonnet with one fist, swinging the bag with the other. It came round fast in an arc and belted her, hard, on the side of her head. Adding to the outrage, her hat was shot violently sideways, together with the gingerish toupee below it. Both hung at a drunken angle.

An onlooker on the pavement had seen the whole episode and burst out with a high neighing laugh, which immediately injected an element of comic opera into the woman's confrontation of only a few seconds. She pulled herself upright, grabbing hat, wig and bag, and marched off into passers-by on the far pavement. They had hardly stopped, unsure of what was entertaining the few who had seen it all.

The examiner leant forward, retrieved his clipboard and very quietly, looking straight ahead, instructed Fraser, "Drive on. First left and back to my office and park there."

Equally quietly, Fraser moved off, the pedestrian crossing receding in his rear-view mirror, and that of the examiner. He parked the car as directed, thinking that's the driving test down de mighty ribbah. Damn and blast. He was sick inside with disappointment in his own quite adequate skills. Had he reacted fast enough? It churned around in a loop of replay upon replay.

After he had switched off the engine they both sat in a silence which spread out around them. The examiner was writing, briefly, on a form. Oh. And oh, again. Drat the idiot blasted bloody creature with her idiot blasted wig.

"Take this form. You'll get your licence in the office. Your emergency stop was, uh, impressive. We shall both remember it."

Whilst there was the faintest flicker of a suppessed smile, he thought, Fraser was equally sensitive to the underlying edge of anxiety in the man's voice. Anxiety that this shared happening must now be safely locked away, as a salutary experience that would remain unspoken by either. You bet it would. Let's just hope that nothing gets stirred up by some unknown witness. The examiner could be out of a job. And I would have to sit the whole dratted driving test again.

Yeah, as good old Wilson might have said, "A beezer of a birthday, man!"

The evening's progression in the sitting room was peaceful, conversation between his mother and father desultory, unforced.

"Alec, d'you think that Fraser has any fixed idea as to what he's going to do, now that he's finished with his Highers and everything? He just seems to be going on forever with this shooting and selling rabbits, over and above this drive to be taking on more work, always farm work, of course."

Alec Baird laughed, dropping the newspaper. Somebody's Scottish dance band was playing on the wireless after the Six O'Clock News. He laughed again, in the good humour of something that was indisputable.

"Oh, to be sure, Mary, the most important thing in his mind right now is putting every pound or penny into My-Own-Farm-Fund!"

"Yes, yes, but what about a proper job if he's determined not to go to Varsity and do a degree or something?" She nearly added, "Or something much more civilised." But that was an explosive area in the minds of both father and son, oh dear, yes.

Her husband put down his paper and was in much more serious vein with his reply.

"Look, I've pointed him in the direction of various openings, not all related to farming, but my bet is that he will already be working something out on the lines of taking a job which will give him experience in something he hasn't tried yet. It will be a job that he needs and he wants to do, not just anything that you or I deem less demanding in the long run." He added below his breath, "And whatever that might be, more than likely a continuation of all his farming forebears." Then he continued, audibly, "And as my good friend Doctor Dallas demonstrated on one occasion to Fraser, there have been whole battalions of those, by God."

Mary Baird looked up from darning a huge hole in woollen stockings (where did the old wool actually go to?') "What did you say, dear?"

"Er, nothing that we don't already know about our, your, my tenacious farming antecedents."

"Oh, yes. I suppose so. What's that got to do with Fraser's ideas or great plans, anyway?"

Fraser just happened to catch his mother's last few words as he came through the hall from having dumped his game bag and gun in the kitchen. Well, if they only knew, he had been working out his great plan for some time, and with the back end of the year drawing closer, matters had to be taken in hand, his hands.

From shortly after having dispensed with the bogey of the all-important Highers examinations, he had taken up the advertised vacancy for a general farm worker on a group of family-owned farms twenty miles north of Aberdeen.

They wanted someone who could handle a tractor (and have a licence), be reasonably experienced in most field work and see them through to the finish of harvest. After having cycled the outgoing distance of about twenty-five miles from his folks' place to meet the farmer (one of three brothers, it seemed),and agree on the terms, he had had ample time to mull over the interview on the return bike ride home, same mileage again.

Fraser had spoken in carefully assembled reasoning with his father before going for the interview.

"Father, what I really need experience in is a good place to learn sheep work, so if I do go to the Hill of Leithen farms for this hairsting or harvest job, I just want it as a fill-in job…"

"…and the money!" both he and his father added silently in their respective minds.

"…so, can you help me in finding a really good sheep place?"

"Hmm." His father took time to think this through, recalling his own father's flock of Greyfaced ewes and the tasks to which he had been put, at much the same age of Fraser here.

"A hill flock or low ground. Have you decided which would be best?"

To be honest, Fraser had not given this aspect enough thought. But he recalled having heard Wilson Watt and some other school pals from further up the country speaking about the ways in which the basic sales and income from, say, a hill flock of Blackfaces, could be augmented by careful breeding of more milky types for sale to the low ground flockmasters, and even some good-priced tups or rams. Well, the more he could get to grips with all this, the better. They also spoke, with some feeling, about the murderous ways of gimmers and hoggs coming to lambing for the first time. He knew nothing about all of this, and felt ill-equipped.

"I think that a hill flock would be a good idea, Father. How would I need to set about that?"

"Right. I think that I might know of the very place. Leave it to me for the meantime, and don't go off setting up something by yourself. By the way, these folk at the Hill of Leithen farms are not the easiest to deal with, so just limit yourself to the harvest, and nothing more, right? And, you would be wise to get your National Insurance card paid up to date, before you start there. Buy the stamps with some of your precious rabbit money!"

Gad, he hadn't thought about that; that would entail money going out from his various payments for casual work, surely? This is all going to need careful handling, hmmm.

311

His time of working at Hill of Leithen had been a testing time for him personally as well as just the straightforward day-to-day farm work. The latter had been fairly predictable and even enjoyable, the former anything but.

On a Sunday evening in early August, his father had insisted that they load bicycle, boots, oilskins and the usual bulky work clothing all into the back of the car and get a lift out to the farm. It would give him, as Fraser's father and hopefully, mentor in the ways of farms and farming, a chance to have a word or two between them, before yet another job was put to the test.

Accommodation for the two single men, Fraser and an older lad called Joseph Masson, lay in part of the steading which also embraced the cavernous potato store, a cattle byre gutted of all partitions or trevises.

The bothy or chaumer was what some of his mother's friends would have described as "Oh, but terribly basic, Mary." On detailed investigation after his father had wheeled out of the yard, how basic it all was at once became more apparent: a wide double bed of uncertain frame for him and Joseph, as yet un-met, an open hearth for the peats which lay in a loose heap on the cement floor. The man running the farrowing sow unit, whose wife Beth was to provide all meals for the two single men, had shown Fraser the single cold tap and a chipped enamel sink in a corner of the one-time cattle byre.

"Nae very fancy, my lad, but you'll manage a skirp of a wash fine that, eence you have a minute efter eating. You'll get het water wi' the thingey on the fire." He gestured to the large black kettle on a chain above the cold peat ashes.

"Oh, aye, fine bloody that, all right," Fraser thought and said to himself.

Once met, Joseph Masson was OK. He was much occupied with steady courting, and warned Fraser ("Ye hinna got a girl yersel'? No?"), that it was quite frequently in the early hours before he would be back in the bothy. He had warned Fraser about the pigman's wife.

"Look, she's paid to feed us three meals a day, and bring out a piece and a hot drink to the field once we're into the hairst. Well, damned little of that do we see; she's never oot of her bed in the mornings. We have to go in through the kitchen window and make for oorsels, and wash a mug and spoon, with the bloody grieve mannie yammerin' to get started. Lazy slut of a woman, I tell you. And she and Bill the pig baillie get paid plenty to feed us. Bitch."

"So, what about dinner time, do we–?"

"Oh, aye, she has the makings ready then, right enough, but that's only because her man needs his meal. She wouldna cross him, faith ye!"

Once the potato harvesting was under way, running in tandem with the grain crop, occupation of the bothy was shared with a burgeoning rat population; they lived in the straw bales lining the potato store, and came through the countless rat holes to share the warmth of the peat fire on nights when Joseph was at the courting. Bill and Beth did not encourage either single man to linger for a moment beside the fire in their sitting room, in fact neither Joseph nor Fraser had ever seen inside it.

The nights grew markedly colder. Whoever was into the bothy first lit the fire with a dash of diesel oil, and kept it banked up should Joseph say that he would be late getting back in. Some nights, it was nearly four a.m. when he did come banging in. The homegoing rats plopped right across the bed with its lumpy chaff-filled mattress, grey blankets and greasy quilt, having made a meal of the dubbin on his, Fraser's, tackety boots and laces, as he soon found out the first morning, pulling on the leather laces. They had been nibbled into short lengths. Bastards. Joseph always wore wellingtons, except when poshing up, cold water and Brylcreem, to go courting. Even allowing for the time Joseph needed to get to and back from where all this courting activity was going on, Fraser wondered, what in heaven was keeping him up to three and four o'clock in the morning?

Sometimes, before weariness claimed him, Fraser attempted to read an old magazine by the wan light of the single central 60-watt electric light bulb. The original 40-watt job was too dismal; in desperation, he had switched it for one in the pigman's store.

Fraser tolerated the hard living conditions. Sometimes they grew to become quite laughable, but the one thing which enraged him with a sullen burning anger was the deceitful practices of this damned woman Beth, who was supposed to be providing three good meals a day. On some mornings when Joseph and he had to throw up the kitchen sash window, clamber in over the unwashed plates and pots in the sink, raid the cupboards for bread, syrup, milk, cheese, any damned thing to cram into their mouths, Beth would appear as they made for the door, feigning surprise that they were in so much of a hurry that they couldn't wait for a plate of porridge, as yet unmade, of course, and the pot yet to be cleaned: "Oh, did I not clean it last night? Oh, dear."

She would make ineffectual sounds of regret, but with a sleepy loucheness about her full-lipped features, even a kind of smirk if she believed neither of them was looking her way. She was not even dressed on some particulary raw and cold mornings, careless as to how much or how little they might glimpse of her nakedness below a slippery dressing gown thing. It badly needed a good wash, Fraser observed sourly, bumping into Joseph in their haste.

"Aye, man, Fraser, a bloody good ride with her man in the mornings means more to her than a' the four shillings and sixpence meals allowances she rakes in for each of us, by Christ, aye, and supposed to be for three times a day at that."

The harvest wore on, putting all nine or ten men into a thirty or forty-acre field with many tractors and binders fairly got things moving. One of them was an older man, whip-thin and bowed and wiry. He drove a big Oliver 90 tractor, one of the wartime Lend-Lease machines from America. He and Fraser struck up an easy companionship, regardless of their age difference; Jonathan Souter was close to sixty odd, but looked a deal older. As a boy, he had left school aged eleven, and been put to work as an ostler in the stables of the small town where the horses of the Aberdeen to Peterhead coaches were changed and rubbed down. Fraser listened intently, their backs to a stook in the oat stubble when they stopped at three o'clock for their 'fly' or piece, and a drink from a thermos flask. When their uncaring housekeeper Beth failed to appear with something for Joseph and Fraser, the other men said little, but unfailingly gave each a part of their own provender and a half-mug of tea. Fraser noticed that the grieve, or foreman, always found something that called him away when this generosity of spirit amongst the other men took place. One of the older farm workers, Harry McWilliam, who had survived numerous savage actions through the war years with the 6th Battalion, Gordon Highlanders, nudged Fraser as he passed a scone with jam in it to him, and spoke quietly, looking ahead:

"Aye, man, Fraser, no piece again for you and Joseph the day, eh? Well, in the normal way of things, a word wi' the grieve would have sorted that out, but, mark my words, there's more jukery-pakery goin' on atween our grieve and the pig baillie, Bill, and his wife, than you might believe possible, and the more plausible of the twa' where money matters and the boss is concerned, is Big Willie. So, tak' my word, and dinna kick up a shinty, you wunna be with us after the hairst, I take it? All of us ken what's goin' on wi' the meals money, but we're a' married, and we've a hoose and bairns at the school to help hold oor tongues."

Not long after this, with the end of the harvest in sight, two events at the farm left simgular memories of his time at Hill of Leithen.

The gypsies or tinkers suddenly came upon the place to gather the potato crop; it covered well over a hundred and forty acres and weather was a driving force to be worked hard against. After the tinks' last day's work, pulling their bonnets as the Boss handed out wages in cash, with hearty expressions of loyalty and satisfaction, the strawed yard holding young pigs coming on to a hundred pounds or some more pounds liveweight was found to be two short.

The police came; the grieve, pointlessly and with absolutely no perception, Fraser thought, questioned all the men one by one, trying to appear important, and the Boss gave Bill, his faithfull and conniving pig manager, a vicious, scurrilous opinion of his inability to either prevent this sort of brazen theft, or to find out where both pigs had silently walked to, all this in front of the men as they dispersed out of the mucky yard on the Saturday afternoon. One of the men, an extremely able and robust tractorman, took hold of Fraser by the arm and demanded of him, loudly, and in full view and hearing of their employer, the grieve and "Pig" Willie as the men now called him:

"Aye, man, Fraser, just because our Willie's wife here finds it awfu' tiring to rise from her bed to give you lads a decent meal in the morning, there's little need for you an' Joseph to keep your bed warm with a couple of fine, swack piggies oot o' Pig Willie's straw court. She must surely be giving over all those meals allowances to you boys, to keep yon twa piggies fed and fine and quiet. Mighty me, so that's where they've been all this time!"

The guffaws rang round and round the central yard, accompanied by a cacophony of grunts, squeals and high pitched noises indicative of supreme porcine pleasure.

Fraser confessed to his parents that the necessary fifty-mile round trip by bicycle on the weekend, in order to take home dirty clothing and go back with clean things, was a bit of a grind, especially so if overtime at corn crop or potatoes required working a full Saturday, or even on a Sunday. On one occasion he had got totally lost in thick fog on wee roads going nowhere near his destination. He had eventually dropped his bike outside the bothy by only a couple of hours or so before yoking time, in a clammy sweat which owed more to extreme fatigue than temperature. He resolved that he would finish up before the onslaught upon some hundreds of tons of compacted muck that had to be taken out of the cattle and pig courts, much of which, he knew, would have to be torn out in black reeking lumps by men such as himself with graips or muck forks. Aye, tireless and brainless, by God.

On the strangely truncated day when the last few loads of stooks of the late harvest were finally led into the cornyard, Jonathan Souter had asked of Fraser, "Would ye be coming with us to lift the peats?"

"Oh, surely, Jonathan, where's the peat moss? Is it near at hand?"

A rare, infectious grin crept across Jonathan's lips and largely toothless gums.

"Na, na, man. We aye gang with the cattle truck; tak' off the body and fit shelvings. Put on a hoor of a load, build it up like a hoose, an' a'body gangs, a' the men, wives, bairns an' a'. We tak' a rare piece and a bottle or twa tae hand

315

roun' and dinna give a bugger what time we land back hame!"

The night air was already creeping in with a grey haar over the peat moss by the the time that Joseph reversed the cattle truck slowly onto a hard stance where a huge stack of dried peats waited, well built to shed rain. They formed two chains of pairs of hands. Two of the older retired men from the Leithen cottar houses had come to build the load. When all was done to their satisfaction, and they had carefully come down off what was clearly "a hoor of a load", nets were cast over the entire dark mass, wives and bairns squashed into the cab with Joseph, driver, cracking jokes and pleasing the little ones in every way (Fraser grinned at his workmate's great good humour, and the way in which the bairns called him "Jovis"!), the men clambered up, with many hands to swing up the last ones, and they set off, backs to the chill wind, lying in hollows amongst the peats as they swept, swaying, through the night air. They had not gone a mile or two when the singing started! It was beautiful.

The voices started in the truck cab, high, clear, desirable, the women's singing light yet plangent. These were songs, Fraser realised with a shiver, that these women of wholly mixed ages had all learnt at school, or maybe at their mother's knee, or at farm or kirk picnics of a different time. 'Ca' The Yowes Tae The Knowes', 'The Bonny, Bonny Broom', 'The Bonnie Lass Of Fyvie', they swept on in the cold clear moonlight.

And then the men started. There were one or two ditties, not songs of any provenance, some army stuff that quickly died away, and then one man broke into 'Dunbarton's Drums They Are Sae Bonny', followed by the 'Eriskay Love Lilt', and every voice rose in the night air, two men harmonising in deep, bass register and all the women in true voices which soared in the silver light, some of them and their children singing descant. As they went easily from the 'Skye Boat Song' into 'Abide With Me', the tears ran down Fraser's cheeks unchecked, dark blots in the peat dust on his dungarees, with old Jonathan's gnarled fingers dug into his shoulder from behind, but connected heart to heart. These were his friends, his workmates, his kind of folk. He would know them, respect them, give his heart and hand to them forever.

I LIKE TO WALK IN THIS FIELD

XXXVI

This business of sheep farming was something that Fraser had not yet managed to become personally involved in. As such, it was an area of not-knowing that was a profound and growing irritation. This had to be attended to, now that that wearisome circus of farm men versus their employer at Hill of Leithen had slipped into the store of experiences gained, some of them, as he was beginning to appreciate, not wholly concerned with farming.

And so, this back-end, with frost and haar starting to lie heavy in the valley at home, and partridges creaking away in the stubbles as they jugged down in their tightly circled laagers, he determined to get on with doing something about a shepherding job. He would ambush his father at a time when he, Fraser, could pin him down as to names and places, before any more time was lost in these fill-in farm jobs which he could clearly see were taking him nowhere gainful in the long run.

To the front of their family home, lying towards the sun, the garden that year had thrown up a prodigious mass of growth after the clammy heat which had invested the whole of August and part of September, making the harvest a wearisome task. Neighbours calling from within the village, his sister Jean's Varsity friends, the postie, all had been obliged to push aside delphiniums, asters and Michaelmas daisies, the heavy dew on their stems persisting until midday or later.

"Right, intrepid rabbit retriever." Fraser enjoyed the interested companionship of Tam, collie cross Labrador, as he set-to in cutting back all the dead growth and exposing the greenish mould on the soil to the late afternoon sun. If things dried out a bit, he would get a fire going and gather up leaves, broken stakes from around clumps of summer plants and have a right good clean-up. The prongs of his graip or fork clattered in the autumn stillness. Lifting the heart of the fire to let in air, Fraser heard the familiar sound of his father's car coming up the drive, to which Tam had already responded by trotting with a circling tail to welcome car and driver at the front of the house.

317

"Poor old beggar's getting stiff on that hind leg," Fraser observed. "Too much jumping off the tops of dykes going after wounded rabbits, you stubborn old thing. But you're usually damned right, by God."

Fraser smiled in recalling how many times, after a tense silence amongst crop cover or bracken or whatever, Tam would come back up over the dyke, rabbit in his jaws, so abundantly pleased with himself, with his vital place in this man, dog and gun team that they shared. How can a dog carry a bird or rabbit in its jaws and yet appear to be grinning in canine pleasure at the same time, Fraser asked of himself? They bally well can and do!

"Well, squire, that should let the light in."

Fraser lifted a bundle of matted stems and settled them carefully over the hottest part of the fire. He straightened up, anxious to get on with bigger matters.

"Did you manage to speak with anyone about a job with a hill flock?"

His father's pipe was going now, blue haze marrying easily with thick greasy coils going straight up from the popping, hissing fire. The late afternoon merged into evening, with a noticeable drop in temperature.

"Come with me on Saturday. We'll go and have a word with James Melvin. If you've no other great scheme in the offing that is."

At first, Fraser could learn little from his father's expressionless face. There was just the faintest of lines of an inner amusement about his mouth, Fraser detected. His father had foreseen and, luckily, forestalled Fraser's growing restlessness for instant action. They both smiled. The humorous rondelay had been played to the satisfaction of both, and enjoyed for its adroit timing.

"James Melvin. Who's he?"

"Farms manager at Whitepark. I've done a lot of work for them there. There's a big Angus herd. Anyway, they'll keep you right about sheep. Two flocks; low ground and hill."

His father coughed suddenly and pulled the pipe to one side, his eyes, quite tired and reddened, watering.

"OK, father, but where's Whitepark?"

"Oh, a few miles beyond the fishers' hotel at the Crook Inn. It'll take the best part of the day, maybe we should ask your mother to make us an early lunch, or she might want to come with us. We'll get away before something or somebody hinders us in this great plan to make a shepherd out of you!"

Fraser tackled the fire with sudden, focussed determination. This Mr James Melvin might just be the very person to open up a very important chapter, one that he, Fraser, had been feeling the need of to get started with for some time now. He would have to have this big sweep of sheep work below his belt when it came to telling a worker on his own farm what he wanted done, or better still, demonstrating by doing it himself.

Their long run up the valley was almost by way of being an expedition, Fraser decided; a going-out from amongst familiar and comfortable horizons, towards a specific objective. There was a feeling about it, Fraser further identified, of certain things which he had wanted to happen for long enough. Well, they were going to happen now.

Slipping into side-roads which led away from the river whose waters they had kept sight of for twenty miles or so, the car now brushed past cow parsley, foxgloves and broom. The drystone dykes channelled them upwards, past farmhouses and steadings, tightly gathered clusters of thatched corn rucks in their lined-out ranks, well brushed and bonny and fat under the lazy autumnal sun.

Fraser's observations of range upon range of blue hills and more sudden outlines away to the north and west took more than just a single sweeping glance. Oh, aye, some biggish hills up there, it was more a continuing process of deep absorption. There was a rolling fullness about them and Fraser felt possessed by the need to be on them, actually doing some task or other that would demand daily contact and familiarity in remote places, in all seasons. It was a hunger in him.

His father's arms, shirt sleeves rolled to the elbow, were warmed by the afternoon sun as they drove due west now. Alec Baird maintained a running commentary to and with Fraser; it seemed that there were few farms of which he didn't know their names, the inhabitants' families likewise. They all held a vast store of personal experience for his father.

"You see yon place with the big dam and millwheel, there?" He pointed with a blunt finger. "Down by the larch wood."

"Aye, set into the ground behind. Why do you ask, father?"

"Well, a place like that, it's the easiest thing imaginable to get up on the roof in your stocking-soles. You needed an accomplice to tie the door of the house really tight, then set a good big grassy divot exactly on top of any lum in the chimney head with reek coming out of it. Hah!"

His laugh was explosive and infectious. Laughing uncontrollably, his father choked and the car swerved in a swoop to one side, threatening a Blackface ewe.

"Hey, get over, you great idle thing!"

Fraser laughed outright, knowing instantly that his father had actually done this, seeing the confusion and smoke billowing from windows thrown open, hearing fury and uproar inside a home with the doors tied shut! Their mutual paroxysms took some distance to subside, catching each other's eye in snorting explosions again.

The road ran on ahead without fences, into an ever-increasing sweep of heather, bent grass and roadside whins and junipers. Blackface ewes were stolid, their yellow-irised eyes uninterested. Wind-stretched Scots pines and a few larches existed only in odd clumps, remnants of a bigger plantation or around a farmhouse, seeking shelter themselves from the wind as much as giving any. One such place down off the road drew Fraser's attention. It seemed to have more buildings than a farm, yet curiously lacked stock or crop. He turned to his father, pointing a finger.

"Oh, yon place? Aye, that's the notorious Netherwhinmill. A bit of everything, really: hotel, pub, even some farming of a sort, but damned little of that these past few years, just a drinking hole nowadays." He took one hand off the wheel to point at the window to one side of the plain, weather-washed door. "Aye, there are probably more downright unlawful schemes brought to fruition in that dirty old bar than the rest of rural Aberdeenshire. And that's saying something, young man!"

As the dreich-looking pub-cum-farm slid away behind them, Alec Baird regarded the place with an easy acceptance, unlawful acts and all, which instantly told Fraser that were they to turn in there right now, and his father walk in through the bar door, there would be an equal familiarity with those already in the room, whose Land Rovers, cars and one or two tractors were parked ("discarded" would be a more fitting term, Fraser thought) nose to the broken stone dyke. Soft blue smoke rose straight up from two of the chimneyheads, bluer than the late afternoon sky behind the spruce trees, thin around the place like an old hen's feathers.

His father glanced at him, jabbing back over his shoulder with his pipe stem. "Peat reek. They have their own peat moss, and probably an illicit still somewhere in amongst the place, for when they're snowed in with drift."

Another snorting laugh. The countryside was still and golden. With car windows open, they could hear a curlew wheeping and bubbling not far off the road.

Drawing up on the gravel outside the Melvins' home, the strong glare of granite blinding to their eyes, roses and honeysuckle released scent around them. The hall door out of the white-painted porch stood open, a stag's skull and antlers blind and bleached above the lintel, a vase of flowers in the low window facing the drive. The late summer afternoon seemed to have stopped, to enfold the visitors with a feeling of comfortable, expected welcome. From behind the house came the compound sounds of a tractor and binder at work; exhaust, chattering knife, packing and knotting of finished sheaves quite specific in detail. Fraser knew exactly what was going on.

"Well, young man, is it a land-drive or power-driven binder or what, hmmm?"

The man in baggy plus fours had seemingly popped up from nowhere to question Fraser's familiarity with important things such as types of binders in those first few seconds.

"It's a power-driven one," he said, with no hesitation, but faintly surprised.

"Why do ye say that?" There was an enunciation, a precision, which spoke of origins farther north than Aberdeenshire.

"Because, when the sheaves come, er, keep coming out, or the knife jams or something, you can hear them giving the whole thing a run-through without the tractor moving off. And, at the corners, you can slip the power drive out of gear without having to stop and–"

"Aye, young man, just so, quite so. I ken all aboot that, for Lord's sake! Right, come away in for a cup of tea, along with your father, eh, Alec? I want to have a word with you anyway, about yon heifers up from Stirling."

By a sort of woolly deception of the eye, James Melvin disappeared abruptly into the cool and tranquil hall. There were flowers in copper jugs, a longcase clock counting off the afternoon sedately, a Farmers Weekly lying on a black oak chair beside the telephone.

There was conversation from the sitting room to his left. Fraser hung back from the others, to savour the sense of tranquillity and care. That was it, a loving care, of the assorted pieces of well-used furniture, pictures and prints, even the low stone fireplace set into the rear wall of the hall, blackened stonework softened by an enormous arrangement of foxgloves, delphiniums and ferns.

"Aren't you coming in with everyone else?"

Fraser swung round from looking at the detail in a hand-coloured engraving of salmon fishers on a brawling Highland river, to instantly see at his shoulder the very form and feeling of these rolling hills, fertile valleys and graceful river in the young woman standing right beside him.

She held the laden tray with one arm against her waist, propping open the sitting room door with one foot and leg, slim and silk-clad. Mrs Melvin's voice came to Fraser from a very great distance, it seemed to him.

"Are you? Oh, there you are. Margaret, bring Fraser along in with with you."

Margaret Melvin looked at him steadily, registering the passage of his eyes over her hair, her face, her birthmark. It had possession of more than one half of her face. They regarded each other silently: the growing youth, almost a man in height and stance, the girl who while patently young, was inescapably a woman in all respects of femininity, form and function.

The flow of hair, neckline, shoulders, swell of breasts, curve of waist into hip, thigh and extended leg, spoke to him with precisely the same sweetness and promise as did the hills and haughs and hidden places ranging away behind the Melvins' home in the sunlight.

Part-sentences from the two men and her mother flowed past them in the quiet hall, suspended in sunlight, to fall gently about their feet like flecks of seaweed separated from the mother-strand. Fraser's eyes did not leave her face, or rather her eyes. The constant flare of the birthmark did not seem to matter. If this was a part of Margaret Melvin, he accepted it.

"Hold on, I'll help you."

He held back the white-panelled door to let her straighten and pass, her arm in a fleecy jumper brushing against his chest. She was about the same height as him, possibly slightly taller, and as she passed Fraser was possessed by a surging awareness of everything that he could see about her, from the crown of her inclined head to her neat brown shoes.

The manner in which her figure was indicated and enhanced by what she wore – openwork jumper, smooth worsted skirt, fine stockings and brown court shoes – created a respect, a fulfilment, almost an intuitive sense of what was right for her. For Fraser, this was a wholly new sensation, difficult to both express and yet suppress! It seemed absurd not to be free to show it, sitting opposite Margaret Melvin, with another magnificent gathering of flowers and foliage in the hearth between them,

Fraser registered details of fallen petals with a silent, pointless intensity while the two men chatted easily. Outbursts of laughter complemented short exchanges of conversation on farming topics in which he would normally have been equally interested. Ultimately, though, things would have to come round to on what basis he might be taken on for shepherding work. Or maybe even not.

The two men suited each other, in spite of or maybe because of their dissimilarity. James Melvin was small, compact, a bird-like person, inside his functional attire of baggy tweed suiting, with his shiny nose pointing like that of a hunting stoat, immediately pursuing any word or half-sentence escaping from the main discourse. His brown-rimmed spectacles slipped slightly askew as he made a vigorous shake of his head to show just how poor was the quality of some cattle or other at the Stirling sales.

Fraser's thoughts, wheeling round on everything other than uninteresting Irish heifers, ran on at random. Mated to someone plump and dumpy like Mrs Melvin, how on earth did the pair of them manage to turn out someone so fine and tall as Margaret, sitting right across from him?

His eyes flicked from one to the other of the three adults, returning always to her, to Margaret sitting not more than one good pace away from him, covering his attentions with quite unnecessary movements of his hands, teaplate, cup and saucer, which deceived no one.

Fraser became aware that he was holding an empty plate fractionally after James Melvin noted the same. He had stopped abruptly in the middle of some story feeding his skills as a raconteur, as though caught in the act of doing something frivolous and unsuited to his position.

"Lorna, give this young man something to eat, for heaven's sake. He's too quiet-like to take it himself, or rather, he's too much taken with our Margaret to speak out, I would say!"

Margaret made no response, pouring another cup of tea and passing plates anyway, but Fraser sensed a clamping-down of feelings from within her, in the deliberate extending of the plate of sandwiches and unblinking expression of her eyes as she swung round offering them to him. Lord, of all places to have a birthmark.

"Och, do come away now, Fraser. You've eaten very little, taken with our Margaret or no'. You'll have to do better than that if you're to withstand her father's inquisitions in a moment, for that's why you and your father have come all the road here. Won't he, James dear?"

Lorna Melvin was not unperceptive, noting everything passing between her daughter and the vet's son. She neatly lifted the aura of embarrassment that had congealed around the two young persons, and to relieve them, dropped it around her husband. Her head on one side, she waited for her husband to get on with the more pressing matter of Fraser's wanting to work with sheep, as she understood it. It would be more of his stories, unless she gingered him up.

"James?"

"You've done nothing with sheep before then, I take it? Why d'ye want to come away up here, tell me, hmm?"

James Melvin grappled with spectacles, pipe and tobacco pouch, to their eventual submission, all the while drilling into Fraser's face with his own eyes, nose and fierce jutting chin. Christ, does he want to take out my very brain, and take a look at it? Fraser bristled internally.

The summer's sounds stilled, as did the two women: the softly faded mother, the beautiful birthmarked daughter. His own father's fingers appeared to be fidgeting their way round the bowl of his pipe, but his eyes watched him, unblinking, through the blue smoke from the match. Fraser felt that it would be best to be direct in his response to this tweed-suited farms manager, or whatever he was.

"I don't know a great deal about sheep, Mr Melvin; all my work so far has been amongst cattle. It would be no use if I was to go for a manager's job, and then work up to a place of my own, to be telling the men what to do if I hadn't done it myself."

"All right, young man, great schemes. Is he a good riser in the mornings, Alec?"

Melvin swivelled round to Fraser's father, who smiled faintly into the bowl of his pipe. What the devil was his father going to say now? Fraser felt his stomach muscles quivering.

"Good riser? Good Lord, he's usually shot a bagful of rabbits and the whole parish rudely awake before first light. His mother and I sometimes wonder if he sleeps at all!"

They all laughed immoderately, the picture in their minds of entire households awoken by shots in the dim light, amusing and infuriating and not unknown. Margaret clasped her smooth silken knees and leant backwards, laughing delightedly. Fraser had a moment's gift of low sunlight striking golden thighs below her lifted skirt, and paler shadows beyond.

Lorna Melvin leant forward, concerned. "That's all very well, James, but where would Fraser be staying and what about meals and–?"

"Just let me finish, woman. Now, Fraser, I'm going to put you away up Glen Annacht, as second shepherd to Jock Wyness, and then on as lambing shepherd in the spring. You'll stay with the Wyness family. They'll do you handsomely I don't doubt. You'll have about eight hundred ewes to go to the tup in a month or six weeks, and two hundred of these will be gimmers. If you've not had anything to do with gimmers and their perverse ways, you'll dashed soon find out come lambing time, mark my words!"

Glen Annacht? Fraser moved the name, the ring of it, around in his mind. Where had he seen it? An old county gazetteer or statistical account maybe? He didn't realise that he was being spoken to until Mr Melvin repeated his question.

"You'll be keen to take it on?"

There was now a kindliness in Melvin's question. The asperity had gone, displaced by his apparent satisfaction at Fraser's reasons and not least of all, his energies. He glanced towards his father, receiving an almost imperceptible nod.

"Oh! Er, aye, yes. That would be fine, only when would you be wanting me to make a start?"

"Well, now, the sooner the better, there's aye a lot of preparation to be done and jobs in the pens. How about you make a start immediately before tupping time, First of November, eh, Alec? We'll say seven pounds a week, all board and keep with the Wynesses, kindly folk, and they'll want a strong lad to make a go of things. Are you at all handy with tools, young man?"

Fraser had a sudden urgent wish not to appear cocky or boastful in the eyes of the girl and her mother, both of whom were alert to this exchange behind their removing of tea things and plates.

"Well, my father's pretty good at making things for all the poultry, so I've learnt a good deal from him, including some of his special terms when things haven't fitted in all that exactly!"

James Melvin hooted and rocked back with his knees as Margaret had done so revealingly minutes earlier. Fraser glanced at her, caught in confusion, and annoyed with himself for being that wee bit too familiar, or something. But there was an air of relaxation in the sunlit room, a relief that the testing time was over, and that all parties involved were satisfied for the meantime. Whatever he showed outwardly, though, Fraser felt tumult within. The nature of these feelings and the degree to which they possessed him was wholly unexpected. Margaret Melvin, with her grace and composure, beauty and birthmark, her richness and invitation of woman's being and body, filled his awareness to capacity. She was the embodiment of what he believed, in his sketchy idea of things, a young woman should, could be.

With an abrupt clap of palms to his knees, James Melvin rose out of his chair, where tweed and chintz had formed a comfortable liaison.

"You'll be casting an eye on those Shorthorn-cross heifers we're putting to the bull, Alec? You'll both be staying for a bite afore you go. Lorna, will you be ready for us in about an hour? Now then, Fraser my lad, you'ld be far better employed having a walk round with Margaret here than trailing round ahin us at the cattle. She would enjoy a talk with you, tell you what it's like to be tucked away up here with two aul' fogies like us, eh? On you go, the pair of you!"

He turned to his wife, laying his arm around her shoulders and hugged her in a way that was not perfunctory, but purposeful.

"Come away, then, Alec. You're aye telling me that a vet's time is that valuable!"

325

The rest of his words were smothered in a flurry of doors, dogs' claws scrabbling and a Land Rover being loudly started on the gravel outside. His leaving gave the impression of a gentle tide of peacefulness flowing back over a dishevelled shore.

With the restoration of tranquillity, Fraser's feeling of tension was broken into by Margaret Melvin's speaking to him, with her father's directness, but with a quietness of her own.

"...little to do once father's got you tucked away up in Glen Annacht, but maybe you know your way around here, anyway?"

Her hands lay at peace upon her smooth-skirted thighs.

"No, I don't!"

They both smiled, suddenly, and she laughed when he added, "My rabbit harvesting hasn't got me up this length yet!"

In some ways, Margaret Melvin reflected, this rather gauche young man standing in front of her held a droll yet captivating turn of language, which, given the right kind of topic, might well enthral listeners with his patent enthusiasm. She stood up, a fragrance coming to Fraser, released by the movement and warmth of her body.

"Come on, I'll show you our great garden. Your father did say that you were a keen gardener, if somewhat ferocious in approach!" There was that sudden sly twinkle in her eyes, matched by his own fluttering of excitement that all this was actually happening to him! "Mum and I do most of the flower beds. We get both early and late frosts up here, you know. We'll take a walk up the hill; you get a great look down into the village, and the river, and–"

"And two wee figures down there in tweed suits, looking at 'my beeyootifull Shorthorn-cross heifers'!"

Their shared snorts escaped into gusts of laughter, tears springing into Fraser's eyes, while Margaret, her own eyes wide in surprise at the felicity of his spontaneous mimicry of her father's tones, shook silently in helpless paroxysms. Putting her palm up to steady herself against Fraser's shoulder, with her head and hair hanging in loose fineness, he felt the warmth and firmness of her arm on his own. At once, urgently, he needed to have this little capsule of intensity enfolded in some secret place, along with the rich smell of sun on stubble, the ruckety-cooing of wood pigeons in the sycamore above them. Oh, Margaret!

"Right then, Fraser-Baird-who-never-sleeps, round by Cadger's Brae! I'll show you the village."

She strode off with a swing of her skirt and hair, having done a quick change to well-worn flat shoes in the porch, took a path through the tranquil garden (behind her, Fraser grinned in what was becoming a surfeit of sheer unalloyed pleasure, noting some pockets of unplucked weeds) and brushed through a honeysuckle clump into the long narrow field that lay like a crescent between the Melvins' home and the wooded crown of the hill overlooking it.

The narrow cattle and sheep track, dusty and tramped hard into corrugations, angled through the last of the summer's grass in its slanting path uphill. Still following Margaret, he watched her slim feet in the old gardening shoes dealing confidently with stones, bits of dried-out branches and lumps of dried dung.

"Look, there's the river!"

There was pleasure and pride in her voice, as her left arm brushed his shoulder. Fraser stopped abruptly and looked back along the angle of her pointing arm. A small brown mole in the pale crook of her inner elbow, rest of her arm brown. Golden, like......

"Aye, our friendly old Don. Even in spate, it doesn't roar like your Dee! Our river always has time to dauchle here and there, and work a few mills and things, but the Dee, och, it's such a very important and impatient creature, with all your fine folk coming to the salmon fishing. Do you think that each river has its own nature, Fraser?"

He chose not to turn from the view of the Don below them, but spoke in reply, quietly. "Aye, a friendly feel about it, just like the folk who bide aside it."

Keeping her hand and arm outstretched for some long seconds, she turned her face fully towards Fraser, the blemish visible in every hateful encroachment of neck, temple and cheek. Inescapably a part of her, and now for him, it did not detract from all the other deliciously enjoyable aspects of looking at her – as a whole person.

"You could say that, Fraser Baird." Her eyes moved up and down his face, "but things are not always fine and bonny like this. You'll know that full well."

Dropping her arm, she wheeled away uphill, the muscles in her lower back and hips working as she leant forward into the dusty track, making for the roundel of beech, larch and sycamore trees above them.

"There you are, now, that's our village: shop, bank, school, doctor's house and surgery, garage, hidden mansion house and all the usual stuff of Life In The Highlands!"

She was smiling and a gleam of humour came into her eyes as she checked her vigorous stride, to half lie back against the stone dyke encircling the wood. She hooked her elbows backwards on to the cope stones, and hoisted one foot behind her skirt, resting the heel on a projecting stone. She smiled at Fraser, with him, happy for both of them.

I Like to Walk in This Field

Fraser stood a few paces back from her, more than a little bewildered by the battering of feelings now sweeping through him. The beauty of the valley below them, the river seemingly arrested in silvered stillness, the swell and thrust of those blue hills guarding its source, the same swell and thrust of thigh, hip and breast of this comely, contactable – ach, what was the word he was searching for? Approachable? No, but utterly friendly and yet feminine woman whose existence here had been totally unknown to him only a couple of hours ago. Now here he was, trying to find words in this gentle storm, yet feeling that there really was not the slightest need to do so, under the late harvest sun on this hillside.

With a tilt of her head and easy flick of her hand, Margaret beckoned to him with definite purpose. This was her personal and familiar world, and she was, it seemed, prepared to take him into it.

"Come away, now, Fraser, if you're going to know all the places that father would have you know, you'ld better pay attention – down there, not up here!"

She laughed wickedly, pointing to herself with a twirl of hand and finger, but without arch coquetry. Their heads were close together. God! Was this possibly happening to him, in broad, no-nonsense daylight, with folk going about their business all around them?

"Now, that's where I started to the wee school. 'Along the way, up the brae, workaday.' That's just one of Miss Gillies' sayings. She's there yet. Said I was one of her 'right good wee lassies'. She's got a hairy top lip!"

She laughed again, not unkindly.

Fraser felt that he had to possess every little particle of Margaret Melvin's life, to instantly amass a bank account of commonplace things that would be uncommonly wonderful for him to cherish. Being older than he was, she already gone further along a path, further into feelings and experiences which he knew to be there, waiting for him too, but which he had not expected to get the measure of. Until today.

Margaret ran on in swift description and anecdote, as though anxious that no one aspect of her life in this summer-sheltered Highland valley should escape being made quite clear to him. Her outstretched hand moved from one feature to the next, amongst the roofs and gable-ends of the village below them, crofts and steadings solid on modest platforms set back into the hill, a gleam of white paint on dormer windows hidden amongst beech trees lining the dusty road winding into the heart of the village.

"That's where the General stays. You'll have seen his cattle floats and things?" Her eyes were already passing on to some other feature.

"Hold on! The General? General who? What's he doing with cattle floats and things?"

Margaret giggled, more at his ignorance than at the reason, then explained, still laughing, "When he first started up here, Father says that would have been in the late Twenties, he would take on any job at all, and some of his forays in haulage were hilarious, but he had 'General Delivery' painted on his first lorry, and has done so ever since. So that's our valiant General, and Katherine or Kate his wife, very much larger than life, I can assure you. If we stand here long enough, we'll likely hear him roaring and bellowing at something or somebody!"

Above their heads, bees mumbled and tumbled amongst late lime pollen or honeysuckle nectar. Fraser very badly wanted to feel the softness of her hair.

"And that's where Piper Glennie lives; he gives piping and chanter lessons to the youngsters and older men as well. You should hear the roars of him when they muddle up their grace notes. So, tell me, Fraser Baird, is there any music in you, hm?"

Quizzically, her eyes assessed his face and deeper, trying to see just what else was in him, never mind all this rabbit-shooting stuff. She waited for him to produce an answer.

"No, I don't play a thing, although I would really like to have a go at learning the pipes. My mother plays the piano, really well, and we have some great musical nights at Hogmanay and times like that, but when I was put to piano lessons, the teacher lost his temper when I tried to work out a tune by ear, and smashed down the piano lid across my fingers, so that was that."

At this brief picture of brutal crushing of a young person wanting to create music, and with something akin to distress in her face, Margaret swung from one aspect of the pastoral scene to another, her grey skirt flaring and clinging.

"Now, there's our great bank. It has a congregation more faithful than the kirk. The Reverend Mr Buchanan's a poor old soul now. Folk were daft with religion here at one time, Presbyterian, Catholic, even a small but superior straggle of Episcopalians, would you believe! And even a Wee Free placie farther down the glen. Gracious me, two kirks, no, three kirks in a place this size around the turn of the century. How daft can folk get? Maybe puffed up with being different to everyone else, as though it mattered, that would be more like it. Oh, there now, you can just see the golden weathercock on Craigannacht House behind those trees to your left. Father says that there are more storms going on there inside than outside. He aye has an awful struggle meeting the Laird's wishes and his wife's wants. She's an American, his second one – wife,

I mean, not American!"

Suddenly serious and quiet with it, Margaret pushed herself off from the warmth of the lichened dyke and then, her hands loose in her lap, inclined her head to look down upon him from where she stood, to ask him:

"Why on earth do you want to work with sheep and lambing and dipping and all that? Are you really all that keen on farming – especially away up here?"

Distant voices came clearly to them from the scene below. A dog barked twice, and stopped to an unseen command from an open door somewhere.

Fraser stood in front and lower than her, his explanations coming tumbling out – he wanted her to know.

"Ach, well, it's just something that has always been in me, all that I've ever wanted to do, to get into a place of my own. And somewhere like this, if possible."

He flung out an arm as she had done, in similar strength of feeling, swinging in the breadth of his wished-for world, and by so doing hit Margaret hard on her upper arm and shoulder. His distress was instant.

"Oh, Margaret! I'm so clumsy, did I hurt you? Crikey, what a daft thing to do!"

Startled, they both took hurried random paces around each other, but seeing the comical part of it.

"No, Fraser, you silly thing! You were that keen on what you were saying and seeing and going to do, a proper one-man band just for me!"

"Well, I didn't mean to thump you in my enthusiasm for all that you and your parents have here. I don't go behaving and telling everyone like–"

"Like that when showing your appreciation for something by walloping everyone or getting excited, like one of Father's special heifers!"

Their mutual relief showed in quiet smiles at the nature of her simile.

As the light lengthened, there was stir in the village. Children were in cheerful dispute along the waterside, a tractor coughed out blue exhaust reek as two men in dark overalls adjusted it, one (presumably) of the General's cattle floats rattled its way through the square, turning in below trees. There came shouts of greeting or enquiry, doors banging, the rhythms of replies. It was close to their evening mealtime and blue smoke rose from homes scattered through the village.

"Margaret, what are your plans for things, things that you want to do? Are you keen to go to University or train away from home, or what?"

She turned, for she had been only just in front of his shoulder in their easy companionship down the track. They halted some paces short of the honeysuckle dyke round the Melvins' garden.

"No, I've no plans, really, not at the moment. I don't fit in with some courses if they're set at a higher level of schooling, but never mind, the Domestic Science course at the college was quite worthwhile. Father, well, both of them, wanted me to take it. One way or another, it'll come in quite useful, no doubt!"

Her fingers (brown, too, Fraser noted) plucked spent flower heads from a lupin's spine, but her level regard of him from below dark eyelashes gave an unmistakeable statement of what she saw would be the more likely pathway for her in years to come. The quiet resignation in her words sank into Fraser's immediate grasp of her vision of what lay ahead for her life, in a bitter, burning pain.

"Come away in for your tea, the two of you. We've waited for you to come back."

Lorna Melvin's voice, kindly, welcoming, bade both of them turn, but Margaret put out a hand, to clasp Fraser by his wrist.

"Like you, Fraser, I have thoughts and wishes which I don't just share with anyone who comes in from outside of the glen. I would really want you to know, and to remember, that whatever you may come to think on our humdrum way of life up here, I always like to walk in this field..."

She calmly laid her arm and hand along Fraser's shoulders, and turned by her in a last look of all that lay around and behind them, he realised that her statement meant something inexpressibly vital in both of them.

With infinite simplicity, she said, "This wee wander has been a good thing for both of us, Fraser," and held the gate open for him behind her.

There was little talk between Fraser and his father on the road home. The engine's hum varied little for climb or descent. There was an almost febrile luminosity about the trees, the quiet farm buidings, even the spent grass in the long-shadowed fields. Everything that they passed on the road home was gilded with a light richer, more dramatic than that of midday. They hardly needed speech. Eyes noted anything of mutual interest with minimal movement, minds stood down, but returned to the events of the afternoon.

His eyelids drooping from the combined effects of the ample evening meal, warm sun and whisky the colour of dreams, Alec Baird glanced sideways at Fraser and reflected, I'll bet he'll have damn near total recall of everything that we've passed on the way up to Whitepark and along our way home now.

Fraser was watching but not seeing. Changing his grip on the wheel, Alec cut the dusty corner fine at Findlay's Mill, the water black in the mill dam where it lay, untouched by the slanting sun. Unspoken, his own thoughts embraced all that had taken place at James Melvin's place. Well, girl or no girl, hundreds of ewes or few ewes, he'll be asking me about every dashed thing back there for the rest of the week. But, he's got his heart's desire about a job with a hill flock, never mind heart's desire of a different nature as well. It'll be hard going for him, up there with Jock Wyness, after the turn of the year. We shall see.

Lodged in Fraser's mind was this group, a picture viewed within a gilded frame, the evening sun low behind the lime trees in the Melvins' garden. James Melvin and his wife Lorna within that precise distance to each other of a comfortable unquestioned marriage bond, each taking the bodily presence of the other as much for granted as the hills behind them. And, slightly apart, their daughter Margaret, fulfilling every desirable aspect of hospitality for visitors to her parents' small world. And in her acceptance of Fraser's need to follow for a certain time, that way of Highland life, readily showing him all those unchangeable prides and prejudices of that small farming community which by her own assessment, were equally certainly going to restrict her chances of escape from it.

He badly wanted to become a part of this enclosed village with its hills and farms, while she harboured the need to leave it. Margaret from Whitepark, Fraser realised, with all of her dark beauty and her birthmark, would always be a girl, a woman, a person apart from others in her own mind. And in his.

XXXVII

Fraser's bond given to James Melvin, Farms Manager at Whitepark, had been that he would get himself up to Glen Annacht and the Wynesses about a month after the tups or rams had been in amongst the total head of Blackface ewes from the first week of November and then on into the short days of December. There were a lot of jobs to be tackled before the turn of the year, Mr Melvin had made clear. He would be paid six pounds per week until lambing started. It would then rise to seven pounds a week, all bed and board found. His home for all practical purposes, would be at Tornaquhil, at the head of the glen, living in with the Wyness family.

Going up to Glen Annacht in his father's car, with all his heavy work-clothing and other stuff stowed in the boot, seemed both familiar and yet strange to Fraser. James Melvin had telephoned the night before to report that the weather had closed in with a wintry vengeance; the Whitepark road out of Roughford was briefly open only for the width of one vehicle. The County Council snowplough had been out working all that night, but that many stretches well-known to his father were filling in as fast as they were ploughed out. And all this wintry weather had only come into the glen still within the first few days of November, with folk still at ease with getting the harvest safely in.

His mother had not been able, or willing, more like, to grasp the fact that he was going to be away from home on a permanent basis now, with no biking home at weekends and so forth. Fraser cast back in his mind to those very long exhausting cycle runs to and from the arable place way out in Buchan; gad, that had been a test of endurance, in all respects. That bloody lazy slut of a woman, the outright theft by the tinks of the two pigs! He burst out laughing.

His father looking across at him quizzically, guessing, "Past events, Fraser, eh?"

There was no telephone away up at the head of the glen, the nearest one being five or six miles distant in the village. So his fond mama would have to accept that, as she would the fact that he was to all intents and purposes, master of his own destiny so far as home comforts were concerned now, and no running home for this that and the next thing, clean clothes and all that.

As the car started to move out from the house, her parting injunction had not been unfamiliar:

"Now, whatever you do away up there, don't work too hard. It's so silly, and only for someone else's benefit after all. But you're getting so pig-headed about anything that I try to tell you, you're probably not listening anyway. I do wish you'ld go on and do something else, other than this farming business. D'you heed me?"

Slipping the car's clutch to accommodate this delivery from Fraser's mother, Alec Baird's features were impassive. Fraser's exasperation coiled and turned upon itself, like an animal seeking the smallest crevice of escape from a trap, to enlarge and burst free.

"Mother, this is a job, a steady employment, not a, a sort of filling-in thing like a blooming student! I'll be writing or give you a ring when I'm able, all right?"

"Well, be sure to thank the Wynesses for looking after you, and let us know if there's anything you want sent up. Just let someone else do the hard work, remember?"

Fraser felt impatience and worse seething inside him. Yes, Mama, no Mama, the last blooming word Mama! Come on, Father, let's get going, or we'll be stuck here all day! He ground his teeth, not altogether silently, as his father turned right onto the main road, heading west.

They came to a stop in deep snow, a hundred yards or so up the winding Glen Annacht road out of the centre of Whitepark. His father reversed steadily back to the open mouth of a large dark peat shed and turned there. The black trunk, his father's old army one from the 1914–1918 War (William Jardine & Co., Military Outfitters, Edinburgh), his game bag bulging with spare oilskins and tackety boots, were set down out of the snow heaped up on the roadside stone dyke. More snow was drifting steadily in from the north-west, from the direction of Glen Annacht itself. From his cheekbones and hands, Fraser felt certain that the temperature was dropping steadily.

"Dinna concern yersel', Alec," John Sutherland, alias the General, assured him loudly in the stiflingly hot kitchen. All his cattle floats and lorries were off the roads in the continuing conditions, he informed Alec and Fraser.

"We'll have him and a' his stuff up to the Wynesses afore nightfall. We'll fairly get up there wi' the auld Major tractor and the hay sledge, nae bother, eh, young man?"

Fraser felt a part of the rich and glorious disorder in the Sutherlands' kitchen as he and his father were noisily made welcome by the General and his buxom, bustling wife Katherine, or Kate.

"Get the Glendronach oot for the vet., Kate, that's the one he aye favours!

And will you be for a dram, then, my loon, Fraser is it? No? Well, try a wee shottie of this ginger wine. We'll both be needing a heat-up in a minute or twa; it's fair dinging on oot there." He nodded at the kitchen window.

With a tumbler of whisky the colour of an evening sun held comfortably on his knee, Alec Baird was chatting easily with this larger-than-life couple, who, Fraser decided after only a brief assessment, were not only at the centre of everything that went on in the village of Whitepark, but also seemed to be archivists of just about every activity in the glens, radiating from it like spokes of a cartwheel.

Fraser perceived that his father was clearly esteemed as a visitor by the Sutherlands. As a local farmer's son who had gone to the Veterinary College in Edinburgh before and after serving in the 1914–1918 war, mind you, and now here he was taking his own lad to make a start in the job of herding up the glen; some use, that! The General and Kate would bask afterwards in the telling of reflected importance of someone who had the college learning and the way of telling folk what to do, with an ailing beast or anything. And here he was taking a dram in their kitchen, with the snow whirling past the window. The tumblers of both men were extended, almost absentmindedly, for Kate to top up.

Within a tightly closed-off division of his mind, into which nourishment and hope had trickled throughout the long snowy run up to Whitepark, Fraser was acutely aware of the fact that Margaret Melvin was at this very moment probably only a few hundred yards separated from him; she in her parents' home overlooking the village, he having to listen to the two men and their hearty, interminable stories. What small tasks would she be choosing to do while the snow whirled and gathered outside? Would there be the slightest opportunity to make contact with her, through some errand or other taking him down to the village, ostensibly to speak with her father? Get settled in with the Wynesses first, that's the best thing. One thing's certain; of course, both the Melvins, and daughter Margaret will be well aware that I'm up here now, no distance from them at this moment. Come to that, the whole dashed village will know that too! He smiled faintly. The two stout-bodied men were still at it, ploughing more furrows of bygone local happenings.

"You'll mind when Mack Middleton was banker at Roughford, Alec? He could fairly size up a body, or cut some ignorant cratur down to size, for that matter! He once hauled up the young laird about his manner of speaking to folk in the Bank, aye, and in shops and ither places as well!"

The two men pursued a rambling and riotous exchange:

"...and yon time the insurance mannie came a' the way oot frae Aberdeen to peer at the horse-shoe marks across the bonnet of Sandy Glashan's auld Austin car – aye, for the second time, for Godsake!"

They all laughed outright at that, and his father rose to go, making his farewells to the Sutherlands with goodwill and a lot of noise.

Fraser felt decidedly strange not to be going with him, along familiar roads home. Giving Fraser a rough shake of his shoulder and a half-admonitory, half-jocular "Now, pick up all that you can, including those great tackety boots of yours!" he was gone, with a drubbing of the car tyres on the snow. The sound was quickly muffled by the large flakes that had been steadily sifting down throughout their time in the warmth and heat of the Sutherlands' kitchen. It lay evenly over the house roofs, stone dykes and trees in the centre of the village, with no sound, unmarked by foot or vehicle of any nature.

The General turned his boots and bodily bulk round carefully in the creeping chill of late afternoon, regarding Fraser with a dispassionate but not unfriendly eye.

"Weel, then, young man, we'd best be makin' tracks for your highland home, otherwise you'll be biding here with us aul' fogies. Come awa' with me. Where did you say you put your stuff down?"

He hawked, gathered and spat into the snow, with the aim and delivery of a practised rifle shot. Fraser was impressed.

The manner in which they tackled the hill road up out of Whitepark was something of an eye-opener to Fraser and hugely invigorating. The Fordsdon Major tractor was cranked up and exploded into roaring combustion deep in the Sutherlands' cavernous peat shed, filling the building with thick blue fumes.

"Give yon bit of wire ablow the manifold a good pull. Aye, that's it, the very thing!"

The tractor settled into a harsh crackle of contained power. Fraser was impressed not only with the twin sets of retractable spade lugs bolted on to the bright orange rear wheels' centres, but equally by the massive, smiddy-made steel box bolted on below the radiator, heaped with heavy drag chains, some fifty-six pound weights and "Some useless auld lumps of scrap, ye ken; it keeps the auld bitch from rearing up, you see. She does that, whiles."

Solidly bolted to the rear of the tractor was a Hesford winch, battered and welded and scarred by its history of battles with trees, boulders and other supposedly immovable objects. Fraser grinned – this was getting more robust and wildly enlivening by the minute!

While the General backed the tractor out on the road, which climbed steeply between walls of packed snow, Fraser was waved to pick up the drawbar of a massively constructed sledge, longer than a field gate, with narrow shelvings and bolsters slotted into the heavy beams along each side. As the drawbar hung heavy in his hands, Fraser suddenly knew the tackiness before fiery pain, of metal freezing to palm and fingers. The drawbar pin thudded solidly into the snow beside his foot from the General's mittened hand. Fraser rattled it into the clevis quickly with a final kick from his wellington boot as the pain dug deeply into his hands.

"Come awa' into the hoose, man. We'll have a quick word with the wife afore we gang up yonder. That stuff of yours'll nae gang very far or we pick it up. D'ye tak' yer tea fine and strong like me, then?"

He rumbled along in front of Fraser, a bulky bear of a man: woollen tammy on the back of his head, red bale twine cinched round an amalgam of two old jackets with greasy frayed cuffs, and a police tunic, with trousers and dungarees stuffed into immense wellington boots. Taking both hands to the door knob and the sneck, the General gave the whole door a forceful wrench, coupled with a kick that would have felled an obdurate horse, and Fraser felt the sudden warmth and kitchen smells penetrate all through his face and body.

"Weel, now, it's Fraser isn't it? Aye, so see you tak' a right good piece. It'll tak' a whilie afore we get up to the Wynesses, but they'll fairly mak' ye welcome, whatever the journey."

Very strong hot tea was noisily inhaled with gusty appreciation. The General's beaked nose filled the mug as he ate, spoke and drank at the same time. Unbelievably thick potato scones were buttered and passed to Fraser by Mrs Sutherland, with a spoonful of bramble jelly plopped in the middle. The three of them were companionably silent. Fraser regarded old, fly-speckled photographs of kilted men in full Highland dress, some with bagpipes under their left arms, tractors of various vintage, men and pairs of horses at ploughing matches, moustachioed men wearing wide, flat caps tilted to one side, more men with proud boots poised on curling stones, ferns at their elbow, and a Blackface ram looking thoroughly bored, front hooves carefully planted onto an artfully disguised (Well, not quite. Fraser grinned slightly.) molehill or hummock. The ever-so-slightly uphill stance was supposed to convey vigour and virility or something, the tup looked as though he'd done all this pushing and posing before, but just wanted a quiet life.

They set off with sustained staccato barking from the revved-up Fordson Major, and Mrs Sutherland's forceful "We'll see you afore the turn of the year, Fraser. Be sure to give us a look-in, you're aye welcome here!" ringing in his ears. Her husband had already settled the black metal trunk, suitcase and game bag amongst bales of hay and six long bags of flaked maize on the sledge.

"Right, come on, then, my loon; we'd best mak' a start, afore the storm closes in again."

Their journey up the winding glen road as yet unknown to Fraser, unfolded into scenes of dramatic interest, albeit under an ominous and leaden night sky. Everything about them was in infinite, precise detail of black and white. Fraser and the General somehow found the exact pitch of voice which permitted their exchange of words over the tractor's blare of noise which, in steady second gear, was considerable. In this gear, the General had the throttle yanked out to nearly full stretch as they clawed, swooped and skied between overhanging wreaths of snow. Deliberately setting the steering so that the front wheel and tyre on one side carved out a spray of fresh snow for the rear tyres and attached lugs to bite into, he explained matters to Fraser, perched to one side behind his shoulder.

"This is damn near the only way that she'll tak' a hold gaun up here. The road's as sairly polished and skity she'ld be offering tae tak' off, man. Gey dangerous, that sort of caper."

He gave the steering wheel another forceful quarter turn, chuckled, coughed and spat, quite assured of his mastery in all matters male.

The sledge hissed along, riding easily on its massive burnished steel runners. Standing high on the drawbar, Fraser could see down into the valley to their left, the hill road with odd yellow-lit windows in the farms or crofts ahead of them. The road made no attempt to pursue a specific contour line, but crawled down into tight bends, angled itself sharply between stone bridge parapets, uncoiling to the occasional level stretch with grazings on the lower side, cropping fields clinging to the flank above them. You'ld never get anything pulled up out of those fields on the low side, Fraser knew. He leant forward to catch the General's next delivery of interest.

"You see yon place at the waterside? Same family there for abeen twa hunner' years. You'll be meeting them. Very fine folk. Desperate place in a time of drift, grows a good-like crop in a half-decent year. That's the old militairy road doon there."

He gave a wave of his mittened hand, black with oil and grease.

From the radiator gauge bolted on below the steering column, Fraser saw that the engine was well heated up, maintained by the old piece of binder canvas tied across the front of the tractor. The engine barking vigorously, they climbed up in the gully with snow walls to a point where Fraser, from his stance behind the General on the bucking drawbar, could see ahead down into a sort of meeting place for road, river and bridge, and by ducking his head down out of the vibrating cab, could see just how far and high they had climbed from the clustered houses of Whitepark behind them. Each place that they had passed, with the exhaust blatting back off steadings and gable-ends, was slightly different from the next place along. Peats spilling out from an open shed, snow battered hard and treacherous in the yard, muck and dung staining yellow in the snow. The blue reek of burning peats lay close about farmhouses, as soft and harmless as a dream, yet pungent.

Speaking with rough clarity above the roar of the throttled-down engine, as they skidded and took hold in slithering down to the bridge, the General waved a fist at the dark buildings capped with snow in the folds of the glen to their left, about a mile or more distant. "That's where we're makin' for, your new home! And a gey snowy brute she can be at times, by God!"

Fraser jogged his elbow.

"Is this hay and maize for the Wynesses? How often do you have to make a run up here? Can they not get it all in earlier in the year?"

John Sutherland twisted round, face expressionless.

"Ach, weel, it's aye a wee jobbie for me when there's damned little else a body can be doin'. This aul' thing is aye the better of a richt good heat-up whiles, and I'm something the same!"

He laughed and coughed explosively, and pulled out the throttle by a few more notches, to take the tractor into some deeper snow and hold back the momentum of the whole assembly. Fraser could feel that the sledge had, by its own considerable free-running weight, been pushing the tractor on. The big tyres were alternately slipping, biting and even making the smallest flicker of attempted movement in reverse, the most dangerous and lethal sign of tractors being pushed or pulled from behind. In conditions such as these, Fraser was entirely happy to have the General doing the driving.

With a barked "Haud on, noo!" they swung left and then right over a high-crested bridge, crossing a water that reflected both silver and black, with snow-capped stones reaching out to each other with fingers of ice. Two hundred yards further on, a wall held a small square of lamplight. It was now very, very cold indeed, with rime thick inside the cab, as well as all over the tractor cab.

Having crossed the trestle and plank bridge, the diagonal battens scoured clear of snow, and with the sledge crabbing sideways, the General took the bend away from the river at high throttle, seemingly heading straight for the hill face in front of them. With a sudden swing to the left and up a short incline, they burst into the yard at Tornaquhil with a roar; dogs barking, buildings holding the high exhaust note and throwing it back at them, figures hurrying, dark against the blowing snow, ewes rising to look from behind the barn.

Fraser stepped down stiffly from the drawbar, the vibration still weakening his lower legs, head and neck tingling, the exhaust drumming in his head. He looked about him, trying to gauge where might be in order for whatever was going to be handled first, conscious of folk looking at him – at least three, no four – two of them young-ish lads of about eleven or maybe twelve.

The General wiped his brow and face generously with a mittened hand, fingers red and swollen.

"Here's your new 'herd, then. Jock just dinna give him a' the abuse that ye hand oot tae me, whiles!"

What an incredibly brown, almost mahogany-hued face this Jock Wyness had! He looked like a being strangely transplanted from a cantonment somewhere high amongst the Swiss Alps.

"You'll be Fraser, then, Fraser Baird. The vet's son, aye?"

At once there came to Fraser the awareness that this must be a difficult and uncertain occasion for the Wyness family, as well as for himself. Making a friendly response, which he had seen his father put forth countless times, Fraser tried to put them at some measure of ease with the same particular blend of warmth and jocular disclaimer.

"That's right, Mr Wyness, and I ken dashed little about sheep, but I could see on the way up that you've some size of handling here. Do these two lads help you at all, or do they just caper about?"

They all laughed, in spite of one of "these two lads" instantly scowling darkly. Mrs Wyness, eager but shy, or maybe the other way about, made to shake his hand, then would have quickly withdrawn, had not Fraser suddenly remembered the parcel of fresh fish that his mother had insisted on buying for him to "take up to that poor Mrs Wyness, all that distance from a good fish shop". "At a distance from any damned shop, more like," he had added at the time.

"Here's something to start off with, Mrs Wyness. It must have been a gey long while since you had the chance of fresh fish."

She nodded, in surprise and pleasure, and Fraser quickly added, not really knowing where he found the words to dispel the faintest hint of patronage, "But dinna get the notion that I do this sort of thing all the while; I'm a much better eater than I am a shopper!"

As he had hoped in that second, the last remark made against himself (intense cold must sharpen the brain, he believed), brought more laughter, and the General was patently diverted by this opening largesse of fish and play on words, wheezing and rumbling mightily, fingers and mittens busily wiping his eyes this time. All this sort of banter, Fraser now knew, flew totally in the face of the stolid refusal, prevalent amongst working folk through much of the north-east, to exhibit any hint of warmth of feeling, even for a moment, unless sorely called for.

They all trooped into the farmhouse and kitchen, Mrs Wyness moving as though to usher him in, but then, in a confusion of arms, hands, legs and eyes, changing her mind, to walk quickly in front of him, half-turning round to begin breathless, unfinished sentences. The lamplight from the kitchen reflected all proceedings on her spectacles. Her rush of words as Fraser stepped into the room made him more than a little uncertain about everything, about his being there even.

"For any sake, Fraser, dinna let our Jock start on about his yowes; that's a' he ever speaks or thinks about. Ye'll be seeing them soon enough. Come away in and meet Granda'. Round to the right now, that's fine!"

With his nose still clenched and stinging from the intense cold outside, the smells of the Tornaquhil kitchen flooded Fraser's nostrils, his sinuses, the very back of his aching head, it seemed: Peats and logs burning, pine kindlers drying, and releasing their resins and oils into the heat of the room, countless wellington boots ranked in front of the Triplex open range, newly baked scones, heavy underwear and shirts drying on the overhead pulley, faint residues of cream and cold damp air from the stone-flagged pantry as they passed the half-open door, the Tilley lamp already hissing brilliantly in the middle of the table, neatly set for their main meal of the day.

The General came rumbling into the kitchen behind their tight procession, speaking to Jock Wyness, who just kept on saying "Aye, aye, man" almost impatiently, Fraser sensed. The big, bear-like figure clapped his hands loudly, giving his summation of matters outside and inside.

"By God, people, that's a ringer of a bluddy frost the nicht, an' no mistake! Ah'll tak' a fly cup with ye, and mebbe a fair-sized dram with it, and syne Ah'll leave a' you sheep fowk tae get on with it. Here's tae ye a'! Hey! You twa lads!" He swung round and boomed back down the length of the passage, "See an' tak' off yon bags of sheep feed an' dinna let them spill – and the bales an' a' when you're at it!"

He swung back to the ring of faces, and backed his rear end to the blaze, grinning at Mrs Wyness' father, who had risen from the fireside, stooped but still a tall man by any account.

"Weel, Donal', man, ye'll not be seeking to venture oot for the hale o' th' lambing noo. Just bide in here and organise a' these swack lads to do your bidding. Slainthe!"

His toast in the Gaelic tongue came out so easily, then the tossing down one half of the deep measure of whisky, a noisy gulp of hot tea, and following that with the last of the golden whisky, letting out a most prodigious belch in conclusion of a needful task well done.

Mrs Wyness turned to Fraser, real concern in her face and voice.

"I just hope that you dinna think that we're all as ill-mannered as this man." She thudded her elbow with force into the General's ribs. "He's an awfu' man, our John Sutherland, eence he gets started. But," she continued, looking up into his big mottled features and smiling warmly "he's aye been a real life-saver for us folk away up here, and that glen road is something that nae any body would care to have a go at! Ach, you'll all be starving, with me going on. Come away, now."

Fraser was just on the point of saying how hungry he really was, when a large, grease-blackened mitten fell on his shoulder, whilst the other seized him by the elbow, and the General lowered his face towards him, woollen tammy at an impossible angle on the back of his head.

"Mind this, noo, we'll no' be lookin' for ye until after the turn of the year, or mebbe efter the lambing's by, but if you're needin' ocht, or get stuck at the wrang end of the glen in a storm, Jock or yersel or whoever, just come awa' in for a meal and a bed. Ye'll be verra welcome, eh, Jock? Mechty, me, if my auld sheddie for the wagons had been a wee thing more commodious, ye could've pitten a' your ewes in there, an' Fraser an' me could've lambed them nae bother. Dash it, that was a verra fine dram. Ah'm for off noo."

And he was out of the warm, stuffy house, humming like a pipe tune as he pulled the compliant tammy down over his ears. They felt the tractor being revved up with a crackle of its exhaust and grinding of low gear as the whole outfit vibrated and drummed its way out of the yard, on the long journey down between icy, glazed drifts and on to Whitepark.

Lacking immediate conversation common to them all in the curiously quietened kitchen, Mrs Wyness, smiling nervously at everyone and anyone, made entirely unnecessary adjustments to the place setting at the table. The layers of different cooking smells came wafting out behind Fraser as he stepped sideways through the kitchen door and into the hall, suitcase in one hand, the bulging old game bag slung over his shoulder.

The only window to the upstairs landing, a skylight, looked out across the burn to a single silver fir on the far bank. Clear white light from the Tilley lamp in the kitchen sliced out across rushes and tussocks along the burnside, with jerky interruptions and lumpy silhouettes of those inside. Fraser could just see where things were upstairs by the reflected snow glare from the land and hills sinking back into the approaching night.

There were two bedrooms, one on either side of the diminutive landing; the skylight through which he had scanned the hill was white-rimmed on the inside, the biting frost was just a thickness of glass away from entering right into the house. As Fraser stepped cautiously across the rag mat on the landing linoleum (Heavens above – was it really purple and green?) there was a sudden escape of voices from the kitchen as someone opened a door below him.

"But he's never had anything to do with sheep or yowes afore. How's he going to be any use to our Dad?"

There was unmistakeable scorn and anger, even contempt, in the young lad's vehement question or rather, demand. Mrs Wyness' tart reply was quick:

"Never mind that kind of talk, you two. Just watch your manners, and you might even learn some–"

The boys' mother's reply was overlaid by a man's tones, querulous, asking:

"So, he came up wi' John Sutherland's tractor? How long is he to be here for, d'ye say? Nan, dash it wumman Ah'm sair needin' ma tea, can ye no'…"

The door was shut with a bang, sounding even more explosive up in his icy bedroom. There was more rise and fall of voices from the kitchen below him. Looking around, Fraser reflected that if sounds came up all that easily, surely some of the kitchen's heat would escape likewise. He grinned faintly in the pale glimmer from outside, standing motionless in the jutting-out window embrasure, a typical feature of all coomb-ceilinged bedrooms in North-East Scotland houses.

Dusk had closed in from the hills surrounding the house and steading. A luminosity came off the snow-sheathed slopes of the steep hill-face across the burn. It was a sort of nocturnal release of that day's light received during scant hours of the working day. Away up on the ridge (two thousand feet, maybe?) there was a jumble of black crags. To define them visually, Fraser had to look to one side, with eyes opened wide, pupils relaxed. Around the angularities of granite black against the snow, there was the slow movement of other, indistinct shapes. They had to be deer.

Clattering sideways down the stairs, he passed an open door to a bathroom off the hall; a clothes horse congested with shirts, socks, underwear, all hanging damply in the middle of the floor. The smells of a much-used, and occasionally cleaned family bathroom, made worse at this time of year by being on the sunless side of the house.

"Come away in, then, Fraser. Am I right with your name? Just sit in and make yourself at home. If you need anything that's no' in front of you, sing out or rax for it!"

Employing the usual Aberdeenshire term for reaching out, with her little rush of words, Nan Wyness half-rose from her seat, then sat down again solidly. She had accepted this business of welcoming an incomer, although the brown and flushed faces of her family swivelling to scrutinise Fraser were ill-at-ease. Yet again, with a muffled exclamation, she rose to give the fire a stirring-up which it did not need. From behind the shoulder of her father's stooped figure rising from the sagging armchair, Nan Wyness nodded in nervous encouragement to Fraser.

"Granda', give Fraser your hand. He's to be here with Jock right through the tupping time, and on into the lambing, and maybe on again for another year or so. And, och, he'll pick up the way of things here in the glen just fine."

The last words she scattered with a rush, hoping that something in them would please her father. The old man gave him a dry and impatient hand, saying nothing, to push past to his accustomed chair at his daughter's left hand at the table. This man, Fraser surmised, was the General's crony, who had been so plaintively complaining about not getting his tea on time. Well, well, some fun and games sure to be in the offing here, if things don't go too well, he decided.

Jock Wyness grinned up at him from the foot of the table, wolfishly, it seemed to Fraser in the Tilley's strong light; eyes crinkled up, almost closed, teeth showing fiercely.

"Sit in, man, and tak' a good meal. It's by your doing that we're having these fine smokies, eh, mother?"

There was mumbled agreement from everyone around the table; they were already eating, plates edged with skin, bones, remnants. Toast from the blazing peats stood steaming on edge amongst scones, pancakes, sliced bread on the scarred board, a tin of syrup, home-made jam, everything.

"Ben! Matt! Less of that capering aboot at the table, d'ye hear? Fraser'll be thinking that the pair of ye have no manners. Now, can ye no' sit at peace, damn it?"

With these words their father grasped the edge of the table and half-rose, scowling at the boys at one moment, turning to Fraser at the next, with eyes crinkled up and that ridiculous gaping grin. One of the boys looked sulky and defiant; the other, Ben, struggled to keep his round red face from bursting into outright laughter. He snorted and fragments of smoked fish flew from his lips all over the table and everyone sitting round it. In a second, they all exploded into gusts of laughter, tears running down Nan Wyness' face and her husband's eyes shut tight as he leant back in his chair and roared like a beast in pain.

In that moment dissolved the tension and animosity of his, Fraser's, entry into the heart of this family, now rendered a moment of utter hilarity. Even the glowering, resentful lad Matt was laughing wildly, imitating his brother's explosive snorts and collapsing in manic cackling, at which they were all set off again.

But Matt was not the father's favourite, Fraser had divined at once. Mrs Wyness darted about, all tension gone, deftly placing boiled eggs for everyone, rattling plates and then sitting down with a gusty relieved sigh and beam of pleasure, in which Fraser felt warmly included.

"You'll surely tak' twa eggs? Breid and loaf in front of you, Fraser. Stick in now." She used the old word for oatcakes, baked on a griddle in front of the open fire. They were broad, three-cornered, salty, delicious.

"So, your father's an auld Deesider, is he? I mind when I started as a young loon at Leyford," said the old man, pronouncing the last syllable as "feurd", "there was a neighbour ca'ed Baird, a gey staunch mannie, he was, too. Would that have been some kind of a kinsman to your father, think ye?" Mrs Wyness' stooped old father was beginning to thaw a wee bit. Fraser was relieved.

By the time that Fraser had gathered more detail from the old man, and his own meagre recall of family branches before the Great War, he could partly satisfy the old shepherd's questioning:

"That would have been my father's second cousin, I think, a Joseph Baird of Nether Slacks."

In his mind, Fraser reeled back to that winter's afternoon with Doctor Dallas and the welcoming Boxalls of the friendly country pub near Melford, with that wonderful employment by the doctor of the concentric layers of an onion to demonstrate where everyone sprang from, where they all fitted in, of a family. That afternoon had been a gift in Fraser's understanding. He smiled inwardly in pleasure.

Fraser kindled to Granda's interest and they pulled their chairs closer, in animated question and answer. As they talked, darkness pressed down upon the glen to enfold Tornaquhil, the croft Auldachourn across the burn, the stark black larches and the restless, hungered deer. The northerly airstream from beyond the Cairngorm mountains dropped, and frost clenched the land and all the snow that lay upon it, in a fist of crushing, creaking intensity.

Lying in bed, knees hunched to his belly, Fraser felt the extreme cold of the night hours invading the dark, unknown corners of this unfamiliar bedroom. The extra blanket handed to him by Mrs Wyness as the family broke up to make for bed had proved a welcome soporific

"Goin' intil a strange bed is aye that caul', Fraser, but I put a stone pig in your bed afore we sat round the fire."

She had grinned at him companionably. The stone hot water bottle had proved a welcome bedfellow. They all seemed very fine folk.

Now, as he felt the dawn coming in with the most minute of sounds, he was putting the rhythms of this isolated farmhouse into some kind of order in his mind. This was to be his home, and what his fond, dratted mother would make of everything up here goodness only knows! At this very moment of the creaking start to the day, how far away was he in miles from Margaret Melvin's fine, sheltered home down in the village? In the way of things common to all farming folk the world over, they, the Melvins, would know that he was up here now with the Wynesses; but would they ever speak of him to Margaret? Or she to them? Did she ever think back to that sunlit, wakening afternoon? He held it to be a precious thing, deeply buried in his sparsely furnished store of things wonderful. Come on, my lad, time to get up.

Smoke coiled down past his window in the bitter cold. He had heard Nan Wyness riddling the ashes with a clattering poker immediately before setting the kindlers going. Three carrion crows were hunched up in the silver fir across the burn from his bedroom window.

Jock was sitting close to the crackling fire, logs blazing and spitting, with his hands cupped round a mug of tea. The shepherd's hair was still in spikes from a pillow's flattening and the heavy stockings half pulled up to meet thick tweed trousers had left uncovered some inches of long woollen drawers extending to his ankles. Jock grinned in silence, nodding at the teapot on the side of the range, and inhaled some more tea, dropping his head and neck to do so, rather than lifting the mug.

"Aach, man, that's better. Help yersel', Fraser, put some bark in a man's belly."

He muttered the last bit more to himself than anyone else, grinning again at Fraser. The kitchen smelled strongly of over-heated pine kindlers, paraffin, methylated spirits for the Tilley lamp and hot, bubbling porridge.

"Come in for your breakfasts in half an hour, you men, an' bring in some mair sticks and peats when you come," came the injunction from Nan Wyness as they passed by the scullery door.

The intense cold made the soles of their wellingtons squeak, clenched their nostrils in crushing pain and encrusted their eyebrows and hair below their caps with the same rime that invested the entire birch wood up behind the steading. Fraser stood slightly behind Jock, waiting for some indications to come to him of what would be useful for him to do. Jock turned to him, speaking quietly but hoarsely out of a corner of his lips, as though it was necessary not to let the subjects of his speaking, the Blackface ewes and tups, hear what he was saying. This is daft, Fraser thought, having difficulty keeping his own face severely without expression.

"This is the main lot of yowes, man. We usually have a ram or tup running with every fifty or three score of yowes, and split them up into aboot a hunner' or so, in different places for seein' what tups are dae'in the maist work. Tricky brutes, these lads; they get favourites, ye see, and jist keep running with the one yowe, which is nae damn use at a'. We'ld best haud on wi' the feeding."

Outside in the clear biting wind, it demanded all of Jock Wyness's two dogs' energies and persistence to keep the ewe flock from overwhelming everything before the rows of troughs were ready. Patch, smooth coated, compact, showing her teeth in furious silent rushes. Moss, of rough coat and flowing circles, shouldering ewes into tumbling reverse with a sudden swirl this way, a headlong impact another way. Any more than a truculent ewe or tup would suddenly be faced with Moss, in a savagely intense jaw-to-the-ground fixation on the animal's very eye, even into her brain, it felt to Fraser. Jock was in full flow of commands, counter-commands, arm and stick beating a tattoo on the packed snow.

"Toast them up, Patch, toast the buggers up! That'll do, that'll DO! Moss, come bye, come bye – lie doon, lie doon! Get oot of that, come awa' tae me – haud awa' back, haud on there!"

Jock was now kicking over the empty troughs with one foot and filling them from a feed sack and shouting to the dogs all in the one breathless spate. Fraser had been so intent upon what the two dogs were doing, most of the time of their own volition, he decided, that he had not immediately acted upon what the shepherd himself was doing. Fraser had the distinct suspicion that he could hear mutterings issued in his direction between the hoarse roars directed this way and that at the dogs. Is the man in a bad temper with me already, he asked himself? He hefted another full bag and ran in the mixture of bruised oats and maize as speedily as he could. Jock nodded to an old fish box some distance from the melee around them.

"That's for the twa tups, Fraser. Gang ower wi' some feed an' they'll follow you, but watch they dinna bowff you aboot the legs, man!"

He did and they did; a working truce was established with difficulty. These old buggers know that I'm different, Fraser muttered to himself, grinning at their bold dark gold and black eyes.

Jock suddenly appeared beside his shoulder, half-speaking, half-shouting, demanding, "Now then, man, have ye ever seen sic' ferocious auld buggers, eh? Ye hinna? Weel, there's days when I'll swear the craturs'll just run ye doon! The ones to look oot for are yon eens that are slow-kind tae come in aboot tae the troughs, or they dinna feed eence they are there. Come oot o' that!"Jock bellowed hoarsely at the smooth-coated bitch Patch. She was slinking round behind the jostling ewes, belly to the tramped snow, with all the look of surprised innocence familiar in any animal, or human, who foments a disturbance and then confidently looks to be credited with suppressing it.

What the devil was Jock going on about now?

"…and the yowes are all up here, that's six hunner' of them, then there's a hunner and seventy gimmers in grassparks at Rhinagaar, an' there's twa hunner stock hoggs tae be wintered; they're a' doon at Waterside, ye ken, then there's a' the tups tae be pitten through their time afore we tak' them oot as weel!"

Ever more and more spilling out from Jock. Mighty me, am I ever going to get the hang of all this? Fraser pulled a wry face at himself.

"We'll not let them lie there, Fraser. Once we have the brak'fast, the twa lads'll hunt them oot the hill as far as they're able. They'll get a pluck where the snaw's aff."

As they passed the open-fronted peat shed, with the tracks of the General's coming and going on the tractor crimped rock-hard in the snow, Fraser recalled the "Aye, and the auld bitch rears up, whiles!" opening to their journey, his first one, up the glen. Jock nodded apologetically, it seemed, at the contents in the dark shed.

"We'd best tak' in some sticks tae the wife; they're fine for a quick blaze."

Fraser hurriedly gathered up some peats into a feed sack, and followed Jock into the kitchen, which was heavy with the smells and aromas of all that was good for appetites and the pleasing of them They all pulled in their chairs across the linoleum to the laden table in the big kitchen, Granda' accepting the split logs and peats for orderly stacking beside the range, then set to his careful task with the shiny, well-used toasting fork, keeping a steady supply of thick slices of toast passing to the table. Some of the slices tasted strongly of paraffin, others had a whang of peat reek; everyone ate of them steadily.

As they consumed all placed before them, Jock Wyness, the two boys Ben and Matt, with Nan Wyness's father preoccupied with toast and firing, Fraser marvelled but did not exactly wonder at the quantities of porridge, creamy milk, fried bacon and eggs, thinking ruefully to the travesty of supposedly being adequately fed by that slut of a woman away out in Buchan. How he and Joseph were perpetually hungered – Christ, what a place that was! Well, my lad, better pack away as much as your belly can decently hold; there's no telling what this day is going to present in unfamiliar tasks.

XXXVIII

On his very first day as a shepherd at Tornaquhil the content of the day was soon made clear by Nan Wyness, hands on hips, asking of her husband, "And what, may I ask, are you lot to be at the day?"

Jock was in the middle of some dramatically needful account of "Yon's a verra special yowe oot there," pointing his spoon coated with congealed egg through the kitchen window with its sashes stuck solid by repeated applications of very thick, very green paint. Jock's growl was as dark as his face, near to mahogany, Fraser decided.

"Ye see yon yowe wi' the brocket face? She's from the Clash, by yon high-priced Beldornie tup at Perth, an' she aye has the best pair o' twins every year, without fail. Noo then!"

Fraser regarded this prodigal mother silently. Well, if she was my ewe, he deliberated, then I'ld have her and any like her away by themselves somewhere, where they could get an extra bite of feed or concentrates or something. And would her or their progeny have this twinning trait in them also? He didn't know enough along this line to avoid displaying ignorance; Jock would surely know. Or would he?

They rose in a great clatter of tacketed boots and swarmed out of the kitchen, the two boys trying to make up for late rising by snatching last great savage bites at the table, cheeks bulging with alternate mouthfuls of porridge, toast and syrup, egg and loud sucking-in of very hot strong tea.

So, Jock did have a plan:

"We'll awa' doon tae th' gimmer flock, Nan, and mebbe have a go at some of these bad feet amongst them, and a tup or two if we get on not too badly."

"Well, that's fine, then, my bold men, but are you to be taking a good piece with you, or are ye to be stopping in bye at the McMillans, or what? You've a long yokin' until dinnertime, mind."

Nan looked at the two boys and their father, already swinging out into the snowy yard, with a forthright kindliness but with a degree of necessary asperity and practicality. Nan was clearly the organiser, marshalling her troops, Fraser reflected.

Then, when they were all striding out for the bridge below the house, came an urgent cry from Nan Wyness, standing out from the doorway:

"Have you got all the footrot stuff in your bag, Jock?"

Jock's jaw dropped, his eyes visibly darkening with an instant annoyance.

"God Almechty! Idle buggers of loons! Awa' back ye go, young Matt, and get the damned stuff, and the cutters! D'ye hear?" he roared, striking at the battered snow with his stick.

"But, Dad," Matt said plaintively, kicking at the snow, "why is it aye me that has to gather up things you hinna mindit aboot? Why shouldn't Ben?"

There was a brief flare-up of hardly contained temper on Jock's part, with a measure of truculence from Matt, neither having good reason in the eyes of the other, and Fraser felt uncomfortable at his being there. Well, maybe this was all part of learning the ways of sheep.

The tension was only exacerbated by Jock's despairing outburst:

"Ach, come on, one of ye, there'll not be a damned thing done afore dinnertime unless one of ye gangs back, now!"

It took over half an hour's steady tramping down the road flanking the Annacht Water, or rather, what could be seen of it in places scoured clean of snow by the wind. They got to the foot of what seemed to be an avenue of old, lichened sycamore trees rising to a line of stone buildings to their left. As they swung in amongst the trees, Fraser spotted the sheep, presumably these gimmers spoken about earlier, in a field largely snow-covered, on the far side of the avenue.

"Are these your gimmers, then, Jock? They must be not this past year's lambs, but from the year afore, and you have tups running with them, is that right?"

Jock's reply was cheery, approving. "Aye, man, the very thing! By the time that they've hin their first lamb, they'll be twa year aul'."

Well, thank God for that, Fraser breathed to himself; the sun has come out to shine upon us again!

Jock was pointing his stick at an upright Blackface gimmer, totally black-headed barring the silhouette of a bell in white on her forehead. "Yon's the best o' the hale jing-bang lot. Ah'll swear. But, man, just look at yon ither; is that no' just the perfect model of a sheep!"

Confused, Fraser looked serious but said nothing.

They wheeled uphill and trudged through between what seemed to Fraser to be an endless row of decrepit farm or estate buildings, more like a deserted hill town than just a long disused steading. Hadn't he seen photographs of places like this, roofs off, on deserted islands, St Kilda?

Jock offered no explanation, so Fraser thought, well, come on, we may as well find out as much as we can about this place. Jock responded immediately, in detail.

"The steading? Ah, weel, at one time this was the greatest place in the hale glen or roun' aboot. Kinchoulie Castle, they ca'ed it. Castle, a mansion hoose, mair like; coach hooses, stables, a rare big mill off the dam up there." He pointed with his stick. "Milling an' bruising oats for cattle, ye ken, a sawmill and a joiner's shop. Then there was the smiddy, the laundry and a host of ither places, all at the heid o' the glen. Fowk tae work the place? Weel, Ah'm led to believe by auld residenters that there was fully twenty-five or thirty estate servants, farm men and staff for the big hoose; that fairly kept the wee schoolie at Ballachmuir gaun wi' bairns!"

Jock laughed, sheep forgotten for a moment, in simple pleasure at having so easily excited Fraser's interest in matters of which he knew absolutely nothing until he, Jock Wyness, had told him in some detail.

Fraser stood, looked but hardly listened, gimmers, hoggs and everything else pushed to one side by his mounting curiosity. Castle? Well, where was the castle? A tall, somehow Italianate clock tower facing across the walled garden and valley beyond, innumerable drives, vistas and walks, but no central residence of any description to be seen. Where? Jock watched him, grinning, impatient to divulge more that only he, not Fraser as an incomer, would know.

"Aye, Ah ken fine what you're thinking: where is the bliddy place? Weel, Ross, they were ca'ed, the family that aiched it, made a big splash time of the Great War, or afore, in fact, the biggin' of a' this." Jock enlarged upon all that they could see with both arms and stick outstretched. "All of what ye see would have been weel on the go afore mebbe even yon war wi' the auld Boers oot in Africa. Syne, the hale bliddy lot o' them went bust in aboot the nineteen twenties. If Ah tell a lie, there was some size o' a redd-up when the hale thing went doon the burn."

Fraser shuffled his feet in his boots, cold as mutton, but this, this was really amazing!

Jock Wyness jabbed at the ground and fouled snow and looked up, eyes wide and staring, in a fashion which Fraser was already getting to know signalled that Jock was preparing to come out with some feat of narrative showmanship, perhaps not entirely supported by fact. Would they ever get round to making a start with whatever was to be inflicted upon the gimmers, the tups or other sheep?

"The wye that Ah've heard tell o't, the hale bliddy ootfit was biggit wi' his money frae een o' the wars, man. Mebbe frae a hale heap o' wars, ye ken, gaun back a while. Masons brocht in in droves, fancy plasterers frae the toun, terrazie flairs frae Italy, a great muckle ballroom. Nae end til it, faith ye!" Jock's eyelids drooped in dramatic significance. "Mebbe no' a' paid for!"

Well, damn me, Fraser thought, this was a dashed sight more interesting than getting stuck into the threatened feet or foot jobs, whatever. Presumably, Jock and the boys would get going soon; it wasn't a day for standing about. But Jock was in full flow. He placed himself directly in front of Fraser, stick and bag getting in a tangle at his feet, and launched into the denouement with relish, so easily having a captive audience for the telling of it.

"Weel, when the crash came," Jock said, his entire face and inclined body animated, his eyes wide and enlarged, "by God, the hale dashed place wis torn doon and awa' in lorries, weeks at a time, man! Aal the fine parks and palings roun' aboot them, a' the fine joiners' shoppies an' doos' doo'cots, a'thing jist wheeched awa' wholesale, or taen doon into pieces. And them that was owed money, they jist gathered up a' bliddy thing they could lay their hands on, aye – even the twa benches frae the curling pond! So, now ye see it, Fraser my lad, there's not a stick nor a slate tae be seen. If there had been any kind of a half-decent bigging wi' a roof to it, we could have gotten a puckle yowes in there come the lambing, faith ye."

Jock stamped the battered snow in triumph at having got through his tale of the toffs' downfall, and stood, mouth open to his gums, waiting for, almost needing, Fraser's response.

"Aye, Jock, quite some affair. Amazing that the Ross family should have put so much into a place like this."

Something lodged in Fraser's brain. The total effacement of the entire fabric of this castle, mansion – well, whatever – had left not the slightest imprint of a family history, of bygone, happier days' events. Surely something of what these people had conceived, constructed and empowered would have rubbed off with small traces, echoes, but in this case, whatever had brought about failure on a grand scale, had left an aura that did not feel good in his bones. Jock had turned away, losing patience with Fraser's moment of reflection.

They set to, all four of them, Jock, his two boys Matt and Ben, and himself, to preparing pens and gates for the gimmer flock, now standing with heads high in suspicion of something out of the normal way of an early winter day, snow or no snow. The three Blackface tups in with them were detached in a sort of stolid observation; they were big, and heavy and prepotently male, above all else, not given to flighty alarum. All in the flock were gripped up to the rails of the pens by Moss's unblinking eye. Now, were they at last going to, as Jock loosely put it, "Have a go at these feet jobs"? Feet jobs? Foot jobs?

With the gimmers and their attendant rams hustled into the pens, Jock's approach consisted of harooshing a score at a time into a long, narrow handling pen, letting them run along one side, spotting the lame or cripple ones, and then catching each one with a leg cleek. It did not take this diving and catching in a great threshing of snow, muck and sodden fleeces, to be repeated more than a very few times for Fraser to stop, chest heaving and arms outstretched to a rail. Might it not have been a better plan that all this necessary and unavoidable handling should have been done before the tups went in? And what about a more controlled method of spotting the ones with bad feet? He wasn't sure how to handle this, or more importantly, how to handle Jock without seeming the complete bumptious amateur at the game. Some bloody game, this, all right!

"Jock? How about running the whole shebang up the shedder race, marking the cripple ones and then working a shedder gate to run all the foot job ones into a wee pen by themselves?"

Jock's response seemed to embrace everything, without specifying anything. He kept saying, "Aye, aye, man," repeatedly, apparently going along with the idea, his mouth and face opening into that now familiar lips-drawn-back sort of facial rictus, nodding vigorously to whatever Fraser was saying to explain a different approach. But still grinning in this fashion, Jock pronounced in a wholly incontestable delivery:

"It's nae use that way o' dae'in'. It wunna wurrk, man."

"Oh? Why's that, then? Have we not got enough pens, or what?"

"Na, na; it wunna work because the shedder's been broken this lang while, an' ye'll nae get they brutes til rin up the damned thing!"

This last bit with almost triumphant defiance of reason.

"Oh. Hmm. Well, now." Fraser's mind came to a complete stop. Clearly, the obstacle lay, not in the intransigence of "they damned gimmers", but in Jock's mind. The two lads nodded in silent support of their father not having anything to do with such a daft idea.

They set to in the catching pens, doing just that again and again and again, Ben spotting and pointing with his father's stick (Matt having faded away somewhere), Fraser catching, holding and upending between his knees, Jock applying the treatment once the foot or cleet had been trimmed of rotten horn, pulpy stinking tissue and impacted muck. Some of the gimmers' individual hooves were a mess of distorted outer horn, concealing multiple, pus-filled cavities. They both cut, pared, trimmed, curetted and whittled away, bent double over jerking, flailing feet and legs.

But the whole laborious enterprise collapsed, literally, Fraser felt, straightening up his aching back, when part of the sheep pens yielded with a splendid cracking of rotten spars, the gimmers having bunched up against the rails in alarm from a sudden lunge of Moss to apprehend a particularly determined escapee from the melee.

So, Fraser thought, repair jobs needing to be done, in order to get other jobs done. Were there any tools, a hammer, a saw, some rails to patch things up, he asked Jock? No, nothing of that nature at hand.

Jock's resolve of the morning to "get on with things" dissolved abruptly:

"Ach, weel, boys, we'ld best make up the road again. We'll get a late dinner frae mother, an' there's aye a puckle things we can be getting on with eence we're fed."

Fraser caught a flicker of irritation in the young lad Ben's face; he was scowling and avoiding Fraser's glance. Of a moment's inspiration, of retrieval of a day's purpose lost, somehow, Fraser suddenly twigged what was important to Jock's younger son, and spoke up:

"Hey, Jock, how about your idea, marking the worst ones that are yet to be done, for tomorrow? Ben knows them, don't you? Save double-handling, eh, Jock?"

Jock grinned suddenly in compliance, and they did just that.

There was a curious sensation of not having put the day, Fraser's very first day at this sheep business, to any good use, but, and all-importantly, Fraser guessed, Jock Wyness's standing as the wise shepherd of the hills had been preserved. In single file, they made back up the glen to home, with little or no conversation. The shrinking day made short work of the fading light and the persistent snow dusted bonnets and work clothing below their faces angled into the wind.

The following morning, there was an impetuous drive swirling around Jock Wyness's movements in his impatient haste to get down to the gimmer flock and make a serious start with, with everything and anything, if even only half-spoken about. Fraser asked of Ben where he could find a hammer, nails and a saw.

"They're in the back of the meal hoose, but dinna tak' Granda's tools, mind; he's the only one that lays hands on them!" Ben warned him. "Ye'll just have tae make do with Father's old bushman saw."

"What about a three-foot rule. Is there one about the place?" Fraser asked, anxious to get kitted out before Jock started rampaging about in the yard.

355

"Well, ye might chance Granda' giving you a wee loan, but only for the day, mind!"

Down the glen they clattered and slipped, Jock allowing Fraser only scant minutes to strip an old gate for rails to mend the shedder and shedding gate. They launched into a crushing system of catching, upending, grabbing sorely infected feet and exercising ruthless surgery with their respective horn-handled knives in order to expose clean, healthy tissue. Jock applied the final treatment to each extended foot, sometimes two on the same animal. In a slim old Camp Coffee bottle, Jock guarded a dark brown, rancid-looking fluid which he termed butter of antimony, with the air of a reverent alchemist.

Using a clipped turkey's wing feather, he jabbed this into the fluid, keeping his eyes and face to one side as he withdrew it, and then brushed the sticky antimony all over and into the diseased and damaged horn. The sheep might well struggle hugely as the acrid fumes arose, causing Fraser's eyes and nose to run mucus copiously, but the coldness and bright sun seemed to mitigate the severity of this primitive agent which was caustic in the extreme. In this fashion, they worked on steadily through all the gimmers, to well past midday – Christ, when are we going to stop for something to eat, for Heaven's sake? Fraser asked of himself, and then perversely thought, I'll not damn well stop until Jock does; keep going, just haud goin'...

It came to the last fill of the catching pen, helped immeasurably by young Ben's adeptness at singling out not only the badly infected ones, but also those with scant signs of incipient lameness, when Fraser felt a distinct unwelcome coldness across his loins, back and legs. The sun was no longer, the hills to the north and west of the abandoned estate buildings were now veiled in whirling flurries of snow.

The very last gimmer to be tackled, upturned between Fraser's legs, its head hanging out below his left elbow, was so thickly plastered with wet snow that he couldn't see if there was that much rank infection in the mal-shaped foot and hooves stuck out in front of his face. Swiping the snow from his eyelashes and cheeks, he clamped the lower limb grimly, cutting into rotten, twisted horn. Someone had been at this one before, Fraser could see.

With a sudden heave and gargled grunt of protest, the gimmer twisted below his arm, the knife blade, already slippery with blood and snow, plunged into the ball of his thumb and the freed leg flailed across his face.

Blood, his blood, flowed down his hand, overalls, leggings, wellington boots, running off face and fingers, clotting on the fleece.

"Come on, Jock, for pity's sake, scau'd the bloody thing!"

Fraser seized the bottle of antimony, thrusting it in front of the shepherd, who was gawping at the mess of blood everywhere. Speechless in open-mouthed surprise, Jock jabbed the feather in with careless haste, the snow now dripping off his face and hands, rendering the bottle difficult to hold firmly. He splashed the fuming solution onto the infected hoof in tangible heat of temper himself.

Feeling the bite of the stuff, the gimmer, a big bulky brute, lunged out in her pain, striking Jock's hand. The contents of the savage bottle jolted out in a liquid arc over Fraser's left hand. The corrosive bite of the fluid ran through his entire body, doubling, redoubling with every few seconds of piercing agony.

"Aaaaagh, you absolute baarstud!" He doubled up in breath-stopping pain. The gimmer flew, to be lost amongst the others.

They moved the gimmers out of the pens quietly, Ben tramping a narrow road for them through mounting hummocks of snow, which covered the muck, blood, crescents of rotten horn, plucks of wool and dark brown hoofprints as quickly as they were impressed.

Fraser stood in the holding pen, his clenched left fist dripping clots of congealing blood into the snow beside his wellington boot and shining and dark across the toecap. The coldness of everything struck into him with alarming potency; it never bothered him normally. This blasted wound needed attention quickly. Oh, aye, away up here at the head of Glen Annacht, in amongst all this clart of muck? He laughed weakly. Well, now, what had Nan Wyness shouted after them yesterday, about going to the McMillans if they hadn't time to wait for a piece and hot thermos?

Jock and Ben came trudging back to him, boots losing purchase in the snow on top of greasy muck. Jock's face showed a kind of rough bravado about Fraser's wound, but his over-dark eyes betrayed the anxiety over this mishap.

"Aye, aye, man. Ye're a'richt then? It could have been waur!"

Fraser's mind, ringing with pain, seethed. Worse? – of course it could have been much, much worse, man. Jock's attempt to brush aside such things as some practical first aid from someone, anyone, struck Fraser as even more ludicrous, but things here needed gingering up into action in some direction; never mind all this belittling humour.

"Oh, aye. Jock. Look, that stuff that you splashed on it; it'll cauterise any damned thing, have no fear, provided it doesn't bloody well burst into flames, for a starter!"

Jock seized the chance to have the laugh that he felt was due, but young Ben had been watching Fraser's attempts to accommodate what must be, by golly, severe pain. He attempted to get his father to see that it could well have been much more serious. A' this standing aboot and laughing, by Christ, man!

"Dad, ye should be thinking aboot what kin' of a bliddy disaster it would have been if yon stupid bitch of a gimmer had smacked the hale bliddy bottle across Fraser's eyes, for God's sake!"

With a sudden flash of assertion, and brushing aside completely Ben's alarm, Jock pulled his cap sharply down across his eyes, canting his dark brown face sideways as though to test the force of the strengthening wind.

"Come away, then, lads. We'll get our fly-cup an' a bite o' something at the forester's hoose, and Robina'll get yon thing sorted at the same time." He unnecessarily pointed his stick at Fraser's gory hand, fingers clenched shut to cover the deep wound.

By the time that they had made their way down the silent one-time carriage drive, it was a tunnel of tormented branches, snow swirling up below their caps and faces. Fraser felt that a grain of foreknowledge would be a reassurance.

"These folk that we're going to, Jock. Do you usually just land up on their step?"

"Oh, Ramsay and Robina? Nae bother, grand folk, aye pleased to have a neighbour in aboot for a blether. We'll get a guid-like fly there, just wait-ye! His folks bide just round the foot of the brae ahin ye." He pointed with his stick. "Where the auld blanket mill was at ae time," he added.

And young Ben looked up from below the frosted cap-brim pulled down over his woollen Balaclava, his round face sorely chapped.

"Aye, but we'll get cake and stuff here!" he said, in straightforward measure of what was more important.

Jock turned to the door, gave the green-painted panel two loud blows with his cleek, cleared his throat with dramatic effect and grinned in cheerful anticipation of what must surely follow. Stooping and bespectacled, the figure opening the door addressed them with feigned severity:

"And what the devil are you lot standing out there for? Do folk have to rise and open the door to you? Come away in, for pity's sake. You should really know better, Jock Wyness!"

They sat around the oval table in the small kitchen of the one-time lodge to the vanished mansion of Kinchoulie. Fraser looked around with an enhanced awareness of the imprints upon this home, firstly from the time of a totally different scale of comforts to be expected in an estate worker's home, and now secondly from the occupation by an ex-RAF bomber pilot and his family, for that was what Ramsay McMillan had been prior to joining the Forestry Commission, according to Jock Wyness's hoarsely muttered intimations just before knocking on their door.

Ramsay's wife Robina was speaking to Fraser, or rather quizzing him in a lively fashion.

"Your father's the vet. We know that from blether-wife Jock here." She gave the shepherd's head a push forward, tousling his damp hair, to which he grinned like a delighted child. "But all this sheep work, is this something which you've not done before? Surely you'ld be better getting into veterinary college like your father? Anyway, never heed me spiering the life out of you; let's get this awful-looking hand of yours seen to. Come away through to the scullery 'til we see what the damage is."

The congealed blood and fibres of wool matted into it from his jacket sleeve presented a gory mess to Robina McMillan. She took a firm stance beside Fraser, holding his arm and hand below the running cold water, easing his fingers open to reveal the wound. The blood began to fall away in large black clots, then ran in fresh rivulets. Fraser was well used to blood from all sorts of farming and country matters, but he suddenly felt light-headed and the voices in the kitchen behind them began to lose volume.

Robina acted with perception and speed.

"Here, hold on to the sink and I'll get a chair. Right, kneel on that, or sit if you can manage to keep your hand over the sink. Are you steady now?"

Fraser nodded, feeling unmanly to have shown such weakness, particularly so in front of this fine, capable woman quite unknown to him until these past few minutes of unutterable pain and weariness.

"Aye, that's fine now – just the cold, and the wound stounding away," he said, making excuses.

Robina looked critically at the gash. The edges had opened; it was deep but not long. Getting any dirt out of it was the main thing. She smiled grimly. Plenty of muck and soss whenever Jock Wyness got going in the sheep pens!

"Right, Fraser my lad, I'm going to have to get this really clean and it will start bleeding again. By rights, the doctor in the village should see this, but it'll heal right enough without stitches, and the blessing is that it wasn't a great long slash up into your wrist. Right, over this towel, and we'll put a really firm dressing on it."

The warmth and concern and deftness of Robina McMillan flowed around Fraser. He yawned, trying to conceal the sudden relief from everything due to her watchfulness, but didn't succeed.

As she tied the crepe bandage firmly around his wrist she winked at him, saying, "Just listen to yon men through there! What blethers they are once they get started! There now, we'll put this arm of yours in a sling, that'll keep the hand up on your chest and keep it from stounding. So, how long are you to be up here in the glen? Have you sisters and brothers or what? Come on through now, and get a hot drink into you. And you haven't told me why you're into all this daft work with Jock, when you should be thinking about veterinary college or something for yourself, hmm?"

The others at the table opened up to have him join them. Jock was in full flow, Ben was crowing in hoarse mirth, his brother Matt had materialised from goodness knows where, knowing where they were ensconced, and a chance of fine sweet things, forbye.

Ramsay, smiling broadly at all this hilarity, noted the firm bandaging and decidedly wan look of this young man come amongst them. Well, his wife was a trained and experienced nurse, and she would have his family history as a bonus, no doubt.

There was companionship and much noise around the table, no one caring about voices raised in laughter, thick steaming broth with tatties in it, and oatcakes heaped up in the middle of the table on a white dishcloth, all this welcome provender on a stormy day being consumed with gusto. Their wellington boots, gloves and jackets gave off rank-smelling steam from around the open hearth, which had a small shield with armorial bearings sculpted into the sandstone of the lintel above the open hearth. They would be of the departed Ross family, Fraser supposed.

In his left hand and arm, there was now a steady, quite deep painful pulse, but it was bearable. He managed to eat using his right hand with a fork or spoon. Robina sat herself down at his right hand, dislodging young Matt.

"Here, you go round a bit 'til I help this poor cratur." She resumed her role of concerned and inquisitive advisor, placing a buttered oatcake and cheese on Fraser's plate. "And how are you going to fare for a girlfriend while you're stuck away up at Tornaquhil, pray? Listen to me, now, Jock Wyness." She took him firmly by the ear. "You'll just have to let this poor laddie down to the village with Ramsay and me and the Land Rover once in a while, or he'll go clean skite with nothing but your sheep nonsense day after day, d'you hear me?"

At the innocent but unforeseen introduction of a "girlfriend" into the conversation, Fraser felt a coil of anxiety in his inner parts, overriding the pain in his hand. Did they know anything of his knowing Margaret Melvin? Of course he would value some time in her company, but the fact that it just didn't fit in and wasn't remotely possible (ha! That was the right term!) and in any case, that was his concern, no-one else's, not even Robina McMaillan's. He held quiet, letting that bit of the conversation slip away unnoticed.

They all laughed at this sally about Jock's obsession; he guffawed, open-mouthed, enjoying the feeling of being accepted as one of this small group whose backgrounds and social levels were all so different from his own. Jock was beginning to feel, after their uneasy start with Fraser, that the coming lambing in the spring, with him helping, might not be such a desperate affair after all. All this silly talk about "the glens being finished" as a way of life, well, just wait or I get my yowes and twin lambs dancing awa' through the grass parks, an' mebbe Fraser'll stay on a good while longer. Jock laughed outright again, in high pleasure at being at the centre of all this, and searched his pockets for cigarettes and matches.

They finished their meal, relaxed and quieter over the last cup of tea – and cake (Ben's eyes gleamed in satisfaction at Fraser). Robina piled the used crockery through in the back kitchen, scene of the dressing station for that ugly wound, happy to have folk and conversation around her. This new lad of Jock's looked as though he might just be one to ginger up our Jock a bit. Goodness knows, Robina reflected, putting cake back in its tin, there were some days when Jock's mind got absolutely stuck over some silly wee thing, and his hands would do less in a day than this Fraser Baird had seemingly pushed them to accomplish this morning, wounded hand or no.

The snow was starting to blow and drift again as they pulled on their gear, soft and heavy from thawing at the fire. There was feed to bag up for the home ewes, Jock reminded everyone, and the two milk cows to let out for a drink before being milked and settled for the night. Chins tucked into wet, scraping collars they all nodded to Ramsay as he bade them, "Haste ye back, you lot. Come back down some night with Nan, Jock. All of you, when it's no' so stormy."

They trudged along in line, lessening the work of making a track. No one talked unnecessarily, taken up with watching their feet and then casting forward to thoughts of whether this weather was going to be with them over the turn of the year, or even after, even on into the lambing.

That would very likely prove the finding-out time for them all, thought Fraser, head down into the scarifying wind, Ben and Matt in single file between him and Jock. Probably a dashed sight more things than just the mechanics of lambing, he smiled grimly. The two dogs tucked themselves in behind Fraser's legs as closely as possible, the dry snow creaking with the deepening imprint of every foot as it passed, but silently filled in at once.

From those first half-dozen episodes of getting-things-sorted-before-the-lambing, Fraser felt fully stretched in an effort to somehow put together the feel of how each person at Tornaquhil was going to fit in with the others once the lambing started. He had to put aside thoughts of getting down the glen, if only for a few hours, to attempt contact with the Melvins, and with Margaret. He knew that she was down there, and her folks in the village, and therefore herself, would have the knowledge of his being up here. It would just have to rest there. He felt a need for a brief time of warmth in her company, nothing more, and didn't attempt to define reasons. Mebbe a chance just before the lambing got going. And what was the weather going to be like then, by God? Who was going to be responsible for this task or that, or were they all just going to muck in together? There took place a number of happenings which could not, by any stretch of imagination, Fraser concluded, be held as likely to recur. With each, Fraser found exposed a hitherto unexpected part of Jock Wyness's skills or knowledge coming into usefulness.

A lightning leap from a common mishap of everyday order, to abrupt cutting off of life, could take place with unstoppable speed. Fraser's first confrontation came about suddenly, and so easily, in its first few minutes.

A mad, and stupid with it, ewe hogg had bolted in escape from Moss's hard-eyed herding, jumped the avenue in two straight-legged bounds, plunged through the level snow blanketing the width of the narrow field beside the river, and in attempting to leap the hidden river in huge bounds across an apparent bridge of snow, had suddenly and silently dropped through the drifts' crust into the water. Below the gaping opening, the water ran deadly cold and black, smoking in its silent lethality.

Glumly surveying the hole, hunched over his stick, Jock nasally pronounced the uselessness of rescue, with almost a casual disinterest, not looking at Fraser or Ben as he did so. Moss should not have gripped up the beast so fiercely.

"Aye, man, damn the chance of yarking the silly brute oot o' that. She'll be jammed up against the water gate." He nodded his head downstream from where they stood. "And bloody weel drooned gin noo. Smothered, more like."

Smothered, drowned or not, Fraser was compulsively sizing up places where the snow-cover would surely not be all that deep. If he was to run down and smash through the wreaths of snow, surely? Jock saw the thought in his eyes and body, and shook his head, superior in long experience.

"Dinna think ye'll ever get at the silly cratur dae'in in that, man. Just one deep hole in the burn an' you'ld never be seen again. It's buggerin' caul' doon there, your heart would just stop. Leave her be, noo."

Daily life and increasing need for this to be done, that to be seen to, always rather late in the doing of it, Fraser felt, threw up even more unlikely and incalculable responses to violence and injury.

But one of the crofts down at the foot of the glen, a poor-like place possessing only a scanty covering of soil overlying glacial debris, had been the scene of a not altogether unforeseen accident.

The fifteen-year-old crofter's lad, a grandson in a sort of sideways fashion (Christ, only a year or so older than Ben or Matt, when you think about it, Fraser turned over in his astonishment), driver of the croft's only tractor, a battered Fordson Major, had been the subject of withering comment around the meal table amongst them all at Tornaquhil.

"Aye, and a right cocky, dangerous devil of a cratur is he, by God! There's nothing he reckons he can do a sight faster than any other body, but one these days, just wait ye!"

Young Jimmy had indeed been close to being crushed in a monumental overturn of the tractor. With throttle yanked out far beyond everyday prudence, the Fordson had swung widely in huge rasping of tyres on ice below snow, the bogey-load of turnips had lashed completely round and past the tractor in that first wide tearing swoop, shearing the drawbar pin with a bang like a gunshot. The tractor's final one rear wheel slew off the scored ice, and the youth was catapulted onto the frozen turnip drills, breaking his teeth, lower jaw, a wrist and one femur and part of his pelvis in three places. Standing in the lodge drive, Ramsay McMillan had seen the entire rapid whirling maelstrom of metal and machine, and ran inside to the telephone, before grabbing the first aid kit and back out again.

In its explosive carom through the fence, dyke and into the burn, the tractor was sheared of its exhaust, steering wheel, fuel tank and one front wheel and both mudguards when it ploughed, belly up, through all the stones, sump and rear axle turned to the sky.

Privately, Fraser marvelled at the dichotomy of folks' outlook at such things: one minute forecasting calumnies of a highly unsavoury certainty for young Jimmy, and any like him, the next day holding forth with a kind of perverse smirking pride that Aye, weel, God sink it, jist the very marrow of his father (or uncle, or whoever), aye up for a caper; just disnae ken when to haud back, the daft cratur! And yet proud for his foolishness, God!

And so the fading year had progressed, not by any measure smoothly; there were always incidents, episodes, things that had not been forseen by any of them away up there at the head of the glen, Ramsay and Robina McMillan included, for they were nearest neighbours.

I Like to Walk in This Field

On the matter of his pay ever coming through or up or something from the estate and farms office outside the village, Fraser had just felt confident that it would either have been allowed to grow as unpaid wages due to weather conditions (but, how did Jock and Nan and family manage, with Granda as well?), or perhaps deposited in the Clydesdale Bank, in his modest account there. Either way, with little need for the actual money, but wanting to find out the situation, Fraser looked for an opportunity to make his way down to the village on foot through all the snow and find out how things were with the Melvin family, even perhaps make time to call at their house, and see... and even chance a few minutes with Margaret, if possible.

How these things got around, apparently without him necessarily speaking openly about it with anyone, Fraser did not know, but Robina McMillan was well aware of his interest and concern for the Melvins' daughter. He had been surprised by her forthright broaching the subject one Sunday morning, he having ploughed his way to their door on a solitary mission to check the overall condition of the gimmers, there having been more snow, and Jock and Granda stating there would be more on the way, by all the signs.

Disturbingly, Robina knew more than he expected about the Melvins' home life, snow or no snow.

"Here's another cup of cocoa for you, my lad, and I'll make up a piece for you. It'll take a while for you to get back up that road, by the looks of things. So, you had wild thoughts of paying a friendly call down at the Melvins? Well, we're hearing that things have not been going all that well with Margaret's folks; there has been some kind of a flare-up between the laird and James Melvin, threats of leaving and so forth."

She regarded Fraser with concern and caution. This was a touchy area; anything could happen, and swiftly, where some lairds and their workers were concerned.

"Fraser, I feel that it would be a good idea..."

(and save you a deal of heartache, young man, she added to herself, inwardly)

"...if you wrote a letter, just asking how things were going, and telling them, and her, of course, of all your fine adventures with Jock Wyness up here in Outer Mongolia. In fact, if you just sit down right now, write a wee letter to James and Lorna, they'll really like that, and it'll take their attention off the other one which you could address directly to Margaret, right? And we'll get them both down to the Post Office with the Land Rover. My feeling is that you appearing like young Lochinvar at a time when things are not good with James and the laird, would not be a good idea. There will be a better time, right?"

Also, Robina thought, any damned thing could flare up with the Melvins' situation, and they could be away, and Fraser here none the wiser. Oh, dearie me: a young man's hopes in spring, tra-la, but this spring's going to be a very long time in coming away up here, and these poor souls trauchled with the lambing.

Fraser did as he was bidden; he really liked Robina, she was kindly and could speak about difficult things with no fuss or flannel. He would speak to Jock and Nan about his pay. Surely they would be getting his bed and board allowance out of it somehow?

"Dear Mr and Mrs. Melvin, This job which you very kindly fixed up for me has proved extremely worthwhile. I am beginning to realise how much there is to be done, every day, to make a successful job of a flock of hill ewes, particularly when conditions are so difficult. If this snow continues to lie, and then be added to after the New Year, the lambing is going to be an uphill struggle. All of us up here will have to do their very best and just keep going. The biggest problem is going to be enough places to shelter the newly lambed ones, and trying to keep the milk on their mothers.

"Once the lambing is by, I would like to come down to visit and say 'thank you' personally, and tell yourselves and Margaret about some of the more entertaining moments of Life At Tornaquhil! There will have been plenty episodes of a very different kind by the time that we get the lambing behind us.

With all good wishes."

The secondary letter, for Margaret Melvin, was infuriatingly difficult to put into friendly and not over-familiar words. He needed to express things for which he had no words. As he sat there, Robina carefully occupied in the kitchen, Fraser realised – this is the very first time that I have ever done anything like this.

THE MERRY DANCERS

XXXIX

Nan Wyness possessed a longer view of things than her husband Jock, Fraser had come to realise. And appreciate. As the meagre daylight shrank cruelly in the latter days of December, and bitter temperatures held or continued to drop, she stopped him on his way out to milk the dun cow before breakfast. The other half-Shorthorn milk cow was dry, coming to the calving in a few weeks.

"Fraser, if you're needing to get away to the town for any reason, or perhaps to give your folks a visit, then this would be as good a time as any. There'll be dashed little chance once we get by the turn of the year, and Jock and you'll be gey hashed to keep on top of a'thing that needs attention, even well afore the first of the lambs."

She regarded him with some anxiety. In her innermost knowing of how desperate a struggle it was going to be to put the lambing through, and her trying to keep her man's spirits up, and usefulness, by God, then it was essential that she persuade Fraser to take the bus into Aberdeen now, this very week, before the usual stramash and things coming to a halt over Hogmanay and a' that. Little chance of much first-footing and stir coming their way this New Year, anyway, the way the snow was set in now.

"Is that going to be OK, Nan? I could get you any messages from the town, and if the first bus is running, that would get me in to make the best use of the day, and get back out again."

He would not complicate things by trying to take another bus out to his parents; his mother would just assume that taking another day away from all this sheep business would be perfectly all right. Ach, the silly woman. And by the same consideration of just trying to get about with all this snow, little point in making tracks to the Melvins' home. They would have had his letter by now. And if Robina's saying that there was some kind of trouble between James Melvin and his employer, and that's my employer too, come to think of it, then better to let things settle. Right, the early bus first thing in the morning. That

366

would mean starting out from Tornaquhil, say, not later than about six, with all this damned snow to wade through.

On impulse, a flooding of relief that Fraser had accepted her plan, of knowing that a wee break for him now would ensure that he didn't get into a guddle of total fatigue as her Jock was prone to do at the height of the lambing, Nan Wyness put out a grateful hand to Fraser's arm and smiled at him, a smile of infinite sweetness, which transformed her face into features moré than just bonny.

"You're a good lad. Just mind and come back up the glen when you've had your fill of the toun!"

Rising to the alarm clock at half-past five, and taking the piece and thermos flask made up for him by Nan last thing the night before, Fraser set out from Tornaquhil, game bag over his shoulder with a pair of shoes for wearing in the town, quite warm inside his blanket-lined ex-army jeep coat, with the deep collar turned right up below his nose.

Coming down the skity brae into the village, Fraser smiled at his own pleasure, almost simple excitement, in seeing lights on in the scatter of houses, peat reek hanging heavy in the intense cold, sounds of human activity. He sat at ease in the first bus of the day, bound for Aberdeen, the diesel engine already started with a throaty rumble. There was a stillness in him as he sat, propped up against the window, now with the weariness of weeks and the difficulty of walking down the glen released in languor as the bus heated up.

He badly wanted to find out what this trouble was involving the Melvin family. There might be time enough to make a call after getting off the bus on the way home from the town, regardless of what the McMillans had warned him.

He watched for a brief sight of the road up to the Melvins' place, set back amongst the trees but no sign of life or Land Rover tracks to show activities of the family, who had given him of their own pleasure, and his, on that golden afternoon.

The bus conductress, Bunty Moir, watched Fraser idly as he slept. Strange to see such a sun-and snow-darkened skin with even darker, almost black hair, and yet him a fair-skinned lad to start with. Aye, this was him she'd heard speak of in the village, the vet's son up at the 'herding with Jock and Nan Wyness, and making a fair go of things, seemingly. There would be a better chance to have a while to speak with him on the late bus. The glen folk didn't seek away from home for more than a day, and they aye talked more freely after getting round a' their jobs in the town. Ah, well, here's the first of them, anyway.

"There now, Mrs Anderson, and it's a return for you goin' in to see Jan on her day off from the hospital, right? Two shillings change, that's the thing."

He slept until the bus suddenly vibrated on hitting the granite cassies leading into the centre of the city. He woke with a pool of saliva in his half-open mouth and a rank taste of breakfast eaten in too great a hurry. God, it seemed altogether like another day, another life. Stepping down awkwardly, one suddenly weak leg numb with the most excruciating cramp or pins and needles or blasted well both, he was strangely stupid and slow in movement. His shoes felt so light, somehow beyond normal control. Released from wellingtons and tackety boots, his feet seemed to flap and leap around of their own volition!

Standing at the pavement's edge, he pulled out his list. Haircut, belt, fish shop for Nan, bookshop. Already, the noise of traffic was something which he did not want to be amongst all day. He swung these ridiculously lightweight legs into a steady tramp up the street, hacking a woman in front of him on the back of her heel before he had even gone half a dozen paces. Momentarily crippled and shocked, she stumbled backwards into him and his involuntary grasp of her upper arm, perhaps more appropriate to catching hold of one of Jock's wild gimmers, made both of them leap apart in alarm at the prospect of more injury being done.

"Ooh! My goodness! That's quite enough, young man!" Her permed hair-do was trembling furiously, and Fraser suddenly cast back to his driving test morning and yon furious woman flailing at the front of the car, hat and toupee sent flying; he very nearly burst out laughing, but emitted or rather snorted in a strangled fashion.

"You are a painfully uncouth brute. Just where have you escaped from, for mercy's sake?"

He made astonished apologies, sidestepping with exaggerated care and hackney-style gait around any other likely candidates for unintentional hamstringing. He glowered at another woman, who stopped dead, nonplussed by this unwelcome overture, and he just had to burst out laughing, rendering any explanation quite impossible.

Of a sudden, he felt an impatience, an unwelcome sensation of being trammelled beyond ordinary sensible behaviour. He pulled back into a doorway, disturbed by this slight upon his own good manners, and looked down at the list, compiled aeons ago, it seemed, in the kitchen at Tornaquhil. Right, a haircut first, then that ex-Government surplus clothing place on Queen Street, maybe leave any parcels and things there; get them on the way back to catch the last bus. Just watch your uncouth bloody feet, my good man! Ach, weel, toonsers and the like! He set off, determined to make the best of the day, the last chance before the run-up to and total giving of himself, and Jock, and the boys, and Nan, and the dogs, too, dammit, to that huge flock, once away from the turn of the year. In Jock's half a-feared prediction, "Aye, it'll fairly tak' the good of you, man!"

"So, you're the lad that's going to do the lambing with Jock Wyness and Nan?"

The conductress gave him back his return ticket with an open bonny smile. Startled out of dream-like registration of images in the windows of the last bus out of town, Fraser nodded. How did she know all this?

His evident puzzlement must have looked out from his sleepy eyes. She smiled again.

"I'm Bunty Moir, a kind of a relation with your Nan. So, this is you having a day away from our bold Jock and a' his yowes? Much need! He's a great lad, with sudden notions, but Nan says it's whiles like trying to get the better of a brute of a horse, but lacking harness!"

They both laughed, as though they alone knew about something that the rest of the bus did not share. Bunty liked the look of Fraser and spoke with an easy friendliness. Mechty, he would still have been sleeping, the same seat as the morning run, if I hadn't spoken. Tired out, no doubt. Bunty recalled how the tainted circumstances of her mother's unwanted liaison and her own appearance to swell the family on the wee croft gave her grandparents the presumption to unpaid labour at any damned time. Aye, tired wasn't the word for it, more like a dragging, down-pulling weariness. Inescapably, she also remembered the less savoury ways of her mother's father, the domineering old bastard.

"You'll be on the go for long hours, once the lambing starts, Fraser. Well, the very first time you're anywhere near Waterford, give us a look in. My man Alan Moir's in the Forestry there. That's us, Alan and Bunty Moir. Old James Dow, you'll have heard tell of him? Well, he's my grandfather. Anyway, tell Jock and Nan that we're asking for them. We'll take a run up after the lambing's by. Alan's a great lad for the fishing."

Bunty Moir patted Fraser on his arm and went off down the bus to lean against the handrail, watching for the setting-down places needed for the easily chatting passengers, mostly farm folk, to be let off in total darkness at unmarked farm road ends.

Escaping back from the town certainly was turning out to be a late affair. He was suddenly weak and wobbly from fatigue and the early morning rush to get down the length of the glen. Struggling up the waterside road in intense frost, knees cold and stiff in trousers thinner by want of the usual layers of overalls and leggings, Fraser was asking of himself just what were his reasons for this impatience, this need just to be back amongst everything he was now happy with at Tornaquhil, when he suddenly, violently, shuddered, with more than just penetrating cold after the stuffy heat of the bus.

The alarm held him rigid, surrounded by an intense crackling in the immense vault of the night sky, above the length of the glen, above the whole of Scotland, for all that he could surmise. He was brought to a complete halt, head back and up, confronted by a display of hanging robes in purple, green, azure, lilac, miles high into the night, rising, flickering, folds shimmering in an essence of indescribable intensity. He had to crane well back, painfully, in fact, to see how far up into the aching immensity it all extended.

"My God! What in Heaven's name?" he said to himself, his voice sounding puny, feebly attempting reassurance of his tiny presence below all this possession of the night skies. The audible crackling and tension shook all of his senses. Almost to the point of, of terror? He shivered, in uncontrollable rigours.

"Aha! 'The Merry Dancers Of The North'! I've got you! Well, get a load of this." Fraser muttered out loud, to himself and to any foxes known to frequent the larch wood beside him. Hadn't Granda' or someone gone on about The Merry Dancers coming swinging down from the Arctic regions before a right bad storm or change to severe weather conditions? Well, here it was, the Aurora Borealis. Ho hum, rumpty tum!

Of a sudden, Fraser felt a deathly chill deep in the very core of his body, not only due to the weariness of a long day, but also the presence of a simple terror well enough described from mediaeval times as a heeded heavenly portent. Trudging on, with his packages bumping in the old game bag, Fraser cocked an eye up at the now totally silent display, and looked away again. A body could go clean gite, or stupid in the head, looking right into the very gates of Heaven. Or Hell

Heat, the smoky sweetness of burning peats, the voices of the boys in bickering mood, strong smells and dampness from the open larder door; all settled around his person like an invisible tea cosy of welcome familiarity. Patch and Moss inhaling smells from his hands and trousers, all the things he now knew of this as home and of his place as a part of it.

Blinking in the strong light from the hissing Tilley lamp, Fraser smiled foolishly, hearing not just the content, but more the warmth and caring of their questioning. Young Matt was at his elbow, pulling at his sleeve.

"Did ye mind to get me yon…?"

Fraser smiled again, recalling the outburst from that daft wifie in Union street: "And just where have you escaped from, young man?" He burst out laughing, and started to tell them all about his day.

XL

Only a couple of weeks before the turn of the year, and not long after young Jimmy Dow had by a whisker narrowly escaped being crushed to pulp by the overturning tractor, Doddie Paterson, the postie, ventured up the glen, riding in the cab of the estate Caterpillar D4 tractor along with the badly needed cargo of bags of sheep feed, some of the items needed to replenish Nan's larder stores, and a gather-up of mail, with newspapers being passed from one beleaguered farm steading to the next on the principle of neighbourliness.

Doddie and Harry the forestry tractor driver crowded into the warm kitchen, along with everyone else at Tornaquhil, noisily supping tea and manipulating large, jammy pancakes held in stiffened, mittened fingers.

"Aye, Jock, man, your neighbour doon the glen, auld James Dow; he's no' very great at all. It's well into his chest. And what a brute to work in his young day, by God."

Aye, and by all accounts, Fraser silently added, a brute to drive everyone else on the miserable holding to total compliance – or leave home. He cast back only a week or so to the quite unexpected foray they had made at Jock's insistence, to visit the Dows in a sort of sudden, well-let's-have-a-go-at-this-Christmas nonsense. It had surprised Nan far more than the rest of them put together.

In all the farm jobs to which Fraser had willingly given himself (and of himself, by heavens, in recall), Christmas Day and Boxing Day too for that matter in Scotland, had always been just another two days given to the usual work of seeing to the beasts and housed cattle, suckler cows and their calves, of milking, mucking and cleaning in dairies, of taking muck out, or bringing in turnips or kale. That was just the way of things in the north-east; it was down in England that all the fuss was made of these Christmas goings-on. But, Hogmanay and the New Year was the time for least possible work on the land or in the byre, and there was a totally different feel to those two or three (or even more!) days of straight pleasure in a dram offered and taken as many times as possible, in a great spirit of neighbourliness.

"That's aye been the way of it" had been Gran'pa Teatime's response to

Fraser's questions as a very wee lad, about his days and times as a young man growing up on the family farm.

Whatever the worlds apart differences between the essentially more family-based English festivities on the one hand, and the hard, yet steel-true sincerity of the lift to Scottish spirits (Fraser smiled broadly to himself at the images of umpteen glasses being raised!) seized and celebrated by Scots folk, there was little chance to make much of either event at Tornaquhil that winter as the scant hours of daylight were scrunched down to a couple around midday, before light began to fade after two o' clock. On a steady northerly airstream, the snow came relentlessly in, the length of the glen and far beyond, adding to the old, tramped stuff.

On Fraser's telling of his pleasing acquaintance with Bunty Moir on the bus into the town, Jock Wyness had suddenly been taken by the notion, fairly typically improbable, that they would all walk down the glen, snow or no snow, and have a kind of a Christmassy gathering with the whole Dow tribe at the croft, Bunty being a part of that family, and even take in the McMillans on their way back up the glen. Nan jumped at this outing with alacrity, the lamplight on her spectacles reflecting everything in the room at the time as she ran around in unusual excitement.

"Good for you, Da! We'll mak' a rare go at it, the 'hale lot of us!"

They put everything outside and inside to rights, and set off about midday, leaving the dogs shut in, the house cow, to her great surprise and confusion, milked by Fraser, and Granda' quietly content, or so he said, at some ploy of his in the toolshed, his pipe going well for him, out of the incessant wind. There was a strong reek of burnt horn about him these days, some private ploy in hand.

The welcome spread about them all, once down at the croft; Jock and Nan, the two boys, and Fraser was uproarious, warm-hearted and very noisy. Old Mistress Dow, her cheeks rosy and brosy with neighbourly surprise and delight, instantly set in motion relays of tea, warm scones from the griddle, slices of a cake that "Wisnae put by just for Christmas, ye ken, mair like the New Year, but, ach! We'll gi'e it a fair fleg afore that. Now, stick in, you folks, Godsake. Ah'd near forgotten your faces since afore hairst!"

Fraser wondered what quantity of a hairst or harvest they would have gathered together on the few acres of ploughable ground on the Dow croft: dashed little over and above cattle feed.

There must have been well over thirty or more folk, with upraised voices (and glasses), between noisy groups of men, women, youngsters in shrill incomprehensible excitement, and two old dogs, grey of muzzle, steadily thumping their tails beside the open hearth, raising pluffets of white ash from the burning peats. Fraser was hugged and kissed by Bunty.

"Aha, young Lochinvar that snored a' the way into the town on my bus! How on earth did you folks manage to get Jock here, to abandon his precious yowes for even a blink? By God, you must be getting soft, or something, Jock Wyness!"

Everyone roared, even louder, and Jock sat, glass tilted dangerously in his hand, savouring it all, his hectically reddened face in perpetual rictus of pleasure.

Old James Dow must be a great age, Fraser deliberated, watching him put down a gnarled arthritic hand to each of the dogs in turn. A big, bearded figure, he was listening to Nan's account of this and that, but hardly giving any replies, focussing steadily upon her face and repeating the odd word of her account. Fraser spoke cheerily with all and any of the company, running a fashion of outward cheeriness, but the same time looking around him, silently asking questions to which the answers were not easily or immediately forthcoming. How on earth did the Dow family survive financially on such poor acreage? How could they produce enough winter keep for their suckler cows tied in the byre, together with their calves from last year? What kept them all in just the necessities of living, with a number of youngsters still at the school in the village, and another two taking the bus every day to the big school down the road into the town? Bunty was at his elbow again, offering a tray of things to eat.

"And how long are you to be with us here, away up in the Abergolian mountains? I hear that you've a notion to take on a lease of a hill place some day, is that right? Well, you must be daft; poverty is no pleasure, my lad. Alan and me, each of us, we need to have a wage coming in every week, away out from all this, this muckle ant heap of trying to make everything pan out, money-wise, I mean."

Standing close to each other in the tide of bodies moving around them, Fraser thought, she's a fine, bonny woman. And funny that she doesn't seem to have an identifiable mother or father here amongst this heap of folk, all related in some fashion. Maybe they have another place like this. He would ask Nan. He peered out through the kitchen window. They should really be making a move to get back up the glen. The track they had made on the way down the glen had disappeared. Snow was blowing steadily, ominously.

As if on cue, Nan was there at his elbow, putting an arm around Bunty's waist.

"Dinna be thinking you're making off with our Fraser. We'ld be stucken without him!"

There was an unspoken warmth of conspiracy between the two women, then Nan put her hand to his shoulder.

"Fraser, the light's going fast, and the weather's aye getting worse. We should be making tracks, and it's nae very bonny out there."

She was genuinely concerned, too.

"Is Jock ready?" Fraser asked. He had doubts about Jock's willingness to abandon his patent enjoyment of this rare event, a while off from the anxieties of the sheep. They were substantiated by Nan's rather apologetic reply.

"He's biding a wee while yet. It's nae often that he tak's an outing like this. There'll not be another chance now, afore the lambing starts, the way things are with this snow, dashed near every day."

Stepping away from the thrang of folk clustered around the scarred open door of the Dows' home, with their strong cries of "Haste ye back!" in their ears, Nan, Fraser and the boys were a file of four dark figures, heads down to the wind-driven snow sweeping across their narrow path, now hardly discernible. Fraser was wholly sensitive to young Ben's anxiety to get back to the ewe flock, Matt's reluctance to leave the chatter and shrill amusement of the young folk, and Nan's concern about her father attempting to tackle outside tasks before the night closed in. Of Jock, the last they heard of him was his high, hoarse repetition of "Aye, aye – the best tup ye'll ever see, just a master, just a master!" as the stories and gusts of laughter flew back and forth in the tightly packed bunch of menfolk, glasses in their hands, being spilled, being refilled, being emptied at a gulp.

Before they had gone the length of a gunshot from the house, the clamour and voices were suddenly emptied from their backward glance by the steadily deadening snow. With Ben leading the way, and Fraser following, Nan requested, "Hey, stop a minute, Fraser, or I get this scarf to one side. My bloody specs keep getting frosted over!"

This done, they set off, Nan half in the lee of Fraser, holding on to his left arm and the heavy blue coat. They plodded on in needful but companionable silence, freshly accumulated snow to above their ankles and beyond. Any speech was pointless; they all had their coat collars hauled up to their nostrils, bonnets and caps pulled down to a narrow slit of vision. Aye, a right Christmassy scene it must damned well appear, Fraser conceded. Anyone nearer to the town would never even suspect this lot, or mebbe even only twenty dashed miles away, for that matter.

Their last pull up, over the bridge, invisible below them, treacherous bar for the single handrail, was a struggle. Granda' spoke to them as they filed at last into the shelter of the steading, his pipe reek being snatched by the flick of the wind and snow.

"I gave the yowes a wee bite when the day started to brak doon. They'll not need mair or morning. The coo's needin' a sup water, and the dogs have a' been oot and fed. So, ye hinna Jock with ye? Ah, weel, he's damned lucky tae have us folk dancing aboot up here. Hmmph. If he's that wise, he'll bide where he is for a day or two or we see the shape of things wi' the weather. Christmas an' sic-like'll not go wrong for his not being here."

Nan clearly heard, but made no reply. They stamped and shook off their snow-plastered coats, scarves, bonnets and gloves. Fraser thought, I should really take the responsibility off Granda's shoulders.

"Nan, I'm going for a wee look round a'thing, give the cows a pail of water and so forth." In Jock's absence, there was a comfortable bond of trust between them, almost as man and wife, Fraser supposed it to be.

"Aye, Ah'll come with ye," said Ben.

Jobs done, they stood shoulder to shoulder in the barn door, looking over the body of the ewe flock, rumps grey and round to the wind, a carapace of snow binding them to the ground in irregular hummocks.

"Fraser?" Ben half turned to him.

"Aye, what?"

"It's just that Dad hardly ever tak's a day off. He gets fine pleased an' happy-like when folk make a fuss of him. Like today."

The boy's statement was more a pleading, a seeking of understanding amongst men. Out of warmth for Ben's moment of trust, Fraser put his arm around his shoulder, with solid agreement.

"Of course your Dad needs a break, and a fine Christmas present that has been for him. Ach, you and me, and Matt and Granda', and your mother, we'll all manage away fine. When we were down the glen at the croft, Ben, we should've left a note for Santa: 'Get a split new Caterpillar bulldozer up here, but dinna try to get it doon the lum!'!"

Bumping into each other, laughing and capering about, they turned for the house, and warmth, and a meal of sorts, and a seat round the fire. Their Christmas night would be just fine, when it came to the time, however modestly observed.

Lying open-eyed in his bed that night, gauging the whip of the wind around the gables of the house, Fraser suddenly grasped that which had eluded him through the rather strange day. There had been no music of any nature whatsoever, and not just Christmas stuff coming through on the wireless, or trying to. Hogmanay and bringing in the New Year was a different matter altogether; whether it be on some farm or other in the course of work, or a gathering at his parents' home or neighbours – by golly, there was music all right! Piano, accordion, fiddles, even a competently played mouth organ, songs, it was all a great delight. Did fiddlers always pop up in pairs, he wondered? There aye seemed to be two, at least! He laughed quietly, in the darkness, and passed into sleep. The wearisome difficulties of the run-up weeks to the spell of lambing was nothing compared to the ferocity with which Arctic conditions burst upon them just as early April inescapably came in, its gentle place on the calendar with the usual bonny pictures of daffodils, catkins and the like, cruelly meaningless to hill run folk in the wilder parts of Scotland.

Fraser had by only a very few last half-crazed efforts held exhaustion and death from claiming him on that night of the storm, trapped in a pit ripped out by a newly felled larch tree, which they were all well accustomed to seeing upright on endless treks up and down the glen.

Shortly before the first week of expected lambing, Jock had burst out to Fraser, "And by God! There's aye a puckle as canna wait. Ye've to be buggerin' quick wi' them or they just die on ye!"

Conditions had plummeted into temperatures well below zero, with strangely, ominously unpredictable winds and storms of snow without end. There were drifts to the depth of a grown man. The difficulties in just getting basic tasks done were draining of all energy.

After holding off from making a start to follow Jock and the boys back up the glen until a particularly wild gimmer had been lambed (with the head out, but both front legs back; it had been a bloody struggle, single handed), the light had vanished in a dark roaring storm of snow directly from the north. Fraser debated with himself, his chest heaving and hands clumsily pushed back into gloves, about going down to the McMillans, but reasoned that would be a mile lost, and at least an hour or more into the bargain. "Na, na, my lad, keep going." With Moss crowding up against his legs by the force of the storm, they set off together.

Three quarters of a mile up the glen, Fraser knew that he had lost any certainty of being on, or following, the hard road. The violence of the wind was continually bringing him to a hunched stop every forty paces or so along the worst stretch. Things happened in rapid sequence after about his fourth stop to take deep, rasping breaths.

I Like to Walk in This Field

In a stumbling uncertain gait, both of Fraser's boots stubbed on what might have been the felled tree root; he plunged head and shoulders into the snow-caped pit left by the upheaved larch tree. As he battered down, arms outstretched in violent and shocked response, one side of his head crashed into a stone in his head-first plunge downwards. Pain overwhelmed him in dark waves. With great whistling gasps, he struggled to inhale against the unremitting mask of snow packed closely around his face, with the wildness of fear.

As Fraser came to realise afterwards, he had lost consciousness, and only the insistent jumping in and out of the blood-splashed hole by Moss, as often as not thrusting fearfully against his lacerated face with his hind legs and claws, gave Fraser the last lashing strength to twist and claw sideways at the lip of the deep pit and gasp in rasping inhalations to secure his life in this bloodied maelstrom.

Well beyond two hours from the time he had set out on the two miles up the glen back to Tornaquhil and shelter and sustenance there, he collapsed into the dark mouth of the peat shed. Hunched upon himself in acute pain, he trailed across the yard with small steps, hide gloves lost, God only knows where, Moss whining beside him. He grabbed once, twice at the door latch, a dull roaring pain gripping his head and chest. He and the dog fell into the passage in a battering of wind and snow, bodies and boots, to the alarmed scrape and clatter of feet and chairs in the kitchen. With one arm holding Moss tightly to him, his slurred injunction through a mask of frozen tears, torn skin and bloody mess to Nan Wyness to "G-g-give M-M-Moss something h-h-hot!" seemed to come from a vast distance.

With each day's inexorable dawning and being drawn into the actual concentration of lambing, the most useful tasks that Jock and Fraser and the two lads could focus their energies upon, were those of seizing any ewe going into the birthing process, getting at least one living lamb out of her and then both heaved and hauled into some scrap of shelter, using every means at their disposal to promote a few drops of milk to flow. There was no drawing of respite from each night's accumulation of snow, be it in inches or more inches or feet. The unlambed ewes fed every morning, the troughs had to be laboriously carried and stacked on their ends immediately after the last hurried lipping of concentrates. They would have been buried and frozen solid in the morning.

Those ewes that had lambed and were mothering their lambs as best they could were penned up in every conceivable place to afford the lambs some scrap of shelter, just to hold on to pathetic resources of body heat.

And by so doing, and by setting up some half-rotten old door in the angle of the dyke, did so convince, Fraser thought grimly, both Jock and himself that life would keep going through yet another day and night of Arctic conditions. Down that long road to the foot of the glen, such vital matters amongst the gimmer flock were decidedly less easily fulfilled. School attendance for the two boys continued to be an impossibility; they laboured mightily with each day's demands upon their father's livelihood, as did the entire household.

Fraser and Ben mostly, his brother always claiming some other thing to be done just at that point, had to rig up pens with old rails and sheep stakes, with gates wrenched off snow-buried hinges, sides and tailgates from long abandoned carts. They tied everything with laboriously fumbled lashings of old coir ropes from the roof-couples of the buildings, the creosoted strands cut deeply into the deep red hacks at finger and thumb-nails. Unavoidably, Fraser had more than thirty gimmers outside, their lambs huddled into any pockets of tree roots or rabbit holes below the spruce trees the length of the deserted avenue, where they just had to be shut in for some protection out of the worst of the storms.

It was a desperate, mind-draining, hellish struggle, a nightmare of inescapable participation: gimmers living but lambs dead when pulled from their wombs, orphan lambs resulting from twins where there was just no milk to sustain one, let alone two, another gimmer attempting to mother and succour her lambs, herself found dead at first light, milk- and heat-starved scraps of lambs hunchbacked in the dawn beside her failed body, a momentarily lost lamb pushing at a post with blind eye-sockets where the carrion crows had ripped out its eyes in savagery, for their own survival.

Fraser came on Ben one grey morning, beating to death a huge hooded or grey-backed crow that had panicked in surprise and become trapped in an old hen coop used to jam a pair of twins and their mother in the angle of two stone walls of a derelict building. The hoody had already damaged one lamb's eye when Ben came upon it with his stick, breaking its wings. He was beside himself, incoherent, tears of rage and fury trickling down his frost-scabbed cheeks as he lashed and slashed the crow's body.

"Hoodies! Bastards of bliddy hoodies. Why canna the keepers nae kill them a', why does God let them flee aboot an' mak' nests an' young an', an' mair bliddy craws?" Ben's slashing stick invoked every curse and depth of impotence. "Ye black fleein' fuckin' thing that ye are!"

Ben put the heel of his wellington boot on its head and mashed it into the snow. Bloodstained snow aye looks redder than blood by itself, Fraser had seen, as the boy stumbled past him, speechless, sobbing. The gimmer's dark brown eyes regarded everything: Fraser, the dogs, her damaged lamb, the inert crow, without movement. Her nostrils were quivering at an uncountable rate. She touched the terrified lamb with her muzzle. It turned to her. Riven from the macerated remains of the crow's carcase, the hard black beak lay in the snow, still exuding its purpose; a chisel for killing.

Being on his own amongst the gimmer flock until late morning, by which time Jock might show up from the main flock at Tornaquhil, Fraser found that he had to allocate his own resources with care. There was no energy to be used up in stupid ways of doing things. When his eye spotted a gimmer close to lambing, rising and lying down, circling this way and that, he learned to to curb his anxiety to have as many lambed and living as possible. Thinking back to those illustrations of veterinary obstetrics in his father's textbooks over which he had pored many times, he was grateful for the confidence which they had given him when faced with malpresentations and the like.

He adopted the practice of closing in, kind of obliquely, with Moss dropped to lie some distance off, to almost casually compel the animal to move to a more sheltered place (Shelter? Shelter?! What an idiot useless term that was, relatively bloody well speaking) where she might lamb by herself and not have to be caught with the cleek and then manhandled by sheer dragging effort into a pen of sorts. Sheltered? No, a mite less exposed. Well, maybe, he would mutter to himself, shaking the drip from the end of his nose.

All too often, it didn't work out like that. Enragingly perverse, she would have to be pursued with dog and cleek until all were exhausted, frequently with a grotesquely swollen lamb's head and tongue walloping about her vulva as she whirled and leapt. Fraser often spoke to Moss, "Christ, Moss, what a bloody business this is! Here, mannie – come bye, come BYE! La' doon!" Once caught, there was the then inescapable need to drag and trail the wild stotting animal to somewhere affording control of getting her lambed and then preventing her, by all and any means possible, from just making a leap for freedom. It all demanded energy, skilful deceit, persistence and a well of indomitable patience, which utter fatigue often did not possess.

Most mornings, there came a pausing, a taking stock, when all seemed for the moment to be under control. Fraser lifted Moss by whistle from his hidey-hole amongst the bales and trudged down the avenue to the McMillans' green door with the stag's head knocker and the warm and cheerful kitchen, where Ramsay and Robina had become his greatest support in just keeping going on really desperate days.

Putting another round of cheese and pickle sandwiches on the table, Robina rested her hand on Ramsay's shoulder for a moment, then sat down in front of Fraser and demanded:

"And just what is all this leading up to, my young man? What good are all these daily heroics going to be? Tell me that, now."

"What good is what going to be?" Fraser echoed, puzzled, speaking as he ate. He almost inhaled a particle of bread and choked and coughed, just like one of those blasted animals up the avenue he envisioned, eyes streaming.

"Yes, my lad, all this endless hashing yourself to exhaustion with other folks' sheep and lambs and every dashed thing out there! What bally good is this going to do you, Fraser? You should see yoursel'. You look utterly drained..."

Her husband interjected, "Clapped out, I would say!"

"Well, if I've done all these jobs myself, especially under conditions like these," Fraser replied, nodding to the drifting snow beyond the window, "then I'll be able to put someone else to do it, when I'm in a manager's position."

Robina interrupted, her usually warm and cheerful eyes flashing with spirit as she wagged a finger, flour and margarine clarted on it, in front of his startled face.

"Oh, aye, and from what Ramsay and me have been seeing, if you've done it all yourself, you're never going to be satisfied with some other poor soul trying to do it for you. I've seen it all before, young man; you'll be dishing out the easier things for them to be getting on with, while you, you silly creature, will be slogging away all by yourself! Am I not right, Ramsay?"

Triumphant, the forester's wife swung round to her husband, quite flushed with the heat of her sentiments. Speaking quietly, almost as though bringing scenes and feelings to his own evaluation, Ramsay took up the opening.

"Fraser, lad, when I was demobbed from the RAF, my greatest wish was to get out on the hill amongst trees and forestry work again, just peace and quiet, easy physical tasks most of the time. Not a lot of that sort of thing around on bombing runs into Germany, night after night."

For a moment, Ramsay McMillan, onetime Sergeant Pilot, was very still, lost to both of them listening, feeling the vibration in the cockpit of the Lancaster heavy bomber, smelling the high octane aviation fuel and the fear in his throat as the German ack-ack came soaring up, searching for a wing, an engine, a fuel tank, a tail gunner crouched in his turret. He shook himself back in amongst the two listeners.

"Well, after a couple of years of wellingtons and clammy overalls all day and every day, and being ordered to carry out as many jobs which shouldn't have needed to be done, and as many again which really couldn't, with any common sense, I decided to quit being stupid or blind, and have a go at achieving some reasonable returns from a reasonable, if not entirely superior, intelligence. So, a deep breath, and back into the books again, and setting my face and energies to getting a degree. Not all that long a haul, in terms of a lifetime, and a position as Forest Officer, which was a hell of a difference to being just one of the squad, out in all weathers."

Fraser was on the point of making a rebuttal or something defensive, but Ramsay McMillan pounced, with the timing of a skilled boxer.

"So, where's the difference, Fraser, between how I started off, knocking my idealistic pan in for no gain, and what you're knocking yourself out for with a load of old Blackface ewes, and carrying responsibility for other folk a lot of the time, hey? Does Jimmy Melvin's fine laird even know that you exist?"

Ramsay tamped his pipe in studied conclusion, regarding Fraser over the frame of his spectacles. Robina looked for any sign of agreement in Fraser's eyes, not just on his face.

"Ah, well, the difference would be..." Fraser started to say, then thought, oh, what would the blasted difference be, in any case, between managing a squad of men as a farmer or as a forest officer? He carried on, "...is that you canna put men to their work, properly, that is, unless they know that you can do the job just as well as they can, or preferably better, and there are always certain jobs which, if you want them done at all, you're better to–"

"To bally well do them yourself! I just knew that's what you would come out with!" Robina broke in, clearly annoyed now, rattling cups as she rose abruptly to gather crockery. "Just you wait and see, young Fraser. Once you're a married man, you'll not be so keen to hash on like a mad thing, and you'll not handle a farm without a sensible wife to knock some sense into you, you daft thing!"

"Look out there; the snow's on again." Fraser broke in on purpose, feeling a wound, to himself and his view of the future, that he could not counter. Anyway, what had being married and all that got to do with putting farm men to their work with authority?

Robina sensed his division, his uncertainty: "Ach, away you go, you're just as blind as the rest of them, taken up with, with sheep, and shooting... and shelter belts!" she exploded finally.

Fraser felt that he had stayed too long with all this talk. What really mattered in winter conditions like this was being able and experienced enough to know what to do and how to do it; that much he knew without question.

"Right, I'll come up with you, Fraser. There's nothing else that I can put the squad to in all this.'

Ramsay pulled on his hooded parka, wellingtons and gloves. They both stepped out into the driving snow. The rank smell, almost a taste, more like, of fire-dried gloves and jackets, all soaked by sheeps' wool and lambing fluids, rose up in Fraser's face, his nose hunched into the deep collar. Ramsay put out a gloved hand to hold Fraser back a moment.

"Fraser, don't take against Robina for her going on at you. She's concerned, we both are, about the way in which your willingness is getting a rough deal; you'll not achieve the things which matter in this life by being a slave to work. There will come a time, as it did to me, thank goodness, when another way of getting there will still be open, but, by golly, Fraser Baird, that time whips past you bloody quickly – you don't get a second chance! Come on, let's see to these precious animals of yours."

They trudged on, heads down, up the brae to the greatest concentration of lambed, near-to-lambing and attempting-to-lamb sheep in the worst possible conditions of scanty feed, negligible shelter and hellish weather that Fraser felt had been inconceivable those months back when he had willingly, keenly, taken on this job. By Christ, tell someone else to handle all this and stand back? He made an involuntary sound of disbelief, which Ramsay heard and immediately understood, each looking at the other without speech, but with the momentary glimpse of mutually grim and determined features that spoke volumes.

XLI

"Christ! Ah thocht the bloody machine was near buggered. We was damn near in ower the burn a couple of times. Man, it's settin' in for a fair storm, Ah tell ye. Auld James Dow is better off where he is noo, aye – deid!"

Harry pulled on the hand clutches of the crawler tractor. It squealed to a stop in the Tornaquhil yard. Delivering his message to all of them standing around in the snow, not waiting even to get down off the machine and into the warm kitchen, he sounded quite beyond normal coherency. (Just as well, thought Fraser, catching a glance from Nan, eyebrows leaping in amusement, both being well acquainted with Harry's usual range and repetition of lurid terms. Not entirely fitting for the death of the respected crofter down the glen!) Fraser smiled broadly in the hubbub around the yellow tractor.

Old James Dow had died, it seemed, the day before. The D4 Caterpillar and sledge had burst its way up the glen, carrying the minister, the Reverend Mr Buchanan, in the cab with Harry, roaring and sliding in the drifts, impacted snow piled high on the radiator cowling.

Fraser and Ben had been down with the gimmer flock before first light. It had taken them over an hour to struggle through. There, with a release of tension that Fraser tasted in his throat, they had only another three lambed overnight, one of which had two dead lambs, devitalised and then crushed when she had lain upon them in the confused cramped night hours. He rode back up to Tornaquhil on the tractor with Harry, after offloading bales of hay, bags of sheep feed and a pitiful amount of turnips into the old estate buildings. Fraser had seen that faithful old Moss was failing in reserves of strength, in spite of extra feeding one way or another by himself, known but unremarked by Mrs Wyness. The dog clawed his way on to the remaining bales for Tornaquhil with a shove from Fraser, who had felt the flesh thin over Moss's pelvis.

"Come on, you poor old thing, here's a wee hidey-hole for you!" Fraser tugged two bags apart and with a goodly wad of hay, still with the blue-green of summer upon it, Moss stayed there, out of the wind, out of sight for the entire journey, sheltered and warm and for the short while, uncaring. The dog's light brown irises stayed faithful to Fraser's presence and movements with devoted intensity.

Dinnertime that day had a palpable feeling of urgency, of everything not absolutely essential discarded or pushed to one side. This delivery by Harry had to be the only chance in the severity of conditions outside, to restore mental as much as physical resources, to take measure of the next onslaught, before it burst upon them away at the head of the glen.

In wholly unforeseen fashion, Fraser sensed, there now arose the imposition of having to consider this funeral business.

"They hinna even gotten him doon th' stairs yet. God only kens whatever fashion they'll mak' it oot o' the hoose. It's drifted in tae th' bloody eaves, man!"

The whole tragi-comic affair was relieving Jock Wyness of his endless worrying about what to do for the best with the ewes, with the feed, with gimmers' lack of milk, with every damned thing a body could think of.

The matter under noisy heated discussion around the littered table was, would he, Jock, prepare for the funeral and go off directly with Harry and the tractor, down the maelstrom of the glen, or would Nan make up a parcel of his good black clothes, and Jock carry them down the next day, in a lambing bag, on foot? Harry, impatient, cut through all their propositions.

"Nae bother, Jock man. Ye can bide with us or wi' the wife's brother. If we were tae tell them you'll be attending on the road doon, we can mebbe mak' up a gang o' fowk," he said, pausing to lick the fragile tube of thin cigarette paper, then rolling it with the fingers of one hand, "an' get the auld cratur shifted oot o' that, ae wye or anither."

A final match to the cigarette, a final pronouncement on the Dow family, or hornets' nest. Fraser substituted in his mind: "There's aye trouble at yon place noo, there's far ower mony o' them for agreement aboot the place, God sink it. Aye, man, they've gotten awa' frae any control by auld Mother Dow this past while."

In the finish, Jock did go down the long snowy defile on the tractor. Nobody at the foot of the glen, so Harry said, seemed clear as to what day the funeral could possibly be staged. They might even hold the service upstairs, Harry Coutts conjectured, in the cramped, coomb-ceilinged bedroom, and then skite the old boy out through the window casement on planks, coffin and all, and it likely to tak' off ower the heids o' the drifts and land God knows where!

There was a great gust of perverse delight at this improbable picture. The two young lads, their mother and Fraser exploded in paroxysms of laughter. Jock Wyness could only grin, wordless, looking from one to the other, put about in his mind that all this unseemly hilarity was focussed on his earnest intention to pay his respects to the old patriarch and family, snow or no snow. By God, he would go down the glen; a funeral of this magnitude was not to be missed. There would be that many drams going, for a surety.

Jock's face, excited, almost childlike, peered out from beside Harry in the cab of the yellow tractor, funeral clothes lodged between the oily seat and diesel fuel tank. The clattering tracks and idlers died away quickly once over the bridge, thinly falling flakes of snow turning the minds of the figures still waving in the banked-up yard to what had to be done for ewes, lambs and cows with the last remaining light, for the immediate present and also for the morning, and whatever that might bring. The high riggings of the hills around them all were entirely closed-in with streaming curtains of thick snow. The coming storm pressed in amongst them in blinding, swirling menace.

As Fraser's outside workload trebled in Jock's absence, so had, perforce, his ability to make mental and physical provision for tasks he could see coming upon them all. It all needed a degree of inventiveness to which young Ben responded in most able fashion, but from which his older brother Matt took refuge, or rather escape from, in Houdini-like disappearance.

Over the previous few weeks, in any few moments of relief from weariness and lassitude, Fraser had begun to realise that the actual birth process took place in cycles, at certain times. A major flurry of lambings at first light, a lesser number in the first half of the afternoon, and only an occasional one around darkness. Sitting watching the puzzled sidestepping of a ewe with a twinned-on lamb thrusting desperately at her udder for a warm nourishing suck, the skin of her own, now dead lamb flopping around the heels of the adoptee, Fraser pondered, was this cycle of giving birth (parturition, to give it its proper term), in any way connected with the pressure of a full rumen pressing on the uterus? There had to be some factor of feeding, or light or moisture content in the air or something common to all of them at a certain juncture. I'm just seeing the results, he said to himself, without fully knowing the causes. Reaching farther back, to a time of non-domesticated animal species, might it not be something to do with the best possible time to avoid or reduce the risk of the young being pounced upon by predators before they got properly footed?

Did Jock know, did old Granda' know, did his own father know? Who the blazes did or would know?

Anyway, together with Ben, he worked out what seemed to be the only scheme possible, so far as the main body of ewes at Tornaquhil was concerned, that would allow them to see to everything there and then allow Ben and himself to make for the the gimmers down the glen soon after light came in.

Long before first light, Ben rose to Fraser's tap on his shoulder in the absolute silence of extreme frost. The very fabric of the sleeping house felt in the grip of bitterly low temperature inside as well as outside. The Tilley lamp squeaked dryly as Ben pumped away at it, his face still red and swollen with sleep, but grinning at Fraser in companionable accord. They went out in the bottomless cold, bumping into each other's bodies as their boots slipped, useless in snow which would not, could not compress further.

Into the long byre, they breathed out coils of instantly condensed hoar as they went round all the lambed ewes, feeding, checking, giving a suckle, easing a ewe's swollen teats for a weakly lamb, terrorising some rebellious old beggar with the sudden appearance up on the bales of Patch, snapping and slavering, to arouse reluctant mothering. As soon as the greyness of another day slid in like a knife-blade from the east, they replenished the troughs from bags filled the night before and let the un-lambed ewes make their own speed up to the troughs, provided that Moss had been put out to run wide round the further out resting places for a start. The entire stretch of ground lying from the steading to the birch hill, normally weary but wiry old pasture at this time of year, was a glazed-over expanse of sheep muck, snow battered into yellow and black-soiled ice, ice in every configuration of instant freezing and denial of what might otherwise lie below it.

"Yours all filled, Ben?" Fraser checked.

"Aye, an' it's freezin' like buggery tae the wooden bits a'ready!"

They spoke to each other from behind gloved hands held to their mouths and noses, the contents of the feed sacks froze immediately with any residual moisture once emptied out. They both stood a few paces back, without speech, watching the ewes stepping quietly (or limping) into the grey light.

Any beast which held back, the two of them immediately ran into an enclosure of gates, old doors, anything at all which made an enclave in the old midden yard. If any single ewe in particular was clearly on the point of lambing, the two of them agreed to grab it there and then for swift assessment of dilation and lubrication and easing of the lamb whilst literally in their hands to do so. If not, well, they had shelter and feed and could do thus until into the afternoon at a pinch. Somehow, this very pragmatic approach seemed to get nearer to the times of lambing likely to take place anyway. Ben and him would just have to push on down to the gimmer flock come what may in their absence.

The key thing for the older, experienced ewes, Fraser justified to Ben's upturned face in the eye-searing coldness, was shelter. Whilst away down at the foot of the glen, what the gimmers needed most was someone at their rear end right at the moment of birth, with no chance of whirling off to leave the mewling scrap in the snow, but banged into fairly tight constraint and shelter, with marrying up enforced upon the more uproarious brutes right away.

"Aye, plus a nasty suspicious mind into the bargain," Fraser reflected to himself.

"Right, come on, Ben, you grab some peats, I'll take in logs. Let's get going." They turned to the house, nearly falling over the circling forms of Patch and Moss.

"Oot o' the way, dammit, dogs! By God, Ben, am I right in thinking it's getting even colder, by Christ?"

"Aye, man, ye'll be right, it's a right bliddy corker."

They barged into the still warmth of the house, clumsy in their layers of clothing, carrying fuel for Nan Wyness and Granda'. Taking an earlier-than-usual breakfast of sorts, but without kindling the fire for toast or such hold-ups, they hastened back outside, bonnets tugged well down against the biting northerly wind.

It crept into Fraser's purview that it was more than provident that old James Dow had died when he did, regardless of difficulties in "getting the auld bugger oot" and had to accept that to Jock Wyness, strangely, the most important thing for him was to get away down to the funeral. It was provident that feed had been gotten up with the crawler tractor when it did, bearing the news of the death; the afternoon of the day following Jock's departure, they saw the sky over the high ridge to the north-west became awesomely black and menacing, darker by far than slate.

The temperature had dropped steadily all day as they worked, and the entire horizon around them, whichever way Fraser or Ben looked, a hand pressed to their aching backs, seemed to exude a frightening fusion of land and sky, with the latter swept into limbo by thickening snowfall in every direction.

By late afternoon, with all possible measures taken for the survival of anything with a single lamb or twins at foot, the two of them, Fraser, novice shepherd and Ben Wyness, eleven-and-a-bit years old, brought up to read sheep like a book, felt little doubt that this was shaping up to be a particularly severe night of storm, quite likely to carry on into the next few days.

With Nan's pieces and jammy scones all consumed, thermos flasks drained, with Moss watching intently for any gratuitous bits of crust or biscuit, which they both donated in good will, Ben and Fraser stood with bowed heads, their backs pressed against the hay bales, already fatigued with what they had done and getting colder and more stiff around their backs where the sweat had gathered. Silent in tiredness, and with few words, they measured the growing sound of the wind, whirling flakes and even deeper drop in temperature by sensors in their faces, ears, eyes and scalps, right up through their clammy wellingtons and down across their shoulders. This was setting in to be a storm of desperate, unspeakable severity.

Fraser came out with what totally possessed his mind.

"Aye, Benjamin, this is going to be the bugger of all storms. Where the devil can we possibly put these poor bloody creatures out of this lot, tell me that?"

Driven in below their headgear, snow hung over their eyelashes and lips and nostrils. Neither spoke. Ben for all his readiness to work along with Fraser, and keep him right on needful points, was neither used nor ready to be asked such critical questions. That was what his and Matt's father aye sorted out. And he was beyond reach, at yon bliddy funeral business. He would have to say something to Fraser at his elbow.

"By God, man, it's nae easy," in his most careful, grown-man gravity of voice. They, the two of them, would have his father to answer for if things gaed wrang at this game, nae twa doubts aboot that. The lad's ambivalence, dratted canniness, whatever you called it, suddenly cleared the way to a decision, the only decision available.

"Ben! Listen here. If we dinna get them out of the worst of the storm, the whole damned lot of them are going to land up in a heap getting smothered: lambs, gimmers, the whole jing-bang lot! And us along with them if we dinna make a move. Now."

In Fraser's mind there arose, all too readily, a vision of multiple humps of frozen, smothered sheep and lambs. Apart from those already lambed and in the shelter they had managed to knock together, the remainder were a substantial body; they would not, could not, hold off from lambing for more than a day or so, whatever the hellish conditions. Christ! There bloody well had to be some course of action that the two of them could pursue. "Think not upon the Act, but Act upon the Thought!" ran the maxim in his great grandfather's tome of farriery, indelibly penned in the mid-1800s Lord Strathcona, no less. I bet he'd never had anything like this to contend with. Well, here we go, m'Lord!' He smacked his fists together in sodden gloves.

"Right, Benjamin! This is the great plan: we'll need yon two field gates off their hinges, and trail them down to the head of the avenue. Come on, let's get yokit!"

Using the north-east word for getting started or yoked into a task, usually demanding, was unnecessary for Ben. They set off at once, upwind into the driving blizzard, caked white from their few minutes' progress. Being bidden to stay well down amongst the bales, Moss whined in uneasiness, watching them disappear in seconds.

Fraser stopped abruptly. Ben bumped into him with his head down and scarf pulled right up across his nose and eyes. They were at the top of the old coach avenue leading down from Kinchourn to the McMillans' lodge, obscured now. Cypress and sycamore trees stood to Fraser's left shoulder, a tossing brake against the steadily roaring blizzard. More sycamores, larches and lime trees to his right. On either side outside the wooded shelter strips, a fence ran right down to the lodge gates. Fraser swung round to speak with Ben, cracking the mask of frozen snow, mucus and scarf stuck to his own scarified skin.

"Listen! We'll bloody well shut them all in here. To hell with closing off the road; there'll be no raving idiots seeking to come up here in all this!" He shouted with renewed force. "We'll need to trail in a puckle bales on that feeding sledge of yours, Ben, to tryst them back in from getting blown into heaps around the old sheds! Close it off top and bottom, put down bales for them in aneth the trees, and haroosh the whole damned lot in here! How's that, then, shepherd?"

Ben's eyes looked into his, expressionless. With equal care not to expose his forever-scabbed cheeks, lips and chin, he enunciated his Granda's stock response to all suggestions hitherto untried:

"Aye, that's mebbe nae a bad idea. We'll gi'e it a wee try. Man!"

They both grinned, cracking open old hacks, not caring once the sharp pain had been accepted, and set off again.

Heaving the gates off their unused hinges and dragging them in the snow with ropes over their shoulders took a long time. They found that they really needed four to bridge the avenue securely. By despair and determination in equal parts, they got them: the two field gates, a half-rotten old thing from behind the roofless smiddy, and a desperately heavy iron one, festooned with curlicues and tendrils for some long-gone walk or avenue in the policies of the destroyed mansion house.

Grunting heavily with the effort of heaving it along, Fraser noted the small scabs of long-ago white paint, echoes of summer tennis, parasols and bustles, shooting parties and carriage drives. And estate workers and farm servants – ha! a very fitting term, that! – getting incredibly meagre weekly pay from the toffs.

Getting their motley collection of gates and things into position needed sheep stakes driven into the snow, ground, whatever, with the pinch bar to make holes, the heavy mel hammer to drive them. At last, with all in place and their chests heaving, going back for the gimmers, now with heads down in total submission to the storm, proved to be the easiest part of the whole plan.

Moss leapt in relief at their reappearance in the horizontally driven blizzard, and was sternly put back in amongst the bales until Fraser and Ben weighed up how to go about the final stage. The sheep could well persist in silly, sullen immobility, and the dog might render them even more obdurate. Ben was already glowering at them and swearing.

"Stupid, thrawn buggers, ye'd better bloody well move this time!"

Fraser had already seized upon the only manoeuvre left to them.

"Ben, see you an tak' an armful of hay, go up through the middle of them, canny like, and start to tramp a track through to the top of the drive. Cry at them to come on once you're to their front, and gie them a few wee wisps of hay. I'll push them on from ahin. Come on, get going!"

Head down, trudging through to the foremost sheep and placing his boots sideways to make a more completely flattened track, Ben Wyness started to call strongly, facing back to the grey mass of shapes behind him. Immobile in the background, Fraser felt Moss's nose slide into his palm, hanging straight down from the shoulder.

"Wheesht, man, lie doon!" Ben kept calling, trudging in reverse. "Sik-sik-sik! Come oan then! Sik-sik-sikkk!"

The gimmers' response was almost immediate; in a caked snow-white file, they stepped into Ben's track in slow compliant silence, frozen fleeces creaking. Once started into the shelter offered by the trees lining both flanks of the steep, disused avenue, they sifted away amongst the branches hanging low with snow, mysteriously, silently, some limping hugely. Fraser and Ben stood to watch them, the tension and drive utterly drained out of their bodies and minds.

"That's it, then, Ben. Let's get that hay down with the sledge, and just close the gates at the foot of the drive. To hell with it!"

Dimly discernible greyish blobs along both sides, fast fading in definition, the gimmers gathered round the bannocks of hay falling away from the slashed bale twines. The blackness of the flailing branches above them emphasised the great thickening blanket of steadily falling snow. With knives in their mittened fists, Fraser and Ben took some suspended seconds to grasp the fact that they had done everything humanly possible for the survival of these silly damned brutes and their soon-to-be born lambs. In shared impulse, both swivelled round to peer at the light further down, in the McMillans' sitting room window, then looked at each other without speech. No weakness, take the initiative for heaven's sake with this lot.

"Nothing for it, Benjamin. Make for home!"

Fraser knew this had to be put into motion, now, this very minute. They settled into a rhythm of clumsy, booted feet, oilskin leggings crackling with ice and frozen muck. Missing the precise placement of his foot in the other's deep print, one of them would stumble and just lie there, collapsed in the relief of being down out of the suffocating flakes. The other would wait, head down, too drained to speak, Moss patient beside them, eyes and muzzle in a grotesque mask.

"You all right, Ben?"

"Mechty aye. Just gie me a minute or twa tae mak' a start."

Fraser felt a quiver of unease; this seeking a moment's refuge was totally unlike Ben. He turned back and stuck out his hand for Ben to grasp it and be hauled upright. They went on, blowing snow from devitalised lips, everything white; even their sticks were sheathed in frozen snow. Two shapes, followed by a lesser one close at heel, all sometimes merging into one uncertain form in the blizzard of Arctic severity. Behind them, those animals whose welfare lay wholly in their hands were entirely blotted out. They would lie beneath the trees the length of the old one-time carriage drive until morning, and whatever that might bring.

All the signs were of the imminence of the unleashing of a blizzard that would defy mitigation in any human form.

Lying in bed, Fraser lay tense in his hearkening to the storm outside, feeling the whole house shudder to the force of the gale, now hard into the north-east, truly a killer of a northerly airstream. Where in hell did all this violence come from? What was the purpose of it in the whole pattern of things, this never-ending struggle to at least temper chaos? His over-full bladder drove him to snake out of the bedclothes, flapping them back again to hold some measure of body heat, and pad across to the window. Immense flakes whirled in the beam of his torch. He made a hurried foray to the downstairs bathroom, feeling grit under his bare feet. On the way back upstairs, he turned to check the kitchen clock: a quarter to five. His own alarm clock had stopped. Maybe the intense cold had buggered up that as well.

Rigid with a core coldness that would not go away, and with the gnawing pressure of his responsibilities in Jock Wyness's absence, he lay curled on his side, while his mind raced, envisaging what must now surely be a scene of smothered disaster and suffocation of life at the end of the glen. By half past five he was leaving the house, a note to Nan on the kitchen table, matches and meths laid out on the oilcloth for the Tilley lamp when everyone else got up. Between them all, the home forces could cope with any births amongst the older ewes; his own need, yammering constantly at him, was now to be down among those poor, blessed gimmers right there at first light. Or before, God wot.

Breakfast was half-warmed porridge, a hurriedly boiled egg (semi-congealed, more like) from a quick flare of dry kindlers and two spoonfuls of jelly from the dish on the milk house stone slab. Patch came twisting and grinning to his legs, but he patted her down and slipped out, snow falling across the threshold with an innocent flop. Resolutely avoiding going anywhere near the home ewes, he stopped to let Moss out of the stable, smelling warmly of dog's straw and dog's body. The two of them struck out for the bridge, then turned right to pick up the waterside road. Huh! That was the great joke. Fraser suddenly gripped his stick in uncertainty. By God, where was the bloody brig?

Of the familiar structure, nothing could now be seen barring a short meaningless length of handrail. The drifts were as high as a tractor wheel. Oh boy, oh boy, and where do we go here, Moss, my friend? Using his stick as a probe to sound the whereabouts of the planking across the bridge, Fraser struck to his left, cutting a slightly easier track for himself and Moss, working at convincing himself that while the wind seemed to be just as high, the snow it carried was slightly less overwhelming. A tightness in his throat and palpable heartbeat were not entirely due to his labours in making a track; to have dropped suddenly down through the treacherous white stuff into the black-running water below would have been the finish for him, and only faithful, wary Moss would be there to signal mutely to whoever came looking for him.

Cutting obliquely round the houlder of the hill, Fraser slowed, to try and get a hold on his racing apprehensions, before cautiously drawing close to the top end of the silent avenue of trees. There was nothing to be seen, absolutely no movement as he moved through between the first two cupressus trees.

For God's sake, dinna say that the gates had been opened by some idiot creature, after all their tugging and heaving to close them? He couldn't see any distance with definition in the slow dawn light. Still convinced that Ben and he had done the only thing left open to them to avoid a mass disaster, and yet with yawning dread cold in his belly, he pushed quietly through below the snow-caped branches into the centre of the avenue. Moss smelled and saw them before he did.

"Sit doon, Moss, mannie, that's a good lad."

His stomach was corded into bowstrings. What terrible things from the night hours of flat out snowstorm was he going to have to accept? Then he spotted the first movement of something grey, and another, and another. They all seemed to be there, settled and undistressed under the trees, and in some cases almost inside the damned things. He muttered to himself, unbelieving. Moss looked up to his voice and pricked his ears. The fact that the roaring wind had partly spent itself against the closely spaced trees seemed to have restored a measure of stolid acceptance to the gimmers' movements through the night hours.

Slowly at first, he stepped amongst them to count. Nine had lambed since last light yesterday, almost thirteen hours without attention. One had lost a twin. The lamb's head was still tightly sheathed in the foetal membranes. Another had a head, forelegs and shoulders of a partly extruded lamb hanging from her rear end, dead and useless. Attempting to lick her first born as it suckled, the gimmer caught sight of Fraser regarding her, and whirled in fright, causing the thing swinging at her haunches to alarm her further.

For the moment, Fraser asked of himself, would there be others in more desperate straits? He stepped on, moving slowly down the avenue, speaking quietly to the shapes that jerked up their heads at his passing, but were reassured by the shape and repeated familiar sounds of care at hand.

"Ho, lass, come away then, ho, lass. Canny noo, canny noo."

Praise be, the rest of them looked well enough suckled and sound. No feet sticking out in mute appeal for correction of malpresentation or worse. Now – he breathed out in massive, almost painful relaxation of tension – now, if some feed could be got to them, carefully and quietly, they would bide where they were for another night, no bother. Nae bloody bother at a'!

With sudden purpose and strength, Fraser wheeled round to trudge back up to the sheep in the old coach houses and steading where the already lambed ones were penned, tethered, held behind doors, gates and even an old bed from the bothy. Then he saw it. Christ, man! Did you have to do that?

It, the whole damned business, was a big, fleshy gimmer with a bumping, bleeding, prolapsed uterus, just what Jock Wyness would glumly describe as "The 'hale bloody lamb-bed hingin' oot, God sink it!"

His stomach plummetted down again. No help at hand; some intense and rapid applied action needed here. He knew what to do, but had never tackled the whole job by himself. "One thing at a time, and think what you're doing, my lad, or you'll have a casualty here." He breathed deeply. JeezUSS!

He tied her flailing hind legs together with a short length of rope, looped it over his left shoulder and neck, straightening up until the animal's head and neck trailed sidewys in the sparse, bloodied muck of her pen. Bracing himself with teeth-grinding effort, he straightened his spine futher, pain flooding down his neck as he squinted down with eyes and fingers to pick off pieces of hay, muck and rotten, devitalised tissue. The bottle of strong-smelling lambing oil was ready in his coat pocket. Splashing it liberally down the inside of an old torn oilskin legging, Fraser slid the whole bleeding mass inside this improvised tube, and started to try and feed it all back from whence it had come, this massive extrusion of vagina, cervix and uterus to about half the length of her own body. Twice, he had to bend down, utterly exhausted with wrenching his body upright against the dead weight.

Only after despair spurred him to make use of the roof truss above his head, putting a rope over it and hauling the damaged sheep up by main force and body-wracking half-grunts, half-curses until its muzzle scraped the ground, did he succeed. Then, a square of sacking tied in amongst clumsy knots of fleece across the purple, swollen vulva to keep everything in, and the huge weight carefully lowered to lie, supine, on the ground (but hind legs not released – "Not bloody likely, my fine fat friend!") did he stand back, hands pressed to his lower back in sweet relief.

By eleven o'clock that morning, with Moss almost manic at his knee from being released out of the only old shed with a door to it, crinkling his upper lip and whirling to catch his hand, everything was under control. Dizzy with utterly spent energy and feeling his heart thudding preternaturally loud in his neck or some blasted where, he distributed the meagre heaps of concentrates in such a way as to save the lambed and settled ones from having to trail new lambs out from under the trees' fine shelter, and made an attempt to clear a watering place in the frozen ditch. Gad, what a morning, and the McMillans going on at him all yon times, about not having to attempt everything himself. What a bloody great joke that was!

Ben had appeared with brother Matt, unusually, at his elbow, mumbling and grumbling and laughing by turns. Ben, his round face red and beaming at his own exertions, grinned hugely in pleasure at finding his absent father's precious gimmers alive and in good order. He stumped up and down the avenue, familiar to and unheeded by the gimmers, exclaiming in satisfaction in his cracked old man's voice, at the survival and hold on life of the lambs and their dams, unlikely candidates for canny mothering at the best of times. He knew all their mothers, where they had been lambed themselves, two years back, the lot. Even more like some diminutive querulous old man, Ben leant on his stick in front of Fraser, and peered up at him.

"Aye, aye, there, lambing shepherd, ye're doin' awa' fine. That was a dashed fine idea of mine to have them a' shut in aneth the trees!"

I Like to Walk in This Field

"You cocky wee bugger!" Fraser exploded, and took a swipe at Ben's legs with his own stick. Moss leapt excitedly from one to the other as they took up exaggerated parrying stances, poking away at each other until nonsense and laughter overcame both, falling sideways in the sullied snow, too weak to struggle up. Young Matt had long since departed to the McMillans' for what he could find in diversion for a mind unpossessed by sheep of any description.

They gathered their limbs and awkward bodies slowly, Fraser's hands still darkly blooded from the prolapse, but now with a certain unlikely sensation swamping both their minds to the exclusion of all else.

"By God, Ben! That's not a fresh wind coming in… is it?"

In stuttered response to the same ridiculous notion, incredulity rendered Ben's voice a squeak, a very young boy again:

"Well, if yon's nae a saft wind, the mannie in the wireless is speakin' a load of shite! Oor Dad kens a lot better nor him!"

Like two pointers on an uncertain but shared scent, they both raised their faces and nostrils to smell and identify something they couldn't see, coming in from the west. Moss stood to one side, looking quizzically from their faces to sticks and caps flung down in the snow. Of their noisy antics a moment ago, he could make nothing at all, but as to the changes in wind direction, temperature and barometric pressure, the dog had been well aware of all these, and other changes, registering in his canine valuation from before dawn. His work would be that much easier now.

XLII

Jock did not return home on the yellow Caterpillar tractor, nor on any other tractor, but on foot, a small and ineffectual figure, apparently making little progress up the slippery and exceedingly treacherous track of battered ice, now awash with brown peat-stained water. The narrowness of the glen and the burn within it, fed snow melt and icy slush into a swirling, roaring torrent in which no living creature had a chance of survival if once caught up in it. Jock's son Matt, always inventive regarding pleasure, and trying to perfect a long icy glissade right down to the dangerous lip of the burn, spied his father's struggling figure before any of them.

"Mam! Dad's coming! He's fair drunk!" He let out a shrill scream, ear-ringing at the finish. Matt's battered bike was flung down as he ran wildly round the yard, into the house and out again, screaming, "Dad! Dad!" bumping sorely into his mother as she ran into the yard in turn.

From inside the peat shed, skinning a dead lamb, to go on another to be twinned on for adoption, Fraser heard all of this uproar. He checked for a moment, knife and hands slippery with birth fluids. The shrieking boy had used the word "drunk" rather than "fu", the diminutive for "full". Fraser had learnt that in this part of rural Scotland anyway, being fu', a measure somewhat beyond normal intake of drink, was nothing out of the ordinary. But to say that somebody was drunk was a much more serious affair, with a real likelihood of behaviour collapsing into chaos or violence for no reason at all.

"Well, Jock Wyness," Fraser breathed to himself and the waiting lamb, "what are we going to be presented with in a moment or two, I wonder?"

Young Matt's continued (and tiresomely repetitive) yelling that this approaching father figure was drunk implied that while the erstwhile funeral mourner was perhaps not in a state of utter helplessness, there might well be aspects of his return home that promised to be a wee bit more difficult to handle. By all of them.

Jock's younger son Ben, Fraser's indefatigable and loyal helper through an uncountable number of draining days, slowly made for the gateway overlooking the bridge, passing Fraser, with his young old man's face set in a mask of dismay and anger. The wound of his total loss of faith in his father's behaviour lay like a deceit revealed across his face.

Nan Wyness's father heard the screaming and yelling from inside the barn, where he had once again been patiently arranging a very young lamb's wry-necked posture into a position where it could suckle its mother's swollen teat. It would suck feebly, once, twice, and then fall back weakly (or perversely, Granda' grunted to himself, biting on the stem of his cold pipe), making no effort at all. With diligent support from the elderly man, it had just made its first spontaneous and vigorous suck when all the screaming and yelling of that damned boy got up. The ewe whirled to one side and kicked savagely at the man's arthritic wrist, tumbling the malformed lamb and bruising its body. Very carefully, shaking with pain and pent-up fury, he set down the mewling lamb outside the pen, and seized the ewe by its muzzle. He pounded her face with his one good hand until he was breathless.

"Makin' a bliddy sound aboot bugger aaal!" he muttered, gasping with the pain in his wrist. "That damned boy's a born troublemaker, tae himsel' and tae a'body else, spawn o' the bliddy Devil!"

He stepped back from the ewe, judging her to be submissive. Slowly, the old shepherd filled, tamped and lit his pipe, and gently folding the diminutive lamb's limbs into a suitable position once more, knelt down stiffly beside the tethered ewe's flank, ignoring the growing commotion outside.

The only thing that kept Jock Wyness from falling down outright on the glazed track was his stick. It spun and scraped in wild swoops upon the snow and water. A lot of times, the stick was between his legs, which did not seem to have anything useful in their functions other than the desire to put as much distance between each other as possible.

Passing Fraser close by as he staggered and swayed into the yard, Jock regarded him gravely, from some remote, echoing place inside his skull. Jock's face was normally brown or tanned, but the only whiteness about his face now was the unnatural glitter of his teeth, locked in an open-jawed grimace, the rest of his face, eyes and neck a uniform suffused livid redness, almost purple, Fraser noted dispassionately. Even the whites of his eyes were as small pieces of torn, frayed canvas, from which two brown discs, violently charged with blood, looked straight ahead with unnerving fixity.

As Jock lurched past Fraser and young Ben, his dull muttering was only faintly identifiable as "Wharra beezer 'f a bliddy fu-f-fooneral. Hunn'ers' o' fowk." He belched loudly and pirouetted on one wild, sliding boot. Jock Wyness had been, still was and gave every indication of continuing to be, very, very solidly drunk indeed, on the afternoon of the fourth – or was it the fifth?

– day of giving a respected neighbour a fitting funeral, a properly celebrated send-off amongst a' that snow.

Near to tears of relief, anger and a strange kind of let-down feeling low in her chest, Nan Wyness pushed back the door, not wanting to get in his way and perhaps not even wanting to help him, drunken sot that he was in front of a'body. Jock missed the worn step with a ridiculously elevated hackney pace, and almost fell over forwards in so doing, then in attempted recovery, lurched backwards upon his wife, arms and legs flailing.

My God, she thought, a smile still set uncertainly upon her trembling lips, we've got this far into the lambing, the weather's hellish, an extra man in the house to be fed and washed for, no vans getting up the glen for months on end, trouble between Matt and his grandfather, and now this bloody disgrace of a creature: hold a bottle of anything ablow his nose and he's just useless!

She followed him along the passage at a safe distance, but stooping to pick up the carefully stacked logs through which her husband clattered, swearing coarsely, her tears of sheer fatigue and weariness escaped at last and ran down her cheeks, unseen by the uncertain and appalled figures halted outside in the yard.

Nan Wyness attempted to mend the situation brought so totally to chaos by her husband's return.

"There's some dinner left for you. I'll heat it up. I'll–"

She was interrupted by a resounding crash, a groan and oaths as Jock turned half round to reach out for the back of an easy chair, missed it completely and fell sideways into the peats and logs at the side of the range.

The cat hissed and spat vilely and fled through between their legs. By the time that she had turned from hastily closing the kitchen door upon the fleeing cat and male figures in the blinding snow glare outside, Jock had slid down the arms of the chair and was lying on his side, an arm over his face, utterly, stertorously unconscious.

Standing motionless in the centre of this crazed destruction in her kitchen, a scattered log still in her hand, and half-prepared baking things dropped on the table, Nan was possessed by a moment's vision of shining truth:

"Oh, if us women could only have just the work from our menfolk, without a' this, this unwelcome trachle and sotter!"

She knelt down to pull off his boots, rising to drop a blanket from the kitchen press over his collapsed inert form. Her tears then ran unchecked, without reason, for every reason, as she looked down at her hands taking up baking tasks. The assembled makings, the griddle ready to smoke with a knob of suet skiffed across it, her place at the centre of the house up here in the hills – these all seemed to mean something far more vital to her sense of wholeness than, than trying to compensate for the unspeakable wrongs of a man, her man, away out of it all for the best part of a week at the very worst time of the lambing, and then blundering in like a demented beast thinking to have it all just waiting for him, ach.

There was a fatigue lying over the entire daily scene and their struggles. It possessed them all, given a moment's respite to know it. These damned sheep and their lambs and their needs in this hellish weather. Would things ever come to normal and folk be themselves in the process? she wondered. Feeling an unutterable weariness throughout every fibre of her body, Nan Wyness closed her mind to not only everything but the floury board before her, but also to the sounds and presence of her husband snoring out his drunkenness behind her.

Nan Wyness lay in obdurate wakefulness, her head clear of the bedclothes, her husband's form beside her totally covered. She harkened to the whip and loom of the wind; she knew it to be the turn of things in the darkness before the dawn comes in. The sour smell of unwashed maleness and stale whisky from beside her did not turn her mind away from a joined up sequence of thoughts running freely now that she was totally awake.

She was looking in her mind's eye at her man's, her Jock's way of doing things. Or rather, his way of only part-doing things.

Tupping time, lambing, dosing, marking, clipping, dipping, speaning, feet, teeth, udders, injections (when the farms manager and her man got it right between them, that is), lamb sales, ewe sales, tup sales and then back into tupping time again. God's sake, was there never an end to it?

How many times had she felt the pressing need to ask of Jock, quite simply, if he was taking heed of tasks she knew to be coming up (or should be), only to be brusquely met with "Ach, haud yer tongue, wumman, it'll be be a'richt." On far too many occasions, it had just turned out to have been abundantly not a'richt.

Oh, Jock, my poor bloody Jock – he knew so much about sheep and their ways, but it never seemed to grow within him, to bear the need for strength when things were going badly. She knew well enough by now, to always present a happy and cheerful face, and for those things of their home and with outside jobs which she understood to be approaching, all would go well. Jock somehow looked to her, Nan well knew, for reflection of what he wanted to see, needed to see, true or false.

Pushing on in her review of everything and everyone involved in just keeping going at Tornaquhil, Nan posed a question to herself that immediately threw up an unpalatable answer, had not a major factor for the whole jing-bang lot of them been entered into the inescapable endeavours of every day, and night, whiles, namely, this young lad Fraser Baird needing to acquaint himsel' with the ways of sheep?

What would things have been like for her Jock, for the poor yowes, for the milk-starved lambs, for those perverse bitches of gimmers, for the sheer drain of energy that lay upon them all, if (Nan drew in her breath involuntarily at the thought) if they had not had Fraser landed upon them by Mr Melvin the farms manager, as a sort of notion by God knows whom? Aye, and at a time of fierce storms that a body would never have thought likely. There had been unforeseen moments of heated temper, but also some small seeds of warmth and companionship, particularly so between wee Ben and Fraser, and unlikely enough for her father's opinion of anyone not born to the job, a bond of shared interest between Granda' and Fraser, in the matter of bygone times up and down a' the glens, but seen from their hugely different viewpoints of age.

God's sakes, what great talks they had, the two of them! And none of her father's scathing tongue with matters that Fraser knew little of, for a wonder.

But wee Ben, there he got on real well with Fraser, barring the episode of the tup. She chuckled loudly, surprising herself! Fancy a vet's son nae kenning that yowes only come into the tupping once a year, about the back end of the year. He had got himself into such a hecht to find one of Jock's prime Blackface rams in amongst the ewe flock, stealing from their troughs, and tried to enrol Ben's help in catching it up there and then, before – what was the term Fraser had come out with? – mis-something or other; mis-sliance it had sounded like.

Ben, bless him! He had just laughed outright and said, "Catch him up yersel', there's little chance they'll get tuppit noo!" and had come in for his breakfast quite red in the face with ill-temper and wonder at siccan fool ideas.

Ah, well, as for young Matt, well, what about him? Nan unconsciously made the smallest movement of shaking her head. As if in accord with his wife, her husband's form beside her mumbled a sequence of sounds below the heap of bedding, which might have been an irritable "Come on wi' them, Patch!", then released a shattering, sustained fart that made Nan almost laugh out loud again.

There was little doubt that Matthew had chanced his luck too far with Fraser on those desperate days of blin' drift down at the old castle place. Buggerin' off like that and nae even telling a body; that was an outright disgrace. Nan turned over on her other shoulder, not easily; wearing vest and knickers in bed to keep warm these bitter nights was an excusable necessity, but they aye got kirned up through the night. Thoroughly wakened now, and wincing at the all-too-familiar clear light reflected upwards into their bedroom from the snow outside, she swung her feet, still in wellington socks, out of the bed on to the linoleum, determined to make a start. Get the fire kindled and porridge on the go.

In the kitchen, trying to clad herself and kindle the fire in the range and avoid stepping on Mouse, the patch-faced cat, who was extending himself languorously from his sleeping place in basket beside the oven, Nan asked of herself again, half aloud and sleepy with it, "Surely to God the weather will break and this giving from within each of us more effort and willpower that we ever have to call upon, will come to a stop? It's aboot bloody well time; we canna go on and on. Come on, fire, let's get something going first go!" She could hear Fraser, or somebody, banging about outside, bringing in split logs and seemingly speaking away to himself, not in the best of humour by the sound of it.

"Mighty God, the twa of us having to converse wi' oorsel's. The hale bloody place is goin' skite! Well, Mouse, it's a right good job that we didnae a' choose tae gang doon the glen to the auld cratur's funeral. Some bloody redd-up that would have been; we'd have all been in the loony bin!"

She burst out laughing at the expression on Fraser's reddened face, he having caught her last few words. Thinking that yet another disaster had only narrowly been averted, his obvious puzzlement prompted her to add, "Aye, young man, never mind the dratted funeral, it would have been a toss up between which of us would've landed in the loony bin, goin' oot of oor minds and a' crammed into the early bus oot o' the village!" She burst out laughing for absolutely no apparent reason at all, at the lunatic reality of the funeral, the endless storms, the chaos and weariness in everything.

XLIII

Their shrill cries piercing the very bones of her skull, Nan threw her head back in a sudden alarm as Matt and Ben whirled back into the farmhouse, kicking and skirling like banshees.

"Mam! Mam! There's a fresh wind comin' in from the west! Dad says it's coming in by God Almighty! Come outside, Mam! The noo!"

Outside, Jock Wyness stamped up and down and round again in a short stretch of the yard, driving his stick with speechless demented force into the snow and ice and muck, battered into grey glass by their daily journeys for so very long now, it seemed. His stick bent and bowed and twanged against the indifferent earth's encasement.

They all stood, Nan, Fraser, the two boys and haltingly, Granda', as prisoners released from a terrible and endless dream; a sly difference was working upon all their senses.

"Aye, man," said Jock, grasping Fraser ferociously by the arm, his lips pulled back tightly, baring his brown-stained teeth, "aye, man, there's nae wind! Nae bliddy wind! And there's a fresh coming in by God Almighty, or I'm oot o' my senses, by Christ! Can ye nae feel it, a' you folk?"

Fraser looked out over and above their variously inclined heads and faces, looking up to the farthest hill tops, back down along the length of the glen, suddenly back to the rim of the hills beyond their own, all seemingly locked in snow glazed upon snow. What was the difference, for God's sake? Jock was at him again, a man possessed.

"Look ye, Fraser! The snaw's melting. We'll mebbe see black groun' by morning! What think ye of that, by Christ?"

There was no wind. Then, then, oh, the softness of it came to them, in all of their starved senses. Out there in the dirty, battered snow of the farm close, Nan Wyness grabbed her man's arm and whirled in a wild whirling reel, did the same with Fraser and skirled with a yell that came back to them all and was redoubled in sheer animal relief.

But in a straight line of six miles from the manic dancing figures at Tornaquhil, in another home, the Melvins' home, there was an explosion of bitter intensity.

403

In a savage baring of bitterness (or shock), and in an uproar of intense feelings owing nothing whatsoever to difficulties of lambing or feeding or utter weariness of sheep and their servants at some remote outbye hill farm or other, James Melvin, farms manager to the estate, whirled round to his wife Lorna for only the briefest of seconds, before flinging himself away from her ashen features, jerking into agitated stamping up and down the length of the low-ceilinged kitchen.

"This is what you get for giving your best, your very last ounce of energy and loyalty, our very best for a damned laird who can only choose to believe the worst of a body when it suits his misbegotten purpose. Damn him to hell!" His fists were clenched into claws, deep in the pockets of his tweed jacket.

"Nine years, Lorna, no, damn near ten years, ten blasted years, and look how I've improved his suckler herd, and his stock heifers and bull sales; buying in the best of blood and changing the calving programme, and then having the whole infernal labour of it thrown back in your face, by an ignorant public school so-called toff that disnae ken a good breeding beast from… from a double decker bus, by Christ! Damn his miserable inbred eyes and the whole lot of them!"

Lorna Melvin plucked ineffectually at a thread hanging from the pillowslip she had been ironing when her husband had slammed the Land Rover to a halt outside and stormed through to her in a crash of doors wrenched open, the old spaniel sworn viciously out of his way, finally to loom in front of her, incoherent in rage and shock. And, she divined instantly, in fear.

"But, James, maybe the factor has misunderstood whatever the laird was in such a state about. You ken fine, he always simmers down once you've explained matters directly to him; he's just not got the farming knowledge you have. Could you not just give him a wee ring, or drop in a letter? Margaret could draft it for you, just telling him that you bought some heifers for yourself at the same time as the Home Farm ones. Surely that would–"

"Look, Lorna." James Melvin delivered his words with huge, clamped-down control, as to a wayward child. "Our great factor knows not one thing about prime cattle, right? But he has always been decent enough to leave that side of things on the estate entirely to me, and the laird has accepted that. Seemingly. The great laird himsel' knows even less about beasts of any kind, let alone registered Angus, but he makes a practice to put it about to all his friends and other lairds at their dinner parties up there, that anything I bring back to the Home Farm has been his selection, his eye, his knowledgeable investment, by God! And over the years, I've been stupid enough to be his wee servant. 'Oh, Melvin's quite a good chap with cattle, y'know.' With me supposedly running to do his bidding at all the sales. And, now this." James Melvin's voice rose, exposing the depth of corrosion, the destruction of trust by his employer. "So, here's our reward, my dear wife, and Margaret's too, for that matter." He flourished the letter he had found lying on the farm office table only scant minutes back and read it out to his wife:

"'The Major has instructed me to terminate the agreement between the Estate and yourself, and to tell you that you and your family will be permitted to remain in your present estate house until the end of next month. You will receive a letter in confirmation from the Estate lawyers, who will be pleased to accept any communications you may now have.' And just listen to this odious sting at the end, by the factor. '...that he, Mr Anthony Leslie, was deeply vexed about this rather unpleasant business.'"

Lorna Melvin registered her husband's words in speechless compassion, while her inner being churned in turmoil; their home was a tied house that went with the position of farms manager.

"And you can be sure of one thing, Lorna, that arrogant bitch of a wife of the laird, with all her American charm and roving eye, will have some fancy bloody ideas about how to run the farms, and the Angus herd, and even the hill places, with something willowy and wonderful straight out of agricultural college in God-knows-where." His eyes and voice were like a whiplash across both of their faces, one white and drained, the other suffused to insuppressible rage. "And then, we're out on the road; no job, no pay and no roof to our heads, in seven generous weeks' time. This day I shall remember, by Christ, I will!"

He was quieter now, but if anything, more intense in his view of something that could never be mended, should never have had to be mended.

"They know fine in the estate office that I buy the odd really good heifer for ourselves, our own wee Angus fold, Lorna, and that my cheque covers it as soon as I'm back here after the sales, but no, the Great God in the Big Hoose must have some yah-yah pal of his, a damned spy, watching at the ring, and telling him that I seem to be using the estate account to buy in a beast for myself, by God! Even the auctioneers can back me up. I've put all the estate's business through their ring these many years, but anything for ourselves is entered in my own, separate account."

James Melvin turned to look out through the kitchen window to the wooded ridge of Cearn na Phealidh, that bonny outlook where their daughter Margaret was so fond of walking, but now not really seeing its crown of trees that sheltered the village.

"God sink and rot the man – and his sleekit wife. They want to ruin my name, our name and our home and our chance of another post at my age now, all through this, this petty-minded drama to let the laird be seen as Major Big, interfering with everything and everybody in his own wee domain. Aye, 'interfering', that's the word for it, by Christ!"

Sitting on the upstairs landing with her knees clasped to her chest, Margaret Melvin had heard every harsh word, every heated explosion from her father. She had grasped at once the full import of their having to leave this fine, settled home. For her especially, it was not only home, but a haven from wounds that went too deep, far deeper than her disfigurement on which these slights were still directed.

There was another thread of not knowing pulling at her mind. Even before the relief throughout the village which folk felt with the unclenching of weeks, months of Arctic conditions that everyone could suddenly feel. Thanks to the various persons who had come in to speak with either or both of her parents, she knew perfectly well that the young man, Fraser Baird, who had so gladdened and pleased her on their first meeting here, in this very house, had been accorded unstinted praise for his efforts with Jock and the burden of lambing away out of things up at Tornaquhil. She would have welcomed the opportunity, any opportunity to find out from Fraser, once the hash of things was by, how he felt about making his life amongst them. Or, just to have some time for a talk and a laugh with him, as they had done before. That would be fine by her. By the same token, in spite of the desperate conditions, it had somehow got about that he had spoken to the General about how to go about and tender for the lease of some hill place that lay out beyond the watershed of their own, fine Don. Was this what he, having had a good schooling and his own father being who and what he was, was this *really* what Fraser wanted to do? Should he not be turning his face to something far better?

In this strange concern, should not she be pointing out other avenues for Fraser Baird, of whom she knew but little but equally strangely, enough? There was another, incomplete wish to see further in her own life. Could, would things of a cautiously personal nature ever possibly come together? In what fashion? And where, and with whom?

In the awful storm of raised voices that now shook her, Margaret railed inwardly at her father's easy assumption of everlasting security, his self-assuredness in his comfy farm manager's tweed suit, his favourite posture in the worn armchair, his sheer complacency thinking that this exclusive state would obtain for him forever, until – until what, pray?

Damn him, damn all lairds and Major This and Colonel That and their grasp on folks' lives in their damned tied houses up and down the land. Margaret Melvin bowed her head to her knees and wept. Her forearms clamped around those nylon-clad knees, which had afforded Fraser Baird such surprise in that confusing vision of this blossoming young woman's anatomy, such shy excitement. They now received a steady silent splash of tears, streaming down over pale beauty and livid birthmark alike.

XLIV

The release from battling, from defying, from the dragging of will and muscle to see through another and another day of storm and driven snow, came upon them in the late afternoon of a day that had fallen silent. The air moved and lingered in a beguiling fashion that all at Tornaquhil just did not believe.

Lifting his nose and face to it, Fraser greeted the lazy pluffets. "Aha, you deceiving bloody bitch of a thing, why should we take this as the change we're so desperately needing?"

Soft currents and clouds, sweeping in from the Atlantic, released a towering drive to sheer ferocity of work amongst everyone within and without the glen. Jock, he, Ben and Matt, their mother and even on occasion, Granda', were in the sheep pens at both ends of the tired grey glen just about every single day. There was no end to the tasks faced, fought with, pursued with energies no one realised they had. At nightfall, with normal mealtimes abandoned, there was no talking amongst the five of them. The boys sometimes just pushed their half-cleaned plates away from them and slept at the table. The evenings were stretching out, but always the promise of more light to do just one or two more tasks never quite gained ground. Jock and Fraser were exhausted by nightfall. With the grey, tired-looking hill road winding down between sullen defeated drifts to the village opened up, both boys were, with every reluctance, gathered back into school attendance again, after weeks of being cut off. They took ill with this inescapable penalty, and trudged dourly down to the old shooting brake at the end of the road.

It was just as Nan had foreseen, but to nothing like the same degree as each dawning day's reality of work, work piled up. Marking lambs, inoculating ewes and lambs (yeah, we got it right this time, Fraser muttered, with some relief as the "instant authority"), cleaning ewes' and gimmers' clarted tails and udders, sorting the tups' feet in their long neglect, mending fences, gathering up rotten lambs' carcases for burial, stinking, discarded skins from twinning-on, casting huge blocks of snow away from collapsed hill fences, and latterly, branding the ewe hoggs. It was an endless whirl of demanding, draining physical hard work. Fraser was secretly impressed at the way in which Jock Wyness just damn well kept going; long past dinner time, long past piece time in the afternoon (not even a quick bite and a laugh with the McMillans), long past a sensible time to stop and make up energies at anybody's welcoming kitchen table.

The day that they burned the numbers of their year of birth on to the horns of the year-old ewe hoggs (next season's gimmers-to-be, realised Fraser, pulling one into his knee as it spun round him), it was hot, really hot. Ben and Fraser had their shirts and vests off by midday, reek from the heavy branding irons and dust from the pens in their noses, eyes, hair. Their faces and forearms, snow-tanned to mahogany, were in deep and startling contrast to the smooth whiteness of upper bodies, free of dungarees, pullovers, shirts, vests.

Whoever was catching would run a hogg hard up to the rails in the catching pen, her flat horn hooked over the second rail up from the bottom, the last two digits of the previous year branded deeply with the smoking iron, and her head and neck then immediately twisted round for the other horn to be given a paint mark, all without losing that first essential clamp-like hold on her horn and rump.

They worked well together as a close-knit team: Ben, his father Jock and Fraser in the pens, catching and holding, and Alick, one of the many young men about the Dows' croft place, branding and Granda' heating the irons inside an old oil drum, red hot with coals and peats. Nan Wyness painted each hogg with the narrow band of colour on the left horn.

Not surprisingly, mistakes were made. It needed only a moment's inattention. Fraser was so surprised at the sudden leap upwards of the hogg in his grasp, that its full horned impact high on his bare chest knocked him flying against the rails, making the one held there for branding buck and twist in attemped escape also.

A number of things happened in quick succession. Jock swore with foul, stuttering ferocity, Granda' stumbled in passing the dull red iron to Alick and charred the length of the horn, Ben cackled with venomous derision at Fraser, and his mother, offended by the vehemence of her menfolks' foul tongues, stepped back and upset the paint tin, the only one left in precisely that colour.

Fraser, mortally embarrassed, face set like stone, grabbed savagely at the same hogg that had escaped him, held it by one manically jerking hind leg, and rammed it into the rails with both knees.

"C'mon then, let's keep going for Christ's sake," he added, not entirely under his breath.

To "Have ye got it right noo, then?" Granda's and Alick's withering query, immediately before setting the heated iron to the proffered horn, Fraser made no reply. Of course he was right, no need to for all this bloody carry-on just because he'd let go that leaping bugger of a beast before they'd...

"Hey, man! The stupid bugger's given Granda the wrang bliddy horn. He's done the wrong side!" Young Ben's outraged yell stopped them all in mid-motion, to look down, angrily, accusingly.

"Christ, man, Fraser, what in hell's name are ye thinking aboot? These are my special ewe hoggs, d'ye hear, and I'll not be made oot tae be a complete bliddy ass by you, God sink it! Awa' hame if ye cannae dae it right."

Jock's sudden explosion of rage, his voice offensively hoarse, was cut short as he curtly turned his back to Fraser, but audibly continued in muttering to his father-in-law, a succession of obscenities concerning handless amateurs, and more. Jock wrenched the offending iron from Granda's hand and flung it back into the fire.

Nan Wyness, hurriedly scraping the thick red paint from the concrete, sheep muck and all, and appearing to be guardedly watching her husband with one eye between the rails, winked hugely at Fraser with the other, silently mouthing something beginning with B at Jock's back, grinning like a mischievous young lassie. Fraser was utterly ashamed at his ineptitude. He retreated into work, catching a hogg and nearly crushing it with iron force. They all drew closer, guarded and careful in sideways looks at one another before taking up the rhythm again.

Fraser determined to have the matter out with Jock there and then, otherwise he may as well just knuckle under to Jock's sarcasm, but that he knew he was not prepared to do. Right, he'd come away up here to learn, and was not anywhere near the end of the process, if there was such a point. What was it that his father had once said to him, about having made some grievous mistake in the company of experienced men? "Look, Fraser, what you have to do at once, is present yourself as entirely happy – no, wrong word – willing to accept guidance, help, if you like, from someone who has the notion to see himself as a giant amongst pygmies! Present yourself to him, them, whomever, as a novice. Get the idea? You will make some awful wrong decisions. Just as I have done, believe me!" Fraser could hear his father's advice in his head. He straightened up as he hooked the hogg's horn over the rail again.

"Jock? What odds does it mak' if the brand's on the other side, anyway? Keep me right, you men. I'm just a bally cowboy, buggerin' about up here and getting sheep-minded in the process!"

The shepherd turned to him slowly, as though imparting a confidence to someone of sadly lesser understanding.

"Ach, weel, when it comes tae run them up the shedder for any reason, the one person can spot them single-handed if they're a' on the one side, d'ye see? Anither thing, putting bonny ewe hoggs through the ring, they aye look better if they're a' the same. A brand or a paint-mark on the ither side aye looks bigger or sma'er than the rest. Ye ken yersel' how stupid fowk can be!"

Jock grinned, maliciously at first, but then laughed outright in a direct sally to the rancour caused by Fraser. They all laughed, but not unkindly. Jock had one more good reason for his way of doing things.

"And mark ye this, Fraser, if it ever comes that ye're putting ewe lambs through the ring in your ain name, a tidy bit of showmanship puts pounds on them, an' something verra important tae me and any ither 'herd – his reputation, and folk ken my reputation, do they not, Nan? Come on, lads, we'll set to again!"

So saying, Jock accepted the apparent harmony of mood and movement amongst them, and to all appearances, they were a team, knowing in the ways of handling sheep and getting on with the job as best and in as good humour as they could. But in all of them, working in the smoke and sun, there was a deep well of utter weariness which they had drained to exhaustion. With care, it did not manifest itself in gross malfeasance, rather in small acts which, with care, could safely be put behind them all.

Now, as the days lengthened, as peewits and curlews wheeped and whauped far on into the spring dusk, Jock, Fraser, the two boys whenever dropped from the dusty school shooting brake, Granda' too, they all toiled tirelessly at or from one task to another. In the stolen moment of a few seconds' breather from whatever was in hand, one or another of them would bring back to all of their awareness that the drifting snow and bitterly low temperatures had taken possession of the glen on the thirtieth day of November, and bare ground was only now spreading and joining up creeping fingers of black ground on the fourth of May. What a desperate time it all had been. But they preferred not to speak about that time.

The hill burns released the smallest of drips, the capes of frozen snow upon clumps of rushes and juniper bushes were suddenly collapsing, revealing all colours of green, refreshing the eye, and spirit. There came the smallest of sounds of release from the rigid land.

The increasingly warm-like shift into spring held up. Some days the bare ground could actually be seen to be steaming, but this was commonly reversed by a hard frost at nightfall. Going up and down and back up again the long glen road any number of times in a day, a good part of the road was free of snow or ice, but painfully hard. No need now for sweaty, clammy wellingtons. Jock and Fraser were glad to get into the tackety boots. With the evening round to check that ewes and lambs were mothered up before last light, shared equally between Jock, Fraser, young Ben and even to a grudging extent by Matt as well, their lower legs and feet were whipped into cords by sheer muscle fatigue and downright soreness.

Jock, leading their noisy column of bodies into the kitchen passage as they clattered home below the dark sky pulling the night's clouds to conceal their deep tiredness, would drag and scrape his nailed boots in sudden utter weariness, while to Fraser, his feet and heels throbbed like hot coals. The white light from the Tilley lamp made them look away and wince. Jock's first action on making for his customary chair, muttering, "Christ, sair tae hell at baith ends!" was to stretch out his legs, half-laughing, half-crying out with the pain-cum-pleasure of being finished for yet another long day.

"God's sake, ma queets are that sair!' Jock intoned down his nose, cigarette smoke and speech in unison, as though comment might mitigate a pain beyond all tolerance.

Queets, queets? This, Fraser deduced from the way Jock employed it, could only be a very old, very local word for feet or ankles or both. With what early folk amongst the glens had this word originated and from how far back? Gaelic, perhaps?

For the moment of blessed relief, queets or no queets, they were companions in having used every fibre of their bodies to put another day to good use. Sitting opposite Jock, with Nan happy to have all her menfolk gathered to the supper table, Fraser squinched up his eyes as he eased off his own boots, falling with a clatter to the floor and pulling off his socks in wonderful easement, to wriggle his toes. By God, sair wisnae the word for it!

"Come away to your meal, a' you girning men. A hot mustard bath'll be just the thing for the twa of ye, once you've eaten!"

Hands on hips, Nan stood smiling at both of them, but with only the shadow of a wink to Fraser. Jock screwed up his features in even greater agony and Fraser burst out laughing. He had noted Jock's impossibly distorted toes, compressed into a row of misshapen lumps. Jock expanded this opening for more drama with even more illogical pride.

"Aye, Fraser my loon, many's the day I've herded hoggs, an' yowes, an' gimmers with just what ma feyther could find for a pair o' boots tae me, nae the best. On with them in the morning, soaking wet or frozen like a board, with whiles a puckle strae tae keep oot the cauld." He looked directly at Fraser, his voice dropping to a meaningful murmur. "Aye, an' many's the time Ah didnae hae socks, just the strae!"

Fraser was aware of the talk round the table, but not as a part of it. There was another, deeper ache in his thoughts that no mustard bath was going to ease, let alone mend. There was a stillness in a secret part of him, that deeply secured store of personal wants and will from childhood; things that were important that he do. He needed some time away from the glen, the roaring, insistent clamour of the unruly gimmers with whom he had struggled to exhaustion to provide shelter, feed, firmness, ach, everything. That part of him that made decisions needed distance to see what things, what plans were possible, but also to recognise those that could not be sensibly entertained.

About the middle of May that year, Fraser asked Jock if it would be in order to take just a half-day on the bus out of the village, to where or for what he didn't specify. Nan would go down with him and make long-neglected visits to friends in the village also, and shopping, of course. They might get a run down with one of the Dows who had a car.

The two of them walked far down the glen, all the way down to the Don valley, for Alick Dow to pick them up in time for the midday bus. As he turned to step into the bus, Nan, in unexpected fashion, put her hand to his shoulder, saying:

"Fraser, you're one of the family. You must realise that and I ken fine some of the things that you've been thinking on this while; so dinna be makin' decisions that'll tak'you as far awa' fae us that we lose you, do you heed me?"

He sat in the bus, at ease, but returning to Nan's caring words and the other, whirling number of strongly related matters clamouring for clearance to make choices, decisions. Crocuses gave way to slim daffodils, flowering currant bushes, a few early tulips. He knew fine from desultory talk around the table, even on occasion in the sheep pens, that strange and unpleasant affairs involving the Melvins, James Melvin the farms manager in particular, had resulted in their moving away from his job, their fine bonny home and their place in the village two or three weeks back. From the talk amongst estate folk generally, there was undoubtedly a measure of ill-feeling and acrimony in the matter, accruing from the laird, the owner of the estate, so it seemed.

All that he, Fraser, could draw from it was that the deep down tenuous hope for warm, heart-speeding contact with Margaret Melvin had now gone. The talk in the village was that they had moved away down into the Borders country, that James Melvin was trying to get into a place, some acres of his own, and good luck to him. And to his fine wife, and that poor lass, too, of course. In a closed-down part of him, Fraser felt stricken. Was there something he should have immediately done on hearing this gathering of threads of comment and speculation, a token at least, of caring, repair?

I Like to Walk in This Field

From the bus, after choosing the seat that offered the view he needed, he waited for a brief sight of Margaret's home (her one-time home, he dourly corrected himself) but there were now no signs of the lives or activities of the family who had given him of their golden afternoon in welcome. A lazy blue reek came from the place further down the road to the ford through the river; Bella must be burning peats. She would know where the Melvins had flitted to. She would have done the last cleaning of the house for them once the removal van had rumbled out of the village, and not one of the General's, seemingly. Aye, Bella would know. He would go and see her, first chance, and maybe get an address for forwarding letters. But only once this blasted lambing business stops going on forever. Come on, man, get on with things that you need to find out about, things that come before anything of a private nature.

Step One: go to this solicitor's office in the market town on the way into Aberdeen, and see about this rumoured upcoming tenancy of the hill place. Go to the bank, and see what it would take to make a start, in even the simplest of fashion. At a push, take the time to go on and speak with his father about this urgent wish to create something, some piece of land that would repay hard work and industry, some thing that would grow, not to be content with, what had Ramsay McMillan called it? – "Working your way into a prison of slavery, without a key to unlock the prison door".

Well, he would see about that.

Tramping steadily up the glen road, Fraser allowed his mind to roam unchecked over the events of the afternoon. Before setting out that day, and wishing not to place a burden of extra work upon Jock, he had risen extra early, and along the bottom fence of a thick growth of birches and juniper bushes he had heard and then seen the blackcocks in their courtship display on the lekking grounds. In the thin mist of early morning, their liquid bubbling "Buhhloo-buhhloo- luhloo" had led him, by stealthy stalking, to actually see the oval patch of short sward free of overhead canopy from the birches. The beauty and grace of the blackcocks' bowing and retreating, drumming of feet and wing feathers, had possessed all of his senses. It was a gentle advance into a heightened awareness of sheer aesthetic delight which he didn't know was in him until that still summer's morning.

Deeply drawn into Fraser's senses in the succession of incoming summer days that year, it seemed that this little-known glen was offering up to him the very essence of experiences, not only from each day's satisfaction from work well handled, but added to by the most simple of things: a walk up to find the source of some wee burn, the quietness of a roofless croft's modest stone walls, or running his palms over the heat-fired stones of a massively constructed lime kiln, long abandoned to the heather. These findings were sometimes with the two boys for company, before supper and bed, but more often with Moss at his heel.

"C'mon, then, old man!. We're not working now, just out for a dander. Away ye go!" he would say, and Moss would describe manic circles of sheer delight, rushing back to press his flank against Fraser's leg, eyes warm and liquid with total devotion.

They saw the brush marks of an eagle's wing tip feathers in a hidden, north-facing wreath of old snow at great height, saw at a higher elevation than Tornaquhil the ploughed rigs of long-dead crofters' toil revealed in the long evening light upon the land, and came upon an old brass strip-wound cartridge for a .450/.500 rifle in the cupboard recess of some kind of a stalker's bothy or summering place for folk with their cattle.

In the endless light of a summer's evening, he would clap Moss to him. They would both sit in a pocket of heather, seeing so far away into the blue hills of Perthshire, Inverness-shire and beyond that it stung the eyes into malfocus. "Aye, man, ye've been looking fair into the very heart o' Scotland," Nan Wyness's father would observe in response to Fraser's tales of sitting and absorbing all those ancient kingdoms beyond the peaks for which he had no name. Granda' was content in his inner vision of it now, after so many years on the hill in all weathers during his own working life as a Highland shepherd.

For Jock and Fraser, with summer laying its promise upon land and livestock, the two of them were out constantly; striding, checking, heeding, herding, ewes and lambs, gimmers and lambs, twins, singles – the lot. It was an affront to their diligence for either of them to find a ewe, bulky with fleece before clipping time, stuck on her back for too long, with a lost-looking lamb nudging her bloated belly and udder in distress. "God sink that!" Jock would mutter.

The last look at nightfall, the speed of getting round them first thing in the morning, were all-important. By the end of each stretching day, their weariness was something apart from other bodily responses.

Late one afternoon, while the two of them were waiting at the road end to be company for the two boys coming off the big old school shooting brake, Jock divulged his anxiety, increasingly obvious to Fraser, of the past two days.

"Ye hinna seen yon bell-browed hogg, aye, the right good Braichlie one, have ye, Fraser?"

"No, I canna say that I have, Jock. They were certainly a' there when I looked them for you, last. Yesterday, about midday. Why do you ask?"

Jock Wyness's face darkened and he began poking repeatedly at a thistle

415

with the end of his stick. His voice dropped, to assume that nasal, half-muttered intonation indicative of dramatic significance.

"Well, then, lad, but she's awa' – and I'm nae sure but that she's been lifted!"

His eyes were open like saucers. Lifted? Jock's suspicions of neighbouring or even beyond-neighbouring shepherds were morbid, continual and frequently hilarious. He would tap his nose, squint through his cigarette smoke, which was always coiling out from places in his brown face that surprised Fraser, and mutter on about sheep disappearing. Nan Wyness usually burst out laughing, her father would hawk, spit and say nothing, pointedly silent, and the two boys would roll around, helpless in parodies of dastardly sheep-stealing at the dead of night, and their father would storm off, raging.

In a swirl of dust, exhaust and hot engine smells, the old pre-war shooting brake on the school run, drew away, and they all clattered up the road, Jock repeatedly glancing at Fraser from under heavy brows.

As they all clumped over the bridge in sight of the house, young Ben wheeled round to demand of his father, "Dad, are you lot to be lookin' for that hogg after we've eaten?"

Jock's suffused face darkened further, before he burst out half-laughing, half-roaring, "Damned loons, there's not a dashed thing a body can keep from them! Awa' in and tell your mother we're awa' tae the hill efter. Me and Fraser'll see to the coo. Hurry on, noo!"

With their meal heavy in their stomachs, Jock and Fraser went straight up the hill facing the house. Ben was predictably with them, matching their stride, grunting with it. Young Matt had offhandedly spoken about, "Going down the waterside" and promptly just somehow faded out of sight.

They each took on a widening triangle of high hill, the starting point, with Tornaquhil house and steading tiny below them, back to where they would each make when the light was gone.

Right up on the high ridge at the crags, Jock set off north-eastwards at even greater pace, with only a sharp word to Patch to "Come in aboot, 'ooman, an' nae raking!" Fraser made sure that with Ben taking the northerly triangle between his father and himself to the north-west, no dead ground would be missed in their search, going off himself to the north-west on a high plateau dotted with juniper bushes, to swing round later directly west once he had seen Ben out of sight, making for the far-out march fence. Fraser knew that Ben would swing left-handed to come round above him as he dropped to investigate wee hollows and lurks between his path and old farm grasslands below.

Jock had muttered at the moment of splitting up, "Aye, man, we're gaun' tae tak' in a hell of a groun' at this caper. God sink her, the damned thing!"

Turning for a last sight of Jock, Fraser felt his familiar strong sensation of being truly a part of all that he could see around him, from range upon range of the far farmlands of Banffshire, round to the dim mountains of Inverness-shire, Perthshire and here, his own homeland of Don and Dee, the infinitely beguiling mixture that was Aberdeenshire. He set off once more on a systematic swing this way and that, Moss clearly aware that they were seeking a single sheep or more likely, a wandering band of two or three. He was a flowing curve of canine willingness, not needing directions. Fraser smiled in greatest pleasure at the black and white body rippling in amongst junipers, rashes, heather, scrub willows, completing each circle of quest to look back to Fraser with gleaming eyes and liquid tongue.

Fraser's involuntary "Get oot, man!" was entirely unnecessary, but he did it anyway, for the joy of seeing his dog's arrow-like streak to full stretch up over the next ridge. A buzzard, probably disturbed by one of the searchers, lofted high on a thermal heated by the mixed Scots pine and larch plantation directly below Moss and he, mewing to its mate. They had found not a solitary beast, had seen only blue hares and a black dot of a grazing roe. The night air enfolding him and Moss had a softness of near-silence which carried small sounds for immense distances.

Of an impulse, Fraser pulled the ever-attentive Moss into his chest and tried to atone for these long hours on the hill again, after a day's work already done, by ruffling up Moss's neck and his ears, stroking firmly down his throat and chest. Moss promptly collapsed against him in sensuous delight, wriggling and catching his hand. Fraser looked down at him, grinning in equal pleasure.

There was this great ache (was? – no, had been for some time back now), a need to be actually in the workings of this part of Scotland, to firmly belong there, to have a home and successes and failures and see land he had ploughed and trees that he had planted and ditches he had shieled out, to come home in the last light to his own house and hearth and have a woman he could hold and talk with and share and love, to have her feel her own need for him grow within her and centre his living and joy of hard working upon her in so many ways he could only guess at just now, to smell the scent of this young woman's hair and body in his head and kindle the early morning fire for her with the blue reek rising to welcome the day, their day, to... his head drooped low in sheer waves of longing.

Fraser pulled himself from pointless reverie over things he might never attain; they were supposed to be looking for Jock's bell-browed God Almighty-mebbe-stolen hogg, dammit!

"Aha! You poor old bugger. No more work in you, is that it? There certainly isn't a great deal in me. C'mon!"

Fraser pulled in his belt a hole, setting his cap to one side to get better vision against the sun's last long rays. He made for Ben's area of search with long strides.

Then, from an immense distance, came a commanding sequence of up-swooping whistles, Jock's unmistakeable command to get away round something and hold it there. Again? Yes! In the cooling night air. They both stopped abruptly in mid-stride, Moss's ears pricked, questing.

"What's he got a hold of now, I wonder, eh, Moss? 'The Great Hogg Stealing Mystery Unfolds' I shouldn't wonder! Get on, Moss. Away to him!"

The dog was a black arrow, splitting shadow and sun.

Jock's face, eyes and voice positively glowed with utter fulfilment. The scattered cups and plates of a midnight homecoming lay before them all, the kitchen over-hot, their bodies uncaring with the languor of extreme effort and success gripping them in wide pleasure.

"Man, Ah just kent the verra place she would mak' for; it's no that far from where her mother lambed her – and skulking aboot nae clippit for a hale season – now then!"

Jock's dark, almost black, eyes gleamed. Nan stood with a hand on his shoulder, shaking her head in wonder and pride.

"Aye, Jock, you're a right crafty aul' bugger, creeping aboot the hills like some aul' fox. If you couldnae find her, then naebody else could. So there, the lot of you!"

Nan rattled the plates into a heap, bonny and laughing, her faith in her husband repaired and generous. Fraser knew perfectly well that he couldn't have found the hogg; it needed someone just as Jock was, full of the ways of sheep and sometimes just as seemingly infuriatingly irrational in the way of doing things himself, to heed his senses and dark suspicions only, go on and on into a dim summer's night, find this flouncy, huffy beggar of a beast, and two others with her, take command of their semi-feral fear and flight with only the one dog, then pen them in a disused bothy and contain them for the night.

Lying in his bed just as he had crawled into it, there came the recognition into Fraser that he, at last, was beginning to know about knowing about sheep! The faint smile was still on his features as he turned once, stretched his limbs luxuriously and slept.

XLV

T he evening before he left the glen, with hogg and ewe clipping, and dipping completed, with great comings and goings between neighbouring sheep places, there came a message left with Nan Wyness by Willie Duguid on his call with the travelling shop, rolling and labouring along roads that made his van creak and sway: Would Fraser kindly collect one of Nan's broody hens, a right good "clocker" and walk down to Ramsay McMillan's folks in the croft house at Waulkmill, halfway down the glen?

This he did, with the Rhode Island Red hen protesting from within the meal bag under his arm. Once over the sun-dried bridge, Moss and he turned directly up on to the path through the larch wood, instead of down along the hard, metalled road by the burn.

The familiar green Land Rover sitting angled up on the grassy bank below the cottage, the welcoming figures standing about the open door with its bower of rose and fuschias, the McMillans' wee boy Fergus running out from the byre: it was indeed a sort of family by easy adoption that took him in, with laughter, questions, willing hands to gently take the fluffed-up hen to her task of bringing out a brood of chicks. They all smiled at each other, as she turned a few times, nudging the eggs below her breast and wing feathers, and emitted a series of low, crooning sounds of contentment in hens' speak.

There was the same feeling of contentment within the modest enclave of trees surrounding the byre and cottage, the old waulking mill and dam, a fine settled home for Ramsay McMillan's folks in their retirement from Perthshire.

"Why did you just bring the one, you lazy thing? This idleness after the lambing is all by is a sore disappointment!"

Ramsay grinned maliciously at his wife's masking of her soft spot for this young man whom they had all come to know and like, with equally spirited ribbing from him, in response.

"Ach, away you go! It's quality of stock I go for, not quantity, and in any case, that cockerel of yours is far too dashed keen on his harem of hen pheasants to be a safe bet. I've seen him at it these early mornings! I'll bet you hardly any of those eggs will be fertile. You just don't know the half of what goes on!"

They all laughed, outraged and delighted at the sallies between the two men and Robina, who was spluttering in frustration.

"What a load of nonsense you menfolk talk!" Robina grasped the back of Fraser's neck, shaking him vigorously but lingering with the contact. "Who would believe one half of all these impossible stories you come out with at piece-time, you daft thing?" She laughed into his face and eyes, but in her own there was this warmth and concern for him. "All this work, work and no fine girlfriend. The very idea!"

They all crowded into the sitting room, a fire of peats blazing in spite of the summer warmth, conversation flowing easily amongst them all, young Fergus happily content to lie curled up against Moss on the hearthrug. Tea, pancakes, scones, red currant jelly offered, passed, consumed; satisfaction for giver and taker. Smiles on faces, in voices. Outside, the July moon rose full and white over the hill, trees, fences and fields alike, the valley silvered now with dew. They could hear the subdued chatter of the river below them as they all moved slowly to end the day, the work and for Fraser, that part, that very significant part of his life for some time, knowing the probability of other events laying claim to his energies, in situations very likely unknown to him.

Ramsay's father, Old Sandy as a'body called him, took Fraser lightly by the elbow, a rare gesture for a gentle, mannerly Highlander.

"It's been a pleasure to have you amongst us. What laughs we've had, and yet troubled times for you, and for Jock too, many's the day. When we see the wee chicks hatch out, well, but we shall be thinking on you and minding all of this."

He took Fraser's hand in both of his own; and Fraser could feel his dry skin and bones.

Old Sandy said, "Haste ye back, and soon," with a shake in his voice. He stepped back from Fraser, smiling in his sadness, dignity preventing more. Robina ran forward and took him by the waist, both arms round, trying in mock desperation to lift Fraser. That way, it hid the wetness upon her cheeks.

"Come on, Ramsay, into the Land Rover with him. Another forester'll not come amiss and I could certainly use his lodging allowance!"

They all laughed at that, faces and eyes softened in the dusk. The fragrance of roses at the cottage gate came to Fraser in heavy sweetness as their feet blackened the moisture on the grass. This sweetness welled up in his nostrils, and then another moisture welled arose, unbidden, in his nose and eyes and throat and he felt torn and stricken. Ramsay bundled his family into the Land Rover and stepped directly back to him.

"Ye'll aye ken where we are, you daft skite. The key will aye be up the muckle china dog's backside. Just look after yersel', man!"

A firm clasp and he, and they were gone, almost silently once the dark larches closed over the vehicle and its small red lights. Old Sandy's wife, the elder Mrs McMillan, was at the cottage door, a gentle soul and diminutive figure in contrast to her tall, spare ex-stalker husband. Fraser turned to her, spoke to his dog Moss once by name, waved slowly and without word, a full sweep of hand and arm above his head, and turned for the path down through the trees, holding in the great ache that was bursting his heart, head and entire being.

His father's car and reassuringly unchanged figure came surprisingly early (how long had he, Fraser, been away now from his parents' home?), but he was ready, and had been so from long before his final breakfast as a part of the Wyness family. There had been too much tension for the meal to be enjoyed.

Jock and his father were chatting together easily, looking at something amongst the nearest ewes and lambs – oh, aye, that old fool with the badger face; he'd dived into the Annacht running high and brown with snaw bree, to scoop up her twin lambs which were bleating piteously and dangerously for their dam; she had crossed lower down, to forage on the other, lower bank. As he had struck out furiously for her, lambs crushed inside one arm, half-bleating, half-drowning, God wot! – he was passed in mid-water by the silly old fool plunging for the bank he had just left, and like to drown with the weight of her sodden fleece.

Throwing himself wholesale back in to drive her back, screaming and pummelling before the lambs sprang in to reach their mother, his heart felt likely to explode out of its cage with the terrifying icy water. He had run up to the house, in socks, shirt and little else, gasping, to be met by Nan Wyness's "Dear God, you'll catch your death!" It was already a memory amongst many score others. What was his father saying now?

"Well, squire, that's your stuff all in, is it? We had best be off, Mrs Wyness. No, not this time. We'll stay for our dinner another time."

Stepping up to each of the two boys, Fraser grasped a hand from each, placing in them a complete set of mechanic's tools in a handy canvas roll, costing twenty two shillings and sixpence apiece in the ex-army place that day in the town. It was worth the carrying of them all the way up the glen that night to see their faces and slow grins! Fraser almost bumped into their mother as he turned. Her hand was cold and limp, the apron twisted in her fingers. On impulse, he put his arms around her shoulders, pressing his cheek against hers, and adjured her loudly, "And, mind, nae running aboot wi' little clothes in the morning. You'll catch your death!"

They all broke into laughing, the boys cackling louder than any others at his use of Nan's now most-quoted term of extreme dire malfortune. Old Granda' strode forward, placed something hard into his palm, and turned about, stopping only to say firmly over the shoulder of his waistcoat:

"Moss'll be fine. I'll be seeing to him, dinna fear."

Where was Moss, anyway? Fraser needed to see him. No, better to get away now, without the feeling of blackness getting worse.

Jock wouldn't, couldn't match any of these expressions of what had grown between them all through those down-pulling months of towering effort, struggle, despair, fatigue, little achievement that they could see at each day's weary end. It was only when the car was beginning to roll slowly out of the yard at Tornaquhil that Jock lurched forward to the open car window, reaching in to seize Fraser's wrist in a fumble of fingers, his stick clattering against the car door. With those big brown eyes of his swimming in that mahogany face, Jock demanded of him, huskily:

"You'll be back, then, loon, you'll be back?"

As they rumbled over the bridge, past the pens, past the ducks' puddle, past the track to the hill he had taken so many, many times, Moss at his heel, these last words rang in his head again and again from the figures finally waving and then dwindling behind them:

"Haste ye back, Fraser! Haste ye back!"

His father drove on steadily, seemingly concentrating on the glen road. Fraser, his whole body in a vice, could not bear, or even dare to look back. Instead he attempted to find out what lay in his palm, blinking furiously, futilely, to dispel the tears. Unwrapped, it was a beautifully shaped and tempered Blackface ram's horn, fashioned and polished as a handle to take a good hazel stick. With precise workmanship and clarity was carved into the horn his own name: 'Fraser Baird', and on the reverse 'Tornaquhil', in deep, unforgettable letters.

Trying to look down or back or see anything at all was pointless after that.

PART FOUR

NEVER VOLUNTEER

XLVI

"Christ! God damn and blast the bloody man!"

Fraser knew at once what was in the buff-coloured envelope flipped over to him by his sister at the breakfast table that July morning.

"It's something official, isn't it?" Jean remarked, her cigarette in predictable prominence and combustion. "Is it something to do with you going on your potato rogueing course?"

"No, it damned well isn't. It's – it's the blasted army call-up!"

He knew perfectly well what this summons was. He'd seen the same document served on school pals and other young men of his age and acquaintance. He opened the envelope savagely in one long jagged tear with his thumb. What he read there made him sit down abruptly in disbelief: "Well, I'll go to hell!" he muttered, reading on.

"National Service Acts, 1948 to 1950.

Enlistment Notice: Ministry of Labour and National Service, Regional Office: Under the Act of 1950, you are called for Service at No.3 Training Regiment, Royal Corps of Signals, Catterick Camp, Yorks. on 23rd. July, 1950.

You will report to the Officer Commanding, Induction Centre. A travel warrant is enclosed, together with travel and reporting instructions to be noted before starting your journey. A postal Order for Four Shillings, representing an advance of service pay, is enclosed."

"Well, bugger me."

Fraser's mind seethed and scythed in rage, in circles, in chaos. Four shillings? Four bloody shillings? That was less than he was getting for just one good, clean rabbit at Laings the butchers, and this morning he had come back with twelve in the game bag; nearly three pounds for that morning's work, with probably more coming in that evening, over and above any normal local farm work pay, all to go smartly into his bank account. Was this pitiful evidence of army pay, army worth, an indication of how things were going to be?

He suddenly felt sick, almost light-headed and went out into the garden, Tam hopeful at his heel. Very clearly indeed, something had gone far wrong with the necessary renewal of his agricultural worker's exemption, but with a pit of coldness in his belly, he knew without doubt that attempting to reverse all that would not be of any use now. The whole damned business had gone too far to retrieve.

The absolute certainty that this slip-up lay at James Melvin's feet during his time of acrimony with the laird at Whitepark, leading to his dismissal, or leaving, or whatever, his job as farms manager, grew into an implacable fact in Fraser's anger. Damn. The annual application for an agricultural worker's exemption should have come directly to him; it had never appeared. This was exactly when James Melvin had been in a fury over being sacked. In his attempts to get the measure of what was going to happen to him very soon, everything that he looked at seemed suddenly different in Fraser's spinning mind.

Would there be a river of any kind at this Catterick place, any fields within sight or smell, any chance of a walk? Standing at his father's desk in the bay window, he had absolutely no way of knowing how this army business was going to turn out.

His mother came into the sunny dining room, looking strangely at odds with the day, and not in a fashion that he could relate to any fairly well-known reason in the past couple of days.

"Are you still going into Aberdeen, Fraser. You said that you might be going in for–"

He swung round angrily, wanting to cut off these silly placatory words, and, oh, stuff.

"Aye, well, the great idea was to go in for a new pair of wellingtons, a couple of boxes of cartridges and, well, there's little blasted need for either, now, is there?"

He glared at her, at the deceitful day, at the system that was now impossible to challenge or delay.

"Och, it surely won't be as bad as all that. You'll get leave or whatever they call it, and you'll likely find some lads just like yourself, I'm certain," his mother said, with no conviction whatsoever.

Her placatory words triggered a reaction that almost made him stammer.

"'Find some lads'?"

Christ, that was the last thing he wanted or needed, to be thrust into the enforced company of a whole damned bunch of, of townsers (that was not the

426

word he struggled to find, but it was the nearest thing to satisfy his rage), not to be free to make your own decisions, not to be able to just escape for a wee while and take the dog out for walk or a shot or something. I wonder if you've made as big a mess of your own affairs (and of Margaret's) as you have of mine, Mr Blasted Melvin? "Signalman Baird" or some such label. Bloody hell!

Two days before "the journey named on your warrant" he stripped down his shotgun and rifle on the old table at the back door used for cleaning boots, shoes and other leather gear. The top was impregnated with shoe polish, dubbin and neatsfoot oil. The sycamore planks of the table top sweated a fine oily exudation in the strong July sun. Muzzle on his paws, old Tam lay under the table, heeding the familiar click and snap of gun parts being stripped. There had been lots for him to do these past days, his master and he always away out by four o'clock, walking, waiting, shooting and retrieving; rabbits, mostly, the odd wood pigeon on flattened oats or barley. Tam felt the years'old security of doing what was needed of him in this strong bond they had together.

Fraser's mother came out from the house with a cup of tea and slice of cake. At first, Fraser took this to be for herself, having cleared away after dinnertime, but she set it down in front of him as he packed away oily cloths and cleaning rods. His mother lit a cigarette in reflective fashion, twirling the half-burnt match.

"How do you feel about things now? Still convinced that it's going to be such a huge waste of your time? You'll be in amongst guns and rifles and things that you know about. There may even be someone you'll know."

Her tone was an attempt to be helpful, to give this strong-willed son of theirs a plank to cross between one way of life and another. She smiled at him tentatively.

"Mother! You ken fine they'll not all be going into the wonderful Signals, in any case. More likely into something a dashed sight more relevant to what they've been doing, I shouldn't wonder."

He picked up the rifle, opened the bolt to check it was truly empty, and aimed at an audible but hidden pigeon in a spruce tree. Tam's eyes and ears followed him, alerted by the clack of the bolt, by the weapon being lifted and swung. The final denial, final imposition had to be voiced between him and his mother:

"Two whole blooming years in the Signals! What use that's going to be for farming purposes, and I'm dashed sure it won't be any better for saving money, either!"

She clearly saw his dismay flooding over his features as he leant over to stroke Tam strongly. They had been a solid complementary pair from child- and puppy-hood.

"What are you going to do with that thing?" she asked, pointing to the rifle with her cigarette, eyes half-closed against the smoke and sunlight. "Will you be leaving it here, for your father to use?"

"No, I'm taking it down to Tom. He'll use it, keep it in good order and the firearm certificate along with it. Father can hang onto my shotgun."

Tom was their village police constable, ex-Royal Artillery gunner from his war service, and good friend and shooting companion of Fraser. Together, they had taken on the rabbit and pigeon shooting on the Lunzie estate. From Tom's everyday speech, it could never be guessed that he was, in fact, a native of Wiltshire; his father kept a smiddy in a coombe-sheltered village below chalk downs.

Tom's wife Brenda was of the same maiden name as his own family, Baird, although no immediate relation that either of them could trace back. Her father had been a grieve or foreman on a biggish place up north, but was killed by a huge mare defying service by an equally immense and hot-tempered Clydesdale stallion. Brenda was a bonny and attractive woman, of course she was, but she had the added appeal of being able to speak and talk with him in the same warm, lively manner as had Margaret Melvin. That was a nice and easy feeling of friendship, with no complications.

"Come on, then, old feller, last round up."

As he gathered up rifle and accessories, on an impulse he laid his free arm across his mother's shoulders, warm to touch in her frock under the strong sun.

"Come away, Mama. It's just the first training bit that takes time and marks for good attendance! I'll be back to plague you in my rustic fashion in, och, in a few months' time. You and father'll get some peace in the early mornings. That should be a change!"

His mother turned, putting her small hand to keep his own one on her shoulder, rose jerkily, and went back inside. Fraser knew there would be tears.

Ach, dammit, why did emotions spill over into everything at a time when a fellow had to try and think clearly? Right, get going and take all this shooting gear down to Tom. One thing less to see to for the time that he was going to be away from home. Bloody business. It did not have a good feel about it.

Tom was on his knees in the front garden. He always put on a spectacularly colourful display in the flower beds surrounding the police house in the village. Brenda was leaning against the warm stones of the garden dyke, watching their two wee girls playing in a litter of dolls, saucepans and clothes pegs on the lawn.

"Well, soldier, turning in your rabbit rifle for something much bigger?" Tom called out, but did not stop what he was doing with a dibber and boxes of transplants.

Brenda waved her hand to Fraser as though to say "Never mind him!" but smiled warmly at him nonetheless. After pushing off from the warm stones with a swing of her arms and scuffling one of the girls' hair with the same swoop of movement, Brenda motioned to him to sit down with her on the green bench seat, her head to one side, and serious.

"What would you be wanting us to send on to you? You've only to say. Tom will be sending on the Shooting Times anyway, you know that."

They bought the weekly magazine between them, Tom and Fraser. Brenda was speaking to him again. There was a patent concern in her words, and her eyes.

"When Tom had to go down south for his last training and then embarkation, he was on that train so long. You'll need some sandwiches and better still, a piece of my special game pie. Full of good stuff from you two fellows' shooting forays!"

At once, she saw that this had not been the best thing to speak about. Oh, dear. She felt that Fraser, usually so kind with the two girls, and helpful to Tom and herself in so many ways locally, was somehow resisting anything from them, from her, from anybody. Oh, dear God, these men, backing off from everything one minute, needing you in umpteen ways obvious or otherwise the next. She felt and fought the urge to pull all these dratted shooting things off him, put her arms around him, tell him that it would be all right, nothing would be changed when he came back. She wondered if Fraser could sense to the slightest degree what was shaking her so strongly? No, he couldn't possibly, always too taken up with more work for this precious farm of his. She stopped speaking to him. In the middle of all this friendly talk of things to keep them in touch, Brenda smiled, trying to mask the sudden liquid pulse deep in her woman's core, causing her to gasp minutely. She jumped up, speaking to one of the girls:

"Yes, on you go, then, Madgie. Let me take off your dress if you're all that hot. Fraser, put all those things in Tom's office and then come back out here to see if there's anything else you want us to look after for you." By his face and eyes, Brenda could see that Fraser Baird was far more troubled than she had ever seen him before.

For Fraser to tell Tam to drop at the house door was entirely unnecessary. He was lying stretched out on his back in the sun, grinning teeth upside down as he relished the heat on his belly. The coolth of the grass, familiar voices in speech and laughter around him, his master's reassuring smell; he had been here often enough. Madgie's sister Joan was gently counting his exposed teeth with her tiny finger.

"There's anuvver lickle one, there's anuvver licklest one, there's..." Tam's tail slowly swept the lawn, eyes soft in pleasure.

Fraser padded his way through the house to Tom's office in his socks, but suddenly finding them too hot and sticky, he pulled them off in the hall. Tim would snitch them up if he forgot. Fraser laid his .22 rifle carefully down on the counter top, bolt uppermost, and looked at it silently, lifting off a grass seed from the oily blued surface. The satisfaction was still all there; saving money frugally from sales of rabbits, saving was one thing, but keeping it intact from the clutches of his cigarette-smoking sister Jean was another matter entirely. "Most buggerin' awful!" would be how any one of the farm lads would put it. He grinned broadly. He cherished the feeling of achievement, something else acquired by his own efforts.

"Aha! So, who's the big ape leaving marks all across my clean floor?"

He half turned, soles obstinately sticking to the linoleum floor, lifting his arms involuntarily. When he dropped them, breathing out in a rush, it was to the even greater shock of having Brenda's arms around him.

"Brenda, you shouldn't do that, it's... "

"Yes, what?"

"Look, Tom's my best friend, it's not the right thing…"

"Just you hold quiet, just for a moment."

Fraser was aware of her warmth and weight as she turned her face slowly sideways. He was flooded by the fragrance of summer sun and perfume and washed hair and newly-ironed dress and woman floating up from her skin in gentle, sweeping sweetness. Tom's voice, a pleasant rumble, lay in the sunlight outside. He was talking to the girls, comfortable and unhurried. Contented.

Brenda took one slow step backwards. Fraser saw how pale brown, almost hazel, were the irises of her eyes.

"Will you be careful, in the army, please, Fraser?" She spoke simply, yet no one else would have heard her speaking a few yards distant.

"Things there will change you. They did to Tom. We don't want… it'll not be fine if you come back different, not for Tom, not for the girls – they dote on you. Not for me." Very gently, she laid her cheek on his sun-warmed brown upper arm. "You'll be in amongst men of all natures; some good, some kind, some just downright coarse and brutes for their own pleasures, some just like yourself, from the country and not knowing the way of things. I saw them all when I was receptionist in the doctor's office, getting engaged to Tom. Just be yourself, never heed what others may try you on to do if you don't want to, such as drinking yourself silly and all that. Remember all the good days shooting with Tom, and coming back here, the two of you full of stories and nonsense! I loved that, all of us round the table."

The two fine lines at the corners of her lips crinkled quite deliciously. He suddenly wanted to kiss them and didn't know how. Brenda quickly brushed his face with her lips.

"The girls will miss you, but this girl most of all!"

With a flick and promise of her summer frock, she spun away. Fraser saw that her feet were bare, like his own. Funny that he hadn't felt them beside his own, considering the way in which they had been standing so closely together.

Climbing over the Andersons' march dyke, as the old dog slipped a wee bit amongst the stones, Fraser pulled Tam into his knee, steadying him, holding his dense hair to his nose and face, and half-growled, half-sobbed into the dog's infinitely pleasurable and familiar head and neck:

"Well, I needn't expect any long letters from you, you silly auld cratur, can I now?"

Tam's tail thumped enthusiastically. Was this hitherto unfamiliar vocal contact meaning that they would be going out together, as usual, in the early morning? Surely so. He would be ready at the first creak of the stairs in the dim light, and willingly enrolled. Tam scampered ahead, mock puppy-fashion, a shade unsteadily, but anticipating something satisfying after the day's heat. They, Tam and his master, always did these things together. They made a productive team, based on mutual skills, acting in silent and practised unison. Of course, they'ld be out together at first light, canny and watchful.

The countless olfactory receptors lining Tam's nasal turbinate bones had already registered two quantities: there would be rain in the early morning, and this release of a strange, rank smell from his master's hands and body. It had not been evident a few days back. He, Tam, anticipated that with some steady gathering of rabbits and pigeons in the coming day, this disturbing and unusual smell would fade and disappear, and the two of them could get on with things as they usually did. Nothing would be different.

So far as he could ensure it so, leaving home for Fraser was a rapid and efficient affair. He knew that the early morning breakfast preparations were the work of his father, who was shaved, fully dressed and had the car standing out at the front of the house by the time that Fraser went upstairs to check everything in his bedroom one final time.

They had to be at the station for eight o'clock. There was little enough to take with him; sandwiches, a book, some money (he had banked the last sales money for rabbits and pigeons at the Post Office, Mrs Lamont looking at him, but saying little), some very ordinary shaving things. He took careful attention to pick up his knife used for all paunching and skinning of game; you never know when a good knife comes in handy. The feel of it in his pocket was reassuring.His father had said quite emphatically that there was absolutely no point in his mother coming to the train with them. Of an impulse, Fraser ran back up the stairs, touched his favourite books, the boxed collection of different cartridges, the shotgun he hoped his father would use (and clean!), and walked out to the landing and down into the hall. The door to his grandfather's room was still closed. The old man slept late these mornings. Better that he slept on today. Good old Grandpa Teatime. He had been a part, a solid useful friend and fund of knowing everything useful for a small boy. In the dimness of the hall, Fraser blinked away tears. Going up to his mother in a sudden deep vexation about all of this and where his rightful position should be in it all, he clasped her, speaking too forcefully:

"Dinna fash yersel', Mother mine, this is just me having an apprenticeship, clothing supplied!"

They both grinned weakly, through these dratted tears. He couldn't see Tam very clearly as he bent down to stroke him, not knowing, not wanting to stop. The dog was unsettled by the tension in folks' movements, at the salt drops fallen on his coat. He licked them off desultorily, keeping his dark eyes on Fraser with intense devotion.

The station was seething, noisy, with lads, young men, fathers, mothers, a few figures in khaki checking travel documents. Maybe his father'd had much the same sort of thing, going off as a veterinary student to the 1914–1918 War. But that had been in Edinburgh; a different feel about it; they'd all enlisted; they wanted to get to where the war was, his father had said. His father's voice broke in, brusquely, getting on with what they both knew had to be a more difficult, more disturbing burden than anything experienced by Fraser in his single-minded drive to be a capable farm worker. He felt it as the cutting off of exposed roots to a vigorous tree, one by one, with the exception, he desperately hoped, of the one central taproot that would nourish him through all this.

"Right, then, squire, you've got your carriage number? Aye, that'll be it right enough. I'll be off. Don't let yon rucksack of yours out of your grasp, particularly once you get out at the other end. And even more so once you're actually in your billet, got that? At least, you'll not be under canvas!"

"Aye, father, I'll keep a close watch on it, and mebbe even try to shorten my stride a bit!"

This was in reference to the long length of stride he had grown into throughout the lambing. His father had remarked upon this only a day or so back, pointing with the stem of his pipe: "That's quite un-military!" and had shaken his head, laughing.

A clap on his shoulder, and his father strode off, a stout figure in a tweed suit, which, Fraser recalled with a sudden deep pang in their parting, his father always called "My best working clothes!"

Fraser saw him turn abruptly at the ticket gate, wave an upright arm once, twice, holding his hand with fingers spread high in the air, and then was gone.

In all of his limited travels by train, Fraser had never felt so oppressed, so battened down by sheer numbers of human beings and their incessant noise and shouting and clamour, all dragging him with them to whatever lay ahead. As the long line of carriages pulled out, flicking platforms and canopies away into separation from a whole way of life, he folded his arms across his chest and dozed and turned in upon himself, holding on to those small but necessary things of meaning that had been his purpose until this day.

He knew from repeated study of the printed forms in his pocket that they had to change at Edinburgh, with twenty-five minutes between trains. Christ, you would think that this was some sort of hysterical joke for these creatures: lads continually seeking reassurance from their pals, running, shouting, braying and laughing, laughing at absolutely bugger all about things of which they knew even less than he did. At least he could shoot and drive, and was competent with both; surely that would come in useful in the army?

Suddenly, their train was standing in Edinburgh. Of a sudden, the imperative need was in him like a storm: go round that loading bay, quickly, NOW, eat your sandwiches while they're all getting on the next train (the announcer was already blaring, over-loud and distorted: "...will be the twelve fifteen to London Kings Cross, stopping at Berwick, Newcastle, Darlington, York, Peterborough and..."), spend some time in the station here, and then get away out of it, into the country somewhere, another farm job wouldn't be all that difficult to pick up, hay and harvest coming on. Fraser disciplined himself to stand, head down, trying to work out practicalities. Only five pounds in his wallet, no working boots or overalls. All the business of trying to claim agricultural worker's exemption again, having to give a false name and address. Not just for now, but for all time. Gad. What-do-I-do-here?

The army would get the police on the go. Likely a big Wolseley or Humber full of bobbies out from Aberdeen. He knew that whole business was called "on the run".

The voice came right at his shoulder:

"Aye, young man, you're surely thinking the same aboot this as I am, right? Corpral McGillivray, Seaforths."

A Corporal, Seaforth Highlanders, double white stripe and red band with "R.M.P." on his tunic sleeve.

"Are ye for a smoke, lad? No? Ach, well, and where might you be from? Going along with this lot, are ye?" He nodded at the over-animated scenes behind them both.

Fraser spoke briefly, his stomach churning. There was something had to be decided and acted upon in the next few seconds. He spoke about his work at Tornaquhil, his gathering of farm experience. The corporal nodded again, breaking in, friendly-like:

"Och, I ken where you're speaking aboot. My folks are nae that far awa'. But hark ye, Fraser, it'll all be there once your time is in, and you'll be in for just the two years, right?"

He stood side-on to Fraser, head on one side as though they were old friends, looking disparagingly at the boys massed for the train, some frenetic in efforts to impress, others stricken in the realisation of inescapable separation from the security of home and family.

"Hmm, not pleasing you very greatly, is it, this National Service nonsense? You've worked on the land then, by the looks of you?"

Fraser provided the barest of details about his taking on farm jobs, with scenes from Glen Annacht haunting him as he spoke.

"Annacht? Tornaquhil, you say? Man, if you'ld only said! My folks' place is just the other side of the hill. Last place up the glen from the other side. There's an old green road atween your place and mine. Miltonshiel, that's it. Well, I'll be damned!"

The train was loading; both of them knew that the bond, the brothership just declared, had little time left now for an abrupt and probably unlawful refusal to board.

"Now, just you hold a wee minute, young Fraser, and listen to me. I came off the land, just like you." He waved away his companion lance corporal impatiently, pointing to the congestion all along the platform. "I was with the Forestry a while, then clippings, lambing, hoeing neeps, pulling the damned things in the winter, tractorman – the lot. That's no life, man. Soaked many a night or roasted, for damn' little. So, it was seven years for me, and I've got these already." He tapped his stripes. "Now, dinnna think that you'll be making a run for it. That's a fool's game. There's better in you than that, and you'll do just fine." He looked Fraser straight in the eye.

The locomotive was blowing off steam and smoke. The clamour was punctuated by doors slamming, whistles.

"You're surely not going to miss rising to sort stupid old beasts at four or five of a morning, are ye? No. You're that bit older and some long days' work aneth your belt – that's a great and valuable start! Get in with the right lads, and it'll be a caker. Two years? Away you go, a right short yoking, that! Now, come away with me, Fraser."

Corporal McGillivray's use of the Aberdeenshire term for an afternoon or morning's sustained hard work was made with the scorn of a man for whom all this outrageous labour was now a thing of his past. He picked up Fraser's rucksack and marched off smartly, with purpose. Fraser could hardly avoid noticing the disparity in length of stride at once; his own was resolutely far longer.

Corporal McGillivray halted, looked into a compartment at the front of the train, and sought a response from the occupants, a sergeant and two infantrymen or whatever Fraser presumed they were called.

"Aye, aye, there, Sar'nt Forbes. Pollutin' the minds of young and ignorant with accounts of your glorious campaigns. On the milk run to Darlington, right? Well, now, that's fine. This is Fraser Baird, from the verra same place as mysel'. Fraser's a teuchter, and a hardy lad at that, so if you bold gentlemen would kindly keep him right at Darlington, Sergeant, "Sir," McGillivray said, grinning in exaggerated servility, "I'll mebbe buy you a drink tonight, an' you young lads an' all. Now, for Chrissake, look regimental!"

McGillivray prodded Fraser towards a vacant seat amongst webbing belts, cigarette packets and a tired looking magazine with a dark haired girl on the cover, wearing high-heeled shoes, a sickly smile and nothing else. Sar'nt Forbes' two infantrymen instantly assumed superior and disinterested expressions indicative of their uniformed, experienced status. Fraser became aware that under cover of making much of throwing Fraser's rucksack up in amongst the soldiers' clutter of equipment, Corporal McGillivray was speaking sideways to him, but without moving his head and eyes in the same direction:

"Just listen to me and mind this: dinna volunteer for any damned thing, save your pay and keep the heid doon at all times. And – dinna forget where you're from!"

An almost undetectable wink, face expressionless, and he marched smartly away from the carriage door as the entire length of the train gave its first lurch. On the platform, as a last, and for Fraser unforeseen link back up to to those hills where he had gone from a young lad's freedom to a man's solid work, Corporal McGillivray, in his blood a man of Glenlivet, made a parody of hooking his lance corporal's leg with an officer's Malacca cane that he had somehow acquired in the last few seconds, just as you would catch up some thrawn old ewe with a cleek.

Then, abruptly smart, military and a signed-on soldier, Corporal McGillivray, Seaforth Highlander now, inspected Fraser stolidly as the train pulled out of the station. On impulse, Fraser stood up to the carriage door, placed two fingers between his lips, but silently, and flicked his hand and arm:

"Cum 'ere away to me!"

With the merest nod of his diced Glengarry, the corporal acknowledged and raised a hand to his forehead. It could have been a salute, but to a nicety, it was the gesture of a hill man, putting his dog away out to gather, shielding his eyes from the sun. Or the wind, or the snow.

XLVII

Darlington Station was a booming cavern of head-splitting noise. The clamour of a woman announcer's impersonal voice, directing "Nashnull Sairvissmen from Ebberdeen and Edinboro' proceed naow to Platform Three" was overlaid by rasping, unintelligible instructions from this RTO, that Marshalling Officer, repeated demands to clear the main line platform at once, endless revving of truck engines somewhere, everywhere, and manic voices screaming "Here! You lot! At the double, I say! Signals, REME! On these markers naahow!"

The system was already beginning to bite; no singing or forced, cackling laughter now, two or more NCOs to each of the carriages on the battered, tired-looking trains making their last haul from Darlington to Richmond and Catterick. Clipboards in constant play by officers, everyone to be in groups, identities unheeded, unwanted. Most of the endless yelling and chivvying was done by corporals and lance corporals, Fraser noted. They did not, for reasons he could not put his finger on at once, give the impression of being men trained in the ways of war, but were more like a rabble of farm dogs, snapping at heels, whose ill-training and inefficiency was masked by their numbers and by making a lot of noise. In apparently casual observation around him, but scrupulously avoiding eye-contact, he identified others who had just the same need to instil fear and swift vicious biting as did certain of the worst type of farm dog. He spotted them right away by the slightly off-centre, poised-for-treachery look in their unwavering eyes. Ho hum. Nasty with it.

Fraser had never in his life seen transport massed like this. The ranks of three-ton Bedford trucks in tightly slanted rows on the cobbles of Richmond Station, all with their tailgates hanging down, were difficult to clamber into and devoid of anything at all to sit on. To Fraser's practical eye, they seemed to be too high and potentially unstable if loaded with thirty or forty men. How could they be of any use going over really rough ground, in serious action, never mind loaded six or seven courses high with bales? His farmer's eye (and inner mind) was coarsely jerked into immediate distaste for the figure bawling at him:

"Get bloody back! Come on! You're worse than a bunch of bleedin' virgins in a nunnery: 'Don't touch me, soldier!' JeezussChristmoveyourbloodyselves!"

437

The lance corporal flailed at them, sending a number stumbling on the canted deck of the truck as they tried to stand up after their awkward climb over the tailgate. Fraser held on to his corner stanchion, rucksack wedged between his feet. Yes, his father's recollection of French rail wagons going up the line in the war, forty men or eight horses, aye, that would be about right.

"Christallbloodymighty, Corporal, can't you get your lot to do anything you want? Let me up there. Move out of my fucking way!"

The sergeant was short, compact, sallow-faced, explosive, with 'Durham Light Infantry' shoulder flashes and two rows of campaign ribbons. He meant business.

"Get your miserable fucking boots out of my way, laddie, or you'll feel one of mine up your bastud arse!"

Between the sergeant's regimental designation and his brilliantly white three stripes, there was a square divisional sign. The NCO spun this way and that to the slightest hesitation in response to his presence. He reeked of stale cigarette smoke and Fraser noted his fingers and nails were deeply nicotine-stained. Fraser held on to his corner position, facing forward to the light, but avoiding the sergeant's look upon him as you would a beast that was more than ready to have a go at you, fast. Aye, man, he intoned silently, but this one is a different kind of beast. In careful, peripheral vision, Fraser watched everything that was happening.

"Right, pay attention! When I speak, when I give you an order, or the Corporal or any other NCO – d'you lnow what that is? Can someone actually speak? Well, your job from now on is to listen and move, not bloody well speak! When spoken to, you will jump to it, and move your precious little bodies a whole lot fucking faster than you've ever dreamed possible or I shall bloody well know why not! Now." He grasped the nearest one of the young lads by his shoulder and gave him a single furious shake. "Get your idiot selves into the back of this idiots' wagon!"

Streaming out on the cobbles in file, transmissions and ribbed tyres whining unlike any tractor, Fraser had to accept that this entire day was going to be one of every dashed thing being quite outwith his world, even down to the noise made by these trucks.

At least the July sun was a known quantity. They'll be at the hay at Tornaquhil! But down here in England, all likely cut, turned and carted. Fraser edged forward half a pace, trying to get a glimpse of the countryside over and around heads and necks. The truck heeled over abruptly, bodies and baggage slithering in a suddenly vocal protestation.

"Are you from Scotland, then?"

This from a chap about the same height as Fraser, to his immediate left.

"Aye, how did you know?"

"Oh, from the way you were coming out with the odd farm word, as we were lying over out of yon corner! You were goin' on just like some of the drivers that come into me dad's place to pick up return loads, cattle floats an' all. We've a farm, small like, but the wagons making back up to Scotland allus call in for what might mek' up a load. What part do you come from, anyroad?"

Fraser was intrigued. He warmed to this clean-looking neighbour who pronounced "come" as "coom", and finished his sentences with a sort of upwards lift in his voice.

"Oh, Aberdeenshire, up the valley of the Dee; ever been up that length? No? Ah, well it's about three hundred miles–"

Fraser didn't get out the rest of his reply; the North Country fellow he'd been speaking to bent down and pulled vigorously at a full knapsack from below another lad behind him, sorting him out in straightforward fashion: "Hey, man! Dunna you think Ah brought it aal the way from whum for you to sit on. Use your own danged thing, mind!"

Fraser reflexly nudged his own rucksack for reassurance, feeling depressed and profoundly irritated that the other lads around the two of them were so quick to adopt and then overuse the same two or three totally meaningless swear words so used to excess by their first army receiving personnel, who were almost like prison warders. For himself, he had been only about eight or nine years old when he noticed the frequent use of "bloody" and "fucking" in some farm men's everyday talk. It grew to be that he just accepted that and allowed it to pass unnoticed thereafter. In his inner, private commentary on the passage of this disturbing day, Fraser muttered to himself that this endless, tiresome, meaningless swearing was highly likely to become a feature of every waking hour for the immediate present and the future. He moved his weight from one leg to the other, feeling depressed beyond words. The air below the canvas tilt on the army truck was stuffy and stale; all the good sunlight and country smells were at a vast remove.

"My name's Colin Bowles. What's yours?"

"Fraser, Fraser Baird. What did you say about your place at home, is it a farm?"

They stood or rather swayed with right and left shoulders at right angles to each other, their belongings in the protective triangle at their feet. Colin Bowles had just started to say something about his home life and farm, when gears were crashed through changes and their truck passed through some sort of a guard point. Even above the whine of low gear and loudly revving trucks came the sound of continual voices of command, demanding attention from points around them; bellowing, berating, words indistinguishable in meaning. Tailgates were dropped with shattering crashes, corporals, well, just about every creature that you could see was shouting at them. The noise ricocheted off walls, buildings, doors, drill squares, acres of tarmac, the very bones in their skulls.

"Colin? Have you–"

It burst upon him, generated of sheer animosity, just as Brenda at the police station had predicted.

"You there! Where are you fucking well going? You don't know? Don't you bloody well know your own names? Can't you fucking well read? Double up, man, double, I say!"

The corporal out of whom this blizzard of abuse poured was on to Colin and Fraser like a terrible human windmill; boots stamping, arms flailing, stabbing, pointing in fury and three different directions at once, yelling "Sah!" at the same time and in the same second screaming demands at Fraser and Colin, and at the boys behind them and at anyone else who turned, momentarily immobile in bewilderment.

"Come on! Move it a bit, for Chrissake, at the double!"

They carried their things to large plywood squares carrying hut numbers, an NCO at each one with lists of names. At a distance from the choleric corporals and their orchestrated destruction of any civilian identity stood a group of four sergeants, all fairly young, Fraser thought, unlike that one smelling of beer and cigarette smoke back in the truck. The sergeants looked relaxed. They had a system, they were in control. One of them strolled forward, hands behind his back.

"All right, all right! Cut it out. Now listen. Listen, I said!" His voice was surprisingly full-bellied, in spite of being a fellow of thin stature. "There are four squadrons in the lines. You already have your troop number and your hut. Be quiet. You there in that fancy jacket! Stand to attention when I speak to you! Out here on these markers when your name is called, listen carefully for first name or initial. And!" His voice suddenly dropped to a steely level, but with total clarity. "We have a punishment fatigue for those who don't know their own name when it is called! Let's be having you, naouww!"

Throughout that utterly strange summer's afternoon, they made files, troops and training groups or sections, after which there was the briefest of entry into huts to stare and smell and move uncertainly around beds and lockers. Then they were summoned outside to be marched (Jeesuss! How the blazes can I keep going at this silly wee marching step and going like the dickens, when a good long pace would cover twice the distance with half the effort?!) to the stores block for issue of kit.

With his lumpy and ill-packed kitbag over his shoulder, the realisation crashed into Fraser's over-worked awareness that from now onwards there would be precious few occasions when anything could be done as a person, as a man quite content and complete within himself.

"By God, Colin, doesn't all this stuff make you think of how wonderfully comfortable our ordinary working clothes are back home?" Fraser asked, seeking the smallest measure of reassurance that things might prove better, as he struggled with gaiters and boots, all as stiff and unyielding as a stack cover soaked by rain. Colin grunted with vexation at the same frustration.

"By gum, lads, this is a reet okkard lot to get pulled together."

A pair of immaculately glossed toecaps came crashing into their peripheral vision.

"Pay attention! My name is Sarn't Whyte, spelt W-H-Y-T-E. You will do three things correctly for me! Speak to me, h'only when required as 'Sarn't' or 'Sarn't Whyte, SAH!' Secondly, spell my name correctly when necessary – you know how to spell my name, don't you, soldier? Well – spell it for me now! Louder! What did you say? I-T-E? Out here, my lad, in front of me. At the double! Now, spell my name! What have you forgotten? Tell 'im what 'e's forgotten! You haven't said 'Sarn't'. Thirdly, you will always address me as 'Sarn't', won't you? You are not in real trouble yet, you miserable little nignog, but when you are in trouble, I need to hear that 'Sarn't Whyte, Sah!' at the other side of this bleedin' parade ground. Got it? Get back in there, move!"

The final spray of this being's outrage was flung at them in an eruption of outflung arm, crash of boots like gunshots, visible swelling of chest and throat to bursting point and hawk-like thrust of head, neck and shoulders. It was all the more threatening that throughout this delivery, Sergeant Whyte remained locked to one point on the tarmac outside the hut. Or so it seemed to Fraser, immobile, watching with his outer rim of vision. Aye, man, we're learning this idiot business fast.

They dressed off to their lance corporal as marker ("Don't bloody well look at me, look at 'im!"), stiffened, relaxed, stiffened again to hoarse bellows of command, had their berets wrenched and twisted over their stunned heads, were put through basic commands again and again.

The corporal in whose hut Fraser, Colin and another dozen or so were billeted

441

was practised in the allocation of sarcasm, malice and deliberate offence, probing for response, any response to which he could become insufferable,and untouchable by rank. He looked over at Fraser for no apparent reason.

"You there! Come here and shift my locker so that you can all see a proper kit layout for inspection."

There was the suggestion of a test in Corporal Swainson's direction. Fraser wrapped his arms around the locker, rocked it onto his left boot, and rotated locker and boot in one silent movement, setting it down precisely where ordered. The corporal, Royal Signals induction cadre, said nothing, just looked. Whoever or whatever you are, the look said, I shall get the measure of you, and there will be plenty of opportunities for me to do so, as full corporal, don't forget that, Squaddie Whatever-your-name-is.

Fraser immediately recognised that he had forgotten the maxim for survival. Stay unnoticed at all times. Keep the heid doon. Bugger it.

"OK. Cookhouse at seventeen hundred hours. Be back here in one half hour, full kit inspection." Corporal Swainson looked at Fraser. "You, what's your number? Ought seven nine five? Right, you will stay here, to be responsible for looking after my model of kit layout, got it? Dis-Miss!"

Colin Bowles conferred with Fraser hurriedly.

"Shall I bring summat back for you, Fraser?"

"No. Look, you get going over there. There'll be long queues, with all this lot. If you can, bring me back some bread and butter or a piece of cheese, on you go!"

"Reet y'are. I'll do me best!"

He ran out of the hut, boots clattering like a newly-shod Clydesdale. Fraser grinned to himself. Colin was a good lad.

The hut seemed even more like a prison, but now strangely lacking in commands, crashing of boots, constant repetition of oaths. This mouldy smell of blanco everywhere – come to that, where was this blessed blanco room? Next to the ablutions? Ah, between the two huts. He took off his boots and socks, to glumly inspect the crimped imprint of army socks; the boots were far too narrow across the way. Not good.

With sweeping mental fatigue, all that he had left behind as the long train had relentlessly snaked southwards away from Aberdeen, the solid but inescapable barrier of Corporal McGillivray's restraint, the blue hills up beyond Laurencekirk, all came through his tensed body and being like a gale. Fraser lowered his aching skull into his hands, trying to massage out all the huge stress and resentment the day had produced to crush him. God, there would be even more of it the next day, and the next, and the next...

Colin's footsteps scrunched on the gravel outside. He entered with evident relief that he had got back to the right hut. His voice was high and angry.

"Look you, Fraser, I've got this for you. The food's awful and my Mam would be reet upset if she saw it. Anyroad, it's only bread and cheese, and a bite o' cake. If you were to go now, you might get a plate of taters and 'orrible beans. I tell you, it's just like muck. Bloody 'ell, the place is that dirty!"

Colin Bowles, reared on the best of farm fare, was deeply offended.

Gulping down torn-off lumps of over-dry white bread and hectically coloured cheese, Fraser could see two things with clarity: If he left the corporal's precious kit layout and was seen by him, there would be trouble, and he felt that Swainson was already a very dangerous quantity. But if he went to the back part of the kitchen place and spoke to a cook, he could maybe bring something back to the hut. He grabbed Colin by the arm.

"Look, all of this stuff, lift it off, blanket and all! Right, on to my bed, as quick as you can, and tidy it a bit before our pocket Hitler comes back!" Fraser swooped on his mess kit, fiercely holding the knife, spoon and fork to stop them from rattling. "Tell him that I've had to go to the lavatory, any damned thing that sounds half likely."

The scene at the rear of the mess hall was appalling and smelled revolting. Below a corrugated iron overhang, a few figures were trying to dodge splashes or any contact at all from the scum-covered slop and spillage around two small tanks with steam rising from them. The soldiers were attempting to clean or do something with their used utensils. On the surface of the water, which was patently not all that hot, there floated scraps of bread, cigarette ends, pale grey beans and curds of grease. The fluid itself was greyish yellow. Around the insides of the tanks were layered ridges of congealed grease. Even the concrete apron, cracked and pitted, was impacted with scum and grease. The steamy miasma surrounding the entire area reeked of rancid, semi-liquefied rotten refuse.

Fraser lingered at the open doorway. No sign of Corporal Swainson, not by his back view, anyway. Ah, but of course, he and other NCOs would be eating proper food somewhere else. He spoke to one of the men behind the steel containers:

"Excuse me, anything left?"

It was plainly visible: potatoes, baked beans, some kind of sauce or gravy.

"What lot are you from, then? Can't you come at the right bleedin' time, mate?"

Fraser improvised, wildly.

"Er, Signals. E Squadron, late getting in."

With infinite contempt, the cookhand, his overalls glazed with smeared-in food residues, flicked away his cigarette butt with a finger exhibiting a crescent of black impacted dirt below the nail, and thudded out potatoes, beans, gravy into Fraser's mess tin, viciously, blobs spraying onto Fraser's tunic. The cookhand wiped his hands over his hips.

"Banger?"

"Oh, aye."

The sausage was beginning to whiten with congealing fat, and looked only partly cooked.

"Don't take too fucking long, will yer? We're not waiting around here y'know. Not for ignorant bastud Scotch squaddies, no how."

Suppressing any response whatsoever, Fraser walked hurriedly to where the tea urns were located. The fluid dispensed was almost orange-coloured and vile. Right, no tea. He was out of the building in seconds.

Avoiding any contact with the so-called Cleansing Point, he ran back in a circuitous loop to the hut, coming into the door cautiously, keeping off those damned horseshoes of noisy heels. Stooping for an instant, Fraser slid the mess tin and crude cutlery, all unwashed, behind the right-hand door and straightened up.

Walking past the corporal's open door, Fraser was aware of movement on the edge of his peripheral vision, but just kept going. Swainson's model kit layout was exactly, precisely, lined up on his bed. Colin was hovering to one side, a boot in his hand. He looked grey, fearful. Without a second's hesitation, Fraser picked up the incredibly stiffly blanco-ed packs in a single, all-embracing body and carried them into the corporal's billet.

Corporal Swainson was sprawled beside his bed, smoking, beret on, displeased.

"Where d'you think you're going with that lot?"

"Safer in here, Corporal – might get marked." Fraser attempted to show respectful concern.

"OK, but set it up exactly as it bloody well should be or else. Understand?" Swainson flicked his cigarette end out of his room, into the communal floor area. Let the nignogs pick it up. "All right, soldier, get your own stuff properly done, or you'll be on a charge. Just a minute. What's your name?"

"Ought seven nine five Baird, Corporal."

"What was your job in civvy street?"

(Oh, ho, keep the respectful bit going, Fraser, me lad!)

"Ah, farm worker, Corporal."

"Really? All right, dismiss, Baird."

Corporal Swainson, not unversed in the imposition of authority from above, at all levels, had the suspicion that ought seven nine five Baird held a little hardness in him somewhere, oh, yes. He, regular full corporal, would make it his business to ferret it out. And then stamp on it.

Fraser felt utterly caged in. The other occupants of the hut just seemed to want to stay in, talking, moaning, swearing. He caught Colin's eye and nodded sideways towards the hallowed blanco place.

"Hey, Fraser, how did you get on at yon mess hall? A reet good name for the whole stinking outfit, an' all."

"Not bad, but at least the bread and cheese you brought back was unpolluted." How quickly these tawdry items of usage crept into your speech. Fraser felt betrayal of his own background of speaking at home, strong though it could be. "Colin, that whole place was absolutely poisonous. And that muck-hole at the back, Christ!"

They came back into the hut, to sit on their neighbouring beds, talking quietly. Colin was talking of his last few days at home.

"We were busy wi' t'hay two nights past; me dad, uncle and Mam came out, too. Didn't stop 'til we had it all, about seven acres, up in pikes. A reet lovely smell to it when it's cured green! Do you have such in Scotland, wheer did you say, Aberdeenshire?"

Fraser was pleased to reply in kind; this was something which would nourish both of them, as a respite from military madness.

"Aye, something the same, Colin. We call 'em coles or coyles, though, and we usually fork them into a loose ruck or straight into the baler once the loose stuff, especially fine meadow hay, has cured. It'll still be in the cole yet, up north."

It did help to talk about such things. He could almost smell the fragrance of fine, natural grasses and wild plants up the backs of the dykes, or along a burn, when he had held a twist of it up to his nose, and the coolth rising as the dew settled on the sheared stubble. Mighty, he did feel really tired now, and weary with it.

"Come on, Colin, my friend. Let's call it a day. You an' me have kept the invading hordes from overrunning the Frogs and the Krauts another day. We'll have the top brass know that, the morn!"

Colin was of similar mind, yawning. He grinned back at Fraser, speaking quietly, just the two of them.

"You, know, Fraser, the best thing that's happened this blessed day, has been meeting up with you. I reckon the two on us'll have a trick or two to keep the likes of 'im more than a little foxed, hey!"

He gave a sideways nod to the corporal's cubicle.

"Good lad, Colin, and I do hope you're right. We'll work on it!"

Sleep did not come easily to Fraser; he turned on his side, uneasy with the presence of others around him.

The last thing which he could retrieve, fleetingly, after his first day and night in the Army, was his realisation of the difficulties the two of them, really only farm lads, were going to have in outfoxing the system. Well, for a start, never volunteer, and keep your head down! And... don't forget where you're from, by God, no. That was the very rock and the roots to which, however forcibly transplanted, he would have to cling from now on.

The long summer days of a hot July dragged on and ate into Fraser's sense of being not a complete person, but something compressed into a mould that his entire persona rejected. By rights, he should have been engaged in timely tasks with cattle, sheep or crops. Instead, in a never-ending welter of drill parades, fatigues, lectures, medical checks, aptitude tests, more drills, filling in of forms, and mindless, manic polishing, he muttered, "Colin, this is no damned use; we should be gaining useful experience at something, not bloody well wasting our time at this endless performance!"

The rituals of polishing were never discharged for even the briefest of let-ups. They were driven to it, it being cap badges, toecaps of boots, soles of boots, the rust-pitted stove, eyelets of laces of boots, window catches, harassed by sundry corporals or the sergeant, in any and all time available, be it only minutes, with items of imperfectly sheened kit and accoutrements thrown violently to the ground, there to be deliberately tramped upon, maliciously and wholly abraded in gravel, dust or brickwork.

Due to the pointlessness of this continually oppressive, nay hostile, regime, Fraser found that he was at a complete loss to know how to counter a suffocating, swelling feeling of being shut in. He sat quietly, apart from the others, listening, trying to soak up a vicarious comfort from Colin Bowles' description of his home way of life and his way of cheerfully meeting queries that cropped up from those lads of urban, as opposed to rural background. The obsessive and slavish polishing became desultory and then ceased.

"How many sheep do you have at home, Colin? Two hundred? How on earth – don't they all look the same?" The young lad looked bemused, disbelieving.

And so it went on round them all: sheep, deer, rabbits, horses, cattle, a whole world beyond their experience or comprehension of the way of life in quiet places. Fraser's mind drifted off, recalling the eerie colours and ghostly crackling of The Merry Dancers in the vault of the night sky, tramping up Glen Annacht.

But not all of them were lacking in a wider acceptance of things. "Polly" Walcott, for example, an Honours B.Sc. graduate from Durham, and another fellow who'd been through Varsity, but in what subject he hadn't said yet. Counting himself, Fraser knew that there were only three from north of the border.

A draughtsman from Stirling, and a fellow from Dundee, called Donnachy, Matt Donnachy. Aye, some fellow if only half of his exploits were to be believed. Or less.

Donnachy set himself to be an authority on football, girls, drinking places ("howffs", he called them, knowledgeably), where and how to get pally with girls, more football and how to get girls to do it once you got them somewhere. He had many relations in the armed forces, most of whom, it appeared from Donnachy's enthusiastic narrative, had contracted, suffered and gloriously recovered from every known form of venereal disease while wearing the King's or Queen's uniform.

"Aye, oor Donal' wis the bizzness. Shagged himsel' oot o' sanity wi' every bint frae Falkirk tae Cairo, so he did!" Donnachy declaimed, with touching pleasure and no small pride. With rising ire at these oft-repeated sagas of self-destruction, Fraser made known to the hut at large that while he and Donnachy were Scots by birth within that country, the relationship went no further. To prove the point, there were times when Donnachy became so febrile in his enthusiasm for anything centred on sex, that his accent was all but totally incomprehensible. Polly Walcott, Varsity man, engaged Fraser on this intriguing (to Polly, for one), disparity in speech. Fraser felt only too happy to emphasise the root difference.

"Now, Polly my friend, I can understand all that you say to me or to the others, even though it comes with a strong County Durham accent, whoo hey, man, and all that! If I was to say the same sentence to you, in the local dialect from around home, you would probably get the gist of it, barring odd words which are peculiar to much of Aberdeenshire, right?"

Polly nodded.

"OK, that's entirely reasonable. I can think of some words, Fraser, which would floor you, if delivered in local tongue."

They both grinned, and Colin Bowles was impatient to get into the to-ing and fro-ing of examples between them all.

"But, hey on, Fraser, that gabble which Matt comes out with, man – it's an unknown language, apart from his two or three universal adjectives. My God, I don't really know what he's saying, but it just sounds so foul!"

"Right, think of Glasgow and five miles round it, Polly. Just a receiving sink for over three hundred years for folk from the outer Highlands, England, the Low Countries and Holland, some Huguenots, poor buggers looking for any kind of work, Irishmen with empty bellies, Liverpool a feeder port for all kinds of dross from Ireland or sun-rotted alcoholics from the colonies – that's where Donnachy's double glottal stottal and vowels flattened out like pancakes come from, so what to him is perfectly normal speech, is really a language of its own, with a vocabulary of its own, not a local dialect such as you, or Colin here, or I have grown up with. Bits of that, bits of this, all squashed into Scouse-speak. Bloody wonderful, and sounds hellish."

Polly had half turned his head towards a commotion at the other end of the hut. "And speaking of Liverpool and Scouses, here's our resident scum from God-knows-what dark hole he was spawned in!"

In all his days before army service, Fraser had never encountered the term "Scouse". Now he knew that the strange and really annoying gang of youths at the top end of the hut (it actually did slope uphill, they had found when scrubbing the gap-planked floor) were all from Liverpool. "Scouse" – the very word sounded like the way in which they spoke, struggling thickly through a sodden sponge at the back of their noses and for a few, it was the way they looked as well, in some peculiar but fitting fashion.

Amongst them was a specimen who was particularly objectionable to everyone, with no exceptions. William Betts was preternaturally tall, and with a lack of breadth that rendered him even taller. In spite of the most draconian drill, Betts always seemed to be slouching indolently ("insolently" according to Sergeant Whyte), beret pushed back over black greasy-looking hair and thumbs hooked into his pockets, the better to support inordinately long angular arms.

Almost upon their arrival and coagulation into a Scouse cohort, Betts' acolytes adopted his tiresome and belligerently repeated catchphrase "Betts is best", throughout a range of nasal intonations, in respect of anything from his self-vaunting prowess as a footballer, to his ability to manufacture, control and raspingly emit loud and noxious wind. In the small community of their army hut, Betts was without doubt the most accomplished in spraying out obscene and foul-mouthed combinations of adjectives, nouns and verbs, more so if focussed upon someone to whom he had taken a loud and vicious dislike.

It had become tiresomely predictable that following a lengthy and argumentative evening in the dreary NAAFI canteen, Betts and his followers would come trampling into the hut at a time when others were already in bed or making moves to do so. Betts wanted to bully, to terrorise.

Beds would be overturned, occupied or not, kit layouts scattered with a sweeping arm, incredibly filthy verse bellowed out, anyone in sight challenged to a fight. Because of his height, Betts in truculent, drink-taken mood looked very frightening with his lank hair falling into his eyes in slavering excitement.

Fraser and Colin Bowles studied him carefully one night, from the door of the ablutions block, blanco kit in their hands. Colin's observation made Fraser smile guardedly.

"For an ill-thriven young beast, my dad would have put 'im away to th'hunt kennels smartish; a reet bloody bad doer. And a bully amongst others."

Fraser's acute dislike was moderated with caution, a wariness of something quite dangerous, about which he had not yet got the measure in terms of any threat to himself. An unlikely candidate, Fraser found the inescapable need to get the true measure of Mister Betts was thrust upon him in salutary fashion, suddenly.

XLVIII

The gathering storm of revulsion and loathing surrounding Signalman Betts' presence came to a violent head on a wet Saturday evening in the hut, about three weeks from intake at Catterick. Thinking back to the explosion of gratuitous violence of that evening, Fraser confided to Colin Bowles and "Moash" Train, another new-found solid soldier who had no time for euphemisms, that the choice of phrase "came to a head" was more than appropriate. The three of them burst out laughing, but with a hard edge to it. Moash added his view:

"You know, Fraser, me old cobber, the vile bastard had it coming to him, so think nothing of it, right?"

In complete accord, Colin rounded it off with his typically very direct, "And if you hadn't grabbed him, some other driven-mad beggar would have duffed him up, but, by gum, that wor a reet fashion to shut the bugger up, an' all! Aye, very neat, I'll say. Knocked his Scouse wheels right out of gear!"

They exchanged slow grins at their oblique and apt humour, and went back into the workshop, Fraser the last of the three, recalling how the "Moash" bit came about. Aye, well – with a name like "Train", logical – "Locomotive, locomotion, motion, moash…" yeah, yeah. There you go, logical, a lot handier than coming out with "Ainslie" for a first name. For himself, he now seemed to be stuck with "Jock". A second identity might come in handy, you never know in the bloody army…

On that evening of steady rain outside, a knot of four or five soldiers had been playing cards on one of their beds. Curiously, as Colin had observed to Fraser, "Theer warn't no table for us to sit around." Harry Curran from Belfast lay on his bed, legs crossed, bringing out one tune after another with his mouth organ, and Fraser lay likewise, listening to the melodies and not really reading the old copy of The Farmers Weekly. He was aware of the magazine falling and his eyelids drooping, to the background of "Radio Luxembourg, on two-o-eight metres, bringing you the Big Band sound of..." He pulled himself off the grey blanket, undressed swiftly and slid into bed already warmed by his body, in rare and welcome quietness.

Fraser shot into tense wakefulness even before the inner door was kicked open, slamming against the flimsy partition of Corporal Swainson's billet. Oh, yes, here we go, "Betts is Best" again, he grated silently, eyes closed to slits. What form of hellish behaviour do we have to suffer tonight?

Stumbling and belching, they all came up the centre of the hut, hitting out at sleeping forms, heaving beds and occupants and kit layouts to the floor. One bed away from Fraser, Noah Oakleigh, a young lad from somewhere in East Anglia, barely eighteen and suffering pain and confusion in every hour of army life, shot upright in his blankets, groping for his spectacles. Yelling and screaming, Betts and his followers lunged through the wreckage to get to Noah, like a rabble of curs tearing at a blinded rat. From where he lay, Fraser saw it all.

As two of Betts' followers tore the blankets off Noah's bed, Betts himself let out a hoarse screech, stretched out a long thin arm and grabbed the young lad's ankle. Oakleigh's own snatching of his foot left Betts with a handful of pyjamas, which he tore with a yell of triumph.

Trying desperately to escape from his bed, from Betts, from everything, Ackers Oakleigh fell heavily out of the total wreckage of his bed, terrified by Betts towering over him, waving the lad's pyjamas like a battle flag, howling hoarsely with spittle flying from his open mouth. One of Betts' "my good muckers" crunched Oakleigh's spectacles under his boot, twisting them into opaque fragments. The whole place was in a yelling, screaming shambles. All due to this braying bastard from loathsome bloody Liverpool, Fraser swore viciously to himself.

Fraser's entire body grew harder and harder by degrees. His arms across his chest corded themselves into the sort of solid muscular tension he hadn't felt nor needed since leaving farm work behind him.

Betts came shambling back down the hut in the grotesque parody of a victor, and then stopped suddenly, disbelieving. Challenged.

"Oo, look 'ere, my lads, who's this 'iding in 'is bed, not joinin' in the fun, eh? Why, it's our sheep shagger from up in the fuckin' 'Ighlands. Lost 'is fuckin' kilt running after them woolly little cunts, I'll bet."

His band of brothers sniggered, "Yeah, sheep shagger an' all!"

He held a hand up to arrest his mob from more abuse of Oakleigh, who was crouched, sobbing, at the ablutions door, trying to protect his young boy's genitals. Fraser sensed Betts coming round the the back of his bed. Fraser's eyes were slits, his body coiled like a spring in barely contained hatred. With malicious exaggeration, Betts tiptoed up the length of the bed and, putting his face close to Fraser's blanketed shoulder (God! The smell was worse than foetid, Fraser registered, detached), commenced his run-up to the terrorising of another, but so far untried, victim.

"Oh, Ah say, booger me, reads books an' all, does 'e, lads?" He read out, with difficulty: "The Farmers Wu...Whe...Weekly. Ay then! All about bulls, an' cows wiv them big titties, and dairymaids an' all that country stuff. Ah bet 'e goes quite weakly, lookin' at them pitchers!"

He looked up, for the expected nasal catcalls, immediately fulfilled. A string of saliva dribbled on to Fraser's blanket.

"Ah bet 'e's just lyin' there, dreamin' about stickin' them sheeps' legs down 'is wellington boots, and stickin' 'is little–"

To the particle of a second, Fraser's restraint fell apart. He felt icily clear on what he was going to do. Clamping down on his churning stomach muscles, and stretching his arms lazily above his head, he turned his apparently still-sleepy eyes towards Betts, who was crouched, slavering and giggling, close beside him.

"Shall we cum closer, then, you Scotch fuckin' farmer's boy. Shall I tell you what we're gooin' to do wiv you?"

Fraser's four words "Aye, you do that!" and instant explosion happened in the same blur of movement.

His left arm whipped right round behind Betts' head and neck and instantly clamped shut in a V-shaped vice, his left fist rammed up below Betts' jaw. With one savage jerk, Fraser shot up in his bed and, crushing Betts' head backwards, pulled it upwards and inwards to his own chest. Betts gave a half-scream, half-groan, and squirmed down on his knees, unable to get room to wield his scrabbling hands and nails.

Fraser's left arm, shoulder and chest muscles crushed steadily inwards, fuelled by a hatred which stretched beyond anything he had ever felt before. He would teach this vile, foul creature some respect for anyone, everyone who had their roots and their living from the land, who possessed dignity and values utterly beyond the comprehension of this loathsome specimen.

So far, Fraser estimated, this wasn't anything like so demanding as picking up a beast's hind leg while someone else trimmed back her hooves, so, he would go bone-crackingly into that very intensity of power! Come on, you black-headed bastard, here it comes, RESPECT! Ever heard of it?

Betts, choking and trying noisily to get freedom to use his fingers and nails on Fraser's face, tried to bite into Fraser's chest and nipple through a bubbling froth of saliva and spittle. That snapped Fraser into total loathing and irreversible action. In a swift part of a second, he shot his left fist upwards, spread widely across Betts' features, took the lower jaw into the heel of his right hand, and pushed abruptly away from himself, screwing Betts' head and neck even further and harder into an acute angle.

The crack was loud, heard above the noises from Betts' mouth as his hands and legs flailed, before his body sagged. Incongruously, Betts broke wind like a horse as Fraser flung him away. It was quite obvious that Betts' lower jaw was wholly dislocated on one side; it hung to one side of his face, which now looked sickeningly ill-assembled. Betts' hands rose, fluttering at his cheeks and then dropped as he collapsed into his own vomit. It had all taken about twelve seconds, Fraser reckoned. Or less.

Without uttering a solitary word to any of the stunned Scouses, deprived of their rabble leader, Fraser slid out of bed and was into his uniform in seconds, ignoring the moaning figure of Betts at the end of the bed. With a single sweep of both arms, Fraser pulled all his bedding into a pack out of contact with this creature for whom he felt nothing but contempt and cold rage. He turned to face the deflated Betts Is Best pack, from which adenoidal protests and promises of what they might attempt were rising.

His outrage must have showed in his eyes, along his rigid jaw. He pulled back his battledress blouse sleeves and stepped to within inches of the fallen god's most vociferous supporter.

"Right, now you just listen to me! If any single one of you has the same loathsome ideas, ever, as that thing crawling about in its own muck, I-shall-break-your-bastard-neck, and by Christ, I mean it!"

In its potent, venomous production, his voice came strangely harsh to his own ears; it clearly appalled the clustered Scouses. ("Now, my bold fellow, keep going – get out of here, fast!" his mind urged repeatedly.)

Fraser jerked his battledress blouse straight and swivelled round to snatch up his webbing belt. His boot toecaps were within six inches of Betts' distorted face. There came an audible hissing intake of disbelief from the sullen Scousers. He spun round, eyes like stone for the few seconds that it took to bore hard into each face, and marched out, boots crashing. To meet Corporal Swainson head on.

Fraser's mind went cold and empty. His tongue took over in detached function, almost as a bystander to some unfortunate mishap.

"Ah, Corporal, the lads might need your help. One of them has fallen quite badly. I've just come in from a walk. It must have happened before I came back in."

Corporal Swainson's features indicated that his own thoughts were not under control. As Fraser spoke to him, registering Swainson's vacant look, one of

Betts' gang suddenly whirled round, crouching, projecting a stream of vomit over a bed in disarray, on the floor, on people's kit, around his own boots. In the uproar that erupted, Fraser marched smartly out of the hut at strictly regimental pace, or even faster, he thought, ironically, to mask the trembling possessing his belly muscles. As he marched out, he made a one-handed grab for the shivering form of Ackers Oakleigh, propelling him with some force through the doors of the ablutions block, sweeping up the lad's pathetic kit from the litter around him.

"Come on! Move yourself! For pity's sake, Ackers, get dressed, get out of this bally place, Now!' he said stabbing a finger in the direction of the other hut. Fraser propelled him with a massive shove, and marched away, very quickly, but as to where, he had absolutely no idea.

Captain Noel Lockley, Adjutant to the Officer Commanding, No. 3 Training Regiment, Royal Signals, looked down at the file again, flicking back to the second page, then to the first. Flies buzzed torpidly, minutely inspecting their own excreta, and buzzed again in the stuffy heat of the CO's office.

"According to Sarn't Whyte, sir, this Betts person, a Liverpudlian of loud voice, it seems, had been behaving particularly objectionably since his draft came on squadron strength. Apparently, he reckons he's a giant amongst pygmies. And with a voice and language to match, I gather, sir.

"But no brain."

Sitting informally around his desk (his own one, rosewood with yew inlay, not one of those ghastly issue things), the CO regarded his Adjutant, Medical Officer and Training Officer (Duties), with speculative interest. Odd and somehow unusual that the cast for this episode seemed to be lacking a cause and a perpetrator, and had defeated them all. So far. Our Provost Sergeant has surely missed a trick with this one. Hmm. Captain Lockley raised his eyebrows across at Captain Sullivan, MO, in silent query.

"Tell me again, Charles, about these rather peculiar marks. Yes, yes, go on, man."

The three officers recognised the well-known indications of their CO being definitely testy this afternoon, watching him shift from one buttock to the other, and then slouch, tipping his chair back.

"Well, sir, I described them as 'non-impact contusions'." Charles Sullivan hastened to say more from his notes as Lieutenant Colonel Moore growled abrasively in the back of his throat, his customary signal of mounting dissatisfaction. "Ah, these are bruises, sir, capillary damage, for which there was no evidence of impact with anything relatively harder–"

Moore broke in harshly, "In other words, he'd been thoroughly belted, but in a controlled fashion, eh, Charles?"

"No, sir," Sullivan said apologetically, then was suddenly assertive. "More like something crushing into his jaw with quite considerable force."

Lieut. Col. Moore swung round in his swivel chair, trying to contain, or dispel discreetly, the stomach gas from luncheon pushing hard against his waistband. He badly wanted to be shot of all these damned National Servicemen, wanted to analyse this episode of petty bruising in some blasted hut, to swiftly guide his senior officers in identifying the causal factors (or malefactors – ha! Neat turn of phrase there!), sort out appropriate action and then chuck it back to them to deal with it. Subject to his approval, naturally.

Moore rumbled deeply, trying to belch. It did no good, so he erupted into quick, abrasive speech in an effort to quell the quite wretched pain in his guts.

"Very well, gentlemen, let me condense all this. Noel, Sam." He nodded sharply at his Adjutant and Training Officer (Duties) respectively. "You fellers check with me, right? Corporal Swainson goes into B Hut, finds the whole place a stinking shambles, but no fight or whatever going on, right? This Betts creature lying in a filthy state, jaw round below his ear. Swainson – ah, I've never cared for that man as an NCO. Too idle by half, and sneaky with it – um, where was I? Ah, yes, Swainson meets this chap, what's his name? Baird? Right, Baird fully and tidily dressed, apparently having come in from a walk, and going out to get hold of an NCO or something like that, so he said."

Moore grunted and belched softly. He badly needed more relief. Get on, before the others start up their interminable wrangling again. Better speak to the mess chappie about these damned over-rich lunches. Irritably, he pushed the file of flimsies away from him.

"No other combatants, everyone else in that hut unable or unwilling or un-some bloody thing to give a statement. Provost Sergeant no wiser. Betts in dock, with sideways lux, er, dislocation," Moore glared at MO Charles Sullivan. "Can't or won't say a word, too bloody painful anyway, other than 'accident'. No witnesses. No one else marked or hurt. Right so far?"

Lieut. Col. Moore steepled his fingers and slid his feet back under his chair. Gad! That eased the blasted wind-pocket a bit. "Come on Charles, all of you; we are beginning to waste our time."

(You are beginning to waste my time, would be more accurate, breathed the Training Officer (Duties) to himself, in silent correction.)

Moore continued peremptorily, "These young lads are here to be trained in a technical, not a combatant capacity. To a certain extent, they or their NCOs should police themselves. Let's go for simple facts." His fingers steepled themselves even more acutely. "Betts is a loud-mouthed bully. Fact. For the moment..." Moore continued, smiling acidly, "he is neither loud-mouthed nor fit to bully. Fact. There is no one else involved as Betts' aggressor. Apparently. There are no witnesses. Apparently. There is no damage to WD property. Fact. There are marks on Betts' face, fact, which he cannot or will not account for. Fact. No one will testify or support charges being laid. Fact. All this is known. Gentlemen, we have a soldier in that hut who put Betts' jaw out of joint, using skills which we are not in the process of teaching him. Betts' Scouse friends will neither attempt redress of injury to their leader, nor are they prepared to say or do anything about this ephemeral, ah, bruiser."

Moore permitted himself a small smirk of satisfaction at that spontaneous and neat label. He looked at Captain Sullivan over his half-rimmed spectacles.

"Charles, how long will it take to repair this young lout and put him back in some capacity or other?"

"Three weeks? Right, he goes into a different training troop, anyway. Sam, you'll see to that. And Sam…"

Captain Sam Weston, Training Officer (Duties), took a small number of seconds to respond.

"Sir?"

"Make it a learning experience for him, understood?"

"Sir."

They all nodded. The Old Man was taking short cuts. Sometimes they worked. They were immediately arrested in any premature anticipation of this session winding up rapidly. At that moment precisely, an intransigent pocket of digestive gas surged noisily into a loop of Lieut. Col. Moore's large colon, and with the instant relief came clear cognisance of what they were all stumbling around. Moore already looked triumphant, while his senior officers were visibly at a loss.

"Gentlemen, when I was assembling the known facts about this blasted Betts fracas, we failed entirely to take account of one immediately obvious fact concerning the whole distasteful affair."

The CO waited, half-hoping that his adjutant or any of them in the room would jump to something so simple, but also half-hoping (or by a margin more than half), that it would be left to him to elucidate.

"Right, pay attention Sam, Noel, Charles. Of course this load of Scouse sycophants know who bashed up their illustrious leader – they damned well saw it happen! It follows that there is one reason only that not one of them has it in him to tell us who stopped Betts dead in his objectionable ways, and that is because every man jack of his fawning rabble will have been threatened with precisely the same treatment if they so much as sneak a name for our RSM to descend upon. The soldier, gentlemen, who so effectively put the frighteners on the whole damned lot has to be on the roll for that hut."

The CO looked round his officers in patent satisfaction that the equation was solved. It just required the blank space to be filled.

"Right? So, he's physically strong, no callow schoolboy this fellow, and determined enough to not just threaten to duff up the Betts creature. And, very clearly, the severity of his action gives us a strong indication of the extent of his provocation. Now, who might this lead us to, Noel?"

Captain Lockley wanted to show comparable acuity of mind.

"This other soldier, Baird, who had seemingly just appeared on the scene, sir, but how?"

"But how nothing, Noel. Don't you see that the whole bad smell of this Betts affair has been dealt with in a one-stop fashion that has taken it out of our hands at one swoop, and that is definitely worth something in itself, ha!"

Moore had the look of some kind of judge who had resolved a difficult case entirely to his own judiciary satisfaction. Captains Lockley, Weston and Sullivan exchanged confirmatory looks. Lockley spoke up – this bally thing was going to go on forever.

"Well, sir, the rotten apple has had his day. I'm sure that Captain Weston will have him reassigned to something that will cut him down to size. And we can put it behind us, sir, at last."

"Right, Noel and Sam, fourteen hundred hours, Baird here on CO's Orders. Advise Mr Oates, RSM, and shirt sleeve order. Let's get on now with more pressing matters, I think. Charles, Sam; dismiss, gentlemen, and thank you. Noel, about this requirement for BAOR in November. Will we have drafts ready for them by then?"

He clamped down, hard, on another dangerously explosive escape of wind. Gad. They consulted briefly on intakes, workshops and special training. Lockley rose to leave as Moore stretched himself, leaning back in his chair.

"One last thing, Noel. This fellow Baird, how old is he, what's his background? Oh, twenty. Hmm, a good bit older than the usual stuff. Anyway, where does he hail from? No, I don't mean precisely, dammit, Noel."

"His home is a good distance up the river Dee from…" Lockley checked with his notes. "From Aberdeen, sir."

Lieut. Col. Moore straightened up in interest. "Ha, indeed? The renowned salmon river, the silvery Dee! We might just–" He belched expansively, with evident relief. "We might just learn something of interest to all of us." He let his chair legs come down with a crash, his face impassive, eyes guilelessly wide open."Leave the door open, please, Noel. Oh, and Noel!"

"Sir?"

"Once Signalman Betts is able to converse again, I shall want to have a chat with him which I would guess will take all of three minutes." He belched profoundly. "And, Noel."

Captain Lockley grated his teeth silently, and swivelled round in the CO's office door a final time, his eyebrows questioning.

"Sir?"

"Whatever you may feel personally about this difficult-to-resolve affair, dear chap, please don't think for a moment that I am abjawring you! Hurrm, Ha! Ha! Ha!"

Moore grew very red in his face from his barking bursts of laughter, from relief in more pockets of wind rasping their way to freedom, and from his sudden delight in seeing a neat way to once again get the last word in amongst his officers. Pretty smart, that! All tension released, Lieut. Col. Astley Moore permitted escape to a whole series of rasping escapes of wind that propelled him forward and nearly off his Chair, Admin. Officers for the Use of (1925), G.S. Smiling broadly, he slackened his tie and took out from a top drawer a much-thumbed volume on Fly Fishing For Salmon & Sea Trout.

Fraser knew at once that RSM Oates had come to march him off for something to do with the Betts business. Damn and rot his vile Scouse existence. He was beginning to feel that keeping the head down and never volunteering for anything hadn't quite done the trick this time. As he put down his tools, Colin grasped him quickly but quietly, intoning his earnest warning round the back of his head:

"If the CO's gaahn on at you about the Betts creature, tell 'im he's a shockin' disgrace to 'is precious regiment. A reet bad un for t'youngsters. We'll aaall back you oop, if need be."

"Baird! Move it, at the double, man!" Oates was watching him closely.

RSM Oates found the whole affair mystifying, and that was not to be accepted. Signalman Baird, double zero seven nine five, just did not have the telltale signs of a troublemaker. Big strong lad, very quiet. Hmm. Well able to look after himself, I would say, Oates pondered, and who started what? he wondered.

Let's see what the Old Man makes of this one.

Outside the CO's office, Oates brought Fraser to Attention.

"Double zero seven nine five Baird, Shah! Hat off, queekmarsh, eftoight, eftoight, left wheel, maaartoime, aarrp!" RSM Oates let his breath out silently, gazing fixedly over the CO's head, saying nothing, noting everything. Mr Lockley here too, was there something that had slipped past them all?

"That's all, Sarn't Major, thank you."

Moore flicked through the brief service record in front of him. Not an iota of suspicion there.

"That's all right, Baird. Stand at ease, stand easy. I'm interested to see that Corporal Swainson and the Provost Sergeant state that you came upon this fracas as you arrived back from a walk. Tell me about it, your walk, I mean,' Moore said, almost casually. Looking at Baird's general physique, he noted that his neatly rolled shirt sleeves were almost too tight across his upper arm muscles and tanned arms.

"I miss the countryside, sir, and the river. I thought it was a fine evening for a walk round and get the feel of the country outside the camp."

Moore checked on the mention of a river in this soldier's background. The Dee, of course. He glanced for a second at his adjutant. Good chap, Lockley, but wouldn't know a fishy-looking bit of water if he sat down in it.

"Ah, good, go on, Baird, tell me about it. Oh, just a minute, which school did you go to?"

Fraser ticked off this giveaway signal. The CO was trying on a wee bit of bland deception. There was definitely a need for "keep the heid doon" strategy on his, Fraser's, part here. He told the CO about the College in Aberdeen. Go on about the river, quickly.

"The Aberdeenshire Dee, sir. You can see it from our house. There's a run of sea trout in it at this time of year. Sir."

Moore got up, came round his desk, to pitch one hip on the dark wood, swinging a highly polished dark tan shoe.

"That's all right, Baird, stay where you are. Tell me, do you or your father go out and take the odd cast?"

In his observer's corner, Noel Lockley relaxed. By God, the Old Man certainly snicks in onto anything to do with fishing, but what's that got to do with…?

"Aye, er – yes, we usually get to have a cast if there's no one on that beat; it's in return for my father keeping the ghillie right with his stock and dogs. Mr McPherson and my father were at school together."

"Spendid, sounds a good chap, this ghillie friend. Anyway, getting on all right with the lads in your hut? Know this fellow, what's his name, Best or something? Is he any good?"

"I don't know him, other than on the drill square, sir. He doesn't do the hut or the younger lads any good. He's–"

Moore pounced.

"Yes, he's what? Spit it out, Baird."

Like a sudden terrier at the kill. Lockley grinned behind an impassive face.

"Well, sir, he's a big mouth and a bully. Some of the lads feel he's going to let the regiment down, sir. He just doesn't do the workshops properly, bullies the others to cover up for him, sir."

"Ah, I see, most interesting. Has Signalman Betts been a particular nuisance in any way to you?"

Captain Lockley observed silently, not bloody likely, CO, sir, just get the solid feel of this young man, for a man he damned well is. Might we be getting somewhere now…?

Moore was digging away. "You're a good bit older than the rest, Baird, how's that?"

Fraser told him about taking all the farm jobs to gain experience, with the firm objective of getting into a place of his own at the earliest opportunity.

"And that's how you're in here, talking about fishing with me, ha! So, you're about twenty. Let me see, your father, was he in the 14–18 War by any chance?"

"Yes, sir. He was a Gunner, Royal Field Artillery. He was badly wounded. His gun took a direct hit at Passchendaele–"

Moore interrupted strongly. "Oh, my God! My God! That bloody awful business, utter shambles. Horribly wrong decisions being taken by horribly incompetent fellers at the top." He was visibly agitated. Moore swung round abruptly, looking directly at Fraser. "So, your father's man got his head blown off, you know how that happened. This Betts fellow got his jaw knocked off, what d'you know about that, Baird, eh?"

Keep your head down, never volunteer.

"Not really, sir. He probably pushed one of the lads too far and got walloped in sheer anger. A number of the men have always said he had it coming to him, sooner or later. Sir."

Moore was gazing out of the window, drill square commands losing their edge in the sultry afternoon.

"Yes, you're probably right. Look, Baird, you can help your troop, and thereby help me in running the regiment by doing two things. Should any of Betts' cronies' idea of fun or filth be pointed in your direction, or any of the other men in the hut, do not be tempted to handle him like one of your wild Highland cattle, right?"

(Was the vital word "again" hovering, present but unspoken in the CO's homily? Fraser maintained what he hoped was an interested but impassive expression.)

"Mr Oates will attend to anything like that, should it occur, right?"

Above Fraser's head, there was some sort of unspoken exchange between the CO and RSM Oates.

"Sah!"

"The other thing is, give your Gunner father my regards, and tell him it would give me great pleasure to be introduced to this ghillie friend of yours, the next time when I'm up north, agreed?"

"Sir."

"Right, Baird, your comments have proved most illuminating, haven't they, Mr Oates? Thank you, RSM, carry on. Captain Lockley, stay a moment, will you?"

Fraser was marched back to the disembowelled tank and its various pieces of dismantled radio equipment. There was a strange, indefinable glint in the RSM's eye as he regarded Fraser in silence for a moment before giving the order to "Carry on!" Then he said, "Double zero seven nine five Baird?"

"Sir?"

"Saved by your friend the ghillie, and his fine Scottish salmon river, I would say, Baird!"

What was that last piece of Corporal McGillivray's advice, which now seemed like a heap of months back? "Dinna forget where ye come from." Well, damned right, he hadn't, and damned right he wouldn't.

XLIX

Towards the end of their third month in training at Catterick, fields beyond the rows of huts became businesslike and active with farm men, binders, and nodding Shire horses taking wagons to steadily growing stackyards. Feeling frustration, almost a pain at being cut off from being a part of what he saw, Fraser soaked up all possible detail of the sprawling farm buildings behind the trees, half–hidden by deep-foliaged Yorkshire elms.

Colin Bowles joined him, recognising between them both the same unaccepted apartness of being tethered to so many pointless procedures as an unlikely soldier or signalman. It was, in fact, a knot of pain.

"Hey up, Fraser, we're to gaun on t'range firing tomorrow, that should give us country lads a chance to show our mettle!"

All of B Squadron troops were posted for range drill and firing (rifle), light machine gun drill and firing (Bren light machine gun), in the coming week. Rifles were drawn for practising dry firing, mostly in the prone position, under the suddenly animated eye and tongue of Sergeant Whyte.

"Remember, lads, when you fire that rifle," he said, smacking his weapon forcefully on the flat of the darkly oiled butt, "you've to reduce and counteract two forces: one, backwards through your right hand, stock, butt, shoulder and the rest of your body, and two: upwards, trying to jerk up from between your hands. It's trying to escape from the explosion in the breech, and the only way for it to go is up and to the right. So, Train my lad, what do you do to counteract this bangin' and leaping around? C'mon, pay attention, soldier."

A stocky fellow from Derby, quite happy with his locomotion-linked familiar name Moash adopted by the rest of the hut, he was at that time hugely bothered with boils, pustular eruptions of livid colour. ("It's this rotten bad food. Ah've fed better to t'pigs an' all," Colin Bowles declaimed at every opportunity, Orderly Officer no exception.) The men could see that Moash was in obvious pain and tension from a fresh crop of dark red and swollen boils around the back of his neck. The most agonising thing for him to do right then, was to have to get down, lie prone and arch his head and neck back to sight along his rifle. They stepped back a pace from round him, silent and anxious.

"Right, when I say, get your body in line. In line, I said! Line that rifle out down your right leg out behind you!" Sergeant Whyte's running flow of instruction was all round Moash Train; the NCO was entering into doing something at which he was abundantly experienced. "Let me see your cheek pressed hard into the butt, just behind your thumb wrapped round the stock."

Train sighed heavily, sweating. "Right, Sarn't."

Sergeant Whyte was dancing around Moash's prone form, eager to show them all how a professional soldier functioned with his rifle.

"Now then, zero nine six eight Train, my lad, pull that butt into your shoulder like you'd captured your girl friend's leg or some bloody thing, and get your whole body locked in behind it."

Whyte was enjoying his task, his experience, his soldierly skills, his teaching them, his family of unlikely lads, serious soldiering.

"Prone, I said, but not with your bleeding right foot and heel cocked up like that! Get the bloody thing shot off, and then you'll be prone, all right. Get that right elbow, left elbow both screwed into the ground, and your fingers pulling that stock back and in! OK, now, sight and relax. If your rifle stays on target when you relax, or drops a little, you're all right. If, howevAH, it waves or wobbles around all over the fucking place, then you've got to compensate with your body until it stays on target. Train, take that rifle what you've been playin' around with, get a grip on it like iron, and let me see if I can move it."

From where they were all standing, the afternoon sun behind them, they could all see only too plainly that Moash's shirt collar was cutting right into the glistening, swollen redness of a fresh boil, hugely inflamed. There were another two close beside it. His neck muscles were rigid and quivering. The principal yellow-tipped boil was close to bursting.

Sergeant Whyte darted about like some malevolent spider, pushing into Train's shoulder with his leg, bending down to pull his rifle muzzle up, trying to cant it over. Moash's head, neck and shoulders were visbly quivering in spasms, his eyes clenched into slits and sweat running down his jaw. But his rifle stayed aligned, and his boils glowed with the pressure of pent-up contents.

"OK, Signalman Train." The sergeant's voice was casual, almost benevolent. "Relax."

As a groan was only partly emitted from the prone form, Sergeant Whyte screamed at him one second later:

"Haarrpp man! Hold your weapon like bloody rock! Don't let it wobble around! Take steady aim, fire and reload and fire again!"

They all jumped and started, conditioned as they now were to sudden yells. Moash's arms, his whole body and that obscene-looking neck were quivering.

The sergeant was down on his knees, taking hold of the muzzle to try and move it significantly in any direction. He could not.

"Right, relax aim! Check your bolt. On your feet, port arms." Whyte's fingers rattled inside the open breech. "Ground arms, stand easy."

As a body, they all let out an audible collapse of breath, looking at each other, at Moash's suffused face, chin sunken to his chest, at those beastly, pent-up boils round his neck.

"That," said Sergeant Whyte quietly, "was bloody magnificent! If you lot can use your rifle in a consistently accurate fashion, whether you're shitting yourself with the trots, or you've got a wound dressing stuck on you, or…" He grinned hugely. "…you've got the biggest bastard boil on your arse or your elbow!"

They all roared with splendid release from tension and Train dodged, with very real alarm, a mock punch on the back of his neck from Whyte.

"Then you'll put your weapon to good use. Any points? Right, my lads, how about my showing how it goes, eh?"

He strode off a few paces and in an instant was a totally relaxed Tommy, fag hanging from his lower lip, beret pushed back on his brow, battledress blouse hanging open, rifle slung on his shoulder. The immediate small arms action was over. He sauntered through amongst them, and then suddenly screamed "Down!"

The rifle came off his shoulder in a flick, even as his whole body came down with a thump that they felt come up through their boots. Left arm and shoulder took the impact to one side, right leg kicked out behind, both hands in place and elbows hardly moving from where he had rocked them into the ground. The bolt crashed open in a motion that had happened before they could register it. The whole sequence was a sort of blur of man and weapon as a single lethal entity, and had taken slightly more than three seconds.

On impulse, Colin Bowles stooped and enveloped the foresight protector with the palm of his hand and tried to pull it up, and then to quickly shove it down. The rifle did not move. One of the sergeant's eyes gleamed at him maliciously, the other continued to sight-in the rock-steady rifle.

"Ee, by then, lads!" Colin muttered, in patent admiration.

They all exclaimed, in recognition of a deadly skill they knew had not come out of a small arms manual, nor yet from repetitive drill in a Yorkshire field disused from forty years back. The tension and curiosity of earlier in the day had all disappeared; in groups of two and three, they busily attempted to equal their sergeant's speed and accuracy of movement, his combat-hardened total readiness to kill.

Rifles slung, they marched to the ranges, going at that ridiculously short pace that irritated Fraser, and it seemed, country lad Colin, to a degree. As they went up on to the banked firing positions in sections of ten, Fraser took a candle end and matches from his overalls pocket, and holding his rifle between his knees, smoked the whole of his foresight blade and protector in the candle's near-invisible flame. The whole muzzle assembly was coated in a densely black coat of soot, any blued or bare metal becoming instantly non-reflective. Beckoning Colin and Moash to come over, he smoked their foresights in similar fashion. From his stance some yards to the rear, Sergeant Whyte noted this, was on the point of telling all three to get back behind their numbers, but stayed silent. Signalman Baird had some decidedly non-regimental tricks in him. They were well known in infantry regiments, combat units to a man. Now, where or how had Baird picked up this old sweat's trick?

"Second rank, stand to your firing positions by number. Ground arms, stand easy! Pay attention. The ammunition detail will supply you with eleven rounds only. Here are your firing instructions."

As the ammunition detail passed along the row of men, Fraser took off his beret, carefully inspected it for the point of maximum overhang and placed the fold low over his forehead and eyes, instead of per King's Rules and Regs over his right ear. Sergeant Whyte watched, noted, said nothing.

"Assume prone firing position, get yourselves set and steady. Right? Open bolts and load one round only. Close bolts, safeties on. You are allowed one sighter. This will be marked for you on the target. But! Listen! Check that you are firing at the target carrying the same number as your firing peg. You will then load your ten rounds and be ready, on command, to take ten shots, in your own time at the correct target to your front, taking the same point of aim throughout. You will not shoot at your neighbour's target!"

Eyes shut, neck relaxed, Fraser waited for the predictable preamble to stop. He moved his body infinitesimally to one side. Grip? Good. Relax. Where does it move to? A shade more to the right. Right, breathe out. Chest, stomach flat, f-l-a-t-s-q-u-e-e-z-e. He registered the dull wummph as he fired. Just like a twelve-bore, so far as sound goes, less kick than his father's old Home Guard Pattern '14 rifle of the war years. Tightening slowly, the rifle came up to the target, locked on to it again; the marker disc had risen jerkily, tapped slightly to the left of the black bull and was quickly pulled down.

"You all have your point of impact now. Your point of aim for your next ten rounds' fire should be exactly the same for all of them, which will not be marked. Put up your arm if you have a problem, rifle laid down, bolt open, to your front. At your target in front, in your own time, fire!"

Fraser pulled his beret even further down over his brow, until it almost touched the cocking piece in front of his nose. He let the rifle lie loosely in his hands, cradled in fingers that could only drop so far. His elbows were solidly into the two heel marks made before he lay down. He breathed slowly, steadily, slower, steadier, and tightened everything by stages, everything behind and below his sight-picture going flat. Firing in sequences of three, his senses shut out the flurries of shots to each side of him. The absolute blackness of the foresight came up again and seemed to nail itself to the target, almost lingering there after each of his shots.

"Firing detail unload! Close bolts, dry fire, open bolts. On your feet for inspection, port arms!"

It all felt good. He turned to look for Colin and Moash, but could not tell by either's stance how they had done.

"Ground arms! Stand easy! Detail will sling arms. Hup! To the right in file, 'ighttahn, march off. Next detail."

Conversation amongst them was excited, with surprise or vexation in voices and faces. Colin Bowles grinned broadly, his North Country vowels strong in satisfaction.

"That were a reet good trick wi' t'candle, fairly made the beggar stand out!" He rubbed his shoulder, peering inside his shirt ruefully. "Worse nor forkin' 'ay all t'day for me Dad, but by golly! What a rare do that were!"

He laughed outright in sheer enjoyment, suddenly doing something properly soldier-like at last and liking it.

The range NCOs and sergeants gave out targets. They were about halfway through when Fraser saw one sergeant pause in handling the cardboard square and nod the others over, looking at one target in particular. Another great balls-up by someone? The nervous fluttering in his stomach churned in disbelief. Both sergeants looked up.

"Seven nine five Baird?"

His target was passed over in sudden silence. His single sighter was at the extreme left angle of the small, black half-round bull. Precisely across the middle of the bull extended a row of interlapping bullet holes, with nothing separating one hole from the next, a series of round notches marching across the bull, with the edges blurred by rounds passing through the same hole.

"Let's have a dek, then. Christ! Another bloody Davey bloody Crocket!"

"Shit 'ot shot Sniper Man! You wouldn't bloody chuckle!"

Sergeant Whyte interrupted the buzz peremptorily.

"Let me see your target, Baird. Hmm." His sharp features glowed with satisfaction. "I think you're in the wrong bloody lot, Baird; you should be out in Korea!" he said, looking round his NCO colleagues, who grinned in assured easy camaraderie.

Sliding the square of warmed cardboard inside his shirt, Fraser looked at Moash and Colin.

"'Korea?' What's he on about, men?"

Sergeant Whyte heard him.

"For your edification, young man, it's where we're currently trying to kill as many Koreans, Chinese and gooks as we can, in the mess left by the Americans when they pulled back, right? Get a grip, you lot might just be on a troopship for sunny Korea!"

They marched back, rifles slung, feeling satisfied with their handling of what had to be every soldier's basic skill.

The corporal came at Fraser like a striking cobra. Colin Bowles, in the file to Fraser's left, and two men behind him, was alarmed by the man's open viciousness. Silently, Colin endorsed his own simile: Eeh, my lad, and you bloody well look like a sodding snake, an' all…

Tall, lanky, bending over Fraser in rampant animosity, the corporal screamed the squad to a ragged halt.

"Look to your bloody front! Nah, then, soldier, think you 'ave to be bleedin' different, rifle on your left shoulder? What do you say, hey?"

"It's just that I'm more used–"

"Ho, don't you fucking backchat me, bloody nignog. Name and number, quickly!"

Everyone in the two files stood stolidly at attention, looking to their front, exuding layer upon careful layer of impossible wariness.

"Right, seven nine five Baird, 'ight taahn! Two paces forward at the double!"

"Nah, then, you address me as 'Corporal Collins, Sah!' – got that? Let me 'ear you say that!"

"Corporal Collins." An imperceptible check. "Sir."

With his eyes completely devoid of any expression, and seemingly directing his vision to a distant object of equally remote significance, Fraser registered the fact that this, this vile being carried no campaign ribbons or skill-at-arms flashes of any kind. Where do pointless treacherous bastards like this come from?

"Ho, so you're a Scotch fucking nignog, hey? Think you're something special, been playin' at real soldiers. Lemme see; you'll 'ave a range card. 'And it over, come on, c'mon!"

Salivating with malicious pleasure, the corporal held it up between finger and thumb, then proceded to tear it into ever smaller fragments, falling around Fraser's boots.

"You must 'ave bin banging away at some other bleeder's target, is that right, all these irreg'lar 'oles?"

He waited, lips open, in the engineered certainty that he could render this idiot National Serviceman even more of a fumbling nignog.

"Right, seven nine five Baird or Braid or Bread..."

He waited for an appreciative snigger. There was none.

"Seein' as you've left all your lying evidence layin' 'ere on the floor, you get down on your knees smartish, and pick 'em all up, and then–"

From fifty yards back came Sergeant Whyte's rasping irritation:

"What's the hold-up, Corporal? You're blocking the whole detail. Move it man!"

Collins thrust his face and darkly glittering eyes to within breathing distance of Fraser.

"Now, then my Scotch clever dick, see all the aggro you've got all your muckers in. Do you hear me? You'd fucking better get that weapon on the proper shoulder, this time, and take up your mate's weapon and all! I'm watching you like a bleedin' 'awk."

"Squaard by the front, queemaarsh!"

Their implacable hatred of this snarling travesty of soldierly leadership invested the two files of men with a tight presence as they marched away in seething, battened-down correct order.

From somewhere in the rear of the firing detail came the faintest breath of a rhetorical question:

"Who are we supposed to be fighting, anyway?"

The slightest of tightly, silently pursed lips marked its passage throught the entire body of men; they had regained their self-respect.

"For Chrissake, men, don't treat that rifle like a pick shaft; it's your best friend!"

Sergeant Whyte offered around an opened packet of smokes to any of them who smoked.

"Let me pass on something which you might use or need, in connection with you soldiers and that trusty rifle. Just remember this: it might turn out to be the one bloody thing that's going to save your skin or some other useful parts of you, if things suddenly get distinctly dodgy. You might well say, 'Ho, but we're Signals, we're not going to get face to face with 'orrible obnoxious Krauts, wogs or little yellow buggers in jungle 'jamas!' Oh, yeah? In action, my friends, more Signals men get shot than the blokes they're attached to; you're the ones they need to kill first of all, the blokes with a radio pack and antenna waving about. They kill you, and then the officer or senior NCO with you."

Sergeant Whyte drew deeply on his cigarette, then took it from between his lips with a pincer-like thumb and forefinger, smoke curling up from between his nails.

"If any of you lot are ever in action, and I mean in the real hard stuff, attached to some infantry mob or even tanks, and you have to deal with some other bugger what's popped up from fuck knows where, it'll all take place in about three seconds. You've got to make sure that your first round nails the bastard and to make that happen, you need to have three excellent rules stamped into your head."

He paused, flicking away the butt of his cigarette without an apparent movement of his hand, and spoke steadily, looking right through them all, with an inward view of figures, firing, yells, confusion in battle.

"Always 'ave your rifle ready. An empty magazine'll be damn little use to you. Have it full, ten in below and one in the breech, with your bolt closed and cocked on it, safety off, by God – no messing! And, a bayonet's no soddin' use to you if it's still in its frog. First sign of trouble, you get it on that rifle, pronto, right? Right hand and stock clapped 'ard into your hip, left hand in that rock-like grip out in front."

His voice rose a pitch, at once harder, higher, flatter.

"So, you're primed to fire at the first bloody twitch he makes. Watch his eyes. They're the dead giveaway. That's Rule Number One: Be Bloody Ready! Rule Number Two is – if you have to move, an' there's little cover, then by Christ, you move that last five or fifteen yards flat out at 'im when both of you least expect it and you fire from the hip like I said; a fire 'ose spewing out bullets at the middle of 'is body and the instant you fire you crash that bolt and you fire again. That's Rule Number Three, and you come in low and fast and you smack that precious rifle into his face or throat as you go down to one side and you reload as you roll and you shoot 'im again, stick it in his ear or eye or any bloody place and you reload and your 'eart's going like a fucking pom-pom and you're alive, 'cos of those three F's: Fire, Fast and Fire Again."

Sarn't Whyte spoke slowly, almost in weariness.

"And remember this, my good lads. A couple of field dressings come in

469

bloody 'andy at times. Keep 'em on you, preferably the big jobs, much more use than some silly bastard looking at you and then saying 'Good luck' and all that when you're dodgin' shot and shell with great speed. You wouldn't bloody chuckle, then, pal."

He chucked the rifle back to Colin Bowles, winked silently and marched off, closing his battledress blouse with his sergeant's stripes and many campaign ribbons.

L

There was something brewing in the matter of postings as they neared the finish of their various training workshops. The top possibilities were Korea, Germany and Malaya, and from what they knew from the Orderly Room blokes, the order of priority changed day by day. So, their training intensified day by day: field exercises, technical instruction on new equipment, more weapon training, individual assessments, getting bashed around hill and dale by the black-jerseyed PE staff.

They seemed to be forever running from whatever they had just dealt with to tackle some other technical likelihood, and general amongst them all, Colin, Moash, Polly, Fraser, "Captain" Cuttle, Vic Yates and the others who were determined to make the best of things, it was felt that they were allowed no time to say amongst themselves, "Right, we've got that particular bit of gen mastered this time."

As this build-up of pressure slid into the frosts and fogs of Yorkshire autumn, Fraser felt the enforced separation from things natural, the strong rhythms of the countryside preparing for winter most keenly.

Each one of the group had developed his own antidote to combat the feeling of adding on more skills not entirely mastered, of not yet encompassing a capability they could then truthfully describe as wholly genned up in their letters back home.

For Fraser, Sunday was his day of escape, by walking, sometimes for hours at a stretch. It was the only way in which he could draw relief, really letting tension out, by striding out at a good long natural pace, easing the thigh muscles that ached abominably from that dratted infantry pace.

Breakfast was an hour later on Sunday mornings in the mess hall, and by getting up at his usual time, he could get shaved, dressed and breakfasted in comfortable solitude. That was a luxury. Colin was on a weekend pass to go the few miles to his home and folks. Fraser and he enjoyed each other's company, sometimes without speech.

To get past the duty guard picquet at the camp gates, dictated being even more smartly turned out than was sensibly necessary; the hovering corporals of military police, sometimes two of them, were invariably of silent hostile manner. Fraser took satisfaction from the fact that they had no inkling of the true persona concealed inside the meticulously prepared uniform. Ha! This provided endless amusement between Colin and himself, giving no pretext whatsoever for hatred from the surly, loathed RMPs.

Fraser had no directions or map. His explorations of Yorkshire farms and villages tended to follow a circular route, keeping the sun to his left shoulder. He stretched out his legs in a steady stretching pace and felt the better, much better of it at once. He had the pleasurable sensation of impressions of every nourishing nature being usefully stored away, but to remain on call when needed in the long avenue of years ahead.

Tall elms, towering up from hedges, with oaks and ashes in equal numbers (and girths); mist lying quiet below hilltop hangers and established woods of considerable extent; large, quietly satisfied farmhouses and attendant ranges of buildings; the settledness and orderly disposition of ploughed land and root crops; the lively industry of folded ewe flocks. The immutable prosperity of this old, honoured land.

Glimpses of things seen between more boles of trees; oak, ash, lime, elm, beech, chestnut, dignified stone gables and chimney heads, the arch of a manor yard ducking his eye to rows of loose boxes beyond – it all drew him on and on, strangely not feeling out of his rightful surroundings (what he very privately called his "home place" in his innermost repository of objectives to be fulfilled) but quite content, even invigorated by all that could be seen, heard and smelled of this well-husbanded countryside.

Walking steadily on between hedges higher than any in Angus, Perthsire or Dumfriesshire, there were ditches to either side, and all were tidy, or in the process of being made so after the growth of summer: hedges and banks stripped and clean of growth, grass and weeds of any kind, ditches scraped to the hard bottom, all by billhook, slasher and spade, as he well knew from his time with Jack Harris, and his frequent and forceful "Hey! Bluggy 'ell! Youm got h'it down to the bluggy bone, Ah'll shay!"

Fraser grinned openly and widely to himself. That had been a good time. He smelled wood smoke and came upon blue haze and thick grey coils rising from a fire of hedge trimmings, trash and leaves from hedging work of the previous day.

All this industrious husbandry restored his own feeling of still having a definite purpose to the years ahead, if not at all in this army existence that oppressed and trammelled him so sorely for the present. At unpredictable moments, this need to be a rooted part of all of this nature of things became an ache high up in his chest, to the extent of proceeding to a soreness that was hard to dispel. He knew that he had to stop walking and take a hold of a gate or stone wall, run his hands along a well put-in strainer post, in massive sawn oak or ash, or walk along a headland to get the feel of soft, tilled ground coming up through his feet again, and then to stop, twist off a handful of dead grass to clean the muck off these over-clean army boots. And then to straighten up, wipe his hands thoroughly with the knot of stems and drop it neatly in a rabbit's burrow.

The voice came strongly from some distance behind him:

"If you care to open that gate, and check my ewes as they run in where you're standing, you can come home with me and get properly cleaned up."

The horse and rider had come padding along the grass verge down in the lane, whilst he had been occupied with bending down in the field. Now, man and mount stood calmly, looking at him from beyond the gate which he had closed on entering the field. Grey gelding, clean-legged, fifteen hands, crisp head, stout barrel. Legs well muddied up and belly likewise. Rider in market boots, old stained riding coat, cap pulled well over his eyes, looking at Fraser steadily. Waiting.

"Aye, er, yes. Good morning! Just getting the feel of things in this part of the country. I hope you don't mind my stepping about in here? Not the easiest of land for ewes in a wet time, is it?"

There was a faint smile about the farmer's face.

"No, not at all; you're perfectly welcome to step about, as you put it." The smile broadened. "Provided you give me a hand to count in these ewes first. What part of Scotland do you hail from, anyway? Had anything to do with sheep up there? Never mind, let's get on with this lot first, talk afterwards. Need my dog? He's holding them a piece back. No? All right."

The rider trotted off in the direction from whence he had come, out of sight. Fraser heard a repeated whistle, then a single indistinct shout in the still autumn day.

Fraser opened the field gate wide on its hinges, back to the hedge, making sure it wasn't going to swing back by its own weight, and then stepped down into the lane as the first scuffling of sheeps' hooves came from round the bend.

Between him and the mounted rider and dog in their rear, there were somewhere close to three hundred ewes or so, Fraser reckoned, nicking them off in roughly a score at a time. Big fleshy sheep, not quite the same as Greyfaces back home, but similar. Mashams, maybe? Without being aware of so doing, Fraser had closed his distance to the first dozen or so ewes until they halted, heads alert, about fifteen paces from the open gate. He spoke to them, just a random contact to get them to focus on him, and not the gate in a wild rush.

"Hoo on, then, ladies, just ca' canny, tak' it easy, tak' it easy."

They made their first scrabbling rush to the gate. He closed even tighter, allowing the first seven past him as a visual encouragement to the rest. He closed even tighter, imposing his presence upon them, counting rapidly, audibly, with one outstretched finger, the other extended behind him to deter any infiltrations from a circular rush of bodies. He succeeded in slowing them down to a steady drumming of grey faces and fleeces, wary of the predictable anxious rush to get past him by the last score. When they did try, very nearly successfully, he yelled out loudly and tenaciously, "Seventy-six, sev'nty-seven, haar! Getback! Getback ye brute! Sevn'ty-eight! Nine, eighty, eighty-one, two, three, four, five, six, Harrgh! Seven!"

And then they were all in the field, including two flighty objects that decided to make a pointless rush back past the collie, which knew exactly their gambit even before they even wheeled to take off back down the lane.

"What did you make it, then, young man?"

"Two hundred and eighty seven."

The farmer sat, relaxed in his saddle, saying nothing, mentally checking flock numbers known to him anyway.

"Humm, do you now? That can't be right. They're four short or you're four short or something. You've been at this before, haven't you?" He was puzzled.

"Oh, aye, right enough. Hill sheep mostly." Fraser gave the name of the Whitepark estate back north.

The farmer cut him off from further detail with a quiet, "You'll be absolutely right, I do believe. The shepherd's got four kept back in the pens with bad footrot; they'll keep there until morning."

No comment between them, just an easy smile at the satisfaction of knowing that they were both proved right. The sheepdog came up to Fraser, smelt his hand and sat between them.

"Right-ho, but what's your name anyway? Excuse my bad manners in not enquiring for a start."

Fraser told him.

"Well, much obliged to you, Fraser. Robert Hesketh." The farmer leant down to shake hands, smiling warmly. "So busy counting these fat old ewes, we didn't introduce ourselves properly, did we? I shall go quietly round this lot and see them settled, and you make down to the house." He rose in his stirrups to point out the line of trees and chimneys beyond. "I shall meet you there. Introduce yourself to Mrs Hesketh."

He pursed his lips to the gelding and dog. Fraser shut the gate behind them, sheep grease, horse sweat and dung from both mingling in his nostrils. This was proving to be a really interesting day!

He had surveyed the house, yard and what could be seen of the buildings for some minutes when the horse and rider trotted past him to the loose boxes along one side of the yard.

"Have you made yourself known yet?" Robert Hesketh asked of Fraser. "No? So, Royal Signals, eh? By choice or wondrous business of putting lads like yourself in the most stunningly un-useful capacities? The latter. Ah well, no surprise there. Look, we have a bite to eat about now, you'll join us, Fraser? Good."

He led the way into the foursquare farmhouse, motioning Fraser to follow on.

"Follow me. In there you'll find the hose, brushes. Hot water and things, towels and all that stuff."

The nature and appointments of the farmhouse were of a generous scale unknown to Fraser. He followed Mr Hesketh into a wide passage, passing through a spacious hall with rush matting upon red tiles. Everything was quiet, clean, orderly to Fraser's wide open senses. He was intrigued about this being the day-to-day or working end of the establishment of this farm. There were innumerable doors opening into rooms all specific to their purposes: coats, boots and shoes, tack-cleaning materials on a broad bench below saddles and bridles. A number of guns in an upright glass-fronted gun cabinet, the smell of gun oil immediately familiar to Fraser's nose. He spotted that which would be his host's so-called everyday or working gun amongst the other best quality English shotguns.

Robert Hesketh strode rapidly through this part of his home, opening one, then another, broad unpainted door – elm or ash, Fraser reckoned them to be.

"Here you are. Hands and hot water brought together here, other affairs in there. Come on through to the kitchen." He pointed. "I'll tell Kitty that we're all needing something to eat. Hmm. Fraser, Fraser Baird, right."

The entire set of things felt so easy, sitting in at the long white scrubbed kitchen table, easy to be conversing with Mrs Hesketh, natural for them to be interested in his own background without any fuss. Robert Hesketh had pulled off leggings and boots and was leaning back in a high-spoked chair beside the Aga, breeched legs splayed to the gentle warmth. Looking about him in turning from one to the other of the Heskeths in the flow of conversation, Fraser saw everything to be neat, clean, and purposeful from many years of use. Fraser thought back to some of the farms, farmhouses and families and farmers' apparel along the valleys and haughs of his home ground, for a moment feeling disloyal about values of which these easily welcoming folk might not be aware, let alone fully comprehend.

Mrs Hesketh passed him a plate with a slice of pork pie, tomatoes, cheese and pickled onions, and smiled at him as she indicated the bread board with rounds of crusty bread already cut. There were slices of cold ham on a platter to one side.

"Robert tells me that you're from Scotland and this is your National Service? Tell me about where your home and family are. Here, Robert, pass the butter to Fraser and stop talking about your old sheep, for goodness' sake!" She expanded, unnecessarily, Fraser at once recognised, saying, "Robert's mind is more with his fat old ladies, as he calls them, than any other living thing on the place!" She gave her husband's hair a vigorous tousle up. Robert Hesketh smiled faintly, but made no reply.

The careful husbandry of the Hesketh fields outside was entirely matched inside by that of their calmly functioning and well-ordered home. Fraser could feel the years, decades of prosperity by prudence in everything around him, silently making the statement that it was entirely proper to be well funded by the good things of life, if that in its turn assured the land timeously and tidily of its needs.

Conversation flowed easily amongst them all. His descriptions of the types of countryside and mountainous parts of his own home area, the various stock enterprises that were most usual, his father's work in the farming community and his own wish, eventually, to farm for himself once gathered of adequate funds – all of this ran on until interrupted by the tap of heels from another part of the house, bringing another of the Hesketh household into the relaxed group in the warm and cheerful kitchen.

"Marjorie, this is Fraser Baird, from up near your father's cousin's place. He very kindly and capably helped your father with his ewe-count this morning. That was a real boon; saved our Robert a bit of roaring from horseback, I'm sure! Fraser, this is our eldest daughter, Marjorie."

Fraser stood up, surprised that the mother's comeliness and grace was almost exactly mirrored in her daughter. Hair near to black, eyes and mouth the same – warm and attractive. Both of them tall, slim, the very kind of woman, of person he so fiercely wondered if he would ever, could ever win.

Marjorie's father broke into Fraser's few seconds' inner attempts to see into the future, his future.

"Aye, Marjorie, he even talks the same language as I do, what your mother terms "sheep-ish!""

The Heskeths all laughed at what was patently a well-worn family joke. Fraser, smiling too, felt entirely at ease with these people. At a deeper level, he also felt equally lacking, or nearly so, in some interesting abilities other than just mouldy old farming. Perhaps this was a good time to go.

"Mrs Hesketh, it has been very kind of you to invite me in. Your hospitality will see me through another few weeks of army life now. Mr Hesketh and Marjorie, thank you for having me join you."

He shook hands with the mother and daughter, a light but warm contact.

To have a super farm such as this, which expressed everything he ached for, and this, this tremendously attractive woman for his wife. Robert Hesketh, Yorkshire yeoman farmer, was fortunate beyond any words which Fraser felt, but could not say.

Making no ceremony of Fraser's going, Hesketh put out his hand from his stance beside the Aga cooker.

"Much indebted for your help with the ewes, Fraser. If you would like to join us for a walk round with the gun nearer to Christmas, just ourselves and neighbours. You would? Fine, let me know, for I shan't be that far away between now and lambing those early ladies. You know your way out. My ladies will see you off. If you're going by way of Strenshall, you'll see a lot to interest you there: the Hunt stables and old coach houses, modelled on some grand old place in Buckinghamshire, I'm told."

He looked across to the longcase clock, whose somnolent ticking had nicely paced their talking and laughter in the kitchen.

"If you go directly there now, you'll doubtless see all us devout Church of England folk swelling the congregation, aye, and the bar in The Hart! Take a head-count between pews and pints, Fraser, it might prove very revealing, ha!"

Laughing, Kitty and Marjorie Hesketh came out with him into the paved yard to say goodbye. How many times had these winter-stilled elms and chestnut trees looked down on meetings, greetings, crises and christenings, weddings and woes, Fraser wondered, looking around him.

"We did enjoy your talking with us, and feel welcome to drop in before your training finishes."

Kitty Hesketh smiled at him with genuine pleasure in her eyes and voice, and put her arm around her daughter's waist. Marjorie leant into her mother's shoulder and side with no artifice in so doing. Fraser turned round for one last look, some way up between the trees. They both waved gaily to him and turned for the house, arm in arm.

Getting into his stride, his own, long one again, Fraser's mind raced backwards and forwards, like a collie let out of its kennel. What was it about the farms and folk in his part of Scotland which rendered them so lacking in the ease and assurance so evident in everything and everybody down here? Even the damned sheep seemed much bigger, bumptious and self-assured, by God!

A carrion crow spying the land from high in an elm at the end of the drive tensed and cocked its eye as the khaki-clad figure below it shouted out loud, and sprang nervously off its roost when the dark, almost black beret was flung, spinning, in the direction of tree and crow, with another wild shout. As soon as he was finished with all this army nonsense, he would most certainly set about all the very important things he intended to be the rock-firm basis to those quantities he loved and needed so very deeply in his life. Aye, man – he damned well would!

Colin was waiting for him at the picquet guard gate. His accent was strong and cheerful.

"Hey, mon, wur postings are h'oop!"

Fraser grinned at his open excitement.

"Reet, mon, let's be gaun on wi'eet!"

They punched each other about the shoulders and strode, fast, to the Adjutant's Office and Orderly Room and its postings.

The overseas postings for everyone who had completed their courses were put up on the board outside the Adjutant's Office, Squadron HQ. There would be a postings parade at 1400 hours. Looking at the various units to which they would very soon be dispersed, there was a palpable feeling of both anti-climax and yet high tension amongst the usual comradely group of Colin Bowles, Moash, Polly Walcott, Spam Selby, Fraser (more often than not, now, he found he was usually addressed as "Jock"), and Vic Yeates and the others.

Staff Sergeant Hannah, Radio and Telemech course, was being questioned by Spam, their inveterate buffoon, as to the issue of insignia for their battledress blouses.

"What I said, Staff, was – will we have our flaming arseholes up for parade?"

There was a great stamping of boots and cheers at this anxious query about putting up their qualified Radio or Telemech shoulder flashes, and the traditional nickname for the dramatic blue bolts flashing from a central red ring. Sergeant Whyte glared at Selby and then failed to smother his barking laugh.

They all cheered wildly again. Staff Sergeant Hannah continued calmly:

"Right, my merry men, you've finished your courses and you're off to whatever units need you most – Gawd help them! But, Sergeant Whyte will advise you about the great regimental passing out parade. Sarn't?"

"Right, this is your moment of soldiery truth, the full strength of No.3 Signals Regiment on parade, and on this orspisshuss occasion, you will have your flashes up; round, square, flaming or otherwise."

The Troop Sergeant, their Troop Sergeant, stepped forward, knowing them all. He moved amongst the benches where they were standing or perched in their work overalls, his head hunched, hands behind his back, measuring every one of them against some inner benchmark of soldier-like attributes. Fraser, having a presentiment that something unlikely was about to follow, winked very slowly at Colin Bowles, and held his breath, avoiding eye contact with Sergeant Whyte.

The explosive transformation into a boot-crashing, command-bellowing, compulsive figure was electrifying:

"Troop! Troop! Shaaaahh! St'ndateez! Shaaahh! Do not think to move a millimetre, you paltry signalmen and lesser orders!"

They were locked into (well, almost, Fraser intoned, letting his breath out by silent degrees), the hammered-in imprint of conditioned response, just like a load of pigs at feeding time. Fraser did not allow himself to look even the slightest degree towards any of his mates.

"That was not at all bad for a bunch of amateur sparkies, but on my parade you're going to be bloody well immaculate, spotless parade ground soldiers for twenty-four hours up to, and during the march past and until you leave the depot, understood? Troops A and B will parade outside their huts at eleven hundred hours, with their markers, for my personal and searching h'inspection. Right. Troop! Troop Haaagh! Troop – Fall Out!"

Nine of them were going to Germany, British Army of The Rhine Districts 12, 14 and 9. Five were posted to Malaya, one to Iceland, two to SHAEF Headquarters, Fountainbleu. Fraser had used what few contacts he had to try and pull a Korea posting, attached to any Scottish or Highland regiment, but with no success.

On the morning of the passing out parade in more than warm sunlight, the entire parade ground and squadrons and troops thereon, waited for over three quarters of an hour for the reviewing officer from Salisbury District HQ to be escorted to the saluting dais. Two soldiers had already fainted, their heads and rifles bumping audibly as they clattered sideways to the asphalt. Fraser noted this minor commotion. His own mind was comfortably passing the slow minutes with inner pictures of what he would otherwise have been busy with at Tornaquhil; ewe clipping, or gathering meadow hay, or renewing contact with the Melvins and Margaret, or arranging contact with the Melvins, and Margaret, before going on embarkation leave. Maybe even finding and looking at some small place as a yardstick against his own start in the future, once this army business was put behind him at last.

When, with rifles suddenly flicked up and across to the slope, the order came, high and clear over the entire square, he was still standing, immobile, asleep, with his eyes open.

"General salute! Preezaynt Haahms!"

The command was heard, but meant nothing for about two seconds. With appalling clumsiness, he dragged his rifle, his precious, spot-on, shit-hot zeroed rifle, through a blur to presenting arms, a substantial part of a second behind every other rifle on the parade. His brilliantly polished boots were not in the correct position for the quivering crashing impact of boots and blancoed rifle slings. Slowly, from behind him somewhere, came a tongue clicking forcefully against teeth, three times. From the same location, deep in Sergeant Whyte's diaphragm, a preternaturally chilling rumble snaked out at about head height, to totally invest, a harbinger of the storm, Fraser's mortified mind and burning ears. Damn and blast and double-blast the bloody bloody army.

LI

The long grey train carried them all that day, deep into Germany, bogies and wheels clacking quietly, halting only to take on German border police at Aachen. They were all either reading, or silently looking, or dozing in the train compartment. They had made the best of mediocre army sandwiches, flattened in tasteless white bread.

"Quite some train. Can hardly hear it." Fraser looked across at Moash, whose father had something to do with locomotive engineering at Derby, so he had said.

"Yeah, look at these materials, better than hotel quality!"

Vic Yeates, going on to SHAEF HQ Intelligence, patted the upholstery in knowing fashion. Fine all round was Vic, but not afraid to refer to his old-womanish ambivalence and make fun of it. They all liked Vic and were used to him and could be implacably protective if the need arose.

Moash was expanding further on railways and rolling stock:

"You wouldn't chuckle, Jock. These industrious Krauts have got things going again bloody quickly. All right, some of it, the freight stuff particularly, is a dead copy off Yankee heavy wagons, but they're making use of the same plant and fabrication lines as they did before the war, knockin' out tanks and heavy armour below our politicians' very noses then. You've got to hand it to them, lads—"

"Holy flaming arseholes! Just look at the bastards!"

Stan Culver was off his seat in a flash, almost incoherent, stabbing through the darkened glass with a shaking forefinger at the scene through which the train was threading its way... clack-clack, clack-clack. They were all up to the windows of the train in every compartment, looking at tanks, heaps of tanks. Moash was stringing together disjointed words:

"Christ! Old Panzer jobs, Mark IIIs and IVs and, er, Tigers, and there's a couple of tank destroyers. Jeezuss! Just look at that bastard, turret opened up like, like a rotten orange!"

German tanks they undoubtedly were, Tigers or otherwise, they couldn't sort out as the rusting hulks slid past them. Their long muzzle-braked barrels, no longer dipping or traversing, to sniff out targets for their red hot steel

481

shells, high velocity death in a frozen second for anyone seeing that round black opening swinging on to them, lay in maximum depression on their hulls, slewed and disembowelled at all angles. Burst tracks, feet wide, ripped back off sprockets in coils. Armoured glacis blasted off hulls in jagged scabs. There were about ten of them, others farther back, all severely damaged, run together into a heap or pushed there. They exuded an air of killing, lethality.

In compartments the entire length of the train, the various army drafts were restless, disturbed, by being confronted with the reason for their being what and where they were. Combat and killing and crackling flame from armour piercing shells, fired by their own Allied tanks or artillery, had invested these snarling behemoths in an atmosphere of dread – Fraser could feel it.

"That's the bastards what me brother got killed with."

All faces turned, aghast, to Colin Bowles. He looked as none of them had ever seen him at any time before in their shared army training. Tensed, rigid, head and neck pulled in, manifestly withered with disturbance by something from which he couldn't turn away.

Polly Walcott flicked an eyebrow at Moash; he shook his head forcefully. The same silent question to himself, Jock? He let it hang a moment. OK.

Fraser avoided looking directly at his friend Colin as he spoke quietly, almost casually.

"Were they in Germany, your brother's lot, Colin?"

"Aye, they were that; Yeomanry, tanks an' all. Got shot up in France, two weeks on from D-Day, rotten panzerfaust, nested in that blasted bocage, couldn't spot the buggers. Whole bloody tank got brewed."

Colin's face was grey, angular in distress.

"One of his mates in t'troop came over and spoke with me mam and dad, on wounded leave, 'e was. Seen it happen. All bar t'bloody details."

They sat very still, minds occupied with scenes of what happened to a tank and its crew when it got brewed up. Sergeant Whyte had told them, explicitly.

Snaking its way into the railway marshalling yards of Dusseldorf, the long troop train presented everyone in it with yet a further spectacle of the detritus of unconditional waging of war.

Tangled heaps of huge, impotent steam locomotives, underbellies of crankshafts and crumpled cylinders, pistons, driving rods hanging from huge fractured driving wheels – all stacked up three or four high. Beside them, on a length of intact track, stood a railway crane of unbelievable proportions, steam down, the monstrous multi-sheaved jib lowered onto a small freight wagon, all dimly visible in the gathering evening's greyness. It resembled nothing more than a huge predator, pecking and tearing at helpless prey. Massive coal tenders were rendered puny by being thrown upside down, cavernous coal bunkers rusting. One massive machine, five driving wheels to each flank, lay punched into the tracks, broken-backed by the impact of some bomb or shell which had ruptured it in one final shattering impact.

They clacked onwards, skirting the death heaps by sudden swings of the carriages on to circuitous tracks, continuing northwards. Closely gabled village farmhouses sealed off from zones of destruction, turned inwards, clinging to their remaining core of quietness and land, however impoverished.

It seemed to Fraser that their moment of actual arrival in Occupied Germany was undoubtedly when they climbed down stiffly from the train in the Munster bahnof, and strangely not when they passed into Germany from Holland with hardly a pause. Now, heavy Germanic script snared their eyes with its convolutions and crossed lettering. There was an impatient efficiency in the movements of the station workers, handling everything that was moveable out of the goods wagon.

"Hey! Fraser! Look out man, they've mobilised our great old LNER trolley! Christ, they're going to push it all the way into ruddy Munster at this rate!"

Moash and Polly were beside themselves in glee. When they had finished loading all their kit at Liverpool Street Station, the whole lot of them had grabbed the railway trolley and flung it bodily into the goods van on top of their kitbags. They could hardly summon up the collective strength to do this, doubled up with laughter and swearing in idiot nonsense. Now, here the bally thing was in banged-up Germany. What would the super-efficient Deutschers make of that!

Their first glimpses of Munster, Westphalia, were that it was snagged by gaps of total collapse from bombs or shell fire, with a sudden shop window in startling bright display, and a few workmen in round-peaked black caps and one-time Wehrmacht field boots. Their small convoy of four vehicles swung left-handed across the steeply cambered, greasy-looking cobbles, jerking to a halt at the red and white pole at the guardroom. Lights of brilliant intensity, very high up, illuminated every detail of men and movement.

"Ee, Jock, man, it feels reet bloody Teutonic already!" Colin muttered as they crowded into the warm guardroom. He was looking a bit better.

"Right, then, lads, respond to your name and number, and we'll have you across to the mess hall as soon as you've got your kit into your billets."

The picquet guard corporal seemed friendly and helpful, to the wary regard of their small group. There was a totally different feel about this place.

I Like to Walk in This Field

"Zero eight seven Train? Block B, room one-o-eight. Nine zero two Bowles? Block B again, room…"

The four soldiers were silent as they skirted one end of the central parade square. The central enclave of the one-time Wehrmacht motorised infantry barracks stamped itself as an immutable presence of German military purpose and architecture. The grey walls and embrasures soared upwards, high and silent above floodlights, to heavily detailed eaves. Shadowed lintels and sills pursued each other in infinite precision across the elevations of all the blocks facing on to the square. Fraser felt visual and atmospheric imprints being stamped into his awareness in rapid sequence. Germany and Germans had built this place expressly for their men highly trained in waging war, preparing for it even some years before the intent of another conflict became undeniable to the outer world. Now, Fraser turned over in his mind, the hated British professionals at arms were visited upon traditionally militaristic Deutschland, to protect them from the savage Mongols in the East, ha! A not altogether apposite remnant of a World War I soldier's song slipped into his mind: "The bells of Hell go ting-a-ling-a-ling, for you but not for me. Oh, death where is thy sting-a-ling-a-ling…"

Their first meal in Germany was in total antithesis to all of their experiences of hateful army catering to date: clean, quiet, efficient service of a brisk but not brusque nature fron German civilian staff, and a far better presentation of food at this late hour, nine in the evening, than they had ever eaten at any time in deplorably dirty, vile Catterick, by God. Two fried eggs? You betcha!

Having eaten, they took a few minutes to sit, weary but relaxed. They each felt a new self-regard in these surroundings. They felt as though they were already assigned to duties in which they would be held as being competent and responsible. They noticed Moash was not in the slightest concerned about imminent responsibilities; his gaze was focussed upon the generous display of firm, symmetrically shaped breasts by the pleasant young German serving woman. Polly Walcott coughed dryly, and regarding this distraction analytically, made his trained (B.Sc. Hons., Durham) scientist's evaluation:

"Gentlemen, be wary of what you see. They may, like those other market goods on which we have been advised, suffer from inflation."

Their burst of not unkind laughter called for some civility in reparation. She was speaking to them, clearly, pleasantly:

"Right, boys, if you finish now, so we do, bitte."

Polly gave Fraser a nudge.

"Come on, bold Jock, let's say 'Thank you' to the kind lady."

484

Surprised but smiling, she gave them all a warm "Ja, bitte, I em heppy to do."

As they rose, politely pushing their chairs into the long table, Colin voiced something that was in all their minds.

"Well, my goodness, that were a reet good feed. We'll not goo wrong here, lads, Ah dessay!"

Following his evident distress at seeing the war material responsible for his brother's horrible death, his companions laughed outright at his regaining practical north country good nature.

The vast blocks making an enclave of the square were dark, silent, as they sought their beds and sleep, all but the largest building where lights blazed out from all windows on the two floors running the entire length of it, halfway up. It loomed over them like some great ship berthed there until a silent tide of water or war would flow back in, then to slip its moorings. Double-banked wireless ops on constant transmission watch, they had been told.

As Colin, Fraser, Moash, Vic, Spam and Polly settled and slept during their first night in Occupied Germany, the receiving sets and fine tuners and headsets lined up in the dry heat of the long radio listening post hummed and crackled in short bursts, searching and sifting even through that pause and slowing of all things natural in the deep rhythms of the night. The dawn light was already coming in, slicing across China, Mongolia, Soviet Russia, Poland and Prussia, and then Germany, the sun's rays a visible vehicle for groups, letters, codes, individual keying styles that had no names or faces, only fingers, speeding out encrypted tattoos.

The glowing valves, circuits, transistors and fine tuners, oscillators and frequency modulators, and the men controlling their electrical energies waited, listening with silent hunger for any sound or signal, however brief or truncated, from the east, in which direction every part of the massively banked receiving equipment along those two long floors was precisely aligned. Waiting, listening...

485

LII

The rapidity with which their small comradely group was targeted and briefed by hitherto unknown officers was surprising, even impressive. By their second day of getting genned up, there was no mistaking that there was, in this particular unit, a definite and watchful purpose; they could all feel it.

"You know, Jock, mein freund. " Polly was sitting cross-legged on Fraser's bed. "This whole business of intelligence gathering is really being narrowed right down to the capabilities and experience of blokes like our friends Captain Eff-Eff and Plum Duff; they make the first sweep, or rather we do, right across every likely frequency."

"Aye, you're right, although you would think that there must be other similar units operating as we do, Baltic to the wily Bulgars," Fraser speculated. "But Christ, I had the most helluva job not bursting out at Plum Duff's notion of 'How To Get On Mit Der Vicked Gairmanns'!"

"Yeah, well, OK," Moash added, "But just at look at the old beggar's campaign ribbons. He's got a system that works when we're out on detachment, or he wouldn't be the effective officer in the field that he is!"

In rapid sequence on day one, they had been through a rapid duties and work assessment by two Captains, Downe and Duff, previously advised to them by Staff Sergeant Allison as known as "Eff-Eff" and "Plum". Captain Edwin Downe had burst upon them in a froth of hands, flying swagger stick and a file of papers only just under doubtful control. He launched into a straightforward rundown immediately:

"Your Staff Sergeant will keep you right on our range of equipment. Our unit here has but one purpose, that of intercepting and plotting all Russian military transmissions from Danzig to the Black Sea; army, naval and air force. We're on watch here round the clock, catching the smallest or briefest burst or group from Ivan. We need to know where he is, what he's doing and even almost what he's thinking of. You're here to operate, maintain and even improve that equipment, to its upmost efficiency."

Captain Downe looked them over, distilling his own intelligence from each soldier's silent response.

"In this wireless regiment, we employ a small number of German civilians. We know that they know what our job is. What they do not know is just how successful we are. None of us, and you, here in Occupied Germany know that in its entirety; everything, every scrap that we gather goes directly to another centre."

Downe banged his stick forcefully on the table top, in slow time.

"Whatever-pieces-you-think-you-know-you-do-not-discuss-with-any-German-male-or-female."

Downe's eyes flickered across their faces, not wasting time with fools or poodlefakers. How was this officer's full temperament going to manifest itself, Fraser wondered? He was speaking to them again.

"This regiment functions as a self-contained unit, along with Intelligence. We do all our own repairs, transport and guard duties and you can be detailed in any of these capacities, especially when on detachment. When that happens, just get on with it. Do not fiddle and fart around."

Faint smiles passed along their faces, now friendly towards Captain Eff-Eff Downe.

"Organise your work, organise your mates, make it a team job, in the regiment, right?"

Downe paused. They did not now notice his buck teeth, his receding chin, the tendency to round shoulders. They noted instead his straight-out sincerity, determination and many campaign ribbons. He continued speaking.

"Two last points. There are very few things which we, your commissioned officers and your senior NCOs, have not experienced. If you have trouble of any nature, see it, or, more usefully, smell it coming, stop, think carefully – is this going to involve and put at risk the men beside you? Ask us.

"Point Two: We cannot stop you from fraternising, but you do so at your own risk entirely, and also of the integrity of our operations here. Leave everything concerning your duties at the guardroom when you walk out. Of course the Germans damn' well know what sort of an engineer or technician you are, and how you do it."

Captain Downe regarded Donnachy with patent extreme distaste as the latter made no attempt to conceal his ever-ready expectations of fraternising.

"But a good technician should always be a good soldier first."

He swung back to focus his whole presence upon Signalman Donnachy.

"And you, young man, stand to attention when I am addressing you! Something in your attitude tells me that you are unlikely to prove either a worthwhile technician or a reliable soldier. I shall make a decision about your immediate future here within the next few days. Staff!"

Captain Downe positively fought his way through the door, after a brief mix-up with the personnel file and his swagger stick, which flew up and whacked against his officer's cap as the errant door swung back.

Staff Sergeant Allison looked at them in relaxed fashion, winding up the morning's spiel.

"One point which Captain Downe did not deal with: our friends along die Strasse at the DP Camp. Listen to me. Do not tangle, tango or anything more personal with anyone out of that place, be it man or woman, they are vicious. All of these displaced persons have had to do things just to stay alive which would make you shudder, and they are still capable of such things. Don't do any black market deals with them, don't do deals of any kind, or you'll land up in the glasshouse, courtesy of the Special Investigation Branch, or the VD ward at Belefeld. OK? Right, dissmiss!"

Going on detachment came upon them far sooner than anticipated. They were summoned to their Officer I/C Workshops with Captain Plum Duff at half an hour's notice. Their close-knit group was curious about this. You usually got three days' advance orders.

"D'you reckon they've lost a detach unit somewhere in Ivan-land?" Colin asked of Moash as they walked briskly in a bunch along to Captain Duff's hideout in the heavy vehicle bay.

Polly Walcott answered for him, for them all:

"No, what's more likely is that we're picking up a lot more stuff coming in from Russki units which haven't moved camp for some time, and they're on the move again. The volume of their signals has suddenly picked up like a running tap these past two days."

Fraser and Moash and the others knew that Polly had been on watch as Duty Radio Mech., Receiving Flat A in the radio flats for the past forty-eight hours; he would know. They crowded into Plum Duff's congested office, their faded blue overalls smelling of oil, tools, electrical plant and a sort of sweetish Germany-in-summer quantity, hard to define. Captain Tom Duff waggled thickly forested eyebrows (independently of each other, they noted), twitched his nicotine-stained moustache, moved his pipe stem from one side of his mouth to the other and spoke to them, all in one integrated, joined-up operation. Their officer did not appear to be concerned with what his hands, fingers, tobacco pouch and matches were doing. That was an entirely separate matter.

"All right, men, find yourselves a perch. Now, listen closely. We've had to bring you fellows on to the detachment roster ahead of schedule, but we've been assessing your approach to the work and you're a good bunch, fully up to it. So, field job coming up, we need to check where Ivan is moving his most northerly motorised stuff to. There is definitely something going on. They could be thinking of making a push, hoping that we make a substantial response with tanks and artillery, which they would immediately claim to be 'provocation'. Same stunt that Hitler pulled."

Duff coughed explosively, eyes red, nose running.

"If you lot can keep things in shape out in the sticks as you're doin' here, shouldn't be any trouble get... get... aheerrgh!"

With his cataclysmic sneeze, pipe, pouch and open tin skidded across Plum Duff's black-ringed desk and a fine dust rose up in the afternoon's sunlight. A few motes lodged in his bushy eyebrows. With surprising speed, he ran through all of their duties on detachment. Having dealt with Polly Walcott, Bowles and Moash, he swung to Fraser.

"Are you a farmer or something in civvy street? Driving tractors, most things, right? You're back-up to Driver Shields, and recce-ing best locations for the grid-wagon and scanners fixed and mobile. Talk farming with the Deutschers, and (a), keep them happy and (b), maintain a very low profile in the country generally, in all respects." A wolfish grin lit up the older, worn officer's eyes and face. "Also, never let the enemy know where you are and what you're thinking. Dead right, useful maxim. Beware of friendly Deutschers who come mooching around your wagons with their hands in their pockets, but their eyes and ears fully operational. They're working for the other side. Be absolutely hostile to them. Right-ho, men. Er, fall out."

They all liked Captain Duff's straightforward and friendly approach. They felt that they could bank on having his support if their detach attracted the wrong sort of attention, never mind from whom. They gathered in a loose bunch outside the maintainance bays. Polly spoke with quiet but perceptive authority.

"Plum is OK, men. We're lucky to be in his troop. He's a likeable old bear."

Fraser added, "Aye, but he's a battle-hardened bear. Just look at his campaign ribbons. Seemingly he kept things together with the gunners when they were having a helluva battle coming up through Italy. So, if any of us do a sloppy job, it'll be O-U-T, make no mistake."

That summer in Germany was one of great heat. Within their small group, they had situations come upon them for which, as Colin Bowles observed with feeling and some exasperation, "Hey, Jock, theer warn't no bally training at evil Catterick for this sort of arse up!"

There had been the episode of Driver Shields and the bogged down 3-tonner

Bedford. Shields had demonstrated his abundantly vicious bad temper to the entire detach by urging the nose of the truck on to and down over the lip of a deep, scummy ditch. Driver Shields ("Ha! That's a bloody joke," Fraser muttered to himself, Colin hearing also and cracking one of his rare mendacious, trouble-for-someone-grins) had got the truck belly-down on the edge of the ditch, and was staring ahead, fag in his lips, revving the rear wheels to absolutely no useful purpose whatsoever.

Fraser straightened up from assembling an aerial frame, and bearing in mind Plum Duff's warning about keeping a low presence in the German countryside, thought, aye, man, unless that mad bugger is stopped dead, we're going to have to call up a Scammell recovery job from tanks, and from God knows where.

Shields continued gunning the throttle, black muck spraying out. His response to seeing Fraser steadily looking at the scene was audible over the whole site.

"Piss off, you bloody 'Ighland sheep shagger. Don't think you're the clever fucker what's going to get this useless cunt of a thing out of this bastard Kraut shit-'ole!"

He gunned all four wheels into the black muck. The entire setting-up of the unit came to a stop.

"What d'you reckon, then, Fraser? Got a plan?" Farmer's son Bowles had a certain look in his eye. "Put a live round up Shields' arse, for starters? 'Cos that's wheer Ah believe his brain is!"

"Aye, Colin, my friend, I damned well do have a plan, and Step One is to get that maniac out of there," Fraser said to Colin, and Moash, and Polly, in fact almost all of the personnel, and walked rapidly, with purpose to where their detach officer, Lieut. Willie Anderson, was beginning to realise that a lot of things were teetering out of his control, and not just the blasted truck.

Fraser strode firmly through all the unloading of equipment to engage Lieut. Anderson, Edinburgh law graduate, directly in urgent talking. A salute was quite unnecessary, Fraser reflected, but he got one off anyway. He knew exactly what he had to say; it was waiting in his mind.

"Sir!"

"Yes, Baird, er, Jock?"

"Sir, if we don't get that maniac Shields out of that wagon, fast, he's going to put it nose down into that muck-hole that's going to need a Scammell to get it out!"

Fraser knew that he was initiating action in a manner that by rights should be being taken by their officer and that his face and manner probably showed this all too clearly, but things had to get moving. If he had been a farmer back home, things would have been dealt with immediately if anyone like Shields showed his lack of know-how and experience. He would have been sacked, by God.

Lieut. Anderson was getting the urgency of it all. "Right, have you a plan, do you know how to get the blasted thing out of there?"

"Aye, I do, but right now, get that idiot out of the wagon, sir, at once!"

Anderson acted with speed, bellowing:

"Driver Shields! Driver Shields! Get out of that wagon now! Switch it off! Sergeant Penman."

"Sah?"

Fraser had spoken rapidly to their officer, along with the first suggestion to get Shields out of the way.

"Sarn't Penman! Get three men and empty everything out of the truck, well back from it, right?"

"Sah!"

Thinking back to one such episode in a steep harvest field on that big arable farm away back in Buchan, with a big Oliver 90 nose down in a fenced-in ditch, more of a burn, really, Fraser recalled how all of the farm men, himself included, with little fuss, had worked the tractor up and out. Using long timber battens, the farm men had simply but cannily driven it across, once unhooked from the trailer, up and out. With a deal more preparation, it should work here.

"Sir, we'll need four lengths of timber about the same dimensions as railway sleepers, no, eight, and not less than ten feet long, preferably longer. Get Sarn't Penman to try that farm over there, sir." Fraser at once recalled Plum Duff's emphasis on good relations with any German locals. "Give the farmer a five hundred pack of fags, and a gather-up of provisions."

By these astonishingly confident directions, Lieut. Anderson at once knew that Fraser had been at this job before. He also knew, with clarity, that this situation was quite beyond anything in his experience or training as a National Service officer.

"Well, it had better damn well work! What men do you need? Pick them now, and tell 'em your great plan. I'll give you all the back-up that you need. And for Christ's sake, Baird or Jock, take great care."

Lieut. Anderson, law graduate, breathed heavily. Fraser was tempted to reassure him by saying, "Dinna fash yersel, sir!" but thought better of it. No, just get on with the blasted job.

Somewhat over an hour later, with Fraser and Colin knee-deep in the vile ditch, they had the truck up, forward and out. By dint of careful, repetitive and

491

filthy movement and with all the men paying silent attention to orders from their officer, relayed from Fraser, they had the three-tonner up out of the ditch, inching it backwards and forwards on increasingly raised baulks of timber, and on to the sward on the other side.

Standing in the greyish sickly-sweet muck, Fraser and Colin looked at each other and burst out laughing in the anti-climax of their successful, farm-bred skills. Colin looked around at himself, scraping off curds of semi-liquid muck from his battledress trousers and flicking them away with huge disgust.

"Fraser, this danged Jerry shit doan 'alf clag on to a lad like nothing Ah've iver seen, by gum!"

Fraser's chest was heaving with sudden sly humour. "Colin, it just goes to show that military training is a great impediment to handling tough assignments!"

"Jock, by golly, mon! By God, you h'are an uncouth bloody object. My mam wouldn't half fettle you back home, aye, wi't shippon hose!"

By now, Colin and Fraser were uncaring about the muck on their and everyone else's hands extended to pull them up and out of the gray scum. There was a ragged and heartfelt rally of "Good lads!" "Tricky job, that, man!" and "Keep it in the Regiment, lads!; Ivan will think that we've gone underground!". Lastly, from some wag amongst them on the blackened bank, a chorus of "Covered all over in SWEET VIOLETS!".

That late afternoon, they laagered all the trucks, having taken the muck-plastered three-tonner for a brush down with pails of water, silently provided from the farmer whose timbers they returned. Sergeant Penman and Fraser made a point of handing over some of their detachment provisions and extra cigarettes and two tins of Lyons coffee to the farmer and his hausfrau. Fraser felt immediate kinship with the couple but annoyingly incompetent, unable to go beyond the most basic of phrases to express thanks for their materials since his schoolboy German had languished in disuse:

"Vielen Dank fur den gut Waren, ja?"

The farmer, grey in years and stubble and work clothes, grinned slowly and speaking slowly, enunciated, "Es ist OK, Schottischer, Sie ist Bauer, Ich sondern auch, ja? Das ist Gut!"

There was good nature in both their laughter.

"Where are you going with that grid wagon, Jock, er Baird?"

Lieut. Anderson was curious to know just what act of independent mind Fraser was going to demonstrate next. Fraser pointed to a small, natural level shelf set down from the pine and beech plantation behind it.

"If I can get it tucked in up there, sir, it's got a clear line of reception a few points south of east, out of sight, and the wireless ops reckon it's a better-than-good trawling point. Sir."

Following the recovery of the bogged-down truck, there was an unspoken concord between the officer and Fraser.

"Go ahead, Baird. Just watch out that those branches don't snag your precious rig of aerials. It's our secret weapon!"

They both grinned.

Picquet duties allocated, a solid meal inside them and only intermittent or infrequent groups coming through on test reception, Stan Culver, duty wireless op, sat in the glow from his equipment bank, the tailgate of the truck down, with a single headphone clamped to one ear as he skimmed a motor cycle magazine. There were gusts of conversation and laughter from the others around a modest wood fire made to deter mosquitoes and midges. His back-up wireless operator looked up occasionally from the men to question Stan on steady careful scanning. No? All quiet.

Around the cheery group, formality of rank was laid aside for friendly banter, exchange of views on all things, and unexpected topics from quite surprising pre-Army experience.

"You look back through sufficient length of history in Europe, and the Jerries have always been at it, beating some poor buggers into a plucked duck, for reasons they don't even attempt to explain after the deed!"

"Go on, Sarn't," Lieut. Anderson encouraged him.

Sergeant Cooke, Catering Corps, and a veteran of getting victuals to men under some vicious combat conditions since 1942, expounded upon his belief.

"Well, they always seem to look round for something like a special iron ore or crude oil, which no other country wants to sacrifice, and then breaking up control of that country by its built-in royal family, or even elected president, crying acts of aggression or murdering the poor beggars, and then – wham!"

He waggled his fingers to an ever-increasing, high-pitched, whistling crescendo, and they all saw the Stukas, splitting the ground with orange and black flowers of death.

Polly Walcott cleared his throat, mouth full of his peeled orange. Not for the first time, Fraser mused. Hey, that's strange. Polly's an honours science graduate, no commission, yet Big Willie's a law fellow, commissioned from the start. How the hell do they work that out?

Polly was speaking in earnest.

"D'you know this, lads? Hitler's so-called Bureau for Cultural Development was actually planning, designing and bulding all these magnificent barracks, vehicle workshops, tanks and what-have-you as far back as 1928." His normally dry voice cracked with incredulity. "Right under the noses of the idiot Allied Control Commission, barely nine or ten years after the 1918 Armistice–"

Stan Culver's urgent shout from the radio truck broke into his rhetoric:

"Sir! Sir! I've got a heavy line coming through solid on band three, fifteen megacycles. We've got him coming in now!"

Chester Allott, senior Wireless Operator on the detach, was up and into the truck at speed, second set of phones clapped on, fine tuning after a look at Stan Culver's frequency. This was their whole purpose; stopping, listening, always listening, co-ordinates sizzling back to them from other units on detach, examining everything that swam through the ether into their fine mesh net. Chester broke in fiercely.

"This is the same beggar with that motorised infantry lot. I'ld know his keying style in my sleep. But he's sending on a different piece of kit, slippery Russki bastard, yahr! I've gotcher, mate. By God he's coming through in volume!"

They all rose quickly from their places round the fire, going to duties that would tighten up the effectiveness of their skills in pulling Ivan's radio traffic out of the evening sky, lots of Ivans by the frequency of bursts of groups. Far to the east, it would already be night, Russian night.

In the tight detach group laagered in woodland, dampers, fine tuners, and beat frequency oscillators were adjusted, hunting with precision and persistence for the slightest whiff of military forces getting moving in the night hours, poised for the first savage thrust into the heartland of Germany. Outside the radio ops' two equipment trucks, the men were silent, controlled in movement, watching their comrades' fingers flicking across the receiving sets. Something seemed to be moving far to the east.

LIII

They were not in an active theatre of war. Any idea of death amongst them, their brotherhood of good lads, would have been incongruous. When death sprang up, literally in front of them, Sergeants Penman and Cooke, Fraser, Moash and two others, in macabre fashion two days after that afternoon's toil and muck with the three-tonner, it did not burst upon them in the long-expected form of a massively mobilised weight of Russian armour from the east, air strikes, artillery, whole armies of infantry riding on Russian T34 tanks. It was there, amongst them with an easy turn of the steering wheel, when they were literally occupied with minding their own affairs on detachment.

They had set off in a light truck, leaving their full wireless ops roster on watch, to reconnoitre the possibility of local purchases to beef up their field rations. Sergeant Cooke was an essential man in the group. The black and white gabled town lay about three miles from their tracking site, in a valley of burgeoning fruit orchards and very domestic-looking farm crops. Many of the farm houses and steadings lay within the enclave of the town's alleys and lanes, in Fraser's eyes a curious form of circumstance for farm buildings.

As Fraser accelerated carefully out of a long, tightening bend to the left, they almost drove into the very heart of violent, explosive chaos. He had just muttered to Sergeant Penman beside him, "Sarge, these glittery wee cobbles are treacherous bastards—"

The object in front of them was not at once recognisable as a human being, in spite of movement amongst the mash of blood and hair, and pulses of gore from scalp to waist. The twin black tracks of locked tyres going straight off the reverse-cambered bend towards a single birch tree, now so much splintered matchwood, and then on into woodland, ended in a jeep that lay upside down, improbably buckled, its occupants lying crushed into the blackened trails left behind it.

Fraser braked in a welter of appalled shouts.

"Jeezuss Christ!"

"Oh, my God Almighty!"

"For Chrissake, man, keep the truck back, Jock!"

He ran the truck further on, hard into the side of the hedge as all of them flung out or jumped sideways to run back to the bodies. Lying at the foot of an ash tree to Fraser's right was a bundle of blackened khaki, much like a scarecrow stuck in a turnip field back home, collapsed in a spineless bundle. The head was at an acute angle to the body. What in all hell's name could they do for this poor bastard? With instant certainty, Fraser knew this man to be dead, already flaccid in less body volume than in life. Was there any point in dragging the body away from the overturned jeep? Not a bloody bit.

He ran clumsily, crouched, all sensors of his eyes, face and ears keyed to snapping point on the ticking, cracking jeep. His all-out concentration was pulled violently sideways by Sergeant Penman's bellowed, "Jock! Over here, man. C'mon!"

From that moment precisely, a number of things seemed to happen at the same instant, with great speed, yet each one contained within it a capsule of sight and sound distinct from the others in the concerto of chaos.

The bloodied and torn object twisting and gouting over Sergeant Penman's trousers broke out in a series of unstoppable screams, abruptly choked off by great bubbling inhalations. The figure's torment rang in the bones of their skulls. Crushed into a travesty in steel, the jeep seemed to pull in the air around it (Fraser felt air being sucked out of his lungs, making him light-headed and foolish in his actions) and hung, silent for ponderous parts of a second. Then it exploded, like a visitation from hell.

Metalwork blew sideways, vertically, into the ground, scything through foliage above their heads, with the dull clang of vicious armoured engagement, to be overtaken by a great ball of black and red flame, lifting the jeep to reveal a third body, which seemed to rise, unbelievably, within the core of the inferno. Fraser felt the surfaces of his eyeballs going dry and hard.

For only the frame of a second, summer frock, yellow hair and fair skin were intact, then fused into flame and were gone. Masking his face with his beret, Fraser made a lunge for the broken bundle lying in front of him. The khaki-clad object on which his fingers closed had exactly the same feel as a rabbit shot at too-close range with a shotgun; a lot of mush, broken bones and smashed guts inside a bag of skin. He registered the black beret in the grass bearing the badge of the shattered men's regiment: KRR Kings Royal Rifle Corps. Fraser also registered the double pips of a full lientenant on the blood-sodden epaulettes. Bent double, he grabbed a gaitered ankle, then Sergeant Penman was beside him with a rush, almost tearing the body from his grasp like a broken relay baton in a furious contest of no purpose.

"Jock, for Christ's sake, man, let's get this poor bastard out of here afore the bloody thing goes up again. It's not all past exploding yet!"

The other tortured shape some yards away, the first one they had come on in their leap off the road, had given up life, in bloodied, monstrously dismembered silence. Head down, gasping with unstoppable heaves of his stomach muscles, Fraser noticed that where blood was mixed with oil, it hadn't clotted. Dragged to pointlessly safer distance, the dead soldiers were mangled spectators along with the living, while the tyres on the jeep burned with high, resonant squeaks and pings, rather like a receiver not quite set on the signal frequency. The men of the detachment were drained, silent, uttering only brief unanswered questions. Sergeant Penman loped back to their truck, now positioned some distance back on the road, lights full on and one of their number posted with it to flag down any vehicles, to send back a detailed message of their location and involvement there to Lieut. Anderson, using the short wave radio set they always carried in the command vehicle when on the move. His orders were to stand down and stay put until Military Police and Special Branch bods came on to them, from about thirty miles distant at least, along Helwigstrasse. Leave the bodies where they are, do not attempt retrieval of tags or discs. Radio watch to continue at their base camp.

The day was lost for sustained radio watch over transmissions they knew had been within their plot of previous traffic from co-ordinates to the east and south.

There were regimental police, red-brassard-ed RCMPs in officious accusative abundance, eyes hostile behind their ridiculously squashed-down hat peaks, and a German Staatspolizei accident team. Of them all, the last-named were the least disagreeable in their approaches to all personnel in the detach group.

A German girl or unknown woman had been totally consumed in the towering pyre of the jeep and its fuel tank. There was a strange and unexplained intensity in the search to establish her identity. The various police assumed that she had been German, but the Staatspolizei captain, a painstakingly polite ex-Wermacht officer, observed in near-perfect English that this assumption was not necessarily correct; she might have been a displaced person. They would have to do a lot of checking. None of the dead KRR soldiers could speak for her personal circumstances, or for their own, least of all the dead lieutenant.

The combined police personnel were hardly an hour into their interrogations when a BAOR Opel staff car, with the Lubbecke District pennant fluttering, swung into the area of blackened grass holding all the police vehicles, the men, the burning jeep and two dead soldiers lying behind them. There was an immediate presence of highest level authority. The tall Lieutenant Colonel of Intelligence Corps and Royal Signals Brigadier stood where they had climbed out of the staff car, their driver marching quickly to Lieut. Willie Anderson with an urgent expression. They marched back to the waiting officers together. The whole atmosphere of the ensuing investigation changed to one of direct authority taking control, of containment of the fact that the Signals detachment unit were the sole witnesses to the sequence of events whilst in the performance of their totally unrelated field duties. A second staff car swung off the road, to be authoritatively halted by an RCMP.

"This'll be the Rifle Corps brass." Moash breathed to the men beside him. "Now there's going to be a lid clapped on the whole business, men."

Lieut. Anderson summoned all of them, his detach unit, to be addressed by the Signals Brigadier.

"Lieutenant, thank you for your prompt intelligence and action. Sergeant Penman, you and your men will prove invaluable in what we can establish internally, in the regiment, at base. Do not answer any further questions from any of the police authorities present here. You are all under the authority of myself, Brigadier Helling, and Colonel Myles of Intelligence. Thank you, all of you. Lieutenant Anderson, carry on. Stay in your existing, er, field location until we advise you otherwise."

An Army ambulance hovered on the road. German civilian vehicles were motionless, the application of authority intense.

On the strength of the episode involving recovery of the three-tonner, and his speed of action at the scene of the burnt-out jeep, Lieut. Anderson later told Fraser that he was recommending he be made up to Acting Lance Corporal and that Sergeant Penman go on to Staff Sergeant, with effect from return to base. There was an easy relationship between Fraser and his NCO that stemmed from his knowing Penman's home area in Dumfriesshire. Privately, both of them had questioned the veracity of calling the jeep business "an accident". Surely, if the driver had not had the wit to feel the reverse camber spinning his jeep off the bend, and he had not had the skill to take his foot off the accelerator, then that would have been careless or negligent driving, and there was something else not quite right about the proceedings at which he, Fraser, had subsequently been called to make statements. There seemed to be an element of covering-up going on; both he and Staff Sergeant Douglas Penman were sure of it. The latter had shrugged and said, "Aye, Jock, my lad, there's some officer or NCO who should have signed that jeep out from their motor pool and didn't, and in the middle of a field exercise going on with the KRR men and tanks, what's more.

Just the very last mob we needed around us on detachment. And there'll be some well-covered Kraut feeding the smallest particles of intelligence about all of us, back to those fellows with the fur hats. That hellishly unfortunate woman was purely incidental to what those KRR men should have been doing, mark my words. Anyway, poor silly bastards, the lot of 'em. We shall never know."

In Fraser's inner repository of matters requiring deep storage until further need, there were a lot of things which just didn't add up, the way that the army handled them.

Following the burnt-out jeep business, and its macabre conclusion, all the men in Lieut. Anderson's detach unit returned from their gathering of Russian radio activity. They now possessed a certain close-knit bonding, a comradeship. They had handled everything required of them in the most practical way at the time, not all to be found in King's Rules and Regulations. All ranks felt a shared solid capability, not experienced by the rest of them back at HQ.

Fraser's mind was not much concerned with the drill and duties course back with the regiment, now to be taken if he was to be made up to full corporal. He had heard of the rather pointless excesses of "bull and bellowing" too many times. It had turned out to be dead right; a demanding two weeks of the physical, fanatical and farcical. For what worthwhile result? He felt entirely content with his place in the regard of the men he knew and liked: Moash, Colin, Polly, Sergeant Penman and the rest. At least the improvement in pay would help his savings towards the farm, this farm where his proper life would begin again.

So, the great D and D course. A recently transferred wireless op to the regiment, who exuded self-satisfaction in every waking moment, succeeded in performing a feat that lived in the recollection of everyone who witnessed it. On a day of frost and fog, it was required of L/Cpl. Morrington, who was thought to be just a bit too concerned with his own perfection, that he march his test drill squad out on the asphalt parade square for his final assessment. Watching this, as they had done with all those up for full corporal, were the CO, the Adjutant, RSM Bateman and the Provost Sergeant. The purpose of all this square bashing was, Fraser understood, to demonstrate effective control of a section of men "in anticipation of, participation in and tactical withdrawal from combat."

Fraser and the others had laughed outright at the printed protocol, Moash in particular.

"You what? Oh yeah? This is more than faintly ridiculous. Christ, under combat, you would either be well prepared beforehand or spread out in situations where you could move a wireless op and his Number 2 at top bloody speed."

I Like to Walk in This Field

"Aye, to get the hell out of it and all!" said Colin Bowles.

Anyway, everybody involved knew that there was an element of showmanship to this tearing up and down on the drill square. The art bit was to demonstrate control of your allotted squad at a distance where no normal spoken close-range command could be heard, and then bring them back in a set piece of masterly control, to halt in front of the examining officers. "Bring it up from the belly, young man," the RSM enjoined candidates.

The supremely confident Acting Lance Corporal Morrington, inwardly smug at the thought of his spendidly whitened corporal's stripes already sewn on his non-issue best battledress blouse, set them off marching in tight precision, coolly turned his back on his squad, hands behind his back, taking some measured, regulation-length paces as if in deep deliberation.

His urgent high "Ayybowttaahn!" was too weak, squeaky and too far away. They marched on with great élan and speed. The fog of that winter morning opened to accept his signal of distress, took it quietly into the greyness, and the men of the drill squad heard it not. Apparently.

As they marched on, moving imperceptibly but unmistakeably to their right, Corporal-to-be Morrington stood locked in disbelief. The drill squad of twenty-one men marched straight into the far goal net and continued to pile rank upon rank, all marching stoutly in the most intimate of relationships until the pressure from the rearmost rank pushed them all into the net, where they collapsed, to muffled sounds. Two or three soldiers in the rearmost rank continued to mark time splendidly, impassive faces pressed to the jerking goal net and its heaving khaki contents. Those terms and isolated words that escaped from the mass were, for the nearest onlookers, not difficult to understand.

From all windows of the entire wireless operators' floors came yells of manic, insane laughter and repeated bellows of "Goaahll! Gooaaal!" Some figures collapsed over the window sills, speechless.

The few remaining marchers, still to the rear of their comrades fallen in glorious combat with a hockey goal net, affected not to hear the puny squeaks of their section leader. It all took some time to restore soldierly discipline. Moash, Fraser and Spam were posted that week in their full corporal promotion. For Fraser the best bit about the whole idiot business was the apoplexy that possessed those hearing about the D and D squad fiasco. It became wonderfully embellished with every riotous retelling.

The bulky letter, AFPO-franked and colourful stamps, was lying in the pale winter sun on his bed in the billet. His father's handwriting was unmistakeable on the envelope. What he read pulled his mind completely away from the prospect of trees coming into bud in Westphalia, the weight of corporal status or regimental responsibilities thereon.

Being sustained by news of farming matters at home, in his own letters from his folks, Colin was wholly cognisant of the fact that this sort of contact was important in its first reading.

"Aah'll ketch oop with ye down at t'workshops, Jock," he said, smiling in shared pleasure.

"Aye, right enough, then, Colin. I'll tell you the best bits later on," Fraser responded, raising his eyes and grinning. Colin was the best of pals; there was a lot of sense in him.

There was a page of strong, flowing script from his mother, much more from his father, and clippings from The Press & Journal. Fraser unclipped his webbing belt and took off his tunic, turning first to the newspaper clippings. The faces of Jock Wyness amd young Ben were there, in one of the grainy pictures:

"Local Herd Takes Double with Glen Annacht Ram".

Aha! The November Michael Fair Sale! He could almost smell the sheeps' urine on sawdust, the steamy floats unloading, voices and crooks raised in excitement, Brylcreem and best tweeds and tackety boots in the sale ring.

He read on, seeing other scenes in the midst of his mother's narration.

"...and Jean has found a great many friends at Varsity. She enjoys most of the lectures, barring those on political economy. She says that the lectures (and lecturers!) in that department are just not in touch with what is really going on in our own country, never mind in others.

"Mrs Barr is a real gem. She is lucky to have digs with her as landlady, but very staunch that the courtesies of Town and Gown should be well observed by what she calls her 'Right clever young ladies'!"

Fraser looked up, momentarily stricken. He could hear yet Margaret Melvin's voice, telling of her teacher's modest praise: "One of my right clever wee lassies." Where was all that golden afternoon consigned to now? He looked down at the letter.

"Your Grandfather is not so able to go with us to St. Andrews, he's quite content to bide at home with the dog. It is sad that he is unable to see his granddaughter in the same setting as your Aunt Rachel, your father's sister, when she was a student there. Goodness knows, his putting two through University from the farm in those times was an act of sustained faith – and economy! Mrs Scott at the dairy farm was asking how you are getting on; she says that the rabbits have been terrible since you left, and do you like being in the kilt?!"

His father's steady hand took over.

"Fraser, something of a random gathering here, but also an unexpected occurrence of something which I know has been rotating in your mind. In the paper, there's your old friend Jock Wyness looking nonplussed with his First at the ram sales, either that or drunk, maybe both. The rain since harvest started has been incessant; ground splunging, beasts not looking good. You will not know of how things finished up with the Melvin family and the estate; James and Lorna, and Margaret, of course; they finally left Whitepark and are away down in the Borders, having taken a smallish place of their own there. The estate and farm staff and tenants were bitter about his leaving, the mechanics of what happened between the Major, his factor and Melvin will never likely be known, but it has done the estate no good at all. The laird's rather difficult American wife had some part in pushing for the severance. Don't forget how useful James Melvin was to you in getting you started in the sheep world. They were all asking for you before leaving. Lorna Melvin said that she felt the move might be for the better where Margaret's future is concerned. One or two other items before I get on with the reason for this letter.

"So far as dog and gun are concerned, I have used your Westley Richards gun a few times (and cleaned it, religiously) but old Tam is getting a wee bit stiffer now. We make a canny but knowing pair! Tim or Tam, he answers to both in your absence, misses your early morning forays amongst the rabbits. I know exactly how you feel about army food, believe me – it was a damned sight worse in the trenches, and as gunners, we were dashed lucky to get anything hot once a day, or even at night. Before my main topic, we don't know how well briefed you may be about what is happening in Korea. Things are not looking good, Chinese troops in huge numbers beefing up their North Korean compatriots, and so-called Russian 'advisers' supplying and training with arms of all calibres. The Americans are not any good at fighting soldiers who can run along the hilltops faster than all the American heavy stuff down in the valley bottoms, and still blow bugles when they overrun the infantry."

Fraser sat on his bed, his mind and scenes therein far away. Margaret Melvin: where was she now, was this going to be the way of things for her, tagging along in the wake of her father's fiery misdemeanours? He felt a stinging in his throat and eyes of frustration, impotence. Ach, damnation, what way ahead could he see to make a life, a secure future for such a super, desirable young woman as Margaret? He felt absolutely misplaced and not where he should or needed to be. His father's writing continued:

"Here is something for you to mull over, as a yardstick of what you are so keen to achieve once you are finished with Army service. I am not at odds with your wanting to get into a place of your own, for all of your forebears on both sides have been farmers or farriers for umpteen generations. Hereditary factors are both compulsive and long-lasting.

"There is a tenanted place coming up for re-letting in about nine months' time. It lies in a valley in Banffshire, about twenty miles from your work place and good friends in Glen Annacht, but lower down and sheltered. The outgoing tenant is elderly, he has run it on the most frugal of stocking and cropping. Fifty acres ploughable (but not for a long time), two hundred upland and hill. It is a kindly place, with goodness in the land, untapped. The family who own it are good farmers themselves. They will be looking for someone who will improve and nourish the place, for a worthwhile lease of say, eight to ten years. Do not, at this stage Fraser, get a bee in your bonnet about this place. There will be others like it. I am fairly certain that this is the kind and size of place that you are so keen make a start with.

"What you must do is start roughing out a budget based on the fixed annual costs, of which rent will be the major item. Ingoing valuation will only be a once-and-for-all outlay, and for a place of this nature, you're looking at anything from six hundred to close to a thousand pounds per annum maybe less. You would only be able to pay extra labour for lambing, say, and bring in a contractor to make sure you've got enough winter keep made when the weather's right. Handling this on your own, making meals, washing your clothes and so forth is a cheerless and draining exercise, only you know who or what might lighten your existence as a young man going flat out to build a future that will last. Once you are demobilised, you might well be advised to to take an under-manager's or foreman's job for at least a year until the right place pops up. When this happens, you will know it, and then you must go for it with all your determination! Remember Doctor Dallas and that young shoot forging up from the heart of the onion? Well, that's where you must picture yourself, and in the most practical and hard-headed way possible. Get objectives and plans into place in your mind; it is so easy to let time drift once the army way of life lets you go. Keep your powder dry, Fraser, you've a lot to look forward to.

With our help, Your Father.

LIV

As winter closed in from "everybloodywhere east of Helsinki", north-west Germany lay in penetratingly cold fog and frost. The barracks, workshops and offices were all supremely, efficiently heated, as befitted beneficiaries of Hitler's "technical programmes" of the nineteen thirties. For many, the regiment was entirely adequate in its provision for their needs, less so for a minority. Of one, it seemed.

Matt Donnachy ("Ah'm a Fifer, an' guid at it – jist ask the wimmen!") came back off eighteen days' detachment sorely stricken from denial of congress with women, any woman. He looked to be in profound suffering. In the most lugubrious of central Scotland glottal-stottal enunciation, he defended his condition to curious comrades.

"Churrist, man, Ah couldnae even get wan o' them tae open their mooth an' gie me a smile, an' me wi' a' yon tins of coffee! It wis downright unnatcherull! Ah tell youse guys, this goan oan detachment is jist a total bliddy disaahster!"

Donnachy was known to all rankers, NCOs and most of the officers in the unit as possessed of, or more accurately by, an insatiable appetite for flat-out repetitive sexual endeavour. Polly Walcott expressed it thus:

"A Knock 'Em Down, Drag 'Em Out Saga of Early Days in The West (and The North, South and East). Matt 'Clap' Donnachy Rides Again, and Again, and Again!"

The others in whosever billet they were gathered would enthusiastically render hobbling horseshoes, splintering doors and tormented bedsprings, before they all collapsed, helpless.

Five days after his return from detachment, Donnachy was not to be seen in his loosely uniformed slouch, cigarette tab-end only just concealed beneath his beret. It transpired that he had been charged with a great many offences, under both British military regulations and German civil law. He did not return from Belefeld military prison. Some months later, at the REME and RAC armoured refit depot at Hanover, one of the Munster Signals men heard that Donnachy had been admitted to hospital with "twenty different kinds of clap", and following treatment had been discharged. He took with him some bizarre and unrepeatable experiences, summarised by Moash and Spam as not only

504

himself but having brothers, cousins, and uncles who had shagged their way relentlessly round the world, in the uniform of the Queen...

"...and getting paid for it!" Polly finished, with some heat. For himself, he was engaged to a girl from Morpeth, whose regular and prim letters bored him to distraction. He had a feeling that some significant aspect of man's enjoyment of life was passing him by, while a creature like Donnachy wallowed in it, with all the drive of a demented buffalo in a mudhole.

There were, fortuitously, other projects to engage all personnel of the regiment, other than the inevitable self-destruction of Donnachy. As was the case in many other units making up the British Army of The Rhine, there was in the regiment a cadre of musicians of professional ability, and their practice sessions for other less favoured units' functions never failed to afford Fraser inexpressible delight. He had lingered one evening, after working in piercing cold to fabricate a particularly elaborate mounting for a wide-span aerial, to watch and listen to the group of five or six running through their dance tunes in the gymnasium. One of them, playing a clarinet, came over to Fraser.

"Play anything yourself, Jock?" He smiled in this friendly contact.

"No. Sadly. Just started to learn to play the pipes at school."

"Yeah, OK, that's a start. You can read and play off a score. Why not try something else that fits in with other instruments? A bit of brass, pal? It's a bloody good skive and time off duties pretty well round the year. Between all of us, we can teach a regimental mascot to play any damned thing! I tell you what, come over and speak with Lance Hewgall once we've wrapped this lot up. Christmas dance coming up. That's him at the piano."

Fraser grinned, delighted, excited.

"Aye, sure – I will!"

The band's easy rhythms and syncopations lifted him and one or two others completely out of and away from army existence, rank and seniority put aside in shared pleasure. As a twenty-year old tenor saxophonist, Doug Dolland from Motor Transport had liquid music and tears flowing from his fingering, which made even the other experienced band members around him grin at each other, shake their heads in assumed amazement, and come in behind him with a pointed finger, a double nod and some excellent harmonising as a platform for his brilliance. It was a very good band.

Fraser found that they were to play in the gymnasium, suddenly and stunningly transformed into the foyer of some quite smart hotel by the expertise of two ex-nurserymen. They had mounted winter berries and foliage, columns and floral arrangements with precision and telling effect. Looking closer, Fraser found that the Hyslop brothers had cut beech sprays of withered brown, and painted them in wild colours: great!

It had been made quite clear by the organising committee, i.e. the Sergeants Mess, plus one officer, that absolutely everyone who shared in the running of the regiment, British forces and German civilians alike, were properly invited, with out-of-barracks couples being collected and driven back.

Feeling nervously inept, yet drawn by the music and the mood of the evening, Fraser sponged, pressed and ironed again, until satisfied that while lacking proper civvy kit, he was beyond being "regimental", he was positively Brigade-of-Guards immaculate. Colin Bowles watched his preparations, intrigued.

"Up to all this dancing an' suchlike, are you, Fraser?"

Together at quiet moments like this, Colin used his proper first name, comfortable and kindly for both of them. "How on earth d'you go about asking some nice-lookin' lass as you've never clapped eyes on afore, to dance with you when the band gets going? That would defeat me an' all, by golly it would."

In his innermost mind, Fraser agreed totally; he hadn't any skills in dancing or ballroom stuff of any kind. He just had a sudden want to be where the music was, where he wasn't just solitary in his bunk, reading The Shooting Times for the umpteenth time.

"Well, Colin, I reckon it comes in useful to be able in such matters, but putting steps to the beat or whatever, never seemed to have the time. So, I'm going to have a bash."

Again in his innermost mind whilst saying such to Colin, he checked this so-easy response. You arch-lying creature, you've always too taken up with slaughtering God's furry and feathered game and working your stupid backside off. There had been dance classes somewhere, after school, but of no account then in his plans. What had Ramsay and Robina McMillan always gone on about, away back there in remote Glen Annacht: "And what's your chances of a fine girlfriend when you're always work, work, working, and to what end, my lad?"

"Crikey, I don't know sometimes, Colin. What about you asking the band to give you a note to start you off with reciting 'The Lampton Wu'm'? All ten verses, by God! That would have all the frauleins salivating over you, big strong country lad!"

Colin smiled. He only performed this legend of home and heath when he'd had a glass or two of ale, "Wi' gurt big goggly e'en!" etc., etc.

His large brogues, sent from home, would have to do, in lieu of smart Oxfords. They were well polished. They were brown.

It was clearly developing into a very good evening for those with partners: dancing, drinking and dancing, just drinking, or eyeing up every woman on the dance floor with the keenest of predatory eyes, letting tensions and tedium go. Their CO was at the end of a story; expansive gestures, flashing bold looks alternating with knowing nose-tapping, eyelids drooped for effect.

"I was a raw subaltern at the time, but, by God! I sprang to attention like a Black Forest cuckoo clock, screaming 'Sah!'"

The listeners' gale of laughter was infectious. Some amongst them had heard this particular yarn before, but never mind, everyone was in a good mood.

Karl Lindt, a staunch helper to everyone in the workshops, be it vehicles or field equipment generally, with his shattered left ankle, a legacy from the Russian Front ("Ja, Ich haf leemp noch, but still I had das Leben, nicht?") was at one end of the bar, drinks brought to him by Warrant Officer Beaumont ("Bo") Horton. Out of his faded grey overalls, the left leg of which was always frayed from the dragging foot, Karl looked wonderfully clean and enjoying things. His wife was a slender woman (over-thin, I would say, Fraser reckoned) of flaxen hair, in whose features the pleasure of this evening smoothed out hard lines of pain and despair ingrained during nights and long months of a very different nature for the wife of a Wehrmacht soldier in Russia.

Karl's face lit up on seeing Fraser; he limped across, looking for all the world more like a modest brown-suited provincial banker than workshop helper to his country's conquerors. His excited words came out scrambled:

"Ja! Jock! Is' meine Frau. You say 'vife' neh? Ist Madeleine, prima vo-man nach haus, ja? Madeleine, Jock iss von Schotland, gut mann, lieb. I haff die Geschichte tell her, Jock, of many schafen, sheeps, ja?"

Karl, survivor of savage invasion of and battered retreat from Russia, clasped Fraser's upper arm with real affection and grinned at him. Madeleine smiled carefully at Fraser, trying to understand the flow of unstoppable earnest goodwill from her husband. Fraser made some apparently pleasing contribution to all this (they laughed eagerly, over-quickly) but could not recapture one word of what he had said after they moved on. The driving tempo of a quickstep was compelling everyone to take to the dance floor.

Good old Karl, Fraser thought; he's not afraid to try and make something of this dancing business, war injury or not. Not having any pretension to dancing skills whatsoever, as he damn well knew would happen, Fraser had to stand anyway, incapable of picking up the music with a partner. He felt the lift and beat of the music, the innate rhythm of it acutely. He tried to give the impression that, yes, this was truly a super evening, and presently, having exchanged jokes and smiles with the other able exponents of the various dances, he too, would be warmly partnered by someone and take to the floor smoothly, easy in pleasure of a woman's close contact. Someone who quite plainly to Fraser, was not there, and unlikely to be so. Trying to push this cynical certainty away from him, and with what he imagined to be a calm and resourceful look, this was perceived by those standing and chatting close by him as plainly being unsure of his solitary place there, tense and uncertain.

Sergeant Keats spun by with his fair-haired willowy wife Sheila, who, being taller than her husband, could see everything and everyone over his shoulder. They danced so well together (much as they performed in another not unrelated activity, Sheila thought, smiling faintly) that she had no need to think about David's movements, once they stepped off. 'Smoke Gets In Your Eyes' suited everyone.

"Who's that dark-haired chap, David, a corporal – no, there, beside the pillar? Come on, round again, that's him. Doesn't look all that happy. Is he one of your lot?" She hummed, waiting for her husband's sideways search.

"Oh, yes, that's our Jock, newly made-up corporal. Bit of a dark horse. The lads all say that he's scared of bugger all except booze and women. Ones like you, I should imagine, coming as he does, apparently, from darkest Scotland. Primitive men, up there, you know."

"Hmm," Sheila Keats speculated. "Some of these slow starters can be rewarding to teach – aarh!"

The sudden impact of his hand on the thin material of her evening dress was sharp, his dark eyes gleaming.

"How about you keep your mind on the man you've got, or I'll reverse you in behind that shrub and give you a private lesson in primitive men, my dear!"

Fraser felt a great longing in him now, to be looked upon with warmth in the eyes of a certain woman, and on a splendid evening such as this. He sensed a strong likelihood that he was forever constrained to look upon Christmas Dances and parties and the like from beyond a barrier through which he was not equipped to pass.

Suddenly, he could not contain the prickle of tears of frustration, rage even, and looked down to blink them away, cursing, barely able to see his knife-edge creases and brilliantly polished belt brasses. Me, Fraser Baird, feeling like this? Over a few silly folk prancing around and probably getting drunk? Huh. He straightened up, squaring his shoulders to depart the scene, the noisy drink-primed hilarity, and swivelled round to look straight into the grey eyes of the wife of their Workshops Warrant Officer, Beaumont Horton.

She was German, oval-faced, straight haired and beautiful. She was very much a woman. Confused with this unlooked-for, almost personal closeness, Fraser could not suppress a whirlpool of feelings any longer. He nodded, politely and punctiliously, to her and her husband, and strode out of the warm, gay gathering, Doug Dolland's plangent saxophone calling to him. The force and directness of his non-regulation length strides was made even more noticeable to those seeing him depart by the impact of his steel-tipped, non-regulation brown brogues.

LV

In warm sunlight, the long drive up to Bad Oeynhausen, with Warrant Officer Beaumont Horton's wife Uta sitting beside him, was curiously pleasing. It certainly didn't feel at all like anything to do with being in the army.

Some time before the regimental dance, regarding other young men drafted into the unit, Warrant Officer Beaumont Horton had noted something different about Fraser Baird. The difference lay in his gait going to and from the workshops, about twice the length of infantry pace, or thrice that of a Ghurka rifleman. Added to this was the fact that he didn't seem to need other men around him for personal or social completeness. Fraser looked, Horton decided, like a man sufficient in himself. That could be useful.

By the same token of noticing things that were different, Fraser recognised that WO Horton, able linguist in what he, Horton, termed praktikal Deutsch, and well liked by all at base, was quite uncaring about much of army protocol. How did he get off with it?

Whacking his swagger stick against his battledress trouser leg and cutting across to the workshops at his loping pace (just about as un-regulation as mine, Fraser was happy to note), Horton had come across Fraser watching something intently at the foot of a birch tree.

"Achtung, Jock, mein freund! And what, may I ask, are you concerned with? Beetles? Beetles?! What are you going to unleash upon them? Breed them, milk them, build up a flock?"

There was this easy familiarity between them of late, each having found a common enthusiasm through small daily contacts and use of shooting terms known only amongst keen shooting men. Fraser passed on his copies of The Shooting Times, despatched as promised by Tom and Brenda back home.

When off duty, Beaumont Horton, familiarly known as "Bo", spoke to Fraser straightforwardly as "Jock", because he maintained that all Scots in army service were part of a larger-than-regimental cunning scheme to render the Ministry of Defence dependent on Scotland for recruitment, and probably had forenames that were totally unpronounceable, hence "Jock" for all.

Bo Horton sat on Captain Plum Duff's desk, swinging a leg, and prodded Fraser in the midriff of his overalls with his leather-covered stick.

"Look here, Jock, I've got a load of stuff, myself and Uta's, all to go up to Bad Oeynhausen. I need a careful, experienced driver, because I'm taking my leaping beast. You've seen The Thunderer? I'm driving it up myself to do a lot of work on it."

He narrowed his hooded eyes at Fraser.

"If you're as handy with tools and making things as my colleague Herr Kapitan Plum alleges," he continued, giving Fraser another prod, "your local leave and my aggregate local leave is going to consist of driving up our possessions and my wife to Oeynhausen, staying with us a while, and helping me with getting on with making the machine roadworthy. How would that suit you?"

He was speaking about the as yet very basic BMW-engined racing car that he was fabricating himself in an empty bay behind D workshops. Fraser had heard and seen it.

"Come on, then, Jock; eat and sleep with us, travel warrant back here, enlarge your Highland horizons a wee bit, ye ken! I would be grateful if you would set your canny Scots mind to do this small thing. Uta loathes the idea of being immured with some strange spotty youth devoid of speech and emitting a fog of halitosis when he does speak. And so do I, frankly! Right, back to your beetle ranching."

He loped off out of Capt. Duff's littered office, whistling and whacking, and then checked, to call back over his shoulder, "Beginning of May, Jock, right?"

Fraser had hardly spoken. It had a good feel about it. A cautious, contained smile lit up his face. "Enlarge your Highland horizons, a wee bit, ye ken!"? What a bloody insult!

So, here they were, the three of them, tooling up the autobahn.

From some agency unspecified, Warrant Officer Horton had obtained the use of a large GMC command truck, US Army Forces white star on both door panels. It had already been loaded with domestic items, one or two crates, their ordnance stencils painted over, and Mrs Horton's personal luggage, when he walked round into the courtyard of their married quarters flat in Munster. His possessions were minimal. The old skinning and gutting knife was in his pocket; handy to have it for all sorts of things, sporting or otherwise. A good knife always came in handy.

Warrant Officer Horton was paying out to a couple of German workers, in their ex-Wehrmacht caps and blue-dyed British battle-dress trousers and blouses. He rattled on confidently in a version of German that did not sound entirely correct to Fraser, but to which the two men responded happily, grinning and saluting. The elder one clicked his heels and inclined from the waist, more of a formality to an officer, but including Horton's wife Uta with the slightest inclination of head and eyes.

Was there the merest trace of sardonic regard in this, Fraser suspected? Was this dark-visaged man saying to himself, "Ja, you have done all right for yourself, madchen, marrying one of our Britisher enemies. Food, clothes and a warm bed can speak louder than the blood of our volk, heute, das versteht sich."

Right, come on, man, get a grip; Bo's giving out the great plan.

"Now, you two, don't go up the wrong alley when we cross the Anderstrasse, watch the double set of lights, for Heaven's sake, Jock. I've heard all about you driving straight over the island strictly for tram points at the bahnbloodyhof! I shall try not to lose you on the autobahn, and just do not lose me!' Horton's eyes gleamed as he gathered Uta with one arm. "I shouldn't let you loose on this simple lad. These Gairmans haf vicked vays, Jock. Just let's get to our destination in one piece, men!"

He cocked his Warrant Officer's hat at a very un-WO angle and loped across to the bare-framed Thunderer. The boom of the unshrouded engine resounded off the high walls and windows of the married quarters. He grinned below his tank commander's goggles, waved a gauntleted fist, and they rolled out.

Uta and Fraser exchanged tight, cautious smiles. It all seemed good to Fraser. This was a task for a dependable man. He felt entirely up to it; the responsibility upon him for all these cherished and useful possessions behind them, this equally much cherished woman putting her trust in his driving.

He tried to assume a look of careful yet mature concentration, making Uta smile inwardly to herself, although her outward smile of pleasure in the day was entirely normal and visible anyway. She knew that she was going to enjoy this drive, and also find interest in the company of their Schottischer friend.

Fraser checked the gear shift and brake lightly, the big American engine grunting in a six-cylinder rumble as he changed up into a long-legged higher gear. Uta made her voice high and clear above the engine's note.

"We both hev the afternoon off, Jock. Shall we run away and loose – ach! – lose thet big schoolboy in front?" She nodded to her husband ahead on his low-slung automotive male object of love.

They came sweeping round a long bend to their first sight of mountains, spruce and pine plantations stretching their dark tree tips upwards, pulling their black trunks further up into the snow. It was all on a rather more grand scale compared to the harder but lower ridges of Don- or Deeside back home.

In a very low key, to Fraser, these surroundings made it feel so much like coming home, albeit in the strangest fashion: driving an American Forces truck on the other side of the road, speeding the temporary nucleus of a married couple's home along the autobahn, this attractive and attentive German woman beside him, who, when he started to whistle a few bars of a pipe tune, smiled broadly and put a hand on his steering arm.

"You are saying 'Hello!' to the hills again, I t'ink, Jock, neh? We shall find many more for you in Oeynhausen," she said, and smiled at his startled pleasure.

The late afternoon sun was streaming into the cobbled yard at the rear of the building when he reversed in, and cautiously followed Bo Horton and his wife up the stairs, carrying two of their smaller cases, following the reasonance of their happy voices. Fraser felt it incumbent upon him to be somehow responsible for organising things if he could, by ensuring a good start for his friends Bo and Uta. As he understood matters, this apartment was to serve as an occasional relief from married quarters with the regiment.

It was a furnished apartment, with good, solid oak and elm evident in construction and principal furnishings. Fraser already knew that Bo wanted to use the time there to both fulfil leave due to him prior to being gazetted in his captaincy and also to push on with necessary work on his auto-creation.

"Bo, Uta, do you want me to go and buy some bread, milk, anything, in the town?" His German would be OK for that.

Uta swung to him, hands on hips, pleasure, excitement in every line of her being.

"Jock, do you t'ink thet I hev not already put all such food things in the big basket there? We hev ev'rything for zwei – two days' eating with us, all of us. But, thenk you!"

As his boots echoed on the hardwood floor, Uta's heartfelt cry of "Oh! Bo! This is going to be so good for us, darling!" came to him from the light, airy upstairs sitting room, then silence as the couple's happiness found added expression.

He went down into the courtyard, checked the strapped-down canvas of the truck, put the ignition to 'off', and walked out into the town.

It came to him almost at once, the difference between the surroundings to the regimental HQ at Munster and this place: vitality and things being done with vigorous steps and lively voices, a world away from grey, battered Westphalia. Again, he whistled the same pipe tune, this time in full sequence of the parts or variations, and a man with a wild boar's tuft in his alpen hat and bristly cleft in his chin, nodded briskly to him, eyes flicking over Fraser's face and form, and back to his eyes again. Fraser nodded in return, a countryman's quick signal of things common to them both, not necessarily declared but there. Do hill men, stalkers, keepers and jaegers and the like, farmers even, do they recognise others of their ilk, even when displaced into another's country, by such things as length of stride, checking of wind direction and so on? It certainly seemed so to Fraser.

He got into his proper, ground-covering pace going up the narrow street, taking in deep lungfulls of this clean air. He would ask Bo or Uta about the significance of the boar's tuft mounted in the man's hat There were lots of things for him to find out about here.

LVI

After a cheerful breakfast, but always not quite enough for him to feel satisfied, each day was given to hard work on The Thunderer. It needed more parts for the water pump, suspended linkages to the clutch and brake pedals and also a set of big end shells for each connecting rod's bearing onto the crankshaft.

"Hear that rumble and knock on overrun, Jock? Not good news if I want to get peak performance out of this lady; she would grab up on me. C'mon, mon brave, nous allons chercher les bits."

Bo took the battered Volkswagen, which bore hardly legible licensing, and they nosed quietly in and out of alleys, semi-empty machine shop floors, workshops, all grimy and echoing in their disuse behind brickwork and steel doors pocked with small arms fire and larger calibre impact.

At each stop, Bo Horton slid out of the Volks in his black tank crew overalls, settled an arm around the shoulder of some initially non-communicative local artisan or mechanic, and flowing into cheerfully imperfect German, had the man riveted with intrigue at the photographs of the rolling chassis and engine, and everyone talking, peering and grinning at once. In most instances, spares were not forthcoming, but names and addresses were. Money and engine parts, once scrutinised, changed hands, and they swung out into sunlight again, Bo grinning hugely as they checked whatever he had bargained for.

"We've got to get the engine parts numbers to match, at least in the same series, Jock, otherwise we've got a bastard product begat of mismatched parents, and she'll blow up on us. You remember that, you dark heathen Scot, once we've replaced all the orginal kit."

"Hey! Look where you're going, Captain, Sah!"

Horton swore, spun the steering a half-circle, and glared viciously at the offending Bussing-Nag truck, which deviated not a flicker of an inch from its course on the crown of the road. He flung out "You're on a course to self-destruct, ignorant Kraut!" without breaking his flow of comment with Fraser.

They responded to each other in this jocular way when things were going well, running to earth some specific and elusive part, or rather the specific and elusive person to whom they had to deliver the usual spiel.

515

With hands still roughened from grease remover ("ersatz grinding paste for piles and pimples" as Bo called it), as much as from the actual work on the engine or chassis, both of them were famished and eager recipients of Uta's cooking skills. The smooth-grained oak table served both as their gathering point to sit and eat, but afterwards, replete, as a support for elbows and arms as they talked, dishes pushed aside in languorous contentment. They sometimes made a rapid effort to wash up and dry before relaxing in the warmth and easy conversation. Uta was surprised at Fraser's readiness to clear plates, wash up and tidy things away.

Fraser found that Uta's favourite position when all was cleared was to prop herself up on the padded bench seat, sideways on to her husband, and slide her bare feet and legs over his thighs and lean back in pleasure as he absentmindedly stroked her feet, ankles and lower legs. Fraser could see that this gave both of them an easement into relaxation and unalloyed sensual pleasure. Well, that was fine by him as an onlooker; they were quite open about the practice and their pleasure in it. Bo broke into his own satisfaction, as he gazed out upon the slopes beyond the town, and the woodland thereon.

"Jock! Good Lord, the lad's dreaming again, Uta. Are you spiking his food with some cunning knockout stuff?"

Fraser was indeed away in a momentary absorption with things familiar to him: the town's intriguing jumble of neighbourly farm and family houses, each with painted eaves boards and gables, with logs stacked neatly in below the overhang. Amongst the conifers that had somehow trickled in amongst the buildings, he spotted some deciduous trees and was instantly keen to get up there and handle and smell them. He swivelled round, embarrassed with his preoccupation.

"Oh, I am sorry. Thinking of something else."

"Ja, roasted kartoffeln, Jock." Uta smiled bewitchingly. "You will get only two on your plate if you do not stay nach haus with us this evening!"

Uta and Bo were by now accustomed to his evening excursions, satisfied to see him go out and content to have him return, whether or not already in bed themselves.

Whatever their effective male partnership in the workshop, once Fraser followed Bo into the warmth of this welcoming home, there was a tacitly adopted shift of bonding, Bo and Uta slipping happily into two closely knitted parts, needful to each other's whole.

Fraser found a new awareness in him now, an awareness of the power a woman's bodily presence could exercise upon the equilibrium of this man at the centre of her life. Captain-designate Beaumont Horton, professional soldier, and Uta Forsterling, German-born wife from Paderborn, took open celebration in their comfort of loving, at domestic and deeper levels.

As the wind coming down the valley became too keen for late-night exploration of the town, Fraser needed scant urging to stay indoors once their meal had been eaten and enjoyed. There was an almost family feeling about their fulfilment in finding out things about their respective backgrounds. Fraser's questions about how Beaumont Horton had started in his army career got all three of them talking in intriguing turns of conversation.

"'Boy Soldiers'"? Would you have such things in Scotland, Jock? No? Oh, well, some of your infantry regiments maybe, that's how I came into things, as one such. As much from juvenile resistance against my dratted father, who could not, would not see beyond probity, pension funds and the 'respectability of a sound bank career'."

"And didn't he tell you, in angry vords," Uta broke in with some heat, while Fraser's neck tingled deliciously at her play with Ws and Vs, and other words, "that you should not hev a home unless you started in the job which he had arranged for you so carefully, neh?"

She felt strongly about this martinet in Bo's home life, and leant forward to blow smoke from her nostrils in angry disbelief. In so doing, she tilted her head and neck muscles, lifting the fullness of her breasts more prominently into view from her V-necked woollen jumper. Each man knew that the other's gaze had lingered there, for a second of purely male pleasure. Bo continued, looking back in years.

"Yeah, my old man really was a pocket dictator, a sort of Oberst right there in stuffy old Colchester. Liberated the old bugger's best suitcase and marched into the Anglian Regiment as a Boy Soldier, with three stripes from my cadet force days, a couple of quid from my mama and a packet of French letters which two of us had bought at school, in great expectations." Leaning to one side, with a black grease smudge in his inner arm, Bo snorted suddenly, "The laugh was that I enlisted as a bandsman, in those days OK for young lads, and an education in skiving, otherwise known as band practice."

Fraser wanted to know more. All this early boyhood stuff was unknown to him.

"Did you have to do full infantry training, even as a bandsman?"

"Lord, no!" Bo smiled wickedly "Played, as you might say, one side off against the other, but got chucked out. For a bet, we tried to get a young WRAC to wear our bass drummer's leopard skin and smuggled her into a band practice night, wearing the skin, spats and nothing much else. Got the book thrown at me for that one. Her name was Elaine, as I recall, ravishing pair of legs, huh! Got a ticket into the Engineers. Yeah, yeah – you learn all the tricks for survival, especially when the war was dragging to a halt."

Uta turned round to Fraser, claiming his attention with feeling.

"Jock, Bo was a Tommee and never got hit, all those hoarruble Gairmans shooting at you, so big and man-like. Mein clever klein Wotan, so!"

She glared at her husband, then was instantly spilling with concern and skilled coquetry, with the flick of an outthrust hip, all in the space of less than two seconds. Aye, man! And there's the really natural Uta, Fraser recognised, saying nothing. Inwardly, he smiled to himself, for a variety of reasons.

Bo Horton was looking at his wife with a strange, distant focus, not seeing her, but picking out things, feelings, in a view over time and happenings past.

"Yeah, Uta, my time of digging holes and filling 'em in again was keeping me safe for you, Uta's Lohengrin, nicht war? The dastardly Deutschers tried to shoot seven kinds of holes in my sergeant's skin in l'Italia, treacherous sods. You know, Jock, these Germans – they are some of the world's most technically able engineers and wonderful composers and philosophers and yet they seemingly cannot resist destroying, totally and utterly, all that comes in their advancing or retreating, the better to vindicate the decisions of the pathologically lethal bastards they choose to come up with as leaders."

Fraser wanted to bring out more of this most able of person's experiences and attitudes. Bo was certainly not the usual Army career-focussed bloke. He held back; things were flowing rapidly in Bo's mind.

"The jolly old Huns are using us, and the Amis, and the vacillating Frogs, to rebuild again, but I'm going to extract all our dee-licious BMW spares out of them with the help of my dee-licious and sensible wife. Then we shall all drive off to Greece in The Thunderer, open a very sloppy hotel, and you will be back in the Highlands, rearing kids and cattle and bullshitting everyone about how you did all the vurrk on this madman's car, while I was as pissed as a large Gairrman goose! Go to bed, Jock, great things to be done tomorrow."

He yawned and stretched his arms prodigiously to the ceiling, as Fraser rose and gathered plates, but was stopped by Uta's smiling and emphatic head-shake. Suddenly, from within her, there was this curiosity springing from being a city girl, a town girl with no knowledge of what went on in country folks' lives, to find out whatever enthusiams this Jock-man had in his head and heart. She could read the book of her Bo's life and loves with ease, but here, with Jock, it was a blank page. Something to do with farming? She was interrupted, to the shared surprise of both in the warm kitchen, by Fraser's straight-out question:

"Uta, did you have men of your family in the Wehrmacht, or forces, or what..?"

Uta sat down abruptly. Her face seemed closed.

"My vater, father, was Kapitan for horses to bring the supplies for infanterie and patronen and stuff, mortars, kennen?"

Fraser sat without movement.

"As madchen, I hev hed no time to know my father. He never came home from Russia and Poland and Byelorussia to my mother and her two sisters. I was born to my mother after the guns, ze panzers, the many t'ousands of soldaten marched to z'Ost, all to be killed, so 'Gott Mit Uns'? Ja, ja. My aunts, end my brudern never did see my poor father ever again."

Things were very quiet between them in the kitchen. Uta rose quickly, calling down the corridor to her husband:

"Bo? Jock ent me, we are going to have a small talk about t'ings in Schottland, ja? OK. I join you very soon, gute nacht.' She turned, smiling, happy, composed again to Fraser. "Komm, we sit here like old friends, and you will tell me so much thet I don't know about your home and everyt'ing you do as a boy, like Big Bad Bo!"

Fraser felt warmly pleased by the frank interest now being shown by Uta in his way of life before the army, his home and his parents, the river, shooting, good old Tam.

"So, there you are, as a young scholar, rising so early." She pronounced it "hurully". There was that shiver of daft pleasure again! "To go shooting many rabbits, hein?" Her grey eyes crinkling at the corners, she planted her elbows on the oak table between them. "So, as a young boy, you were going out with your papa, your father, in his car, making so many stops at farms – was this with cows, cattles – ah, cattle! In Schottland, no? Ah, home in England for some years, when our two countries were at war. Your father, did he hev to go to the army?"

"No, Uta. He was too old and we had Reserved Occupations for veterinary surgeons, er, TierArzt, and doctors and so on. He was wounded in the 1914–1918 war, in the artillery, at Passchendaele." He decided that this was not what Uta wanted to hear about, and cut it short. "We came back to Scotland, to my father's home country, and I worked in farming, sheep, dairy cattle, all kinds of work–"

Uta interrupted:

"Did you not go to a gymnasium or college examination – ach, what is the word, Jock?"

He knew what she was searching for, the term for a young person to qualify for a university entry and degree.

"No, I didn't. My target is to go flat out for a farm of my own."

"Oh, really?"

He slipped the conversation sideways into such things as the courtship lekking display of blackgame ("This vurd 'lekking', does it come from Norvege, ja?"), the very male pleasure of expeditions at an early age and an early hour, going shooting and trapping rabbits with Argo, and then Tam (oh, touchy bit there, Russian general!), the smells of the countryside, and the river in the back end of the year, the curl of new soil from the plough's mouldboard, saving oystercatchers' and peewits' eggs from crows and field work for crops. He spoke with animation and depth of knowledge, but retained unspoken within himself lay the deep fibres of belonging to Tornaquhil, with Whitepark, with far-off Margaret Melvin and her marred beauty. She was the only young woman who had, at first acquaintance, abruptly tumbled his male pursuits into a different ranking of importance, of what he should be doing with his life.

Uta perceived all of these intensely felt and valued emotional imprints passing at depth through Fraser's mind and eyes – a richly composite something, but no someone it would seem, has really laid its life-print on this oh-so-serious young man of this Schottland place, with its hills, trees, doodlesaks, even some words which are so like German. On an impulse which came from she knew not where, Uta put her hand across the table, taking Fraser's left hand in her own.

"Is there no someone very important for you beck there, Jock, ja?"

There was no need for the brief contact of hands to linger between them, yet she let her hand and fingers stay for seconds where they were. Mensch! What warmth flowed from it, from him! Uta knew then that there existed values and visons of which she, a city girl, knew nothing, as equally clearly neither did her one-time Boy Soldier husband. His voice unexpectedly returned from going to bed, breaking into her whirl of thoughts:

"What are you two going on about? Couldn't settle to sleeping, so I'm going to have a quick dekk at the parts manual"

He had it in his hand, a greasy, much-thumbed workshop manual of pre-war BMW engine components. Exasperated by want of undisturbed sleep, by want of getting the right bits for his machine, Bo talked to himself, to Fraser, to Uta:

"My guess, Uta, is that our dour Jock must have at least a brace of Highland madchen back home, distracting him from annihilating God's furry creatures. Oh! Bugger me, just why do your German brudern have words absurdly long for something simple like 'big-end shell', huh?"

He flattened out the page of the manual once more, then proclaiming "verfluchten Krauts" with cheerful malice, and came out triumphantly with "'Verbindende rutenlagersschale', mein Gott! All that just to say 'big-end shell'!"

Suddenly serious, Uta felt a need to find out what set this quiet young soldier apart from so many she had noted in and around the regimental HQ.

"Jock, do you hev heart. Ach, what do you call it, heart–?"

"Ache," came her husband's dispassionate suggestion.

"Ja, this heartache for all this great beauty of your trees end hills end Schwarz, neh, bleckgemm birds which you tell me?"

What her eyes were asking of him, Fraser picked up, was were his deepest feelings for something more than the admittedly enthralling features of a country she had never seen?

"So." She picked up Fraser's hand between both of hers, clapping them together in time to her summary of things now known to her, as she rose and stood over him, still seated. In so doing, she knew full well that the inviting, shadowed division between her breasts was inescapably presented to Fraser's attentions – if he so wished. Nothing wrong with that.

"Well, there you are; hunter, Jaeger, bauer or farmer, sheep man, tree man, hundmeister, but, no wonderful girl, no? No Scotch lassie, hein? Kommen, Kaffee for all of us!"

This unusual evening of talk and finding out things was coming to a close.

With certainty, Uta perceived that those things to which Fraser Baird had given himself with vigour and strength had this far not included really loving a woman. In her book of what was important in a young man's powerful life forces, that was very strange. Turning to the electric cooker with a pan of milk for their coffee, she shook her head slightly, mystified.

HARDWOOD, SOFTWOOD

LVII

Next day, in that early summer morning, there was the promise of heat. Fraser slipped out of the apartment in his socks, boots in hand. He wanted to feel the pulse of the countryside, draw in the smells as the sun released them. For anyone driving through these comfortable German townships at this time, there would be the rising, lingering tang of wood smoke, too early for hay smells from the steep meadows, but perhaps a softly thudding Lanz tractor giving purpose to the day, work to be done.

Bo smacked his wife across her buttocks with great cheerfulness and the tattered workshop manual.

"Goin' up to Bergdorf, meine schmutzie, for these crankshaft shells. Verbindende rutenschalen to you, my love. All-day job finding them. Wanna come, Utie? No? OK, boring stuff. Where's our Highland enigma, by the way?"

Uta kissed him carefully. "Outside, smelling and stroking his beloved trees, I t'ink. What do you want him to do here, or are both of you going?" she asked.

"No. Tell Jock to clean all the tools, and run a half-gallon or so of flushing solvent through the engine at tick-over revs; he knows where it is. I may look up Dandy Durward in Tanks, at Celle, and have a beer or two. Ask Jock, no, you tell him your Deutscher names for these trees he's always gazing upon, and he'll very likely come up with the equivalent English ones, even though he's a dour bloody Scot. It'll all come in useful when you're charming the wits out of these retired old desk colonels who are goin' to laager down in our hotel and buy me drinks every night! They wouldn't know a panzerfasust from a plate of prunes. I shall tell them, and you will dispense tea and sympathy and… and whatever." Her husband poked a finger in her nether regions. "And do not terrify Jock with any more searching questions about his lack of love life; you'll frighten the poor laddie into Celtic celibacy, or worse. See ya, baby!"

He went off, Uta watching his entirely unsoldierly lope and then his lean figure fold itself into the battered Taunus which had appeared in place of the Volkswagen and chuck his WO's hat and stick onto the rear seat. She smiled, easy in her mind that she, a moré than ordinarily attractive woman, could confidently compete with big-end shells, torsion struts and beers with good old Dandy Durward and his tanks, or whatever.

How do these things arrange themselves in a man's mind? All these matters of machines and engines and manifolds were certainly not overriding passions in their Jock's mind she realised, casting back to the warmth in his eyes and voice as they had found in discussion between them in the previous lengthening evening's light, picturing his home life and places and persons in it, even his old dog! And yet, no great love at, how old was he – eins und zwanzig, zwie und zwanzig? She knew from Bo, at a similar age, that he had already had casual sexual explorations in number, which troubled her not. How was any person, man or woman, to gain knowledge in such things, hein?

In a light blue skirt, white blouse and simple slip-on flat shoes, Uta took long, easy strides beside Fraser, commenting on various small features of the mountain town. Any silences were shared, with sometimes a sideways look along her outstretched finger and a nod. The sun was more than hot upon them. As the cobbled road became steeper, with its square little paving stones, treacherous when greasy with dew or rain, Fraser was curious to encounter again the small but prosperous-looking hunting and shooting shop to his left with 'Jaeger Loden' in heavy Germanic script, black lettering outlined in gilt on highly varnished dark green.

"Kommen, Jock, we hev to talk of trees now, you and I, up on the berg track. For us, I hev made something to eat." Uta's pronounciation of "hev" sounded fantastically delicious to Fraser's ears, as did her way with "eckshully", being much more expressive than dull old "actually", oh, yeah! "Then, when it comes sehr heiss, you will do the engine vurrk for Bo, and I shall be the heppy hausfrau, nicht?"

More of her squirrelly pronounciations; rrrgh! It made his spine curl!

The proprietor of the shooting and stalking goods shop was at his door, in rolled-up shirtsleeves, oiled leather waistcoat and loden breeches, considering the modest display of Kettner hunting apparel and copies of Wild und Hund in the window. As Uta and Fraser climbed past him, the man looked over Fraser's entire person, needing to establish something of the innate nature of this interloper in British Army clothing. Was he looking for some kind of international countryman's code, Fraser wondered?

"Up here, Jock!"

Uta took his left hand and arm, tugging him off the hard road into a cool forest ride only a few paces wide. It was agreeably quiet, heavy with the scents of sun-warmed conifers. There were bees, mumbling and bumbling deep in the foxgloves along the side of the track. Shafts of gold summer light carried a fine dust of pollen. Fraser felt that it was a day of great promise to be amongst woodland. He hoped that his own response to such things, as they had spoken of it the previous evening, would not prove boring for Uta. English names of trees? OK, he would have a go.

"Now we come to our Schule, and you must be mein Lehrer, teacher, ja? Your tree place, so. My father tell, uh, told me of the names of many trees, but not all and not heving the English names for t'em, but, you hev the same in Schottland? Look, this is a good thing that we do together, no?"

Enfolded in the day's tranquillity, they stood, shoulders angled to each other, on a level grassy platform, looking over the valley's receding waves of blue-grey forest. Some were hardwoods; Fraser picked them out, like meeting familiar faces of old friends, making space for their limbs in the mainly coniferous canopy.

He turned to step away from the chestnut-haired person beside him, to be halted by the most gentle of touches on his arm, and by the incline of her head, hair and eyes into his line of vision. Fraser smiled in recall of Uta's protestations that her brothers had always called her "horse hair" because of its straightness and strength of colour.

"I am to say the German vurrd, and you will give the English to me, yes? OK, say, 'Yes, I will do thet thing for you, Uta.' Good?"

"Aye, of course I will, that's how we'll do it!" He smiled at this so-punctilious approach.

"So, you will learn. No, I learn, you will teach me. Go on, what is this one, please?"

She pointed him round towards what Fraser had already noted to be a whitebeam. With a grin of pleasure on his face, he turned to her.

"That's a whitebeam, Uta. Look at the silvery underside of the leaves. It'll be heavy with orange berries later in the summer. What did your father call it?"

She was touchingly child-like in her eagerness to add her bit of knowledge.

"Ja, I know he told me the same t'ings. In German is 'mehlbeere'". She grinned and laughed with a young person's happiness. "And so, now what is thet big one like a queen hinter. You say 'behind'?"

"Yes, Uta, we have such bonny big ones in Scotland, beech by name. What is the German for it?"

"Ha! Easy, 'buche', and in my parents' home from here, we always use it for the fire. 'Buche' in Deutschland, 'beech' in Schottland, is the same thing."

"Now, Uta, did your father say anything about the differences between hardwood and softwood trees? There are both kinds here, and at my home. You can usually tell what kind they are by the colour when it is felled or cut down. Did you know that?"

"Oh, Herr Professor. All this kennen-lehrnen!"

There were quirky puckerings at the corners of her lips and Fraser nearly laughed, but mindful of the task set by her husband he carried on, sternly.

"When you cut down a hardwood tree, Uta, the kind that drops its leaves in winter, the centre is often a dark colour, very hard to saw." Fraser stretched his arm towards a tall conifer about thirty yards away. "That one's a softwood. They grow quickly, have soft spaces in the centre, saw easily. Nearly always needles instead of leaves. Much lighter in colour, a bit pinky, got it?"

Uta smiled, sensing Fraser's confidence in himself, nach haus – at home with all his friends in the forest. Any moment now, our Jock will run up to one of these good trees, softwood or hardwood, and put his arms around it!

"Look, Uta." He stripped off a spray of needles from a low branch and crushed them in his fingers. "Look at the silver stripe below and a notch at the end. They smell like orange peel. Smell." He held out the crushed needles to her. Standing to one side at his left shoulder, she looked at him gravely, took his hand and raised it to her nose. And then, with the smallest possible movement, to her lips.

"And what is this your name for this one?" she asked, looking at him.

"Ha! Es ist abies alba, Uta, European silver fir. And in Deutsch?"

"Is it fichte? No? You look heppy, Jock, you know the name!"

"Aye, I em heppy as you say, Uta. It's 'weisstanne'. I learnt these names from other countries from a forestry book. Come on, Uta, I'll run through some more."

He identified an oak – eiche - below them, majestic after an untidy elm – ulme. She repeated the German and then English names after him. Moving not very far into the quiet green canopy of mixed hardwoods, they came to a stop, Fraser silently peering into a wide-branched tree of open spread (might it be a chestnut?), sunlight splintering his gaze to fragments. Wood pigeons ruckety-cooed momentarily, a tractor exhaust thumped from across their valley, then rumbled and bumped to a stop. It was really hot.

Sensitive to the physical presence and closeness of Uta slightly behind his shoulder, Fraser turned his head and shoulder slowly, curious as to a whisper, to a sound, then to the absolute stillness of her person. He was at once aware in his peripheral vision of the reflection of sunlight, a glow from surfaces of soft, luminous quality.

Her rich woman's body utterly naked to her waist, Uta stood erect, regarding Fraser with quiet composure. The whisper of friction had been that of her pulling the white blouse free of her waistband. It slipped from her arms and wrists to the ground, innocent of sound.

The wood pigeons were still in muted dispute, somewhere above them. As Fraser's gaze passed from her eyes and face to her naked shoulders, to her breasts, areolae, nipples, swell of belly and hips, she exhaled gently, as of releasing a burden, and turned towards him, content in his wonder at her body and beauty.

Raising a finger to her parted lips, she beckoned Fraser to turn fully round to face her, and then come closer. Undoing the buttons of his washed-out work shirt and discarding first one tightly rolled sleeve and then the other, Uta gave the gentlest of sighs, passing her hands over all the musculature of his twenty-one-year-old man's chest.

"Mein 'Ighland man, you teach me about your trees; they are your family, you really love them, ja? Now, I give back to you, this love."

Her words flowed through all of his senses, like the downy flutterings of a brood of nestlings, but not attempting flight. Her body exuded warmth, fragrance, invitation to touch, to feel. Resting her hands on his bare shoulders, Uta spoke quietly to him.

"Mein Jock-man, you know the Amis hev this Thenks Giving thing?" She spoke it as two separate words. "Well, now." She took his fingers in her own, guiding them steadily to the fastenings of her skirt. "This is my German 'Thenks Giving'." She stepped clear of her pale blue skirt and nothing else. "And, you will be my Schottische 'Delight Giving'."

Her sensible flat, slip-on shoes were already neatly shed and placed to one side. Tidily, thoughtfully.

With the smooth, silky warmth of Uta's right thigh lying across his groin, both gently flickered by sun and shadow, Fraser traced the areolae of her breasts with a gentle finger. "Why are these bits so broad and brown, and yet these," he asked, as both her nipples became erect and brilliantly pink to his touch, "are so wonderfully different, Uta?"

She nuzzled into his neck, cat-like in sensual pleasure.

"Jock, mein leibe Jock, it is all somet'ing to do wit' trees, hein?"

Trees? How? Hornbeam, weissbaum, buche, scented needles? All the wonder of Uta's "Thanks Giving" swirled and swam in golden light and sun-smell of woman.

Uta raised herself, eyes hooded and dream-like, screened by her swinging glossy chestnut hair. Slowly, she brushed the tips of her breasts and nipples across Fraser's face, eyes, lips.

"Jock, you ask me why are they so different, the colours of these 'bits', hey? Well, you teach me sehr gut; it is all about hart-wood und soft-wood!". In uncontrollable laughter, she collapsed upon him, long legs, belly and breasts in deliciously sun-warmed fulfilment.

He lay, his hands gently stroking her body with an intuitive skill he didn't know that he possessed. He was stilled, beyond anything in his life. He wanted to hold this happening ("heppening"!) secure in his deepest, most inviolable store of things known only to him. That could never be of his own memory alone, this precious jewel of giving, loving; the wonder of it would always have Uta at its core. Sensing his gentle smile on her cheek, Uta accepted its imprint and returned it in drowsy warmth. The wood pigeon above them checked its song of summer, but briefly, finding no cause for flight from the most gentle of movements below the dense foliage.

POINT OF AIM

LVIII

In the late afternoon, shadows lengthening, Bo Horton blew in upon the calmness which lay upon both Uta and Fraser at their respective tasks, in apartment and workshop respectively, with a gale of shouted, urgent queries, great excitement, things to be done at once, by him, by them, by all of them. Above it all was his surging jubilation.

"Utie, the bloody big-end shells. I've got a complete set, and a gash short block for a spare, and some rare and wonderful packs of gaskets, all unused high performance stuff. Mein Gott! This old engineer feller was a find from a different age. He lit up when I showed the photos and gave him the whole goddam spiel! Hey, Jock! Got everything done, how about we fit these shells tonight and give her a blow through?"

Involuntarily, both Uta and Jock warmed to his impatient excitement; it was infectious. Fraser was uncertain how Uta would handle the need for normal contact in the course of him just being there, good old dependable Jock with the tools and interest in completing her husband's driving project. All that remained of their well of loving was the deepest of gleams in a passing glance, a small fire unquelled.

Good, he would make no presumptions upon anything.

"Right, I'm ready. We'll have a go with the shells, I got her warmed up and flushed out twice; no swarf, nothing in the pan. She's clean."

They made a rapid meal, mostly standing up near the stove, with Uta handing out helpings of a sort of pottage, with grated cheese on hot toast, some sweet preserved plums in syrup, lots of coffee.

"I will bring more to the vurrkshop once all is cleared here. Off you go, get cracking, boys!" Uta commanded, in happy mood. Clearly, she thought, Dandy Durward and his tanks didn't get the time and attention he was supposed to, early this morning, ha!

"Right, Jock, let's get this funfair on the road. Come on, we're off to the vurrkshop, Uta." Bo was at once the commander in the field; seeing everything, marshalling back-up support, delegating with total authority. "Jock, no room for us both below the beast. I'll fit the shells, you set them out in matched pairs. They may have serial numbers, OK? When I say, you turn the crankshaft through twenty degrees. Give me a little pot or dish with some engine oil in it. Let's go!"

As Bo's and Fraser's feet clattered in noisy partnership to the workshop, Uta reflected to herself that quite a number of things of that day had not been according to any earlier plan. Or any plan at all.

In the circle of light around and below the machine, their quiet exchange of parts, tools and the odd grunt of controlled effort was good and companionable. Squatting on his haunches to pass down whatever Bo needed or passed back up, Fraser suppressed images that were forever closed down, set at a necessary distance from this man's world.

Looking at the opened packaging for the new set of shells, thrown up out of the pit by Bo, Fraser noticed engineering drawings of size and section. He set each pair of shells in careful apposition.

"Top one, bottom one, top one, bottom one. Here you are, Bo. Number three set. Are you numbering from the front of the engine, or by the firing order?" Fraser asked. He knew that all engineers numbered and marked all engine parts as they were stripped out. Had Bo felt this was unnecessary? His thoughts were cut short by Bo rolling out from below the chassis.

"Come on, Jock! Oil in. I'm taking this baby out tonight!"

Everything was tightened down with a final clatter of tools. There was still enough light in the evening sky to make the next declaration of intent irresistible:

"You or me, Jock? At low revs, my friend, we shall put our priceless Deutscher verbindende rutenschallen to bed in their new home. Ha! Uta, does that sound good to you?"

She had stepped into the work area around the car and bench and tools. Short leather jacket, plain but slim skirt, those neat flat brown shoes again, Fraser noticed. He shivered, slightly.

She set down the thermos flask and sandwiches, and held up both arms, encompassing the poised machine and everything around it.

"Bo, she is your baby, neh? To you should go the first proper driving. It is important. So much vurrk, you two! Be careful, Bo. You hev lights, ja?"

The Thunderer's exhaust boomed as Bo reversed it out into the alley. Bo spoke slowly, with chopped-off clarity.

"Slip road to Paderborn, make a turn at the 'bahn junction. Back here, six or seven kilometres. Nothing fast, keep her new bits cool."

With a subdued blip of the exhaust, it and he were gone, rear lights seemingly attached to nothing.

Fraser felt mentally and physically drained. Uta moved quietly to stand before him. She placed her hand on his arm, then down to his hand and fingers, enclosing them. A delicate peacefulness seemed to hang, suspended around them in the near-darkness.

"Jock, meine Jock, I hev great heppiness, special memory – memories? And for you? It was a nat'ral thing, for you and me. No talking, just holding so close."

She leant forward, put both hands to his face and turned him to her, to kiss him softly, a number of dream-like contacts, and stood back, hair and head to one side.

"You are special to me, Jock, now. Always."

She walked to the opening on to the alley and lit a cigarette. Fraser needed something practical for his hands to be occupied with, to smother the pain. He picked up a pair of the original big-end shells, discarded by Bo in his impatient refitting process, in his suspicion that the originals would start that noisy knocking so feared by all mechanics.

Oh. Am I seeing something or not? There it was – a small difference in the sectional drawings of the new ones, now flashing round the oil-washed crankshaft at God knows how many revs, but this detail was not present in the old ones. The new ones had a minute shoulder to each side, towards the web of the crankshaft.The discarded ones did not exhibit this projection to fret against the limit of the machining of the actual crankshaft where the connecting rods were tightened down. Christ, man! They were all going to overheat. Oh! Mein Gott!

There was no way to contact Bo now, certainly not by chasing up and down with the old Taunus; he had been gone over half an hour, in solid darkness. Uta at once understood his alarm.

"I think that the best thing to do is for me to stay on here. This'll be where he will make for, either driving slowly, or someone helping," he said to Uta, thinking through likely explanations as he spoke. "You go on back home. A hot meal will be what he will need, OK?"

They kept a distance between them in the darkness. They both felt too much tension about things unknown now, Bo's prolonged absence, the demands of this auto obsession ruling them all, their giving to each other now a world unattainable forever. She sounded desperately weary when she spoke:

"Ja, mein leibe Jock, I will do thet. Jock?"

"Aye, what?' He knew what she about to say, milliseconds before she spoke in the darkness. "I hev great love for you."

Then she was gone.

Bo Horton's sudden appearance was savage, awful in his towering anger. The machine had run only a few kilometres, he spat out, before overheating and then seizing up completely, solid. Jeezussbloody hell! Watching Bo carefully, Fraser felt the likelihood of him erupting into violence, at the same time he breathed to himself at a profound undetectable inner distance. Thank God Almighty that he, Fraser, had not taken the machine out on its first refitted run. Ooooh! He knew all this and other wildly circulating consequences of everything on that night, when Bo reappeared in the lights of the workshop, towed in by another car and driver, the Thunderer impotent behind it. They pushed it into the empty work place, Bo snapping out, "You get in and steer the bastard thing, Jock! No! Don't fucking argue, just do it!"

While the driver had some notes pressed into his hand by Bo, brusquely, Fraser felt the various external surfaces of the engine, allowing for cooling off as it was towed. Not good, still desperately hot.

"Bo?" Fraser seized the need to be entirely open about what he had seen on the packaging, just minutes into the tidying-up after Bo had taken the machine out for its run. Bo was standing in wounded silence and disbelief. He looked up but didn't speak.

"Look at these drawings. These shoulders are not on the old shells. The new ones must have been bearing beyond the limits of machining to accept them–"

Fraser was in total disbelief at the fury and vilification unleashed on him in volume.

"And just when did you notice this, this minor fucking difference, for Jeezuss' sake? Nothing hit you when you were passing them to me?"

"Bo, I did not see the packaging and drawings until you opened them here!"

Horton turned on his heel and strode off to the apartment, head down and swearing acidly.

When Fraser followed him up the stairs and into the warm kitchen, the scene that ensued was frightening and degrading. The soon-to-be-commissioned-officer was shouting hoarsely, coarsely:

"Yes, Uta, the bloody thing is locked solid, propably a total rebuild job, at God only knows what cost, all due to–" He checked himself with difficulty, speaking through his rigidly clenched jaws. "All due to my not checking what Jock, what both of us, had in our hands was the right bloody specification." His voice rose to an anguished roar. "You just cannot get these bastarding parts any more!"

He glared at Fraser, his face suffused and ugly.

"I would have been better served with a Hitler Jugend youth than this farm-bred amateur! And with no long discussions going on between you two at night, Uta!"

His wife, white-faced, drew in her breath with a gasp.

In that moment of searing accusation flung at him, it was at once granite-clear to Fraser that the most compelling quantities in Beaumont Horton's life were his racing car to-be, his impending captaincy, his easy authoritative use of all persons within his remit, be they British, German or any background, provided they were compliant, but not his wife Uta. She was just a suitably attractive accessory to every other damned expression of her husband's unquestionable and unchallenged maleness.

Fraser felt a second line of visceral fire hit him with cruel penetration: "Use?" Use of, of – Uta, by God? Had he, Fraser Baird, been the unworldly young soldier to respond, unwittingly, to the unspoken invitation, or even trap, by the giving of himself to something that had absolutely nothing to do with building a blasted old car, nothing to do with old German men slyly selling old German spares?

He felt ice-cold, yet consumed with implacable fury. He faced up to Bo Horton and his insults, speaking with ice-clear clarity. Icily, Fraser knew at once what he had to state if he was to retain some particle of self-worth in the face of this man's raging madness.

"Mister Horton, sir, Mrs Horton, I shall be leaving with the first available train. Thank you for the invitation to drive up, and for your hospitality. I do not accept that I am responsible for what you are alleging; my first sight of your purchases was only after you had the packaging in bits on the floor. I shall pack and clean my room now, and make my own way to the station in the morning, Mrs Horton. Good night."

He turned on his heel, acid biting his stomach, his tongue, his heart, unfed, unwashed, desperately tired, emotionally in chaos.

Aye, and what heed should he have been paying to Corporal McGillivray's guiding maxim in this blasted army business? "Keep the heid doon, and never volunteer." Had he volunteered, or had he been traduced by something indefinable?

By Christ, right again, damned right.

Uta came to him, silently, in the kitchen.

"Bo will be taking you to the station. This is for your travel."

A neat packet of sandwiches and a small bottle of apfel saft, apple juice. She knew of his liking for it. Fraser extended a hand, both hands, choked with impotence in his sense of destruction of trust. Silence between them, her husband's feet impatient in the corridor. She brought both of his hands together within her own, clasped them with tenderness in her own long fingers, and then stood back.

Only in the last few minutes of the run to the bahnof did the old camaraderie surface. Horton passed a heavy carton over to Fraser.

"Here, take these back to bonny Scotland with you. I've little use for them."

On cursory inspection, "these" comprised an assortment of German and Belgian shotgun and rifle cartridges. At least six or seven of them were Brenneke, full-bore lead slugs for shooting wild boar at close range with a shotgun. Fraser looked across at Bo, and for a moment, it was all still there, the satisfactions of working well together in amity.

"OK, Jock, you mad bugger, we were a good team. Yes, you were right, I should have checked every damned bit of information on those verfluchten schallen. I've really paid dearly for that bollocks-up. Between all of us."

At the station, he swung round to regard Fraser silently. He, Bo Horton, was perfectly aware of Fraser's innermosr feelings of care and respect and affection for his wife, all these probably as a mask for the well-smothered but inescapable sexual attraction that was there too.

A good job that some of these fellows from the Highlands were quite held back socially; there had been too many undercurrents starting up between the three of them.

"Get going, then, Jock. I shall fit replacement shells from somewhere, and think of you with every bloody scraped knuckle! You're a good worker. Stick to tractors and things with horns on if you want a peaceful life! Wiedersehen, Kaporal!"

On the hard bench seat, as the train jogged on, back to the flat lands of Westphalia, Fraser was cruelly beset by feelings of betrayal, betrayal of his bonds to his Scottish land, the farms and farmlife he was so familiar with, betrayal especially of all those farm workers of great simplicity of purpose – to do a really good job. Betrayal of any future with Margaret Melvin by the giving of himself in a relationship which was now forever tainted in his silent mind. Betrayal of the values he wished to hold true to for himself, that he needed to be able to offer to whoever would come to him as his chosen wife and lover, in the way of life his whole being ached for.

After he was dropped at the long-deserted Munster bahnof platform, what happened outside the Displaced Persons building was short, savage and wholly unpleasant. They came at him as a pair of sly predators from the shadows.

"'Allo, Tommee, lost your wo-man, ha? You come to me, hey?"

The voice came from above as he strode steadily past the building, another one-time Wehrmacht barracks. There were always lights on in the huge place. He remembered the warning they got about the DPs on arrival in the regiment:

"Stay clear of 'em, dangerous and diseased bastards; they'd kill you for money or your paybook."

Well, that's not a part of my plan. His pupils dilating in the poor lighting, Fraser was aware of two forms: one behind him, the other silhouette immobile in front. He flung over his shoulder, "Nein, miserable bitch, get lost." Just keep on marching.

Matters changed abruptly, as did the now strident woman leaning out of the window:

"Fucking bastard Tommee; my boys get you now!"

And that was what was immediately attempted. Of a sudden, it all exploded out of him, a savage need to be shot of this grudging, barely combined function of two countries, with the chaos of lesser countries all shot to hell by every other warring nation, and the human detritus jammed in the middle.

The figure behind him was closer, mouthing obscenities, the usual stuff. Without breaking his longest possible stride, Fraser swerved to the wall and came back like a charging animal upon whatever this thing was. He had his horn-handled gralloching knife that he always took with him everywhere, closed in his fist, hard end protruding from within his crunched-in fingers. He made a swooping thrust towards the man's belly with his left hand, which made him or it or whatever, hunch down, head and neck forward. Fraser tensed his stomach muscles and smashed his right fist and that hardness within it backhanded into the man's eye socket, with a hard-grunted "Miserable bloody thing!"

He then about-turned and marched directly to the person in front, in towering implacable rage.

With uncertain movements, the youth half-mouthed, "You give me ten mark, Tommee."

At this, Fraser stuck out his face and chest and bellowed into the creature's features, still crashing his boots down:

"Oot of my way, you useless ill-thriven thing, or I'll break your bastarding neck!"

The youth made a move as though to grab at Fraser's tunic pocket. Now enraged beyond all caution, Fraser belted him backhanded across the face and kicked him hard in the groin. With prodigious outraged strides, he kept on marching towards the brilliantly lit guardroom and duty picquet. Away from treacherous damned DPs, away from seized-up Thunderer (what an idiot bullshitting name that was, anyway, huh!), away from a confusion of friendship gone sour, with its betrayal of personal values to which he couldn't put a name, and in essence being something less than soldier or mechanic or spare driver when wanted. Nothing amongst this military miscellany now seemed to have a clear-cut purpose in his idea of self-worth.

What was it that Robbie McIntosh the old roadman used to go on about? "A stone dyke's nae damned use without a solid foundation to it, man." Well, his, Fraser Baird's personal stone dyke currently seemed to be in a very poor state of repair, with little or no solid foundation on which to build any damned thing. This being used to fill gaps in other folks' lives was not the furrow he should be in; he should be back in farming, with experience and skills of which he was confident and proud. There was an inexpressible need for him to get back to the cold, hard, clear granite – "Dinna forget where you come from."

The lights were bright, soldierly, welcoming. The picquet guard, alerted by Fraser's outraged bellows down the street, had taken paces out into the roadway, rifles across their chests, the picquet sergeant behind them. All this is going to go into the roster report for the Orderly Officer, too bloody right it will. Well, to hell with it.

"Seven-nine-five, Corporal Baird. C'mon there, Sandy, you're half abloody sleep!" Fraser felt suddenly cheerful, he was going to clear the decks of all unnecessary, non-productive demands.

"Yeah, Jock, had a good leave then? Get ol' Horton's sports job up and running? Any super-sexy bints up in the mountains, Corp?"

The duty signalman at the desk was suddenly flustered, covering up:

"Oh, er, yes, Sergeant. No, Sergeant, no, I wasn't talking, sir! Baird signing hisself in, Sir."

The duty sergeant said nothing, face impassive, and turned on his heel.

"Go on, then, jammy bugger, shacked up with someone's Jerry crumpet, an' all, I bet, eh, Corp?"

"Sandy."

Fraser felt too tired, drained by emotional weariness.

"Yes, Corp?"

"Cool your fevered mind, it's like a dung midden."

Fraser hardly registered Jack Connor's artfully held back piece of regimental news.

"Now hear this, you men: the regiment is on to supply a draft for service in Korea. The great choice is that you either say "yes" or be drafted anyway! More time in, more pay."

Fraser looked at Jack and then Sandy.

"Straight up, you two?"

"Yeah, gook-shooting getting serious out there. You're on the provisional draft. Go on, man, get into your billet, get your head down."

It sounded as though this might just be the kind of job he could handle very happily indeed, gook-shooting contributing indirectly to the hungry fund for the farm. God, he felt utterly weary. As he folded himself into sleep, his inner view of what shape and form the immediate future could hold was blank. He felt in sore need of nourishment from figures like Jack Harris, and Watty Taimes and, and Eleanor and even Jock Wyness (for goodness' sake!) and Ramsay and Robina McMillan. He really needed folk like them, all of them, back in his life.

LIX

Beneath the roof girders of the Hanover hauptbahnof, echoing where bomb-blasted glass had been replaced, men filtered in from units all over Germany. Shoulder flashes of boars' heads, flaming shields, tartan squares, regimental or corps insignia: they were all comrades for a common purpose. The four soldiers from the Signals regiment had postings for 27 Commonwealth Brigade: Moash, Fraser, Spam Kirby and Polly Walcott. Fraser had asked of the Signals Adjutant if he could extend his National Service for a further six months or a year, if need be, without the commitment to a long-time signing on, and what would be his pay while serving in Korea? "Yes" to the former, bumped up a good bit to the latter. Some disclaimer forms were signed; not less than six months' extension, not more than twelve months. Quite a bit of manipulation and reference to King's Regulations and Rules regarding service beyond time. "Subject to written confirmation", Fraser had been warned. Oh, aye? Out in Korea?

"Yeah, you wouldn't bloody chuckle, mate."

The orderly sergeant had looked Fraser straight in the eye. He added:

"When you get out there, Jock, watch your bloody back, man."

"Aye, I'll do that."

By ordinary train from Munster, they had clacked quietly on through sparse fields and hedges crippled by severe cutting-out of anything that would burn, farm women in drab headsquares and faded army coats bearing away tight bundles of hedge trimmings. Figures in a latter-day Breughel, Fraser thought them, but damned little dancing in the market platz these days. At those stations where the engine stood, chuffing in cold sunlight, the tired German land was too severely cold to release any farm smells.

Later that evening, with faces and nostrils stinging in the rank coldness, they started to entrain for the Hook of Holland. Knowing that they were to be posted to armoured units in the main, the small party of Signals personnel had formed a friendly liaison with one such armoured detachment. They clambered up in a bobbing line of black and dark blue berets, helping impartially with each other's packs and kit.

A driver from Hawick with whom Fraser had chatted idly, drawn at once by the broad Borders tongue, elbowed him in the ribs as they waited for others to pull themselves up and into the carriage.

"Hey, mon! Traverse left and depress ten. There, by the trolley!"

Their eyes were caught by a tall, fair-haired woman with striking facial bones, dramatically offset by the shadows of the station and her shining, swinging pony-tail. She was talking animatedly with the child holding her right hand, but craning neck and head beyond the shoulders and kitbags filing past.

Fraser was silent. Inside his head, the words "She is so very beautiful!" seemed utterly superfluous.

Another poke in his ribs. Driver Turnbull again:

"Man, isn't she one helluva looker? Ah just huhp it's nane of woor lads that's leavin' her wi' the bairn and promises, eh?"

More to himself than to Turnbull in Tanks, Fraser muttered, "God, if I ever had a woman like that to cherish and care for, I'ld be damned sure I wouldn't be pushing off for bloody Korea."

Ah, she had found the man she was searching for. The little girl was tugging at the sergeant's sleeve and hand. Her mother was smoothing his tunic lapels, pushing a neat parcel into his other hand, laughing at him, with him, with the other soldiers who had swung round to look. They were envious, shy of showing it. It was the ache of soldiers departing, aching with the sudden need for somebody like this golden girl to remember. Alan Turnbull exclaimed, with relief and vicarious pleasure:

"Christ, man! It's Leo's wife, giving him sandwiches an' all. Now, there's the woman of your dreams, by aaahl!"

She put an arm round her husband's shoulders and called out quite clearly:

"OK, boys, you go shoot up these Ko-Ree-an fellers, ja? I keep this man here for the back-up force!" She grinned widely.

Squeezed in beside Fraser, Spam Selby was beside himself in wonder.

"Hey, Fraser, every bugger here seems to know we're going to sodding Korea!"

There was a sudden blast from the locomotive, venting steam and smoke, Redcaps trying to look all-important below their severely flattened hats, station staff standing back to blow whistles. Fraser and Moash were jammed at the entry into the carriage, back to back with the sergeant whose wife and child were level with and below them as the whole train heaved forwards. The woman's face gave of its beauty and youth (she can't be much older than I am, Fraser felt sure). She was waving now, waving to all of them with wide sweeps of her pale arm in the uncertain light.

"All you boys, hey! Do the good job, ja!"

As she called out, high and clear, her eyes locked on to the man, her husband and child's father with all of her woman's being.

As she ran alongside, there was no boyish grin, no calling, no tears, only her fingers touching, stretching and then breaking apart as the train gathered speed, bearing them away to this puzzling, little-known war in Korea.

LX

They would always remember the smell of Korea. It stayed with them in deeper imprint than all the unclear shipboard briefings for all ranks, convoluted lectures on "Halting The Tide of Communism in Asia", and "Command Procedures in American Land Forces". The land of the chrysanthemum? Oh, yeah. You wouldn't bloody well chuckle.

The more bruised and shattered this land was, as they jolted east and then northwards by train and truck, the more it reeked of ordure, rank filth, crumbled mud buildings, a reduction of everything to muck, mess and helpless humanity and all they voided amongst it. There did not seem to be sufficient clean air in volume to accommodate the sourness of destruction.

They journeyed forward, Moash and Fraser, with Polly Walcott and Spam dropped off before the final spine-jolting arrival at 27 Brigade HQ, in company with assorted infantry and artillery replacement drafts. There was dispersal to individual units: batteries, armoured troops, machine gun and mortar sections. All these were dug in, laagered around or in close support of hilltop positions long fought for and retaken by American, Commonwealth and Communist forces alike, over two draining years. From brief conversation with the men they travelled with, the four from Munster had gathered that regardless of how high and well defended a section or platoon was, the predictable approach of the North Koreans and Chinese troops was to simply overrun any position with limitless hundreds of yelling soldiers, racing up and over their own dead and wounded.

"Ah tell ye, the wee hoors come at ye in tens and twenties, aye, even hun'ers at a time, a' jabberin' awa' like Paddy's market. Shoot the buggers up and the next five hun'er or so come trampling ower the heids of them!"

So spoke the Black Watch sergeant riding in the truck with them, with American issue jeep jacket, long-snouted cap with the ear flaps tied up, heavy overall trousers, three-fingered mitts pulled up behind his webbing belt.

Across the legs of his overall trousers was spray of dark, almost black splashes, hardened into the material. Blood. This soldier, Fraser recognised, was a wholly competent-at-killing NCO in his own area of the ground held by the Black Watch infantry.

540

They pulled themselves up as the truck rumbled into a command compound of sorts, the battle group and infantry battalion HQ.

"You Signals men to your troop commander, over there. Keep the heid doon, lads, and dinna let the wee bastards get in ahin ye."

With a hard slap to Fraser's shoulder, the NCO was down from the truck, grabbing a South Korean to carry the two stencilled boxes on the tailboard, saluting an officer with the minimum of effort, speaking sharply to a private, running his hands over his belt and ammunition pouches. He was Black Watch NCO back in line, back in action. As they all damned well were now. Something that the Black Watch sergeant had said about not letting the Koreans get in behind the defensive positions: has no one thought about the practicalities of putting a really strong, maximum firepower couple of hard no-nonsense battalions in behind the Commies, and shoot their replacements all to buggery?

By dint of direct questioning, Moash and Fraser were directed to their respective armoured troops, following a sorting-out by radio of the needs of infantry, machine gun and mortar sections. A strong, fast handclasp was all that time permitted with Moash, their eyes hard, giving comradeship in silence.

There were probes, counter-patrols, sudden envelopment in intense, savage mortar attack.

"It's not random stuff, either, Corporal," the troop commander commented to Fraser. "They've pretty well got every fire position ranged, apart from the heavy stuff farther back. So, you see, us tanks, we're the only ones the jolly Chinese can't plot through the night and that's why they send in the expendable stuff to try and spot our positions just before first light. Now, for Christ's sake, speak to me immediately you feel unhappy about where we're hunkered down or laagered, any of you, right, men? Speaking of what we can't see, let's take a gander forward to spy out that gully. There's dead ground there we can't see into. Baird, you come with me. Todd, take off your black overalls – they'll know you're a tank man at half a mile off."

Lieutenant Saunders' own tank, as troop commander, one of three Centurions as Fraser saw, was under maintainance, a tarpaulin pulled out along one side. Men were working on a drive sprocket and idlers. The other two tanks lay some distance off, both crews clustered round a central figure with a mapboard. All three Centurions looked well-used, thought Fraser, noting the hard packed mud like concrete behind tracks and shields.

The dispersed tanks and their crews waited behind them, twenty-pounder guns slightly elevated, muzzles slewed, awaiting sector co-ordinates to come in over their radios, engines warm. They to it, or it to them; action was sure come upon them. The men could smell it coming. And, now, Fraser realised, so can I.

The savage frenzy of another Communist forces' attack exploded upon all positions central to and flanking the Hook in the dusk of a day later in May. They were clearly determined, whatever their losses, to dislodge the relieving infantry, Duke of Wellington's Regiment, while they were still coming into line through the Black Watch.

Bitter, flat-out fighting invested not only all of the battalion's north-facing trenches and machine-gun pits actually dug into the Hook's forward slopes, but also those to the equally important rear, with Koreans and Chinese clawing their way in like running tongues of ground fire, between sections, platoons, behind strongpoints on to anywhere with some feet in height, gullies choked with bodies, broken weapons and wire.

After rapid radio consultations with infantry and battery commanders, the three Centurions had rumbled off into hull-down positions to the rear and west of The Dukes' flank machine guns, each in location chosen for giving covering fire upon its mates should it be overrun and distances in their main fields of fire suddenly get pulled up closer to them.

Lieutenant Saunders, "Sonny" to his crews, spun round on his heel.

"OK, Baird. What do we call you, by the way? Jock? Right, listen to what I'm telling my drivers and tank commanders. This is my grip in case things get a bit twitchy: See that gully? I want the gun layers to be spot on to the killing ground immediately below there, in the bend of the river. That's where they'll bunch up before taking a run at us."

Each crew acknowledged, and moved into careful disposition, snouts depressed and silent, in ground out of sight of the Dukes waiting in their revetments, and scarcely visible to the Turks on the salient west of them. Sonny Saunders continued filling in Fraser as to his rationale in setting out his fields of fire.

"I'm fairly certain, Jock, that we're out of sight of the gooks or Chinese artillery spotters or their up-front mortar pits."

Grimly, from Driver McQueen:

"Don't you be so sure, sir; the wee buggers'll be stacked up on each other's fucking shoulders, like bleedin' acrobats!"

Saunders smiled faintly, still looking to his front, binoculars in use.

"Jock!"

"Sir?"

"You've got our frequencies locked on? A spare set with you for anyone whose set goes duff? Do not go any distance from my tank. What've you got for a weapon? Your own rifle, not a Sten? No. OK."

They all waited, the same gut feeling of action near at hand growing steadily in the tank crews as the positions along the Hook were mortared without stop. All that could be done in preparation had long been checked and rechecked: racks and bins filled with shells, belted machine gun ammo in narrow boxes, tops off, radios locked on and tested, on frequency common to the Dukes and the troop of tanks, quick-change replacement units for the main gun lock-on device clearly labelled, with connections exposed. There was the unmistakeable smell in the air of killing to be done. Above them the atmosphere was disordered by the flight of high-explosive shells from the battery some hundreds of yards behind.

Drivers, loaders and gunners were taking turns to stretch leg muscles, urinate quickly against the tracks, trying to ease the yawny feel of tension in their stomachs by kicking shards of stone where the track-plates had slewed. Fraser felt more than restless; he was positively uneasy. Something was twigging at his deeper, insistent mind. Acting as standby radio man for command between infantry and armour was good, but there was a serious gap in the fence down there somewhere. Now, if he was a Chinese platoon leader in this treacherous half-light, where would he…? Where would he what?

"Lieutenant Saunders, sir!"

"Yes, Jock?" Saunders' eyes flicked constantly through all degrees as he turned to Fraser's upturned face.

"Well, sir, if I really wanted to brew up any one of the three, but particularly this one, your tank, that ridge running away north from us has a gully on either flank which you've seen, but very much closer in both are dead ground. You can't see what's going on there, sir. Until they're on you – or the others."

Troop commander Saunders had learned something of Fraser's background from his posting: a keen stalker and rifle shot and, not surprisingly with a farming background, an eye for the lie of the land. Lieut. Colonel Moore, 3 Signals Regiment, had said so in his original postings bumff. Hmm. All the way from goddawful Catterick to here, would you believe, Germany in between.

"Right, make it snappy; tell me why you think this needs our attention."

Lieutenant Saunders, tank commander, listened carefully, aware of a prickling in his scalp as he listened.

"You reckon that you could look down into these two gathering places for the brew-up boys?"

"Aye, er, yes, sir. I'll take the spare 88 set. That'll be 'Brown Cow'," Fraser said, nodding to the long ridge to their front, "and my call-up can be 'Hillman'.

I Like to Walk in This Field

If I take Lloyd's torch, and the set is no damn use, I'll give short bursts of singles for 'Nothing doing' and multiples of longs for 'Coming in', and in hundreds of them, two longs for two hundred and so on. If they should show up. Sir."

Lieutenant Saunders chewed his lower lip. They all knew this sign of furious thought. A brewed-up tank was a sickener for all the lads' morale. He poked a finger into Fraser's chest.

"You may well have Scottish second sight superior to those fellers in their bunkers," he said, poking Fraser again and looking him directly in the eye, "No bloody heroics. Speak to us, by set or by lamp. If there are no occupants in your two hidey holes, come back in here bloody smartly, got that?"

Fraser extrapolated this by adding to himself, and if there are loads of 'em preparing to swarm all over you lot, does this mean I stay out there, just watching them?

Saunders picked up his handset.

"Raven to Castor and Pollux. Do you read me? We have a probe going out; single, visual, bearing thirty west of north. Radio watch on net from now, also alert for visual that bearing. On signal enemy closing, I shall call up star shell. Acknowledge."

Within fifteen minutes of working his way forward from the tanks, stooped and canny, and then waiting, he had picked up, tracked and shot the first Chinese soldier. The others took more time.

He had lain on the shoulder of Brown Cow for a good while, with shootable light fading fast, when they invaded his senses. Chunky, near-black objects in a continuous bobbing file, pegging up the valley floor, a long rifle shot below him. How now, Brown Cow, indeed? What was it that Willie McClusky, retired stalker, used to come out with?:

"A beast of any kind aye looks bigger in the evening light!"

Wary of the Chinese practice of enveloping targets in a wide V, base open to the objective, sides running past the flanks, he swung across the flat ridge in great loops with splayed-out fingers and legs, spider-fashion. The rifle walloped badly on its shortened sling, his heart thumped like a triphammer, the 88 set was a plague.

Letting his breath out slowly, Fraser froze, flattening like a hare in fear when caught out of its form.

Not more than two hundred yards from the sloping far end of the ridge, the other end of the file of Chinese or North Koreans was padding obliquely to his right, into the valley bottom, where it would then split, to form that deadly, all-enveloping vee. Where no bugger could see them, except me, Fraser was sure.

544

With total certainty, Fraser knew that this was the point of rapid dispersal from which the Chinese would sweep up him, tanks, Uncle Tom Cobleigh and all. Savagely, he pulled the set round to lie below his chest, holding down the aerial in a loop.

"Hillman to Raven."

Slowly, mouthpiece cupped. How many of the treacherous wee buggers would there be down there?

"Receiving you. Come in Hillman."

"Enemy crossing north of Brown Cow, west to east. Estimate two hundred. Now swinging south, into dead ground. Closing at less than two hundred yards."

Fraser's breath came out with a rush, he was gripping things too tightly. The set crackled.

"Raven to Hillman. Message understood. Pull out to Raven, I say again pull out to Raven now. Starshell four minutes. Acknowledge. Over."

He thumbed the set and got a lot of mush. There was a series of crackling explosions to his far right. The Dukes must have called in H.E. on the ground to their front. As he tried the set again, Fraser was sure that he heard the whine and deep thrum of one of the V12 tank engines. He took satisfaction from the vibration of their exhausts, just like a really large tractor at full power. They must be readying for starshell coming in – come on, man! He cut the squelch to minimum, and onto "transmit".

"Hillman to Raven, Hillman to Raven! Watch your front, I say again – watch your front! Closing fast at two hundred east, do you read me?"

As he released the transmit key, three things happened in front of him. Starshells popped high overhead, giving stark substance and shadows to everything in the valley; the 88 set squawked an angry Yorkshire voice: "They're too bloody close for mortars, we're going to hammer 'em with–"; then one of the tanks opened up with machine gun tracers, searching across the valley floor.

The Koreans or Chinese had stopped. Very carefully, Fraser wriggled away from the 88 set, pulled his rifle into his chest, snicked the bolt open to check the round in the breech, closed it on cocked and laid it directly in front of him, safety off.

All of his senses were clamouring at him, get down off the Cow and pull out fast, NOW. But, one last contact with his mates in Raven, his tank commander 'Sonny' Saunders, Driver Tubby and all – no damned miserable brew-up if he could sabotage it.

On-off, on-off to his rear with the torch so long as the shapes on the near valley floor had their heads down. From where he lay above them, in a kind of soft vanilla light, Fraser saw muzzle flashes from two of the tanks' guns. The noise overall was tremendous. From mortars, artillery fire, machine guns and tank rounds, he felt the rock-hard phwoomfwock as both tank shells exploded amongst the rough growth in the valley running up to the folds of ground behind which the troop of tanks lay hull down. Some of the Chinese soldiers' shapes below Fraser moved, then collapsed. As the starshells' light waned, shadows elongated and the tank guns came in again, low, flat trajectory, searching, slashing in vicious penetration. Almost certainly now, the Commies below him would split and make their V approach to overrun and cripple the tanks, any tank, along with its crew. Rolling to one side, Fraser half-crouched, half-ran to the other side of the ridge and slipped down over its edge.

Aaargh! Down!

The file of black silhouettes came round the hill in a ragged jog trot. He lay to one side, bobbing his head low down to pick up better definition. The last man down off this side would hardly be expecting to meet a Jock on top of this piece of barren ground. The skiving wee bastards are keeping their heads down, good lads!

The last two Chinese stopped, one to hitch something around his middle (a bag full of bloody grenades, my friend?), the other to gesture and move on. Peripheral vision yielded no others. He watched the hunched-up figure, to one side of central focus. There was a useful splatter of small arms fire behind him. Fraser let his breath go completely out of him, held low to the middle of the man's chest and shot him, cranking in another round at once.

The object on the ground did not move. Wait, always wait, wait a–

Lying flattened into the rough ground, Fraser's awareness of a head and shoulders above the rim of the plateau stopped his breathing.

Absolutely stilled, mouth breathing at less than a whisper, no eye contact, his eyes felt as though the pupils were straining to widen to tearing point, to signal the slightest body movement in his direction.

Aaaah, you miserable Chinese specimen, just k-e-e-ep on coming, that's a wee feller. At only seventeen or twenty yards distance, the platoon leader or whatever stopped, seemed to look at or over Fraser's position, and then carried on, with a rolling gait, shouting.

Keeping his head motionless, and straining every optic fibre to follow the man's outline to his right eye's limit, Fraser swivelled rifle and body by small degrees, lung movement stopped. More carronades of mortars, burp guns, some heavy HE coming in – try it in one go, now!

In the most unlikely lull in firing, his left boot scraped on stone. The figure downhill turned round. Fraser fired and missed.

The Chinese soldier ducking from sight, his own cranking in another cartridge and furious backwards and downhill scrabble, the cautious but shocking reappearance of the same man at a different angle all took only about ten seconds. Fraser inched his woollen comforter right down over his eyebrows, slid the rifle out in front, held every inch of any movement until the bulky figure was only a couple of gate lengths from him and punched him backwards with a heart shot. He was up in a rush on one knee and shot him again, hearing the solid impact of the bullet – no misses this time, my friend! As he ran in a crouching rush to the Chinese soldier, Fraser heard more whip-like cracks from the tanks' twenty-pounders. The man was still moving at his feet, almost foetus-like in coiled limbs and torso, burp gun mixed up with hands, blood, clothing. In an instant decision Fraser fired point-blank into the base of the man's skull.

Like a ferreted rabbit punched on the neck, the Chinese soldier arched in a sustained rigour of the entire body, kicked once and fell back. In the now near-darkness, the smell of blood and voided gut contents was warm, foul. Fraser ejected the empty cartridge case, jerked his feet and legs back and wiped the muzzle of his rifle with his sleeve, crabbing downhill at speed to anywhere with an inch of concealment.

Firing was erupting, boiling over in great crescendos, checking only to release voices, yells, single shots, whole magazines being released into the ruck of attack, then gathering in volume and viciousness. He picked up voices, then outlines of figures in front. He tried the trick of moving his head up and down, trying to get a solid target with light behind it. At that moment, artillery put up two starshells and at once there was a muzzle blast of orange flame a hundred yards to his front, with simultaneous sustained machine gun fire. Tail End Charlie was about seventy yards out, looking in the same direction, when Fraser's spine shot put him down. Ahead of him, already registered at much the same distance, was a knot of soldiers' forms, some on their knees. Fraser squeezed off three more shots into the humped and halted bodies, with rapid deliberation. There was a clamour of yells, tinny trumpet noises somewhere and violent displacement of air and earth as tank fire came in amongst them. There was one more figure, upright, gesticulating, urging. Allowing for bullet drop, Fraser brought the smoked black foresight slowly to the top of the man's head and hat, and squeezed off all breath and one more shot.

"If you're not up, you're bloody well down, and if you're down, I trust that you're bloody well dead!" Fraser commented to himself, with satisfaction.

"Right men, you'll get your silly head blown off. Time to load up, make off the ridge and lie up. Get the hell out of the way of these mad, multiplying bastards if you're wise. Good old Brown Cow, you did us proud!"

Skulking like a fox, it was all-night evasion of Chinese or North Koreans, lying doggo for long, edgy spells, easing round scraps of scrub willow or similar, which had to be touched to be seen. Move like a wraith, pal, you're not quite ready for a wreath, ho hum, clever bugger!

Fraser already realised that he would have to go as far as possible to his right, come first light, and transpose himself from a single figure somehow insignificant to both sides, and then – tricky bit, this – reappear much closer as a Commonwealth and British soldier. But, minus the foul-smelling quilted jacket he had taken off a Chinese body to maintain body warmth through the night hours.

The detachment of Turks would not accept his approach and shouted for identity in spite of his hoisting his No.4 Enfield rifle high in the air by its muzzle. He had an increasingly anxious feeling about openly presenting his rear view to mortars from the Chinese across the river, whilst, at last, exchanging questions and responses with a Canadian mortar team sergeant brought in by the Turks.

"OK, Signals, come in nice and steady. These goddam Turks are all set to cut you in half, so keep that rifle up a ways."

Fraser's stomach muscles ached with downright liquid fear of that first nervous rifle shot – or a blasted mortar salvo from behind.

Back in the command post near the tanks' laager, one of them with blackened metal around the turret, the smell released by the warmth from the Chinese jacket and his own overalls was strong and vile. He was greeted by an astonished Lieutenant Saunders with, "Holy Moly, Mother of Christ, I don't believe this! The Phantom of The Bloody Opera!"

Saunders was near to speechless with relief, raging anger and the pressing need to back-pedal, play down and somehow tidy up the entire episode of Fraser's apparently wilful disappearance in the thick of the night's action. The troop commander regarded him, chewing his bottom lip, not a good sign to the interested tank crews. Their errant bloody Jock had undoubtedly alerted them to that devious load of gooks, who had spilled out from real dead ground, trying their usual trick with petrol-soaked rags, and had then by all accounts, crept round behind them, shooting them up the arse – had there been one or two moments when, inexplicably, the bugling infiltration had strangely faltered?

"Baird, you bloody well listen! Do you realise that I am on the point of posting you as 'Missing, presumed captured', to Brigade? No, how could you? We'll have to muffle up your midnight wanderings with some inspired reporting in my Engagement and Action report. So, come on, pay attention: where exactly on this map did you get to, what did you notice about last night's lot – Koreans, Chinese or what? And how many of them did you nail, for sure? Incidentally, is that one of the deceased's clothing? What a vile smell, for Chrissake!" Saunders seized his clipboard and shook his head in disbelief.

"Sir, I thought that maybe Intelligence could make something of the jacket? Anyway, I dropped three spot on, and shot up a bunch of them under the starshell stuff, and–"

The troop commander interrupted his account tersely.

"My God, Baird, what in hell's name have you been standing in?"

Fraser looked down at his left boot. It was crusted with dried blood and hardened excrement. "Oh, that? Must have been the last wee bugger, or the one before that, maybe. Spotted him having trouble with his bag of grenades, or having a shit, or something. Not a bad shot, sir!"

Fraser looked up from untying the offending boot, delicately, and met the eyes of Driver McQueen, who winked at him hugely from behind their troop commander's back.

"By the way, Jock, Challener got badly burnt on both hands; they were all over Castor like maggots, trying for a brew-up. We had to hose them off with emm-gee fire. You may have to stand in for him. Christ what a bloody awful smell!"

McQueen busied himself, rattling tools in a canvas holdall, singing in low key, to the tune 'When It's Springtime In The Rockies':

"When It's Springtime In Ko-Ree-ah, Ha! Ha!

And the gooks come running past,

Look to your front, for the wee trumpeting runt

And shoot him up the arse!"

Saunders swung round, exasperated, shouting at both of them, all of them:

"My God, Jock, what a most diabolical smell. Just get out of here and produce a written report, OK?"

"Sir!"

"And Baird." He jabbed Fraser with his pipe stem and pointed it. "Get yourself another set of overalls; you've got it right up inside one leg!"

Holding his nose in fastidiously arched fingers, McQueen added nasally but clearly, "As the actress said to the bishop!" and collapsed in uncontrollable silent mirth.

I Like to Walk in This Field

There was another "Hold it, Baird!" from Lieutenant Saunders. "There's a letter for you, Jock. Good job we held it here. It's in the Signals shack. Get all that muck off and back here expressimo."

Aye, these overalls do reek a bit, Fraser had to agree. Now, who might be writing to me here? And why and what? Ach, well, all in all, it had been a good wee shoot. As you might say.

LXI

Throughout the tedious stages of journeying back to the U.K. for demobilisation, Fraser had plenty of time to pull out his father's letter and re-read it:

"Fraser – I am tempted to address you as The Good Soldier Schweik, but will refrain; he was a comic figure, the archetypical unwilling but very practised exponent of standing army rules and regs on their ear, and bending them in the process! Where you are, matters are a deadly distance removed from that light-hearted opera. Here is why I am writing to you.

"First of all, family matters. Your grandfather is failing. On good days he sits in the garden with old Tam at his feet; they are happy companions. On not so good days, he sleeps into the morning and is then a bit confused as to whether it is breakfast or dinner time (or, more appropriately, Tea-Time!) and whether he should be outside working at something or other to justify his keep. I believe that it is the work ethic of a lifetime which keeps old farm folk like him going on. For the present, he is contented, and seeks wee bits of news about yourself. As do your mother and I.

"Your mother is fine. An anxiety some weeks back, concerning a bang on her shin which would not heal; one of her coffee-drinking ladies gave her a 'preparation' (!) which made matters worse. Doctor Wilson is happy with it now. Jean is going like a train at St. Andrews for her Honours degree; she has the incentive of promise of a job as private secretary to an MP in Perthshire. Now to what I expect will give you cause for thought.

"The Melvins, James, Lorna and Margaret, are now down in the Borders, near Melrose, where not only did Jas. land a lucky strike managing a small fold of Galloway cattle, but has bought a comfortable cottage with a few acres which they could just afford. No more terrors with a tied house. We understand from friends at Galashiels that Margaret is now on a course in Edinburgh which may enable her to qualify in advising farmers' wives on various small farm business enterprises – she would be excellent at that. But things of unwelcome nature happened ten days ago.

"Margaret was in Edinburgh, her father was out all day, and Mrs Melvin was only discovered by the postie when he found the house open in the afternoon.

551

She had collapsed with a cerebral haemorrhage or stroke at God only knows what time through the day, and had lain in the kitchen for untold hours before she got medical attention. Lorna is in hospital in Edinburgh, she has severe disabilities, and cannot speak. Margaret has had to abandon her course and come home to help her father make daily visits to the hospital and generally take charge of the Melvin household. Oh, dear. What a tragedy and a trachle for them all. I felt that you should know the situation there before you actually get back up here after handing in your kit, etc. At least they, and Margaret in particular, now have the security of their own home. The unpleasantness at Whitepark really hit that fine young woman very hard. The way things are for her now, she will be feeling very cut off and isolated. James Melvin is not a very domestic person at all. A visit from you might cheer them all up, preferably with a letter beforehand telling them you would like to call in and when would be suitable.

"With this Korea business, you have had added time, between dodging mortar attacks – 'stonk' is a very apt term, isn't it? – to see clearly what you would like to do and most importantly, at the staging point you are at now, whether what you would like to do is also at the heart of what you plan by way of earning a living. The Melvins thought a great deal of you, persevering as you did away up in Glen Annacht, with Jock and his tantrums! As did everyone else up and down the glen. Your mother and I thought that you did a really good job there. It was quite plain to all of us that there was a warmth between Margaret Melvin and yourself, and her folks, for all your brief contacts with them and with her.

"Now sit down and think very carefully, about what you can take on your shoulders in the next few years, and what equally clearly cannot be sensibly entertained. Remember your good friend Doctor Dallas's advice about staying clear of propositions which carry a burden of problems or failed endeavour behind them? Fraser, you have made all the right decisions about your life so far. Now, if something does not sit comfortably in your mind or you feel that you HAVE to do something because people expect it of you – STOP! Your steady inner mind will tell you in its own time what is the best thing to do.

"I have bent your ear for long enough. God speed your journey home. It will be fine to have you back where you belong.

"From both of us, and Grandpa Tea-Time and a loyal auld dog that seeks his master every morning,

All our love and support,

Your father."

Fraser withdrew into intense and distant thought throughout the journey home. Surely this was not yet another application of his far-back friend Corporal McGillivray's maxim "Keep the heid doon and never volunteer"? Surely that was all to do with army life and survival, surely he was finished with all that, surely there were other more optimistic and rewarding ways of looking at things, of bringing a job and a home and hopefully another person in the heart of it, all together?

There was a warmth and directness in his father's letter. Curious, Fraser realised, that I know so very little about what events and unforeseen factors in my good old father's life, growing up as a young man on his father's farm, had shaped important decisions in his own life. Would he have stayed on the family farm, with no veterinary degree, if the 14–18 War had not marched him off? Why had there been such unswerving purpose in, firstly, his grandfather determining that his son, Fraser's father Alec, be put to veterinary college, and likewise, that his own father showed similar determination in coming back to his studies after more than four years in the killing fields of France? There were great gaps and silences in his father's life about which, he, Fraser Baird, had never had any conversation. Out loud, out of earshot of the others around him returning from army service, his will sharpened on that very point of stating:

"Father, I would really like to get to know about, about how you decided to do the things that you did. I guess that it is not easy being a father, and I am finding it difficult being a son – different things pulling at me. I need to have some good long talks with you just as soon as I get back home; that will be of some use!"

Sprawled in the stuffy heat of the train compartment going north from London, Fraser felt the clack-clack-clack-clack of the carriages picking up their rhythm on to the Forth Bridge as his closed eyelids soaked in the strong sunlight.

The events of the past few weeks had jostled for his attention following his low-key departure from Pusan: the excessive pointless discipline of the demob camp in Devon (with that sudden, effective beating-up of the provost marshal by "persons unknown"; he deserved what he got, malicious bastard), Colonel Oldacre calling him in for the pre-demob grip about what was he aiming to do following demobilisation and had he thought about signing on for a Regular commission, short or long term? He had decided against it, as he knew full well he would do all along. What decisions would good old Colin Bowles be making now? He had a fairly good idea of what was important in Colin's mind!

He would really be cheered to meet up with Colin again. Yes, he would do that; they had been the best of companions, with his 'Lampton Wu'm' and all!

With his eyes pleasantly warm and closed, Fraser smiled to himself, hearing again Colonel Oldacre's dry enunciation:

"I understand," he had paused and coughed delicately, "that you exercise a certain predilection for independence of action, Baird? Could prove a testing point in your early stages for a commission, y'know. I would approve, others might not. Think what matters most to you in the long term, Baird. Your background is different to most, and no bad thing."

I should bloody well think so, Fraser muttered to his inner self, surprised!

"Look, you tell me that your father was a Gunner in the 14–18 war, why not give the Artillery a thought? I can move things along for a commission in that respect. The present system is all going to change; we're going to need officers who can see that mobility of men and firepower is critical, and can make it happen fast, right? The days and nights and months – by God! – of digging into filthy trenches for weeks on end are past – they have to be."

The Colonel turned round. He was speaking with him man to man now.

"We need really strong-minded fellows, well able to enter into combined ops with air, mobile dressing stations, reconnaissance from off-shore, and really top quality communications between everyone in an action."

With some heat, Fraser thought inwardly, aye, and refusing to bog down into total vulnerable immobility, with decisions needed on the spot. Suddenly, Fraser wanted to distance himself from this blinkered persistence of practices in "the system" that suppressed any independence of thought and action, any seizing of opportunities to do things boldly, differently and with results. Carpe diem was, in his experience, an unknown maxim in the Army. Never mind the diem bit, once meticulously planned, action should be leapt into on the minute for things to happen. Cut out all this waiting for orders. Christ, now he was beginning to sound like a one-man recruiting team himself!

He had made a serious attempt to appear polite and attentive. Colonel Oldacre had smiled broadly and clasped him on the shoulder, added, "Good luck with your farming plans, Baird. Contact me if at any time you change your mind and decide to make a go of it. I can help you with some planning beforehand! We need men with your sense of purpose, by God, we do."

His eyes twinkled but were serious behind it.

Aye, make a go of it, maybe so, but of course, then only according to King's Regs and all that. The building storm in him was to get back to the land, the ways of doing things with men whom he respected.

One way or another, he was going back to where he belonged. And between all the money he had saved from all of his farm jobs, some good and some bad, and his untouched army pay, and his carefully guarded Post Office account from rabbits and game, that in itself nearly three hundred pounds, he knew that the eighteen hundred pounds or more that he had earned and saved, was going to go into something that mattered more to him than anything else, even going for an officer's career and pay. Once you were in there, in the good old army system, that was it; no stepping back into your true, heartfelt identity, which might get lost along the road.

Working up at Tornaquhil had led him to Margaret Melvin, to that sunny afternoon, for so long deeply held and cherished. He had to just go on and arrange to go down there, soon, and find out for himself what might yet be entertained, how the pieces might be brought together. Or not, for that matter. Well, he would do his very best with everything, by God he would, and damn the fears of getting stuck! Like getting that three-tonner out of that vile bog in Germany; it wasn't the army that had taught him how to tackle things like that. As Colin had said, grinning in all that muck: "Aye, you an' me, we fairly fettled the beggar, an' all!"

He smiled openly and yawned, stretching arms, legs, wash-shrunken khaki shirt. The lance corporal opposite, bound for Dundee, smiled too.

"Got something nice waiting for you up there, then, Corp?"

"Aye, well, you could say that, I suppose."

"Been keeping in touch all this time, have you?"

"Oh, aye, very much so, Ken, dead right."

Yes, he had been keeping in touch, deep in his private, unswerving mind, from that last moment of leaving Aberdeen Joint Station.

No more blown RT sets, sullen Germans, strange undercurrents in a marriage, with betrayal and a feeling of loss of place and true identity in his careful plan, no more screaming Chinese, chaos of war going nowhere in bettering things, class and blind tradition dictating his army life, all army life, an existence lacking roots, lacking the bonds with the land to which he longed to give all of his energies and – aye – love for it in every season, even with the rain water and snow running off your nose!

Hey, old Tam was going to go puppy-wild when he walked in through the door!

He smiled again, against the tears of nearing reunion with old Tam, narrowing his eyelids against the glare from the Firth of Forth below. The long train steamed and laboured northwards, pushing steadily between fields shaved and the hay in rucks. Cheviot ewes with lambs at foot looked up quickly from impatient plucking at the stubble, their lambs racing and leaping like demon footballers. Aye, he was returning to his homeland with all its vigour and values, just as he had done all those years back as a much younger fellow still at school, but what a range of experiences he had gathered unto himself for his plans since then. Bluggy 'ell h'indeed! He smiled slowly, bringing into his recall all those remarkable men: good old Jack Harris grinning in his lopsided fashion, "Bluggy 'Ell!"–ing away at every turn, all the other farm men (Watty Taimes, Stiffy, Jock, the General, Ramsay!) and their wives and women who had cheerfully sown seeds in him, carefully garnered to sustain him along that path and furrow calling to him, for so long now!

Soon, the locomotive drawing the long line of dusty carriages would be trailing its plume of smoke through the Angus uplands, within sight of the blue hills once again, as he slept. No, he had never forgotten where he came from, faith ye. With absolute certainty, up here would hold that very field that he yearned to walk in.